Also in paperback by K.R. Griffiths

Wildfire Chronicles: Volumes 1-3

MUTATION

Prologue

"Movement."

The word was a barely-audible hiss, like air escaping from a slow puncture.

"Where?"

"One o'clock. Five hundred yards."

David sighted the rifle, scanning the dark, empty fields that radiated outwards from their elevated position on the stubby hill. Nothing. He switched to thermal.

Ah, there it was.

One man. Shuffling toward them slowly.

"One of them?"

David squinted. The thermal scope turned the landscape into an artistic impression, messily daubed in shades of black. The figure, little more than a dot at this distance, hovered in the gloom like a spectre, a bright white splash against a dark background.

It was heading toward them slowly, but it didn't move like one of the Infected; didn't have that strange animal gait. And then there was the fact that it was alone: increasingly, the Infected tended to move in packs, sometimes numbering a handful, sometimes many, many more, though it had been a while since David had watched a herd moving past in the distance; an army of sightless death that numbered in the hundreds, and remained oblivious to the presence of humans nearby. Thank God.

He shook his head.

"I don't think so. Difficult to tell."

To his immediate right, David heard his spotter sigh impatiently, and he grimaced. He would shelve the rebuke for now, but later - when noise wasn't such an issue - he would have a word. For a member of a sniper unit patience wasn't just a virtue. It was everything.

He glanced at his partner. Larry had good eyes - a prerequisite for a spotter - but he was raw. Never tested in the field. Until 'the field' turned out to be the very lands that surrounded the barracks; training areas abruptly turned live. Suddenly *everyone* was getting tested. *Ready or not, here they come.*

David and Larry were stationed on a hill overlooking the northern perimeter of Catterick Garrison, or at least one sector of it. The garrison itself was huge, and had slowly developed in a moderately-sized town of around fifteen thousand nestled near the northern border of North Yorkshire. It represented one of the UK's most formidable strongholds; the largest British Army garrison in the world.

Catterick had survived the initial encounter with the virus. Just. When the dust finally settled there were a little over a thousand survivors left, trampling on a carpet of the rotting corpses of their former comrades which covered most of the 'town' itself.

The centre of Catterick comprised a small area of buildings - living accommodation and barracks; a school; a recently-installed commercial area - surrounded by thousands of acres of training ground. That huge empty space had provided a buffer from the worst of the violence that had swept through the country, but when the infection made its way into the population at the garrison, the soldiers stationed there had quickly found that all their weapons and training hadn't quite cut it.

When the enemy attacked at a microbial level, what good were bullets?

They had taken heavy damage.

It had only taken a handful of the Infected stumbling through the stretched-thin, panicked defences. Just a handful that had ended up reducing the numbers of what David increasingly felt was a resistance movement by as much as ninety per cent before bullets had finally done enough to stop the infection in its tracks. The only way to fight death was with death. When the infection knocked at the door, the only prudent response was to blow up the whole damn building.

Whatever biological apocalypse had been unleashed on the UK, there was no treating it; no hope of quarantining the afflicted. It was as incurable and uncontrollable as it was ravenous. The only hope was to cut it out like a tumour, and that meant killing. A whole lot of killing. Infected or not: they just kept killing until the violence stopped. There was a grim, terrible irony to their survival.

He squinted through the scope, sweat beading on his brow; stinging as the sharp night air hit it.

One figure. One pale ghost in the night. Could be human. But if he was wrong, one would be all it took to start the cycle of mayhem all over again, and this time David doubted they would be able to fight it off. There was only so much killing that could be done.

Catterick Garrison was still regrouping after the infection had decimated its numbers days earlier, and pulling itself together despite the sudden absence of all high command. That vacuum told David all he needed to know. High command had known what was coming, and they had evacuated like cowards in the night, slipping away like phantoms, leaving the grunts to fend for themselves. In the end, there were a few who had thought themselves important, but had been left behind to die. As it turned out, with the exception of a very select few, they were *all* grunts.

All forms of communication had been cut off, but even if they still had phones and satellites, David was certain there would have been nobody listening. The radio still seemed to work; but the frantic transmissions they sent were met with static and silence. The infection was part of a co-ordinated attack, and those at the top of the military had either been part of it, or had fled.

David knew they weren't the type of people that fled. Not from anything.

He grimaced as the thought about the motto of the Royal Air Force, the one that one of his buddies used to repeat ad nauseam. *Rise above the rest.* As it turned out that motto had been cut short. They had omitted the part which said *and then cut them loose.*

What was left at Catterick after the bloody battle with the plague-ridden creatures - a few broken regiments that had served on active duty, a lot of trainees and some families - would still have represented a formidable force. If they could shore up their defences, they might stand a chance of putting together a retaliation that could attempt to take back North Yorkshire one mile at a time; to at least push the infection back.

The Garrison represented a safe zone. Possibly the only one that remained in the UK. It had to be maintained. The infection had to stay *out.*

Despite the chaos and confusion within the garrison following the collapse, that was the one thing *everybody* agreed on. That meant hyper-vigilance.

Letting someone in, human or not, was a risk. David and Larry were just two of the snipers manning the boundary. They had orders, but also an unusual level of autonomy. This was David's call; no one else's.

"Sorry, buddy," David breathed, focusing on the figure shuffling toward them. His finger found the trigger.

And suddenly his scope was empty.

"What the hell?"

He shot a glance at Larry, brow furrowing, and got a bemused shrug in return.

Returning to the scope, he swept the area where the ghostly figure had been. The spectral image had melted into the night; the thermal now offered nothing beyond the blank, dark canvas of the Yorkshire countryside.

Great, he thought, *now I'm losing my-*

He didn't get to finish the thought.

At his side, Larry croaked and gurgled, and when David's eyes travelled to the right, they settled on a sight his mind couldn't comprehend.

The figure he had been watching through the scope stood over the two men. It had somehow travelled hundreds of yards in an instant. It was huge, over seven feet tall. Deformed; bulbous. *Grinning.*

Its enormous hand was buried in the small of Larry's back, withdrawing slowly, with a sound like flames licking at wet wood.

Tearing out Larry's spine.

David began to roll onto his back and tried to bring up the cumbersome sniper rifle that he knew would be worse than useless at such close quarters, but it was plucked from his grasp even as his finger began to squeeze the trigger, so quickly that his mind thought he was still clutching it, like the ghostly itch of an amputated limb. His finger squeezed on nothing.

The creature - there was no other word for the thing: it looked a grisly parody of something that had possibly once been human, but wasn't any longer - dropped a foot like an anvil onto David's chest, crushing him into the soft, wet earth, and lifted Larry's dripping spine into the night like a trophy.

Licked it.

David's mind retreated from the horror; cowering. He felt like crying for his mother to save him. Years of training, years of combat; nothing had been enough to prepare him. His thoughts froze like a cornered animal as his sanity began to collapse.

The creature dropped Larry's severed spine and looked down at him, and David saw utterly inhuman eyes; saw a dark and terrible future written in the savage gaze, and realised that all that was left now was to pray for a quick death.

God didn't listen.

1

This is the end.

Darren Oliver shivered a little as the thought crossed his mind, yet it wasn't the crossing itself that caused the tremor, but the relentless cold. The truth was that Darren had been looking forward to the end for quite some time. Ever since his sixtieth birthday had lumbered across the horizon. Something about that milestone made his bones feel old. Fifty-nine hadn't felt that way.

He had made the decision months ago to make the current expedition his last: his body was still strong, but it was also fatigued, and when it came down to it Darren had simply grown tired of being cold all the damn time.

Even so, the thought of retirement was a troubling one, when it was to be a solitary undertaking. Nothing to look forward to other than daytime television and microwave meals and a slow deterioration, until one day you found yourself walking down a street in your underwear with no idea how you got there. After twenty years of carefully avoiding spending any time in his own head, retirement was going to trap him there until the bitter end. A different sort of cold.

No, he wasn't looking forward to that part at all. But clambering up mountains was - if not a young man's game - definitely not an old man's game. The last couple of climbs had taken their toll. It wasn't so much that his strength was waning, or even his fitness, really. More his power of recovery: it took a lot longer now for the cold of the mountains to seep away from his bones; longer for the energy and the appetite to return. It was time to call it quits.

Still, it was disheartening to end on a low note. In nearly twenty years of taking groups of enthusiastic young climbers across the mountains, he had only been forced to cut a couple of trips short, and on both occasions the decision had been foisted upon him by illness. Not his, but those he led. Darren hadn't suffered anything more than a mild cold in decades. Probably something to do with spending most of his time at altitude, closer to God. Or maybe the big man upstairs figured Darren had suffered enough for one lifetime without adding illness to the list.

This trip was cut short for an entirely different reason. One that sat heavily on Darren's broad shoulders, making them slump more than the searing low temperatures and biting winds ever had.

Fear.

Darren had been away from civilization for three days, leading the team of semi-experienced mountaineers across Mount Snowdon. It was the highest peak in either Wales or England, a vast rocky wilderness that beckoned all the climbers who had experienced everything else the UK had to offer and wanted one last challenge before moving on to bigger peaks on foreign shores.

It was an easy climb. After twenty years of regular visits, it was his climb.

The expedition was meant to last a week: Darren's specialty was preparing climbers for the much longer ascents they would face when the siren song of the Himalayas or the Alps or the Rockies finally wormed its way into their consciousness and put down roots. No serious climber would be happy until they at least attempted one of the world's more formidable ranges. By comparison Snowdon was straightforward, and it had been many years since Darren's expeditions had been troubled by anything more than a little frostbite or the occasional missing piece of equipment.

Until this time.

This time they had lost all communication at the end of day two.

There had been a little freaking out among the members of the group, of course. Most of the twelve people Darren led toward the distant peak presented themselves with the typical bravado that came with not-quite-enough experience, but the sudden death of their mobile phones and the silence of the radio was not quite the same as a vertical climb. Communication was their safety net: the removal of that net brought the vertiginous drops and the jagged rocks into a sharper sort of focus.

It was not the first time Darren had been without communication on the slopes; not the second or third time either. He knew the phones were an illusion: under most circumstances, if climbers needed to call for help it was because they were faced by a danger that probably wouldn't wait for the arrival of rescue. The best thing to do on the climb was forget about whatever you had in your pockets; forget everything that wasn't either your feet or the next foothold.

Maybe it was weather disturbance, maybe some satellite problem. It didn't matter. The phones were down; the rocks were still the same. Debating it when you were clinging to lethal terrain was pointless.

Eventually Darren had snapped, and roared at the group of young men and women to shut the fuck up and watch their footing, or they would end up discovering that mobile reception was far worse at the bottom of a ravine. He hadn't meant it to sound like a threat, but that's the way it came out. It got the job done, though, and a pregnant silence fell on the group until Darren finally called them to a halt.

It was only then, as they had made camp at two thousand feet on a wide plateau that shivered under the first traces of the snow that covered the peak itself, and Darren had sat next to the fire, half-listening to the younger climbers turning over theories about their dead phones that ranged from the mundane to the fantastic, that he noticed something. Or more accurately, the absence of something.

Where are all the planes?

Snowdon was a busy peak, although it didn't seem that way when you were clinging to some stubborn part of it. There were a lot of trails, a lot of climbers, and generally there was a lot of traffic in the skies above. Darren had long since stopped noticing the gleaming cylinders that made their way across the sky from the airports of northern England toward Ireland and the

Atlantic Ocean beyond: they were just background noise to him after twenty years.

But suddenly that noise had been silenced.

When the rest of the group finally retired to their tents, Darren slipped away from the camp to find a perch that offered a panoramic view of the endless night sky. For almost an hour he scanned the blanket of stars that took away the breath of those that travelled to Snowdonia from the light-polluted cities, searching for the tell-tale blinking lights of aircraft. The night was cloudless, and he knew he should have seen several planes in the time he spent watching, but there was nothing. It was as if the flight path had simply ceased to exist.

When Darren returned to his tent, deep in troubled thought, he retrieved the satellite phone from the bottom of his pack. He hadn't ever needed to use it, but the device was faultlessly reliable. He would look like an idiot using it to ask why there were no planes in the sky, but so be it: the crawling sensation in his gut needed to be halted.

The satellite phone was fully charged, and as the dim green grow of the screen illuminated the tent, he thought for a moment that he had been getting worried about nothing, letting the infectious fear of the younger climbers get to him. Only when the phone had been scanning for a connection for a full five minutes without success did Darren's gut finally get its point across to him.

There was something wrong out there beyond the barren wastes of the Snowdonia National Park.

That's when Darren finally gave in and labelled the crawling sensation in his gut; gave it a name and made it real.

Fear.

As much as he had tried to deny it; to lay it squarely at the feet of the inexperienced climbers, fear had him in its clutches, and that could only end badly. There was no place on the slopes for fear.

He made up his mind then to cut the expedition short and get off the mountain. At the time it felt like the safest option; like the sensible way to keep the group safe and healthy.

At the time. But that had been before they packed up camp and left the plateau, heading back the way they had come. Before they followed the winding trail down to the foot of the mountain. Before the bus station.

The *Snowdon Sherpa* was the ostentatiously-named bus that orbited the base of the mountain, making stops at each of the six main routes that wound up toward the peak, and delivering groups of climbers to the remote region from the nearby towns. The stations themselves were small and unremarkable; just squat concrete buildings and small car parks stuck in the wilderness like thumbtacks. Most were staffed by only two or three people; hardy souls who scraped a meagre living from the rocks and cliffs, and looked to have been there almost as long as the mountain itself. It had been years since Darren had paid either the stations or the staff any attention; they simply hadn't warranted it.

The tiny bus station took his full attention the moment the trail he had been following down the mountain brought it into his line of sight. Once he saw it, he could not look at anything else.

Darren made the sign of the cross in the air in front of his chest. It was a gesture he hadn't performed in years, but it was programmed deep into his muscle memory, and his shocked mind ran backwards at the sight laid out before him; all the way back to a time when he had believed in something greater, hoping to find some comfort in the old routine and discovering that there was none.

A single bus stood in the parking area at the front of the station. It wasn't a full-size coach: those were very rare sights around Snowdon. Only a couple of times a year did a large group of climbers make their way from one of the bigger cities to the Welsh mountains.

The bus, a cheerful green machine that looked to have been built in the seventies and had seen the last of its better days in the same decade, seated around twelve people. Darren's party had taken a very similar vehicle from the coastal town of Caernarfon three days earlier. The vehicle stood dormant, with the door at the front, next to the driver's seat, wide open like a silent scream. Yet it was not the bus that held Darren's gaze like a magnet and made his breath catch in his throat. It was the passengers.

What was left of them.

It was impossible to count the bodies; as futile as trying to guess how many animals had been used in the processing of a packet of minced beef. All across the car park around the bus, Darren saw recognisably human parts mixed with frozen streaks of gore that he didn't want to recognise. For just a second the sight of the blood gave life to an ancient memory, one he believed had been buried deep in the monochrome past.

Suddenly he was staring at the broken bodies of the two people that mattered most in the world to him, trying to comprehend that his young family had been alive one moment and fused terribly with the steaming metal of the car the next, and that it was all his fault.

"Darren?"

Lexie. One of the young women he had been leading toward the summit of Mount Snowdon. She stared at the car park in horror.

Lost in his memories, Darren had forgotten the group of climbers was even there. He blinked, tried to keep his lower lip from trembling. Almost managed it. Lexie looked like she was almost scared out of her mind. She suddenly looked very young. No bravado left.

"What do we do?"

There's no wild animal in Wales capable of this, Darren thought. No other damage; this wasn't some accident or explosion.

Darren's mind swam, grasping for an explanation for the carnage that lay only thirty feet away.

Find the next foothold.

He dropped into a crouch, letting the bushes surrounding the bus station block out the sight of the car park.

"People did this," he hissed at the group, raising a warning hand to stop any debate in its tracks. One by one, the group dropped into a crouch beside him. "More than one, to kill a group that large."

He saw something in Lexie's big, frightened eyes snapping.

"They might be gone. They might not. We stick together, okay? We move slow and quiet, and we get to the landline in the station. Once we're inside, we're fine, right? We call the police and barricade the door until help arrives. Stick together."

He put a finger to his lips, and unzipped a pocket, sliding out a sleek multi-tool and releasing the small blade with a faint snap.

You'll only cut yourself with that, you idiot.

Darren silenced the voice in his head. There was no room for doubt. Not now. Even as he looked at the small blade, Darren was dimly aware of a thrill coursing through him. A feeling of excitement - of life - so unfamiliar he almost did not recognise it. The climbing and the rocks had long ago lost their thrill, the edge of danger blunted by experience.

With gritted teeth, he eased himself up and crept forward, twisting his neck with each step to search for a sign of movement.

The station was nestled against a crescent in the road that meandered around the base of the mountain. Darren was approaching from the trail at the rear, passing rocks that obscured most of the building. Each step brought a little more of the place into sight, and with every passing second as he approached the car park to the left of the station, he expected to see something charging toward him. A psychopath with an axe, perhaps, like Jack Nicholson in The Shining, a manic grin and murderous eyes, coming at Darren swinging and shrieking. There was nothing.

When he reached the horror that stained the floor around the bus, his brain wanted not to look, but his eyes just wouldn't co-operate. All around the vehicle, the passengers had died grotesquely, their bodies sundered by some sharp instrument and, worse, some looked to have bite marks, ragged tears in their flesh that exposed muscle and bone. Several looked as if their eyes had been ripped out.

Freezing sweat ran down into the small of Darren's back.

Most of the bodies were clustered in one spot; a couple had died further toward the front of the building.

It's a trail. They were running for the bus.

Needles of fear slowly pierced down into Darren's mind.

Running from what? What would scare so many people?

He stepped past the bus and headed for the main station building, pressing himself against it to provide cover. Darren paused there for a moment to heave in deep, quaking breaths. Just being able to press his back to something made him feel a little less exposed. As the team joined him, he peeked around the corner, taking in the front of the building in a quick snapshot. It looked deserted.

He held up a hand.

Wait.

He listened, imploring his ears to rise above the insistent pounding of his pulse.

What is that noise?

The sound was faint. A sort of soft scraping, like something wet being pulled along metal. He looked quizzically at the team, trying to confirm in their eyes that he wasn't hearing things.

He leant close to Lexie's ear. Smelled a trace of exotic perfume diluted by sweat and dirt and terror.

"Where's that coming from?" He breathed.

Lexie started to shrug, but then her eyes fixed on a point over Darren's right shoulder and widened in horror, and he heard it.

Thump.

Darren turned slowly to face the bus, and the sight of what had dragged itself out through the open door made his blood run cold. They had walked right past it, assuming the vehicle was empty.

His thoughts froze as he tried to understand what his eyes were seeing, and one of the little sayings his wife had been so fond of threw itself up from a pit of long-forgotten memories.

You know what happens when you assume...

A blood-soaked woman was hauling herself toward them using her arms to lever herself forward, dragging herself along the floor.

Both the woman's legs had been severed at mid-thigh height, like some movie assassin had sliced them away with a sword, and her passage left a chunky streak of red-black gore on the cold tarmac. Both her eyes had been ripped out, and one hung uselessly against her stained-red cheek, like it had frozen there, sticking in place.

For just a moment, Darren's mind went completely blank, just for a split second, and he lost his foothold; felt like he was tumbling away into some endless ravine.

"Jesus, get some help, go call an ambulance!"

The words entered his mind slowly; foggily, like he was hearing them through thick walls.

One of the kids he had been leading, one of the ones Darren liked the most - Trevor, a nice sort of guy who would have been more tolerable if he hadn't spent the whole trip trying to win Lexie over with a little-boy-lost act - completely lost his fucking mind and ran to help the woman.

Darren watched in horror as the thing on the floor grabbed his legs and pulled him down, clamping her teeth onto his flailing hand and clenching, tearing away a finger with a sharp snap that cleaved the still morning air in two.

Trevor screamed and tore his arm away, sending an arc of blood across the floor.

And then abruptly the screaming stopped, and Darren could almost swear he heard the kid let out a sigh and then Trevor was tearing his eyes out and snarling and leaping on top of Lexie and the little-boy-lost routine evaporated in a storm of teeth and blood, and Darren was running for the bus station door and all around him there was screaming.

Darren was weak; scared. Certain he was going to die. He ran blindly, like an animal terrified by the shriek and pop of fireworks, smashing his way through the door and into the station. Footsteps followed him inside; he had no idea whether they belonged to the group of excitable kids he was meant to be leading or the hideous monster that Trevor had suddenly become.

There was no time to think about that.

In the gloomy half-light of the bus station, teeth were aimed at him, driving toward him, snapping and tearing.

Darren crumpled backwards, slashing at the eyeless horror wildly with the tiny blade, driving it deep into its neck.

It's not stopping, he thought dully, as the creature pushed its snapping jaws closer to Darren's face, forcing its flesh further onto the blade, apparently oblivious to the grievous injury, immune to the pain as it impaled itself to get to him.

With a roar, Darren flexed his old, weathered muscles, mustering all his strength to keep the mouth of the thing at bay. He couldn't find the energy he needed to throw it away from him, and so he was left there for seconds that felt like hours, feeling the creature's blood pumping steadily across his arm, holding it in place while it died slowly atop him.

Even when the life had pulsed from the thing, its final action was a weak, pathetic snapping of its jaw.

It took a full minute for it to weaken enough that Darren was able to push it away from him.

He screamed the whole time.

When he hauled himself upright, he saw that seven of the kids had made it inside with him. None of them seemed to be injured; all of them were pressed against the door, holding back the relentless attempts of their former friends to get inside the building and kill them.

Darren saw Lexie outside, eyeless and enraged, throwing herself at the glass panel on the door. He heard the splintering of the glass and knew there was to be no barricading themselves in.

The small room was filled with sobs and shrieks. For several long moments Darren simply stared down at the small blade, at the blood which drenched his forearm, and he thought about the lack of planes. The empty skies, and the satellite phone that found no signal, and he shuddered as his nerves blazed like wildfire.

For the first time in twenty years, Darren felt alive. Truly alive. It looked like he wasn't going to be forced into a lonely retirement of gardening and bland quiz shows after all. The world had thrown a curveball, and he would catch it and run.

As the handful of kids pressed themselves against the door and shot terrified looks back toward him, Darren realised they were waiting for him to tell them what to do, and he mumbled a few reassuring words.

And grinned broadly into the gloom as a plan formed.

*

That had all been days ago. Enough time for Darren to lead the mountaineers to safety, as his contract with them had promised. Well, all but one. But that one had been a noble sacrifice. Without the distraction he had provided, how else would Darren have got them all onto the bus and away from the mayhem in the car park?

Enough time for them to realise that the world itself had become a vast mountain, and they needed a guide more than ever.

Enough time for Darren to find the perfect place for them to stay and slowly expand their numbers with fresh blood. Enough time to plot out a future that would require every last one of them to look to *him* before they chose to do anything. Enough time for him to have been responsible for at least ten deaths.

And enough time to discover something extraordinary. Something that would give them a shot at survival, and Darren a shot at being someone far more important than a guy that teenage climbers spent a week with and promptly forgot.

A lot can change in a week.

Not the excitement, though. The thrill of the new world still coursed through Darren's veins like a powerful drug.

And more excitement was headed straight for him, propelled by large white sails and the choppy waves of the Irish Sea.

Darren had been so lost in thought that he jumped when the man with the binoculars appeared at his side.

"Sir, there's six of them," the man said. "They've docked further down the river. Looks like two men, two women. Couple of kids."

Darren nodded. Six was a lot. There was a definite threat of...*dilution.*

Kids, he thought. Children had great value in a world riddled by death.

"Then get ready," he said. "I think we'll let this group inside."

"Yes, Sir."

Sir, Darren thought, and smiled.

2

It looks like they want company.

Those had been Michael Evans' words when he first saw the light that lanced the sky from the stone guts of the castle as they skimmed across the pitch-black water.

John Francis had stared long and hard at the beam of light as he wrestled against the sails and guided the boat from the open sea toward the mouth of the river that funnelled into the town of Caernarfon.

Three fast, three slow, three fast.

John knew what the sequence of flashing lights meant, of course; anyone with even the most rudimentary military training would. He also knew how an *SOS* could be employed as a lure in a trap. That they wanted company was in no doubt. What John needed to know was why. In a warzone, you don't just stumble forward blindly.

He made up his mind before the boat got anywhere near the shore. If he was going to walk into that castle, he would do it on his terms.

"You stay, I go," he said when the boat reached the dock.

John kept his voice low and his tone harsh. He expected a frown from Michael, and he got it.

"We should stick together."

John finished tying the boat off, and played out a few feet of line, letting it drift away from the harbour wall, just far enough that only someone with Olympic prowess would have a chance of jumping anywhere near the hull. He clenched his jaw in frustration.

Of course he wants to argue the point.

"Michael, I hate to be a bastard about this, but I'm not carrying you through a strange fucking town that is probably heaving with psychopaths to find out whether or not the people in that castle mean to do us harm. We need the boat, and if I come back running I want the fucking thing untied and ready to go, right? There's no possible outcome for me that would be helped by being accompanied by two kids, a grandmother and a cripple. No offense."

John hadn't mentioned Rachel. He saw Michael making a mental note of the omission and stifled a sigh. One way or another, Michael absorbed information and found value in it.

Or maybe 'leverage' is more accurate, John thought. He could see why Michael would have been a good cop, back when law and order had been words that meant anything. Somehow Michael Evans had survived the apocalypse despite his paralysis, and had surrounded himself with people willing to go to great lengths to help him. John had seen men he would have considered far better equipped to deal with a world of relentless savagery fall at the first hurdle. Somehow Michael kept clearing them almost effortlessly. Maybe because he wasn't jumping. He was being carried.

"I'll be back," John said flatly and, giving Michael no time to respond, hauled himself onto the rope, wrapping his legs around it and shimmying across toward the harbour wall.

As he made his way across the improvised rope bridge, John let his mind dwell on his own words for a second. He would be back, though as they had made their way up the coast he had again spent half his time considering the best way to ditch the group of people that had become his travelling companions. To let them all follow Michael down whatever path best suited him.

And what's stopping you?

The answer was obvious, though he didn't let it settle in his mind. Didn't want to admit it to himself, he supposed. Forming attachments was only going to weaken him, and the woman had been badly damaged even before the horrific events at the harbour in Aberystwyth; before she watched her last remaining relative get torn apart in front of her.

He reached the wall and carefully swung a foot across, using the strength in his arms to lever himself upright with as little noise as possible. When he was safely on solid ground, he dropped onto his haunches out of habit and his face contorted into a wry grimace. There was little point trying to keep a low profile: the Infected were blind; hunters that used preternatural hearing to track down their prey. Crouching low would have no effect on whether they were going to swarm toward him. And if the people signalling for help in the castle were keeping lookout - as they surely must be - they would likely have seen the boat approaching long before it actually reached land, and they would be expecting company.

John took a moment to study Caernarfon's picturesque waterfront, trying to gather enough data to form a rough map of the place in his head. Their approach by sea had obscured most of the town behind rolling hills that swept away from the ocean toward the foothills of the Welsh mountains.

When the town had finally hovered into view, John had been forced to admit a grudging respect for Michael. Caernarfon had been his idea, and it wasn't half bad. The crippled man was self-serving, but by luck or judgement his decisions had kept them alive.

But not undamaged.

John shook the thought away and reminded himself sternly: *forming attachments* will *weaken you.*

They had approached Caernarfon from the south, skirting up the coast under the vast, cloudless sky. The castle jutted from the landscape like a clenched jaw, with the town at its back. A river that curved inward around the castle made it virtually unapproachable by land, save for the bridge connecting it to the town.

The town on the inland side was huddled close, small buildings leaning over narrow streets that were typical of old Wales; all crooked angles and glowering claustrophobia. Blind corners and hiding spots everywhere. A great place to defend; not so great to enter alone.

Caernarfon's concessions to modernity were daubed across the ancient buildings like paint; chain stores and high-street brands crammed into narrow structures on cobbled streets. John saw a number of shops that sold fashionable clothes and gifts for occasions no one would be celebrating any time soon; mobile phone shops suddenly rendered obsolete. A market, a handful of pubs; a tiny church. The castle dominated them all, towering far above the rooftops of every other building. Eight huge stone towers clustered around a central node behind a wall that had to be at least fifty feet high.

The place looked about as defendable as any John could imagine. Warfare had been set back hundreds of years. The enemy didn't use guns and planes and warheads anymore; it used fingers and teeth. Huge walls were suddenly a tactical necessity, as they once had been. The violence of mankind had come full circle: eventually weaponry had become so advanced that the only place left for it to go was right back to the start, right back to bare fists and blades and slow, agonising death.

With the mountains of Snowdonia at its rear, cutting off land approach from the south and the east, Caernarfon was a town surrounded by natural fortifications. And then there was the castle itself: a building that had died centuries before and become a tourist attraction had been given a shot at a full resurrection.

The place was perfect.

But someone else had taken it first.

John scurried to the cover of the nearest building and searched for the beam in the sky, among the brilliant carpet of stars. After a few seconds he spotted it and reoriented himself.

There was no doubt in John's mind that the approaching boat had been spotted, but he thought it unlikely anyone would have seen him making his way alone onto the harbour. He had the cover of night and dark clothing, and of course the streets were completely dark: the electrical grid serving the UK had wheezed out its final breath hours earlier.

Only if someone had been studying him carefully with binoculars would they know that he was heading for the castle.

It was a recon mission, and it wasn't John's first. He had to know what they were dealing with. But the castle was a few hundred yards away and there was just one way in: across a long, narrow bridge that spanned the river which stabbed deep into the belly of the town. It would be impossible to get very close without being spotted, but that was a puzzle to solve later: for now, the crooked, narrow streets needed to be traversed, and any number of Infected could be lurking in the shadows.

John had a small flashlight in his pocket, but dismissed the notion of using it immediately. He had to retain the element of surprise and conceal his approach. It was his only tactical advantage.

He slipped into the nearest street and out of the castle's line of sight, and then stopped for a moment to survey his surroundings.

A narrow shopping street, pedestrianized. Blood on the cobbles. John felt tension rising and his jaw clenching involuntarily, and he slipped out the larger of the two knives he carried on his belt.

Where are they?

The streets looked deserted; the windows at the front of each store displayed nothing but empty, dark spaces. John had expected the place to be crawling with Infected: he knew from experience that they seemed almost magnetically drawn toward humans. The castle should have been surrounded, yet Caernarfon looked like a ghost town.

Keeping his steps as light as possible, John made his way through crooked alleys in the direction of the castle, slowly arcing around it, ensuring the beam of light stayed to his left. Several times he caught brief glimpses of the bridge. It didn't look like anyone was crossing it to cut him off.

Maybe they really do need help after all, he thought as he turned a corner and entered a small market square.

And then he was stumbling backwards, and the only thing on his mind was the eyeless creature that stood right in front of him.

*

Before the world had collapsed into violence and chaos, Rachel Roberts had been known for her temper. Her friends had laughed about it and pretended to be afraid of her and made her giggle helplessly about it, but the truth was that Rachel's tendency to lose her cool was generally a source of trouble. Throughout her school years her teachers had bemoaned that her focus on doing good work was punctuated by violent altercations, and Rachel's penchant for defending her actions rather than offering humble contrition left them shaking their heads and predicting a troubling future for her.

When she moved from St. Davids to London to find work and her boss had finally had enough of staring at her butt and decided that some things simply *had* to be squeezed, Rachel had responded with a straight right that broke his nose and effectively cleared her desk.

As she had been escorted forcibly from the building her only regret had been not following the straight with an uppercut or, better yet, a solid knee to the groin. It had taken many hours for the red fog in her mind to finally clear and a semblance of calm to return.

In retrospect, that episode had turned out to be little more than a tantrum.

Sitting on the boat, barely even aware of John's absence and the fact that they had reached their destination, rage consumed Rachel, twisting around her gut like fire; writhing and spreading in the shadows of her mind like a malignant tumour.

The loss of Jason had landed like a nailbomb, devastating every part of her. It was the latest shattering blow delivered by the faceless suits that had turned themselves into gods, smiting the land with a flood of insanity and murder.

She had lost everything. Her parents, her brother, her home, her dignity. Her belief. No part of Rachel Roberts had escaped injury at the pitiless hands of the architects of Project Wildfire. They had destroyed everything that mattered to her like bored children plucking the legs from an insect. Because they *could.* Just to see what happened afterwards.

They had to pay.

"Rachel...Rachel?"

I was supposed to protect him.

"Rachel, are you okay? Rach?"

Rachel snapped back into the present and drilled her gaze into Michael. When she spoke, her voice simmered with unrestrained fury.

"Don't call me that. *Never* call me that, understand?"

Michael flinched and nodded. His daughter, Claire, gripped his torso, her eyes widening in fright. The sight of the young girl's fear poured a little water on Rachel's white-hot core, pulling her back from the precipice before she tumbled down into a destructive, all-consuming rage.

"Are you okay?"

"No, Michael."

She didn't want the words to come out drenched in bitterness, but they did. Michael meant well, of course. And it wasn't his fault, although Rachel could tell that John sometimes thought it was, and that they had all followed Michael on a reckless mission that ended up getting Jason killed. Effectively exchanging her brother for Michael's daughter.

But even lost in bottomless anger at the way things had turned out in Aberystwyth, Rachel couldn't find it in herself to blame Michael. He had not forced any of them to help him find Claire; they had all gone willingly. Rachel herself had been dedicated to finding the girl and proving that there was still some hope left in the world.

There was nothing to indicate that if she and Jason hadn't tagged along with Michael that they wouldn't both be dead already anyway because that was how the world worked now. Death lurking around every corner, waiting to pounce. Every step rich with dark opportunity. A multitude of ways for everything to end without warning.

No, it wasn't Michael that Rachel blamed. Wasn't John either, despite his limited involvement with Project Wildfire. She blamed the men who had created the disaster, the same men that caused wars and economic collapses and guided the world recklessly with only their profit in mind. People with power. *Allowed* to have power and to wield it across continents.

In the past, Rachel's only option to strike back at them had been *voting*. A pointless charade that boiled down to choosing between whether you wore a red hat or a blue hat.

Rachel had never bothered with it.

But they hadn't killed her entire family before, and now only one thing mattered: tracking them down, however impossible a task that seemed.

And killing them.

She blinked at the castle that loomed over the town. John and Michael wanted a place to defend; a place to stay and be safe. As the rage boiled away inside her, Rachel no longer thought that would be enough for her.

*

"Please, don't...I know you are there, don't. *Please.*"

John's mind retreated and he froze, stunned.

It's talking.

He raised the knife.

In the small market square, tied to a lamp post, stood a girl of about thirteen. She was shivering with the cold or terror or both. She looked weak; on the verge of collapsing to the cobbles.

Infected.

Her eyes were gone, ripped from their sockets.

The knife shook a little in John's grip.

"I'm not like them, please, I'm-"

Her plea dissolved in a whimper of fear, hysteria ripping a meaningless jumble of noise from her throat. It was an animal sound.

What the fuck...

"Afraid I have to stop you doing that, mate."

A man's voice, deep and clear.

Behind him.

John span around, dropping low, smoothly pulling out the smaller second knife and slipping his grip down to the blade in a single motion, readying the throw that would land at upper chest or neck height.

Someone *had* crossed the bridge, someone who knew a thing or two about staying quiet.

John hated surprises.

A few feet away, stepping out from behind a wall with his arms raised in surrender, John saw a guy of around sixty. He was mostly bald, and had a white beard that still looked vaguely well-trimmed. He was big and looked physically fit. He reminded John a lot of some of the guys that had made their way to the top of the army, just before they reached the age where politics and meetings and sitting at desks took over and bellies began to expand.

John had seen plenty of those guys, the once-active men embittered by age; more dangerous with a pen and a smile than they ever had been with a gun.

"Didn't mean to startle you," the man said, raising his arms higher. "Exact opposite actually, that's why I came alone. But I can't let you do that."

He motioned to John's knife and the shackled girl. "It's important. Vital."

John's eyes narrowed, and he shot a glance around the square, quickly calculating the possibility of more shapes lurking in the shadows. He dismissed the idea. One man might be able to creep up on him, but John couldn't imagine that he would fail to notice himself being *surrounded.*

"There are more of you? How many?"

"Enough," the white-haired man said. "But I don't want it to come to that. We don't need to have trouble here."

John jabbed a knife at the Infected girl tied to the post.

"The fuck is that? You people keep the things as pets? Why does she fucking *talk*?"

The bearded man smiled affably, but John didn't see a hint of it reflected in his eyes.

"It's a long story. I imagine you've got one of your own, right? So get your friends and come in, and we'll trade tales of the apocalypse. What do you say?"

The smile widened, and the man dropped an arm, holding it out for a handshake.

"Darren Oliver," he said. "Welcome to my castle."

3

It was something to do with the blood.

Even that tiny taste of it had sent a surge of power coursing through Jake McIntosh's twisted muscles, lighting up his veins like an electrical storm. Just a few delicious droplets on his tongue. He wanted more. *Craved* it.

It hadn't been like that when he had killed and eaten animals. The blood of the humans was different somehow, like distilled energy that lifted him to a place of endless euphoria; making him feel like a god.

Am I a vampire?

The thought amused Jake, almost made him laugh out loud. The cretins in the underground base had tried to lay waste to humanity with some sort of virus based on a hundred clichéd zombie movies, and had ended up creating a vampire instead. It was just too funny.

Except that he definitely was not a vampire. He could eat a deer or a rabbit and feel the energy and vitality the food provided. Sunlight had no effect on him whatsoever, and Jake had no doubt that silver or holy water or garlic would do nothing to him. Vampires did not exist, just as zombies did not exist. Only humans that had been twisted and remade, driven back to their savage, primal beginnings.

Some side-effect of their tampering with human DNA, then. They had created humans that were driven by a need to taste the blood of their own. Some part of that programming had made its way into...whatever Jake was now.

In the end it didn't matter. The blood was like a powerful drug delivered in its purest form, and he needed more.

Jake had tried drugs, of course. Back when he had been a serial killer rather than a force of nature, he had experimented with any number of ways to increase the delirious high he felt when he tortured and killed the helpless. Ultimately he had discovered that cocaine and ecstasy and crystal meth only served to pollute the purity of the experience. Killing was far less fun when your mind was swathed in a numbing fog. Drugs flattened out all the glorious nuance, and rendered the wondrous process mundane.

He never felt the remotest danger that he might become addicted to any of the drugs he tried. He was already addicted to something far greater. Murder was a delicious elixir. Pure, dizzying power.

The blood was different to the other narcotics, though. As he licked the traces of life from the spine of the man he had killed, he felt a sense of intense acceleration, a powerful rush that felt as if the air itself was trying to drag the cells of his body in a hundred different directions. Everything became wonderfully vivid and the dark landscape around him shimmered, like the world had been daubed in fluorescent paint.

He stood for a moment, drinking the sensation in. He was, he realised suddenly, shaking with pleasure, every muscle twitching in unison as a tsunami of adrenaline surged through him.

In the distance his hyper-attuned senses detected a large group of humans, and he could sense their terror wafting toward him on the breeze, and he very nearly charged forward immediately, throwing caution to the wind in his desire to taste their blood.

Only the memory of the way his energy had drained so suddenly back in the underground prison in which he had been birthed gave him pause. His body was uncharted territory. The thought of blacking out among the humans and leaving himself vulnerable was too much to bear. To die at their hands simply because he could not control his urges would be a terrible waste.

You should proceed with caution, he thought. *There's no need to rush in blindly like the pitiful eyeless creatures that they created to kill themselves.*

He inhaled deeply, a ragged, shuddering breath, trying to calm his racing nerves and clear his mind.

Just another taste...

*

Gillian Harper had been there right at the start. She had been one of the fortunate ones holding a weapon when the infection had walked in the front door at Catterick Garrison a week earlier and laid waste to the remnants of the British Army, felling the once-mighty force before the majority of them even knew there was a battle to be fought.

She'd seen the first bite at close quarters, the utter insanity of it; the way the bitten soldier dropped to the floor for a moment, like a boxer floored by a sucker-punch. She saw the man rise and rip out his eyeballs with a yelp that sounded terrifyingly like *relief* and sink his teeth into the nearest stunned onlooker. Gill was there when the coruscating chain reaction of insanity began; one of the few who truly knew how things had escalated beyond anyone's control in *seconds.*

After that initial moment of shock the fearful images became a smeared memory, a grisly collage of teeth and blood and bullets fired indiscriminately into a wall of bodies that had belonged to her brothers in arms only moments before they were transformed into death made flesh.

She knew of only one other soldier that remembered it all beginning. Just *one.*

Thousands had died.

Her survival was blurry and indistinct. She remembered staggering backwards, expecting that at any moment the rifle would *click* instead of *bang* and her time would be up. She remembered the chopper roaring over her head, the soldiers inside pouring bullets into the crowd from automatic weapons, a fuel tank somewhere going up; the impact of the blast slamming her back onto the ground as she tried to scramble to her feet.

And the thing that had grabbed her while she was down, and the feel of the knife in her hand; Gill remembered *that* part with crystal clarity. She had a feeling she always would.

Death is the only quarantine that can be trusted.

Gill straightened with a weary sigh and a click in her back that sounded like far-off rifle fire. Every muscle complained, more than she had ever experienced on one of the pack marches she had hated so much during basic training, when she had been expected to carry half her bodyweight on her back mile after tedious mile. That had been a breeze compared to her current task: she had spent days carrying and stacking heavy furniture to fashion a rudimentary wall around Catterick.

"Ouch, that sounded painful. Want me to rub it better?"

Gill rolled her eyes toward Neil. Of all the people that might have survived the attack on the garrison, Gill was sort of glad to see Neil when the dust settled. The guy would probably have responded with a feeble quip on discovering his own legs had been blown off.

Most of the people trying to come to terms with life at the garrison after the attack were pitched somewhere between solemnity and total mental collapse. Lame pick-up lines and innuendo at least carried an echo of normality.

Neil's outdated sense of humour had apparently survived the apocalypse, but Gill didn't think it had done so without taking damage. Usually his lewd jokes made her grin despite herself, but she could tell that this time his heart wasn't quite in it; like the script had gone stale. He still winked, but the cheerful mask he wore could not hide the haunted look in his eyes.

Neil hadn't spoken in hours before he delivered the half-hearted quip on autopilot. And Gill had not minded that silence at all. Being alone with her fearful thoughts was bad; constantly turning over doomsday scenarios with other terrified soldiers was far worse, and all anyone had talked about since they fought off the infection was death.

They had been building the wall non-stop for a week, ever since the spread of the virus had finally been stopped, piling the structure higher and reinforcing it with everything they could find that hadn't been nailed down. Three roads led into the centre of the garrison, and they barricaded each with vehicles and furniture and even bodies, walling themselves in. The centre of the tiny town had suddenly become their world.

Only snipers went beyond the wall, sneaking through the parked truck that served as the only gateway into the hastily-remodelled Catterick, and heading out to establish an outer perimeter. They only went because they had to. *Someone* had to. The thought of the Infected appearing without warning on their doorstep again was too terrible for anyone to contemplate.

The snipers had been given orders to engage at will. If they saw movement, they were to stop it forcibly. If they saw *a lot* of movement, they were to get the hell out and warn the remainder of the troops at the garrison.

The remnants of the army were clustered now around two main buildings: Harden Barracks and the medical centre. Thanks to its shape, they all called the ramshackle fortress they had built *The Heart.* Gill wondered if the name had stuck because the place offered them life, or because they all knew that a strike on The Heart would be a killing blow.

"I think we're done here," Gill said, hammering a final nail into a thick piece of wood and testing the result with a shove.

The makeshift wall didn't move. If it came to it, it could be defended. But if the things attacked in large numbers, the wall simply would not matter. It was far from impregnable, and their numbers were not sufficient to cope with a large-scale attack. Either the wall would fall or the bullets would run out. Most likely the former. Much of the protection the wall offered, she suspected, was symbolic. There was precious little hope left in Catterick, so they had been forced to build some.

Gill jumped off the wall and landed heavily on the ground, and when she thought about returning to the others, her spirits continued to fall.

With the exception of the snipers, all of the survivors of the massacre at Catterick were crammed into The Heart; into one sweat drenched, claustrophobic space. The tension in the air was palpable. Gill felt like she was choking on it every time she took a breath. Maybe when it came down to it, The Heart was most aptly named because one day it would stop beating. The place would not need to suffer an attack; it was collapsing from within, weakening as confusion and indecision raged among people that had relied for so long on a defined command structure.

It had not taken long after the guns stopped chattering for the paltry amount of people that were left to divide neatly into two opposing factions; somehow humans found a route to conflict no matter what.

As far as Gill was concerned the factions could be summarised as those who still thought they were an army, and that they should somehow mobilise and get out there to defend the civilian public, and those, like Gill, who *weren't* completely bat-shit crazy.

The army was gone. The public was gone. There was nothing left to protect, no one left to save. Gill knew it. Anyone who had not leapt feet-first into denial knew it. Any chance of continuing to function as they had before the apocalypse walked in had evaporated when the ranking system had collapsed, leaving one man with outdated symbols on his uniform with the chance to fill the resulting power vacuum. One man. The wrong man.

If history had proven anything, it was that when people were terrified and disorganised, they would happily let a monster rule them just to have *someone* prepared to call the shots.

The Heart was proving no different. Being away from the rotting centre and working on the wall was a blessing, no matter how concerned she might have been about what horror might approach from the other side.

Gill was just thinking that it would be nice if she could crawl back to one of the overcrowded dormitories they had set up in the two main buildings and fall into bed without being dragged into some heated debate when the object sailed through the air and landed at her feet with a wet *crunch*.

For a moment she stared at it, stupefied.

A human head. Tossed over the wall.

Like a medieval siege, she thought, and the notion seemed to form slowly in her mind, like all of a sudden she was having trouble thinking. She tried to turn her head, tried to search for some reassurance in Neil's eyes, but for some reason she found that she could not move. And then she felt it: a crawling sensation, like insects had just hatched in her head and were scurrying about. She couldn't recall ever having felt anything like it. Couldn't, in fact, recall that part of her body ever feeling *anything*. Like straining a muscle you weren't aware could be strained.

She opened her mouth to speak, but no sound came out.

Just liquid.

Warm and thick; clogging the back of her throat uncomfortably.

Her vision flicked off, like the plug that powered it had been pulled out abruptly.

Her last thought was not a thought at all. It was a smell, a fragrance that made no sense amidst the stink of blood and death that hung over Catterick. Fresh lavender, just like her mother always used to put all over the house. She was trying to understand that smell, trying to comprehend why she felt like a little girl again, when the muscles in her face began to spasm wildly and death took her.

*

With a shudder of pleasure, Jake pulled his hand out of the woman's head and licked his fingers clean, shivering as the blood set his nerves alight. Her brain had felt *wonderful*. Moist, and firm. *Fresh.* He had enjoyed the tender caress before the squeeze.

Almost as much as he enjoyed the look on the man's face as he watched Jake killing her, the sheer unadulterated *awe* of it; the distilled terror.

He enjoyed it so much that he didn't kill the man.

At least, not right away. There was no one there to see Jake and alert the other creatures hiding away in their pathetic compound. He needed to taste the man's fear-soaked blood; needed it like his deformed lungs needed oxygen.

But there was always time for fun, so he ripped out the man's tongue to silence his whimpering and then tried his hand at *skinning*. He had never skinned anything before, and he did a far from perfect job, but it was definitely *fun*. All the better for the fact that the man lived through it, gurgling like a baby.

When Jake finally tore off the man's head, he drank deeply, until his mind span, making him feel giddy.

When he was done, the urge to press on, to simply charge into the mass of creatures he felt milling around in the near distance, was almost impossible to resist. Jake had always had severe problems with delaying gratification. It was, he would freely admit, the only flaw in his character. Yet for the first time in as long as he could remember, he managed to suppress his desire to rush forward and begin killing.

This was clearly a military installation of some kind. They would be armed, and already he felt a slight twinge of fatigue as the unnatural movement of his muscles took their toll. It was taking him a long time to adjust to the rhythms of his new body: the extraordinary, explosive bursts of energy he was capable of came at a price. Like a cheetah, his fuel tank emptied quickly and left him vulnerable.

There was no point in rushing things. Better to pick them off slowly, better to enjoy the hunt as he always had even before the scientists in the underground base had turned his body into a glorious weapon.

There was much more fun to be had in terrorising the army garrison. Now that he was closer to them, he could taste the bitterness of their terror on every breath. They were scared of the Infected, even though Jake could tell there were none for miles around. The humans' fear was outdated. When Jake revealed himself their terror would multiply exponentially. An intoxicating shudder of anticipation rippled through him, right down there in the twisted DNA, and it felt almost as good as ingesting their blood.

He took the bodies of the two soldiers he had killed and arranged them precisely, and wondered how the terror among the soldiers might taste when they stumbled across his work and realised that the Infected - shambling, mindless critters that they were - were now the least of their problems.

When he was done, Jake strolled away from the place, congratulating himself on his admirable restraint. As he headed out into the dark, empty fields he tried to affect a cheerful whistle, but the noise that his deformed lips allowed out was more like a distant tuneless shriek.

He kind of liked it.

4

Welcome to my castle.

The words echoed and reverberated in John's head as he left the market and the Infected girl. Darren had offered assistance, smiling warmly as he said he could spare a couple of his men to help John and his friends carry their supplies up from the harbour. John had politely declined, even as the alarm bells rang in his mind.

My castle. My men.

John knew a threat when he heard one. He had heard plenty, and the worst ones were always delivered with a smile. The bizarre meeting with Darren had merely amplified the disquiet he had felt on approaching the castle. Something in Darren's eyes reminded John of the man that had led him into St. Davids. Jeff had been obsessed with structure and leadership. He had also worn a look of unhinged insanity in his eyes the minute the shit began to hit the fan.

Some men, John knew, were not born to lead others though of course that did not stop them. The military had been rife with men promoted solely because of their experience, with little consideration given to whether they might, in fact, be raving lunatics.

If finding an Infected girl tied up in the market like some grisly totem to ward off passersby had not quite been enough to persuade John that Caernarfon was bad news, Darren's smile and cold gaze had finished the job. The castle was trouble. Every fibre of John's being knew it instinctively.

As he wound his way back through the narrow streets, he wondered how he was going to break the news to the others that he thought they should turn the boat around and get as far away from Caernarfon as possible. His heart sank as he thought about Michael. Convincing him was not going to be easy.

As he thought about the crippled man, John noticed a small care home for the elderly nestled alongside a small square park, and he headed for it, hoping he might find a wheelchair for Michael, and trying to persuade himself that he was not going to use it to try to bribe the man into agreeing that they should move on. Either way, John would be damned if he was going to carry Michael around on his back as Jason had.

When he reached the building, he tried the door and found it swung open easily. He slipped inside, nerves racing, and pulled the small flashlight from a pocket, piercing the darkness with the narrow beam.

He saw the blood immediately, a vast pool of it that had leaked from the sad body of an old woman who had probably been waiting to die peacefully before someone came along and ruined that by ripping her throat out. John played the flashlight over her corpse for a moment. She still had her eyes. She had died human.

He crept forward and found two more bodies in a large communal room to the right. One of them appeared entirely unmarked, and it took John a moment to realise that the old guy had probably died of a heart attack when he saw the world descend into madness.

You got lucky, old feller, John thought. The woman who had died in the same room had not been so fortunate. Her guts had been ripped open, and a long slippery string of intestine sat across her lap. He wondered if the old guy had sat and watched his friend being shredded as his heart began to explode in his chest, and John knew the truth when he saw what the old man was sitting on. A wheelchair. He must have been powerless to move, doomed to sit and watch the horror up close. Wondering whether the explosive pain in his chest or the virus would kill him first.

"Sorry about this," John muttered, and he grabbed the lapels of the old man's jacket and shoved the corpse to the floor with a dull thud.

For a moment John paused to listen intently as the noise of the body hitting the floor reverberated through the silence. He expected to hear snarling and the thunderous approach of feet, but there was only deathly quiet.

It was somehow almost more disconcerting. How could Caernarfon be free of the Infected? Clearly they had been there. Where had they gone?

The question weighed heavily on John's mind as he pushed the wheelchair out onto the cobbled streets and made his way toward the dock. When he reached the rope tied to the harbour wall, he set the wheelchair aside and put all his strength into pulling the boat towards him.

Michael looked at him quizzically, as though he had expected to see John return with a horde of Infected at his back.

"We can't stay here," John said.

Michael's brow furrowed.

"Why?"

"Look, Michael, I want you to trust me on this. There are people in that castle. They don't need our help. I spoke to the guy running the show. He's a bad guy, Michael. I know it. They've got an Infected girl tied up in the town centre like a warning sign. We need to turn the boat around and get out of here. We need to find somewhere else."

"What about the Infected?" Michael said. "They've got one tied up outside the castle? Where are all the others?"

John shrugged.

"I didn't see a single one, other than her."

"That makes no sense," Michael said. "The virus didn't make it here?"

"Oh, it made it here alright," John muttered. "There's blood and bodies everywhere. It's just like Aberystwyth. Crashed cars, smashed windows. Plenty of places look like they've been burned."

Michael frowned.

"But there are none here now?"

John knew exactly where the conversation was going from Michael's tone, and he felt his spirits drop.

"No," John said. "But-"

"But you want us to leave so we can find somewhere that there *are* Infected?"

John sighed.

"John," Michael said. "I get it. You think this place is weird. You don't trust the people inside. Believe me, I don't either. Hell, I don't even trust you."

John looked up sharply, and Michael held his hands up in apology.

"I'm sorry, but I don't. I don't trust anyone. How could I? How could any of us - you included? But we have children here. We're exhausted. Injured. We have almost nothing in the way of supplies. Where else are we going to run to? Wherever we go, they will find us, and they will kill us. For whatever reason, all we have to deal with here is these people, who may or may not do us harm. I think at this point, I'd like to take the element of doubt over certain death."

John rubbed his forehead, his expression pained.

"We have a gun, John," Michael said in a low whisper. "We can hide it from them, make ourselves look helpless. That should be pretty easy, really. Just look at us. But if it comes to it, we can defend ourselves against people. I don't think our luck is going to hold up out there much longer."

He waved a hand at the dark countryside beyond the town.

"Do you?"

John stared at Michael for several long seconds.

Just go, John, he thought. *If they want to stay, let them. Take the boat, and get the fuck away. You don't need to deal with this.*

Torn by indecision, John stared at their expectant faces. A helpless cripple, an old woman, two kids.

Can you really leave them to fend for themselves?

John knew the answer immediately, knew it just as he had known that when it came down to a choice between himself and the other men that had landed with him in

St. Davids, there had been no decision to make. Jeff had died so that John could live. Michael and his ragtag group were no different.

But then John's gaze fell on Rachel, sitting quietly at the back of the boat, her furious eyes burning a hole in the deck.

Fuck.

*

They slipped the rifle into one of the rucksacks they had managed to cling onto during their panicked flight from Aberystwyth. The weapon was too large, and the barrel protruded from the bag, but when John placed it on Michael's lap as he sat in the wheelchair, Michael contorted to hide it from sight. It would do.

"Don't worry," Michael said with a smile. "No one is going to feel threatened by the guy in the wheelchair."

John nodded, and his eyes narrowed a little. Michael had already caught John flat-footed once by portraying himself as a harmless victim. He suspected the trick would work again on the people in the castle, but he could not help wondering if it might work again on himself. Was Michael manipulating him, even now?

"Okay," John said, raising his voice a little for them all to hear. "This place doesn't feel right. Everyone stick together. Stay close. We go in, we thank them for taking us in, and we tell them we need to rest somewhere on our own, right? Don't let them separate us, no matter what. Agreed?"

For once, Michael simply nodded.

When they reached the huge door that barred the castle's main entrance, the heavy wood swung open to meet them, and John could not help but feel like he was stepping into the jaws of some monstrous, malevolent beast.

Darren was waiting for them with wide arms and a wider smile.

"Welcome," he said warmly. "I'm glad you decided to join us."

John stared around the castle with interest. He saw a couple of large fires, and small groups of people sitting in the glow of the flames to keep warm. Only a couple of them bothered to look up to study the new arrivals. None seemed to be speaking.

John's jaw clenched. Everything about the castle and the people inside seemed...*off* somehow. Under the circumstances, how could the people inside be anything *but* intrigued to see who was walking in the front door?

"As you can see, we have fires if you'd like to warm yourselves up, and there's food and water-"

"Where are all the Infected?" Pete blurted out.

John smirked. The kid hadn't spoken much since they left Aberystwyth, but clearly he could not keep a lid on the question that everyone else was trying not to ask any longer. *Good lad,* he thought.

Darren waved a dismissive hand.

"No Infected left here," he said almost breezily. "Caernarfon had been hit when we arrived, but mostly they seemed to have moved on. So we took the castle, and we haven't been bothered since. It's safe here."

He smiled.

Bullshit. John knew the smell all too well. He had been steeped in it his entire life.

"You haven't had any come to you, not even a few?" Michael said, his tone dubious. "Not even with that thing running?"

Michael pointed to the generator that provided power to the spotlight in the centre of the castle's wide, open interior. The same one that had shot the distress signal up into the sky. It chugged away like an idling truck with an ancient engine that badly needed servicing.

Darren shrugged.

"Like I said, we haven't been bothered. Not for days."

John remembered the way the Infected had pursued him through dense forest, the way they had come streaming from the trees when they had heard the chopper engine as his team landed in a field outside St. Davids. The creatures possessed extraordinary hearing, and the generator was loud enough that voices had to be raised to be heard above it. It should have acted as a beacon to the Infected for miles around.

John caught Michael glancing at Gwyneth and saw the old woman shake her head slightly in response.

John grimaced. He did not believe any of Gwyneth's story about being able to sense the presence of the Infected after she herself had been bitten. *Couldn't* believe it. But he had been very clear to warn them not to bring it up in front of Darren as they approached the castle. There was no way to predict how the man or his strange group of followers might react, but John had spent a lifetime watching people kill each other over things that they perceived as valuable. If Gwyneth *could* do what she claimed, or even if others simply believed she could, she would be in jeopardy.

They all would.

He glared at Michael.

Michael pressed his lips together, catching the warning.

"Okay, Darren, thank you so much for taking us in," John said. "We've had quite a journey. Is there somewhere we can sleep?"

"Of course," Darren said with a benevolent smile. "There are plenty of rooms in each of the towers, we can-"

"Just one will do," John interrupted. "We'd like to stay together. We're all family. You understand."

John's tone left no room for further questions.

Darren's eyes narrowed, just a little, and John thought he could read in the man's gaze that he knew bullshit when he smelled it too.

"I completely understand," Darren said amiably. He pointed to a tower at the southern end of the castle. "That one's empty, you'll have plenty of space in there."

"Thanks, Darren," Michael said. "We'll talk in the morning, okay?"

Darren smiled, and nodded. He strode away without another word.

*

Michael wheeled himself into the tower with a wariness that was beginning to feel like second nature.

The tower was cold and bare, but it seemed uninhabited as Darren had promised, and as he made his way inside, just being surrounded by the thick stone wall made Michael feel safer than he had at any point since driving to a café for bacon and eggs and finding a bloodbath instead.

A winding stone staircase led up. Michael figured there might be as many as six or seven levels to the tower, and he was grateful that no one seemed to even consider suggesting that they should ascend. The castle had been built a long time before wheelchair access had become a law, and though some concessions had clearly been made when the place had become a tourist attraction, getting wheelchair-bound people to the top of the towers had obviously been a step too far.

John shut the heavy wooden door behind them as they entered the large circular space. The others made for the wall opposite the door without speaking, sitting with their backs against it, facing the entrance.

Even now, Michael thought, *we're putting ourselves in the safest place, burrowing deep. Getting as far away from the entrance as possible.* It had not taken long to condition human beings to think like hunted animals.

Michael watched as John stood for a moment at the door, listening intently, before apparently satisfying himself that Darren was not lurking outside listening to them.

"What's on your mind, John?"

John left the door and slumped against the wall alongside Gwyneth. Michael saw him cast a glance at

Rachel, whose silence was obviously worrying him as much as it did Michael.

"Two things," John said softly. "One: this place is perfect. Two: at least, it would be if *they* weren't here."

Michael nodded.

"How many of them are there, you think?"

John's eyes lifted to the ceiling as he counted the memories.

Rachel beat him to it.

"I counted twenty-three," she said flatly, and the two men blinked in surprise.

"You don't need to worry," Rachel said bitterly. "I know what you're all thinking. But I'm not Jason. I'm not...broken. I'm *angry.* And the subject you two are skirting around is that the guy out there is trying just a little too fucking hard to appear friendly. I've seen that fake smile before."

She shuddered. Didn't need to say the name.

"They're afraid of him," Pete said suddenly.

They all stared at the boy.

"You can see it in their faces," Pete continued. "They all look at the floor when he looks at them."

Michael clapped a hand on Pete's narrow shoulder and smiled at him. He had feared that the whole group had been damaged psychologically by the events of the day, but putting a stone wall around them was gradually encouraging them to open up. Pete had a habit of vocalising what everybody else was thinking but seemed unwilling to say.

"Kid's right," John said, and Pete beamed. "He's got some hold over these people. They're here because it's safe, but they are still afraid."

"The question is," Michael said, "afraid of *what?*"

"Not the Infected," John said, and rolled his eyes when Michael looked at Gwyneth.

"Gwyneth, can you...uh...feel them out there?" Michael said.

John sighed loudly.

"I can't feel anything at all," Gwyneth said. "I think Darren was telling the truth. If they are out there, they must be a long way off."

Michael felt his shoulders slump. Every time he thought he was getting a grip on the world, something happened to rip it away again and plunge him back into confusion. He knew that John did not believe in Gwyneth's proclamation that getting bitten had imbued her with some sort of second sight, but after everything Michael had seen, he was not willing to rule anything out.

Back at the farmhouse, when they had watched a small army of Infected marching past the windows, they had all got the impression that they were communicating with each other. It wasn't beyond the realms of possibility that they could sense each other, just as some animals could sense the presence of others, or the onset of a storm. And if they could, maybe Gwyneth could too.

One thing was certain: Gwyneth believed it.

Maybe you just want to believe it, Michael thought, *because then Gwyneth will be like an early warning system, and God knows you need something like that.*

"On the boat, you said you felt something else out there," Michael said. "Something different."

"Something worse," Gwyneth said in a low voice. She looked at the children, and Michael realised the conversation was likely to be scaring them. He should have realised it sooner. But he had to know.

"Can you still feel it?"

Gwyneth shook her head vigorously.

"Not since the boat."

Michael rubbed his aching temples, and realised suddenly just how tired he felt. It wasn't just the constant fear or the seemingly endless pursuit of the Infected. His mind was weary of the constant attempts to make sense of a world that he was beginning to believe could not be understood.

He nodded, and let silence fall over the group. After a few moments his eyes closed slowly, and as sleep took him he thought that everything would make more sense in the morning, but he knew deep down that he was lying to himself.

*

In the end, John was surprised that Gwyneth remained awake as sleep took the others. The kids had fallen asleep early, and Rachel had waved away the attempts John and Michael made to engage her in further conversation. *Not now,* her shake of the head seemed to say, and both men were content to leave her alone. In truth, John thought, he didn't know what to say to Rachel. *Keep your chin up* just wouldn't cut it.

Eventually they realised that she had dozed off, and they lowered their voices.

Even Michael did not seem to be up for talking much, and John could not blame him really. The fact was that there was only one subject that needed discussing, and it was the one they needed a break from. They seemed to have spent every spare moment speculating about the virus, or contemplating which angle of attack death would take when it next came at them. Just thinking that way got wearing. John knew that well enough from his years spent in the desert.

But that had been a different sort of dread. At least there the enemy was something that he could comprehend. Every time he felt like he was getting to grips with the death rattle of British civilization, a new horror coughed itself up to take him by surprise.

Not always a horror, either, he thought as he looked at Rachel, who even in sleep wore a troubled frown. *Surprises around every corner.*

"How are you holding up, dear?"

John felt his jaw slacken a little. He had thought Gwyneth had fallen asleep. She had looked the most exhausted of all of them.

"Uh, I'm fine."

"Pfft."

The wrinkles on the old woman's face deepened as she smiled.

"You're troubled."

John gave a shrug.

"Aren't we all?"

"Not just by...the world. By me."

John arched an eyebrow in surprise. Apparently Gwyneth could read minds now too.

"By what I can do. By my...ability."

She smiled again.

"You should have a little faith."

John sighed; kept his voice low.

"Look," he said. "I don't want you to take this the wrong way. You seem like a nice person, but I don't believe in ghosts. Don't believe in magic. I don't believe in mind-reading or psychics or any of that bullshit. Asking me to believe that you can somehow sense the things out there, or see them in your mind, or whatever, is like asking me to believe in Father Christmas."

John shrugged.

"For all I know you're just a crazy old woman," - she smiled at that - "and maybe you were crazy long before any of this happened. It doesn't matter. What matters is that you have been bitten, and you haven't changed."

Gwyneth opened her mouth and John held up a hand.

"What I mean is you haven't turned into one of *them*. That changes everything. That's not *meant* to happen. None of this has anything to do with special powers or magic or fate or *God*. Man did this. It was designed and planned and executed by very powerful people. By *the* very powerful people. This isn't what *they* intended. *Faith* has nothing to do with this, just people with a plan they couldn't carry out. Maybe you believe in all the other stuff. I don't."

Gwyneth chuckled softly.

"That's all very interesting, John, but I didn't mean faith in *God*. I meant faith *in me*. In the people around you. You can believe in anything you want, but if you're not going to believe in the people around you, I don't think you'll go too far. And even if you do, what would be the point of the journey?"

John stared; he had no answer.

"My Steve was a soldier, just like you."

This time it was John's turn to get a pre-emptive *shush*.

"I know, I know; the company line is you were a *driver*."

Gwyneth rolled her eyes.

"But I know a soldier when I see one. Steve was a soldier for thirty years. How often do you think he *believed* in what he fought for? You don't have to believe - in my ability or anything else for that matter. But you have to fight. And that will be a lot harder if you choose to do it alone."

John could not come up with a response to that.

"Glad we got that sorted out," she said with a wink. "Wondering when you were going to skip out on us was getting tiresome."

It took a moment for her words to sink in, and by the time John had opened his mouth to protest, Gwyneth had laid herself flat, turning away from him.

John could almost swear he saw her bony shoulders shake a little as she chuckled to herself in the darkness.

After a moment, he settled back onto the floor, certain that there was no chance he could possibly sleep, and then exhaustion overwhelmed him.

*

Darren stood in the warmth of one of the castle's two large fires for a long time after everyone else had departed for bed, staring at the tower that the newcomers had taken through eyes that narrowed in suspicion.

Family, he thought, and his lip curled in a sneer. The man with the knives was selling lies, and Darren wasn't buying. He seriously doubted whether any of the group of people that had just entered the castle was related. Maybe the little girl that clung like a limpet to the guy in the wheelchair, but the others?

No chance.

Most of the people that Darren had allowed into the castle thus far were weak; broken by the savagery of the world long before they found their way to the safety he offered, and Darren had fallen into the task of leading them easily. Much more easily than he had expected in fact. He suspected that most of them longed to have someone to tell them what to do. People, it turned out, would choose almost anything over helplessness and confusion. Even tyranny was preferable.

Of course it helped that he had muscle backing him: a group of young men that followed him without question, men whose loyalty he had secured through a combination of fear and their own complicity in Darren's sacrificing one of their friends so that they might escape the bus station where it all began.

Few things could hold a man's tongue as firmly as guilt. Darren knew that only too well. It was guilt that had driven him away from society decades earlier; guilt that condemned him to eke out a living in the mountains, where few ever asked him about anything at all, let alone whether he might have a wife and child somewhere. The mountains were a place to forget.

Once the six people that had escaped the bus station with him had made their way into Caernarfon and saw the astonishing bloodshed, Darren knew for sure that the world had gone. Or maybe he had died and finally gone to hell; it didn't really matter. As they stumbled through the narrow streets, Darren had not realised that he was leading them to the castle until they stood right in front of it, and only then did he see a foothold, and a way to keep climbing.

When they had secured the castle, Darren only allowed in those that he could see would be no trouble. There had been a few murmurs of dissent at first; pleas for an open border policy that Darren knew would result in chaos and power struggles. The protests finally died out when Darren had suggested that any one of the young mountaineers could leave if they wished and fend for themselves outside the walls. It had been as simple as that: staking a claim to leadership and seeing who baulked at it. None had been willing to meet the challenge he threw down.

After that, once Darren had set up the light to draw in survivors from the lands around the castle, he had turned several away if he saw that they were armed or if they looked remotely hostile, aiming weapons at them from the battlements until they decided to try their luck elsewhere.

Only once in the week that they had occupied the castle had Darren truly felt like their position might be under threat, when a large group that reeked of trouble had pounded at the gates insistently until Darren himself had taken the shotgun and blown a hole through one of them to show everybody that he meant business.

The other group had departed then, spitting and cursing and hurling threats about coming back for Darren, but he hadn't been unduly worried. The castle was all but impregnable, unless someone turned up with explosives. Even then, Darren had a plan that would ensure that nobody would take his castle away from him.

That first genuine *murder* had turned out to be the moment when everyone in the castle understood that Darren meant every word he said. He had not been questioned since.

But the guy with the knives made Darren's skin crawl. The manner in which he had moved when Darren first approached him; the smooth way he had lined up the knife to throw at Darren. The guy was trained. Military, maybe. That would have made him the most useful of all, if Darren believed that he could be trusted, but there was evasion in his eyes; defiance and threat. Darren couldn't abide threat. Not *within* his castle.

Darren thought he could find a use for the rest of them; the young woman and the children especially, but that one? John? Letting him inside the walls felt like a mistake, and Darren knew he could not afford mistakes.

John had to go.

5

Rachel awoke first and grunted softly as she stretched out limbs that had seized up in protest at yet another night spent on a hard floor. Cold seemed to have seeped into her bones and spread outwards like an ink stain, until every cell felt as if it had frozen solid.

Castles, it turned out, had been cold places in which to live. If she was to spend another night in one, she would insist that the large stone fireplace that dominated the oval room at the base of the tower be used for something other than decoration.

A bed would be nice, of course, but it seemed like beds had gone the way of electricity and safety and sanity.

And Jason.

The loss of Jason ached like a fracture, and the more she thought about her baby brother, and how ill-equipped he had been to deal with the way the world was now despite his hulking physique, she felt a magnetic sort of sadness settle on her, and drag her down toward a deep depression.

There was no room for that in the world now, and Rachel knew it. Knew that Jason had died to protect her, and that if she let herself fade away into self-pity she would turn that gift into something toxic.

She stood, shaking away the pain of the uncomfortable night's sleep, and looked around the rest of them, still soundly asleep and some distance away from waking up to the same bone-deep ache she had encountered.

She glanced at the door, and for a moment she stood, debating with herself.

John and Michael would insist that she stay in the tower, obviously. That she wait until they were awake before she ventured outside. So that they could keep her safe.

They hadn't done a great job of that so far, she thought bitterly, and then admonished herself. They had tried: both had done their best, but the situation was beyond anyone's control.

And besides, since when did you sit around waiting for a man to protect you, Rach? Who protected you from Victor?

The voice in her head sounded a lot like Jason, and her eyes shimmered with heavy tears.

Rachel pressed her lips together firmly and pushed the door open, stepping out into the cold morning.

Most of the castle was open to the elements. Only the towers provided any shelter from the weather. The rest of the building's huge footprint consisted of manicured gardens and the occasional ancient piece of machinery that had been part of the building's life when it had been a tourist attraction, displayed for people to marvel at, back when humanity had time for such trivialities.

Barely more than a week ago.

The whole place was wrapped in a thick stone wall, into which were set heavy doors that led to tiny rooms that Rachel surmised must have served as cells once; and bare stone steps that led up to the battlements.

The castle was a hive of activity: several women were in the process of tearing out the flower beds and planting what Rachel presumed were vegetables. Others were tending to a large pot that sat over a fire. A handful of men were struggling with wooden beams, putting together the skeleton of what would be a large wooden building that would take up around half the courtyard once built.

Rachel gathered her thin jacket about her and shivered, though she could not be sure whether that was due to the cold, or the finality of the work she saw being undertaken around her. The people in the castle were building a community that they obviously believed would have to stand for a considerable period of time.

She hadn't had much opportunity to think about the future: the hours since she first stumbled across the virus, hosted in the once-friendly body of her family's pet dog, had been spent running for her life, or being tortured, or killing.

The battle with Sniffer seemed a lifetime ago; like it had happened to a different person. That much was true, Rachel thought glumly. She certainly didn't feel anything like the Rachel Roberts who had had stepped off the train at St. Davids worrying about how her parents might react to her losing another job.

"Sleep well?"

Rachel jumped a little. She hadn't seen Darren sidling up beside her.

She ignored the question, and wondered briefly if she would ever have a use for small talk again. If the world would, come to think of it.

"Looks like you're preparing the place for a long stay," she said.

Darren nodded, his expression sombre.

"You could say that. I don't really know what happened, but it's been over a week. If there were people out there, government or army or whatever, I'd say we'd have seen them by now."

Rachel dropped her eyes to the floor.

So it is the same everywhere. Of course, she had known it must be. But there was a difference between knowing something, and *seeing* it.

"Did you see it happen, how it all started?" Darren said, and the eager look on his face made something in Rachel squirm.

"I didn't *see* anything," she said bluntly. "There was nothing *to* see. Just normality one minute and chaos the next. I've seen *that.* Over and over again."

"I don't even know when it started, really, other than what I've been told," Darren said almost wistfully. "I was in the mountains. Everywhere was...like this when I came back down."

"You're lucky."

Ah, there it was. Just as the word *lucky* reached his ears, a crack in the friendly façade. She saw Darren's eyes narrow a little, just enough to tell her that whatever the man might say, he'd *seen* plenty too.

"Lucky," he repeated flatly, as if the word was somehow unfamiliar to him.

"To have found the castle," Rachel said, and without another word she turned, and strode back into the tower.

*

"I've got no time for *liars,*" Rachel hissed.

When she had returned to the tower, Michael was already awake. The others looked to be slowly circling consciousness, approaching it reluctantly. Rachel didn't blame them for that.

Michael shot a glance at the door as she spoke.

"Keep your voice down," he whispered. "So the guy doesn't want to talk about it. Do you? I know I don't. If he wanted to harm us he would have done it already. We wouldn't be able to stop him. They outnumber us, and that's before you take the fact that only two of us could actually fight into the equation. If he was going to do anything, it would have been last night, wouldn't it?"

Count to ten, Rach.

Rachel breathed deeply.

"He can't be trusted, Michael. You do see that?"

Michael sighed, and glanced at Claire. Still asleep.

"I see it, Rachel. Of course I see it. He's hiding something from us, big deal. So did John. So have...a lot of people. Nobody trusts *anybody* and I don't blame them. When whatever that guy is hiding becomes a danger to me or Claire...or any of you, I'll do something about. Right now his act seems a lot less dangerous than being out there with *them*. The best we can do is wait and see, okay?"

"I wasn't asking for your help or your *permission* to do anything, Michael, and the next time you condescend to me..."

Michael flinched at the unbridled aggression in her tone, and Rachel caught herself, just before the rage took over.

She breathed deeply again; letting the air out slowly, allowing it to leak from her lungs. Her heart was hammering. She looked away from Michael and locked eyes with Gwyneth. The old woman looked exhausted, like she had spent the night battling demons. She had problems of her own.

We all do, Rachel thought, and felt the fire that had erupted in her nerves slowly being extinguished.

"Fine," she said, and rose to her feet. "But I'm watching him, and you should too. Everybody should. I'm going to find something to eat."

With that, Rachel turned and marched out of the tower, slamming the heavy wooden door behind her.

It was only as she left the tower and followed her nose to the fire and pots of something that smelled delicious cooking over the flames that Rachel's temper cooled enough to allow Michael's words to sink in.

I'll do something about it, Michael had said.

I'll.

Rachel stalked toward the fire, lost in thought.

She slumped down heavily next to the flames, and a young woman stirring a large pot of what looked like vegetable soup.

The woman looked about the same age as Rachel. In another time they might have made small talk about the weather, or fashion, or whatever topic was dominating the news. Probably they wouldn't have talked at all.

But the world had changed.

"Is it safe here?" Rachel asked bluntly.

The young woman dropped her eyes to the pot, and Rachel knew even before she opened her mouth. Even before she whispered the words.

"Please help us."

*

"Please help us," Michael repeated. "What do you think she meant?"

Rachel's brow furrowed. Once again she had returned to the tower, and once again Michael was frustrating the hell out of her.

"Isn't it obvious? Have you actually *looked* at the people here, Michael?"

Michael glared at her.

"Of course, and what about them?"

"There are twenty three that I've seen. Seven men. A couple of them just young boys. Sixteen women. Most of them young, all of them scared to death. Nothing about that strikes you as a little odd?"

To her right, Rachel saw John's jaw clench.

At least John sees it.

"When she said 'us', she meant the women. Please help the women."

Michael's gaze dropped to his useless legs.

"You're sure?"

Rachel crossed her arms and glared at him.

Michael's head dropped.

"Christ," he said.

"Most of the men are carrying weapons," Rachel said grimly. "They've all got blades on their belts. I haven't seen any guns. I haven't seen a woman carrying a weapon of any kind."

She shrugged, and the gesture was clear.

You do the math.

"If anyone here has a gun, it will be Darren," John said. "And if Rachel's right, he's got himself a group of people loyal to him, and they are controlling the rest. And she *is* right, Michael, the make-up of the place is all wrong. Like it or not, men are generally stronger and faster. When the shit hit the fan, it's more likely that a greater number of men would have been able to fight off the Infected. This is more like...I don't know, they've been drawing people in here with that light, and they're only keeping the women."

Michael nodded glumly as he saw Rachel's expression darken. He knew exactly what she was thinking. *Victor.*

"So I guess the question is what are they doing with the men?" Michael said.

"And the women," Rachel snapped hotly.

John nodded.

"That's one question. And it's an important one," he added hastily when he saw Rachel's head whip sharply toward him. "But the biggest question of all, Michael, is *where the fuck are the Infected?* And since we're in the mood for questions, why do these people have one tied up in the town centre...and why the hell does it *talk*?"

Michael massaged his temples. He had only been awake a few minutes, and already he wished he could crawl back into oblivion.

Before he could respond, the door swung open, making them all jump. A young woman, barely older than a teenager, stood in the doorway and regarded them all with barren, empty eyes ringed by dark circles. She looked like she had been crying. Looked, in fact, like she had cried until she had no tears left.

"Darren would like to see you now," she said, and her tone, flattened to a whisper by fear and damage, reminded Michael of the way Rachel had sounded in Victor's bunker, and made his blood run cold.

6

When dawn broke over Catterick, bullet-grey light and freezing wind chasing away the shadow of the night, it was only a matter of time before the screaming started.

Nick Hurt was a first year Lieutenant. Or perhaps *had been* a first year Lieutenant was more accurate. What he was now, he wasn't quite sure. Other than shit-his-pants terrified, of course. But in some ways that was nothing new. The army had terrified him long before its members began to eat each other.

Typically, *Lieutenant* was a position held for about three years before promotion to Captain was considered. It was a chance to lead a platoon of thirty-odd soldiers, and to get some command experience before taking on bigger tasks.

To an outsider at least, Nick had made a promising start to his career as an officer; his uniform had barely been emblazoned with his current rank before his superiors started dropping hints about what a fine Captain he would make. It helped that he came from a fighting family: his father had been a Lieutenant-Colonel, his uncle a Major. Both had trained at Catterick, and the Hurt name became a legacy that game him a powerful boost of goodwill, and meant the many mistakes he made along the way were overlooked.

His family had served with distinction in conflicts across Eastern Europe and the Middle East. His father had led a force of over six hundred heroically in the brief war in the Falklands.

And I lost my entire platoon while I was safely stationed at the largest garrison the British Army has to offer.

If dear old Dad was looking down from Heaven (unlikely) or watching from below (far greater chance of that) he would have snorted with derision. *Of course* Nick had lost his entire platoon without even going to war.

Nick knew that if Lieutenant-Colonel Colin Hurt had been able to give his opinion on matters, he would say that the best thing his son could have done was to die with them. At least then he might have brought *some* honour to the family.

The pressure to join the army had been present since Nick, pink and soft and pudgy, had chewed noisily on his first rusk. It didn't matter to his father that Nick was a terrible fit for the role right from the start. There was no chance in Hell that Colin Hurt going to raise a thoughtful, sensitive boy. He was going to raise an *officer*.

Nick had never quite found the courage to tell his father he wanted no part of the army, and once he was in, there seemed to be no escape from the preordained torture. Nick had a feeling that the army would keep promoting him until one day he found himself in charge of the entire damn thing, and still with no clue what he was doing. Even being inept had no effect: all he got was affectionate slaps on the back and conspiratorial winks from grey-haired warriors who had to 'do right' by the memory of Colin Hurt and take care of little Nick. Even in death the old bastard had managed to exert complete control over Nick's life.

And then, after a battle in its own backyard, a shrieking, howling, terrifying hour spent killing people that wore the same uniform, the army looked to have unexpectedly died, and maybe, just maybe, Nick was finally free.

In the chaos that followed the arrival of the virus, leadership seemed to have disappeared. All high ranking officers were gone or dead. All communication was down. There was, Nick thought, a real danger that the people at Catterick were going to start thinking for themselves and behaving like *people* rather than soldiers.

Unfortunate, then, that the highest ranking officer left alive had decided that the army must prevail, and that anyone caught so much as *thinking* that maybe the army had had its day would be punished as a deserter.

Unfortunate also that Colonel Dave Hopper was a raving lunatic; even more so that enough people still feared him sufficiently to propel him to power.

Nick sat on the low wall that had become his regular perch in The Heart and glowered as he saw Hopper pass by in the distance, chest puffed out in self-importance, flanked by a ridiculously unnecessary security detail. Doubtless the man had found some ultra-important task that required his personal attention. Maybe someone, somewhere, had veered too close to independent thought.

Nick had left the crowded dorm as soon as his eyes opened that morning. The proximity of hundreds of others, piled in sleeping bags almost on top of each other left him feeling claustrophobic and he slept terribly. He spent as much time as possible outside, on the low wall in the square, trying to find some space to breathe.

He drained a thermos of almost-cold tomato soup, and grimaced. The soup was fine, though it made a poor breakfast. Still, Nick did not think the bitter taste in his mouth had anything to do with their food supplies.

In their attempts to block out the nightmare outside, the citizens of Catterick had simply kick-started a different nightmare *inside*.

Colonel Hopper had been universally disliked even before his sudden ascension to the position of God-King of Catterick. His was the lowest of the staff ranks, but that had never stopped him browbeating all around him, regardless of their seniority. He was belligerent, abrasive and intimidating, and he seized power with fervent relish.

It made sense that Hopper would survive the apocalypse. Nick had a feeling that if he were one of only two people left on the planet, Dave Hopper would be the other.

Hopper had quickly rallied a unit of terrified loyalists to his cause, and had then successfully argued that with tensions at Catterick rising like sun-blasted mercury, the carrying of weapons should be restricted to what, in effect, became Hopper's own personal guard.

FUBAR didn't do the situation any justice.

All debate about whether or not the people that remained after the grisly battle with the infection were still an 'army' or just plain old 'survivors' was quickly shut down, or at least marginalised and pushed into the shadows. Those that King Hopper decreed were 'trouble' - even those that he believed *might* cause trouble - were locked away, and the rest began to build a wall around the centre of the Garrison, providing the new king with a fortress. Hierarchy had to be maintained at all costs in order to avoid The Heart sliding into chaos, of course.

It seemed that only Nick could see the insanity inherent in locking able bodies away for 'crimes' they hadn't even committed when a very real threat could stroll up to their front door at any moment.

The area they had chosen to wall off was a cluster of the larger buildings at the centre of the town. The ridiculously-named Heart. The town centre was the wisest choice, strategically speaking. Hopper might be a slavering loon, but he was far from stupid.

At the nucleus of the makeshift fortress, the open space between the large medical centre and even larger barracks had been turned into a sort of public square. People gathered there, murmuring in small groups. Tables were laid out with food - the lukewarm soup mostly - and cold drinks. It made the walled-off fortress they had created feel a little like a small community, as if the creation of a public space represented them clinging to society, or civilization, but Nick knew that wasn't the reason for it.

It wasn't a need for civilization that drove the soldiers to huddle together in the square; it was terror. It was the illusory safety of the herd that brought them together; the need to see that they weren't facing the horror of the world alone. Strength in numbers.

And Nick had a feeling it would tear them all apart.

Already there had been a couple of fist fights, and Hopper's personal police force had stepped in to restore order by jabbing the butts of their weapons into the faces of the men who had 'broken the peace'. The first shooting was inevitable, and once it happened, civil war would rip the place in two and give Hopper the insurrection he clearly longed for.

Nick had taken to hanging around the small square, like so many others. The two main buildings felt cramped and claustrophobic: every square inch seemed to be taken up by improvised dormitories, and the atmosphere in them stank of sweat and despair. But it wasn't a desire for company or the safety of the herd that brought him there each day when he awoke.

Nick sat apart from all the others on the low wall, and stared longingly at the real reason he kept returning to the square.

There was a helicopter sitting on the roof of the medical centre, which had mainly used as an emergency vehicle for ferrying members of the public to distant hospitals rather than for army business. It was far from being a gunship, but it didn't need to be.

Nick was no pilot, but he knew enough to get that chopper off the ground. And so he sat on the low wall in the square day after day, and waited. When the opportunity arose, Nick was going to take that helicopter and get the fuck out. He felt no remorse about the prospect of leaving his comrades, or taking the vehicle. The world had changed.

Let the deluded fools who still thought of themselves as an army stay and play politics while the world burned around them. The last place Nick wanted to be was cramped into a tiny prison with a thousand people suffering serious mental trauma, under the control of a man who was only one loose screw away from authorising public executions, and daubing messages on walls in his own excrement.

He glanced up at the roof of the medical centre. It was stupid, to keep checking that the helicopter was there. Reminded him a little of his days as a cadet, and how he would spend hours cleaning and checking his weapon unnecessarily.

Just checking to make sure it's still there.

Nick tried to reassure himself that he had the courage to follow through on his plan. It sort of worked.

When he dropped his eyes back to ground level he found that his stare had not gone unnoticed. Across the square, a broad-shouldered man with a hard face was looking right at him, his steely eyes locked on Nick through the crowd of passing bodies.

Shit.

The guy stalked toward him slowly, never taking his gaze from Nick, and sat heavily on the low wall with a sigh.

"You a coward, Lieutenant Hurt?"

Nick blinked; said nothing.

"Yeah, I know who you are," the man said, and Nick thought he heard a chuckle in his voice. "Bit older than you, see. I served under your father for a while. Brutal old bastard, he was. No coward, though, I'll give him that."

"What do you want?"

The big man leaned close.

"Name's Drake. Saw you looking at that chopper. Seen a few people looking at it, truth be told, but no one looked quite the same way you did. There's a countdown written on your face, Lieutenant Hurt. A timer in your eyes."

Nick flinched a little and cast a furtive glance around him.

The big man's face split in a grin that made Nick's blood run cold.

"Don't worry there, Nick. I'm not here to tell everyone that you're planning to steal that helicopter."

The man's eyes twinkled wickedly.

"I'm not planning to-"

The man guffawed.

"Sure you are. And I don't plan to stop you. Just hope you've left room for one more, is all."

"And if I were planning to run, why would I take you with me?"

"Ah, there's Daddy's little treasure. Figured the old man might have raised a coward, but he'd also have raised a ruthless fucker. You'll take me because Colonel

Hopper owes me a favour. And I could easily make that favour dealing with *you*, if you know what I'm saying."

He winked.

Nick glared at him.

"So what do you need me for? Why not take it yourself?"

The man shrugged.

"Call it settling a debt with your old man."

Nick's chin dropped. He should have known.

Dad. Of course.

"And besides, I can't fly the damn thing. And I'm not entirely sure there are any actual pilots left here. But *you* can fly it, can't you Nick?"

Before Nick could respond, the sound of raised voices froze the retort in his mouth.

He glanced at Drake, who shrugged and leapt to his feet, heading in the direction of the noise. Nick followed, cursing Hopper for locking up all the guns. When he made it to the street beyond the barracks, he saw a group of people gathering near the wall they had built out of debris. He heard anxious voices raised; the sound of panic gathering.

Fear knotted in his stomach.

The infection? Inside the walls?

Even as the thought crossed his mind, he knew it could not be true. The crowd seemed scared, but there was no sign of the violent explosion of chaos that had accompanied Catterick's first skirmish with the virus.

As Nick drew closer to the group, he saw Drake turn to greet him. Already the big man's face was becoming depressingly familiar among the crowd.

"I'd say you need to step up preparations for that plan of yours," Drake said, and nodded at the people gathering behind him.

Nick shoved his way past a couple of the onlookers, and felt his stomach lurch when he saw what had caught their attention.

On the floor next to the wall they had spent so much effort building were the remnants of several bodies. Nick saw four heads. All the bodies had been ripped to shreds and rearranged, bones and organs twisted and stretched like putty to form a single grisly word.

Die.

*

When Colonel Dave Hopper called a general meeting in the square and made it clear that attendance was compulsory, Nick knew deep in his gut that the place had gone over the edge of the slippery slope, and the journey downward was gathering momentum.

"I think it's safe to say we have a murderer in our midst, yes?"

Hopper had declined the use of a megaphone to address the thousand-strong crowd that filled the square and leaned out of the windows of the nearby buildings. Instead he filled his ample torso with air and bellowed until he was red-faced and showering those unfortunate enough to be close to him with spittle.

A faint ripple ran through the crowd. Even Hopper's staunchest supporters - or more accurately, those most scared of him - had serious doubts that the obscenity they had discovered near the wall was the work of a *murderer*. For a start, the couple of medics who had examined the corpses had been clear on one thing: the bodies looked to have been ripped apart. There was no sign that the victims had been *cut* to pieces.

The medics went to great lengths to stress that they were not coroners and so their judgments included an element of guesswork, but that didn't matter to Nick. He was no coroner either, but he had fucking *eyes*. Whatever had killed the soldiers was not human. He had no doubt there were enough psychopaths within The Heart to commit murder, but it seemed unlikely any of them would be able to *rip people to pieces*.

Unfortunately, the opinion of the medics did not seem to matter much to Hopper either; he apparently didn't see a terrifying mystery in the destroyed bodies. He saw plotting and insurrection.

"Someone here is trying to frighten us. Are we frightened?"

No one spoke.

At least, Nick thought as he saw a flicker of self-doubt wobble across Hopper's jowly face, he had the decency to recognise the ludicrousness of *that* question.

Yes. Of course everybody was frightened. *Terrified.*

"For the security of everybody in this compound, we will be implementing a curfew. I want everyone confined to quarters until this mess is straightened out, yes? Clear?"

A louder murmur.

Hopper had always spoken like that. Virtually every sentence had a built-in demand for acknowledgment. It was a habit that made Nick's teeth grind involuntarily.

Nick thought from the tone of the mumbling in the crowd that he detected a fair amount of acquiescence. Most people clung to the inside of the buildings anyway. Few cared that Hopper had essentially just turned Catterick into a prison, as long as they got to remain safely stationed behind solid walls. Nobody wanted to be out there with the snipers.

Nick stifled a sigh, and glanced around him. To his left, through the crowd, he saw Drake staring at him pointedly, nodding his head at the roof of the medical centre.

Nick already had difficulty imagining how he might get the key that opened the door to the roof of the medical centre, let alone the possibility of making it to the chopper without being accosted by Hopper's men. A curfew took what had been a difficulty curve and lifted it until it was practically vertical.

"Patrols will be set up. Every corner of this place is going to be under scrutiny until the perpetrator of this atrocity is found and brought to justice. Clear?"

Hopper was rising in pitch, heading toward hysteria at breakneck pace. Nick tuned him out. He didn't know for sure, but he was willing to bet that Hopper had the key he needed. Securing it would have been the first thing the Colonel did to prevent 'deserters' stealing the helicopter.

The old bastard probably kept it on his person.

Nick looked for Drake again, but couldn't spot him in the crowd.

You a coward, Lieutenant Hurt?

Drake's first words to him came back to Nick, settling into a familiar groove worn deep in his mind.

Coward.

His father's last words to him, croaked out on the old fucker's deathbed.

Don't be a coward all your life, boy.

The trouble was that Nick *was* a coward; always had been. Which made the realisation that he was probably going to have to kill Colonel Hopper all the more terrifying.

7

Michael hated leaving Claire in the tower. Hated letting her out of his sight for even a second, but Gwyneth had persuaded him that whatever they would be discussing with Darren was unlikely to be suitable for young ears, and Michael had found it difficult to argue. Claire had already been through enough. A break from the constant stress - even if only for an hour or two - might be the best thing he could do for his daughter.

Eventually Michael had reluctantly agreed to let Claire stay with Gwyneth and Pete while he, Rachel and John went to see Darren.

He had expected an argument from Claire, maybe even tears, but she surprised him.

"This is the safest place I've been in days, Dad."

He couldn't argue with that. He hadn't seen much of his little girl in the previous two years. Not nearly enough. Hadn't seen the spirited streak that had grown in her until after the world fell apart. She reminded him a lot of her dead mother, and Michael smiled sadly.

Gwyneth nodded encouragement, and Michael wheeled himself outside to find John and Rachel waiting with the young girl that had delivered Darren's invitation. She stood slightly apart with her head bowed, as though she was unable to meet their gaze.

The strange girl gave Michael chills, and for a moment he considered heading back to Claire. The castle might well have been free of the Infected, but Michael was not sure 'safe' accurately described the way the place made him feel. He looked around at the small groups of people working on their various projects in grim silence. John's instincts about the place had been right.

Michael expected the girl to lead them to wherever Darren was waiting, but she simply pointed at the castle's central tower, the largest of the eight, and whispered in a voice Michael could barely hear.

"He's in there."

She wandered away, moving slowly and slightly unsteadily, as though she was in some drug-induced haze, or a deep state of shock.

Michael watched her until she disappeared out of sight behind one of the towers, and felt the acid burn of stress building in his stomach.

When Rachel turned to head for the tower the girl had pointed out, Michael reached for her arm.

"Wait," he whispered, glancing around to make sure they were out of earshot of anyone that might be trying to listen in. "Look, you're both right, okay? There's something...off about this place. I don't know what it is, but I don't want us to antagonise the situation unnecessarily. We have our story, and we stick to it, right? We play it dumb and helpless. For now," he added hastily when he saw Rachel's expression darken.

John shrugged.

"Wasn't going to play it any other way, Michael. But we're going to need answers."

"And we will get them. I promise you, but for now we're just a family in need of shelter, right? Nothing more."

John nodded.

"Rachel?"

Michael stared at Rachel until she sighed in exasperation.

"Yes, Michael. I'm not going to walk in there and punch him, don't worry."

"Lucky for him," John said with a wry smile, and just for a second, Rachel almost grinned back.

*

"You were a driver."

Darren wasn't buying it for a second. In a way, John couldn't blame him. There had been that fatal split-second of hesitation in John's answer, and the not-subtle-enough glance from Michael when Darren had asked what John did for a living before the collapse. The moment of pause before the answer had not gone unnoticed by the bearded man.

The interior of the castle's central tower was markedly different to the one they had spent the previous night in. This one was much wider: the ground floor of the tower comprised of a single room with a radius of around seventy feet.

Ancient wooden benches lined the stone walls, making it feel like the interior of a church. It had been, John guessed, a sort of throne room or great hall, though there was no throne to be seen now. Doubtless it was on display in some museum somewhere. John was grateful that at least they hadn't found Darren sitting on a throne. The sight might have been too much for him to take.

Instead, the balding man was waiting to greet them just inside the doorway with a wide, easy smile.

Darren had smiled and nodded politely as they told him that they were an extended family on the run from the horror that had befallen St. Davids. He absent-mindedly acknowledged Michael and Rachel's words. Only when it came to asking John what he had done before the virus hit did Darren's interest suddenly seem piqued.

"Like a taxi driver?"

John suppressed a sigh. Darren seemed pretty sharp. He asked John the questions, but kept looking at Michael and Rachel, encouraging them to jump in.

Testing whether we've got our story straight, John thought, and he knew they had not. They had come up with their cover story for Darren, but it was just flimsy theatre. None of it would stand up to detailed questioning. John had to be the one to answer, and quickly; before either Michael or Rachel gave the game away.

"A personal driver," John said.

Darren gave an impressed nod, hamming it up.

"Must have been someone important."

John knew where this was going. Had to shut it down.

"That depends on whether they were your employer," he said, and dipped his tone in just enough vitriol to convey that he didn't want to talk about it. Just enough that even Darren's butter-wouldn't-melt demeanour had to register it. To continue the line of questioning would have been a naked challenge, and John was betting Darren didn't want to go that far. Manipulators usually didn't.

Darren smiled coldly.

Didn't buy it, John thought.

They had told Darren some of the truth about their journey from St. Davids to Caernarfon, but glossed over most of the details. Michael had insisted they say nothing of their encounter with Victor, and that they give no hint of the knowledge they had of Project Wildfire, or of John's involvement with it.

They had to play it as a family, and offer no threat. At the time, when Michael had argued the point, John had thought the man was just being cowardly, ready to throw himself at the feet of the people in the castle and beg for shelter.

But as John glanced at Michael as they stood before Darren, he saw a different truth in the man's eyes. Pretending to be weak was the way to get in to the castle, and it was also the way to get close to Darren. John could practically *see* the bearded man's ego leaking out of every orifice. He thrived on the belief that they were weak, and he was strong.

John knew then that Michael was gambling on the man becoming over-confident and leaving himself vulnerable. There was nothing particularly wrong with the strategy, yet John could not help but wonder what Michael planned to do with it.

"We've told you our story, Darren," Michael said. "What's yours?"

Darren smiled.

"It's probably easier if I show you," he said. "This way."

Darren turned and led them to the winding stone stairway that led to the upper floors of the huge tower, and stopped at the bottom, as though something had just occurred to him.

"Oh," he said innocently, turning to face Michael. "You can't walk at all?"

Michael's eyes narrowed.

"I'll wait here," he growled, and John could read the expression in Michael's eyes clearly. First he had allowed himself to be separated from his daughter, and now from John and Rachel. To a man so reliant on the people around him, being left alone at the bottom of the tower must have been a sharp reminder of just how fragile his position was.

Even the rifle, which Michael had gone to great pains to take ownership of, was out of reach: buried under their bags back in the tower they had slept in the previous night. Without it, Michael was as helpless as a new born. John felt a stab of sympathy for the man, and nodded at him reassuringly before turning to follow Darren up the stairs.

*

"I imagine you have a lot of questions," Darren said as they climbed the winding stone steps. "And I will answer them all in time. But the important thing is that you know what we are up against. Then you'll see there is only one question that matters."

The steps ended abruptly at a heavy wooden door. Darren pushed it open with a grunt and stepped out onto the battlements.

"This is the highest point of the castle. It's the only place high enough to see it."

"See what?" John growled. The guy was clearly loving the pantomime of it, the big theatrical build-up, and John felt his annoyance growing. Glancing at Rachel's face told him she was a little further down the road toward outright hostility, and having difficulty keeping a lid on her temper.

Darren walked to the edge of the battlements. A small chair and table had been set up, turning the roof into a lookout position. Someone would have sat there and watched our boat approaching, John thought, and the notion made him uncomfortable. Darren snatched up a pair of binoculars from the table.

"You wanted to know where the Infected are. See for yourself."

He handed John the binoculars.

When he lifted them to his eyes, it took John several seconds to see it, and a further couple to understand what he was looking at.

Beyond the limits of the town, a dark stain blotted the countryside. It looked like someone had drawn a dark circle around the town that stretched from one side of the peninsula to the other.

What is that?

Even as the question formed, John knew what the answer was. The Infected. Thousands of them, ringing the entire town from coast to coast, gathered at some invisible boundary. His mouth dropped open, and he lowered the binoculars.

"As you see, they have us cornered," Darren said.

John passed the binoculars to Rachel, and grimaced when he heard her sharp intake of breath.

"So why aren't they attacking?" Rachel said.

"Ah," Darren said. "*That* is the question."

8

Confined to quarters.

It would not have been so bad if Nick's quarters were not also currently 'confining' a couple of hundred other people. Some chattered in low voices, some leafed through old books and magazines. After an hour or so, Nick decided that oblivion was the best way to spend the time, and he pulled the thin blanket over his head until he fell asleep.

He woke to find Drake standing over him, silently watching.

"What?" Nick slurred as he struggled toward consciousness. "How did you get here? What do you want?"

"Shhh."

Drake put a meaty finger to his lips and flashed Nick a conspiratorial grin.

"Follow me," he whispered.

Nick stifled a groan, and glanced at his watch. He had been asleep for about an hour. His limbs felt heavy, his eyes gritty.

He sat up, pushing back the blanket that did nothing to keep the cold at bay. Nick's bed was in an overcrowded dorm on the third floor of Harden Barracks. He glanced around the large room. There were sleeping bodies everywhere, crammed together, almost on top of each other, like animals huddling for warmth in a nest. Everybody else looked to have opted for blissful oblivion too.

Drake had picked his way carefully between the sleeping bodies, displaying surprisingly light feet for such a big guy. He beckoned at Nick to hurry.

With a final glance around to make sure no one was watching him breaking the curfew, Nick carefully lifted himself to his feet and followed the path Drake blazed through the bodies, wincing a little every time one of them sighed heavily, or turned uncomfortably in their sleep.

When they were clear, Drake pushed the door that opened out into a corridor beyond, closing it carefully once Nick joined him.

"I think I've found our murderer," Drake whispered in a breathless tone.

He grabbed Nick's arm and led him to a large window that overlooked the newly-built wall and the empty moors beyond. He passed Nick a small pair of field glasses and pointed outside.

A thick, low mist hung over the fields beyond The Heart like a veil. It took Nick a moment to find what Drake was pointing at. He swept the binoculars left and right, and finally saw a small, flickering light.

Fire.

It looked like it was moving. Coming toward The Heart.

Nick looked at Drake, puzzled, and then returned to the binoculars, adjusting the focus in an attempt to understand what he was looking at. As he watched, the fire split in two, and one half of it seemed to grow. It looked like a tree had gone up in flames.

"I don't understand what I'm looking at," he whispered. "A burning tree?"

He looked again.

Why is it moving?

Nick's mouth dropped open as he saw the tree suddenly lifting several feet into the air, drawing back in an odd, mechanical motion, like it had been loaded into a catapult.

And then the tree was arcing through the misty sky, becoming a flaming missile, fired up and over the wall, and smashing into the medical centre opposite the barracks with a crash that sounded like a drum pounding in Hell.

He heard faint screams emanate from the other building, and saw people start to scurry from the building, scampering left and right in confusion, searching for an enemy they could not see.

Something just threw a fucking tree at us.

He looked at Drake, his mouth open. The big man's face had paled.

"Wasn't expecting *that*," Drake mumbled, and then his eyes widened, and Nick saw flames reflected in them.

In the gloom beyond the wall, another fire had sprung up, and another. Nick swallowed painfully, shrinking away from the window as another of the trees lifted into the air and launched itself toward them.

And then the sky seemed to be raining fire down on Catterick.

*

Jake had uprooted about thirty of the trees, tearing them from the ground like dead flowers. At first he had thought about just tossing them over the wall, to scare the people cowering inside as much as anything. But then he had remembered an old survival tip one of his foster fathers had shown him on an extremely ill-advised camping trip.

Fire was just a matter of creating friction. The only difficulty was getting the wood moving quickly enough to generate heat. On that camping trip, when his foster father had smiled patronisingly at Jake's futile attempts to create fire from nothing, he had wished for nothing so much as to be big enough to wrap his hands around the man's throat and squeeze the life from him.

He remembered the sudden look of dark understanding that passed over the man's face as he looked into Jake's murderous young eyes. They never went camping again, and four months later Jake was back in the care system; back on the wheel of misfortune, wondering what might be in store for him when the spinning stopped.

Friction wasn't a problem for Jake now. He lazily twisted the piece of wood in his enormous mangled hand and flames burst into life almost instantly as the stick became a blur of impossible motion, like the fire was eager to be born.

He held the trees in his enormous hands, edging them toward the flames like cigarettes. Once the fire took hold on the wood, he drew the trunks back like a javelin thrower and speared them through the foggy air into the tiny walled settlement. With each throw he cackled as his extraordinary hearing picked up the distant cries of panic and pain. On the ninth throw he hit something that sent a ball of fire up into the sky and his mouth dropped in delight even as he clapped his hands over his ears in a futile attempt to keep the pain of the deafening explosion at bay.

*

When the propane tank went up, blowing out every window in The Heart and sending a shockwave of liquid fire through the crowd, Nick knew that the time for planning was over.

He stared down into the square, slack-jawed, as he saw several figures stumbling from the blast, shrieking human torches that cast a grisly glow on the horror being unleashed below, before they finally dropped to the ground, smouldering. The sickening stench of their cooked flesh floated on the air like confetti, so thick that Nick could taste it, and bile rose in his throat.

He turned to Drake.

"Hopper," he choked. "Where's Hopper?"

Drake shrugged and nodded his head down at the square.

Of course Hopper would be down there, in the thick of it. His rank had taken him away from the action of war and into what was largely administration. He would be right in the middle, barking orders, loving every minute.

Nick would have killed for a job in administration. He had been a coward all his life, shying away from the merest hint of confrontation, let alone any that might involve firearms. Even when he had been appointed as leader of a group of thirty soldiers, he had led by suggestion, never by command.

As he smashed open the cabinet that held the fire extinguisher, he wondered idly if his actions would still be considered cowardly. He was about to do the bravest thing he'd ever done in his life, and all so he could run away once more.

A huge flaming tree trunk crashed through the window at which he had stood with Drake only moments before, crashing through the door opposite and into the dorm, ploughing into the terrified mass of people that huddled inside, where they had believed themselves to be safe.

Nick's eyes fell on the fire axe that sat next to the extinguisher. He grabbed that instead, and hurtled toward the stairs.

When he reached the ground and burst out of the barracks and into the warzone that the square had become, Nick heard Hopper's voice immediately, screaming at no one in particular, barking out the order to get to the wall and open fire.

Mostly Nick saw people milling around in confusion and terror; most were unarmed thanks to Hopper, and Colonel's words fell on deaf ears. He saw a few, the ones he had come to think of as King Hopper's royal guard, hoisting assault rifles and heading to the wall, and moments later the chatter of gunfire fractured the night.

Heart hammering, his breath exploding from lungs that tried in vain to choke out the acrid smoke filling them, Nick cast his eyes left and right.

Where the fuck is Hopper?

*

Jake had loved killing ever since he had been four or five years old, when he had meticulously pulled the wings off a butterfly, slowly and deliberately, relishing the notion that if the thing had been capable of screaming, it would have. The insect hadn't been delicate and pretty. At least not until Jake had finished with it.

That first kill, tiny and insignificant as it had been, had sent an unforgettable shudder of pleasure through his small frame. He had been chasing that thrill ever since, on each and every occasion that he had managed to struggle free of the prison in his mind, the sickness that meant he had to share headspace with a tedious bore.

He had chased the thrill across the deaths of increasingly larger animals, and eventually human beings, and on each occasion he had been fascinated with tearing them apart; with seeing their insides and remaking them.

Even the killing of seventeen people in his previous life had turned out to be a case of thinking small, though. The gift given to him at the underground base; the transformation of himself into an apex predator: that had changed everything.

The battle with the puny creatures at Catterick felt just like killing that first insect, all those years earlier. It felt *new.*

He was powerless to resist the lure of their blood now, reduced to a creature of impulse, as hopelessly directionless as the mindless prototypes that wandered the earth blindly trying to spread their pathetic seed by biting and tearing.

It troubled him a little; that he was drawn toward the people at Catterick as if his actions were predetermined somehow, almost as if he had no say in the matter. He felt a little like a bee that made for pollen mindlessly, with no concept of *why* it was fulfilling its destiny.

Those concerns were cast aside in a haze of shuddering fury when the pathetic creatures lined the wall in the distance and began to fire their weapons in his direction. All thoughts of caution were abandoned to the addiction. He *had* to kill them all. Philosophy did not enter into the equation.

When the pitiful weapons the creatures held poured bullets at him through the misty air, Jake McIntosh had already moved. To him, the squeezing of their fingers on the trigger seemed to last forever, bones and ligaments creaking loudly in their flesh like rusted hinges, firing off long, slow warnings long before they fired projectiles. He saw the bullets heading toward him slowly, like a distant storm.

He was weakening; getting tired. The prudent course of action was to retreat, to leave them with the terror and damage he had inflicted and rest until he could return and attack at full strength.

A bullet whined past his head, the whining song of its passage an insult that bored down into the bubbling chaos of Jake's mind and scattered his thoughts like dust on the wind.

He would have their blood. Every last drop.

With a roar of pure, unhinged fury, Jake put his head down.

And charged.

9

Michael could not hide his relief when he saw John and Rachel descend the steps unharmed. Fantastic scenarios had played out in his mind, of Darren locking them in some room at the top of the tower like characters in a fairytale, or worse; pushing them from the roof before returning to kill the helpless cripple.

He immediately noticed the stunned look on their faces.

"What is it?" He said sharply.

John shook his head, his eyes far away.

"This place is under siege," Rachel said grimly. The Infected are all around Caernarfon, thousands of them, just waiting there."

"What? How is that possible?" Michael tried to keep a lid on the hysteria in his response.

"Not *waiting*," Darren said. "That's not it at all. They aren't waiting for anything. They are there because they can't come any closer."

"I don't understand," Michael said, frowning.

Darren sighed dramatically.

"Neither do I, not really. You wanted to know my story. I'll give you the truth, despite the fact you didn't pay me the same respect."

Michael opened his mouth, but Darren waved away the protestation before it began.

"*Please*," he said, his tone heavy with sarcasm. "A family?"

He jerked a thumb at John.

"A *driver*?"

He snorted.

"I wasn't born yesterday. It doesn't particularly matter where you came from or what your story is. What matters is what you intend to do *here*."

He sat heavily on one of the wooden benches, and gestured for Rachel and John to follow suit. After a moment's hesitation, they sat.

"As I told you earlier, Rachel, I was on Mount Snowdon when...whatever this is began. I first encountered the infection, the virus, when I led a group of climbers back down after we lost communication. We were set upon."

His voice cracked a little, his eyes lost in a terrible memory.

"Half the group were lost immediately. I didn't have the faintest idea what was going on, just that all of a sudden the group I was leading began to kill each other in...horrible ways."

He lifted his jaw and stared at them defiantly.

"I ran. Maybe that makes me a coward. I don't know. I'm not sure that even matters now. The only thing that matters is survival, right? I survived, along with six of my group. We got away by...well, we got away. Still didn't grasp the full extent of this thing though. We thought it was just happening there, at the bus station."

He shook his head ruefully.

"We took a bus, thought we were heading toward safety. Going to get the *police.* All we seemed to do was draw them to us. Eventually there were dozens of them chasing the bus. Every time we thought we'd lost them, more would appear. They ran in front of us, threw themselves under the wheels..."

He trailed off.

"We've seen the same thing," Michael said. "They are drawn to noise. They...hunt by sound. Travelling in a car, well, it hasn't worked for us."

Darren nodded.

"Smart to travel by boat," he said. "I wonder what happened to the people out there who were on boats when this started. Are there ferries out there? Battleships? Holiday cruises full of people wondering what happened? Or just boats full of insane killers, floating around aimlessly."

He shrugged.

"I don't suppose it matters. Unless one of them appears in the harbour. Anyway, as I was saying, we took the bus. We ran. And then, all of a sudden, they stopped chasing us. They just fell back. It was like some forcefield had been thrown around us."

John broke the man's story with a sigh.

"So now it's *forcefields*. And zombies. I don't believe any of it. What is it then? God? Extra-terrestrials?"

"I said *like* a forcefield," Darren said, and his tone lowered, revealing just a hint of menace. "Because I don't know how else to describe it. But I do know it's got nothing to do with aliens, and I don't think God is involved either."

He stared at John.

"The girl you saw? The one tied up in the market outside?"

John's eyes narrowed.

"It's *her.*"

*

"Do you think there will be other kids here?"

Gwyneth smiled. Pete had been asking questions ever since Michael, John and Rachel had left the tower. She liked the boy's spirit, but she could also see the damage in his eyes. When the others were around, particularly John, the way Pete clammed up was noticeable.

Gwyneth did not like to think about the horrors the two children had been exposed to, or to dwell on how young minds might be affected by the violence that soaked the world now. Of course, the TV news had been full of dire warnings that children were becoming desensitized to murder and mayhem. Video games and movies and the internet were supposedly creating a generation of monsters.

She hadn't paid much attention to the news, other than to cluck at it disapprovingly at times. Every day was a relentless barrage of information that seemed designed to terrify everybody, and parents especially. If it wasn't paedophiles and gangs, it was videogames. As it turned out, the television had been completely oblivious to the coming apocalypse. The generation of monsters had nothing to do with children hooked on cartoon aggression. The real monsters were the generations that went before them, the ones old enough to own the news stations, and to wilfully ignore the real dangers that grew in the shadows.

"Do you think this place has a *dungeon*?" Pete said in breathless excitement.

"Of course it does," Claire said. "It's a castle isn't it? It even has a moat. There's bound to be a dungeon."

Claire looked at Gwyneth for affirmation.

"I've no idea," Gwyneth said with a smile. "But it could have. It's certainly old enough. But that's just the river, not a moat. A moat would surround the whole castle. Moats are man-made."

Pete's face lit up, and for a moment he looked ready to burst with excitement.

"Can we go see it? The dungeon? And the battlements?"

Gwyneth frowned.

Michael had asked her to watch the children, but he hadn't said anything about keeping them locked up in the tower until he returned.

She glanced around the room. It was barren and featureless, just a circle of cold stone and steps leading upward. It was no wonder the children were getting restless.

"I don't know if that's a good idea, sweetheart," she said. "We should probably wait until the others return before we start exploring the place. It might not be safe for us out there. If Claire's dad comes back and finds her gone, he'll worry himself to death, won't he?"

Pete looked devastated.

Gwyneth smiled sadly.

She had a child once. A little boy. She hadn't seen him reach the age Pete was now. Thinking about him still made a part of her heart ache, a part that felt like the wound there had only happened yesterday, and it might never heal.

"Tell you what," she said. "I think we can at least climb *this* tower and see what the battlements look like, how about that? And later on, once the others are back, we'll go find the dungeons okay? Promise."

She smiled broadly as Pete brightened and leapt to his feet.

Gwyneth took a moment to haul her old limbs upright.

"I want you both to stay close to me, though. Deal?"

Pete nodded furiously, and Claire rolled her eyes a little at the boy's eagerness.

"It *is* safe though isn't it Mrs Blake?" Claire said. "I mean, you can't feel any of the crazy people out there, can you?"

"No dear, I can't. Can't feel anything at all as a matter of fact. And I thought I told you to call me Gwyneth? Now come on."

She ushered the children to the foot of the winding stair, and kept her face low as they rushed past her, so they wouldn't notice her troubled expression.

The truth of it was that Gwyneth could not feel that familiar itch that indicated the presence of the infection nearby. But she could feel *something*. Something that troubled her deeply. Something far away, yet faintly connected to her somehow, in some way she did not understand.

She told the others that what she could feel when the Infected were near was their rage, and it was true. Whatever was out there though, it did not feel like the Infected.

But she felt its rage, and the enormity of it terrified her.

*

"What do you mean it's *her*?" John said. "How is that possible?"

"How is any of this possible?" Darren snapped. "I said I would give you all the answers I could. That one, I *can't*. We found her in the middle of the road. Thought she was just sitting there, crying. Only she wasn't crying, she was ripping her eyes out, just like they do. She was bitten. Infected. We were about to kill her when she started talking. Whatever she is, she hasn't turned into one of them."

John exchanged a troubled glance with Michael and Rachel, and hoped they understood the meaning in his gaze.

Don't mention Gwyneth.

"She is something else," Darren continued. "And whatever it is, *they* don't like it. She acts like...repellent. As soon as we got her on the bus they dropped back, and they've stayed back ever since. But more of them seem to come every day."

"So she's human. She is...immune somehow," Michael said flatly. "Why do you have her tied up out there like an animal? Why not bring her in here?"

Darren shook his head.

"Two reasons," he said. "One: whatever this effect she has on them is, it doesn't extend very far. A few hundred yards. If she were in here, they'd be in the town, and for the moment the town is our only source of food and supplies, and even that won't last long. And two: whatever she is, she certainly is not *human*. Not anymore. She's not worth the risk."

Michael could feel anger begin to radiate from Rachel, like her rage was beginning to increase the temperature of the air around her.

"How long can this place hold out?" He asked hurriedly, anxious to move the conversation on before Rachel got involved.

Darren shrugged.

"As long as that girl is alive, I suppose," he said. "We are planting vegetables, as you saw. Building shelters. We have stockpiled some weapons. Nothing too lethal unfortunately, but we can fashion petrol bombs using the fuel from the generator if we need to, and there are plenty of blades here if we do need to defend ourselves against attack. Hopefully more people will join us, just as you did. We can go on looting the town for supplies until they run out. After that, your guess is as good as mine."

"It's not sustainable," Michael said. "You must see that. Everything hinges on a sick girl that you've got chained up in freezing weather, and you don't even understand what this effect she has on them is. You have to fight them. Clear them away before they find a way to get to the walls of this place. Once that happens, once this place is under siege, it's just a matter of time."

Darren nodded.

"Of course," he said. "But our numbers are small, and not many people are willing to go out there and start executing the Infected. No one wants to get close. We're not certain that they won't decide that they can tolerate the girl's presence after all if we get too close and provoke them, or if we'll expose ourselves to infection just by being there. If you have any suggestions as to how we go about killing *thousands* of them, please, be my guest."

Michael sighed.

"It's the same thing we have experienced everywhere," he said. "No clue what we're dealing with. Maybe you're right, and the best thing we can do is wait it out in here. Eventually the Infected have to starve, right? They don't eat, that we've seen. At least, not beyond whatever they bite off *us*."

"Exactly," Darren said. "For now the castle is our only card and we have to play it. Wait until the situation changes. Hope the thing in the market doesn't fall down before the Infected do."

He shrugged.

"I'm glad you agree."

Michael shot a glance at Rachel, whose face was slowly turning bright red. He saw her jaw clench and unclench, and hoped she understood the look he sent her way.

"Right," Michael said. "I guess we could use a little time to process this, and besides I have an even more pressing need. Do you, by any chance, have a doctor here?"

Darren smirked.

"Afraid not," he said. "Why? Are you sick?"

His eyes narrowed in suspicion.

"Not sick," Michael said. "Just...I need some help with these."

He gestured at his useless legs.

"Oh," Darren said in a faltering voice.

Bingo, Michael thought. *The world hasn't changed so much that disability has lost its power to make some people squirm.*

"We have a science teacher from the local high school," Darren said. "I'm afraid she is the nearest thing we have to medical knowledge now. She has done a decent job patching some of us up, though to say she's not fond of needles is an understatement."

"That will be fine, she might be able to help," Michael said. "Can I talk to her?"

"Of course," Darren said, and led the way to the tower entrance. "And maybe John and Rachel, you two could help with a supply run into town? Should be no danger of course, but a few of the guys will be heading out soon, and I'm sure they could use your help. The more food we can get back here to the castle, the better we'll eat, after all."

He smiled warmly.

John glanced at Michael and Rachel, and gave a curt nod.

"No problem," he said flatly.

Michael stared at Darren as he exited the tower. The old guy was doing an *excellent* job of separating them from each other. For a moment he wondered if John and

Rachel would be okay, and almost laughed. If anyone was vulnerable, it was likely to be the helpless cripple left alone in the castle full of strangers. John and Rachel could take care of themselves just fine.

Rachel dropped back and made a show of pushing Michael's wheelchair. When Darren was far enough ahead, she leaned in close.

"What are you doing?" She hissed. "You're not actually *trusting* this lunatic?"

"I don't think he's a lunatic at all," Michael whispered, and winced at Rachel's sharp intake of breath. "I think he's something far more dangerous. I think he's a pragmatist, and he's had a taste of power and wants more. He'll cut any of us down to keep his hold on this place. As for what I'm doing, I'm not entirely sure yet, but I'll tell you one thing."

He lifted his chin and stared into Rachel's troubled eyes.

"If we're staying in this castle, it won't be under Darren's command."

Rachel's eyes glittered.

*

The tower looked to have five levels. The first couple had clearly been used as part of the tourist attraction: the rooms were presented as state bedrooms, preserved to look exactly as they must have, back when the castle had been in use in its previous life. Gwyneth saw ornamental mirrors and heavy wooden furniture that reeked of age and opulence, all cordoned off behind a polite rope that encouraged tourists not to get too close, or to touch the precious antiques.

Small plaques were dotted around the rooms, giving potted histories of the objects and the historical names that had once occupied the rooms. On one, she saw a description of a fabulous four poster bed that lay beyond the cordon, which claimed that the lumpy mattress was a far cry from the modern versions that offered cushions of springs or foam. The mattress, the plaque stated, might have looked plush, but would have been highly uncomfortable to sleep on.

Hmph, Gwyneth thought, remembering the night she had just spent on a cold stone floor and the paralysing ache in her old joints when she awoke. Of course the tower had been pitch black then, without the light streaming through the narrow slits that served as windows, and Michael's wheelchair made it impossible for him to ascend the stairs, but still she couldn't quite stifle a mirthless chuckle at their failure to investigate whether the upper floors might have offered more comfortable living accommodation.

She stared at the bed, draped in expensive-looking fabrics.

Dibs.

Both Pete and Claire seemed fascinated by the old rooms, and Pete especially seemed overjoyed that the barriers that had prevented tourists from touching the historical treasures beyond were now effectively meaningless. He cooed and grinned as he ran his hands over the ancient surfaces and ornate decorations.

Above the two floors that held the immaculate bedrooms, Gwyneth opened a door to find an old armoury, filled with wicked-looking weapons from a bygone era. Maces and pikes and broadswords, some encased in glass display cabinets. She let the children look, but told Pete not to touch anything there in case it was dangerous. Pete looked a little crestfallen, but nodded, and Gwyneth rubbed his shoulder affectionately. He was a good kid. They both were. Claire moved around the rooms of the tower wide-eyed, but Gwyneth could see the intelligence in her gaze, and she imagined the girl was probably picturing the tales she had read in storybooks being played out between the old stone walls.

Gwyneth took a last look at the weapons. Most looked old and fragile, the swords mostly appeared to have been blunted by age, but she had a suspicion that John especially would be interested in the contents of the room.

The final floor was just a short curving corridor that led to a door which presumably opened out onto the roof, and another door set into the wall that must have been the entrance to a small circular room that comprised the top floor of the castle. Pete rushed forward and tried the handle, but was disappointed to find that one locked.

"Never mind," Gwyneth said. "It's probably empty. That one over there should lead out onto the battlements. Try that. But be careful!"

She lifted her voice as Pete scampered forward, followed by Claire, and opened the door rushing out into the morning air and a breathtaking view of the town below and the crashing waves that tried in vain to reach the stone walls.

Gwyneth was just about to join them when she heard it.

A soft shuffling noise.

Frowning, she put her ear to the thick wood of the locked door and listened intently.

There it was again, another shuffling, getting louder. Closer.

When the shuffling ended with a soft thump on the other side of the door, and a low, muffled moan, Gwyneth nearly screamed in surprise.

She tried the handle, just to ensure Pete had not been mistaken.

He was not.

Someone had been locked in the room at the top of the tower.

Gwyneth's eyes flicked to a small cubbyhole bored into the wall next to the door, and the heavy iron key that sat inside it.

As if in a dream, Gwyneth reached for the key and slid it smoothly into the lock, twisting it and feely the vibrations of the heavy click in her bony hand as the lock disengaged.

She gave the door a gentle push, and it swung halfway open before hitting something on the other side and stopping with an abrupt thump.

It took Gwyneth a moment to process what was on the other side of the door. When finally she did, she put a hand over her mouth to stifle a scream.

10

The wall exploded.

Nick saw it, but he had trouble comprehending it. They had spent a week laboriously piling up everything they could find at the centre of Catterick, creating a perimeter that stood around twelve feet high. Even the most pessimistic of people - and there were plenty of them, hadn't argued with Hopper's logic in creating the wall. It was the one thing that made them feel vaguely safe.

It wasn't meant to be torn apart like wet tissue.

One moment the pile of cars and debris that they used to build the wall was standing, and several armed men were perched atop it, rattling metal into the fields beyond, the next moment it was...*gone*, radiating outwards in all directions, sending a cloud of deadly shrapnel across the crowd gathering behind it.

Nick watched, stupefied, as several of the figures that had manned the wall hurtled through the air like ragdolls, and felt a crawling sensation ripple across his skin as he saw something *else*, something that moved almost faster than his eye could catch, snatching them out of the air and slamming them into the ground where the wet sacs that had been their bodies exploded against the tarmac like children's water bombs.

He saw one of them caught mid-flight and ripped in two and the pieces *flung* apart; a man's torso suddenly separated from his legs by eighty feet in the blink of an eye.

He froze.

When he had been a young boy of around seven or eight, Nick had been delivering newspapers to earn a pitiful of money that amounted to buying a couple of comics and some chocolate each week, only to be confronted by a snarling, snapping dog that seemed, to his young eyes, to be roughly the size of a small horse.

He hated delivering to the houses that had dogs. There were five on his route, mostly small, yapping dogs that bounded excitedly around his ankles, but usually made him afraid that their playfulness was going to translate into his ankles getting savaged.

There was one though, that always made him sweat even before he approached the driveway that it sometimes inhabited. Most of the time the huge black pitbull was nowhere to be seen, yet still the mere possibility of its presence induced a state of dizzying fear in him.

The fear always proved unfounded, until the day that he opened the gate and saw the dog, and realised too late that it wasn't chained up. When the beast had hurtled toward him, a cannonball of teeth and muscle, Nick had frozen, torn between horror and shame at the warm wetness spreading across his legs and the terror at the raging approach of the dog.

Time had seemed to slow almost to a stop as his mind raced onward, supercharged by the rocket fuel of blind panic, urging his muscles to do something; *anything.*

He'd been bitten then. Not too badly, hardly even enough to break the skin. Barely more than a nip that the owner of the dog nonchalantly described as *playful,* but for that moment, as the jaws of the thing closed around his calf, Nick had felt all-consuming, paralysing terror. He gave up the newspaper deliveries that day, and didn't manage to walk anywhere without casting fearful glances around him, expecting an attack, until he was in his late teens.

As he watched the people around the wall begin to erupt in impossible fountains of blood and gristle, one after another, like dominoes falling at terminal velocity, Nick was for a moment just an eight year old boy again, rooted to the spot, his mind blanked by a mortal fear of a monster that was far worse than a savage dog; something beyond his comprehension that made him feel small and vulnerable.

Again his mind raced as his muscles locked up, and he followed the unfolding massacre in mute horror. Whatever had charged through the wall *shrieked* as it moved, and Nick couldn't be sure if that was the thing's voice, or simply the astonishing speed at which it moved, like water shot from a cannon; a liquid blur that *poured* through its next victim, tearing and dissecting, before the previous body had even hit the ground.

Nick implored his muscles to move, to give him some sort of a fighting chance, but the ballet of death was dreadful and hypnotic, and he couldn't look away.

What is it?

For a half-second the creature paused, and Nick got the impression the slowing of the atrocity was nothing to do with the creature *needing* to stop the assault. It was humanoid; huge. Blood-soaked. It's face was misshapen but from the look in the thing's dead eyes, Nick got the impression it had stopped for a brief moment to enjoy the swirling vortex of death it was creating, like a tourist pausing to take in the sights.

It *grinned*, and then it was gone, and the screaming and the ripping and the wet snapping resumed.

Blood sprayed across the road barely twenty feet beyond Nick's feet, trailing behind a severed head that bounced across the tarmac like a hellish bowling ball and Nick stared at it and blinked slowly, dully, like his eyes were gummed together. Like his brain was passing on the message that it didn't want to see any more and was fully prepared to shut down and wait for the end; to accept the snapping of the jaws.

Piss yourself and die you coward.

And then Drake was in front of him, screaming words into his face that Nick couldn't hear, but he understood. There was no mistaking the message, because there was only one thing *to* do, and as energy finally lurched through his muscles Nick did the only thing a lifelong coward could possibly do.

Run.

Nick took off like an Olympic sprinter, moving faster than he had thought possible, streaking past Drake. The far larger man was taking time to get up to speed, like a heavy vehicle, but in a few seconds Nick felt the man's presence behind him.

There was no way to outrun the thing; it moved at the speed of thought. Nick searched frantically as he ran for something - anything - they might be able to use to defend themselves, but he saw nothing.

"We have to get out of the open," he gasped breathlessly, unaware whether Drake could hear him or not, and Nick charged into the nearest doorway, spluttering in relief as he found the door unlocked.

With Drake trailing yards behind him, Nick raced down a featureless corridor, emerging into a mechanic's workshop.

For a moment he paused. The place was full of weapons that would have been formidable to an ordinary opponent: huge wrenches, welding torches, a range of deadly tools both blunt and sharp.

All were useless. How could you take a swing at something you couldn't even see?

Faintly, in the corridor behind him, Nick heard the door he had entered moments earlier exploding from its hinges and he took off again, expecting that at any moment he would be plucked from the floor and ripped apart. He burst through the next set of doors into another corridor, and saw several others branching from it.

Maybe we can hide?

He dismissed the thought when he heard another shattering crash somewhere behind him, and he rocketed down the corridor toward the doors at the far side, charging into the huge space beyond.

The cavernous room was home to a host of vehicles, some undergoing repairs, others waiting for their next period of use, which Nick realised dimly might now be *never*. Vehicle use might just be a thing of the past.

He saw Drake shoot off to the left.

Feeling a terrified whimper bubbling over his lips, Nick realised that the huge motorised garage door that led to the outside world was shut. It took almost a full minute for the thing to slide up. Pressing the button would be useless.

There was no time.

Nowhere left to run.

11

Michael wheeled himself toward the tower that Darren had pointed out as the one that they were using as a medical facility, "*for whatever it's worth*".

Narrow paths criss-crossed around the interior of the castle, and only weeks before the paths would have been trodden by families of tourists. Michael could imagine sullen teenagers trailing around after enthusiastic parents, focused on playing games on their phones, uninterested in the history of the place, or the manicured flower beds, remaining stubbornly oblivious to their parents' attempts to generate interest.

Michael didn't blame them. The history of the place didn't interest him either. Maybe it never would have; but now history only had any use if it included lessons on how to deal with the entire population of the country suddenly turning into ravenous monsters.

Maybe we've reached the end of history, he thought. *Maybe all the chronicling of the progress of mankind will just stop here.*

He imagined future descendants - new species maybe - finding the books and artefacts that suggested a thriving civilization and wondering what might have happened to halt the progress of the creatures that dominated the planet so abruptly.

Something Rachel had muttered came back to him.

Our evolution came with an expiry date.

For a moment he was lost in a fantasy. Had humanity risen time and time again, only to ultimately destroy itself, leaving a legacy in books and buildings and bloodstains, slowly eroded by time, only for the process to begin again?

As he passed he saw some women planting seeds; a group of three men sawing long pieces of wood into symmetrical shapes. All of them seemed unwilling to meet his gaze, though whether that was because he was new there, or because of the wheelchair, he had no idea. Some part of him suspected neither possibility might be the truth.

He watched them working for a moment, and felt the old cynicism and depression bubbling away inside.

Is there any point in trying to rebuild, he thought, *just so we can begin to destroy ourselves all over again?*

Somewhere in his gut, Michael knew it was not just abstract philosophy. Darren had gone to great lengths to welcome them, but Michael could see through the facade. Despite his best efforts to think otherwise, Michael's group was on a collision course with Darren's. Collision was what humans did best. In some ways, the Infected were the more civilized species. They didn't seem hell-bent on destroying themselves.

Just us.

He was grateful when he reached the door to the tower he was headed for. Time spent alone had always meant sinking into destructive introspection for Michael, even before the world had gone to shit. The worst thing he could possibly imagine was being the last one left alive, just him and his bleak thoughts. If it came to that, if he somehow lost Claire and survived alone he would take the infection and the oblivion that went with it, happily.

For a moment he paused at the door, wondering if he should knock, and the notion made him flush a little. Knocking on doors suddenly seemed oddly archaic.

He pushed it open, and the stink of blood hit him immediately.

The bottom floor of the tower was identical to the one in which he had spent the night with the others, save for the addition of a single mattress, which was being used like a hospital bed. The occupant, a young woman with what looked like a severe head injury, appeared unconscious, her breathing rapid and shallow.

A rudimentary intravenous drip had been set up above her, and Michael saw a low table next to the mattress which held a pitiful range of medical equipment: bandages, salves, painkillers. Most of it looked like the sort of stuff any ordinary household would have in a bathroom cabinet, and he realised that was probably exactly where it had come from. It was a far cry from the sort of the treatment the injured woman looked like she needed.

The enormity of the new world crashed down on Michael then. So much of his time had been spent fleeing from the Infected or dealing with the psychopath in the bunker and his own subsequent paralysis - and now with the bizarre community at the castle - that he had found little time to ponder what life would be like if they were somehow able to find somewhere safe to live out their days in peace.

No electricity, he thought. *No medicine. No knowledge of anything beyond running and fighting and being terrified.*

An image formed in his mind, of trying to deliver a child. Trying to further the human race without the faintest idea what he was doing.

Even if we live through this madness, how can we possibly survive?

"You're one of the new people, right? You came in last night?"

Michael jumped. Lost in his thoughts, he hadn't even noticed the woman descending the stairs from the floor above.

"I'm Michael," he said, and stuck his hand out for a handshake, before realising how ridiculous the gesture appeared. He withdrew his hand, embarrassed.

"Are you hurt? There really isn't much I can do here," the woman said, and Michael saw the dark rings under her eyes. She had a haunted look about her. He would have guessed she was in her early thirties, and if he'd seen her a week earlier he might have said she looked plump and jolly. Now her face was gaunt and hollow, and exhaustion made her look more like forty-five.

"I'm fine," Michael said. "Apart from the legs. But I doubt there's much anyone could do about that."

He smiled warmly.

"How are you?"

For a moment the woman seemed taken aback, and Michael got the impression that it had been a while since anyone had asked her how she was holding up. She smiled weakly.

"I've been better, Michael. I'm Linda."

She offered her hand with a wry smile and Michael shook it with a sheepish grin.

"Darren said you were a teacher, before all this?"

He watched her carefully; scrutinised the way her eyes flickered a little as he mentioned the man's name.

"I taught at the high school. Science. It's funny, I never wanted to be a teacher. Don't really know all that much about science. I just needed a job. You learn the curriculum, learn the bits you need to teach. You don't think you're going to end up trying to perform operations on people with kitchen knives because you know what a double-helix is."

She smiled sadly.

"What about you?"

"I was with the police," Michael said. "Small town. Never did much more than take drunks home. My first murder case was a guy that beheaded his wife and then started trying to eat people. Things have been sort of going downhill ever since."

Linda flashed a tired grin.

"Sounds about right," she said. "You have any idea what happened? What caused this? No one here has a clue. Couple of people have been talking about the end of days, you know, like God's had enough of us."

Michael snorted.

"I don't know how it started, but I know it's got nothing to do with God," he said grimly. "In fact, that's why I wanted to talk to you."

"Oh?" Linda looked surprised.

"I was hoping you might be able to tell me a little more about that double-helix."

Standing in the shadow cast by the castle's huge main gate, John felt his pulse quicken, just a little. It was the shotgun that did it. He hadn't seen any sign of firearms at the castle until he and Rachel met the four men at the entrance, preparing for the supply run into Caernarfon.

When he got close, the shotgun was *all* he saw. That was no accident: the big guy who presumably was under the impression that he was going to be *leading* John into town brandished it brazenly. The gun was a statement. It clearly said *don't fuck with me.*

When John found the big guy's gaze, he saw a sort of smirking confidence there; a smug, knowing sort of stare. It reminded John of the look that people had when they knew a secret that they weren't going to tell you. They just wanted you to understand they knew *something.*

This is going to go badly.

John didn't waste any time wondering where they might have got their hands on the gun: Wales was full of farmland. There would have been a few rusty old double-barrelled affairs out there, just like the one the big guy held so casually.

He saw John looking at the weapon and smirked.

Very badly.

"Sam," the big guy said with a cold smile. "This is Brian, and that's Jack and Glyn."

He pointed at the three men who stood behind him like young children lurking behind a parent. They all nodded. None of them met John's eye.

"You know," John said, "five of us is probably enough. Not sure we need you to come along, Rachel. You won't be able to carry that much anyway."

That was a mistake, and John knew it even as the words left his mouth. He tried to clamp his teeth down on them, but it was too late. Rachel bristled.

"Bull*shit,* John. I'll carry whatever I need to. Worry about yourself, okay?"

John sighed.

Sam rested the gun on his shoulder and snorted a mirthless laugh. He winked at the other three men.

"Obvious who wears the trousers here, ain't it?"

The three of them laughed in unison, but the sound was forced. The sort of laughter that cowards choke out in the presence of a bully.

John had heard it many times before.

Rachel opened her mouth, but apparently thought better of starting an altercation and snapped it shut. She was still glaring at John.

"Let's move out, guys," Sam said. "You know the drill. Food. Medicine. And maybe we can get a collar to put on this guy for his missus, eh? A nice one, mind, with a little bell." He barked a harsh laugh. "No offence, feller."

Sam winked again, and looked slightly crestfallen when John stared at him coolly and said nothing in return.

With a grin, the big man turned and unbarred the gate, striding through the arch and onto the bridge beyond, followed by the other three.

John watched Sam leading them away confidently with interest.

You're the alpha dog here, he thought. *And you've got the gun. So why is Darren in charge? What's he done to earn your loyalty?*

John shook his head at Rachel, letting her know he didn't think it was worth making anything of the man's attitude, and with a nod of his head, headed off after the others.

*

"This is a virus, right?" Michael said. "You know anything about the way they work? Generally, I mean."

Linda smiled.

"Generally is pretty much all I can give you, I'm afraid. I didn't specialise in any of the sciences. I taught the younger age groups. A little physics here, a little biology there. You get the picture."

Michael nodded.

"As I understand it," Linda said, "a virus takes over a host cell and replicates itself to take over other cells. It has to move fast in order to keep growing, before the cells develop a resistance to it."

Michael thought all the way back to his partner, Carl, crashing to the gravel in a remote car park with a placid fisherman sinking his teeth into him; about the way Carl changed so *quickly*. It had taken mere moments for the affable guy to turn into a killing machine.

He shook his head, clearing away the memories. It had been a week; it felt like a lifetime.

"But when you say 'fast'," he said, "how fast are we talking here? I mean, if you get a Flu bug or something, it takes a while to take hold, doesn't it? You start coughing, sore throat - whatever. Then a couple of days later is when it really hits?"

Linda shrugged.

"Sure, with Flu. I suppose it would depend on the virus. Sorry, I really don't know enough to-"

"But a virus could be manufactured to move quickly. Quicker than usual," Michael interrupted.

Linda blinked.

"Manufactured? Is this thing man-made?"

Her eyes widened.

For a moment, Michael said nothing. Project Wildfire, John had called it. *Wildfire.* The thing had been designed to move like lightning.

"I think so," he said with a grimace. "And what happens when a virus meets a cell it can't take over?"

"The virus will die. Or it will mutate."

*

It was no supply run.

John knew it as soon as they passed what looked like a well-stocked pharmacy without even stopping to peer into the window.

The man with the gun led them through the narrow, twisting alleys, taking them deeper into the heart of Caernarfon until the castle was out of sight. John's nerves began to dance in anticipation.

When they passed a corner that John recognised, he slowed his pace, putting a light hand on Rachel's arm to stop her.

"The market is that way," he said, nodding down an alley to the left. "You think you can slip off and talk to the girl?"

Rachel stared at him.

"What are you up to, John?"

"Nothing," John hissed. "I think the girl knows something about what's going on inside that castle. Darren was very quick to stop me talking to her last night. This might be our only chance to find out why. I can't go, the big guy has his eye on me. But I don't think they are paying much attention to the little woman."

He saw Rachel's hackles rising, and he knew he had her.

She glared in the direction of the men leading them, and saw Sam turn and stare at John.

"No time for dawdling back there, feller," he called out. He hadn't even looked at Rachel.

"Fine," she spat.

"Coming now," John called. He shot a glance at Rachel.

"Be careful with her," he said. "Don't get too close, just in case."

He saw the simmering anger in Rachel's eyes, and was grateful when she turned without a word and slipped down the alley John had pointed out. Rachel could handle herself, John did not doubt that. But against four men, he did not think it would be enough. And he knew that if the four men turned on him as he expected them to do at any moment, Rachel would rush to his aid, and they would probably both wind up dead. At least this way, if things went bad, Rachel would have a chance to get away.

Gritting his teeth, he quickened his pace to catch up to the group.

Sam looked at him quizzically.

"Call of nature," John explained. "I think she's a bit shy. She'll catch up."

The man with the gun rolled his eyes, and turned. The road they were on reached a dead end some sixty yards away. If they were going to do it, it would be there.

Hopefully they want to do it quietly, John thought, eyeing the shotgun Sam held casually at his side. If the intention was to execute John, to just blow him away, there would be nothing he could do.

He stalked after them, muscles tensed.

Ready.

*

Mutation.

Michael frowned, trying to recollect Victor's vague words in the bunker, right before Jason had crushed the life out of him.

The virus is in all of us. We've been breathing it in for years and it has lain dormant, waiting for someone to push the button and activate it.

Maybe they had poisoned the water. Maybe they had genetically altered food to include some insidious gene that would lurk in the human body, unnoticed, until the time was right. Maybe the atmosphere itself had been tainted. It scarcely mattered now. John had said the people that designed the virus believed it had failed somehow; had been corrupted by Victor's interference. In fact the opposite was true. The virus was a raging juggernaut of success, far more effective that the people behind it had planned. Relentless and unstoppable. An efficient, invisible predator.

The weight of realisation crashed down on Michael, crushing him like a sudden increase in gravity. Somehow the bastards behind the apocalypse had poisoned the human race, altering the very structure of human DNA, preparing it for the time when they finally decided to push the button and start the end.

Victor's attempt to create immunity had failed. All the lunatic had accomplished was to ensure that in certain people, the virus would mutate wildly, changing them into something else.

Not everyone would become the eyeless monsters. But everyone, once exposed, once activated, would become something. Everyone was susceptible. There was no stopping it. No fighting it.

No immunity.

The only hope was to find somewhere to hide, somewhere the teeth and tainted blood that activated the virus could not reach. Try to live out a semblance of a life in perpetual quarantine, and hope that whatever the key to the virus was, it would die out naturally, or never find them.

He had thought the castle would be safe.

And it might have been, if they were just dealing with sightless hunters; with something they could fight. But Michael knew that was no longer the case. He felt the truth of the revelation squirming in his mind.

The Infected weren't the enemy. Even the people behind Project Wildfire weren't the enemy. The virus was the enemy.

And even now it coursed through the system of an old woman that he had left in charge of his daughter. It had already breached the castle walls. They had brought it in with them.

Gwyneth was not immune.

She carried the virus. Activated. Deadly. Contagious.

She was a timebomb.

12

Another crash, closer this time.

The creature that had single-handedly laid waste to Catterick Garrison, stabbing deep into The Heart that the soldiers had believed was their fortress, was heading toward Nick and Drake unerringly. It sounded as though only a couple of doors now stood between them and a guided missile that would tear them apart. It was approaching slowly, and for a moment Nick was confused, until he remembered the way the thing had grinned; its dead eyes and psychotic stare.

It's enjoying the hunt, he thought. *Getting a kick out of terrifying us.*

Nick bit his tongue painfully, trying not to scream, and desperately searched the vehicles in the cavernous garage, hoping that somehow he had missed a tank sitting among the jeeps and flatbed trucks; wondering if a tank would even be any use against an enemy that seemed to have been spat into the world from a vengeful Hell.

There was nothing. He saw useless crowd control vehicles that had been employed during the last round of riots in the UK, when people finally began to wake up to the idea that the politicians dressed in designer suits were spoon-feeding them bullshit about prosperity while poverty crippled them. Trucks with armoured radiator grilles and water cannons intended to intimidate and disperse crowds of terrified people.

But this had nothing to do with *people,* and it seemed that only Nick felt terrified. Water cannons might as well have been water *pistols.*

"Here," Drake hissed, leaping into the largest vehicle in the garage. It was a heavily armoured crowd control truck, and it was probably their only chance. But Nick knew even as he leapt into the cabin that it was nothing more than a death trap; a bolthole that would do nothing to hide their presence from the predator stalking them.

Nick had seen what the creature did to the trucks they had used as a wall: *obliterated* them; shattering the thick metal like a mini-nuke. The steel frame of the truck might slow the monster for a second, maybe just long enough for Nick to look again at its dead eyes before he was torn apart.

The door they had sprinted through moments before exploded from its hinges and travelled across the room like a deformed bullet, lodging itself into a Jeep that sat with its engine exposed for repairs with a crash that sounded like a god roaring in the enclosed space.

Nick whimpered.

The thing wasn't running anymore; wasn't moving at lightspeed.

It doesn't need to, Nick thought. *It knows we can't harm it.*

He watched, teeth gritted, as the enormous figure ducked its head and *sauntered* through the ruined doorway. Even now Nick's mind tried to conjure up some reason for the creature's existence, but he found it coming up short.

It stood roughly seven feet tall, naked; rippling with twisted muscles that bulged like swollen infections. It looked like some insane scientist had tried to crossbreed a human with an enormous bear. It moved slowly now, with deliberate purpose; a swagger that came from being in absolute control.

It never took its dead eyes from Nick.

I am going to die.

Nick's hands began to move independently, stabbing at the controls on the dashboard wildly, flicking on the truck's lights and wipers, arcing a jet of screen-wash over the windscreen that made the hideous image approaching him ripple, lending it an even more alien look.

Finally he hit a button that sent a powerful jet of water at the creature from a side-mounted water cannon.

For a moment, as the jet hit the creature, it seemed to take a half-step backwards in surprise, and then Nick's stomach dropped like the stock market, crashing all the way down to the bottom, and the bubbling chaos that lived at the edge of insanity.

The thing *laughed.*

Nick was unaware of his own whimpering, unaware of the tears that streamed down his face. His entire consciousness was swallowed up by that laugh, by the evil cruelty of the sound. By its twisted *humanity.*

And then, as Nick continued to slap wildly at the dashboard, his fingers landed on the most hopeless button of all: the sonic generator that sent a low frequency rumble into crowds of protesters to instil headaches and gently persuade them to move on.

And his jaw dropped in astonishment as the terrifying creature collapsed to its knees, clapping its club-like palms to its ears, and screamed in pain.

Nick turned to look at Drake, and cried out in surprise when he saw the passenger seat was empty, and the big man had apparently dissolved into the air.

Losing my mind, Nick thought, and this time it was he that cackled as he understood. There was no Drake. Never had been. Somehow, in the absence of his abusive father, Nick had dreamt up a bastard moulded in the old man's image to get his cowardly arse moving. He didn't know whether he should finally thank Lieutenant-Colonel Colin Hurt or curse him for the mental damage he had inflicted on his little boy.

Framed by the windscreen, he saw the creature struggling back to its feet, shaking its head wildly, as though it hoped to shake the sound out of its mind.

Still cackling, Nick gunned the engine and stamped on the accelerator, and the truck roared forward, smashing into the hideous mutation at waist height and driving it into the wall behind it with a shattering crash.

The creature slumped across the bonnet, sending a shiver through the truck that felt like a distant earthquake.

Nick jumped out and stared at it in terrified curiosity. Its fearsome eyes were shut.

Is it dead?

Nick decided the only prudent course of action was not to hang around to find out. With a final glance around the garage to confirm that Drake had been nothing more than a figment of his imagination, he sprinted through the wrecked door and the twisting corridors that were now filled with debris, wondering idly if hallucinating a carbon copy of his father meant he had gone completely insane, and emerged onto the street that was awash with blood and sundered bodies.

Nick heard a few low moans: a mixture of terror and stupefied pain. Not everyone on the street had been killed outright: the creature had ploughed straight through the middle of them like a tornado, leaving a trail of devastation in its wake.

He frantically scanned the twitching flood of gore on the ground for some sign of Colonel Hopper, unsure whether he expected the man to be alive or dead, and hoping fervently it would be the latter. He was certain Hopper would be carrying the key that would enable Nick to get to the chopper on the roof, but the more he searched, the more hopeless he felt. It was difficult to distinguish which parts of the horrific scene splattered before him had even been human, let alone which particular human they might have belonged to.

He thought back to the garage, and briefly considered that he might be able to head back there and find a jeep or a truck to flee in, but he quickly discarded the idea. The notion of going anywhere near the monster pinned beneath the truck left his stomach attempting to perform cartwheels, and in any case, a truck would not be safe in the long run. The Infected were still out there, a blight that stained the entire land, and sooner or later he would either run into them or run out of fuel. Either scenario would mean his death.

He felt like screaming in frustration.

And then he spotted the fire axe.

He tried to picture the door that led to the roof of the medical centre. Was it steel? Would swinging an axe even leave a dent on it?

He was just bending down to retrieve the axe when he heard it. The low hum of the helicopter's engine, the whipped-air noise of the blades slowly beginning to rotate, picking up speed, and Nick knew what the sound meant, knew it deep inside, where there was no room left for doubt.

Hopper.

Nick was running then, crashing through the wide double-doors that led into the medical centre, a rectangular building three storeys high, expecting that at any moment the creature might pop into existence right in front of him and that the first he would know of it would involve the sudden tearing away of some vital part of his body.

The ground floor of the medical centre was filled with equipment that had been rendered obsolete: all the stretchers and intravenous drips in the world weren't going to matter now. The game had changed.

At the far end of the building, an elevator door stood open, wide enough to accommodate up to three gurneys comfortably, and effectively killed by the sudden loss of electricity. Even if the lift had worked, Nick would not have trusted it. He veered through a door to the left and onto a featureless grey stairway, hauling his aching legs up two steps at a time.

When he reached the third floor he was greeted by the sight he knew he would see: the exit door leading to the roof unlocked; standing open.

He charged through it and out onto the roof, dominated by the helipad and the chopper that wobbled as Colonel Dave Hopper wrestled ineffectively with the unfamiliar controls.

Hopper's eyes lit up when he saw Nick streaking across the roof toward him.

"You there, soldier! Can you fly this thing?" The Colonel hollered above the roar of the engine.

"Absolutely, Colonel," Nick snarled with a savage grin, and he grabbed Hopper by the lapels of his meaningless uniform, and hauled the old man from the chopper.

"Take your hands off me soldier, that's a direct order!"

Hopper screamed, showering Nick's face in hot spittle, and for a brief moment Nick looked into the old man's eyes and saw the fear there. Saw the terrified gaze of an eight year old coward paralysed by the impending arrival of the beast.

"I'm done taking orders, Hopper," Nick hissed, and threw the spluttering old bastard off the roof, grimacing as he heard the man's scream of terror end in an abrupt crunch.

He jumped into the pilot's seat, slamming the door behind him and took a second to study the helicopter's controls. He didn't know how to fly it; not exactly, but he knew enough. A damn sight more than Colonel Hopper had known, apparently.

He yanked on the collective control lever, a little too hard, and the chopper lurched violently into the air, tail down, threatening to collapse back onto the building. Alarms began to sound, frantically chiming to catch Nick's attention. Gritting his teeth, cursing the weight and size of the chopper - large enough to serve as a medical vehicle for much of North Yorkshire - he grappled with the pitch, getting the nose down, and finally lifting clear of the building.

As the front of the chopper lowered, he got a clear view of the disaster on the streets of Catterick. He saw a couple of figures staggering to their feet, a further few emerging from hiding spots that had only proven marginally successful. He saw one man wandering in a daze, clutching dumbly at the oozing space that his left arm had occupied minutes earlier.

For a moment Nick wondered if he might be able to land, and pick up the few that weren't dying slowly of their terrible wounds, but then he saw something that made his gut lurch in unison with the unsteady chopper.

On the ground sixty-odd feet below, one of the stumbling figures suddenly erupted in a cloud of blood. Another quickly followed.

It's still alive.

It's free.

Sweating, panicking at the belief that at any moment the unfamiliar controls would betray him, Nick lifted the chopper higher, his only thought to get the hell away from the massacre.

He was perhaps a hundred feet above the ground, eyes still fixed on the carnage below, when he saw it approaching. A body, hurled through the air toward him like a guided missile.

It's trying to bring down the chopper, he thought, and then: *Oh, Jesus, he's still alive...*

The screaming man hurtled toward the chopper, casually tossed away like crumpled paper, and Nick saw the terror in his eyes, saw the incomprehension as he shot past the windscreen, narrowly missing the body of the vehicle.

And then the man hit the blades, and Nick's view was obscured by a sudden, heavy red rain, and he gunned the throttle blindly and screamed.

*

Jake collapsed to one knee. Getting away from the truck, and the infernal beam of terrible sound that had pinned him in place and made his head feel like it might explode had taken every ounce of his freakish strength. In the end he had been forced to crawl like an insect, dragging himself away from the nightmarish noise, until the sound of it was muted enough to allow him to stand. Even then he had felt crippling pain erupt in his lower back, where the truck had smashed him into the wall.

When he reached the street outside, the chopper was already in the air, lurching upward clumsily, and a tidal wave of rage tore through Jake at the prospect that the hateful human that had humiliated him was getting away.

Tossing one of the screaming creatures at the vehicle took the last of his strength, and he shrieked in frustration when he saw the throw had been good, but not good enough.

The chopper continued to rise, and headed south. The face of the man that had bested him was burned like a brand onto Jake's memory.

I'll find you, he thought, and then, as he sensed movement stirring around him, the few dozen-or-so humans he had failed to kill starting to emerge from their hiding spots, Jake summoned a final burst of power from his aching limbs, terrifyingly aware of the implacable darkness riding toward him on a wave of fatigue and damage, and he bolted away from the wreckage of Catterick Garrison and ran until the darkness caught him.

*

Nick flew until the fuel alarm on the helicopter began to ring out incessantly, and only then did he begin to panic.

Getting away from Catterick had been one thing. But he had no idea where he was actually heading *to*, and as darkness fell outside the narrow windows he realised that might just be a grievous oversight.

His original plan as he had put the horror of Catterick in his rear view mirror, had been to fly south to Birmingham or Manchester, and to land the chopper on the roof of the tallest building he could find. There was, he figured, less chance of encountering the Infected on the top floor of a skyscraper. Plenty of opportunity to work your way down, securing the place floor by floor.

Not a great plan. But a plan, at least.

When the low fuel alarm began to shriek in protest at Nick, he had no idea where he was. He had flown blindly into the darkening night, not registering any detail in the land below. Power was out across the whole country: there was no light to navigate by. No glowing cities, no snaking lines of streetlights to follow. The chopper floated across an endless black canvas.

Only once had the terrain given him any indication where he might be, and then only because it soared up dangerously toward him and he was forced to get the chopper up quickly before it smashed into the jagged face of a mountain.

That must have been the Pennines, Nick thought. *How long ago was that? Shit.*

The alarm pierced his thoughts, and a cold terror seeped from his pores. He was going to have to land, and the chopper was *loud.*

Shit.

He lifted the nose up, slowly stopping the chopper's forward momentum, and then allowed the cumbersome vehicle to drop, as slowly as he could, which translated into jerkily plummeting for what felt like an eternity before he regained control. He descended in increments; jarring, stomach-churning drops of fifty feet at a time that made his already chewed-up nerves scream.

The fuel light blinked rapidly, red and ominous, and still he could not see the ground.

What if I'm over the sea?

Terror clutched at him.

None of the instruments on the dashboard meant much to him: working out how to move the chopper had been one thing. Navigation was entirely another.

He let a shuddering yelp loose as he saw rocks and trees looming below him, and then something even better: four wide lanes of tarmac. A dual carriageway. A landing even he could nail. Nick couldn't believe his luck.

It might have been his imagination, but Nick thought the chopper's engine died even as he descended the final twenty feet or so, hitting the ground with a thump that sent a savage shudder through the vehicle, rattling his bones and almost making him bite off the end of his tongue.

The lights on the chopper didn't illuminate much, just enough to be sure that he had not landed in the middle of a herd of the Infected - though even if he had there was not really much he could have done about it without fuel. The road looked empty, featureless in either direction, but he thought he saw the merest hint of light glinting over the horizon to the west. The last scraps of sunset.

He had come from the east, so he put his back to it, and trotted away from the chopper, trying to maintain a narrow balance between speed and sound.

He'd barely travelled a hundred yards before he heard the noise in the distance behind him, a sound that simultaneously bewildered and terrified.

Snarling.

He turned and looked back at the chopper, an island of light in an ocean of inky darkness. After several moments he thought he saw something there; just a hint of movement. His feet began to creep backwards of their own volition, apparently reaching conclusions his mind had yet to find.

A shadow moved in front of the chopper, and then another, and Nick was at last able to make out what he was looking at.

Dogs, he thought, *it's just dogs.* He almost laughed in relief.

Then he saw another. And another. Five dogs in total. The hairs on the back of Nick's neck began to stand to attention.

Only when the dogs roared as one and tore toward him did Nick's mind finally catch up with his feet.

Propelled by blind panic, Nick turned and sprinted into the darkness, his feet pounding painfully against the tarmac. Behind him, he heard the snarling closing on him inexorably. Running was not going to matter. There was no way to outrun a pack of dogs.

Climb!

Nick veered to the left and hurled himself at the first tree he saw looming in the darkness. There was no time to judge how climbable the trunk was, no time to plot a course upwards. He wrapped his arms tightly around the trunk, ignoring the biting pain as sharp bark cut through his uniform, and began to shimmy upwards, every vertical inch gained feeling painfully slow, until he became aware of the thick branch above him and leapt for it, pulling his feet up and away from the first set of snapping jaws. He felt the teeth grip his boot for a brief moment, before slipping away, and he let out a cry of triumph.

The elation was short lived.

Nick was several feet off the ground. Ground that had now become a seething mass of furry bodies, all of them stalking around the trunk relentlessly.

He was trapped.

And worse. The dogs were making noise. *A lot* of noise. Snarling and howling and barking viciously. Nick stared down at them as horrifying realisation dawned. There was no way down. And anything in the vicinity would hear the noise they were making, and soon he might have to worry about more than dogs waiting for him to fall out of the tree.

Nick fixed his eyes on the road, and the distant pool of light provided by the helicopter, listening to the snapping jaws below and the thundering beat of his heart, and waited for the Infected to find him.

13

Rachel felt growing horror as she cautiously approached the girl tied to a post in the market. It wasn't the girl's appearance that made a cold dread seep into the furthest corners of her soul, though that played a part: like all the others Rachel had seen, the infection had caused the girl to claw out her own eyeballs. The cavernous, weeping orifices left in her face, and the long, ragged furrows her fingernails had ploughed in the soft flesh of her cheeks were bad enough, sure.

No, not her hideous appearance. Rachel was already becoming desensitized to that.

It was the fact that she was whimpering in terror.

It was the fact she was human. A frightened little girl.

All of a sudden the sickness of the new world slammed into Rachel like the shockwave from a dirty bomb, a concussive blast that left a dark burn on her mind that she feared might never fade away.

It only took a week for us to become barbarians. Only a week to sacrifice a child to save ourselves.

When Rachel got close enough, she heard the abject, whimpering terror of the girl take shape, forming words that sent icy daggers into Rachel's heart.

"Please don't, I don't want to, please..."

For a moment Rachel stood, swaying a little, feeling like the world was swimming in an endless pool of nausea.

"What have they been doing to you?"

Rachel's voice emerged as a hesitant whisper. It was a question she was compelled to ask; powerless to avoid, but some part of her didn't want an answer. Suddenly Rachel just wanted to curl up somewhere, in some dark corner. To squeeze her eyes shut and clap her hands over her ears and pretend that the world was anything but rotten to the core.

The girl's frail body was wracked by heaving, choking sobs that made Rachel's blood curdle and her soul shrivel in fear.

And then the girl told Rachel.

And her words made the rage pulse in Rachel like hot lava, rushing up, searching for an exit.

Rachel took a half-step back, feeling like she might vomit or pass out or both, and then a noise in the road behind her swallowed up her attention.

A cry of pain.

Breaking glass.

John.

*

Four to one. Not great odds.

John hated gambling. Hated being put in a position where the outcome of anything was uncertain or left to chance. He stayed away from casinos; he avoided card games. He had never played the lottery. Unfortunately he always seemed to end up in a position where he was forced to gamble with his life instead.

He glared at the four men walking ahead of him. It was doubtful that any of them had the sort of training he had; probably not even anything close to it. But there were four of them. All young. All looked physically fit. All carried knives at the least, and the biggest of them, Sam, the one that smouldered with dark intent, carried a shotgun and a look in his eyes that said he was fully prepared to use it.

Terrible odds.

The big man was slowing the pace, heading for the dead end, making a show of pointing out a small convenience store. They had already passed by two.

If you wait, you die. If they get to start this however they planned to, you die.

Rachel was safely out of the way and John was already moving, letting animal instinct take over, trusting that surprise would prove a more deadly weapon than the two rounds in that gun.

He barrelled into the back of the one called Glyn, sending him crashing into the man holding the gun from behind. The smaller man yelped as he connected with the back of the leader, a pitiful sound that was one part surprise, two parts fear at the physical collision with someone he so obviously feared.

Pathetic, John thought as he dropped low and swept out the legs of another of them. As that one - *Brian? It doesn't matter* - crashed to the ground with a thump, John heard another sound; one that gave him a slight chance, just a sliver of light in the dark.

The shotgun, clattering to the floor ahead of him, spilled from the big man's fingers.

The third of the men - Jack - was still staring, stupefied, at the sudden chaos that had broken out around him. As John rose to his feet, he smoothly withdrew the bigger of the two knives he carried on his belt: a wicked eight-inch blade he had taken from the hardware store back in Aberystwyth. The thing was well-balanced; solidly made. It was a high-end knife designed for use in industrial kitchens and for cutting through stubborn hunks of meat.

The knife slid into the lower back of the man smoothly, like the area around his spine was a purpose-built sheath. John barely felt any resistance as the metal penetrated him, felt nothing beyond a jarring scrape as the blade nestled into its new home alongside the man's vertebrae.

He shot a glance at Glyn, the whimpering coward he had pushed into the big guy at the front.

Not important, John thought, but his muscles were already ahead of his mind, and he launched himself into Sam even as the big man stooped to retrieve the gun, catching him around the waist in a tackle that powered the man's breath from his body in an explosive gasp.

With a deafening shatter, John drove Sam's thick torso through a window into a small fashion boutique, and felt his heart drop a little as he felt the breaking glass shear a deep gash into his thigh.

He had only managed to disable one of them.

Shit.

Worse still: the big guy was fast, way faster than John had expected, bouncing to his feet like a goddamned jack-in-the-box and delivering a heavy kick to John's ribs. It felt like a truck had sideswiped him, and a field of shimmering stars burst across his vision. He felt something cracking in his chest, and the pain erupted, blossoming outward remorselessly from the point of impact.

He tried to rise to his feet, only to collide with a meaty fist travelling at pace in the opposite direction, sending him crashing back to the ground. He groaned as the hard floor conspired with his cracked rib, hatching a plot to send him into darkness.

John grasped at consciousness; clung to it like a liferaft, and desperately tried to reach his other knife, planning to whip it out and sever Sam's Achilles in a single motion, knowing that his only hope was to bring the fight down to the deck and end it quickly.

But then, before his fingers could even grasp the handle of the small blade, the heavy workboot filled his vision, and his head snapped to the side, and white-hot pain exploded in his mind.

For a moment that felt like a lifetime, John lay with his cheek resting on the cool laminate floor, and he saw the boot approaching again, saw it connecting, but this time there was no pain, and he knew then that he was going to die.

He couldn't lift his head, but his eyes rolled upward to see the big man pulling a small knife from his belt.

Make it quick then, you bastard, he thought, and then the room was filled with the sound of the shotgun roaring, and an impossible hole tore open across Sam's chest.

When Sam fell, dead before his skin kissed the ground, John saw Rachel standing over him, the barrel of the shotgun pouring smoke and framing her face, twisted into a mask of pure rage, and he allowed his eyes to close, and let the darkness have him.

*

Rachel felt bile rising in her throat as she looked at the torn body of the man she had just murdered. It felt like the world was slowly twisting her, melting away all the parts of herself that she recognised.

How has it come to this?

She heard a groan behind her. One of the two guys that she had found on the floor when she sprinted up the dead-end alley. Presumably John had already gone to work on them. One looked to have smacked his head into the ground, and was sitting on the floor, staring dumbly at his feet and shaking his skull like a dog trying to shake water out of its fur.

Another was laying still, face down on the cobbles, the handle of a large knife protruding from his lower back.

The other one had just stared at her in mute apprehension. He hadn't looked damaged; just terrified.

He had almost appeared grateful when Rachel stooped and swept up the shotgun in her shaking hands, like the thought of picking it up himself and taking charge of the situation scared him more than anything.

Neither of the two John had left alive had followed her through the broken window, but both would have heard the result of her entry into the boutique. Their response would be either fight or surrender.

She turned quickly, lifting the gun and pointing it at the stricken face of the man called Glyn as he peered through the window to see the guts of his former leader splashed across the wall above the unconscious body of John.

"Pretty sure I only used one barrel there," she said. "Not a hundred per cent, though."

Her eyes narrowed.

"How about you?"

Michael crashed through the door and into the tower, and almost lost his mind when he saw that neither Gwyneth nor the children were there. He frantically wheeled himself to the foot of the staircase, and hollered a *hello* up the gloomy, winding steps.

He gasped in relief when he heard Gwyneth answering, her voice distant and muffled by the stone walls.

It took a few moments for Claire and Pete to bound into view, and Michael knew immediately from the look on his daughter's face that something was wrong.

"Claire? What is it?"

He tried to keep the panic from his voice. Claire's eyes were wide, her jaw slack. She looked terrified; *haunted.* She threw herself at Michael, wrapping her arms tightly around his neck. Michael could feel her rapid breathing, and the pounding of her heart against his shoulder.

He returned the hug, and stared quizzically at Gwyneth as she appeared on the staircase.

And then he froze.

The old woman was not alone.

Michael stared in astonishment at the man who descended the stairs slowly behind Gwyneth. He looked skeletal, and his steps were faltering. In the gloomy stairway, lit only by the narrow slits that served as windows, it was difficult for Michael to tell at first what was odd about the man's gait. He moved slowly, like simply balancing himself and remaining upright was a challenge. When the light fell across him, Michael saw why.

Both of the man's arms had been amputated at the shoulder. He was young, but looked frail and weak, and his skin had a sickly pallor. The stumps where his arms should have been looked slick and rotten. He looked close to death. Michael could smell it upon him, a stink that followed him like a shadow.

Michael's mouth dropped open, and he turned to look at Gwyneth, trying to frame a question that would make sense of the confusion he felt. In the end, he didn't need to ask.

"The girl in the market, Michael," Gwyneth said.

Michael stared at her dumbly.

"They've been feeding him to her."

14

Nick hated dogs.

He prayed the pack below might get bored or distracted, but God hadn't answered any of Nick's prayers thus far, and it didn't look like he was about to start now.

He shimmied up the tree a little further, as far as the narrowing branches would allow, until he was high enough to see a good distance around him. As moonlight filtered through the thick blanket of cloud above, he saw mile after mile of trees bisected by the wide road, and not much else. He thought he could see a tall steeple to the west, which likely meant a town, but it looked several miles away, and he couldn't even be sure that a town was what he needed right now.

He cursed his foolishness. He should have landed the chopper as soon as he was far enough away from Catterick. Should have flown low until he found an isolated spot and waited for daylight. At least that way he might have been able to scout out a safe spot to land, or maybe to locate a place where he might be able to refuel.

Stupid coward. Running blindly until there's nowhere left to run. When will you learn?

Below him, the dogs' snarling intensified, as though they were reading his mind and had decided that his terror and self-recrimination needed a soundtrack.

He stared down at them through the branches. With the shards of moonlight on the dogs at last, he saw their eyes, the livid red infections that they had become, and his heart sank. *All that time you worried about them drawing the attention of the Infected*, he thought. *The infection was down there the whole time. It's in the animals too.*

For a while he had toyed with the idea of snapping a branch from the tree, as thick and sturdy as possible, and leaping down there among the slavering beasts swinging; showing them there was a good reason why they were pets and humans were their masters. The idea had been pure fantasy, of course, and now that he saw their eyes, Nick was glad that fear had held him back. The creatures carried the virus. All it would take was one little nip, a scant breaking of the surface of his skin, just as he had suffered all those years earlier.

The effects of that bite had been psychological. A bite from one of the dogs that now cornered him would have a dramatically different outcome.

After a while, when the complaints of Nick's bladder began to get too loud to ignore, he contorted himself awkwardly to lower his fly, and relieved himself all over the pack below, relishing the sudden surprised yelps he heard in the darkness.

"Take *that*, you furry bastards," Nick mumbled, and he felt a smile creep across his lips. As he pulled the zip back up, he considered the way the tables had turned, the world twisting until a man was left in a position where he was pissing all over dogs, instead of the other way around, and he began to chuckle to himself; short snorts of laughter that he was dimly aware were veering close to full-blown hysteria.

He leaned back against the rough trunk of the tree, squeezing his eyes shut in frustration, desperately trying to imagine a future that didn't involve him either starving to death up a tree or being ripped to pieces at the base of it.

He heard an odd yelp below him, and grinned a little.

Not so nice when it's you getting pissed on, is it?

The grin widened as he heard another yelp that sounded almost like a response.

Suddenly, the growling and snarling below increased in intensity and Nick's eyes flicked open.

Two more abrupt yelps. Now it sounded like there was only one dog growling and barking, and the noise sounded like it was receding away from him at pace.

He peered down at the ground, trying to make out the shape of the dogs between the leafy branches of the tree. He saw no movement, but heard another squealing yelp, which sounded like it was definitely further away from his position, and then *silence.*

Nick held his breath and listened intently.

"That all of them?"

The voice below nearly made Nick fall out of the tree in shock.

"Looks like it."

Nick froze, squinting through the branches, trying to get a glimpse of them. Two voices. Both male. He felt cold sweat running down his back as indecision tore him in two. Someone had killed the dogs, someone that now stood right below him. Whoever they were, they had weapons, and they thought nothing of taking on a pack of infected dogs. They were probably every but as dangerous to him as the animals.

Nick swallowed painfully.

Best to stay hidden, he thought, but as soon as he made up his mind to shrink back against the tree and wait for the strangers to move on, he realised the choice had been taken away from him.

"You coming down then, mate?" A voice called up to him. "We're not gonna hang around here all day."

Shit.

15

Michael felt Claire's grip on his neck tighten.

He tried to grasp the words Gwyneth had just said, but they slipped away from the surface of his mind.

"Feeding him to her," he repeated slowly.

"Pete, why don't you take Claire up to the bedroom upstairs, okay?" Gwyneth said. "I need to talk to Michael. I'll be up soon, okay sweetheart?"

Gwyneth stepped close and ruffled Claire's hair affectionately, not noticing the way Michael flinched slightly. Claire nodded, and released her grip on Michael, following Pete upstairs. Gwyneth waited a moment until she heard the door above open and close.

She led the amputated man over to the wall, and gently guided him down to sit on the floor.

Michael stared at the man in horrified fascination. It wasn't just the grisly stumps where his arms should have been, not even the way the wounds seemed to have been burned extensively, presumably to stem the blood loss.

It was the man's eyes. A sort of madness lurked in those eyes, a screaming, clawing darkness that made Michael's skin crawl.

"He doesn't talk much," Gwyneth said. "I managed to get a few words from him. It was enough."

She rubbed her temples, as though trying to ward off an irresistible headache.

"They think the girl needs human flesh to survive, Michael. To keep the Infected away, if that makes any sense. If anything does. They think we're dealing with *zombies*. This man was locked up in a room at the top of the tower. They've been...keeping him. Taking parts of him..."

Michael held up a hand to stop her. For the first time since he had first stepped into Ralf's cafe on the outskirts of St. Davids a million years earlier, he felt his stomach do a barrel roll, and the meagre scraps he had eaten tried to force their way up into his throat. He choked the bile back down.

"Darren said she was bitten," Michael said weakly. "She has some effect on the Infected. Like a repellent. She's what's keeping them out of Caernarfon." Michael's voice sounded as weak in his ears as his stomach felt.

Gwyneth looked stunned.

"She's immune?"

Michael winced.

"She's just a child, Michael. Just a little girl. Bitten, just like me, but she is still *human*. This is monstrous, we have to stop-"

He held his hand up again and nodded, and Gwyneth paused.

We die fighting them, not each other. Michael had said those words, back in the retail park outside Aberystwyth, said them to avert the disaster that would have been John and Jason killing three innocent, terrified people.

Those people had died anyway. Jason had died anyway. The world was death now. There were no peaceful solutions. He had hoped he could make it through the disaster with his conscience intact. He had been a fool.

Michael felt the room spinning around him, felt the image of Gwyneth standing in front of him dimming, and then he was back there, all the way back in Cardiff, locked in the memory he had tried so long to suppress, confronted by the version of himself that he had tried for years to outrun. The version whose clutches the brutality of the world seemed determined to stop him from escaping.

Cardiff.

The nightmare corridor of blood and bone and screaming.

The darkness.

*

Michael killed the engine and unbuckled his seatbelt.

"Just another domestic," Michael said. "I was here a few weeks ago. The guy beats his wife. The neighbours call us. The wife sends us away."

He sighed, even as his partner rolled his eyes. The story was all-too familiar.

"It's alright mate, I'll go. I can see you're busy."

Michael stepped out of the police car. His partner, James, waved a dismissive hand, preoccupied with his mobile phone and a burgeoning text relationship with a girl he had met in a bar a couple of weeks earlier. The girl, James said, was a 'nine'. He always ranked women like that. Didn't hide the fact from the women either, and Michael was continually baffled that James seemed able to pick up girls almost at will, when he made no effort to conceal his nature. He was a sly bastard, but a good officer. He had taught Michael a lot in the three years they had been working together.

Michael was still in uniform. He had been overlooked for promotion on the two occasions that he had been certain he would get the nod. It was baffling, a source of constant frustration. When his last application had been rejected, they had told him he would make a fine detective. He just wasn't ready yet. They did not said *why*.

Michael shut the door, leaving James alone in the car with his phone.

He remembered the house well from his previous visits; this would be the fourth time that Michael had personally visited the place. He knew other officers who had been there even more often. The joke around the station was that uniformed officers spent more time visiting number 44 Queen's Drive than they did in the staff canteen.

The road was one of the rougher in Cardiff's poorest neighbourhood, far away from the harbour front that was undergoing significant redevelopment, with foreign money and Government investment pouring into designing sleek buildings that offered a marvellous and expensive view of the crashing waves of the ocean. Queen's Drive felt like another world entirely: riddled by poverty and petty crime. There were some nights that James and Michael joked that they might as well just park the squad car on the street and wait.

He stepped up to the terraced houses, not making eye contact with the faces he saw peering at him from behind twitching curtains. Number 44 had a cheerful red door, although Michael always noticed the scratches around the lock. Gavin Edwards was permanently drunk: his key appeared to miss the lock more often than it connected.

Looking at the familiar scratches, Michael wondered with a heavy heart how often Rhiannon Edwards sat in her living room, listening to the key scratching around the lock, praying that her husband wouldn't make it through the door that night to unleash his latest drunken rage upon her.

He knocked loudly, and the door swung open. That wasn't unusual. Neither was the stink of liquor that washed over Michael as the door opened.

But something was different, and Michael noticed it immediately, and felt his nerves jangling in silent warning.

He couldn't hear Rhiannon Edwards crying and screaming at her abusive husband. Whenever Michael had shown up in the past, the woman had been locked deep in retaliation against the bastard she had married too young, and without any insight into the sort of man he might turn out to be. Usually Michael had to separate them physically, and it was rare that he escaped from number 44 without a few cuts and bruises himself.

Never had a problem with Gavin, though. Like most wife-beaters Michael had encountered, the guy was a coward when another man entered the equation, let alone one in uniform.

Michael stepped across the threshold, and saw it immediately.

Blood.

A long, thin trail of it smeared along the wall to his left, leading around a corner and into the living room, beyond his sight.

Shit.

For a moment he thought about signalling James to join him, but then he heard it, and all thoughts of caution and following protocol deserted him.

A baby, screaming.

The Edwards' didn't have a child.

Michael started to run, but his legs felt like they were locked in quicksand, and he knew he was going to be too late.

As he rounded the corner he heard Gavin Edwards snarling.

"Here's what I think about having a baby, you stupid bitch."

I'm too late.

When Michael entered the living room, his eyes took in the horror of the scene even as his mind retreated.

Rhiannon Edwards lay on the floor in a pool of blood; an impossible ocean of it, black and toxic like an oil slick in the dim light provided by a lamp that had been flung into a corner. Her eyes were open; fixed and sightless.

Gavin Edwards stood over her, gripping a large kitchen knife in one hand, and the screaming baby in the other.

For a moment Michael froze as Gavin's eyes locked onto him, and Michael had a second to see the insanity there before the man screamed - a horrific, chilling noise that filled the room and made Michael's gut squirm - and dragged the blade across the child's throat, sending a spurt of arterial blood across the room; a spurt that was both tiny and all-consuming.

The darkness welled up inside Michael, tearing upwards and obliterating everything in its path; erupting like a volcano. He wasn't even aware of launching himself at Edwards. Later on the evidence would prove beyond a shadow of a doubt that Michael had beaten the man to death, but that part of the memory was difficult to access, like corrupted data.

He had no memory at all of James entering the building minutes later to see what had happened to his partner. No memory of the immediate steps taken to ensure the cover up. The public couldn't know. Some of them might understand *why*, his superiors had told him, but the fallout for the South Wales Police would be enormous. There had already been skirmishes on the streets of the city following supposed police brutality as the poor were driven back from the burgeoning wealth on the coast. Michael's actions could well spark a riot, and there was a lot of money being poured into Cardiff. No one wanted a riot.

So it was self-defence. And the end of Michael's hopes of progression in the force. He would have to undergo extensive, compulsory therapy. He would eventually have to relocate to a quiet town where there was no chance of him ever again encountering unspeakable acts of violence.

He was to live with the knowledge that a murderer lived inside him, to suffer the yawning chasm of depression that claimed him as it had claimed his father. He was doomed to dream of the corridor of blood and bone every night, and to wake terrified and shivering, drenched in sweat and praying that he might not remember the dreams, but he always did. He was to tell himself that he could never again allow the darkness at the heart of him to break free, for fear it might take over everything and consume him.

"Michael, are you okay?"

Gwyneth's voice. Tossed to him like a life-preserver. He clutched at it, dragged himself away from the horror of the memory and back into the present. When he spoke, his voice didn't sound like his own.

There was no room left in the world for conscience. There was only action. Only killing. He saw it now, as he had seen it years before, lurking behind the red door.

"Darren has to die," he said.

Gwyneth's wrinkled face paled.

"I don't think that we can-" she began to say.

"I'll do it," Michael said, and the flat emptiness of his tone made him shrivel a little inside. The Michael he had tried so hard to leave behind. That Michael had never truly gone anywhere.

"Well, now, that sounds interesting. How do you think you'll manage that?"

Michael squeezed his eyes shut in despair.

Darren's voice.

Behind him.

16

Nick descended the tree clumsily, and all hope of retaining a semblance of dignity evaporated when he finally lost his foothold and fell the last few feet, landing heavily on his backside with an involuntary yelp. As far as first impressions went, Nick doubted he could have done much to make this one worse.

The two men waiting for him laughed, and Nick saw a helping hand dangled in front of his face. He grasped it, aware as he was hoisted to his feet that his bottom was now damp.

Landed in your own piss, Nick-yyyy. Nice touch.

Nicky. Nick didn't want to think about why the voice of his internal thoughts would now address him using the name his father had used so witheringly. To many people, 'Nicky' might have sounded endearing. Colin Hurt had developed a way of making it sound like a girl's name. Nick hated it with a passion.

He studied the two men carefully, and the first thing he noticed was the crossbow. At least the mystery of the disappearing dogs had been solved.

He gestured at the weapon.

"Thanks, " he said. "For getting rid of the dogs."

"Didn't do it on your account, mate. But glad to be of service. You with the army?"

The man gestured at Nick's crumpled uniform.

"Yeah," he said.

"Come to save us?" The man grinned widely.

Nick shook his head and flushed.

That was rhetorical, Nick-yyyy.

"Nick Hurt," he mumbled, extending his hand.

The grinning man shifted the crossbow to his left hand and shook Nick's hand solemnly.

"Bet you do," he said cheerfully. "Reckon you'll have a bruised arse for days."

They both laughed again, and Nick couldn't help but smile.

"I'm Ray. The shy one behind me is Gareth. Reckon that's your chopper back up the road, right?"

"Uh, yeah," Nick said.

"Can you fly it?"

Nick nodded. "I could," he said. "Until the fuel ran out."

"Ah," Ray said. "We'll have to sort that out, then. Shouldn't be a problem. After all, this is the land of opportunity now, right? No credit card required."

He clapped Nick on the shoulder. Nick blinked in confusion.

"Aren't you worried about the Infected?"

For a moment Ray looked puzzled.

"The Sockets, you mean? That's what we call 'em. Nah, there's none left here mate. They all upped sticks and headed west from here days ago. Get the odd straggler here and there. Animals too, they operate on a different wavelength, I reckon. Nothing we can't handle."

"They headed west?" Nick couldn't keep the confusion from his voice. He had only just learned that animals could carry the virus, and now this strange man was asking him to believe that the Infected were somehow...*organised*. "Why?"

Ray shrugged.

"Beats me," he said. "But that's why we need the chopper."

Nick stared at him blankly.

"We're heading west, too," Ray said with an easy grin. "And you're going to be our pilot."

Nick stared into the man's eyes, drilling down past the grin and the easygoing manner. Something smouldered in the man's gaze. Something that left Nick in no doubt that anything other than an affirmative answer might see things end badly for him.

"Sure," he said weakly, and Ray clapped him on the shoulder.

*

Ray and Gareth led Nick a mile or so down the road, before following a narrow trail through the trees. Neither spoke, and the resulting oppressive silence made Nick clench his fists so tightly that his fingernails dug painfully into the flesh of his palms.

After a walk of around fifteen minutes, they emerged into a small clearing and Nick was surprised to discover that they were near a cliff overlooking the ocean. It looked like the place had once been a spot for ramblers to stop and admire the view. Now, a small, messy camp had been set up in the clearing. It made sense, Nick supposed, to put the ocean at your back.

He saw a handful of other men milling around the camp, and several large motorbikes propped on kickstands in the swaying grass. A group of bikers. Suddenly the devil-may-care attitude seemed to make a little more sense to Nick.

He pulled Ray aside.

"Where are we?" He asked. "I had no idea I was near the ocean."

"Flying blind, huh?" Ray said with a grin. "Reckon we all are now, one way or another. North Wales coast, mate, near the English border. Not too far from Liverpool."

That made sense. Nick had flown southwest for a long time. Any further and he would have been landing the chopper in the sea. He shuddered involuntarily.

"Ray," he said. "Something doesn't make sense. Back there you said all the Infected had gone west. But then you said you wanted to go that way too. You meant east, right?"

Ray shook his head.

"West, mate, that's right."

"But why?"

"To right a couple of wrongs, mate," Ray said, as if the answer was as straightforward as simple arithmetic.

Nick frowned in confusion.

"We had a place we could have been safe," Ray said. "About as good a place as you could get in this nightmare, I reckon. It could have worked, but the guy in charge decided he didn't want our sort mixing with his sort."

Nick stared around the group of men as Ray started toward the camp again. They all looked huge and intimidating. Covered in rippling muscles under weathered, tattooed skin.

"This person made you leave?" Nick couldn't keep the astonishment from his voice as he trotted along behind Ray's loping stride. He tried to imagine what sort of person would be able to intimidate a group of men like the ones now standing in front of him.

"Aye," Ray said. "He did. He had a couple of guns and a big wall to hide behind. We had fists and bad language. But things have changed now, right?"

Nick stared at him blankly.

Ray winked.

"Now we've got a *helicopter.*"

17

Six had definitely been too many. Darren should have listened to his instincts. It was the children that did it. How was he supposed to turn away children? The youngest of the people he had managed to gather together in the castle was seventeen. If they were to survive what was beginning to look like the end of days, they would need children.

If it came to it - to repopulating and trying to build some sort of life for the future - children would be just about the most valuable thing Darren could imagine. They had been worth the risk. But even then, Darren had only permitted the opening of the castle doors because the people with the children looked harmless. An old woman, a cripple. Another young woman to add to the growing numbers he had already secured; God knew she might be valuable as well. He had only permitted a handful of men to remain in the castle, just the ones he could control. They would need lots of women if they were to avoid veering too close to inbreeding.

There would be little point in surviving the apocalypse, living on through dreadful squalor, only to discover that the children you produced were damaged. Not *viable*.

He had thought only the one who stank of military training - John - would be a problem to the continued harmony in his castle. And John was being dealt with at that very moment, out there in Caernarfon. Killed and stored away out of sight. Future meals for the guardian at the gate; the thing that kept them all safe, for as long as Darren kept her alive.

And then, just as Darren thought the situation was under control, he had walked in on the old woman and the cripple plotting to kill him. And worse, they had freed the man from the tower's top room and were no doubt jumping to all *sorts* of conclusions.

Darren stepped into the room and swung a solid fist into the cripple's face, toppling him from the wheelchair onto the stone floor.

"*This* is your gratitude?" He spat the words out like rotten meat. "This is the thanks I get for allowing you in here?"

Michael spat out a mouthful of blood, and twisted awkwardly until he was on his back. He glared at Darren.

"You want gratitude?" Michael barked a harsh laugh. "Do you even see what you are, Darren? Forcing a child into cannibalism? Killing off men so you and your buddies can terrorise a bunch of women you've turned into prisoners? That's the price of safety?"

"That's *my* price of safety," Darren roared. "Because this is *my* place. Who the fuck do you think you are to come in here and think you have the right to preach to anyone? You think I swallowed all that bullshit about you all being a family, and making it all the way up here without getting your hands dirty? I didn't question it because it's not fucking important. My hands are dirty. Fucking *filthy*. But we are safe here, and we can continue to be safe. And now you're in here talking about killing me because of *that*?"

He jabbed a thick forefinger at the amputated man.

"Do you know how dirty *his* hands are? Did you bother to consider it before you started making judgments? That fucker over there is the only one here that has touched any of those women, and that's why he lost his arms. Anybody else here follows his lead and I'll do the same to them. Nobody touches anyone without my say so, understand? He didn't understand and he is paying for his crimes, and we are still fucking safe!"

Darren was screaming now, losing all sense of control. He sucked in a deep, shuddering breath.

Michael looked stunned.

Darren snorted a laugh.

"Oh, what, you thought I was some psychopath, right? Doing this for the fucking *fun* of it? I've had to do terrible things, because *someone* has to do terrible things or we'll all end up dead. We'd be fucking dead already. What about you, Michael? Done anything terrible? Done anything you'd rather you hadn't? Or you, old woman? Are your hands clean?"

Gwyneth took a step backward, as if stunned by Darren's sudden ferocity.

Michael rubbed his hand across his lip, winced a little at the sharp pain.

"She's a *little girl*, Darren."

"She's not a little girl," Darren thundered. "She *was* a little girl. Now she is the only thing that keeps *them* from swarming over this place and killing us all. She is the only weapon we have against them. What would you have done with her?"

Michael stared at him, and said nothing.

"Exactly," Darren snarled. "You have no answer because there *is* no answer. I'm not going to waste time wondering if I'm going to Hell for my actions, Michael. There's no need; I'm already there. I move from one foothold to the next. It's all I can do. You want to live according to some moral code, you do it somewhere else. I want to *survive*. This castle is *mine*, understand?"

Michael shook his head.

"There are ways to survive without us becoming the monsters, Darren. Killing people that threaten your life is one thing, but feeding people to the Infected to stay alive? That's not surviving, not in any way I recognise. If all you want to do is go on living, why not just go out there and get infected yourself? That way all you lose is your eyes, not your soul."

Darren sighed.

"I'm sorry you feel that way, Michael. I hoped you might see reason."

He withdrew a multi-tool from a pocket and unleashed the blade with a sharp *snap*.

"I can't allow you to divide this place, not now. It has to be this way."

Michael laughed softly.

"I never thought you were a psychopath, Darren. I think you're a sociopath. You'd have to be to end up running this place as you have. You'd have to understand that there are some situations so terrible that choice goes out the window. As it happens, I don't even blame you for keeping the girl outside. I would have done the same, had I known the whole story. I *will* do the same."

Michael reached under the pack at his side and pulled out the rifle, aiming it at Darren's face.

Darren froze.

"You are right about one thing, though," Michael said. "This place can't be divided. Not if there is to be any hope of survival here. But the castle isn't yours. Not anymore."

Darren's face dropped.

"We do what we are forced to do, don't we Michael?"

Darren held up his hands, but to Michael it didn't look like a gesture of surrender. More like acceptance.

"We do," Michael said, and blasted a hole through Darren's skull.

"I'm sorry, Gwyneth," Michael said.

Gwyneth nodded slowly. She looked stunned and frightened.

"You had to do it, Michael," she said in a trembling voice. "He was going to kill you."

"No," Michael said. "I'm sorry that you're infected. It's too dangerous to have you here."

He swung the rifle around, aiming it at Gwyneth.

"B-but I'm not-"

Michael didn't let her finish.

*

Gwyneth didn't feel the bullet ripping through her heart. It took her a second to die, but a second was long enough.

In that long, meandering moment, she understood something about the virus that had mutated her cells. As the darkness claimed her, she felt that strange connection being made once more, just as it had when she had been unconscious on the boat.

It was all to do with the blood, she saw that suddenly and clearly, like a flashbulb pointed at the truth. The sharing of the genes with those closest to you. With family. The infection reserved a special savagery for that bond. It attacked it with howling, relentless ferocity. In that split-second as death wrapped her in its cold embrace, she pictured all the mothers out there hunting down their children. All the sons and daughters chasing down their parents; siblings that turned on each other with blinding ferocity, not understanding why their blood raged at the very existence of family; just programmed to kill the bonds that tied them to their old selves.

She understood then what she had felt on the boat in her dark dream.

The last thought on Gwyneth's mind was the son she and Steve had created when they had been far too old. The son they had taken to London and left there, after they saw the twisted darkness in his young eyes, evil and malevolent and inherent. The little boy that they tried so hard to forget; just a whisper of guilt in the shadows.

Gwyneth had always hoped the little boy had found the care and stability she and Steve could not provide.

As the light faded away, and the connection was made once more, linking them together across hundreds of miles, and she felt the endless abyss of his rage, she knew he had not.

*

Rachel was on the bridge when she heard the gunshots, distant and muffled, the sound barely wriggling free of the castle's stone walls.

She had improvised a stretcher for John, instructing the two men she now held at gunpoint to load him onto a surfboard she found at a small shop near the waterfront. John's face was a mess: battered and bloody, his left cheek already beginning to swell. He had a deep gash in his leg that refused to stop leaking. Rachel had dashed into a pharmacy and loaded everything she could think he might need into a bag: bandages, antibiotics. Even a needle and thread, though who might actually sew the leg up she had no idea.

If it came to it, Rachel thought, she would do it herself, but she didn't fancy she would make a very good job of it. Still, she owed John that much. It was obvious to her now that he had tried to get her away from the trouble she hadn't even seen brewing.

Idiot, she thought, as she leant in close to check his breathing when they loaded him onto the surfboard. He was unconscious, but he seemed to be breathing okay. For now, Rachel had done all she could do for him, wrapping his leg in a bandage that quickly soaked through with blood.

They were returning to the castle, and Rachel was just wondering if she was going to have to walk in there brandishing the shotgun without any real idea whether it was even loaded, when she heard gunfire inside.

"Move," she said, jerking the barrel of the gun at the two men. Without the big guy to hide behind, they suddenly looked like frightened boys, and for the first time Rachel noticed how young they were. Younger than her: twenty, maybe; twenty-one. Just kids. No wonder they looked so scared.

When they reached the gate, she pressed the barrel of the gun into the face of the youngest-looking of them, the one that had been too frightened to pick up the gun himself. He had a scrawny, underfed look that Rachel guessed had been with him long before getting hold of food became a matter that required thought and planning.

"Get the gate open," she said in a low, steely voice.

"Uh...hey? It's Glyn, we're back, open up!" He called out in a voice that shook almost as much as his trembling hands.

After a moment, the gate opened, and Rachel entered the castle, holding up the shotgun, expecting to meet trouble immediately.

Instead she saw several people staring in shock toward the sound of the gunshots. Toward the tower they had slept in the night before.

Michael.

*

Rachel burst into the tower and stopped in her tracks. The atmosphere inside felt like the aftermath of a violent storm.

Michael was toppled from his wheelchair, clutching the gun, his face anguished, his lip split and bleeding. In front of him: the body of Darren, his hand curled around a small blade. Gwyneth was crumpled against the curved wall with a hole in her chest; the two kids stood halfway down the staircase, looking terrified. A guy sat propped against the wall close to Gwyneth's body. Alive, though just barely by the look of it; both arms amputated, leaving hideous stumps that looked burned and possibly infected: Rachel could smell the sweet, sickly odour that poured off the man, who sat and stared vacantly through her.

Something about the man's gaze was broken. It reminded her of the way her brother had looked, after he had been forced to kill his mother to protect his sister.

Dimly Rachel was aware that the fact she found the scene inside the tower confusing rather than sickening or horrifying was a sign that something was slowly being stripped away from her soul, flaking off like old paint. A thin veneer of something that she hadn't even been aware of; something necessary.

"What happened?"

Michael shook his head.

"Darren," he said, his voice trembling. "Came in and pulled the knife, knocked me out of the chair. I got the gun, we struggled."

He looked at Gwyneth's open, fixed eyes, staring straight at him.

"It just went off," he said.

Rachel spat on Darren's corpse.

"They tried to kill John, too," she said. "Beat the shit out of him. I had to shoot one of them. John killed one."

Her voice faltered, just a little.

"At least you got this bastard," she said.

Michael nodded, and pulled the wheelchair upright. He levered himself up and onto it."

"It's not all of them," Michael said. "Just Darren and a few others."

"Just the men," Rachel said with a grimace. "And I think a couple of the ones that are left aren't in the mood to cause trouble. Darren had these people terrified of him."

Neither of them needed to say it. Rachel knew what needed to be done, and the message in Michael's eyes was clear. They both had guns. Whether they liked it or not, they had just staged a coup.

Rachel nodded at the man propped against the far wall.

"And him?"

Michael looked at the amputated man. "They had him locked up," he said, and shook his head. "You don't want to know."

Rachel grimaced again.

"I think I already do," she said grimly. "I talked to the girl they've got tied up in the town, Michael. Whatever she is, she's not one of the Infected. She's terrified."

Rachel stabbed a thumb at Darren.

"Why try to kill us? Why even let us in here?"

Michael laid the rifle across his lap.

"He wanted the kids," he said.

Rachel felt the cold, toxic rage washing through her again.

"Just another fucking psycho," she said bitterly.

Michael paused a moment, then nodded.

"I guess so," he said. "Better gather everybody together. Tell them we need to talk."

18

Aviation fuel was going to be a problem. Nick had told Ray that immediately. One of the few things he knew about the chopper was that you could not just dump a load of unleaded petrol in the tank and expect the thing to fly. He sort of hoped that would be the end of their plan to get the chopper back off the ground.

Ray had looked dubious, and only accepted the argument when Nick painted a picture of the helicopter's engine dying at altitude. *I can fly that thing in the same way you can bake a cake, Ray. You might get the job done, but you won't be catering any weddings.*

That had seemed to tickle Ray, and he roared with laughter.

Can't be trusted to cook toast, mate, he had snorted, but Nick's point stuck.

They sat around a small fire for a couple of hours and Nick soon felt that he had misjudged the bikers. Mostly they laughed, usually at each other, although Nick came in for plenty of good-natured abuse when Ray recounted his attempt to descend the tree. Laughter rippled through the group, and became a roar when Nick glumly confessed that he had landed in a wet patch of his own making.

Several times, Nick almost forgot that the world had gone to shit, but every so often a snapping of a branch or a rustling in the trees would bring a dead silence upon the group, and Nick saw the bikers' hands hovering near the handles of their knives. Ray kept the crossbow close, occasionally reaching out to pat it like a pet, perhaps reassuring himself it was still there. The group had obviously managed to attain a sort of equilibrium with the horror of the world that had been birthed a week earlier. Able to relax and remain alert simultaneously.

That came from being out in the world and surviving, Nick supposed, rather than hiding behind a wall in a state of growing terror, as he had at Catterick. Everything felt new and bewildering to him.

Mostly Nick just sat and listened to their conversation, which meandered across many subjects, but sooner or later returned to music, and the prospect of a world without it. They listed album after album solemnly, like a roll call of the dead. Music that would be dead and gone without electricity to give it life. Soon enough, they miserably agreed, there wouldn't even be anyone left that remembered the melodies.

Nick felt a sudden depression descend on him as he thought about it. He hadn't even considered the loss of music, the great soulful hole its absence would leave in the lives of humans. Most of the stuff the bikers listed sounded like what Nick thought of as heavy metal: *Back in Black, Appetite for Destruction, Master of Puppets.* Nick had heard of a couple of them, but had never thought to check them out. Now he would never get the chance.

For a moment the weight of the world that had been lost threatened to crush Nick. All the things he had assumed he would experience at some later date. All the movies, all the books; the music. He wouldn't ever get a chance to meet a girl and take her to see the Eiffel Tower, and see her eyes light up at the pure romance of the place. Wouldn't ever see a tropical sunset. Probably he wouldn't ever leave the UK. *Maybe*, he thought darkly, *I won't even get to leave Wales.*

He lapsed into silence, staring at the flickering fire, and let the chatter around him become background noise.

If the world was just fear and violence and struggle, was there any point to it? It took him a long time to become aware of the silence around him. When he dragged his eyes away from the fire, he saw all of them looking at him.

"Someone take your batteries out, mate?" Ray grinned. "Looks like you're on standby mode."

Nick shook his head.

"Just thinking," he said.

"Never a good idea," Ray said with a wry smile.

Nick shook his head again.

"I guess it's just all hitting me now. I've been hidden away this past week, haven't really seen what it's like out in the world at all. I suppose you've all had a week to adjust to it. You're lucky."

The jovial atmosphere snapped away, as though it had been sucked out of an airlock into deep space.

"Lucky?"

Ray's tone was a mixture of bewilderment and flat-out aggression.

Nick began to stammer.

"No, no, I just mean, you're all here, and-"

"We are *not* all here," Ray hissed. "Not by a fucking long shot. Can you count Nick? Because there should be fifteen of us. How many do you see?"

The sudden hostility in Ray's voice hit Nick like a train.

Six, he thought.

"That's right," Ray snapped bitterly. "Next time you get to thinking any of us have been *lucky,* you remember that nine of our brothers and sisters aren't here. If we seem cheerful to you, Nick, it's because the alterative is throwing ourselves over that fucking cliff. You get me?"

Nick nodded and swallowed painfully.

"Sorry," he said, "I wasn't thinking."

"You were thinking too fucking much," Ray said. "Don't."

Silence descended. After a few moments Ray lowered his eyes and nodded to himself.

"So where are we going to get our hands on aviation fuel, soldier?" Ray said gruffly.

Nick scratched his chin thoughtfully, grateful for the sudden change of subject, even if it did mean returning to the troubling idea of heading west.

"We need an airfield," he said. "Birmingham, Manchester and Liverpool would guarantee fuel."

"That's not all they'd guarantee," growled a huge, tattooed man who went by the name of Shirley. Nick had taken *that* piece of information in straight-faced, and hadn't asked. He told himself he never would.

Nick nodded.

"Agreed," he said. "Cities are out of the question. I think there are a couple of places in North Wales that might hold annual air shows. Mostly they would just do displays of old aircraft, but they would have a runway, and anywhere that has a runway is our best shot at getting fuel. Failing that, we'd just have to get lucky and stumble across a tanker on the roads."

"I think we've established that *luck* doesn't really figure for us," Ray said. "You know where any of these places are, Nick?"

Nick shook his head.

"Not exactly. But any of the local towns would have a tourist information bureau. They would have maps and local points of interest. We'd be able to find out there."

Ray stood.

"Looks like we're heading for town, boys," he said grimly.

*

In the end getting the fuel looked like it was going to be easier than Nick had anticipated. He still wasn't sure whether that was a good thing or not.

When the bikes had roared away from the ramshackle camp, Nick rode with Ray, clinging to the man's wide back for dear life and feeling a heightened terror which he suspected might be more to do with being perched on the speeding bike rather than the outrageous noise the machine made and the possibility of it attracting the Infected.

They made for the nearest town: a tiny one-road place called Mostyn, that was notable only for housing a surprisingly large dock that built the wind farms placed in the Irish Sea.

When Nick saw the bones of one of the huge wind turbines laying in the dock, he thought wryly that at least the apocalypse had done some good: there would be no more human-induced climate change. He wondered if future generations would venture out into the seas and marvel at the massive, bewildering forests of steel jutting from the ocean, wondering what their purpose had been.

The infection looked to have passed through Mostyn almost as everyone else had over the years: like an afterthought. Just scenery that blurred past on the route to some other, more meaningful destination.

As the bikes slowed to a throaty growl, cruising into the tiny town on high alert, Nick saw a few scattered bodies, but on the whole the place looked almost untouched. There just hadn't been that many people there, Nick guessed. Just the few whose corpses now rotted on the streets, and the rest, who had doubtless joined the eyeless herds heading west. The *sockets*.

That strange exodus puzzled Nick more than anything, but when he asked Ray about it, the biker simply shrugged, as if to say *they gotta go somewhere.*

The group piloted the bikes to what looked like the centre of the 'town': a handful of tiny shops that mostly served food and supplies to the docks. When they killed the engines the staccato thunder of the bikes gave way to a roaring, deafening silence that was broken only by the soft whisper of the waves that lapped gently at the dock.

For a full minute they waited, their eyes scanning every direction, their hands on their weapons, searching for some sign that the infection was creeping toward them.

Nothing.

"Looks okay," Ray said finally. "You can stop hanging on to me now, Nick." He grinned, and Nick flushed for a moment, before hopping off the bike, and biting back his gratitude at making it back onto the ground in one piece.

He looked around. There was no hope of a tourist information bureau - Nick doubted the concept of tourism had made it to Mostyn - but he saw one possibility and pointed at a tiny gift shop, the sort of place that mostly sold plastic beach toys and faded memories.

"There," he said. "If anywhere is going to have information on local attractions, that will be the place."

"Local *attractions*," Shirley repeated in a low growl. "I'd say the only attraction here is the road out of this shithole."

Ray chuckled.

"Shirl," he said. "Why don't you go grab us some food from that store?" He pointed at a small grocery shop. "Nothing that will have gone rotten this time, okay?"

Shirley snorted and heaved his bulk from the bike, delivering an ironic salute.

"Come on, Nick," Ray said. "Let's get what we need and get the fuck out of here. This place gives me the creeps."

Nick nodded. He knew exactly what Ray meant. It was the stillness of the town. Even before the virus it would have felt like a sad and isolated place. Now it felt like a relic.

The inside of the gift shop felt dusty and claustrophobic. Even light struggled to find space inside: the windows were piled high with the sort of low-quality beach items that only the truly desperate would ever think to buy. Most of the stuff looked like it had been there for years; faded and tired.

Nick saw what he needed immediately: a rotating rack that held postcards and leaflets espousing the virtues of attractions like *Prestatyn Sands* and *Rhyl Seaworld*. The leaflets tried their best to make the North Welsh coast seem exciting, but only succeeded in making Nick feel sad.

He twisted the rack until he saw a pale blue pamphlet with a an ancient biplane emblazoned on the front.

Visit Mold International Air Show!

"Mold," Ray said, peering at the flyer over Nick's shoulder. "They have a place called *Mold*." It wasn't a question. Nick could tell from Ray's sardonic tone that if anything, he expected the name of the place was probably pretty apt.

"About ten miles south of here by the look of this map," Nick said with a nod.

"Hmph. Not so far. Further than we've travelled since we set up camp, but there's a good chance that place will have emptied out too. Come on."

Ray turned and strode to the door, and paused.

"Just how *international* you think this air show will be anyway?"

"I think it probably means they have a picture of an old German bomber somewhere on the premises."

Ray grinned.

"That's what I thought."

*

With the sad little town shrinking fast in their rear view mirrors, Nick let his mind wander as he chewed on one of the stale pastries that Shirley had decided was the best food he could find in the grocery store.

Not that Nick would complain about the dry, tasteless cake. It was, he realised, the first time he had eaten in hours. Days, maybe. The sugar rush seemed to give his tired mind a shove, and soon it was racing alongside the bikes.

He liked the group of bikers. In truth, he felt more at ease with them than he ever had in the army. But they were on some mission that Nick thought had a faint whiff of *suicidal* about it: some strange yearning for revenge on a guy that had forcibly turned them away from the place they wanted to stay several days earlier.

But there were plenty of places. And with a helicopter, they could take their pick. Whatever the place was that the bikers had lost, it surely wasn't worth heading *toward* a large number of the Infected to get to it.

"Ray," he shouted, straining his lungs to be heard over the roar of the engine.

"Yeah?" Ray hollered back, slowing the bike a little.

"When we get this fuel...you certain you want to go back to this place that kicked you out?"

For a moment Ray was silent, and Nick was not sure the man had heard him.

"It's not a case of *wanting* to go there, Nick. It's about doing what's right. And it's not that they kicked us out."

Ray twisted the throttle, and the bike lurched forward.

"It's that they didn't let us in."

*

The air strip was exactly what Nick had expected: a single short runway surrounded by empty fields and a solitary hangar, just large enough to hold a small dual-propeller plane. He imagined that when the *Mold International Air Show* was in full swing, there would be a few hundred people from the local towns filling the fields, probably eating picnics; playing with their kids. It was the sort of idyllic scene that was probably now consigned to history.

The bikes roared to a halt outside the chain-link fence that surrounded the place, and they waited a moment while Shirley took a couple of heavy swings at the locked gate with his boot, smashing it open on the second attempt to a round of ironic applause.

The bikes cruised inside, each rider still keeping a keen eye out for movement, but Nick could tell from the stillness of the place and the locked entrance that the airstrip was clear of the infection. He doubted anyone had been anywhere near the place when the virus erupted in the population; certainly there would have been no reason for the Infected to head for it. No prey inside.

Prey, he thought. It was odd to consider human beings as the *prey* of anything. Mankind had conquered all but the most isolated parts of the planet completely. The only time a human became *prey* was when they were stupid enough to put themselves in situations that involved sharks or bears or poisonous snakes. Even then, the right equipment made such an encounter meaningless.

It was following that train of thought that made him remember the way the monster at Catterick had responded when he had switched on the low frequency emitter.

Every predator can be stopped with the right equipment, he thought.

"Hey, Earth to Nick. You in there buddy?"

Ray snapped his fingers in front of Nick's face, making him blink in surprise.

"Sorry," Nick said. "Just thinking."

"Ha! I thought we already discussed that," Ray said with a grin. "You think this place has got the fuel you need or not?"

Nick pointed at the hangar.

"In there, if it's anywhere," he said.

Ray strode to the large sliding door. Padlocked.

"Don't suppose you brought a hacksaw?" Ray quipped.

It took them a few minutes to smash the lock away, Shirley bringing a large rock down on the metal with a jarring clang repeatedly until the padlock finally gave up its stubborn resistance. Inside they found a small plane, exactly as Nick had imagined they would. The type used most frequently for giving lessons to would-be pilots. Stacked at the back of the hangar Nick saw a wall of shelves lined with small tanks of fuel, and his heart sank a little.

Some part of him, he realised, had still hoped they wouldn't find the fuel; that maybe the bikers would give up on their thirst for revenge and find somewhere safe to settle down. The fuel was there though, and Nick knew as he watched the bikers heaving it from the shelves that safety was the furthest thing from their minds.

Like it or not, Nick was going to be a soldier again, flying a team off to battle. The familiar fear swelled inside him, and he did his best to throttle it before it overwhelmed him.

"Didn't figure on these being so difficult to transport by bike," Ray said, nodding at the fuel tanks. "How many you think we need?"

Nick stared at him a moment, lost in thought.

You just need the right equipment, Nick-yyyy.

"Take one," Nick said. "That will give us enough fuel."

"For the whole trip?" Ray looked dubious.

Nick shook his head.

"Enough to come back here with the chopper," he said. "Then we can take them all."

Ray's eyes widened.

"All?"

"You never know when we might need them," Nick said.

Ray arched an eyebrow, and Nick could tell from his expression that it wasn't the information that surprised the biker as much as the confident way it was delivered.

Nick slung a leg over the back of Ray's bike, clutching one of the small fuel tanks to his chest, and the bikes roared away toward the setting sun, and the chopper, and what felt like the beginning of the end.

19

The pain was like an insistent alarm clock: it let John know he was awake even before his eyes opened. Eye, more accurately: his left eye was swollen shut, and that entire side of his face felt like someone had to gone to work on it; someone with a grudge and a hot poker and *oodles* of energy. He tried to open the eye and found that even the merest attempt sent a shockwave of pain through his skull.

Still alive, then.

He breathed in deeply, letting the room swim into focus, and the breathing revealed a secondary pain; no less terrible: one of his ribs was cracked. It wasn't the first time he had suffered such an injury, and he gave silent thanks that at least he hadn't punctured a lung even as he told himself that being able to diagnose yourself because of familiarity with a multitude of types of pain probably meant your life wasn't going so well.

Still, a cracked rib would heal just fine. Anything more serious than that, he was not so sure about.

He lifted himself into a sitting position, wincing as his injuries voiced their displeasure at his decision to move. He was in a plush bedroom, resplendent with ancient-looking furniture and ornate decorations. After the hard floors and discomfort of the previous few days, the room felt strangely surreal, and he allowed himself a delicious moment of fantasising that it had all just been a bad dream.

If only.

One wall of the room was a stone semicircle, the window just a slit. The kind that once upon a time people had probably fired arrows from. He was still in the castle. He swung his legs over the side of the large bed, and felt a stab of fire in his thigh. He pulled back the covers, and saw the deep gash in his leg. Someone had stitched him up. It wasn't exactly masterful work, and it would heal to leave another scar on a body that already told a long tale of violent encounters, but John couldn't complain.

The real question though, was *who* had stitched him back together. He remembered the fight in the boutique. Remembered Rachel appearing with the gun. After that, nothing.

Judging by the way his face felt like it had swollen up to twice its usual size, he had probably been unconscious a while. When he pondered what might have happened in the castle while he was passed out, an apprehensive dread settled on him, and for a moment he considered curling up under the covers again, and trying to pretend that he was somewhere else. Anywhere. Even back out in the desert. At least there, he had a vague idea of what he was dealing with; what he was supposed to be fighting.

Turns out you preferred having someone tell you what to do, John, he thought. *Whether they were idiots and arseholes or not.*

He glanced at a dresser at the side of the bed. A glass of water sat atop it, alongside two small white pills. He eyed them suspiciously, and was still pondering their possible effects when the door to the room swung open and a tired-looking woman walked in.

"Nice to see you up and about. John, right? I'm Linda. I'd say pleased to meet you but, well..."

She shrugged, and John snorted a chuckle that sent a wave of fire coursing through his head.

"Feeling's mutual," John said. "You the one that stitched me up?"

Linda's weary face fell. She nodded.

"It's good work," John said.

She smiled a little, apparently pleased. "I preferred being a teacher. And I doubt 'good' is the best way to describe that mess. It'll scar, I should think."

John nodded.

"I'm still here. Makes it good as far as I'm concerned. Thanks. Are these painkillers?"

"Yes," Linda said. "Strongest we've got for now. They have Codeine in them, might make you a bit drowsy. I'm afraid we don't have many, so-"

"Keep them," John interrupted. "Likely someone else is going to need them far more than I do."

"You sure?" Linda asked, sounding dubious.

John smiled.

"I've had my arse kicked before, Linda. I'll survive. Speaking of which, what's the latest out there regarding our ongoing attempts to kill each other?"

Linda smiled despite herself.

"Darren's dead," she said, and her tone left John in no doubt that she was happy about that turn of events. "Sam and Jack, too. Jack's the one you stabbed."

John said nothing.

"And the elderly lady you came in with, she's dead. I think that about covers it. I hope she wasn't someone special. The truth is I feel a bit numb to all the death now. Condolences, I guess."

John waved the words away, and bit down on the sadness he felt at hearing the news.

I liked her, too. Fuck.

"How did she die?"

Linda leaned past John and picked up the painkillers, slipping them back into a small bottle she withdrew from the pocket of her jeans.

"Gunshot," she said, and noticed the arching of John's eyebrows. "It was quick. Your friend in the wheelchair, he had the gun. Darren tried to kill him, she got caught up in it. That's all I know, really. You'd be best off asking your friend. He seems to be the one in charge now."

John's head shot up, and he stared at Linda's face, his good eye narrowing.

Oh, really?

*

When Linda left to tend to her 'other patients' - she couldn't keep the sarcasm out of her tone - John stood and tested his legs. The cut in his thigh had been deep, but he doubted it had done serious damage. Hurt like hell, though, and for a moment he considered dropping the bravado and chasing after Linda to get those painkillers.

He was on the first floor of one of the castle's towers, and the steps took a little negotiating, but as he moved, John felt the pain recede a little.

On the ground floor, he saw a mattress and the body of a young woman. He stepped closer to see if she was alright, and saw the nasty wound on her head that looked like it had become infected.

He wondered if that was what had killed her. It was a reminder, John thought, that there was not only one virus out there that they had to worry about. There were others, far older; hardened and evolved by skirmishes with the human immune system that had lasted for hundreds of years.

Something else to add to the list of things that will try to kill us, John thought. He wondered how many other unforeseen dangers were out there; dangers than humanity believed it had conquered, only for Project Wildfire to give them a new lease of life.

In the end, John doubted any of them would be as dangerous as other humans. With a heavy heart, he pushed open the tower door, and stepped out into the morning air, with only one thing on his mind.

Find Michael.

It didn't take long. In fact Michael was in the first place John looked, exactly where he expected to see him. Back in the tower they had occupied that first night. Where he kept the rifle.

"Congratulations," John said as he stepped into the tower. "I hear you're in charge now."

"You heard wrong," Michael responded. "I'm not in charge of anything. I told all these people what Darren was. I don't think it was news to any of them. We'll take a vote on what to do next."

"A *vote*?" John sneered.

"Yes, John, a vote," Michael snapped. "These people have been scared into submission enough already. I'm sure as hell not going to start threatening them. Are you?"

John sighed.

"I don't want to be in charge of anything, Michael. Least of all...whatever this is."

He jabbed a finger at the doorway and the castle beyond.

"I do want to know how Gwyneth ended up dead, though."

Michael's face dropped, and John scrutinised the man's eyes. John had a fairly evolved bullshit detector, but Michael was a good actor. Maybe too good.

"I suppose I killed her, John," Michael said. "That what you want to hear? I was holding the gun, and she got shot, but I didn't mean for it to happen. I had no choice."

"Got your hands dirty, huh?" John said. "Just like Darren. No choice."

Michael opened his mouth to respond, and shut it abruptly when he heard the noise.

A helicopter.

Approaching fast.

*

"There's your Infected," Ray said, and whistled softly.

For a moment Nick forgot that he was responsible for controlling the helicopter and stared open-mouthed at the endless blanket of bodies below them. Thousands upon thousands of the Infected, pressed together, lined up like an army preparing to lay siege the castle in the distance.

Nick's mind span, and only when Ray clapped him on the shoulder did he realise that he was letting the chopper drop down steadily toward the sea of flesh and teeth. He yanked on the pitch control, bringing the nose up sharply and making the vehicle lurch dangerously.

"Watch it, boy," Shirley growled behind him, and Nick nodded an apology.

"What is this, Ray?" He said in a trembling voice.

"Beats me," Ray said. "I guess they want the castle too."

"I could turn around," Nick stammered. "We can find somewhere else."

Ray shook his head.

"There is nowhere else, Nick. Not until we've done what we came here to do."

Nick clenched his jaw in frustration.

"Why are they holding back like that?" Nick pointed at the strange boundary that seemed to be keeping the Infected from entering the town.

Ray shrugged.

"Aim for the big tower," he said, pointing at the castle. "Land on the roof if you can. If not, go for the gardens. If they start shooting, just focus on not crashing, okay?"

Nick shot a horrified glance at Ray.

"You'll be fine," Ray said with a grin, and hoisted the crossbow from his back. His eyes were filled with eager anticipation, and a grim determination that made Nick's heart sink.

The chopper powered over the last of the Infected, and Nick saw a bank of eyeless faces lift toward the noise of the engine, and wondered how long he had left to live.

*

John raced out of the tower and watched the chopper approaching clumsily, the argument with Michael forgotten. It was an army chopper, but it didn't look like a gunship. More like a medical vehicle.

What now?

The chopper roared over the castle wall, and hovered unsteadily over the main tower, descending in jerky installments. Whoever the pilot was, they had more ambition than skill, John thought, and he began to back away, expecting the helicopter to plough into the stone walls and drop right on top of the stunned people watching from below.

When he saw it land gingerly on the tower, with a shriek of metal scraping on stone, John wasn't sure whether he should be preparing for a fight or applauding the landing.

The engine continued to howl for a few seconds, before dying away into a heavy silence, weighted down by anxious expectation.

John looked at Michael, and from the look in the man's eyes, John could tell he was thinking about the rifle that he had left behind in the tower.

"The guy in charge," a voice roared from the top of the tower. "Send him out."

John and Michael exchanged blank stares. John shrugged.

"Uh, we don't have a guy in charge," Michael yelled.

"Bullshit!"

John saw a face peering over the battlements.

"The guy with the beard. Old guy. Where is he?"

"Dead," Michael hollered.

There was no response from the roof for several seconds. Michael stared at John and shrugged.

"You're lying."

"I killed him myself," Michael shouted back. "You can see the body for yourself." He paused a moment, and then added: "He deserved it."

Again there was no response. Michael and John were still staring up at the roof expectantly when the door at the base of the tower opened, and a man emerged, aiming a loaded crossbow at Michael's face.

"Show me," the man growled.

*

When Nick caught up to Ray, the man was already standing in the doorway to one of the castle's towers, staring grimly down at a corpse.

Nick saw several other people looking on: a man in a wheelchair, a slightly older guy who looked like he had just received a savage beating, an attractive young woman who held a rusty shotgun and glared at Nick as he approached with open hostility.

"Uh, Ray, is that him?" Nick said.

"That's him," Ray growled.

Nick had thought Ray would be happy to see the man dead, but he seemed, if anything, to be a little disappointed. It took Nick a moment to realise that Ray had wanted to kill the old man himself, and had been robbed of his revenge. For his part, Nick gave silent thanks that the castle hadn't erupted in the violence he anticipated the moment the chopper set down.

Not yet, at least, Nick thought. The tension in the room was so thick he thought he might choke on it. He saw the injured man staring with interest at Ray, and Nick realised that despite the man's swollen face and bandaged leg, he was sizing Ray up, maybe even wondering whether trouble was about to start. The man looked ready if it did, and Nick coughed noisily, drawing everyone's gaze to him.

He swallowed painfully.

"Uh, I hate to ask the obvious question here," he said, "but are you guys all going to start killing each other? Because I've had a rough couple of days and...well..."

He trailed off, and for a moment they all just stared at him, until finally, Ray's face split in a grin, and he put his crossbow on the floor at his feet.

"I don't think there's any need for that, Nick."

He looked at John, Michael and Rachel.

"Is there?"

*

It took a long time for Ray and Nick to explain their story, but Michael knew instinctively it had the ring of truth. Ray and the band of bikers had been to the castle before, and Darren had turned them away, forcing them back toward the Infected that had pushed them into Caernarfon in the first place.

When Ray described how Darren had shot one of them, and how they had lost more than half their number trying to escape, Michael saw tears welling in the man's eyes, and Ray didn't strike Michael as the crying sort. Only the truth would hurt that much.

"You came back to kill Darren," Michael said bluntly.

"Aye," Ray said. "And I'm kind of sorry you beat me to it. Gunshot was too quick for that bastard, I reckon."

Michael nodded.

"I wasn't really in a position to do much else," he said, and gestured at his useless legs.

Ray snorted a laugh.

"You people do know you've got thousands of Infected out there, right? We came along the coast, and I'd say you've got every single one within fifty miles waiting out there. Any idea why?"

"Actually yes," Michael said. "Darren was keeping a girl prisoner. She's infected, but she...repels the others somehow. Some sort of...mutation, I suppose you'd call it. The virus acts differently in her."

"I thought we decided she was immune," John said stiffly.

Michael shook his head.

"I'm not so sure there is any immunity, John," he said. "I think the virus just...changes people."

"Like Gwyneth," John said, and his eyes burned into Michael.

"Maybe," Michael said. "Probably. I don't know. But what we think of as immunity, well, it can't be can it? The virus is affecting people, even those it doesn't turn into the Infected as we know them. It turns them into...something else."

Nick drew in a sudden, sharp breath, and they all turned to stare at him.

"There's something I have to tell you," Nick said.

*

"A monster that becomes invisible and throws trees around like paper planes."

John's voice was loaded with sarcasm. He stared at the guy in the army uniform with barely disguised contempt.

"That's what you're telling us."

"Not invisible," Nick snapped. "I think it just moves so quick you can't see it."

"Right," John said. "I can see how that would be more believable. My mistake."

He rolled his eyes, and looked at Michael and Rachel.

"Please, tell me you don't believe a word of this."

Rachel shrugged.

"Is it that much more far-fetched than what we have seen with our own eyes, John?" Rachel said. "A week ago I would have drawn the line at the human race being turned into insane cannibals. How about you?"

John massaged his temples. The conversation was turning a persistent headache into a raging inferno.

"And this...creature," he said gruffly, staring at Nick. "Decimated an entire garrison. Killed everybody. Except for you. Why?"

Nick flushed.

"Look," he said. "I get it. It sounds crazy. I got away, because..."

He trailed off, and his cheeks darkened.

Here goes, Nick thought. *The most unbelievable part of all.*

"I stopped it with a crowd control vehicle," Nick said hurriedly. "With a low frequency generator. It directs a beam of-"

"*Noise,*" Rachel interrupted, her voice tinged with wonder. "You stopped it with *sound.*"

Nick nodded, and waited for the ridicule that was bound to follow, but it never came.

Michael, Rachel and John looked at each other, stunned.

"Noise," Rachel repeated. "Just like we saw at the retail park."

Even John reluctantly nodded.

They believe me, Nick thought in astonishment. Hearing the incredible tale that had fallen from his own lips, he was not even sure he believed it himself. He remembered Drake. He had believed Drake existed too.

And look how that turned out.

"Fine," John said. "I'm sick of operating in the dark."

He limped to the door.

"Where are you going?" Michael asked sharply.

"I'm going to get the girl from the market," John said. "Because we won't find out anything with us in here and her out *there.* Isn't she what all this was about anyway? Isn't she the reason that Darren's dead? And Gwyneth?"

Michael stared at John.

"John," he said. "I don't think you can do that. She *is* infected. We would all be at risk."

"You sound exactly like *him,*" John snarled, stabbing his finger at Darren's corpse. "We're all at risk right now. Right fucking *now.* And if this guy is to be believed, sooner or later we'll have fucking *monsters* after us that we can't even see. Who says whatever strain of the virus this girl has wouldn't be the only thing that could save us? I sure know I'd like to be infected with something that keeps them *away* if it comes to it. I'm bringing her in. Because she's a terrified little girl. Got it?"

"John," Michael began, but John cut him short.

"Michael, *enough*," John thundered. "I've had it with debating every fucking decision to death with you. You might think you're in charge here. Everybody else might be happy for you to tell them what to do, but not me, understand? I've had a lifetime of following orders, and there's a reason I put a fucking stop to it. Keeping that girl out there was Darren's way. Not yours, and definitely not mine. She's no less human than Gwyneth is, or was before *you* fucking killed her, and so I'm going to get her, and I'm going to bring her back. If you don't want that to happen, you'd better stop talking and start fucking *shooting*. Just make sure you don't miss."

John left a shard of steel in his voice, but he knew Michael would not reach for the rifle. Even if he had it in him to kill John, there was no way he would do it in front of everybody. No way he would risk losing their confidence. If Michael had working legs, and wasn't totally reliant on the people around him, things might have been different.

But you don't.

John turned and strode to the gate, yanking on the lever that released the counterweight to lift the portcullis. It shot upwards with a grinding shriek of metal, and then John pushed the enormous door with all his might and stepped out onto the narrow bridge.

He didn't look back as the door shut behind him. Let Michael maintain his feeble grip on control. John didn't care. He didn't want to *lead* anybody, but he would be damned if he would let them lead him.

The altercation with Michael raged in his mind as he marched to the market, dominating his thoughts and blanking out the world around him. He barely noticed the bloody streets as he passed through them, and only when he reached the girl did the anger clouding his mind lift a little.

She whimpered and started pleading with him as he approached.

"It's okay," John said, "It's okay, I'm not going to hurt you. I'm taking you back, you won't be tied up anymore okay? Just hold still. If you make any sudden moves, I'll be forced to react, understand?"

The girl whimpered.

"I don't want to go back, please don't make me-"

"The man who did this to you is dead. Nobody's going to hurt you," John said, grabbing her narrow shoulders firmly. "Trust me, okay?"

He took his knife and sliced the rope away from the lamp post.

"I'll lead you back, just say if I'm pulling too hard, right? Once you get back we'll get you cleaned up, I promise."

John took the rope and led her toward the castle like a dog. He hated doing it, cursed himself for treating her like an animal, but even in his determination to defy Michael's wishes, he felt a faint stab of fear at the girl's appearance. She looked *exactly* like the Infected.

He played the rope out so she wouldn't be too close to him, and led her to the narrow bridge, ignoring her increasing hysteria.

For a moment he thought Michael would tell the others to keep the gate closed, but as he approached it began to swing open, and John felt relief flood through him. Michael had seen sense at last.

When the gate was open, John found himself face to face with the man in the wheelchair.

"I thought you were going to lock me out," John said.

"You didn't give me much say in the matter," Michael said grimly.

"I don't suppose I..."

John trailed off.

Michael's eyes were widening, his mouth dropping open, his hand lifting, pointing at something behind John.

John realised what was happening, but it was a beat too late. He had taken his eye off the girl. Handed her the element of surprise.

You should know better.

He span round, but she had already snatched the knife from his belt, and even as John started to scream, started to throw himself at her, she plunged the blade into her own throat and sliced her life away.

Time seemed to stand still as an impossible torrent of her blood poured across the bridge, drenching her chest, and then her frail ankles gave way and she collapsed to the ground.

For a moment everyone beyond the gate held their breath, as though all the oxygen had been sucked from the castle. For a brief second John's eyes flicked from Michael to Rachel, and he saw her eyes widen in horrified recognition as the sound reached them.

It sounded like approaching thunder.

Thousands of voices raised in unison.

Humming.

20

"Shut the gate!" Rachel screamed as John hurtled into the castle, heaving the heavy wooden door shut behind him. She should have known, as she watched Michael and John butting heads, that things were slipping out of control. Should have done something to stop it.

Michael wheeled himself to the mechanism that dropped the portcullis behind the door, and began to spin the handle, lifting the counterweight. It moved at an agonisingly slow pace.

Rachel heard the first thump of the Infected on the wooden door as the portcullis locked into place, and began to back away slowly, staring at the group of terrified people standing around her. Bikers. Terrified young women who had fled to the castle when it all started, believing that they might be safe there. A couple of guys leftover from what had been Darren's crew, now just terrified boys.

She doubted many of them had actually battled the Infected up close and personal, where only the blade of a knife and willpower would separate them from death.

One of the bikers, the one with the crossbow, appeared in front of her.

"Is this place secure?" He roared.

"I think so," Rachel said. "That's the only way in."

The man grimaced, and hoisted the crossbow.

"And the only way out," he said grimly, and sprinted for the steps that led up to the battlements. Rachel watched him ascend, saw him take aim with the weapon, and then shake his head in frustration, and she knew exactly what was going through his mind. He had ten bolts for the bow. Maybe fifteen. Firing them into the mass of the Infected would do nothing.

She stared at the gate, wincing as frantic blows rained down on it.

The gate has to hold, she thought. *Or it's all over.*

She saw the wood shivering as more and more of the Infected threw themselves into it, and she started to step backwards involuntarily. Again she stared around at the people standing alongside her. All seemed to be in a state of shock, and she realised they were all doing exactly the same thing as her. Staring at the gate. Praying.

Waiting.

Only John moved.

"Weapons," he snarled at no one in particular. "We need weapons."

Michael caught John's arm in a steely grip, making him flinch.

"Petrol bombs," Michael said. "Darren said they could make petrol bombs. They have bottles somewhere. And the fuel from the generator. Fire is our only chance."

John nodded.

"Where?"

Michael looked at him blankly.

John frantically searched the faces of the people around him, and saw the girl that Darren had sent to fetch them to meet him. Her face was the most haunted of all, and John knew as he looked into her eyes that she had been Darren's favourite, and he felt a stab of sympathy that he quickly shut down.

"You," he yelled, jabbing a finger at her. "Where did he keep the fuel and the bottles?"

The girl looked at him, eyes widening in fright.

"Where?" He roared, and when she pointed at one of the towers on the opposite side of the castle, John forgot all about his injured leg and sprinted toward it.

*

To Nick, the atmosphere in the castle reeked of terrible familiarity, and he once again found himself staring up longingly at the chopper, and wondering if he might be able to get to it without anyone noticing. All hope was dashed when Shirley appeared in front of him, brandishing an honest-to-God *broadsword*.

"Don't even think about it," Shirley rumbled, and tossed a heavy mace at Nick. Nick caught the ancient weapon and stared at it dumbly.

"What am I supposed to do with this?" He stammered.

Shirley grinned widely under his heavy moustache.

"*Fight*," he said with relish, and pushed Nick toward the steps that led to the battlements.

When Nick reached the top and saw what waited beyond the wall, he felt like his heart might drop from his open mouth.

Thousands upon thousands of the Infected were flocking toward the castle, smashing into the wall below, crushing their brethren against the unforgiving stone. There seemed to be no end to them. Everywhere he looked, the winding streets of Caernarfon were filled by a torrent of the creatures, a wave of death rushing toward him with single-minded purpose.

The urge to vomit was suddenly overwhelming.

I'm standing in a castle under siege, he thought. *Holding a mace.*

The notion made him feel a little like laughing and he might have, but for the fear that he might never be able to stop.

He stared at Ray, standing a few yards to his right. The man was aiming the crossbow, but reluctant to fire. Only when he saw one of the Infected trying to scramble up the stone wall, and making it a few feet off the ground did he unleash a bolt into the thing's forehead.

"Spread out, Nick," Ray yelled. "When they get up to the top, knock 'em back down."

Nick stared at him.

When?

He stared down again, and saw that as the Infected at the front of the crowd were slowly crushed to death, the ones behind began to climb over the corpses. The tide was rising.

Oh fuck, Nick thought, and then a petrol bomb flew across the wall to his left, landing on the Infected crowd and sending a pool of liquid fire across it. And then another.

And then John was at his side, flaming bottles in each hand, raining fire down on the seething mass of horror below.

More bottles arced over Nick's head, and he turned to see Michael and Rachel below, filling bottles with rags and generator fuel and passing them out to people. Michael was roaring at the terrified girls and the stunned bikers to get to the top of the battlements and defend themselves.

It all felt like a dream, a strange, surreal vision that couldn't possibly be connected to reality. Until Nick saw a bloody hand reaching over the lip of the battlements and an eyeless face appearing in front of him.

And then Nick swung the mace with all his might and felt the crunch and snap of bone as the terrible weapon connected, and he knew that it was all real, every last terrifying bit, and Shirley had been right. There was only one thing left to do. The thing he had avoided doing his whole life.

Fight.

*

For a while there, John had thought it might actually work. But the Infected did not respond to fire in the way any other creature would. They didn't shrink back in fear from the wall of flame the petrol bombs had created. They simply charged into it, hurtling to their deaths, oblivious to everything except the prey they had been kept from for so long.

And worse: the burnt, smouldering bodies of what John thought of as the *first wave* simply provided a ramp for the others to climb. Already some were reaching the top of the battlements, only to be knocked back by one of the people defending the place with ancient swords and clubs.

It was only a matter of time before one of the Infected got across and broke their defences, and then the game would be up. One was all it would take to kill them all. John jabbed his knife through an eyeless face, sending it plummeting back onto the carpet of bodies below and stared about him blearily, wondering which of the people now fighting at his side would be the one to sink their teeth into his flesh when the time came.

When the Infected broke all resistance, when the onslaught finally breached the castle, would it be one of the bikers that ripped their eyes out before pouncing on John? Would it be Michael? *Rachel?*

Will I have to kill her myself?

Will I even know I'm doing it?

He saw the biggest of the bikers swinging a huge old sword into the neck of one of the creatures as it hauled itself over the wall; saw the blunt blade lodge deep in the creature's flesh and get torn away from the man's grasp as the thing fell away.

We have to retreat.

"We can't hold it," John roared, trusting that someone - anyone - was listening. "Get back to the main tower. Fall back."

He saw the one dressed as a soldier streak past him first, followed quickly by the bikers and the handful of Darren's group that had made it up to the battlements. Below him he heard the pounding of feet as the rest of them turned and headed for the tower. He couldn't be sure if they had heard his cry, or had merely seen the thing that he had missed.

There just hadn't been enough of them to hold the entire length of the wall. John should have realised it sooner. They never stood a chance of defending the castle. It was too large. The confirmation of the fact was right there.

Streaking along the battlements toward him, snarling.

Infected.

He saw three, and for a brief, dreadful moment he prayed that they would continue running *along* the wall, straight at him. If they leapt down, the game was up.

Even as he thought it he saw it happening, as one of them veered to its right, utterly oblivious to the drop, throwing itself down at the group of people retreating toward the tower. He heard the savage crack as the thing's legs met the floor, and had time to see Rachel sprinting toward it, brandishing a blade, and then he was rolling backwards, frantically evading the deadly lunge as the first of the two Infected still on the battlements reached him at full tilt.

As he rolled, he swivelled his hips, employing a leg sweep that had always worked on humans. It was a move born of desperation. Bringing the teeth down towards him as he rose.

The thing snapped like an animal; caught his jacket as it fell.

Missed his flesh. Just.

John stabbed down with his knife. *Hard.* He threw every ounce of strength gained during a life spent in battle into the thrust, and didn't even hear his own roar of triumph as the blade cleaved itself a new home in the thing's brainstem.

His hand was already moving, grasping for his second knife.

And finding the sheath empty.

His knife was buried in the back of one of Darren's men.

Kind of funny, John thought. He couldn't even remember the kid's name.

The third of the Infected was throwing itself toward him, and time seemed to slow for John, and he realised the old cliché about your whole life flashing before your eyes wasn't true at all. It was just this one scene. This one hideous image, slowed down to a sickening crawl and intensified until it made his eyes hurt. It felt unbearably long.

Gamble, John thought, and threw himself backwards off the wall.

*

Nick was the first to reach the top of the tower. Most of them were still on the ground floor, wailing and waiting for someone to tell them what to do. None of them seemed to realise that you didn't stop running until there was nowhere left to run.

Nick wasn't going to wait. He knew *exactly* what to do. What he did best.

He sprinted for the chopper.

He would get the engine running. He would give them thirty seconds. Whoever made it to the top of the tower, he would save.

Thirty seconds.

He stabbed the controls and sighed in relief as he felt the steady vibration of the engine roaring into life.

Nick was going to live.

He stared at the mass of Infected that seemed to stretch out endlessly below him, and glanced at his wristwatch.

Thirty seconds.

*

John tried to roll as he fell, tucking in his arms and legs, but he hit the ground *hard.* Breath exploded from his body and for a moment his vision flickered and blurred, like there was a bad connection in his brain somewhere. He saw the Infected creature land beside him, smashing into the floor knees-first, driving its legs up behind its head and snapping its spine in two. The thing's hipbone drove itself all the way from flesh out into the open air, and for a moment John dared to hope the fall had killed it.

And maybe it had. But not instantly.

The creature whipped its broken body over and threw an arm forward, dragging itself toward John even as its life steadily drained out onto the ground around it.

John stared at it in horror and tried to drag himself to his feet; knew his stunned muscles were not working quickly enough.

This is it, he thought, and shut his eyes.

And opened them again when the rifle roared, and the top half of the creature's skull detonated.

John sucked in a deep breath, and jumped as he saw a shadow fall over him, and a hand extended in front of his face.

He grabbed Michael's hand and hauled himself up, almost screaming as pain lanced through his legs; grateful that he could still *feel* them.

"Go," Michael said, and John realised they were the last two in the courtyard. He staggered toward the tower and heard the rifle roar again; didn't need to look to know the Infected were pouring over the wall now, flooding into the castle. The rifle roared a third time and then clicked, and John heard the whirring of Michael's wheelchair, moving behind him at pace, and knew he had run out of ammunition.

They entered the tower almost simultaneously to a chorus of terrified screams and Michael slammed the door even as the first blows began to rain down upon it. He engaged the deadbolt and drew back, gasping for air as the door began to shake under the impact of frantic, thunderous blows.

The door would hold for a while. It was thick wood locked by a heavy iron bar. Better yet, it was narrow. There was only so much force the mass of Infected could exert on it. But he didn't think it would hold indefinitely. There was only one way left to go.

He pointed at the stairs, and the people crammed into the tower began to run toward them.

John dragged legs that felt like they were burning in acid to the base of the stairs and began to climb, praying that the door would hold long enough for the chopper to ferry everyone away from the castle before it was completely overrun. He hadn't seen the pilot anywhere, but if it came to it, John would figure out how to fly the damn thing himself.

Every step was a fresh bout of torture that felt like it would snap his shins in two, but he gritted his teeth and forged ahead, picking up as much pace as possible until finally he reached the door that led to the roof and burst through it and roared in impotent fury.

The chopper was gone.

21

Well done Nick-yyyy, got away clean again.

Nick grimaced as the chopper continued to lift into the air, and the castle below receded to little more than a grey dot. With the dark stain of the Infected swarming around it, it looked like the nucleus of a rotten cell.

Got away clean, he thought, repeating the words his father's voice had just croaked in his mind. *So why am I crying?*

It was not just the tears running down Nick's cheeks either; he could not stop the great, heaving sobs that rattled his chest and throat painfully.

Because you're a cry-baby coward, Nick-yyyy.

Nick squeezed his eyes shut. He wasn't getting away clean. He was getting away stained by the lives of at least thirty innocent people. Stained by the lives of Ray and Shirley; good guys who had helped him, and who he had left to die.

The chopper began to lurch dangerously as the tears blurred his vision.

"What was I supposed to do?" He sobbed.

What you always do, Nick-yyyy. You don't stop running until there's nowhere left to run.

Nick blinked as realisation hit him.

There is nowhere left to run, he thought. You keep running, or you stop and fight. Where is there to run to, that won't be exactly the same as this? Or worse?

He thought of the monster that had attacked Catterick. If he hadn't been safe there, walled in and surrounded by the army, then nowhere was safe. There was no point in running, not any more.

All of a sudden, Nick felt strangely euphoric, and a calm peace washed through him like a drug.

He glanced over his shoulder at the drums of aviation fuel that filled the cargo hold of the fat chopper, and finally he knew exactly what he had to do. To kill a monster, you just needed the right equipment.

That's the coward's way out Nick-yyyy.

Nick slammed the pitch lever forward and sent the chopper into a delirious nosedive.

"Fuck you, Dad," he said with a laugh, and then the chopper smashed into the narrow bridge that connected the castle to Caernarfon and everything went dark.

*

John watched in astonishment as the chopper hurtled toward the bridge, and he realised that the pilot was not a coward. Quite the opposite. But he was definitely a fool. Crashing the chopper into the Infected would kill many of them, but not enough to change anything, not unless the vehicle was carrying a powerful bomb. Even if he was trying to destroy the bridge and give the people in the castle a fighting chance, the chopper was unlikely to get the job done.

When the chopper hit, John could scarcely remember a time when he had been more wrong about anything.

The explosion was gigantic, decimating the Infected in a huge fireball that continued to grow as it mushroomed up into the sky. As the smoke began to clear, he saw that the bridge had been completely destroyed, cutting the force of the Infected in two. Many on the other side of the river plunged blindly into the water and were swept out to sea.

John leaned carefully over the battlements, peering down at the base of the tower. The Infected that had surrounded it had collapsed to the ground, clutching their palms to the ears in agony as the deafening roar of the explosion rolled across them.

He didn't have time to think. His legs were already moving, all thoughts of the pain in his shins forgotten. John charged down the stairs and into the great hall, and snatched a sword from the grasp of one of the stunned bikers.

"Now!" John roared, and threw back the lock on the door. "Take them NOW!"

He didn't wait to see their looks of confusion. There was no time for debate. He simply had to trust that they would follow his example.

He charged out into the smoky air already swinging, smashing the blade through the hateful flesh, decapitating and killing in a frenzy of bloodlust, and after a moment he heard the others begin to emerge from the tower behind him one by one, gradually summoning up the courage to join him. Executing the Infected before they could recover their senses.

John swung the sword until his arms ached; until merely holding the weapon became a problem for his fatigued muscles, and only when he heard Rachel screaming triumphantly at his side did he allow the blade to fall from his fingers, and to collapse to the ground in exhaustion.

*

When John came round, he found himself sitting on a carpet of lacerated bodies. It felt oddly familiar, and it took him a moment to remember the forest outside St. Davids. He wondered how many more times he might find himself drifting on a lake of blood and exposed organs. It wasn't, he thought, the kind of thing you wanted to turn into a routine.

He glanced around. Some of the people left in the castle - to John it looked like there were about thirty of them, all told - were on their knees crying. He couldn't tell whether it was relief or shock that caused the tears; not even when he felt them coursing down his own cheeks.

The rest were on the battlements. Even Michael had somehow got himself up there.

Found someone else to carry you, John thought, but he let the bitterness drain away from him. In the end, he owed the man his life. One way or another, Michael found leverage.

No one was swinging a weapon. No one was screaming. Somehow it almost didn't feel real.

John hauled himself to his feet and groaned as the pain in his legs shrieked. It took him a while, but he made it to the top of the battlements, and the sight beyond lit a small, flickering flame of hope in his heart.

The town was lost to the Infected, for the moment at least. The streets heaved with them, and John guessed there must still be hundreds out there. Maybe even thousands.

But of the ones that plunged into the river, only a few made it across.

Some can swim, John thought, and the revelation should have shocked him, but he was too tired to care. Or maybe the strange, evolving habits of the Infected had simply lost their power to surprise him. It didn't matter. The ones that made it all the way across arrived in small bunches, or alone. They could be dealt with easily enough. The wall slowed most down long enough for them to be killed. The sea would take care of the rest.

He headed toward Michael and Rachel, leaning over the battlements with Pete and Claire. If it hadn't been for the bloodstains, John might have been able to imagine them as just another family taking in the sights at the castle.

"Wasn't sure if you made it," Michael said as John approached.

"Guess I got lucky," John said, and Michael smiled at that, and nodded wearily.

"So, you have your castle," John said. "And here's your army, for what it's worth." He gestured to the group of thirty or so people gathered in the castle's courtyard below. "So now what?"

Michael frowned, but it was Rachel that answered.

"Now we fight back," she said. "We know how to hurt them. Now *we* are the virus, and we will spread from here."

Her eyes glittered with intent.

"Let's go make some *noise.*"

Epilogue

Jake awoke with a roar of triumph building in his throat.

Deep in the syrupy dark, after unconsciousness had taken him, he had once again felt the strange connection with the distant intruder in his mind. Exactly as he had when he had escaped the underground base, only stronger this time. For a moment the connection had built toward a blinding intensity, burning with the brightness of a dying sun.

He knew exactly where the intruder was, and exactly how to get there. He would move through the countryside like a rocket-propelled train, and he would taste the strange old woman's oddly-familiar blood in a matter of hours. *Minutes.*

Even as Jake had blacked out after fleeing from the strange weapon that had damaged him at Catterick, he had retained the presence of mind to bury himself under debris, nesting like an animal; hiding away from the world in his vulnerable state. With a grunt, he flung the heavy slabs of concrete that had served as a protective blanket away from him and rose into the morning light. He was so excited by the prospect of heading south that he paid no attention to what was around him. No attention to the activity his extraordinary ears picked up.

"My, look how you've grown!"

A familiar voice behind him. Jake turned and his misshapen jaw dropped in astonishment.

"You've been a very naughty boy, *Misters* McIntosh."

Jake laughed; a low, rumbling sound that heaved with menace.

"Did you come here to die, old man?"

Fred Sullivan grinned broadly and lifted a crooked finger.

Four strange, square devices had been placed around Jake's resting place. He hadn't seen them. Not until it was too late. On Sullivan's signal, the things hummed into life and slammed agonising blasts of low-frequency noise through Jake, making every cell of his body shriek in agony. He dropped to his knees in anguish, paralysed by the wall of sound, locked into an invisible prison.

Jake's vision pulsed and blurred and throbbed as he drifted helplessly on a river of pain. He saw the old man in the silver suit strolling toward him, his expression jovial.

When he was close enough for Jake to breathe in his musky scent, Sullivan leaned in until the bristly hairs of his moustache scratched against Jake's cheek.

"I did *warn* you that we were not amateurs, Mr McIntosh," he hissed into Jake's ear. "I'm afraid you ran away before we were quite finished with you. The scientists are having a little problem with your blood, so they tell me."

Sullivan shrugged.

"Turns out they need more of it."

Sullivan chuckled, and signalled again as he strode away.

Moments later a helicopter began to descend above Jake, lowering a huge steel cage over him. Jake seethed in agony and impotent rage as he watched tiny figures attaching the hateful sonic weapons to the bars of the cage, before sliding a sheet of thick steel underneath him, trapping him like a spider in a jar.

The terrible noise beat at him, sapping his energy, and he felt himself slipping backwards into the dark, sinking like a weighted corpse.

Fred Sullivan beamed as he watched the abomination slip into a coma. Tracking him down had been tiresome and time-consuming, but it was, Fred decided, all worth it. Just for the look on McIntosh's vile face. Fred knew a thing or two about priceless treasures. That look was up there with the best of them.

"Shall we return to base, Sir?"

Sullivan stared thoughtfully at his new head of security.

"I think not," he said. "Best to take him where he can't do any harm, and I've had rather enough of watching this clusterfuck up close. The fleet is waiting in the North Sea. Take him there. I'll follow."

Fred watched the chopper lift into the sky, hauling the cage underneath it, and felt his hair begin to whip against his forehead as his own ride landed on the grass behind him.

The UK was lost, for the moment at least, and it was likely that *Wildfire* had collapsed in much the same fashion across the entire globe. It was a setback, but hardly a time for panic.

After all, Fred thought, *a good businessman should always be able to adapt to unforeseen...mutations in the market.*

As the chopper lifted Fred up into the sky, he smiled at his own pun. Project Wildfire had failed spectacularly.

But it was hardly the end of the world.

Trauma

Prologue

There was a lingering stench in the van. Something that went beyond the dubious stains left by the previous owner. To Kyle Robinson it smelled like *fear.* The van was ripe with the stink of it.

"I'm not sure about this, mate."

The voice might have come from Kyle's subconscious. Instead it came from the rear of the van.

Kyle grimaced. It wasn't the first time since they had entered the van that his brother had voiced his concerns. For a guy who talked as little as Tom did, repetition of *anything* was generally a bad sign. Kyle loved him, but he was under no illusions: his younger brother was intense and awkward; the kind of guy that made other passengers uncomfortable on buses.

Not that Tom ever took the bus.

The truth was that Tom was the life and soul of the party, as long as the party in question took place in the virtual world. When online he had a presence, and an impressively comprehensive knowledge of where and how to get at information that others didn't even know existed. He revelled in drilling down to the virtual truth, and ultimately in feeding his bottomless cynicism and distrust of everyone that wasn't Kyle.

Tom had retreated to the safety of his house not long after the twenty-first century became the age of terrorism and insidious fear. Fed by the internet on a steady diet of paranoia and hysteria, he slowly became a virtual shut-in, hoarding supplies for what he anticipated was the impending end of the world. Some people called themselves *preppers*, and kept one prudent eye on the possibility of trouble; Tom lived the fear every single day and let it consume him.

In fairness, when Tom had shown Kyle the evidence he had amassed, Kyle had been forced to admit his brother might just have a point.

It was Tom's obsession that started the whole operation, way back when. Yeah, Tom was great online; a bona fide genius with a mouse and keyboard. Not so great if you were sitting in a van with him, counting out each trembling breath and wondering what number you'd be at when the violence started.

The operation.

The word seemed ridiculous to Kyle now. It wouldn't be the first time Tom's theories had led Kyle into trouble, but if things went as badly as they could, it might well be the last. Kyle wished he had paid a little more attention to just *how* ridiculous the *operation* was back when he could still have called it off.

Now it was way too late. They had been parked on Hatton Garden for several minutes already. It was, like apparently everywhere else in London, a *no parking* zone. That fact was making Kyle more than a little nervous. By the look of the sweat trickling down Tom's brow and his wide, fearful eyes, it was giving his brother something like the Chernobyl of all panic attacks.

Kyle stared at Tom in the rear view mirror. The guy looked miserable, which wasn't exactly *news,* but the look of intense worry on Tom's face told Kyle that this bout of anxiety went a little bit deeper than usual. Kyle knew Tom believed implicitly in what they were doing, or at least in their ultimate goal. Which meant Tom's concern was actually two things: the manner in which they were going about it, and the guy sitting in the passenger seat. The guy that was making the van stink.

Kyle slipped the man in the passenger seat next to him a sidelong glance, and looked away quickly when the man noticed his stare.

When Tom had jokingly said that you could get hold of anything on the deep web - even *mercenaries* - he had only really brought it up for effect. Kyle knew that. But once the conversation was started, there had been no stopping it. Tom pulled on the loose thread relentlessly, until it all unravelled.

What if we can stop it before it happens, Kyle? Tom had said earnestly, and against his better judgment, Kyle had allowed himself to be persuaded. He told himself at first that it was just because it was so good to see his brother focused, and able to leave the house for the first time in years, but the truth was that there was more to it. Tom had stumbled onto something *big.*

All of which meant that somehow here they were, sitting in a stolen van in a no parking zone on Hatton Garden with what Kyle could only describe as an Eastern-European *hit-man*, and they were about to kidnap one of the UK's most famous socialites. Somehow it had been easy to think of it as fantasy when it was all happening in a foggy future on the other side of a computer screen.

It was real now. Nothing could be more real than sitting next to a man named Volkov and knowing pretty much for certain that no, that bulge in his pocket had nothing to do with him being happy to see you.

Volkov's phone trilled, splitting the nervous silence like a cleaver.

He pressed it to his ear without saying anything, and then looked at Kyle and said "Go".

Thick Russian accent. Barely-penetrable. It came out as *g-ho.* For a split second Kyle toyed with the ludicrous notion that he should pretend he hadn't understood the man, but the Russian's dark eyes left him in no doubt: they weren't playing a game now. What started on the computer was going to finish on Clerkenwell Road, one way or another. Volkov was in it for the money.

It felt like a dream, like someone else's foot was stamping on the accelerator. Kyle heard Tom whimper in the back seat. At least, he thought it was Tom, but had to concede the sound might have spilled from his own lips. With a sickening lurch the van shot forward, and left Kyle's stomach back in the illegal parking area.

Fuck me, this is actually happening. I'm driving a fucking getaway vehicle.

Naturally they had devised a *plan*, and it was deceptively simple, really. There was no way to get at the man Tom said they needed, so they would settle for taking his daughter. At various times she was hard to reach, surrounded by an entourage that loved to bask in the reflected glow of her spotlight, and sometimes a bodyguard or two. But she was also hell-bent on being Britain's *wildchild*, and sooner or later she'd end up giving her father's men the slip and tracking down a way to appear in the public eye, which generally involved drugs and alcohol. That was what she *did*. Getting hold of Isabelle Sullivan was just a matter of patience and good timing.

As the van rounded the corner onto Clerkenwell Road, Kyle saw that there was nothing wrong with their timing: Volkov's men - *hired goons, for fuck's sake, what are you doing here, Kyle?* - approached the restaurant just as Sullivan emerged a little woozily, and Kyle saw that she was alone, and allowed his hopes to rise, just a little. Of course, the plan succeeding would mean him becoming an actual *kidnapper*, but Tom had promised him repeatedly that the end justified the means. When it was over, Tom assured him, they would be the *good guys*. No harm would actually come to the girl.

Gripping the wheel in white-knuckled fingers, he weaved through the traffic, aiming to pull up alongside Volkov's men as they got control of Isabelle Sullivan.

Tom opens the door, she gets bundled inside, we get to the underground car park just half a mile away, switch vehicles and it's over. Home free.

A simple plan. All it required was good timing.

But as Kyle saw the first of Volkov's men grabbing hold of Sullivan, he understood that it wasn't timing that was going to thwart them: it was a bike messenger. Coming from nowhere, smashing his bike into Volkov's men at full speed and then leaping to his feet and taking them out in a blur of violence like an honest-to-God *ninja*. Kyle's stomach finally caught up with him. It wasn't happy.

The crack of gunfire in the seat next to him nearly made him steer the van directly into an oncoming bus.

His mouth dropped open in horror as he saw Volkov leaning out of the window, peppering the restaurant with bullets as the Sullivan girl disappeared inside with the bike messenger. Behind Kyle's seat, Tom's nervous whimpering had graduated to all-out blubbering.

Kyle fixed his eyes to the road, struggling to rein in the van's insatiable desire to smash into traffic.

"Volkov, what the *fuck*?" He screamed as he took a left onto a narrow side street and accelerated down it.

"This is wrong way," Volkov said in a flat, clipped tone that suggested Kyle had just asked him what he'd had for breakfast that morning, rather than why he'd just opened fire on a crowded London street at rush hour.

"Wrong way?" Tom's voice, in the back, squeezing its way through a wall of hysterical wails to reach Kyle's ears. "Wrong way for *what*, you crazy fucker?"

"For get the girl," Volkov said with a shrug.

"*Forget* the girl is right, you maniac," Kyle snarled, surprising himself with the venom in his tone. Apparently all his fear of the man had evaporated the moment he heard the first of the sirens in the distance. "We've got no chance of getting Isabelle Sullivan now."

He saw the entrance to the car park and swung the steering wheel, almost too late. The side of the van missed the wall by inches. He forced himself to ease up on the accelerator, cruising down to the basement level, where they had parked two cars. A simple plan. Get the girl, split up and get away clean. Only half of that equation now existed.

Kyle pulled the van into an empty parking bay and glared at Volkov, who responded with a disinterested shrug.

"My boys did job. You want let girl go, is your choice. My payment is same."

"Your *payment*?"

Kyle couldn't keep the astonishment from his voice. He opened the door and stepped from the van, shaking his head in disbelief. Volkov followed a moment later, and the dark expression on his face left Kyle in no doubt the Russian did not consider the conversation to be finished.

"Your payment was dependent on us getting the girl, Volkov. Not on you going on a killing spree in central fucking London. How are we supposed to pay you for *this*? And with what? Any money coming from this operation was going to come from the girl. That was the deal remember? We get the girl, you get her money."

Volkov grimaced, his face wrinkling in distaste like he'd just taken a bite of something rotten, and his hand dropped to his hip. There was no mistaking the threat in the gesture. Kyle raised his hands in surrender.

"Look, we'll work something out, okay? But right now we have to get out of here. Cops will be swarming over the whole area."

The van's sliding door opened and Tom stepped out into the car park. He had, apparently, stopped whimpering and come to the same conclusion as Kyle: it was time to go. Kyle heard his brother suck in a lungful of oil-tainted air.

"Right now is time to '*work something out*'," Volkov said in a menacing tone. "You think I am stupi-"

The Russian's eyes bulged suddenly, and Kyle's mouth dropped open as Tom demolished the back of Volkov's head with a tyre iron. The rest of the man's words were ejected in a gurgling bubble of blood as he hit the ground like a dropped sack of meat. Kyle stared at the twitching, dripping lump that Volkov had become in mute astonishment.

That was the other thing about Tom. Guy was a genius, but he was damn sure unpredictable.

Kyle glared at him.

"I guess we're leaving evidence behind, then," he snarled.

Tom shrugged.

"It's not going to matter," he said quietly. "You know what's coming. Worst that happens is we get caught out there and end up in prison. It'll probably be the safest place when it happens."

Kyle shook his head angrily and swallowed his response. Standing next to the rapidly-emptying body of a

Russian gangster was *not* a good place to get into an argument.

"Come on," he said, and ran to one of the cars they had stashed for their perfect getaway. He didn't say a word to Tom as he gunned the engine and left the car park at a moderate pace. Outside there were sirens everywhere, and it took all of Kyle's willpower not to stamp on the accelerator and flee blindly.

When they had been driving for several minutes, Kyle finally broke the silence.

"So what now?"

Tom looked thoughtful.

"I don't think we'll be able to get hold of Isabelle Sullivan now," he said.

"No shit."

"It was a long shot anyway. I doubt the old man cares enough about his daughter to blow the whistle."

Tom fell silent, and Kyle glanced to his left. From the look on Tom's face, he was running through a number of options. He had a brilliant mind, but Kyle couldn't help thinking that it might have been better if Tom was just a *little* less intelligent. Safer, anyway.

Kyle focused on the road. Of the two of them, it was Tom that did the thinking. Sometimes, Kyle had discovered, it was best to just leave him to it.

Tom had always been a fan of conspiracy theories, but he wasn't the blindly credulous type. According to Tom, the world was clearly *not* run by shape-shifting lizards, or by aliens or Elvis Presley; just by organisations that knew the most powerful weapon on earth was a fat bank balance and a pathological willingness to use it. The conspiracy theories Tom devoured online sooner or later became less theory and more fact. Police cover-ups. High profile paedophile gangs ring-fenced by power and authority. Massive financial fraud sponsored by the State.

And then, courtesy of the Deep Web, and a vague post from somebody that called himself *final_victory*, Tom had stumbled across something that dwarfed every other conspiracy he had uncovered. Something called *Project Wildfire* that involved a company called Chrysalis

Systems, headed up by a dead-eyed billionaire pensioner by the name of Fred Sullivan.

The further Tom delved into the company's affairs, the more convinced he became, and when Tom became convinced of something, Kyle had learned to pay attention.

One way or another Chrysalis had managed to insert itself into the manufacture of almost every single satellite that orbited the Earth, a process that stretched back over decades and continents, often overspending wildly to ensure they won contracts. Virtually every person of enormous wealth and power that Tom investigated was connected to Chrysalis by no more than two degrees of separation. The company had undisclosed ties to the military. The more Tom looked, the deeper the rabbit hole went, and the more it became clear that Chrysalis was on the verge of doing *something*. Gearing up for an event that had nothing to do with stock portfolios and everything to do with a military installation in Northumberland that was suspected of bioengineering chemical weapons, and the recent purchase of a number of decommissioned navy vessels that were converging in the North Sea on what was described by the company's vague website as a 'research expedition'.

Uncovering it all was Tom's shot at being a hero. He chased the information ravenously, all the way to Clerkenwell Road, and Volkov's pulverised skull.

"It'll be happening soon," Tom said finally. "I think there's only one thing we can do."

"Which is?" Kyle had a sinking feeling.

"The fleet," Tom said. "There's no way we'll get near the Northumberland base. We've got to get on board one of those ships."

Kyle shook his head in disbelief, and eased up on the accelerator. The conversation was getting to him, and the pressure transferred directly from his mind to the growling engine. He forced himself to relax his grip on the wheel. His fingers ached.

"You're insane. How the hell are we going to do that?"

It was a bad choice of word. Kyle knew it, and immediately felt a wave of regret wash through him. Tom had been called crazy plenty of times in his life. He'd never grown to like it.

"The whole fucking *world* is insane, Kyle. And those that aren't soon will be. Just drive. I'll do the rest."

1

It wasn't the first time the sea had given birth. Again and again across the endless centuries the rolling waves had delivered, until the miraculous became the mundane. First the oceans had created life that was barely-there, single-celled; just a faint whisper that broke the yawning silence that had existed before. As time flowed on and the cells divided, the sea became more ambitious, and the creatures it created became complicated and intricate, delicate webs of life that thrived in the dark cocoon the water provided.

Eventually the creatures born in the depths crawled from the cold safety of the water to claim the land, but the oceans never stopped creating life, churning relentlessly; the idling engine of the planet. It was the energy provided by that engine that allowed life to flourish. The sea took credit for all.

Not this time, though.

The sea had little to do with creating the figure it spat onto the beach. It had created the core of him, sure, but no more than the scaffolding. The final design, that was all the work of humans. All the sea did was carry him.

For two days the man remained unconscious on the sand, and the rising tide lapped at his feet, nuzzling him like a protective mother before falling away again and leaving him to rest.

When he finally opened his eyes and saw steely skies above, the man felt a serene calm descend upon him, but there was no escaping the turbulence in his past; the raging inferno of death and destruction. Even his cells had been at war, a bloody battle fought in a microscopic theatre, as his DNA broke and violently remade itself; invisible and catastrophic. Externally, the man looked unchanged, despite the vicious conflict that had occurred within. For him, the extraordinary had taken place below the surface. Just like the ocean.

For a long time, the man had no idea where he was, or who he had been before the empty beach and the rolling sigh of the waves. His past was a mirror in the shadows, images that loomed and faded, nimbly evading him when he grasped at them. None of the fragmented images in his head made sense; nothing stacked up. The events of his past seemed linked by only one common thread: there was death and blood everywhere.

The beach was calm, and the man wanted to stay, but he knew he could not: something wanted to drag him to his feet. An insistent *something* that pulled at his thoughts, demanding his attention like a fresh wound. He tried to ignore the impulse, and he stubbornly stayed on the damp sand for a long time, just staring up as the skies darkened over him and the temperature dropped. He clung to the brittle sense of serenity for as long as possible, relishing the silence.

Until he heard the voice, and the fleeting sense of peace rotted away and became toxic.

He squeezed his eyes shut, hoping the voice would let him be, but it was futile, because the voice was inside his head, familiar and venomous; an infection of the soul. It whispered at him, clawing and pulling at his memories, determined to knit them together into a terrifying whole.

He pulled himself upright, and the motion was like stepping into a wall of fire. Pain exploded across his body, and the man looked down in anguish to determine the source of the agony, discovering that his entire body was covered in livid bruises and lacerations. He let out a wordless yell of horror.

What happened to me?

As if in response, his body offered up a different sort of pain; crawling and insidious. An itch that burned like poison, making his left arm feel like it had been set alight. The man stared at his arm, his brow furrowing, and saw a patch of angry flesh. He scratched at it furiously, like an animal, thinking of nothing beyond easing the irritation. All the scratching seemed to achieve was transformation in the source of the itching, driving it inward until it felt like it was in his mind. The man squeezed his eyes shut, and clawed at his temples, but the itch worsened, increasing and increasing until-

The man's eyes flared open and he saw the eyeless creature shambling toward him along the beach, and the memories finally came together, clicking into place, and he saw everything he wished he could forget.

Memories of blood and fire.

He knew what the eyeless thing was, but its behaviour made no sense. Every time he had seen one of its kind, they had charged towards humans relentlessly, crazed with the desire to kill. But not this one. It stumbled around aimlessly, swinging its head back and forth, searching for the source of the sound it had heard, but apparently unable to locate it. The creature emitted a low moan that sounded almost like *confusion.*

It can't see me.

None of the creatures could *see*, at least not in the traditional sense of the word. But that didn't stop them hunting: they seemed to track their prey by sound alone, visualising the world around them almost like bats.

Yet somehow this one was completely oblivious to his presence mere yards away from it.

The man walked slowly toward the infected creature until he was standing right next to it, breathing in the sickening stink of blood and shit, and threw it down onto the sand, placing a foot on its neck. The thing gurgled and shuddered, but made no attempt to free itself, as though it was struggling to comprehend what had just happened.

With a hollow roar, the man raised his fist to the stars, and dropped it like an anvil into the creature's already ruined face, decimating it. Again and again he drove his knuckles through the flesh, down toward the bone, until the creature became still, and its blood clotted the sand.

The voice in the man's head screeched in delight; it cavorted in the blood and the violence.

It gave him a name.

Jaaaaaaaasssssssssssooooonnn...

2

Emergency town meetings were unusual in the tiny town of Newborough.

Isolated at the south-eastern tip of the island of Anglesey off the coast of North Wales, the town was distant enough from the pressures of modern-day life that the word 'emergency' very rarely cropped up anywhere other than on television.

Annie Holloway relished being the one to call the meeting.

The Holloway family had been a big deal in Newborough for the best part of two centuries. Holloways had always been the principal land owners, and had sat on the town council for generations, wielding huge influence over their little corner of the world since long before electricity came to town.

To be a Holloway was to be a part of a fine old legacy.

Thus it was, as Annie had been repeatedly told by her long-dead father, a terrible shame that Annie had no siblings - although what he meant, of course, was no *brothers* - because the family name would die when Annie married.

It will be the end of the Holloways, her father used to slur in despair, as though his daughter would simply cease to exist after his death. Albert Holloway would die and the family name would be left with a *woman*. When she married the name would die. When finally she opened her legs and spat out a child, the Holloway coffin would receive its final nail.

Annie was grateful that the old bastard clung onto life bitterly, until she had not one but three children; long enough for him to blame his impending death squarely on his misery at his own failure to continue the family name, rather than his diseased liver.

Annie had picked her husband - a good-looking but simple-minded idiot with a stutter - purely to spite her father, and she revelled in the distaste that soured the old man's face whenever he found himself in the same room as his new son-in-law; at the knowledge that the Holloway name hadn't simply faded away. It had been demolished.

When her father did finally die - of what she hoped to God *was* a broken heart - Annie had the good fortune to bury her husband less than three months later. She reclaimed her name.

She had ruled Newborough with an iron fist for nearly four decades since, and she spat on her father's grave once a year for luck. It seemed to work, but luck was only a tiny part of it, and Annie was smart enough not to rely on something as flimsy as fortune.

Power was just a matter of patience, and Annie had it in abundance. Mastering the fine art of power accumulation, she decided early on, was all about longevity and straight-up willpower. Opposition always faded away, given enough time, and faced by enough trouble. All that was required was stubborn resolve.

By the age of seventy-one, Annie had expended several decades of her life to occupy a number of key roles in the tiny town, and each added a layer of influence. As a school teacher, she had the children of the community - and by extension their parents - under her spell. She let the headmaster of the school, a watery sort of a man by the name of Patterson, have his name on the throne, but everyone in Newborough knew who truly sat on it.

Annie more obviously sat on the town council, as her father had before her.

During her first years on the council she attended every committee, debating every topic to a standstill with an almost religious fervour, precisely because she knew that eventually everyone of Newborough's several hundred residents would get used to the fact that if they wanted to get anything accomplished, they'd have to go through her. So she sat and mulled over itineraries that held no discernible interest: vague nonsense about road closures and town improvements that would almost certainly never come to pass; petty land disputes and tedious event planning, and she conjured up a strong opinion about every single one.

That had been just the start of her reign though, that long period of taking control of all the matters that seemed unimportant to everyone else. Influence crawled toward her from a hundred different directions, and she collected it all. By the time anybody realised there was a silent coup in progress, it was already done and dusted. She won by default, by attrition; wearing her adversaries down like the tide until they crumbled away and she consumed them.

Her father had everything handed to him on a plate simply because he was born with the right genitals. Annie had it all taken away, and so she took it *back*.

Once Annie's sons - Rhys, Bryn and Hywel - were grown, and after Annie had put the fear of God into them whenever one expressed a desire to leave Newborough someday, she got them installed in positions of power around the town. Rhys and Bryn comprised the entirety of Newborough's police force. Hywel - the runt of the litter - Annie provided with the job of landlord of the town's most popular pub, where he at least proved useful as an eavesdropper.

Newborough nestled at the edge of the Warren, one of the UK's largest sand dunes, and the expansive Newborough Forest. The island itself was separated from the Welsh mainland by the Menai Strait, a strip of water only a half-mile wide, but it might as well have existed in a parallel dimension. Few strangers ever found their way to the town, and the rest of the UK either forgot Newborough existed or didn't care in the first place. The latter, most likely.

Occasionally - usually when a new government settled into power in distant London, brimming with enthusiasm and as-yet unbroken promises - edicts about this or that initiative would arrive at the tiny council offices, and Annie would promptly ignore them, unless they could be turned to her benefit. No one from the government came calling to ensure their policies were being implemented. The place, Annie thought, was perfect.

Patience.

Power.

It had all been going so well until the world ended around her and the majority of the population died in a storm of blood and torn flesh.

Annie had survived the initial assault of the virus precisely because of her status in the town, and because the town was so remote.

While the rest of the world collapsed into violent chaos, the most the residents of Newborough knew was that their phones and televisions had stopped working. It was inconvenient, rather than apocalyptic. So isolated was the town that for almost a full day after the communications network went down, business proceeded as usual.

Only a handful of the people of Newborough commuted to jobs on the mainland, and when their spouses began to report to the police that they weren't returning home word reached Annie quickly, and an intuition bred of a life spent with her ear to the ground, watchful for change, made her suspect that Newborough's long and comfortable separation from the world might be at an end.

Her response was to ruin everyone's day, and call the emergency town meeting.

Most town meetings were poorly attended, many of the residents having long since given up putting their point of view across on any matter. It was far simpler to do away with the charade and simply let Annie decide what was best. The addition of the word *emergency* swelled numbers, but the numbers had been anaemic to begin with. So there were a little less than seventy people sitting on uncomfortable wooden chairs in the town hall when the virus reached Newborough like a pebble dropped into a still lake, just one creature stumbling onto a farm outside town and giving birth to three more, that quickly became seventeen.

As the ripple of destruction flowed toward the town hall, it left a trail of dead behind it, sloughed across the fields and the cracked roads. It approached implacably, like light breaking across a distant horizon.

By the time Annie heard the screaming outside and scurried to the front door of the town hall to see something that made her mind feel like it was leaking somehow, there were dozens of Infected in the streets, and Annie did the only thing that was sensible for the town.

She barricaded the doors and let them all die, thinking to herself a little numbly that it had turned out to be an *emergency* after all.

While the rest of the people locked inside the town hall were wailing and sobbing, Annie was calculating. All her sons were safely inside. She had lost nothing. All she had to do was survive whatever strange apocalypse was unfolding beyond the sturdy wooden doors. When the bizarre event had passed Newborough would rebuild, and the influence of the Holloway family would be unassailable.

The makeshift barricade - chairs wedged under the door handles and piled high around the entrance - looked passable, but Annie knew that if that assumption proved to be incorrect, her death would immediately follow, and while she was many things, she was no taker of unnecessary risks.

"Upstairs," she hissed at no one in particular, and made for the narrow stairway that led to a large function room that occasionally hosted Newborough's small wedding receptions. They would all follow her; she didn't bother to look back.

When they were all safely on the first floor, Annie had them barricade those doors too, and made her way to the nearest window to survey what was happening to her beloved town. From an elevated angle, the carnage on the narrow streets made no more sense than it had at ground level.

She watched, open-mouthed, as she saw familiar faces - some of whom she had liked well enough; others who were cretins that few would miss; and certainly not *her* - twisting into masks of pure hatred. Watched as they ripped out their eyes and leapt onto their former friends and family, tearing and ripping at them with teeth and fingers.

"Some kind of sickness," a voice at her side mumbled, and Annie jumped a little. "Blood-borne. But I don't know of anything that acts so fast."

Annie turned and flashed a withering smile at Doctor Turner, who stood behind her, trying to peek through the window. What the town GP *didn't* know could fill an entire shelf of medical textbooks. In fact, beyond prescribing antibiotics for all his patients and industrial-strength painkillers for himself, Annie doubted the man was any closer to being a genuine medical professional than she was herself.

"Could it be airborne?" She asked, though she knew even before the doctor shrugged that the question was merely wasted breath.

"Could be," he said uncertainly. "But it seems like they're only affected after being bitten. Could be, though."

Vague as always, Turner. Antibiotics and painkillers won't help us here.

He shrugged again, and Annie turned back to the window. She saw several corpses cooling on the road, their lives leaking away underneath them. For some, the wounds they had received had proven fatal. But there were many, many more that seemed utterly oblivious to the chunks the infected teeth had taken from them, and they bounced around the buildings like pinballs, hunting down the remaining people of Newborough remorselessly.

"Shouldn't we go out and help them?"

Annie sighed.

"Take a look, doctor," she said. "Exactly what help do you think *you* can offer?"

She stepped aside to let the doctor get a better view.

Outside the window, Hell had come to Newborough.

3

The first floor of the town hall had room to spare, though when it came to sleeping there was no option but to curl up on the cold, hard floor like cats.

On the first night everyone had kept a respectful distance, but when they woke in the morning frozen to the bone, the seventy-or-so people hiding in the function room realised they would have to start huddling together for warmth. In some ways, Annie thought, dignity was the first thing to go.

Dignity and sanity.

At least half of the people trapped in the function room appeared to be undergoing some sort of catastrophic mental collapse. Some sat against the walls, hugging their knees and staring in horror at the past. Annie didn't mind them so much. Their oblivion, although unsettling, had little impact on her. Others mewled and whined incessantly, offering nothing but misery. She dearly wanted to push those people outside and lock the door so she could hear herself think.

Thankfully there were working lavatories; mercifully there was one each for male and female. The bathrooms provided running water, but there was no food.

The lack of food hadn't even occurred to Annie as a potential problem, because there was no way that whatever catastrophe had befallen her town would be allowed to continue. Word would spread, surely - even if the strange affliction that had slaughtered most of Newborough's small population covered the entire island, and the police would come from the mainland. Or the army. *Somebody.*

Nobody came.

By the fourth day the town hall echoed to the endless rumble of empty bellies, and Annie began to understand that everybody was waiting for her to tell them what to do to prevent them starving to death. It was time, she decided, to be proactive.

On day four, Annie lost ten people.

The streets had looked quiet, if grisly enough to turn the strongest stomach, and so Annie had proposed that a group make a dash to the nearest convenience store, just a couple of hundred yards away.

Everybody filed downstairs to remove the barricade from the main entrance; they did it quietly, their actions muted by cold terror, and when Annie eased the door open, she made it clear that they should all be ready to run back upstairs, retreating to their final bolt-hole like hunted animals at a moment's notice.

When the door was open, she saw no movement on the street beyond, and ushered out the ten people she had 'volunteered' for the job - none of which went by the name Holloway, of course, because Annie wasn't *stupid*. The group stuttered outside and disappeared from sight.

Annie never saw them again, but she heard the screaming. They all did, and the wide-eyed fear on their faces said everyone in the town hall had reached a silent accord: they weren't *that* hungry. Annie had them restore the barricade, and the remaining residents of Newborough returned to their hiding place, and the slow crawl of insanity and starvation.

After a week, when the ravenous hunger made the group feel weak and sick, they mostly spent their time sleeping. No one had given voice to the fear that soon they simply would not wake up, but it hung over them all like a bad memory, fraying the edges of every hushed word they muttered to each other.

Annie stood at the window and searched the streets day after day as a dark shadow blossomed in her mind like a tumour. Mostly the streets looked quiet and empty, and sometimes it was almost possible to believe it was all over, or that the massacre had taken place in her imagination. But the Infected were still out there; Annie saw them occasionally stumbling around, as though they were searching for something they had lost. Over the hours, she was able to detect a pattern: the same horrific faces would fumble their way across her field of vision, almost as if they were somehow patrolling.

Or hunting.

Annie had lost count of the days when she noticed that she had begun to absent-mindedly drag her nails across the withered flesh of her hands until they bled.

Something had to be done.

When the creatures outside disappeared from sight, the streets would again become still, and usually remained so for a couple of hours at least. It gave Annie a window of opportunity.

By the time desperation took hold, and the men and women hiding in the town hall began to think they would gladly walk through fire just to get something to eat, Annie had already decided that the convenience store down the street might lead to death, but the row of houses next to the town hall surely did not. None of the houses would contain enough food to sustain seventy - *no, sixty, now. That's something, at least* - people for very long, but the situation had reached a dire point at which no one was thinking about any sort of long-term future. Nothing existed beyond the possibility of the next meal. Some had even said they would happily eat dog food, and Annie understood: her own hunger was a gnawing, sickly pain that had come to dominate her every thought.

Even the fevered speculation about what sort of disaster might have befallen the world outside the town hall had quietened, and Annie wondered how long it would be before people started talking about that movie that had been popular a few years back, the one about the survivors of a plane crash that were forced towards cannibalism. Those people at least had the excuse that they were stranded miles from civilization. The notion that the people of Anglesey, just a half-mile away from the north coast of Wales, would *eat* each other simply because they were afraid to go outside seemed ridiculous.

On that day, Annie began to hallucinate; waking dreams of devouring Doctor Turner and enjoying every last bite, wishing only that she had a little salt and pepper to season the man's bitter, flabby flesh.

I've lost my mind, Annie thought as she sized up Turner's limbs and decided that he had remarkably hairless arms, which might not taste so bad at all.

"We have to go outside," she said loudly and abruptly, surprising herself.

The response to her statement was a collective moan, low and sickly.

"We'll die out there, Annie," Turner moaned weakly.

"We're dying in *here*, Doctor Turner," Annie snapped, surprised to find she had enough energy left to pour scorn into her tone. "Help is *not* coming and we *are* going to die in here. It may be more peaceful than dying out *there*, but I'm not really prepared to choose which death I prefer. Not yet. Are you? The store is obviously too dangerous, but those things don't seem to come around here more than once every two or three hours. We can go next door, to the first house we see, break in and get their food. It won't be much, but if we get that far we can plan our next move."

Turner snorted.

"By 'we' I'm assuming you don't mean *you*," he said pointedly.

Cheeky bastard, Annie thought, *hunger has made you brave.*

"No, Turner. I mean *you*. Consider yourself volunteered."

"Says who?"

Annie hadn't expected Turner's response, and she blinked in surprise. The closest thing the man had to a spine sat in his surgery, propping up an example of the human skeleton that fascinated the children who visited him with various illnesses and infections.

"Boys," Annie said sharply, and her sons immediately rose and moved to her side. They knew the tone all too well. When Annie Holloway's voice dropped an octave, sinking into an animal growl, disagreement was no longer an option.

"Says *me*, Turner. Perhaps you've forgotten who's in charge around here? I haven't. In fact, let this be a lesson to all of you. Times have changed. But *I* haven't. You understand?"

Annie's voice was rising back up. Hunger was making her sound a little unhinged. She reined her fury back in, fearful that once she lost herself in hysteria she would never find her way back.

"You'll go, Turner. Your only choice now is whether you walk through the front door or I have my boys throw you out the fucking window. Got it?"

Annie very rarely swore. It was, she believed, a crude and overused method of attempting to intimidate anyone. Curses were far more effective when used sparingly, when the unfamiliarity of the words gave them an edge like a blade. Most of the people in the town hall had, in fact, never heard her swear.

Turner flinched, and Annie noticed with satisfaction that the flinch passed from person to person like a rumour. No one argued, though, and Annie realised with satisfaction that there was no longer any need for her to concern herself with couching her orders in politeness and politics. Newborough needed a different sort of leader.

Times had changed.

4

The beach seemed endless, stretching away from the water and becoming expansive sand dunes that sucked Jason's feet down and made walking difficult. He felt exhausted, and his body ached and throbbed, demanding that he rest. Just when he began to believe that maybe he had died after all, and that Hell was an endless desert, the sand gave way to grass that shuffled softly in the coastal breeze, and then to a thick forest. At the edge of the trees, Jason sat down, breathing heavily.

I should be dead, he thought. The way things had unravelled back in Aberystwyth, so suddenly and so chaotically, left him unsure as to what exactly had happened. He remembered pushing the boat away from the harbour, and the expression on Rachel's face as she understood what he was about to do was etched deep into Jason's mind. The horror and remorse and fury in her eyes.

He remembered turning to face the Infected as they rushed toward him, and swinging and stabbing as they overwhelmed him, and he remembered getting trampled before the memories abruptly cut off.

Trampled, he thought. The Infected didn't trample things. They bit and clawed at them.

They couldn't see me. Ran right over me.

He stared again at the dark scar on his forearm, and his eyes widened a little in understanding. The farm outside St. Davids. A seemingly insignificant bite from an infected rat. He had expected to die then, too, but all he had experienced was an extraordinary pain, like his innards were dancing a messy jig, and then that strange phantom itch.

We'll figure it out, Jase, Rachel had said, although Jason had barely registered the words at the time. But he knew, now. He'd figured it out all by himself. He was immune, like the old woman in Aberystwyth. And somehow his immunity meant the Infected couldn't zero in on him like they did everyone else.

If only I'd known before. Things would be so different. I'd still be with-

Rachel.

Jason stood, and began to slide his massive frame between the tree trunks, over tangled roots that seemed to grasp at him in the dark.

He had no idea where he was, or even if his sister was still alive, but Jason had to find her.

Jasssssssssssonnnn...

He grimaced as he heard his mother's voice, thick and gloopy; a noise that bubbled, like it was seeping up through a deep pool of something foul.

*S*he's already dead, Jassssssoonnnn. You couldn't protect her, because you're just a little baby, and you left her to die. She's out there now, looking for you, but her eyes are gone and she can't seeeeeee yoooouuuu. Jasssssoooooooonnnnnnnnn...*

Jason squeezed his eyes shut and shook his head, trying to clear out the poison that lurked in the shadows. For several long moments the world around him seemed to dim, as though his mind was slipping through the cracks, back towards a state of catatonic bliss. With an effort, he focused on blocking out the hideous vision of his mother swinging from the trees around him, dropping chunks of flesh from her rotting body like falling fruit.

He breathed deeply.

Opened his eyes.

And heard screaming.

*

Bob Turner hated Annie Holloway; hated her with a passion that burned like the surface of the fucking *sun*. He always had: the seeds of his enmity germinated long before she became the person that forced him from the safety of the town hall out onto a street stained with blood and broken bodies; alive with the fizzing potential for sickening violence.

In what now felt like a previous life, Bob had hated Annie simply because of her enormous influence over his small town, and her relentless snide asides about his professionalism, or lack of it. She prodded and needled at him mercilessly, and she seemed to be *everywhere*. And if she wasn't physically standing in front of him, it seemed one of her hulking, simple-minded offspring was. There was no escape: no part of his life she didn't spread into like a growing, malignant tumour.

Even Bob's marriage had collapsed because of Annie Holloway, when his wife, Kate, had finally decided that she couldn't take another moment of her husband's incessant and impotent complaining about the woman and walked out.

Often Bob imagined that Annie Holloway was a giant, squatting over the town of Newborough, shitting on the residents and somehow persuading them that it was raining. It seemed only he saw it. Or maybe they all knew it, every last one of them. They just weren't willing to be the ones to say it. But being trapped in the town hall had finally forced the woman to show her true colours: no one would be in any doubt now that Holloway was poison. It was too late, though, for anything to be done about it. Her three sons were now her private army, more than powerful enough to dominate the few dozen cowering, broken souls in the town hall. Even when the entire world had gone up in smoke, Annie Holloway still found a way to shit on him.

When Annie had threatened to have him thrown from the window, Bob had looked pleadingly around the people that silently stared at him, praying that they would rush to his side and offer their support.

What he got was blank-faced stares that reminded him of the way people pretended to be oblivious when a drunken vagrant began ranting in their immediate vicinity.

I'm the vagrant, Bob thought sadly, as he let their cold stares usher him down to the ground floor. *But I'll take some of you fuckers down with me.*

When they had cleared the messy barricade of wooden chairs away from the entrance, Bob turned toward Annie and drew himself up to his full - and disappointing -

height, and mustered every ounce of hatred he held for the woman, letting it fuel his courage.

"I'll go," he snarled, "But if you want me to come back with any food, I won't go alone."

Annie blinked.

"Because if you push me out that door alone," Bob continued, "I won't be coming back. If I make it into that house alive, I'll stay there and eat every scrap of food I can find. I'll eat until I'm sick and then I'll eat some more."

Annie rolled her eyes.

"Even your threats are weak, *doctor*." Annie laced that word with venom. That was nothing to do with their predicament, though. She'd placed special emphasis on that word for twenty years.

Bitch.

"Who wants to go with him?"

Bob watched as Annie turned to face the hateful crowd that gathered behind her, and smirked when he saw their smug, complacent expressions dissolving into stunned fear.

He watched all of them running through potential objections in their minds, and saw them all come up hilariously short. Everyone had seen how Annie responded to her authority being questioned. She didn't reserve disdain for Bob alone; there was more than enough for everybody. Arguing would be as pointless as it was likely to be incendiary. They had all feared Annie before; now they acted as though they were trapped in the lion enclosure at a zoo.

"You," Annie said, pointing at Patrick Dunn, a slow-witted barber whose face slackened in anguish.

Bob grinned savagely, but his triumph was short-lived, crumbling away immediately as Annie stepped past him and threw open the door to the street, staring at him expectantly.

"Good luck, Bob," Annie said in a tone that sagged under the weight of insincerity loaded on top of it. Bob opened his mouth to respond, though he had no smart comeback, and was more than willing to settle for a simple *fuck you*, but he didn't get the chance.

He felt a meaty hand on the small of his back - one of the woman's obnoxious sons, no doubt - and then he was shoved out into the night air.

He forgot all about Annie Holloway immediately, as soon as he caught the metallic stink of blood on the faint breeze. *Tasted* it.

For a moment Bob stood alongside Patrick in frozen terror, straining to hear or see some evidence of death rushing toward him. The streets looked quiet. Almost peaceful, Bob thought, if you discounted the ruined corpses that decayed slowly in the cold air.

He waved frantically at Patrick to follow him, and set off toward the row of terraced houses to the right of the town hall. They were only the width of a small car park away, but it felt like the longest journey Bob Turner had ever endured, like a slow crawl through Hell on his knees. With every step his heart felt like it was about to plunge into cardiac arrest.

I'm actually whimpering, he thought dully, twisting his neck from left to right as he ran, almost sobbing in gratitude at the empty streets that greeted him.

When he reached the first house in the terrace, Bob pressed his back to it as he fumbled at the door handle. Locked. *Obviously.*

"Shouldn't we go around the back, in case they see us?" The fear-laden whisper came from Patrick, and nearly made Bob jump out of his skin.

Bob wanted to shake the man for breaking the silence; wanted to scream at him that the creatures stalking around Newborough had no fucking *eyes*, and that it wouldn't matter whether they moved to the rear of the house, away from the street. The only thing that mattered was that they might hear them, and Patrick was a fucking idiot for doing anything louder than breathing. He had to settle for giving Patrick the best withering look he could muster, before turning away.

"Do we need to smash the window?" Patrick breathed, "Because they might hear-"

Bob clapped his hand over Patrick's mouth, clenching his fingers tightly on the man's loose cheeks, squeezing until he saw pain on the dumb bastard's face. With his free hand, Bob put a finger to his own lips and glared at Patrick until he saw recognition in the man's eyes.

Bob released his grip on Patrick's jowly face, and scampered lightly to the next door in the terrace. Also locked. He didn't wait for Patrick to process the disappointment, moving along to the next door without pausing.

When the third door swung open silently, Bob very nearly let out a triumphant yell of relief.

He stepped inside cautiously, and immediately stopped, nearly screaming in fright as Patrick stumbled clumsily into his back.

The hallway that led into the house was pitch-black. Unable to see anything other than the dim outline of two doorways and a staircase, Bob froze, waiting for something unseen to come at him in the dark, and tried very hard to keep a lid on a rising wave of hysteria that sloshed around his empty stomach. Forcing his legs to move, Bob stepped forward, carefully avoiding a low table that held a dish and some car keys, pointing it out to Patrick as he passed.

It took two paces for Bob's eyes to adjust to the lack of light. By the third he saw the blood that smeared its way up the stairs. His eyes followed the dark smear all the way up, bulging and unblinking.

There's something up there.

By the fourth step, Bob's legs were already turning, way before informing his mind that they were getting the fuck out. *In fairness to Patrick,* Bob thought dimly as he bumped into the barber and saw him stumble into the table, *he couldn't have known I was going to do that.*

It was an odd thought, Bob decided, as the dish smashed on the floor and the keys skittered noisily across the carpet. Odd to focus on something so mundane even as the door behind him crashed open and he heard snarling. Odder still that when the air shrieked behind him, and teeth sank into his shoulder, deep enough to scratch bone, the only thing Bob could think was that he'd been wrong. It hadn't been upstairs. It had been right in the next room.

Stupid, Bob. Just like she always said.

As Bob Turner began to plunge his fingers deep into his eye sockets and proceeded to twist, Patrick Dunn screamed loud enough to wake the dead, and then Newborough came to life.

*

Jason didn't stop to think. Thinking meant enduring another conversation with his mother, and the nightmares of the real world were infinitely preferable. When he heard the scream, he trundled forward, building momentum slowly like a heavy locomotive, and burst from the trees at full pace onto what looked like a kid's playground.

Across a muddy field that hosted two lonely goalposts, Jason saw a row of terraced houses. He charged toward it, even as he heard the shrieking start in earnest. It sounded like there were dozens of them. The dull, ghostly itch returned, growing stronger by the second as he crossed the field.

When he reached the street, he saw the man stumbling backwards from the open doorway immediately, but he was already dead; already crashing to the ground under a scrabbling figure that drove its jaws down onto the screaming man's neck. It didn't matter. Saving the man wasn't Jason's goal. Never had been.

With a hoarse bellow, Jason snatched up a heavy rock from a carefully-sculpted garden and sprinted at the Infected creature swinging his massive arm in a wide arc, nearly taking its head clean off. He saw others swarming onto the street, bolting around corners and through broken windows, slipping on the gore-slick streets as they frantically hunted for the source of the noise.

Jason yelled again, and lifted the makeshift club, and smashed skulls until his bones ached and his voice cracked. None of the Infected reacted to his presence.

When he drove the rock through the brain of the last of them, Jason dropped to the ground, overwhelmed by the pain wracking his damaged body, and the world began to spin and fade.

I am the cure, he thought, and darkness claimed him.

*

Jason didn't see the heavy wooden doors swing open behind him. Didn't see the old woman emerge into the massacre, oblivious to the steaming, leaking bodies that scarred the ground in front of the town hall. Her eyes were fixed only on his comatose body, her mouth open in astonishment.

5

"Is he here to save us, Ma?"

Annie rolled her eyes. Rhys was her eldest son, and he was meant to be the smartest, but unfortunately only fifty per cent of the ingredients that had made him came from Annie. The other half came from a man long-dead, who had been her most enduring mistake.

"He didn't even know we were here, Rhys," she said wearily.

Rhys nodded, as though the answer was sufficient, but Annie thought it was far from it. Whatever had happened to turn the quiet people of Newborough into demented cannibals seemed to have no effect whatsoever on the huge man.

Why are *you here?* Annie thought. *What are you?*

Annie had instructed her sons to carry the comatose man into the town hall. It had taken all three of them to do it; the guy looked like he weighed half a ton. She had watched in amazement from the first floor window as the huge man moved through the crowd of the Infected, hollering so that they came to him, and executing them. None of the creatures seemed to know or care that he was among them. He was the bolt gun, and they were cattle. But he was much more than that. Annie recognised it immediately.

The strange man was *power.*

She had Rhys tie the man up, and then led her people forth from the town hall like a prophet, delivering them through the ruined bodies to the convenience store where they took virtually everything that sat on the shelves and carted it back to the place that had kept them safe. Most ate as they walked, lost in a happy fog of calories that gripped them like powerful narcotics.

Annie had half expected that the people - at least *some* of the people - would head away from the town hall; maybe to search for loved ones or simply to go home, but it seemed as though it occurred to none of them to go their separate ways. All shuffled silently back toward the town hall like animals returning to a nest. To Annie they felt like a strange, nightmarish family; bonded by violence and death rather than blood.

While the rest of them pillaged as much food as they could carry, Annie took Rhys, along with his younger brother Bryn, to the pharmacy opposite the convenience store, and she filled a bag with everything that looked potent enough to affect something large.

In a way, it was a shame the doctor was dead, Annie thought. He would at least have been able to tell her what some of the medications were for. In another way, of course, Bob Turner had been an insufferable coward, and it wasn't a shame that he was dead at all.

Every cloud... Annie thought, as she dropped opaque bottles of pills into her bag, and let a rare smile break her wrinkled features. She found herself hoping that Turner had the time to feel truly terrified before he died. Once it would have been the kind of thought that society would have judged harshly.

Not anymore.

The changes in the world were, she thought, of great interest, but nothing interested her quite like the unconscious man. Once she had eaten and the resulting wave of dizziness and euphoria passed, she motioned at Rhys to follow her into a small room adjacent to the main hall, and stared at their saviour. He looked young - younger than all her children - and even comatose, his face wore a sad, anguished expression.

She slapped his face sharply, hard enough to make her palm sting.

His eyes opened, but they were unfocused, lurching around the room like a drunk. He tried to get up, and found that the chair he was tied to had other ideas. He grunted.

"Get him some water," Annie said, and smiled at the bound man benevolently.

"Who are you?" She asked gently.

The man didn't respond, instead railing against the ropes that bound him. For a moment, as his muscles bulged, Annie took a half-step backwards in concern, expecting the rope to snap. After a moment of furious struggle, the man seemed to deflate.

"Why am I tied to a chair?"

The man sounded oddly boyish.

"I haven't decided if I can trust you yet," Annie said. "Who are you?"

He shook his head as though trying to clear it.

"Where am I?"

Annie stared at the man, planting her hands on her hips and waiting for him to answer her. After a moment, the man cocked his head to the side, as though listening to a distant voice that she could not hear, and then he nodded.

"Voorhees," the man said. "You can call me Voorhees."

Annie opened her mouth to speak, but again the man cocked his head to one side, as though he were listening to something else. He emitted a sickly moan that dissolved into a wheezing cough.

"Voorhees," Annie repeated absently. The name seemed familiar to her somehow, but she couldn't place it. It certainly wasn't a Welsh name, but the man's accent was South Wales through and through.

Rhys reappeared with a mug of cold water, and Annie took it from him and stepped directly in front of the bound man, putting her bony fingers under his jaw and lifting it up before tipping the water down his throat. Voorhees drank greedily. It was, for Annie, an oddly tender moment that reminded her of her youth and happier times, when her children were small and hadn't yet disappointed her.

For a brief moment her eyes were lost in memories, until Voorhees coughed and ripped her back into the present.

"Look," he said, "I don't know you people, or what you want, but I have to go. You have to let me go."

"I was afraid you'd say that," Annie interrupted. "That's why I had you tied up. You're not well, child. You're injured. You have to stay here for now."

Voorhees shook his head.

"There's somebody I need to find and-"

"I said *no*," Annie said sharply, and the man blinked in surprise at the sudden venom in her tone. He struggled against his bonds again; gave up a little quicker this time.

"Let me go you crazy old bitch!" He roared, and Annie smiled. *A tantrum*, she thought. She had learned to deal with tantrums *decades* earlier.

"I think you need something to relax you, Mr Voorhees," she said benevolently, and pulled a small bottle of pills from a pocket, holding them in front of his eyes like a hypnotist's watch. His eyes followed the bottle warily.

Annie made a show of reading the warning label on the bottle.

"Take two daily. May cause drowsiness."

She poured out a handful of the pills. Red and black. They looked like poisoned pellets designed for eradicating vermin.

"Big guy like you probably needs more than two, though. And I'd prefer something a little more definite than 'may cause drowsiness', if you know what I mean."

The man's eyes filled with a burning fury. Annie paid it no attention, grabbing his nose and squeezing, waiting for the inevitable opening of his mouth.

"Open wide," she said with a grin.

*

It didn't take long for the man who called himself Voorhees to slide back into oblivion, leaving Annie with something of a dilemma. There was no way she could let him go, not when he had just displayed the strange effect he had on the creatures that had killed everyone else they had encountered. Annie didn't understand how the man was different, but she didn't need to. It had been over a week since she had last understood *anything*, and yet still she survived.

No, letting him go was absolutely not an option. But keeping him tied up was almost as useless: if the eyeless cannibals returned to Newborough, she would need him to fight them off, and he couldn't do that as long as she had him drugged and tied to a chair. Only one option presented itself to her: the man would have to be trained, like a dog. Dogs, in Annie's experience, responded best to a cycle of punishment and reward.

She beckoned Rhys to come to her side.

"We need to make sure the town is clear," Annie said, ignoring the fact that Rhys nodded and looked confused simultaneously.

"I need you to organise people into groups and move them out slowly. Search every building on this street first, one at a time, and come back here, understand?"

Rhys nodded again, though at least this time his eyes weren't fuzzy with bemusement.

"Slowly," Annie repeated. "If you think you hear anything, anything at all, you bring everyone back here."

Rhys turned to leave her side, stopping in surprise when Annie grabbed his arm tightly.

"And bring me back a sharp blade, and some salt," she said, and pushed him away.

Rhys left with a final puzzled look at his mother, and Annie heard him ushering everyone out of the building, and leaving her alone with the drugged man.

*

Jaaaaaasssssssssonnn...

Jason sank into a clawing darkness that gripped him more tightly when he tried to break free of it. His body felt heavier than it ever had before, and yet simultaneously it felt like he was being propelled forward; like he was dizzy and off-balance.

Once he had got so drunk that the room literally span in front of his eyes, but this was more like it was *him* that was spinning, like his cells were riding a hellish carousel that he was powerless to stop.

Bring me a sharp blade and some salt, Jassssssoooonnn...

His dead mother's voice made cuts of its own, worse than any blade; invisible and devastating.

When he saw his mother in the dark there with him, and saw that she looked strangely like the old woman that had drugged him, and that she was rotting away, her ribcage exposed and the diseased organs pulsing underneath, Jason wanted to scream or run or *anything*, but the darkness had him, dragging him inexorably towards her fearsome wet embrace.

His mother chuckled as she wrapped her rotting arms around him, and he did scream, then.

*

The scream startled Annie, pounding into her old heart like an adrenaline shot, and she glanced quickly around the empty town hall, fearful at what the noise might bring. After a few moments she heard footsteps pounding along the road outside, coming straight for her. She froze.

The door opened, and Rhys charged in, his face twisted in fear and concern.

Annie laughed.

"You okay, Ma?" Rhys gasped breathlessly.

"Fine," Annie chuckled. "Just our guest here screaming in his sleep."

She stared at Rhys.

"I suppose we'll have to get used to hearing that."

6

Things fall apart.

Michael Evans had come to understand that intimately. His career, his family, and then finally the entire world itself had all been ravaged by entropy; ground away by time until they were little more than dust on the wind; memories that had already begun to fade.

Michael sat on the battlements of Caernarfon Castle, staring out across the river at the dark town beyond, and shivered. The cold on the west coast of Wales was unrelenting, and the wind drove it home like a hammer. He didn't mind the wind though: watch duty on the battlements meant that at least he was out of the towers, away from the rest of them.

You have your castle, and here's your army. So what now?

John's words to Michael after they finally secured the castle following the Infected attack clung to him like Velcro.

What now?

In the euphoria of evading what had appeared to be certain death, Michael hadn't thought of anything beyond the fact that they were safe. All he wanted was to rest. The frantic chase that began outside a cafe in South Wales had come to an end at last, and his daughter was safe behind thick walls designed hundreds of years earlier to repel enemy attacks.

The *what now* turned out to be endlessly defending the gate against the tail end of the ghoulish army that had besieged the place, and slowly starving to death. Darren Oliver, the maniac that had dominated the castle right up until Michael blasted a hole through his forehead with the rifle he kept at his side, had never bothered to stockpile supplies. There had been no point: he had a living scarecrow to keep the Infected out of Caernarfon, and his team went on daily runs for food.

Darren had thought long-term, focusing on planting seeds and building shelter and numbers within the castle. His short-term plan had always included access to the town, but access had slit its own throat and bled to death right outside the gate.

Inside, they had found enough food to last for a couple of days at most. They rationed it out until nobody was eating any more than a few mouthfuls a day. There was almost none left. By the time Darren's seeds bore fruit, the inhabitants of the castle would be decomposing corpses.

Few people in the castle spoke much beyond the monosyllabic. When they did talk, the conversation usually veered toward theories about the Infected; about how the virus had come about, why some swam and others didn't. Whether the creatures would also be starving out there.

It was Michael's eight-year-old daughter, Claire, who solved the puzzle of the swimming Infected, informing Michael that she had seen one acting like a conductor in Aberystwyth, leading one of the large herds that now roamed the countryside as a general might lead troops to battle.

Michael had seen the same thing from a farmhouse outside St Davids: one leader with a small army marching at his back. Some of them could communicate, rallying the others behind them.

It fit with what they already knew: the virus did not affect everyone equally. Some of the Infected seemed able to adapt in some way, to evolve and learn. Or maybe they were all evolving at different rates: the ratio of swimmers to non-swimmers seemed to increase as the days passed. When the conversation turned to speculation about what they might all evolve *into* eventually, talk dissolved into brooding, fearful silence.

But it wasn't the Infected or even his painfully empty stomach that dominated Michael's thoughts. It was a number.

Twenty-nine.

When the Infected assault had been turned back by the exploding helicopter, the occupants of the old building had numbered thirty-four, but the injuries sustained in the attack were taking their toll. Five had already died.

The number felt like it was branded on Michael's mind. Painted across his forehead; daubed messily in an old woman's blood. He told himself Gwyneth's death - *be honest, Mike, her murder* - was justified by the mathematics. As long as the number of uninfected people in the castle rose or remained steady, as long as Claire remained safe, he could square it off.

But the number wasn't rising.

"You thinking about food?"

Michael blinked; lost in his thoughts, he hadn't even noticed Rachel ascending the steep stone steps that led up to the battlements. She was, he suspected, coming to see if he needed help to get down, but couching the offer in friendly conversation.

"How did you guess?" Michael asked with a rueful smile.

"I don't think there's anyone here that *isn't* thinking about food right now."

Michael snorted a bitter laugh.

Rachel sat beside him, and for a while there was a comfortable silence; just the two of them and the wind and a view of distant monsters.

"Lot of history in this place, you know," Michael said eventually. "They've got little plaques on everything here. Everything in the castle seems to have a story. Did you know this place has been under siege three times?"

Rachel shrugged.

"Last time was back in the civil war. Nearly four hundred years ago. Three times, and it was held every time. Nobody ever took this castle."

"We did," Rachel said.

Michael nodded morosely.

"And look what good it's done us," he said. "It might as well be a prison. There's no way out past *them*." He waved a hand at the dark town over the water.

"Then we have to go *through* them, Michael," Rachel said earnestly. "We can't just hide in here and wait to die. We have to *fight*."

Michael dropped his gaze to the black water that flowed past the castle walls.

"And then what?" He said. "Fight our way to where? I know you want to get out there. I know John doesn't think this place is safe-"

Rachel interrupted him with a snort.

"John doesn't think *anywhere* is safe. I don't think he knows the meaning of the word."

"And maybe he's right," Michael said. "But then what's the point? Going out there, fighting. Where do we go? Where would be safer than here?"

Rachel had no answer.

"People are getting worried about you, you know," she said finally.

Michael arched an eyebrow.

"People?"

"Me, John. Everybody."

"They don't even know me, Rachel. *You* barely know me."

"They know you killed Darren. They saw you save John. Like it or not, they believe in you, and they need somebody to give them some *purpose.* If we aren't all in this together, things are going to fall apart pretty quickly."

Michael felt Rachel staring at him until he finally dragged his eyes from the river and looked at her.

"I know you blame yourself for Gwyneth," she said, and he flinched. "But frankly, Michael, you're going to have to get over it. You've got a lot of people looking to you now. Including Claire. Including *me.* You can pull them all together. We have to take Caernarfon back. *Have to.* Or this place won't be a prison, it will be a tomb."

Rachel hugged herself, shivering in the cold night air. She stood.

"When you're ready, everyone else will be too. *I'm* ready."

Michael stifled a sigh. He had only known Rachel a couple of weeks, but even in that short time he felt like she had changed drastically, and he wasn't sure it was for the better. When he first met her she had seemed impetuous; following the death of her brother at the hands of the Infected that impulsive streak had twisted and darkened into something a little more like recklessness. It wasn't safety that Rachel wanted. It was revenge. With no chance of bringing justice to the people responsible for the catastrophe, she seemed willing to settle for killing the Infected.

She wasn't ready. She was *eager*. A subtle distinction that made Michael's nerves jangle. He saw the thirst for blood in her eyes, heard the dark inflection of it in every word she spoke, her restless tone simmering with undirected anger.

Rachel was like a ticking timer. She had influence in the group that ran deeper than the fact she had taken possession of Darren's shotgun. The men and women all liked and respected her. Sooner or later, when their hunger and desperation matched her desire to go out and kill, she would mobilize them to charge out of the castle to their deaths.

Even worse, Michael would be powerless to stop them going, and his useless legs meant he would be left at the castle with the weak and the injured. With the vulnerable. Better to manage the situation himself. Take Caernarfon on his terms. It was the only way, whether he liked it or not.

He had believed taking the castle would be the end. Finally admitting it was not made his heart ache and sink into a deep well of depression.

He nodded.

"We'll need to be careful. No margin for error now," he said grimly.

"We know how to hurt them," Rachel said. "We have a chance now, at least."

"Sure," Michael said. "We know *how* to. We just don't have the means to do it. No electricity. No way to make a loud noise beyond screaming, and we've already seen how the Infected respond to *that*."

"We don't have the means *here*," Rachel agreed with a nod. "But over there? Fuel, batteries. Who knows what else?"

Michael squinted at the dark town again, and sighed. He had hoped that securing the castle would be the end of it, that the security the stone walls provided would see them through, but he knew now that he had been deluding himself. The Infected weren't going to starve to death, or wander away and leave them to live out peaceful lives.

Without supplies, they had no chance. Hiding away in the castle was simply making the choice to die slow instead of dying fast.

"Where's John?" Michael asked.

"I think he's at the gate trying to teach people how to defend us," Rachel said with a crooked grin. "Though by now he might have killed them all himself."

Michael arched an eyebrow.

"Slow learners," Rachel said, and the grin widened.

Michael cracked a weary smile.

"If you see him, better tell him we need to talk," Michael said, and gave a final look at the town before turning away. "We'll need a plan of attack."

Rachel nodded and turned to make her way down the steps. As he watched her descend, Michael thought about how she had done as he asked without question, and he stared down at his paralysed legs, lost in thought.

It wasn't just the fact that he had killed Darren or had saved John. His paralysis had given him a bizarre power over the people there; a strange sort of authority that he didn't fully understand. Not for the first time he wondered if the trust they showed him stemmed from the fact that he was disabled, and they perceived him as no threat to them. In a world that hummed with constant menace, maybe seeming harmless made them naturally gravitate toward him.

Maybe they think I'm a hero.

Or maybe Michael was reading too much into their willingness to follow him. Maybe it was nothing to do with his paralysis. Maybe it was the rifle. The one he'd used to kill Darren, and which never left his side.

"Oh, Michael?"

Rachel had stopped halfway down the steps, and turned to look up at him, breaking a train of thought that he suspected was headed to a dark destination.

"Yeah?"

"The guy Linda was looking after? Colin?"

Michael knew what she was going to say, and he felt the urgent pressure building once more in his skull, like his brain was expanding, trying to break free of its bone prison.

"He just died. Thought you'd want to know."

Michael nodded, and Rachel turned away, heading toward the largest of the castle's towers. He watched her go with a grimace.

Colin, he thought. It took him a moment to place the man. One of the bikers that had joined them just before the Infected attacked the castle. He had been injured in the attack, and had circled the drain ever since, dying slowly from wounds that any doctor would have been able to patch up with their eyes closed only weeks earlier.

The castle didn't have doctors; it had Linda: a former schoolteacher with a general grasp of biology and little in the way of equipment and medication.

For those bleeding internally like Colin, there was nothing to be done. Their lives trickled away like sand in a timer, and everyone at the castle was powerless to do anything beyond easing their pain and watching them die, and wondering when their own turn would come.

Twenty eight.

Was thirty four.

He wondered how many would die before he could even reliably match their names to their faces.

Alone again, Michael returned his gaze to Caernarfon, and he saw it immediately.

Shaking.

Just a hint of movement, barely noticeable. Certainly not enough for him to feel. But he could *see* it. The coastal wind was bitter; whipping his haggard face like a slap, but it wasn't anywhere near strong enough to be blowing his leg around. When Michael took a turn on watch - grateful for any chance to get out of the stifling confines of the castle's circular towers - he was primed for movement. It was something John had drilled into him, to let his gaze fix on a point and gradually force himself to focus on his peripheral vision.

Just look for movement, John had said, but Michael hadn't expected movement *there*, at the end of the dead limbs that hung uselessly from his torso.

Michael furrowed his brow, staring at the errant limb. Had he really just seen his paralysed leg move?

Focusing on his feet, Michael summoned up every ounce of concentration he could muster and told his legs to move, but they hung, as dead and immobile as they had been ever since the car crash outside St. Davids that pushed a thin piece of wood into his lower back.

Wishful thinking, he thought.

7

Annie guessed that the strange man that had saved them all would be out of action for several hours.

For a while she watched him sleep, surprised to find that despite the quantity of drugs she had given him, which she reckoned would be enough to drop a large horse, Voorhees twitched and writhed while he was out cold. It looked to Annie like the man's slumber was disturbed by nightmares at least the equal of those that now existed in the real world. Several times he mumbled a name - *Rachel* - and his voice was filled with a terrible anguish.

His wife or girlfriend, Annie supposed. Dead somewhere, most likely, or wandering around the countryside with no eyes killing whatever she came across. Annie made a mental note of the name. If the man proved to have a spirit that was difficult to break, she'd use it when the time was right.

After a few minutes, she turned her attention to more pressing matters, and beckoned Gareth Hughes to join her at a shadowy corner separate from the others.

Gareth was one of the few people of Newborough whose opinions Annie gave any credence to. He worked alongside her on the town council, dealing mainly in financial matters, and had always been loyal to her. Alongside a good head for figures, Gareth had a good deal of common sense which in Annie's opinion made him rare for a resident of Newborough and rarer still for a man.

"What's up Annabel?"

Gareth eyed her with concern.

No one else called her *Annabel*. The truth was that she didn't like it much, but she always let it slide because Gareth Hughes was *useful*. It earned him a little leeway.

"Just about everything, Gareth," she replied in a low voice. "Most of these people are only one scare away from a heart attack or some kind of mental break, and I'm afraid our doctor is beyond helping them."

She smirked.

"It doesn't look like anybody is coming to help, does it? I think we're on our own. So I'm wondering: do you think this place is secure?"

Gareth pondered the question for a moment. He always took time to answer even the most rudimentary of questions, a habit that Annie found faintly irritating, though far less so than getting a response from the type of idiots who jumped at the first answer that popped into their minds, spewing it out into the world without thought.

"I'd say no," Gareth said finally. "The town hall itself is fine, but Newborough is too exposed. The forest, the dunes. Nothing but fields the other way. The town is too open to...uh...defend."

Gareth faltered on the last word, and Annie saw his thoughts written clearly in his eyes. The man was in his late fifties, plump and comfortable, more used to worrying about whether he had milk in his fridge or not. The notion of having to *defend* a position, like they were suddenly somehow at war, was no doubt galling to him.

"Too many ways into the town," he continued. "Obviously we could keep a lookout, but I don't think we have enough people to watch everywhere."

"Is there any way to shore the place up?"

Gareth lapsed into thought again and shook his head firmly.

"We could barricade the streets, I suppose, cordon off an area around the town hall, but the...things could just come through the buildings themselves. And besides, building a barricade like that would make a lot of noise. Doesn't seem like there's any of them nearby right now, but I'd bet there's more out there. If they came at us while we were trying to fortify..."

He shrugged. Didn't want to finish the thought, and Annie didn't blame him.

"And if this is countrywide, God help us," Gareth continued, "then we run the risk of them coming over the bridge from the mainland. I can only imagine what it's like in densely populated areas. If a large group finds its way here..."

He trailed off, apparently unwilling to finish the thought.

"I think based on everything you're saying, that if we stay in Newborough, sooner or later we'd end up trapped in the town hall again," Annie said.

"What about...uh...him?" Gareth pointed at the drugged man.

Annie pursed her lips.

"He wants to leave. I think it's going to take a little *persuasion* to make him stay. We can't count on him. Not yet."

Gareth nodded slowly.

"What can I do to help?" He said.

Annie smiled. The response was precisely why she considered Gareth to be worthy of her time. There was no petty arguing, no wrestling for superiority. Gareth backed her when she needed it.

"Can you think of a place we can go?" Annie said.

Gareth' eyes disappeared into the middle-distance for so long that Annie began to wonder if he was suffering some sort of episode.

"Penryth," he said finally, with a beatific grin.

Annie's brow furrowed. Penryth was at the south east corner of Anglesey, and contained almost nothing of interest. The only reason anybody ever visited the tiny village was because of the golf course nearby and...

Ah. Well done, Mr Hughes.

"The hotel," Annie said, and Gareth nodded brightly.

"The hotel pretty much only hosts golfers," Gareth said. "At this time of year, it's probably empty. The golf course all around it means there probably won't be too many of the..uh...Infected nearby. And it's on the shore. We'd have the sea at our back; only have to watch one direction."

Annie warmed to the idea immediately. The hotel was one of those weekend-break type places that had become so popular in recent years: a plush spa, pool and gymnasium, all wrapped up in solid walls designed to mimic an old stately home. The place would likely have plenty of food. Even better, there was a jetty. If they had to run, Annie couldn't think of a better place to flee than the sea.

"We'll go across the dunes," Annie said more to herself than to Gareth. "It'll take longer, but it will be quiet."

"When?"

Annie blinked. For a moment, she had forgotten that Gareth was standing beside her.

"Now," she replied firmly. "Tell everyone to take whatever they can carry. And whatever they can use as a weapon. I want to be there before *he* wakes up."

Gareth nodded, and left Annie alone. She dimly heard him passing on her instructions to the people sitting on the floor eating, convincing them all that they would be safer at the hotel than in Newborough. Very few objected, and those that did so, did only very weakly. Nobody, Annie guessed, particularly wanted to stay in Newborough, where walking anywhere meant stepping over the decomposing corpses of their former friends and neighbours.

Annie let Gareth take care of rounding everyone up. Lost in thought, she stared at the man who called himself Voorhees, wondering how much torture it would take to break him and make him useful.

8

"Swing low," John Francis said, for what felt like the hundredth time, and suppressed a sigh when he saw the looks on their faces: like he'd just told them the earth *was* flat after all.

Each morning, when he took a group of people to the courtyard and tried to train them on how best to defend the gate and themselves, he ran up against the same set of problems. Everything they knew about swinging a sword came from the movies. None of it was helpful.

John had never received any formal training with swords, of course. His years as a soldier had mostly been spent destroying enemies with weapons that didn't *cut* so much as *evaporate* the target. Wars were won by whichever side had the better weapons. Always had been.

Right now the arms at John's disposal were pitiful: the castle had a small stockpile of ancient weaponry that was for the most part fragile enough to be useless, but they had a crossbow and a working longbow that wouldn't shoot far, but still held some potency at medium range. Beyond that the only option was close quarters combat with swords, clubs and maces.

John had been forced to kill at close quarters with a ballistic knife on more than one occasion, and he knew that training went out the window when a battle came down to blades. Winning was sometimes determined by speed and survival instinct; more often by luck. The notion of actually *planning* to use a sword would have struck him as ridiculous, until guns became more trouble than they were worth.

He trained the others by default: he had already killed with swords, and they had not. It made him the expert. Most had guessed that John had spent time in the army, but he told them nothing.

"You don't need to end the conflict with one blow," he continued. "You aim to decapitate them and miss, and you've lost. Aim for the biggest target. Put the blade in their gut and you put 'em down. If you really want to chop off their heads, you do it when they are on the floor and the threat is minimal."

A few of the attentive faces paled. A couple looked like they were trying really hard not to retch.

He demonstrated a wide swing that began low at his hip, rising a little as it arced through the air. If the blow had been aimed at an average-sized adult, the blade would have nestled deep in the gut, somewhere between the barriers presented by the hipbone and the ribcage.

"Worst case scenario, you hit them too low," he said, swinging again from a semi-crouch. The blade was now just a couple of feet from the floor. "Do that and you take their legs."

He straightened.

"Same result. You put them down. That's your focus. Get them on the ground and the fight's done. Get to thinking maybe you're some kind of *ninja*, and things might reach a different conclusion."

At the word *ninja* the tension that had been building as John spoke dissipated a little, and a few half-smiles broke out among the group of six young women that John hoped to turn into competent warriors.

"And what if there's more than one of them?"

The question came from the back of the small group. Emma. The girl John had come to think of as Darren Oliver's favourite. She hadn't spoken much for the first few days, just drifting around the castle with haunted eyes, but seemed to be coming out of her shell slowly when it became clear that the men now living at the castle weren't lunatics intent on doing her harm.

"If there's more than one, you run."

"Is that what you'd do?"

John blinked at Emma's question. Her tone suggested she thought maybe he was being condescending.

"Running is my *plan A*. These," - he lifted the sword - "are a last resort. If you can get away, you get away. It's exactly what I've been doing, and so far I'm still alive. The way to survive is not by becoming skilled at conflict; it's by learning how to avoid it."

Emma flushed and looked at the ground, and John felt a little guilty at the harsh tone of his words. It was easy to forget just how *young* these women were. Most were barely out of their teens; hand-selected by the maniac who had run the castle before they arrived. According to the terrified women he had left in his wake, Darren Oliver had claimed to be running the castle with an eye on repopulation, on continuing the human race in a practical manner.

Maybe the man even believed his own rhetoric, but John had seen the truth in the bastard's sly eyes the moment they met.

The end of the world was, to some people, an opportunity. Hell, that's exactly the way it had been designed by Fred Sullivan and Chrysalis Systems. Darren had turned the castle into his private harem, and given the young women a stark choice: *stay and lose your freedom and dignity, or go and die.*

It was a tactic straight from the playbook of the politicians that had ruled the world up until just a few weeks earlier; the rule of terror. Control maintained by manipulating the fear of the enemy at the gates, trying to get in. Just like the politicians, Darren's motivation had been self-interest.

John wondered for a moment how many more were out there like Darren, finding grim, brutal ways to survive, clawing their way to power in their own little fiefdoms. Many would take the obvious route: the exercising of physical power. Mankind had once more been reduced to the rule of brawn, and many people would look to strength in numbers to rule by force.

Not all though, John thought, casting an eye up at the battlements. Michael had spent his time avoiding John as much as possible, and whenever they did lock eyes, John saw something in the man's gaze that he couldn't quite identify.

As he stared up at the wall, he saw Rachel making her way toward him across the courtyard, chewing on the remains of a breakfast that looked like it was causing her physical distress.

John grinned. The remaining food consisted of rock-hard bread, tins of sardines and a few cans of beans that they were *saving*, as though for some special occasion.

She nodded at him as she approached, and John felt grateful for the opportunity to call the training session to an end.

He told the group of young women to take a break for now, and to remember what he had shown them, and they filtered away.

Rachel waited until she was close to speak, keeping her voice soft.

"Michael wants to see you."

John felt his hackles rising. Being summoned had always had a way of doing that to him.

"Is that right?" John's voice came out bitter. "You his personal assistant now?"

Fire sparked in Rachel's eyes, and John immediately regretted saying it. Rachel had been a P.A. before, and he knew the experience had left her pissed off, though he wasn't entirely sure why.

"Was I *your* assistant when I saved your life, John?"

John sighed and lowered his eyes in silent apology.

When he had been just a young boy of around six or seven, before he had even really comprehended that girls and boys were different in any meaningful way, John had pushed a girl off a wall and into a rose bush. Only later did he understand that he'd done it because he *liked* the girl. He never understood why that affection had manifested in the way it did.

Echoes of that first disastrous flirtation with the opposite sex came back to John every time he spoke to Rachel: increasingly the two of them picked at each other, and rarely seemed far from a full-blown argument or, in Rachel's case, the delivery of another punch to John's face. Their altercations made him feel like that small, confused boy again. He knew he liked her, but he also knew he was perilously close to dumping her in the nearest rose bush.

Even worse: his growing affection for her felt more dangerous than any amount of time spent playing with swords.

"Lead the way," John said weakly, and withered for a moment under Rachel's burning gaze before she turned and strode away.

Stick to killing people, John. At least then you'll know what the hell you're doing.

As he walked, John banished the thoughts of Rachel that made him feel off-balance, and focused on Michael.

Mostly the crippled former policeman sat alone on the battlements, staring out at Caernarfon. When he spoke to anybody - and to John especially - he kept his eyes pointed at the floor. It appeared to John that Michael was slowly fading away.

The man's goal had always been to get to somewhere safe. John could only imagine how it must be tearing him up inside that having finally found somewhere that fit the bill, there was a good chance he would either have to starve to death there or leave the place behind.

The notion of leaving the castle was already lurking at the edge of John's thoughts, had been ever since he arrived. It wasn't something he could exactly put his finger on, but some nagging sensation that the place was more dangerous than it appeared had been with him since he first set eyes on it. Killing Darren Oliver, and even stemming the attack of the Infected that had amassed outside, had done nothing to change that. People had been dying ever since they arrived, either killed in the struggle to get control of the place or succumbing to injuries sustained in the assault. John wasn't much of a believer in omens, but he figured that if a quiet, gentle old woman like Gwyneth could wind up dead in the castle, *anyone* could.

As was usual whenever John thought about Gwyneth, and the way she had conveniently died at Michael's hand, concern uncoiled in his gut. Only later did John learn that Michael believed the woman to be - in her own way - a carrier of the virus. John thought it made the old woman's death especially convenient for Michael, and his sole focus on keeping his daughter safe.

Michael's words to John as they had debated whether or not to approach the castle came back to him. *'I don't trust anyone. Hell, I don't even trust you.'*

As John began to climb the steep steps that led up to the battlements he reminded himself, not for the first time, that the feeling was mutual.

9

In daylight Annie could see just what a brilliant idea Gareth Hughes' suggestion had been. The hotel was dramatic and picturesque, but it was also sturdy and large enough to easily accommodate them all. Better yet, it afforded a clear three hundred and sixty degree view, and the small jetty turned out to be home to a single boat that Annie and her sons would take charge of if the shit hit the fan.

She began to dream up ways in which to fortify the place further. The sea took care of one side of the building. Along the other, she thought, they could dig deep trenches to stop any of the crazed cannibals getting too close. There was plenty of room to grow food; plenty of fish in the sea when the hotel's extensive larder finally ran dry. The hotel could sustain plenty of people for a long time.

If it was - as some of the people of Newborough were now claiming - the end of the world, Annie thought she was doing pretty damn well. And when she broke the strange man who was currently her prisoner, things would look very positive *indeed.*

*

Jason's alarm clock sounded strange. The noise was barely loud enough to wake him, but that wasn't the truly strange part. It was the way the alarm clock sounded *alive* rather than electronic. It wasn't the tuneless beeping he was used to hearing on weekday mornings. This sounded more like an animal; like a puppy whimpering after being kicked by a cruel owner.

As he began to break the surface of consciousness, he noticed something else that was unusual: a searing pain in his shoulders, like a terrible pressure was being exerted upon them. When he finally unglued his eyes the tiny mysteries were immediately solved: the pain was a product of the fact that he wasn't actually sleeping. He had been *unconscious*, and someone had hung him up by the wrists like a slab of meat in a butcher's shop window.

The noise he heard was no alarm; the whimpering was coming from his own throat.

He lurched from one nightmare into another, no longer certain which was real. Maybe he really was dead, doomed to roam Hell with the horrific presence of his murdered mother trailing his every step. Or maybe he was really still alive, lost in a world of insane violence and held captive by a demented old woman and her gang of silent, terrified followers.

Maybe both.

He shook his head slowly, but the poison in his mind wasn't something that sat on the surface like a shallow pool of water. There was no shaking it off; it clawed down into his mind like the roots of an ancient tree, stabbing deep into him, festering and corrupting.

The world seemed to tilt and sway, though whether that was down to the drugs he had been forced to consume or the fracturing of his mind, Jason had no idea.

Frantically, he tried to thrash against his restraints, but he had been tied with his arms raised high and wide, like a gruesome mockery of Christ, and he was unable to gain sufficient leverage in his burning limbs. The restraints were solid and unmoving, and even the slight motion he was able to manage just seemed to tighten his bonds until it felt like some huge creature had snapped powerful jaws shut on his wrists.

His head dropped, and he stared down at the floor, watching as it seemed to liquify and pulse under his feet. Darkness tried to claim him again; a terrifying gloom that was pregnant with a corrosive presence that whispered his name eagerly.

Jason bit his lip, and his eyes flared open at the sharp pain.

Don't fall asleep, he thought blearily, and tried to focus his thoughts. His gut ached terribly, like a poison-tipped dagger had been plunged into his flesh. He leaned forward as much as the ropes holding his arms allowed, and checked his torso. No wounds. At least. No *fresh* wounds. The pain was most likely a result of the handful of pills that had been forced down his throat. He remembered the old woman's bony fingers pushing the pills into his mouth; how cold her fingers had been, like those of a long-dead corpse, and he shuddered. The more he focused on the image, the greater his nausea became, until finally his stomach heaved painfully and he vomited out a thin string of spit and bile.

The pills were long digested, but the mere act of vomiting acted like an electrical charge passing through his body, and he felt a little better. A little more alert. He focused on his surroundings.

It seemed like waking up with no idea where he was had become a habit. He remembered the claustrophobic town hall, stinking of fear and sweat, where he had been drugged, but his current surroundings were vastly different.

He was tied to a handrail that ran along a hallway above his head, but the room he was in was expansive and airy. Directly in front of him he saw plush-looking leather chairs and beyond them an enormous floor-to-ceiling window that offered breathtaking views of the sea. It was misty beyond the window and he saw very little, other than a strange light in the distance, hovering in the air like a flickering star.

He squinted at the light, but could make no sense of it, and turned his gaze back to his immediate surroundings. To his right he saw a small bar area. There was nothing close to him that might be used to free himself. He seethed in frustration, until one possible solution hit him.

It was the last thing he had ever thought he would end up doing voluntarily.

Bring the Infected. Fuck these crazy bastards. Bring the Infected to kill them all.

The thought made Jason feel strangely woozy, like some part of his mind was slowly being dissolved in acid; parts of him disappearing that were vital, and that there would be no way to reclaim.

Doooo it Jasssooonnnn...make some noise...

Jason filled his lungs with air and roared a wordless scream with as much power as he could muster.

*

The scream made Annie jump, and she knew instinctively what her prisoner had hoped to achieve by it. She grinned. It would do him no good.

The hotel had a well-stocked shelf of pamphlets and guide books on local attractions for guests to visit when they weren't busy either golfing or enjoying any of the various beauty 'treatments' on offer. Annie had eagerly grabbed some maps and was busily poring over them with Gareth and Rhys when the scream echoed through the hotel. Most of the 'guests' were in far-off rooms, and almost certainly hadn't heard the man. Certainly no Infected people would have: the journey from Newborough across the sand dunes had been entirely uneventful, and they had found the hotel dark and abandoned. It seemed there wasn't a soul - with eyes or without - for miles. Voorhees would have to do a lot more than *scream* to bring danger to the isolated hotel.

"Rhys, fetch your little brother. It's high time he did a little work around here," Annie said affably, watching as Rhys nodded and left her alone with Gareth.

"I think I'll have a little chat with our guest," she said, and slid her chair back with a loud squeal of wood on marble. "Let him know that the hotel doesn't tolerate noise pollution."

*

"Sleep well?"

Jason stared at the old woman with hatred in his eyes as she stepped into his line of sight. She waddled over to him, until she was less than an arm's length away. Jason wriggled helplessly, pouring all his energy into his biceps once more, desperately trying to snap the ropes that held him.

The old woman looked crestfallen.

"I was sort of hoping you'd wake up...*friendlier.* Things really would be a lot easier for us both."

Her eyes narrowed.

"Mainly for you, if I'm honest. My name is Annie. You, apparently, are named after that guy in the horror films."

She shrugged.

"Cruel parents." Annie nodded with sad understanding. "What's that saying? Something about parents passing down all their flaws to their children and adding a few new ones? Poor boy."

Jason drew in a deep, shuddering breath.

"You have to let me go," he said, trying in vain to keep his voice even.

Annie rolled her eyes.

"There's nowhere *to* go, child," she said kindly. "We need you here."

"I *helped* you," Jason spat. "I *saved* all of you. What the fuck are you doing here, why do this to me?"

"Surviving," Annie snapped. "What else are we supposed to do?"

"You're supposed to let me *go!*" Jason roared in frustration. "There's somebody I have to find. I have to help-"

"Rachel," Annie said with a sad nod, and smiled when she saw Jason's jaw drop in astonishment. "I'm afraid Rachel's dead, Mr Voorhees. Pretty much everybody is dead. But we're not, and we need your help."

"No!" Jason screamed. "You don't even know her. She's not dead, and I need to find her."

Tears streamed down Jason's cheeks.

"Hmph. You'll forget all about Rachel soon enough, child. We'll keep you occupied, don't worry."

Behind the old woman, a young man stepped into view, carrying a bag and an eager expression that made Jason's gut twist in apprehension.

"One of my sons," Annie said pleasantly. "Hywel, meet Mr Voorhees. Mr Voorhees, Hywel."

Annie stepped aside.

"I'm afraid Hywel here has...a bit of a nasty streak, Mr Voorhees. It always used to bother me somewhat. Takes after his grandfather a little too much, I'm afraid. Still, it seems like that will be useful to us now. You boys play nice, and I'll be back later with your pills, Mr Voorhees. They'll make you feel better."

Annie smiled, and waddled away, leaving Jason staring at the slight, balding man in front of him.

Hywel's face split in a toothy grin, and he dropped his bag on the floor, pulling back the zipper and taking out a straight razor and a bag of salt.

"We'll start with this, I think," Hywel said, and his smile widened.

*

Annie found listening to the man's agonised screams distasteful, although she did congratulate herself on at last finding a use for her youngest son. It figured that when Hywel finally found something he was adept at, it would be *torture*. Still, it was better than nothing.

She stepped out onto the manicured gardens that surrounded the hotel's sea-facing side and breathed in the cold air deeply.

It felt like she hadn't been alone for a moment in weeks; probably she actually hadn't. It seemed like wherever she turned now there were people looking to her for something. Her newly extended family, it turned out, was something of a burden. As she stood in the cold morning air, alone at last, Annie let her hands tremble, and stared at her shaking digits in concern. Age was catching up with her rather faster than she would have liked.

"Uh, Annie?"

Annie stiffened, and clenched her hands together to mask the trembling.

"What is it?" She snarled.

The man stammered. It took Annie a moment to place him. Clive Baxter. A limp-wristed teller at Newborough's only bank with a bald head that shone in the cold morning light like a polished billiard ball. A man suddenly *less* useful than her youngest son. She never thought such a moment would come to pass.

"I was just, uh, wondering...about that light over there." Baxter pointed across the Menai Strait in the general direction of Caernarfon. "I saw it last night. It...uh...it kind of looks like a signal fire, don't you think? I was just thinking maybe I should take the boat and check it out. There could be people there. Other survivors."

Annie felt a headache brewing. Judging from the pressure building in her temples, it would be a doozy. She might even have to take some of the painkillers she was pouring down Voorhees' thick neck so liberally herself.

"Why are you bothering me with this Baxter? Do you need me to hold your damn hand?"

Baxter stammered, and blew air from his cheeks explosively. The look on his face said that her response had been the last thing he expected.

"So," he said cautiously, "should I go?"

"Go, Baxter, but if you don't come back with that boat, don't come back at all, understand?"

Clive Baxter nodded and hurried away, scurrying like an animal retreating from a forest fire.

Seconds later, Annie heard his footsteps on the small wooden jetty and then the chugging of the boat's small engine, and the noise made the pounding in her head feel worse. She turned away from the sea, rubbing her temples and setting her mouth in a firm line, and headed back into the hotel, and the screaming.

10

The castle had a signal fire burning up on top of the highest tower, which Michael insisted be kept burning constantly. The generator Darren had used to aim a floodlight into the sky was too loud, he reasoned, but the basic principle was sound: let others know that the castle was occupied by humans, and was safe, and they would come.

Nobody came.

Michael spent a lot of time up on the battlements. Every day he found someone to carry him up there, and spent several hours staring out at the creatures that had them pinned down in the castle. It didn't take long for the brooding silence of the man to percolate throughout the castle, slowly poisoning the faint tendrils of optimism in the people that had believed Michael would lead them to safety.

Whenever John saw him, the man looked deep in thought, but John wasn't sure he was thinking about their current situation. Mostly Michael had a faraway look in his eyes, like he was looking at the past.

He didn't turn when Rachel and John approached.

"We have to go out there," Michael said softly, almost as though he was addressing himself.

We?

John had an idea that Michael wasn't referring to himself. Those useless legs came in handy surprisingly often.

He did save your life.

John bit back on the bitter reply that was ready to spill from his lips.

"We've got enough food left for a day. Maybe two. After that, things are going to get...difficult," Michael continued, and finally turned to face them. He didn't look John in the eye.

"From what I've seen, the number of Infected out there has thinned a little, but I think waiting and hoping they would all wander off or starve has turned out to be a bad plan."

John snorted. It had never been his plan in the first place. If John had his way, the castle would have been firmly in his rear view mirror. He was still there purely because of Rachel.

"How do you propose we do that?" John asked. "I'd say there's maybe ten people here that I trust to swing a sword and not chop off my head by mistake, or stab themselves. Barely enough to defend the gate if it comes to it. Going out there is a suicide mission. I've never been much of a fan of suicide missions."

Michael nodded wearily.

"If we move slowly, we can do it, John," Rachel said.

"No, Rachel, we *can't*," John snapped. "Anything that seems like a good idea in here is going to look very different when we're out there. You and me, sure, maybe we're experienced enough or crazy enough to go straight at them and not lose our shit. But everyone else here? The first scream will bring it all down. We don't know how many of them are out there. It could be tens, it could be hundreds. The odds are against us, whichever way you look at it. There's no way for us to kill every one of them in the town. No way it doesn't turn bad."

Rachel glared at him, but Michael responded first.

"He's right, Rachel. But I'm not thinking of attacking them. In fact, I'm not thinking about killing them at all."

John shot a confused glance at Michael.

"So what are-"

He didn't finish.

What is that noise?

They all heard it. John saw the confusion on Michael and Rachel's faces; saw them working their own way to the conclusion he was reaching.

An engine.

The noise was distant, but getting closer, and with each passing second it became more and more unmistakable. A guttural drone that oscillated in pitch with almost clockwork regularity.

An outboard motor.

John turned to face the sea, all thoughts of the town behind him forgotten. It was misty, impossible to see anything other than a vague hint of a dark shadow flitting across the rolling waves.

As John squinted into the distance, the noise of the engine abruptly cut out, and a heavy silence fell, broken only by the endless white noise of the ocean.

"Why have they stopped?" Rachel whispered. "I can't see anything. Can you see them?"

John shook his head. Visibility was no good. All he saw was the grey canvas of the ocean under a blanket of mist. Still, he had a feeling he knew why the engine had stopped out there in the fog, and the knowledge made him clench his jaw until it ached.

Recon.

No sooner did he think it than he heard the engine buzz back into life, slowly receding into silence as the boat moved away.

"They're leaving?" Rachel said. "If they saw the fire, why not come to the castle?"

John felt his stomach drop, and he knew what it meant. Like everything to do with the damn castle, it meant trouble.

"They *will* be coming," he said grimly. "That was a scouting mission. If they needed help, they'd be at the gate right now."

"How long do you think we've got?" Michael asked in a low voice.

John shrugged.

"Impossible to say. But we know one thing."

Michael arched an eyebrow.

"There's a lot of them. Figure a boat that size holds four to six people. If they're thinking of taking the castle it means wherever they are now is less safe than here. So if they are able to send out a group of people on a recon mission, they must have strength in numbers."

"Could have just been one person in the boat," Rachel said, but her tone said even she didn't believe her own words.

"Could have been," John agreed. "But I'd expect it to be more."

A dark shadow passed across Michael's eyes.

"You're sure?"

"No," John snapped. "I'm not sure of *anything*. But we have a castle and twenty-nine people. How many groups have *we* sent out on recon missions?"

Nether Michael nor Rachel said anything.

"Exactly," John said.

A heavy silence fell over the three of them as they calculated the possibilities. Holding the castle against the mindless onslaught of the Infected had been one thing - and even that had only been accomplished through luck, though no one really wanted to admit it. Holding it against a large force of people felt like a very different proposition. One that might have a drastically different outcome.

"Twenty-eight," Rachel muttered in a low voice.

John looked at her quizzically.

"Colin died last night," she explained.

"Great," John growled. "We don't have many people left that I'd trust in a fight."

"I don't get it," Michael said suddenly. "Say they do have a large number of people. Why come here? Why look to take on a castle full of people?"

John snorted.

"You tell me, Michael. Why did *you* attack the castle?"

"I didn't att-"

"Sure you did," John interrupted. "Not head-on, maybe, but you had a chance to walk away from this place and find somewhere else. You didn't take it."

Michael flushed angrily.

"I just wanted us to have a safe place to-"

"Yup," John cut in. "I'm sure that's what *they* want, too. Like it or not, the way the world is now, the castle is a pot of fucking gold. There will be others that want it."

"But we're practically advertising that we want people to join us," Rachel said, pointing up at the fire on the castle's main tower. "There's no need for anyone to come here aggressively."

John shrugged.

"Tell that to Darren," he said wryly.

It was Rachel's turn to flush. John saw the heat of anger burn across her cheeks.

"Darren was-"

"A psycho," John finished. "Sure. For all they know, we're psychos too. Don't trust anybody, remember?"

He stared at Michael pointedly. The crippled man looked glum at hearing his own words repeated back to him, and said nothing.

"Look," John said, "I doubt they saw much, even if they have binoculars. Maybe they saw the three of us up here, but they have to figure there's more of us. If it were me, I'd be planning another recon mission, trying to find out what sort of force we've got in here. So we should have a couple of days. Next time they come, I'd suggest we get everybody that can stand up on the battlements, and have them all holding weapons. Let them see taking this place won't be easy. If we're lucky, they don't have many more bodies than us, and they'll think twice. Maybe they'll decide talking is the best option."

"If we're *lucky*," Michael repeated grimly.

John shrugged again.

"We won't be. But for now it's all we can do, unless you feel like running and letting them have the place."

Michael stared at John in disbelief.

"Thought not," John said flatly. "No one wants to give up the pot of gold."

"Fuck it, then," Michael snapped. "We need Caernarfon cleared. We need supplies. Will you go?"

He stared at John, who in turn glanced at Rachel.

"Of course, as long as I'm not walking right into the middle of trouble," John said.

Michael nodded his gratitude.

"You won't be," he said. "Get a team together. Whoever you need. You leave as soon as possible."

John took in the words impassively, but Michael saw Rachel's eyes flash with eager anticipation.

11

John stood in the shadow of Caernarfon Castle's main gate, lost in thought.

He had to admit, Michael's plan was pretty good, under the circumstances. There were far too many Infected in the town itself for a frontal attack to be anything other than a suicide mission. So Michael argued that the best idea was not to fight them at all, but to sail down the coast a few miles and set off an explosion loud enough to draw them away.

At first John thought generating an explosion large enough would be beyond their means. It wasn't as though they had a ready supply of C4 or dynamite, and John had serious doubts that blowing up a car would do much more than bring the nearest batch of Infected down upon him. Only after speaking to Emma and asking about the area surrounding Caernarfon did a flicker of an idea begin to burn in John's mind. He told Michael and Rachel enough of his plan for them to trust him; not enough for them to suspect, as he did, that what he was planning was completely insane.

Once the Infected left Caernarfon, following the noise John planned to make, there would be a window for the people in the castle to descend on the town and loot everything they could carry. Michael had argued that the Infected would likely come back, and John didn't disagree: they had all observed the way the creatures acted when there was no external stimulus to give them direction. They wandered in ever-expanding circles, until some noise gave them purpose once more. It was a bizarre and unsettling sight, watching them prowl around, like cats patrolling their territory.

Michael estimated it might take as much as a couple of days for the Infected to circle back to Caernarfon, and even then their numbers were likely to be drastically reduced as some wandered off or got distracted by alternative prey. Relying on the town to be empty would be foolhardy; there were always likely to be a few that wandered in after the decoy explosion was detonated, but he hoped their numbers would be small enough to handle.

They'll have to be, John thought as he stared up at the towering gate that kept the horrors of the world outside.

It hadn't taken long for John to pick the team that would head out with him; in truth his choices were severely limited. Ray and Shirley, two of the bikers, had already seen their fair share of fighting. Neither was particularly skilled, but they came with a fully-loaded *fuck it* attitude that John much preferred to working alongside terror and anxiety. Neither of the men volunteered for the mission, but neither refused when he asked them. John got the impression they were going a little stir crazy in the castle and would have leapt at any chance to get away from the atmosphere of despair and gradual decay that hung over the group of survivors.

One of the young guys that had tried to kill John in Caernarfon at Darren's command actually *did* volunteer, most likely because he was desperate to demonstrate that he was now firmly on John's side. The tactic was slightly pathetic, and the way he had tried to worm his way into John, Michael and Rachel's good books so soon after conspiring to kill him made John cringe a little, but he let it slide. Without the fear of Darren to motivate him, the kid seemed harmless and enthusiastic.

Nevertheless John resolved to keep an eye on him. If anyone was going to let fear get the better of them, It was Glyn.

And then, of course, there was Rachel, who John had tried to convince to stay put, but who had shot him down almost before the words left his mouth.

The last thing Michael did before wishing John good luck was tell him to keep an eye on Rachel, but he needn't have bothered. Rachel's thirst for blood and vengeance was plainly written on her face. Of course, John told himself, he would have kept an eye on Rachel anyway, because he was pretty sure he was falling for her.

He blinked at the gate. It was the first time he had fully acknowledged his growing feelings for Rachel, even to himself. The abrupt realisation that despite his best efforts to remain isolated he had developed such a strong bond with Rachel should have made him happy, and maybe once it would have. Under the current circumstances, admitting the depth of his emotions to himself just made him feel sick with worry.

Those feelings, and the potential they held to induce John to make bad decisions, felt more dangerous than any number of Infected.

Already he had evidence of that: without Rachel, John knew he would have been long gone already, leaving the castle and all the fucked-up problems that came with it far behind him.

Not for the first time, John resolved to keep his mouth shut, and to keep Rachel at arm's length. It would be safer for them both that way. And it wouldn't be difficult: they could barely hold a conversation without getting under each other's skin. John didn't think Rachel had ever forgiven him for lying to her about who he was when they had first met. He couldn't blame her for that.

"John?"

Rachel's voice broke John out of the prison his thoughts had imposed on him. He dropped his gaze from the gate to her. She fixed him with a frustrated look.

"We're ready to go, you know, if you're done daydreaming?"

John grunted, and evaluated his team with a feeling of distant dread. He'd been a part of teams he considered ill-equipped before, more than once, but the ragtag collection of survivors he was about to lead into enemy territory made him more than a little nervous. The fact that he was the one leading them, assuming responsibility for their safety, made him most anxious of all. If a life of violence and death had taught John anything, it was that people were generally safer when they were as far away from him as possible.

They all looked at him expectantly, and he was suddenly struck by the notion that they were waiting for him to deliver one of those rousing speeches that the leaders of armies always made in the movies. *You'll never take our freedom* or some such nonsense.

"Stay quiet," he growled, and turned to release the portcullis mechanism. The metal bars slid upwards with a faint squeal that made him wince, and he pushed open the wooden gate as quickly as possible, scanning the river for any sign of the Infected.

During their time in the castle, John and Rachel had tested out just how much noise they could make before they drew the attention of the Infected, standing up on the battlements and gradually raising their voices until they found a level that crossed the river and sent a visible pulse of activity through the creatures on the other side. Talking in low voices, they discovered, was fine. Any voice raised above room temperature caused eyeless heads to whip in the direction of the castle.

As ever, making as little noise as possible would be paramount.

The first step was to circumnavigate the town by swimming downstream, around the point, and to the boat that John had left tied to the harbour wall. The screech of metal as the portcullis rose wasn't loud, but it could have carried across the water. Maybe, John thought, the noise was not sufficiently *human* enough to cause anything other than mild curiosity in the Infected. Either way, he was grateful that he didn't see any of the creatures come charging toward the river. Having company in the water would *not* be good.

There was no time to waste. John set off at a light jog, moving as far downstream as the rocky ground around the castle would allow before plunging into the icy water.

The cold took his breath away, despite everything he had done to mentally prepare himself for it. He paused a moment as his body acclimatised, turning to make sure the others were behind him, and then he aimed for the open sea, cutting through the water with a long, powerful breaststroke that barely made a sound.

When he reached the mouth of the river, and was able to see the harbour in the distance, he paused again, waiting for the others. All had promised him they were at least decent swimmers. Turned out they had different definitions of the word *decent*. John had already opened up a fifty yard gap on the others.

As he waited for them to catch up, John studied the harbour carefully. It looked almost as quiet as it had the first time he had approached it from the sea.

Almost.

It took him a minute of scanning each building in turn, but it was there: a patch of darkness that moved in the shadows that clustered between the tightly-packed buildings. *Infected.*

The swim meant John was travelling light. They all were; none of the group was carrying anything heavier than a knife. Any fighting that took place would be at close quarters. Far too close.

Ray was the first to reach John's position. He looked grateful for the chance to catch his breath. John put a finger to his lips and turned Ray in the water to face the harbour. He pointed at the shadows and stared into Ray's eyes until he was certain the man had understood. When Rachel arrived, both men had their fingers to their lips. The message transmitted loud and clear.

Once they were all together, John gave them a few seconds to ease their burning lungs, but not too long. The sea had a way of sapping strength, but it wasn't the fitness of the others that motivated him to move them on quickly. It was the paralysing fear that he knew would breed in their minds every second they waited and thought about what they had to do next.

He gathered them all in close, and whispered rhythmically, trying to mask the words under the noise of the rolling waves.

"The hull of the boat is too high. We have to get up to the harbour there," he pointed at some stone steps that dropped down into the ocean about fifty yards to the left of the boat. "We move silently, we stay together, but be ready to run. Stay behind me. Clear?"

He waited until they all nodded, and turned for the harbour, slowing his pace and keeping his eyes focused on the waterfront. He almost hoped the creatures would hear them coming. At least then they'd have a chance to turn back before things got out of hand.

He saw no movement before the looming wall filled his vision and blocked his view of the buildings that huddled along the waterfront.

John dearly wanted more than the one small knife he carried on his belt. Even punching the things with his free hand seemed a risk. All were drenched in blood. All it would take was a small cut on his knuckles, and the mixing of bodily fluids would end it all.

He pulled himself up onto the steps, trying to move as silently as possible, but he knew the game was up almost immediately. The pattering sound of the water that dripped from his sodden clothes was enough to unravel everything. As the first of the Infected shrieked, John cursed himself for not realising how flawed the plan was before he carried it out. He had hoped they would be able to get to the harbour and cross to the boat silently, but there was no way to move quietly enough when the creatures were only a matter of feet away.

Stupid.

John heard answering shrieks from the crooked streets close to the harbour, and then others in the distance. A few drops of water landing on the cobbles had been all that was required to set off a chain reaction. The whole of Caernarfon was coming. The time for silence was already over.

"Back!" John roared. "Swim out into the bay. I'll get you."

He didn't have time to check whether they had heard before he was driving his knife into an empty eye socket and the world exploded into motion.

12

The torture was unending. When Jason was awake, Hywel Holloway sliced endless shallow cuts into his flesh with the razor and rubbed rock salt gleefully into the open wounds until Jason howled like an animal and his brain disconnected from the horrifying reality his flesh was forced to endure.

When Annie appeared and spoke to him softly and gently, her presence was like a soothing balm. She gave him drugs to ease the pain, but then the darkness took him and the carousel of agony started up again. This time the cuts were invisible, laced across his mind by the poisonous words of his dead mother who scolded him for a coward and promised that Rachel was dead.

It was, his mother crooned, no more than Jason deserved. He was, after all, a murderer of the worst type: a boy who had killed his own mother. Jason twitched between reality and unreality, moving from one searing pain to the next, until his mind snapped like a brittle twig. He spent his time - awake and asleep - screaming, until eventually he couldn't be sure whether he was conscious or not and the endless agony swallowed him whole.

For his part, Hywel Holloway seemed to enjoy his work. No, he *loved* it, as he had never loved anything in his entire life.

Hywel had always been a profound disappointment to his mother. He was slow and stupid - *the runt of my litter* - and apparently was the spitting image of dear old dead Dad. Hywel wouldn't know; he had never met his father, but the shadow of the man his mother held in especially low regard had loomed over his childhood anyway, tainting the days like rust. Hywel took far more in the way of beatings than either of his older brothers, both of whom quickly came to realise that their mother hated Hywel, and so they began to beat him with impunity too.

He never cried, though, not once. Eventually his brothers stopped their attempts at torturing him because every time they put him down he would bounce right back up and stare at them defiantly until they became unnerved. Yet nothing stopped Annie. Even now, with her over seventy years old and Hywel in his early thirties and a good six inches taller than her, he still feared that she would lash out at any moment.

Torturing the huge man was the first time he had ever seen anything remotely like *pride* in his mother's gaze, and so he approached the task with relish. Being on the other end of the pain he inflicted was deliciously intoxicating.

He enjoyed slicing with the razor most of all, because his wiry limbs lacked the strength to damage the heavily-muscled man with punches. He felt important, like a surgeon, as he carved out delicate patterns on the man's hard flesh. He was particularly proud of a smiley face he had drawn in blood on the man's chest: very nearly a *perfect* circle. It made him feel like an artist, and for a while he had simply stood back and admired his handiwork.

When the front of the man's body was covered in lacerations, Hywel told his older brothers tie Voorhees face down on the ground so that Hywel could work on his back, and they *did it*. They followed Hywel's orders to the letter. He had never been so happy in his entire life.

Who's the stupid runt now, you bastards?

Annie had been very clear that Hywel should give Voorhees time to rest, and told him the pain he inflicted would have a much greater effect if the man was given periods of calm in which he could foster hope that his torture had finally ended.

Hour after hour Hywel returned to the man, waking him up and breaking him, before retreating. It didn't take long before Hywel began to cut into the rest periods just as he had cut into the man's flesh. Before long letting the man rest at all seemed impossible to Hywel. When Annie poured painkillers into Voorhees' slack mouth, Hywel would wait until she was gone and jam his fingers down the man's throat until he vomited up the drugs.

Voorhees was no fun at all when he was asleep.

In the end, Hywel only took breaks from the torture to relieve himself in the bathroom.

As he stood in front of the mirror, washing away the blood that caked his hands, Hywel Holloway grinned at his reflection and didn't recognise the proud, purposeful face that stared back at him. The change in his features made him feel euphoric, and he hurried back to the bar, and the prisoner, whistling cheerfully.

What began with a razor blade and salt quickly evolved. In a storage cupboard next to the bathroom, Hywel had found a small toolbox that contained a pair of pliers and numerous other items that he could think of a million ways to use to inflict pain. The possibilities seemed endless; it was going to be a *great* session.

Except that the man on the floor was dead.

Hywel knew it as soon as he stepped back into the bar and saw Voorhees, flat on his stomach with his head facing Hywel and his eyes sightless; fixed and empty.

Ma is going to kill me.

Hywel felt like wailing. He knew the man had lost a lot of blood in their last session but he was *enormous*; surely he had plenty to lose?

Stupid runt.

Hywel heard Annie's voice in his mind so clearly that for a moment he thought she was standing right beside him, and he felt like running away. He glanced around the bar. Empty. He had to sort out the mess he had made all by himself.

Panicked, Hywel followed the lead of the doctors he had seen on television: *pump on the chest and blow into the man's throat,* he thought. He retrieved a blade from his bag and sliced through the rope that secured the man's right arm to a pillar several feet away and rolled him over onto his back. The man's tongue lolled out of his mouth, and his gaze fixed on the ceiling.

Oh shit, oh shit, oh shit...

Hywel straddled the man's wide torso and began to press on his chest with all his might.

One, two, three, four, five...

He pinched the man's bloody nose and blew deeply into his mouth, feeling the man's wide chest expand underneath him.

One, two, three-

The man's eyes weren't looking at the ceiling anymore.

They were looking straight at Hywel.

He pushed again on the man's chest feebly.

Four...

Hywel didn't get to five.

*

Jason stared at Hywel Holloway impassively as he clamped his bear-like hand onto the man's scrawny neck and squeezed away his life like juice from an overripe fruit. Thin, reedy arms beat ineffectually at Jason's thick forearm, and the blows simply made Jason squeeze tighter, until Holloway's face turned puce and his eyes bulged out of his head, blood vessels bursting and turning the whites a deep shade of crimson.

Hywel Holloway didn't die with a scream, nor even a whimper. He died with a gurgle and a *click* as his neck snapped. Jason kept his grip on the man's throat for several long seconds, pulling the dead face near to his own and staring deep into the now-empty eyes, before finally tossing the man aside. Unblinking, Jason stood and began to walk away, jolting to a halt when the rope attached to his left wrist pulled him backwards. He fumbled at the knot without really seeing it, finally succeeding in freeing himself, and strode away toward the window that dominated the room. Lifting a chair and hurling it, Jason created a new doorway for himself and staggered through it, charging away from the hotel as blindly as the Infected that wandered the distant countryside.

13

John ripped his knife from the brain of the first of them and ducked low as the second leapt for him, twisting aside and letting the creature's momentum take it past him and over the wall into the sea.

He heard Rachel scream in what he hoped was surprise rather than pain, but there was no more time to think about the people he'd left behind in the water. He took off at a sprint, aiming for the boat, pounding along the cobbles as close to the edge of the harbour as he dared.

The Infected burst from the alleys and buildings like heat-seeking missiles, making straight for him. He threw himself into a forward roll to avoid two that leapt at him and heard them splashing into the sea to his right.

As he came up to his feet he found something for his free hand to do: an abandoned bicycle on the ground near a bench that offered a peaceful view of the ocean. He grabbed the frame, using his momentum to propel the bike into the gathering swarm of Infected as they converged on him, and then he was running again, holding the knife in an outstretched hand like a relay baton, feeling the blade slicing through their flesh until it caught on bone and the handle was torn from his grasp.

Keep moving.

John poured every ounce of his energy into his legs, pumping them explosively. He had always been quick, since he was a kid; invariably he was the fastest in the various teams he had been a part of over the years, and his pace had kept him alive on more than one occasion. He felt grasping fingers claw at the sodden material of his shirt and didn't slow at all, letting his speed tear the fabric away and leaving the creature roaring impotently behind him.

The smell and the sound of them filled his senses, all guttural snarling and fetid meat, and the fifty yard dash seemed to take an eternity before he saw the length of rope he had left as a makeshift bridge to the boat that bobbed several feet away from the wall. With a final burst of energy he leapt for it, knowing he had only one chance to grab it. Knowing that missing meant death.

Time seemed to slow to a crawl, and he focused all his attention on the rope, pulling his legs up toward him like a long-jumper as he left the wall, straining to gain extra distance.

Behind him, he heard the Infected leaping from the wall; heard the outraged shrieks as their bodies slapped into the freezing water below.

His fingers found the rope, and he clenched them tightly as he swung from it, very nearly catapulting himself away into the water.

The rope sagged, and John's legs dropped into the sea, the cold water claiming his knees.

He snapped his hips upwards, aiming to hook his legs over the rope and start to clamber toward the boat.

His left leg complied, but his right didn't. It felt like it was glued to something heavy under the surface of the water. Something that was trying to drag him down.

Something that snarled.

*

It took a moment for Rachel to process John's shout, and to realise that she had to turn and swim away from the harbour. In that instant one of the Infected rocketed over the wall, landing with a splash right next to her.

She screamed, thrashing wildly at the water, desperately dragging herself away from the flailing creature.

More of them were pouring into the sea as she turned and pulled away from the wall, ignoring the shrieking complaint of her burning muscles. All around her she saw the others turning as well; heard Glyn's almost comical yelp of surprise at the sudden attack, and then she was clear, focusing only on the next stroke until she was twenty feet away from the wall and the Infected that dropped into the water like depth charges.

"Everyone okay?" She gasped at the others as they reached her. "Anyone bitten?"

As the others responded one by one she saw the movement of the Infected take on a rhythm that made her nerves howl. Several of them were thrashing in the water. No, more than thrashing. *Swimming.*

"Go!" Rachel screamed, and then she was swimming again, a powerful front crawl that felt like it was going to make her muscles cramp at any moment. The Infected were slow and clumsy, but they were coming. More and more of them; inexorable as the advance of age.

Swim out into the bay, John had roared, but the safer option would be to head back to the castle, where they might have a chance to fight off the group chasing them. The safer option meant abandoning John.

The retail park outside Aberystwyth loomed in her memories, the way she thought John had abandoned them all to die. The look of disdain on his face when she told him she had thought he had skipped out on her.

I was coming back, he had growled in an offended tone.

Rachel grimaced and turned away from the castle.

And swam.

She poured her last drops of energy into the swim, and headed out into the bay, praying with every stroke that the others were matching her pace, and that the Infected swam as clumsily as they walked.

She speared through the water for what felt like an age, until a raging inferno built in her lungs and she felt her vision doing a little swimming of its own. She had to stop. Panic could only fuel her engine for so long.

She turned, surveying the scene behind her. Ray, Shirley and Glyn were following close. All looked unharmed, and all looked utterly exhausted, their swimming reduced to feeble grasping at the incessant waves. She heaved in a few deep breaths, but the oxygen just seemed to stoke the fire in her chest.

Bobbing on the surface of the Irish Sea, Rachel scanned Caernarfon's picturesque waterfront and felt a cold seeping through her that had nothing to do with the freezing water.

The small yacht looked like a child's toy in the distance, but it was close enough for her to be sure that it was floating away from the harbour, and that its movement was aimless. The boat was under the spell of the waves, drifting away slowly.

He didn't make it.

She shot a glance at the Infected cutting through the water toward her. They had fallen maybe a hundred yards back, and they moved slowly, like a learner thrashing through the water for the first time. But they were coming, winding in the yards tirelessly. They either didn't feel fatigue, or they didn't care about it. Or maybe the compulsion to kill was so strong in them that nothing else mattered. It was the latter, Rachel realised with a dull sort of terror building inside her. The Infected cared only about killing humans. Nothing would make them stop. They would follow until their bodies gave up. Until death took them.

Rachel knew she was too far away now to make for the castle. Her muscles felt like they had been hammered by a meat tenderiser, and it was all she could do just to tread water. By the looks on the faces of the others, they faced the same predicament.

This is how it ends. Choose to drown or get torn apart by the sharks.

It was no choice at all. Rachel would dive to the bottom and stay there. If somehow that failed she would cut her own throat. The infection would not have her. Project Wildfire, and all the bastards behind it had inflicted enough on her already. She wouldn't give them that.

She felt for her knife, and slipped it from a makeshift sheath at her hip.

And cried out in triumph.

In the distance, a flash of white blossomed in the misty sky as the sails on the boat unfurled and shot up to catch the wind, and Rachel felt tears of relief running down her cheeks, finding their way home to the ocean.

*

It had taken three kicks for John to dislodge the Infected horror that clutched his ankle in the depths. Each time the water muted the force of the kick, neutering its potential for damage. In the end he had to pull the trapped leg with every ounce of strength he had, hauling the creature up to the surface, before he was finally able to deliver the blow required to shake it loose.

By the time he had pulled himself up onto the boat, the frantic battle on the rope had dragged the vessel much closer to the harbour wall, and one of the creatures leaping at the boat landed on the deck at the same time he did. He mustered up the last of his energy and shoulder-charged the thing, putting all his weight into knocking it over the side, and almost following it over before he caught the low handrail to steady himself.

Several more were leaping from the harbour, slamming into the hull and falling away, and John wasted no time in untying the rope, and unleashing a hoarse, victorious roar as the yacht bobbed away and out of their reach.

John wanted nothing more than to collapse to the deck and rest, but a nagging voice at the back of his mind had other ideas.

Rachel.

He rushed to the rail and leaned over it, scanning the grey waves for movement.

It took him a moment to see them, and it was the Infected that pointed the way. The chaotic splashing of their attempts to swim was easy to spot. Ahead of them, pulling clear, he saw the figures that made considerably less noise in their passage. He counted four. They had all made it. So far.

With a struggle, he turned his mind inwards, trying to remember how to get the sails up.

John despised the boat; had hated every minute of his first journey on the thing, hours spent pulling on ropes that seemed to do nothing, or pulling on ropes that had the weight of the sea and the wind pulling in the opposite direction. It had been exhausting and frustrating, and it wasn't an experience he had ever wanted to repeat. Yet now he had to, and he had to do it quick. By now the others would be suffering extreme fatigue. One way or another, they wouldn't last long.

John knew the basics of sailing. He knew that to sail into the wind meant *tacking* - sailing in diagonal lines toward the target to maximise the energy of the wind - but the boat was large and unwieldy. It almost certainly needed a crew of at least two to manoeuvre it and keep the sails positioned properly. He was going to have to wing it.

He repeated the steps that he had taken to get the main sail up outside Aberystwyth, and felt like punching the air when it released with a loud *whump* and caught the wind, rocketing the boat forward.

The wind was intense, and the boat began to pilot itself, heading to a point something like thirty degrees to the left of the spot that he saw Rachel and the others pull up at. Trying to turn directly toward them would be a disaster, and the oncoming wind would likely either capsize the yacht or drive it back into the harbour wall. Instead he aimed further left, and once the boat had the wind at its back, it bolted across the waves.

He glanced at the group in the water, gritting his teeth as he realised they probably thought he was leaving them for dead. The Infected were closing in on them. Time was running out.

Sending up the *spinnaker* - the smaller, second sail - would make the boat even harder to control, but he needed the speed. With a curse, he released the mechanism and felt the speed of the boat increase. Once the sails were secured, he bolted into the cabin and heaved the wheel to the right with all his strength, shaking and sweating at the effort required to battle the howling wind, drawing the boat around in a huge, looping arc that seemed to take forever, until he was approaching Rachel and the others from the opposite side of the bay.

The Infected now blocked his approach.

With a savage grin, John mowed them down, feeling a powerful rush of satisfaction as the hull echoed to the impact of their bodies. He doubted he had stopped them all, but he had scattered them and left choppy waters in his wake that would slow their progress dramatically. It was the best he could do.

When he got close enough to see the fatigue etched on Rachel's face, he twisted the wheel hard, sending the boat into something approximating a slow, flat spin. The sudden deceleration threw him against the wheel, and his ribs - which had only just begun to heal after the last torment he had put them through - sent a white-hot pulse of pain up into his mind.

Gasping for air, he ran from the cabin and threw the rope ladder over the rail and into the water below. When he saw Rachel's face appear, it was all he could do not to laugh hysterically. Her expression somehow combined anger, relief and terror all at once.

"Fuck the Infected," Rachel stammered through chattering teeth. "Next time, we get a boat with a fucking engine."

"Or a submarine," Ray gasped as he hauled himself onto the deck behind her.

John couldn't hold the laughter back any longer.

14

"Hywel is dead, Ma."

Annie hadn't thought it possible that four words could do such damage, but each one hit her like a hollow-point bullet, expanding on entry and devastating her.

For a moment she just stared at Rhys blankly, unable to pull herself out of dark thoughts that sucked her down like tar.

"Dead," she repeated slowly, as though saying it again might somehow throw some light on it.

"The guy - Voorhees - he got out. He killed Hywel."

Even Rhys looked downcast. Or maybe just scared; it was difficult for Annie to tell the difference. Rhys had hated Hywel ever since the runt of the litter fell noisily out of Annie's uterus, but family was family. Annie had drilled that into all her sons; that one thing above all others. Family was the *only* thing that mattered. And now one of her family was dead. Not just one of her family; one of her *children.*

Something shifted deep in Annie's mind, something that slid away from her grasp into a yawning black crevasse.

"How?"

Rhys shrugged, and the gesture made Annie want to slap him. Hard. The fury his apparent indifference stoked within her pulled Annie back into the present more efficiently than an electric shock.

"*How?*" She repeated, dropping her voice to a dangerous whisper that her son should have known *very* well.

Rhys blinked and took a step backwards. He towered over his mother physically, but sometimes threat radiated from the smallest of foes. He began to stutter, a habit Annie had always detested, and had forcibly broken him of more than thirty years earlier. Her eyes flashed dangerously.

"I...I don't know. I heard breaking glass and...Hywel must have untied him for some reason, and he broke Hywel's neck. I'm sorry, Ma, I should have kept an eye on him, but he was doing so well, I didn't think even he could fuck it-"

Annie did slap him, then. Hard enough to make his cheek sing, and his head snapped to the side violently. When he brought his eyes back to her, Annie saw tears in them, and told herself that if he began to cry, she might just have to lose another son.

"Where is he?"

"Uh...Hywel? He's in..."

Rhys trailed off when he saw his mother's expression reach a dark place he hadn't seen since he was a small child. Not since his barely-remembered father was still alive.

"Voorhees. Where is *Voorhees*?"

Rhys squeezed his eyes shut.

"He's...gone."

Kept them shut. He didn't need them open to see his mother's anger. He could *feel* it.

Annie glared at Rhys for a moment, and then stepped past him, heading for the stairs that led down to the ground floor. When she reached the bar area and saw her dead son, her breath caught in her throat and her eyes shimmered.

Somewhere deep at the back of her mind, she could hear her father cackling, taunting her from beyond the grave. She wanted nothing more than to be alone with her dead boy, to scoop him up in her arms and cry, but Annie knew that showing weakness was not an option, and so she focused on the smashed window, and crouched down to put a hand on Hywel's forehead.

"Still warm," she muttered absently.

"Ma?"

Rhys' voice, behind her. He sounded scared. Annie ignored him and stepped to the exit Voorhees had created in the large sea-facing window. In the soft earth outside, she saw footprints that led north.

"Go get your brother, Rhys. Round up as many people as you need. Quickly. He's gone north, and you're going to bring him *back,* understand me? Bring him back alive."

Rhys stared at his mother for a moment, apparently trying to process the order.

"How should-"

"Go," Annie interrupted in a flat, dangerous whisper. "For your brother. Go. *Now.*"

Rhys nodded, and left her.

*

By the time Rhys and his brother Bryn left the hotel, along with Gareth Hughes and a burly farmer by the name of Stan, Annie had covered her dead son's body in a sheet, and vowed to make the man who had killed him pay. Not with his death: even as her emotions raged inside her, Annie knew that she needed Voorhees alive. But she would make him pay nonetheless, with an endless barrage of pain and suffering.

She stared through the smashed window at the rolling sea, and didn't even hear the engine of the boat as Clive Baxter returned to the jetty. When he found her, and told her that there were people in Caernarfon Castle, Annie was so lost in dreams of bloody revenge that she barely heard him.

15

"Strip," John said, and kept his tone carefully neutral.

Shirley and Glyn - especially Glyn - looked at him dubiously. Looking at the kid's horrified expression, John doubted that Glyn had ever taken his clothes off in the presence of a woman. The notion that such an act would concern anybody who had just been through the sort of ordeal they had nearly made him burst into laughter again.

"Don't worry, kid," John grinned. "This isn't a *sex boat*. It's freezing, everyone's clothes are soaked. You want to warm up and avoid hypothermia, you gotta get those clothes off. Wring them out, let 'em dry a little. You'll thank me in the long run."

Glyn's eyes maintained a firmly horrified look, and his cheeks flushed.

"Christ's sake," Rachel snapped, and stripped off her soaked shirt without hesitation.

John couldn't take his eyes off her, but the stare had nothing to do with attraction. As she stripped down to her underwear, John saw a sickening network of scars that laced her torso and thighs. It looked like someone had repeatedly taken a razor blade to her. He knew who, and for the first time he thought - really *thought* - about what Rachel had been through. Five days spent at the mercy of a man that made Darren Oliver sound sane. He stared, and his heart broke a little.

When he lifted his eyes, he found Rachel staring back at him, jaw clenched, eyes clear and defiant, daring him to say a word. Somehow she looked proud and dignified, and John found himself struggling to resist the urge to kiss her.

John had seen plenty of guys in the army that functioned on pure bloodlust and the need for vengeance. He had grown to understand it: for many it was simply what held them together. Revenge was the sticking plaster that kept the cracks in their mind from spreading and pulling them apart.

It was, he realised abruptly, the same for Rachel. Had been ever since her brother died. Focusing on getting even was no more or less than triage for her, a necessary band-aid. At least he could understand it. He understood also that there would be no chance of him getting close to her. It was embarrassing that he had even thought about it. After Victor, any sort of romantic involvement would be the last thing she wanted.

In another time and place, maybe John and Rachel would have had a shot. But in the aftermath of St. Davids and Aberystwyth, John imagined that Rachel was as far away from thinking about him as anything other than a comrade as it was possible to get. There was no hope for him, not with her. There never would be.

The knowledge hurt, but it was a good sort of pain. It helped him let go. Helped him focus.

He looked away from Rachel, and got an eyeful of Shirley's pasty white body, at the wobbling, tattooed flesh as the man struggled to peel off the sodden t-shirt that clung tightly to him. If nothing else, it helped clear his mind.

John stripped too, and began to wring as much water as possible out of his clothes. In moments, the floor of the small cabin was soaked.

"Better all stay in here, out of the wind. Try to get as warm as possible," John said.

"You want us to hug or something?" Shirley responded in disbelief.

The man's tone made John chuckle, and went a long way toward diffusing the tense atmosphere building in the cabin.

"Sure," John said, "If you've got any takers, go for it." He grinned widely. "I was thinking more like keeping moving, jogging on the spot, or doing some push-ups or something."

Shirley pouted in mock disappointment, and they all laughed.

For a moment it was possible to forget that they were being hunted to the point of extinction. Out there on the boat, safe from any possible attack by the Infected, John almost felt a sense of normality, just for a fleeting moment.

It would, he realised, probably be the last time.

They sailed south. John kept the boat as close to the coast as he dared, and kept his eyes peeled for rocks and shallow water. When he had taken the boat in the other direction after leaving Aberystwyth, he had spotted a small beach that he remembered being a few miles south of Caernarfon. He leaned on the wheel, staring out keenly, determined not to miss it in the fog that clung to the sea.

After a while, a vaguely comfortable silence fell over the five of them. Most likely, John thought, they were all relishing the rare sense of safety, as he was. He felt a presence moving alongside him at the wheel. Ray.

"Reckon you're a hero, then, mate. Right? One of our brave soldiers fighting for Queen and country and all that?"

John smirked.

"Or you're a *driver*," Ray continued sardonically. "Don't know too many drivers that could pull off the type of shit you did back there, though."

A hero. It wasn't the first time John had heard the phrase, of course: soldiers were routinely described as heroes by those who had no idea what the armed forces actually did.

He hadn't heard it applied to him specifically, though. When he had left the army, his departure had taken place under a thick cloud of disgrace. *Dishonourable discharge.* Somehow, whenever he thought about those words now, he heard them in Fred Sullivan's smug, gravelly voice.

He dearly wanted to get his hands on the old bastard's wrinkled throat.

"There are no heroes," John replied distantly. "There was never even a hint of heroism about anything I did in the army. I believed in it all when I signed up, because I was a kid who didn't know any fucking better than what the TV told me. *Protecting Queen and country.*"

He spat the words out bitterly.

"I believed it right up to the moment I was ordered to infiltrate a family home and wound up killing two children. The fucking Queen didn't need protecting from *them*. I executed people with no way of defending themselves, over and over again. That's what I was. Not a *hero*. Not even a villain. Just a weapon. I was the finger on the trigger. That's all I was."

Ray seemed a little taken aback by the venom in John's tone.

"Didn't mean anything by it, feller," he said, raising his hands in apology.

"I know," John muttered. "Sorry. I don't like talking about it." He shrugged.

Ray nodded solemnly.

"Reckon it's a good job I'm a pacifist," he said.

"A pacifist who carries a crossbow," John replied. "Yeah, I'd say that worked out well. You're a soldier now, whether you like it or not."

Ray looked like he hadn't really considered that at all.

"Seems like it'd be pretty hard to get over being a soldier, if it was like you say," he said.

It wasn't a question, but John answered it anyway.

"You don't," he said. "You live through it, or you die and get your name on a fucking plaque somewhere. Only it's not really your name, not anymore. It's the name of the guy that went in. The war kills all those guys, one way or another. No one gets out in one piece."

Ray rubbed his jaw thoughtfully.

"Doesn't sound too good for us, then mate, if we're all soldiers now. How do you get through it without getting fucked up? Getting, uh, stress disorder or whatever?"

John grimaced.

"You don't," he said, and turned the wheel sharply. "This is the place."

16

It had taken a little less than an hour for them to reach the small beach John had remembered as being the closest place to Caernarfon that he could make land. He would have liked to be closer to the castle, but the forbidding cliffs of the Welsh coast wouldn't allow it, and there was no fighting nature.

As the crow flies, he thought, *we're probably seven or eight miles away from the castle. Too far.*

The small strip of pebble-strewn sand was deserted, and he hoped the chances of encountering the Infected was slight: the beach looked isolated. No sign of any buildings, and if Ray had been right, most of the Infected within a huge radius had converged on Caernarfon, diluting the numbers in the surrounding countryside.

Isolation might just be the only way to survive, he thought idly.

He blinked as his mind suddenly raced, solving a puzzle he hadn't even been aware of. *Isolation.*

It was probably the only reason *any* of them had survived. The cities would have become hell on earth. The UK was a small island that heaved with people, heading rapidly for claustrophobic overpopulation. There were few parts of the country that *weren't* teeming with people, packed together densely like battery chickens. He stopped on the beach abruptly, and turned back to face the sea, lost in thought.

The nagging sensation he had felt back at the castle, like the answer to an important question hovered just beyond the boundaries of his understanding, suddenly made sense, and his blood cooled in his veins.

"You look like you're trying to remember if you locked your car or not," Rachel said. She turned and followed his gaze. Only the rolling grey ocean filled the horizon. "What's up?"

"We *have* been lucky," John said in a distant tone.

Rachel frowned.

"Huh?"

"The only reason we've lived this long is that this part of the country simply doesn't contain that many people. The virus is actually *weak* here."

Rachel snorted.

"You could have fooled me," she said flatly.

"Can you imagine what London is like?" John said in a tone laced with dread and wonder. "Birmingham? Manchester? All those people piled up on top of each other when the virus hit?"

John let the image float in the air for a moment, until he saw Rachel's eyes flicker with recognition.

"So?" Rachel said. "It would have been worse in a city." She shrugged. "Of course. What's your point?"

"Project Wildfire was an aerial attack. Like a bombing. When you hit a target, you don't just spray bombs everywhere. You focus your fire on the place you need it. On the land. On the cities. The high-value targets."

Rachel nodded slowly, and John gritted his teeth at his inability to frame the words that tumbled in his mind.

"Darren was right," he said suddenly. "What about all the people on the ships?"

Something lit in Rachel's eyes.

"No one dropped bombs all over the ocean. It would make no sense. The target was the land, and even then you'd concentrate fire on the places with the highest population. Places like the Welsh coast would have been low priorities, and the bombs would have been widely-spaced. Nothing would have hit the sea at all. So where is the navy? Where are all those ships that were out there when the virus dropped?"

"Not Infected," said Rachel, and John knew she'd got it.

"The safest place is the sea," John said triumphantly, jabbing a finger back at their small boat. "There will be aircraft carriers, battleships. Thousands of soldiers stationed at sea."

"Like I said," Ray interrupted. "Next time get a submarine."

Ray's words melted slowly into John's mind, entering his consciousness by osmosis.

The sea.

All of a sudden John knew exactly where the navy was, and exactly why he had seen no trace of it. And he knew immediately that they *had* to leave the castle.

Or die there.

"We have to go back," he said suddenly.

"What do you mean we have to go *back*?" Rachel snapped, and John thought she did an admirable job of biting back the vitriol that her eyes clearly revealed she wanted to pour all over the question.

"Sullivan has control of the navy," John said.

"So?"

"So his little project has fucked up, big time. And if they haven't stopped it by now, it's because they *can't*. Hell, even *my* being here was a last throw of the fucking dice, and look what good that did them. There's only one other way for him to get this country back under his control." He stared at Rachel, his eyes wide. "He'll nuke the whole place."

"And then what?" Rachel said. "I thought the whole point of all this was to take over the country, not blow it up."

"Sullivan only cares about control. If he has to destroy it to own it, he will absolutely do it. Losing his grip on the project, abandoning it; *failing*...that would...*offend* him. He won't allow it."

John knew it in his bones, knew it from every minute he had spent in the company of Fred Sullivan. The man was ruthless; cold as the edge of space. And suddenly John knew something else, too: Sullivan would have a backup plan. The old bastard was razor sharp. He was a billionaire precisely *because* he hedged his bets. Which meant that somewhere out there, across the ocean, there was a country that Sullivan had left untouched. Somewhere...isolated. A place to retreat to if everything went wrong, and there was no way back. John had a feeling he knew where that would be, but the knowledge was useless. Just getting there seemed insurmountable. He dismissed the train of thought, filing it away in his mind for consideration later.

"Fine," Rachel said, dragging his attention back to the present. "But that changes nothing about this. We can't run from the castle without any food, John. With no supplies. It's not like we can just pick up what we need from the supermarket after we set off."

She's right.

John nodded.

"Let's do this quick," John replied.

"Say's the man stood chatting on the beach," Shirley growled. "Are we moving or what?"

John nodded.

"We're moving," he said grimly.

"Good," Shirley said. "Which way?"

John glanced around the beach. When he had described the narrow strip of rocks and sand to Emma, after the girl at the castle finally opened up a little, she had told him she knew the place. Sometimes, she said, she'd skip school with her friends and end up out there. The statement had stuck in John's mind like a thorn; the sudden revelation that she was so *young*. A schoolgirl one minute, a survivor the next.

All the way out there? John had said in mild disbelief. *Hell of a trek just to skip a few lessons.* She had shrugged, as if it was nothing.

When everybody nearby knows your parents, word would get back home quicker than I did, she had explained. John understood: if you wanted to play truant in a town as small as Caernarfon, you had to go far enough away that no one would see you.

There was, Emma had said, a small village to the north of the beach. About halfway to Caernarfon.

If Emma had been right about the village, John knew making a big enough bang to draw the Infected wouldn't be a problem. *If* she was right, he could make a bang so loud it would shake the walls of the castle itself.

That wasn't the problem. The roughly three-mile hike to get there *was*.

Find the road and follow it north, Emma had told him. *You can't miss it.*

She made it sound simple.

As John climbed the hill that led away from the beach and thought about what travelling three miles in the open actually meant, he cursed himself for his complacency. Somehow, back at the castle, it had been easy to forget just what being outside was really like. Three miles felt like three hundred. He shuddered when he thought about the way they had spoken back at the beach, barely bothering to keep their voices down at all. The place looked deserted and they had let their guard down.

But three miles was a long way to travel and hope they wouldn't run into the Infected at all.

Too far.

He knew it as soon as they had left the beach. As soon as he saw the Infected shambling around in the strange, circular way he had come to think of as their default mode. Only two, and they didn't seem aware of the presence of humans nearby. The conversation they had must have been drowned out by the noise of the ocean. Somehow, John's luck seemed to be holding.

He made a mental note not to stand around casually discussing *anything.*

He held up a clenched fist, and dropped into a crouch. He had spent time at the castle teaching everyone a few basic gesture commands, mindful of just how important such skills might prove for the future of humanity. John had hoped to make the three-mile journey north to the village Emma had mentioned in absolute silence. It looked like that hope was going to be dashed immediately.

He drew Rachel in close, whispering in her ear like a lover.

"Two Infected," he said. "I need two knives. And I need all four of you to stay *right here.*"

He checked to see Rachel had heard him and understood, and held out his hands while she passed him her own knife and gestured to Ray to hand over his. When John took the weapons, he saw Rachel leaning in close to Ray, passing John's message along. The group froze.

Turning away from them, John prowled toward the two Infected in the distance like a panther, moving every muscle in agonizing slow motion, dividing his focus between the creatures and his next footstep, painfully aware that breaking a twig or kicking a stone would almost certainly take the next minutes in a vastly different direction.

John thought he could handle *two*, even if they rushed him, but they tended to shriek, and that would bring more. Maybe *lots* more, depending on whether the countryside was as sparsely populated as it looked. If it came to running, the boat was anchored many yards from the beach, making any chance they had of a quick retreat slim at best.

He imagined another round of swimming with the Infected chasing. They had all survived that once, but John didn't want to push his luck too far, worried that sooner or later it would inevitably push back.

Got to get this right.

The Infected were around fifty feet away, and it felt like it took John forever to close the distance, edging toward them inch by inch. Forty feet.

Thirty.

John's heart hammered.

At around twenty five feet, one of the Infected whipped its head in his direction, pausing its endless, circular shuffle, and John froze, holding his breath until his lungs felt ready to burst.

Still too far.

Finally the creature seemed to decide that whatever it had heard did not constitute prey, and resumed its aimless wandering.

John crept forward.

Twenty feet.

Close enough.

His left arm was nowhere near as accurate as his right, so John knew he'd be unable to take them simultaneously. The first shot was all-important. He had to take the closest creature down; had to ensure it made no noise while he aimed at the second.

Whipping his arm forward from his hip, as though throwing a frisbee, John let the first knife fly, and felt relief wash through him as he saw it land exactly as he had intended, burying itself to the hilt in the throat of the nearest of the two Infected. The creature let out a soft gurgling sound, but the second knife was already arcing through the air, cutting deep into a windpipe of its own. Both of the creatures fell almost simultaneously.

When their bodies impacted on the ground with a soft thump, John remained stock-still, his senses hyper-alert, waiting for some sign that other creatures nearby had heard the noise.

Nothing.

After a minute, he allowed himself to breathe easier.

Only for a second, though, because even as he gestured to the others to follow him, John heard a sound in the distance. A sound that made his blood run cold.

Humming.

A herd.

Fuck.

Every one of John's instincts shrieked at him to run, and warning fires erupted in his nerves. It felt like his very cells quivered in response to the rumbling hum. He ignored the impulse to flee with an effort, forcing himself to stand still. He raised a warning fist to stop the others running, and listened intently.

The herd wasn't close. Not right on top of them, at least. Most likely a mile or two away. Proximity wasn't as much of an issue as direction. The bellowing wind, and the answering sigh of the ocean rendered the noise muddy and difficult to pinpoint. After a moment he shut his eyes. Looking at Rachel's wide, terrified eyes and Ray's gritted teeth was a different sort of noise, and he needed to tune it out.

He frowned.

Seconds later he opened his eyes and let the noise of the group's terror back in. It looked to have gotten louder. He wasn't entirely sure, from the expression on Rachel's face, that she wasn't considering slapping him.

Probably would have, if it wasn't almost certain to draw the Infected here, he thought.

"Okay," he breathed. "We're okay. They're south, a couple of miles away I think. Heading north, coming this way."

Rachel looked horrified.

"How is that okay?" She hissed in disbelief.

"Because we're heading north too," John replied with a grimace.

"Are you crazy?"

"North, Rachel," John whispered. "They're going *north*. Caernarfon is north. The castle won't withstand another herd. We *have* to stop them."

Rachel stared at him, open-mouthed, and he saw her eyes flicker with understanding as the weight of his words settled on her.

"Move fast, but don't run. Watch your step. Light feet. Eyes open. *Quiet*." John delivered the words as he might to a platoon preparing for a mission. His tone left no room for doubt or debate. There was no time.

Thank God Michael isn't with us.

John blinked the thought away, and set off at a light jog, weaving and crouching to retrieve the knives from the throats of the dead Infected as he passed. He didn't look back. He had, he supposed, taken away any choice they had by simply going, but it didn't matter. Any seconds he spent talking it over reduced the distance between themselves and the herd, and increased the chances that they would all die. Or worse.

The terrain was tough. Lots of rocks in the soil, dense shrubbery, trees. Running would have been all but impossible even if silence wasn't John's primary concern. Several times he was forced to clamber on all-fours across twisted roots, but he kept moving, making sure the coast remained to his left. It was just as he began to think the journey would become impossible that he burst from the trees into open space, and onto the road.

When he felt tarmac under his feet, John paused, and held up a fist, halting the group once more.

He scanned both directions for any sign of Infected, but the mist and shadows gave up nothing. He could still hear the humming, though. He couldn't be sure, but he thought it sounded a little fainter. It made sense. The Infected weren't *charging* toward them. There was no need to panic, and flee blindly. They just had to keep moving.

He waved at the others and set off again, keeping firmly to the middle of the road, scurrying along on his toes; whispering along the tarmac. Rachel, Shirley, Ray and Glyn followed, hustling along single file, like a train transporting terror through the misty afternoon. John still held both knives. He ran with them raised.

Ready.

17

The end of the world had barely registered as a blip on Ed Cartwright's radar. His mother had always said - in a tone that increased in exasperation when it dawned on her that her twenty-four year old son might never leave home - that Ed would probably sleep through an earthquake. She hadn't been far wrong.

Ed had spent the last night of human civilization in much the same way as he had spent every other leading up to it: delivering virtual headshots on his favourite online shooter. The hours drifted past on a haze of marijuana smoke and were only really notable for an outburst of uncontrolled rage when an eight-year-old from Iowa spent ten minutes team-killing Ed and screeching laughter and insults across the chat channel. Finally, after a mostly successful night of gaming, Ed crawled into his unmade bed at around 5am, collapsing into a deep, druggy sleep.

The canisters that changed everything fell as dawn's light broke faintly across the horizon. The world began to end around six. Ed slept on.

Ed was used to waking up in an empty house. He lived alone with his mother, whose job in nursing meant she often had to work through the nights. Most days Ed woke up between two and three in the afternoon, but on the day that everything changed, his eyes flared open at around midday. He stared at the alarm clock - which was, in truth, just a clock; the alarm function hadn't been used in years - in bleary surprise as the digits swam into focus and informed him of his unusually early start.

His head was thick and foggy, and his throat felt like someone had taken an industrial sander to it, so Ed groaned his way out of bed, threw on a stained dressing gown and staggered downstairs to the fridge like it was an oasis in a hundred miles of parched desert.

As usual, his stomach complained that his habit of stuffing three or four chocolate bars down his throat right before falling asleep was bad form, and as usual he ignored it, and twisted the cap off a half-empty bottle of cola, grimacing in pleasure as the cold liquid fizzed over his fuzzy teeth and throat and delivered a sugar hit that hauled him toward full consciousness.

He belched and made for the living room, and his first joint of the day. His mother hated the fact that Ed smoked so heavily, and nagged him constantly about giving up. The weed was, she said, the reason he couldn't get a job. It was ruining his chance at a decent life. Ed nodded politely and agreed, but of course he didn't want a job: he just wanted weed and late night porn and the latest iteration of *Call of Duty*.

He had the same argument with his mother about marijuana almost every day, and in the end she barred him from smoking in the living room, threatening that if he turned her house into 'a drug den' she would be forced to kick him out. Ed doubted she was serious, but all it took was not smoking downstairs to defuse the debate, so he paid the price. Better not to rock the boat when he could just go smoke in his room or in the garden instead.

Unless she was out shopping, or at work. If that was the case Ed stretched out on the couch and blew lazy smoke rings, watching the sunlight that filtered through the window as it caught them and made them otherworldly.

He slumped onto the couch and belched again, painful and acidic, as he flicked on the television. Static.

Ed frowned and surfed through the channels. They had approximately nine hundred - the majority of which tried to sell miraculous household cleaning items to the viewer or encouraged them to gamble away their money on rigged games of chance. Nine hundred channels should have yielded *something*, but static blared on every one.

Ed sighed. They'd had problems with the satellite dish before, and it usually took a couple of days to fix. Frustrating, but in no way as earth-shatteringly important as a loss of internet.

He flicked the TV off and slipped his tobacco and a small bag of weed from the pocket of his dressing gown, rolling a fat, untidy joint. The TV wasn't necessary. It was a crisp, clear morning. A joint in the garden always made him feel a little virtuous. Getting some of that fresh air his mother always raved about. It was practically *healthy*.

When he was done, he slipped out the kitchen door into the back garden and lit up, inhaling deeply.

The house was a part of a small community nestling out of sight in a sparse forest far away from Newborough, the nearest town. The collection of houses was nowhere near large enough to count as a town in its own right, nor even a village, really. It was no more than an exclusive enclave that allowed those with enough money to buy the huge properties to avoid the riff-raff and live out a quiet life close to the sea and an expansive golf course. It went by the name Orchard Grove, which Ed thought was nice and poetic, but pretty misleading given that the 'orchard' in question was made up entirely of Ash trees.

Only nineteen other houses were dotted around Orchard Grove, each dripping wealth and sitting in acres of unused gardens. Ed's mother would never have been able to afford the house, but her ex-husband could, and the judge presiding over the divorce took an instant dislike to Ed's father. The house, the judge said, was the least the man owed her.

Nobody ever complained about Ed's pungent smoke: none of the neighbouring houses was close enough to be bothered by the smell, and he figured most were probably busy with more expensive drugs of their own, high on the narcotic rush of accumulated wealth; on their new *Porsche Cayenne* or their next trip to a distant exotic beach.

Orchard Grove was always quiet - in fact the whole of Anglesey could have been fairly described as soporific - but as Ed exhaled a cloud of smoke that drifted up into the cloudy sky, he felt oddly unnerved at just *how* quiet it seemed. Although the collection of houses was hidden from the road that led to Newborough by a smattering of trees, it wasn't so far removed that the sound of traffic couldn't be heard. The road wasn't exactly busy, but it led right across the north of Wales and into England, meaning there was generally some traffic at least. And there were the usual noises from the neighbours as well: lawnmowers and barking dogs and the sound of young children having fun; the suburban symphony was always playing in the background.

He inhaled again.

Nothing seemed to break the quiet of the early afternoon. Even the birds didn't seem to be singing.

Exhale.

Ed had issues with paranoia, of course. For a dedicated marijuana smoker it went with the territory. Sometimes the drug made him happy and dopey. On rare occasions it made him dissolve into hysterical giggles and blissful euphoria. But the more he smoked, the more it simply made him feel numb and slow, and his mind became a fertile breeding ground for paranoid fantasy.

Inhale.

No sound.

Exhale.

Something was nagging at Ed's gut. Something that ran deeper than the indigestion that went hand-in-hand with late night attacks of the *munchies*.

Inhale.

Frowning, he retrieved his mobile phone from the pocket of his dressing gown, staring at the screen as it lit up cheerfully. No signal.

Exhale.

Inhale.

He tried to connect to the internet, and found that both the *wi-fi* and the *3g* service seemed to be out of order. The unsettling dance in his nerves increased in tempo.

Exhale.

The paranoia had its claws deep in his mind; the insistent feeling that somehow he had slept through something important. He took a step back toward the house, dimly wondering if the radio in the kitchen would work - and come to think of it, when had he last needed to use the radio for anything?

Inhale. He flicked the half-smoked joint away, suddenly strangely conscious of the smell that had never bothered anyone before; feeling oddly concerned that it might draw attention to him.

It was as he turned that he saw it. A splash of colour through the gap between the wall of the house and the fence that ran alongside it. A splash of something red. Something that didn't belong.

Ed took a few faltering steps toward the front of the house, cursing his inability to bring his racing mind under control.

Come on, Ed. This is crazy. Freaking out because the internet is down?

He took another step and realised he had been holding his breath. His pulse hammered in his ears and his lungs burned.

Exhale.

Ed choked out the cloud of smoke, feeling himself becoming light-headed. He took another step, and then he saw it, and realised that the squirming feeling of apprehension in his gut was nothing to do with paranoia or late night snacking. It was more like some genetically hard-coded instinct for danger that screamed at him through the gathering fog in his mind.

In the middle of the quiet road that snaked around the expensive houses, Ed saw one of his neighbours.

Or more accurately, what had *been* one of his neighbours. Mr Wallace was now little more than a smear on the road, his throat and abdomen ripped to shreds. It looked like he had been dragged along the tarmac like a grisly piece of chalk, as if someone had interpreted *street art* in the most horrific way possible.

A long streak of gore stretched back from Mr Wallace's prone body for about twenty yards, like he had been trying to crawl away from something terrifying, leaving his life stained on the ground behind him, before he finally succumbed to death.

Ed's mind wanted to stare in open-mouthed astonishment, but his stomach had other ideas, and he bent double and vomited up a foul-tasting brew of half-digested chocolate and cola onto his mother's neat lawn.

Panting, Ed lifted himself upright and choked down the morning air, desperately trying to quell the heaving retches that ripped painfully through his abdomen. He couldn't take his eyes from the corpse. Ed had killed tens of thousands - millions, maybe - of virtual adversaries, and each time he saw explosions of blood erupt across his television screen, his eyes lit up in glee. The real life corpse spread across the road in front of him was nothing like the thousands that littered the save files on his hard drive. It was so still. So *wet.*

What the fuck happened?

Has nobody else seen this?

Where is everybody?

Ed's mind offered up question after question, but no answer was forthcoming. It looked like Mr Wallace had been ripped apart by wild animals or butchered by Hannibal fucking Lecter.

He slipped his phone from his pocket once more. Still no signal.

His gut squirmed.

Ed was only a few yards away from the corpse, drawn toward it by gruesome fascination, when he saw the most horrific aspect of all.

Mr Wallace's eyes were gone, almost like vultures had descended on the body and ripped them out. Ed took another step forward, and then he saw the missing eyes, clenched in the man's dead hand like those spongy stress balls office workers sometimes used to keep themselves from punching their co-workers.

Ed's stomach heaved again, but there was nothing left in there but acidic bile that made his throat burn.

Ed whimpered, and then his mouth dropped in mute horror as he saw a bubble of bloody saliva inflate from the dead man's lips and burst over his ruined face.

Ed's mind had time to process two words - *not dead!* - before the ghastly mess that had been Mr Wallace reached for him feebly, and Ed screamed.

As the high-pitched wail of fright pierced the still air, Ed saw movement everywhere. The small neighbourhood woke as one, crashing through windows and sprinting around corners. All blood-soaked. All snarling.

All coming for him.

Ed's eyes flicked across the mass of furious fleshy motion as it streaked toward him, and he saw immediately what his neighbours had in common. All of them had torn out their eyes.

Ed was running then, his feet racing beyond his dope-wreathed mind. He crashed back into the house, slamming the kitchen door behind him and locking it, snatching up a pathetic butterknife before realising that the blunt blade was useless and tossing it with a shriek.

Panic had him.

Inhale. Exhale. Inhale. Exhale. Inhale. Ex-

The living room window imploded with a deafening crash and Ed heard something impact heavily on the coffee table. For a brief, ridiculous moment, he thought about the bag of marijuana he had left there and felt a dim sort of outrage, but then the thing was in the kitchen, leaping at him, and Ed was falling backwards, watching it tear through the space he had just occupied as he fell. The creature - *Mrs Atkinson? Oh fuck me, that's Mrs Atkinson* - slammed into the kitchen counter with a brutal thud and fell to the tiled floor, writhing and bucking. The noise of the impact seemed to echo through the house oddly, until Ed realised that it wasn't an echo at all. It was another of *them* in the living room, hurtling through the broken window, scrambling across the couch toward the kitchen.

Towards me.

Ed hit the stairs, taking them three at a time, his smoke-wrecked lungs burning in complaint at the unfamiliar imposition of physical movement. He felt fingers grasping at his ankles; felt one of his comfortable house slippers torn away, and he shrieked, pouring every ounce of his energy into ascending.

He made it another three steps before the grasping fingers became clutching fingers and his trailing leg was suddenly locked behind him, bringing him down onto the stairs so heavily that all his breath exploded from his lungs and he saw a brief starburst across his vision.

Ed twisted onto his back and kicked out wildly, connecting the slippered sole of his free foot with the blood-soaked, terrifying face that loomed below him. He put more determination and focus into the kick than he'd put into anything else in years and the creature's nose *exploded*, sending it crashing back down to the base of the stairs where it collided clumsily with two more of its ghastly brethren before popping back to its feet like a jack-in-the-box and making for Ed again.

Ed screamed, scrambling up the rest of the stairs on all-fours in blind terror, throwing himself into the bathroom and slamming the door behind him. He threw across the deadbolt, but he knew the measure would be temporary. The bathroom door was flimsy; the lock even more so. Both were built more for privacy and decorum than keeping a pack of insane killers at bay.

No sooner had the bolt engaged than the door shuddered in its frame under the weight of a solid impact from the other side. Ed watched in frozen horror as the door buckled inward and a small but terrifyingly significant crack appeared in the wood around the lock.

It had been maybe five minutes since Ed had stumbled blearily downstairs into another ordinary day. Five minutes since his greatest concern had been the possibility that he might need a new packet of tobacco. In that five minutes, the entire world had changed into something he couldn't begin to comprehend.

Ed threw open the window in his mother's perfectly-kept bathroom and hurled himself from it without giving a second thought to the drop, or the enormous potential for pain it represented. Seconds later, when the bathroom door splintered and groaned and finally crashed open, the Infected creatures poured into a room that contained a solitary bloodstained slipper.

Outside, Ed was already running.

He hadn't run for anything in years, but on the day everything changed Ed Cartwright ran like a target in the crosshairs.

After only a moment of hesitation, the Infected followed.

*

Pure, dumb luck was what saved Ed that first afternoon.

As he ran, barefoot and terrified, around the twenty houses that made up Orchard Grove, he realised he was fleeing with no destination. If he veered away from the buildings and out into the open, there was nothing but fields and the road that led ultimately to Newborough in one direction and the bridge to mainland Wales in the other.

He doubled back around the houses, back into Orchard Grove, hoping to put enough distance between himself and his pursuers to at least give himself a chance of hiding - in a neighbour's garden shed, maybe, or up a tree. As he continued to loop back and forth along the single winding street, through gardens and over fences, he was suddenly struck by a memory of the old *Benny Hill Show* sketches, the ones where the comedian ran in circles from a crowd of half-dressed women to a jaunty theme tune, and he felt a hysterical sort of amusement building in his mind. Ed couldn't remember whether Hill ever escaped his pursuers - although escape probably wasn't the point of the gag - but he knew he wasn't going to escape the grisly crowd pursuing him. They chased the noise he was making, but if he stopped to remain quiet they'd be right on top of him. It was an horrific catch-22.

He had been running forever, until every muscle burned like it had been dipped in acid, when luck intervened and a vehicle screeched past on the road to Newborough before ending its journey noisily at the base of a tree. The resulting crash drew the Infected away from him, and Ed slowed his pace a little, trying not to gasp explosively for oxygen, and slipped into an open garage, crouching down behind the large Range Rover that sat inside.

He heard a man's voice screaming in the distance: a bloodcurdling yelp of horror that twisted into a ear-bleeding screech of pain which he guessed meant the driver had survived the crash, for a few seconds at least. Ed wondered briefly if the man had been engaged in a twisted Benny Hill sketch of his own. Probably.

Ed hunkered down behind the vehicle for several hours, terrified to move. Once he saw a couple of the Infected shambling past the garage, their mouths and chest drenched in what looked like fresh blood, but it appeared that they moved without purpose.

Nothing to hunt, he thought, and the notion terrified him. With nothing to draw the creatures away, would they simply continue to circle around the houses until they eventually stumbled across him?

When a couple of hours passed without any sign of the creatures, Ed padded to the open garage door, grateful for his bare feet despite the painful bruising the soft soles had suffered in his frantic flight. He wondered idly how humans had coped before they had learned to fashion shoes for their feet.

You have to learn to focus, Edward.

His mother's voice came back to him, a phrase she had used so often that all the texture had worn away from it. Ed had never listened. Only when the world ended did he realise she'd been right all along. Daydreaming suddenly looked like an activity that might get him killed.

Ed cleared his mind of everything but minimising faint noise he was making, and the clammy search for movement on Orchard Grove.

He moved slowly and noiselessly, until he could see the street. It looked empty in both directions.

He made his way silently back to his mother's house. Every fibre of his being screamed at him that he was in the open and exposed; that moving slowly while being hunted was all wrong, but he wrestled the runaway panic under control. The creatures couldn't see. That much was obvious. But they could hear, apparently well enough to track him accurately.

Once he was inside, he shut the door to the living room and barricaded it with a chair placed under the handle. The smashed window meant the living room was like ground lost at war: reclaiming it without further bloodshed looked impossible, and the only blood around to get spilled belonged to Ed. He wanted very much to keep hold of it.

He secured the kitchen door in a similar fashion. Neither barricade would stand up to a concerted attack, and of course the windows were easily breached, but the mere act of fortifying the house made him feel a little better. At least he was doing *something*.

When he was certain his actions hadn't brought any unwanted attention upon him, he retreated up the stairs to his bedroom and sat in silence. Occasionally he checked his phone, though that was an increasingly forlorn exercise.

Days passed.

After a week, when the electricity suddenly stopped working, Ed was certain beyond doubt that no help was coming. For a while he cried softly over the loss of his mother, and wished with all his heart that he had been a better son. And then he cried for himself, for the terrified hopelessness and paralysis he felt. Then he just cried because it seemed like the thing to do, until the tears ran out.

18

Ed took as much food from the kitchen up to the bedroom as possible, working his way through the bread and milk and fruit at first, before eventually resorting to eating uncooked beans and drinking water. He pissed in the bathroom sink so he wouldn't have to flush the toilet. He defecated in a waste paper basket, and soon the house was filled with the overpowering stench of it.

On a couple of occasions he heard distant screaming. Once he heard what sounded like a far-off explosion.

With no food left, the problem of remaining hidden became an issue of surviving or not surviving. Ed had to leave; had to at least get to the next house and hope they had a healthy supply of canned food, or resign himself to starving to death.

He spent a full day debating the situation while his stomach growled at him, frozen in place by doubt and fear. It was how he imagined a terrified first-time parachutist might feel when the plane they travelled in finally reached the necessary altitude and the doors opened.

It's time to go, Ed. It's now or never.

Ed moved lightly, a process which was made easier by the fact he had dropped several pounds in the two weeks since the world ended. Unrelenting terror, it turned out, was a better diet plan than anything *Weightwatchers* could come up with.

He felt comfortable moving softly around the house: at no point over the previous days had the whisper of noise he made as he walked up and down the stairs threatened to bring the Infected to him. It was only when he reached the kitchen door and removed the chair barricading it that his heart started to pound relentlessly.

He scooped up a large knife from the rack on the kitchen counter and held it in trembling fingers. The knife was a good weapon; large and deadly, but Ed had no faith in his ability to use it. It was hard to tell whether clutching the handle made him feel more or less secure.

He opened the kitchen door.

The first thing he noticed was how fresh the air outside smelled. He had, he supposed, gotten so used to the stink of the house that he had stopped noticing it. The crisp air beyond the door tasted incredible, and he paused for a moment to drink it in.

Slow, Ed. Slow.

He forced himself to stand still for a moment, craning his neck left and right to search for any sign of movement and finding none.

Almost in slow motion, he began to creep to the spot at which he had smoked his last joint two weeks earlier, and moved silently toward the front of the house.

Mr Wallace still lay in the middle of the road, but he was definitely dead this time. Ed could see the signs of decay on the flesh, and the rigor mortis that had set in, leaving Wallace's arm pointing toward the sky like an accusation. When he got close enough, Ed could smell him, too; sickening and rotten, like chicken that had been left in the sun for days. He stared at Wallace's body for a few moments, composing himself.

Ed knew all about zombies, of course. He'd popped open thousands of their rotting heads on games like *Left 4 Dead* and *Resident Evil*. He'd watched all the zombie classics. The similarity to the circumstances he had found himself in that first day had not been lost on him, and he had spent a good deal of time since pondering the possibility that an *actual zombie apocalypse* had been unleashed on mankind.

Ed had fantasised about the zombie apocalypse before, idly conjuring up possibilities in the clouds of marijuana smoke. Like many of his peers, he had watched the rise of zombie culture with gleeful appreciation. There was just something so damn *cool* about the concept: something magnetic about the thought of the world being rebooted and everyone getting a chance to start again. The zombie apocalypse would make the world his playground, just like the shopping mall in *Dawn of the Dead*. A world without people. It had always sounded just plain *awesome*.

He had believed that he'd be just fine if the dead rose from their graves. He knew all the tricks, he knew which weapons to use. He knew to aim for the brain.

Turned out the zombie apocalypse was less like an online shooter and more like hiding in your bedroom crying and eating cold beans and breathing in the stink of your own shit.

But in any case, this wasn't *zombies*.

Wallace was as dead as Latin, and he wasn't coming back to life no matter how close Ed got. Ed didn't know if that was something to be thankful for or not. If it had been zombies, he would have at least been reassured that he had some clue what was happening.

Zombies don't exist, Ed. You're losing it.

Glancing around furtively to make sure nothing was creeping toward him, Ed gripped the knife tightly and slipped it into Wallace's torn throat, just to make sure. There was no response. The wet, pliant feel of the man's dead flesh made him gag.

Wincing at the noise he was making, Ed squatted next to the body and searched the dead man's pockets, feeling relief flood through him when he discovered Wallace's keys.

He withdrew them slowly, making certain not to drop them. When he was done, Ed lifted himself upright, and mentally ran through the layout of Orchard Grove. Wallace, he was certain, had lived at number eleven. Only three hundred yards or so along the winding road to his right.

Can't stay here, Ed thought as his tensed muscles did their best to root him to the spot. He set off carefully, paying attention to every footfall, scanning his surroundings and the road in front of his feet with equal concentration.

Ed had no idea how long it took him to negotiate those three hundred yards; it felt like forever. Every step he took was like walking barefoot across broken glass with his eyes closed.

All of the houses on Orchard Grove had been built to individual specifications. There was no uniformity to the designs: some were sleek fabrications of glass and wood; hyper-modern attempts to fuse the buildings with the landscape. Others were low and expansive complexes that looked more like plush public buildings than private homes. Still others were modern twists on old themes, fresh interpretations of stately homes.

Mr Wallace's house was one of the latter: a huge, domineering mock-Georgian mansion that boasted a front porch held aloft on four huge and unnecessary stone pillars. It looked more like a scaled-down museum than a home to a family of four.

Ed slipped under the ostentatious porch, grateful for the cover the pillars provided, and paused a moment to search the gardens for any sign that death was streaking toward him in the dark. His luck seemed to be holding. He cautiously tried to twist the door handle and found it locked.

Ed concentrated on the set of keys he had fished from the dead man's pocket. Thankfully it was a small bunch: one of the keys was very obviously made for a vehicle, and Ed carefully separated that one, making sure he didn't accidentally press the button that would activate the central locking of Wallace's car with a loud *beep*.

Three other keys. Most likely front door, back door and garage. All looked virtually identical.

Turning his back on the world to try each key in the lock felt like painting a neon target on his back, but it had to be done. He tried the first of the keys in the door, and it slid part-way into the lock with a faint *snick* before he met resistance. Not that one.

He shot a sweat-drenched glance over his shoulder. Still no sign of the creatures.

The second key slid into the lock smoothly, and Ed twisted it. The door unlocked with a clunk that made his heart race, and he grasped the handle and looked over his shoulder again. Still nothing.

Ed pushed the door open, and cried out in horror when he saw the eyeless child that had been trapped in the house streaking toward him down the expansive staircase, snarling.

Ed scrambled backwards blindly, slamming the door shut just as the child reached the other side with a solid crunch. The noise reverberated around the quiet street like gunshots, and Ed had time to hear his heart beat once before the sound of footsteps erupted around Orchard Grove. They were coming for him in the darkness.

Which direction?

Ed turned left and right in terror, whimpering, unable to discern the direction of the danger. It sounded like it was coming from everywhere.

It probably is.

He saw the first of them, a fat old woman rocketing toward him like a sprinter; a wobbling mass of flesh and blood and teeth, and Ed took off in the opposite direction.

Straight toward another.

He veered away from the grasping fingers, missing them by inches, trying and failing to stop himself from shrieking in terror, certain that at any moment one of the creatures would leap from the shadows and claw him to the ground, and it would all be over.

The figure came out of nowhere. It was huge, heavily muscled, charging toward him, unleashing a hoarse bellow. Ed didn't know whether to feel terror or relief. The stranger had eyes, at least. He also had a large piece of two-by-four, and he was winding up to swing it at Ed's face. Horrified, Ed ducked low, and heard the whistling wind as the wood arced through the air just above him; heard the wet crunch as the wood connected with bone a fraction of a second later.

Were they that close behind me?

Ed's mind felt like it was breaking apart.

The huge man grabbed hold of Ed's t-shirt and dragged Ed behind him.

He's helping me, Ed thought numbly as the big man focused on swinging the wood at the incoming creatures, winding up like a baseball pro to dispatch home run after home run. Ed watched open-mouthed as his saviour killed six of his former neighbours, savagely crushing their skulls, leaving a trail of twitching corpses on the ground.

When it was done, the man stood for a few moments, his weapon readied, until it became apparent that no more of the Infected were coming toward them.

"How-" Ed began to say, but his voice caught in his throat when he got a good look at the man that had saved him. The guy was big, but every inch of his body appeared to be covered in wounds and livid bruises. Some of the lacerations looked old, healing and scabbing. Others leaked, and Ed caught the scent of them on the breeze; a sickly sort of sweetness that he knew meant infection.

Ed's mind stumbled when he saw that somebody had carved a *smiley face* deep into the man's bare chest.

The big man staggered a little. He looked like he had been at war.

Maybe he has, Ed thought abruptly, *maybe while you were hiding and crying this guy has spent weeks fighting for his life.*

The big man staggered again. It looked like hitting those gruesome home runs had used up his last drop of energy.

Ed opened his mouth to take a second attempt at the question that was trying to take shape in his mind, and closed it again when his saviour's eyes rolled up in their sockets and the big man collapsed.

Ed stared at the prone body for a moment, wondering whether it would spring up like one of the creatures, trying to kill him, or whether the man might just die there on the tarmac. He did neither.

Ed knelt next to the man and gave him a gentle shake. The man's eyes rolled around for a moment, unfocused.

"They're after me," the man slurred, before once again lapsing into unconsciousness.

The man's words drilled down into Ed's nerves, and made them rattle uncomfortably. Whoever was after the guy, it presumably wasn't the horrifying eyeless zombies. He apparently had no problem dealing with them.

Someone else was out there. Ed glanced around the empty street nervously, half-expecting to see someone rushing toward him. There was nothing.

He shook the unconscious man again, but it was like prodding a sack of potatoes.

He's out cold, Ed. He needs your help.

Ed eyed the man's heavy, inert body, and stared back toward his mother's house. The place had run out of canned food, but there was plenty of medication there. The house was three hundred yards away, and the unconscious guy looked like he weighed a ton.

That's just great.

19

The village Emma had described took John by surprise. Not just because it appeared out of nowhere as he rounded a blind corner, but because it was bigger than he had anticipated. He had come to expect that when a Welsh person labelled something a 'village' what they actually meant was 'a few houses'. This was different, though. It even had a small high street. Once it had probably had a population of several hundred. Most of whom, John suspected, had ended up dead on the riverbed next to Caernarfon Castle.

Darkness was falling, and John slowed up abruptly, furtively searching the gloomy houses and gardens for the Infected. It all looked quiet. He could no longer hear the humming, but dismissed the notion that the Infected would have turned inland. Just too convenient. They were still coming, he knew it deep in his writhing gut. He'd be able to hear them in a few minutes.

"We don't have much time," he hissed. "The petrol station."

He jabbed a finger down the main street. About halfway down it stood a small, four-pump fuelling station.

"Look for any vehicle that looks solid. Look for keys. We'll have to get out of here *fast*. Move."

John took off down the street, keeping a wary eye on the windows and doorways as he passed them. If they stumbled across Infected now, he thought, the game would be up. Any more than a couple would be too many to handle, and reinforcements would be arriving at any minute.

John found their escape route right next to the petrol station.

In a side street next to the fuel pumps he saw a small schoolbus. A twelve-seater that had probably delivered all the village's children to the school in Caernarfon, back when education hadn't revolved entirely around surviving by learning to kill.

For a moment John wondered whether Linda had taught the kids who travelled in the vehicle. He dismissed the unhelpful thought immediately, and focused on the bus.

The vehicle looked undamaged, discarded in the middle of the street at an incongruously jaunty angle. A long smear of blood ran from the door at the front, down the entire length of the bus. John's mind wanted to conjure up images of the horror that had almost certainly befallen the passengers, and he told it in no uncertain terms to shut up.

John approached the bus at a canter, slipping inside and sighing in relief when he saw the keys dangling from the ignition. He dearly wanted to test the engine, and ensure they weren't all about to die because of a flat battery, but he didn't dare risk the noise. Against his better judgment, he was going to have to roll the dice. He grimaced.

"In the bus," he whispered, and waited until the others had filed silently into the vehicle before speaking again.

"Rachel," he said finally, "I want this bus ready to move, okay? The minute you see my signal, get that engine running and *go*. Don't stop for anything."

Rachel nodded firmly.

"What's the signal?"

"Fire," John said through gritted teeth. In the distance, he heard the approaching hum of the Infected. Time was slipping away far too quickly.

He leapt from the bus, pausing outside.

"This isn't just about drawing them away from Caernarfon. We have to cut this herd down as much as possible, and that means waiting until the last minute. Everyone stays quiet until the signal. No matter what."

He turned away, jogging lightly around the front of the bus and onto the petrol station's small forecourt. There were a couple of cars near the pumps, abandoned much like the bus. John checked quickly to make sure neither vehicle held any unpleasant surprises for him, and turned to the pumps, lifting the nozzle from its cradle on the nearest of them. He figured it wouldn't take much: a quick spray of petrol around the forecourt, and as long as he left the nozzle resting on the ground the fire would do the rest.

He squeezed the pump's trigger, and heard a dull click and...nothing.

For a moment John stared at the nozzle, dimly wondering how the petrol station could possibly have run out of fuel. He squeezed the trigger again, and again got a click by way of response. No fuel.

Oh shit, John thought as realisation dawned on him. The pumps needed electricity to haul the fuel up from the underground tanks, and electricity had gone the way of the dinosaurs.

He dropped the nozzle to the ground, and began to frantically search the petrol station, hoping desperately to find a container of fuel that he could use to soak the pumps.

Nothing.

The humming was closer now, shaking the air. It sounded like the Infected were right on top of the village. Leaning out onto the street, John peered down the road, but couldn't see any movement. Not that it mattered: the blind corner in the road might spit an army of the Infected up at any moment without warning.

Think.

The answer arrived slowly, sinking into his consciousness, and then he was running, pulling out a knife and slicing through the rubber hose that provided a jet-wash facility for the cars that carried the dirt of the coastal road with them. He cut a length of the hose that measured about three feet, and sprinted back to the first of the two abandoned cars.

Locked.

Who locks an abandoned car?

John felt like screaming, and the urge only increased when he caught a flicker of movement in the corner of his eye. The blind corner had become a terrible pun: Infected filled the width of it, marching straight at him.

As John's heart began to pound out a dreadful rhythm, he scurried to the second car, and breathed a sigh of relief when the door popped open easily. For a frantic moment he scrabbled under the driver's seat, searching for the lever that would release the fuel cap and came up empty. For a horrifying second he thought the car might be one of the older models that needed a key to get at the petrol tank, but then his fingers found the lever and he clenched and pulled.

The fuel cap opened with a soft *pop*.

He slipped the hose into the fuel tank even as the first of the Infected appeared in his line of sight. Panic swelled in his mind, and he fought hard against the instinct to run for safety.

There is no safety now. Not even the castle. If this herd gets through, everyone dies.

John sucked at the end of the makeshift hose, gagging on the foul taste of the air in the petrol tank. For several long seconds nothing happened, and John's mind sagged under the notion that the car had no fuel whatsoever.

That's why it's at a petrol station, you fool.

The petrol surged into his mouth without warning, and it was all he could do to suppress the urge to cough. He badly wanted to spit the fuel out, but even that minimum of noise concerned him, so he let it leak slowly from his lips. Placing the hose on the ground so the fuel pouring from it would remain silent, John stood.

And saw Infected everywhere.

20

Shit.

John had planned to get back onto the bus before the Infected appeared, but he saw immediately that the creatures would block his route to door on the other side of the vehicle.

Wincing and cursing inwardly, he sprinted for the bus, landing on his toes, praying the noise he was making would go unnoticed; knowing beyond doubt that his prayers would go unanswered and that only speed would save him.

A ripple of awareness passed through the first cluster of Infected visibly, beginning with the one leading them. Noise was no longer an issue: John sprinted.

With a final burst of energy, John threw himself at the side of the bus, scaling it and landing on the roof in a single smooth motion. He flattened himself to the surface of the roof, gritting his teeth as the herd began to swarm around the vehicle, searching for the source of the noise.

He dearly wished he was inside the bus, as much to keep the four people hiding inside calm as to get away from the creatures that pooled around it.

If any of the four people separated from him by a thin sheet of metal so much as whimpered, the Infected would tear the bus apart, and then blood would flow like the fuel spreading slowly across the petrol station's small forecourt. There would be no getting lucky this time.

John held his breath while the bus rocked underneath him as the Infected began to stumble into it, and forced himself to wait.

*

Inside the bus, Rachel had watched John scurrying around the petrol station in a rising state of confusion. Only when she finally saw him appear with the hose and drain the fuel tank of one of the parked cars did she understand that John's plan was to blow the place up while they were sitting right outside it.

No wonder he wanted me ready to drive, she thought. *The crazy bastard.*

It was little wonder, either, Rachel realised abruptly, that John hadn't filled any of them in on exactly what he planned to do. It was the same stunt he had pulled on Michael back in Aberystwyth, when he turned a tower block into a gigantic bomb while they all hid inside it. She had understood John's actions then, knowing full well that Michael would have disagreed, and that John's plan had been the only way.

Maybe he was right this time as well, Rachel thought, but that didn't make being left out of the loop any less irritating to her. She wondered briefly if John's *modus operandi* had always been to leap headlong at danger without any planning, and to do it alone. He had done just that back at the retail park. She couldn't decide whether the man was insane or lucky.

When she saw John stand, and fuel pooling around his feet, the look on his face drove all thoughts from her mind beyond one, a single dreadful question that filled her mind.

What's he looking at?

She knew the answer even before she followed his gaze. Before she saw the Infected rounding the corner and appearing on the street in front of her.

She clenched the wheel so tightly that her knuckles ached.

Stay quiet.

From the corner of her eye, Rachel saw John scurrying toward the bus, and felt the vehicle rock slightly as he leapt onto the roof.

He is *crazy.*

Moments later, the bus rocked again, and to Rachel's left, an eyeless face thumped into the window, leaving a streak of gore and gristle behind on the glass as it turned and shuffled around the back of the bus. It was followed by another. And then another. All of a sudden, the windows were full of the Infected, a shambling, dark stain of them that blocked out the light and made Rachel's throat constrict, until it felt as though they were pressing on her neck, cutting off her air supply.

Beads of sweat broke out across her forehead, and the seconds became hours, and with each one that passed, Rachel wondered which of the people in the van would be the first to make a noise and unleash hell upon them all.

Come on, John. What are you waiting for?

*

On the roof of the bus, John remained prone as the Infected swarmed around and underneath him, searching for the source of the soft footsteps they had heard. He heard a strange hissing noise that took him a moment to decipher.

The noise of dozens of nostrils. *Sniffing.*

John's blood froze in his veins. Hadn't Michael said something about one of them trying to locate him by scent?

John had wanted to delay setting the petrol station alight until the creatures surrounded it, giving him a chance of killing as many as possible, but when he heard them sniffing, and realised they were beginning to focus on the bus and would soon be looking for a way in - or *up* - he knew the time for waiting was over. He wanted to kill them all, but he had no interest in doing so by way of suicide.

Holding his breath, he eased himself up from the flat roof, and focused on the ground beyond the Infected, carefully avoiding staring at the animated insanity their faces had become. Fuel had stopped seeping from the car - *didn't have much left in the tank after all* - but there was enough: it had spread across the ground around two of the pumps, and the pumping nozzle he had left on the floor rested in a puddle that would do most of the work. The fumes in the pump would have to do the rest.

John slipped the lighter from his pocket. It was the same scratched *Zippo* he had acquired a thousand lifetimes ago, from a pilot he'd liked at first glance, and had later been forced to kill by jamming a flare gun into the man's open mouth and pulling the trigger. Staring at Ash's burnished gold lighter, John remembered thinking, what felt like an eternity before, that the man's usefulness had ultimately boiled down to him possessing the lighter; no more, no less. He smiled sadly. There was every chance the same could be said of John himself.

Funny, he thought, and thumbed the lighter into life with a soft *snick.*

A shriek multiplied rapidly around him, wrapping him in invisible insanity that clutched at his mind.

The engine roared below him as Rachel decided that waiting for a signal was no longer an option and twisted the ignition, sending a wave of boiling outrage through the creatures flocking around the vehicle.

John tossed the tiny, insignificant flame over the fleshy wall of infected bodies, where it landed with a faint metallic thud in the shallow lake of fuel and began to breed with ravenous hunger, and then fire was everything, and everything was fire.

*

There was no time left to wait for a signal. Rachel saw the Infected swarming around the bus, concentrating on it as a hunter might concentrate on a trap set at a natural choke point. They *knew* there was something in or around the bus. It was a matter of time until they decided that smashing their way through it was the best way to determine just what that something might be.

Sorry, John, she thought. *Hold on.*

She released the handbrake gently, and then twisted the key in the ignition, letting out a scream of pure terror and adrenaline as both the Infected and the engine roared into life simultaneously. In the empty space next to her seat, she saw two knives penetrate the thin roof and realised John was using them as anchors to keep himself on top of the vehicle. Rachel stamped on the accelerator and the bus lurched forward, smashing into the Infected in front, even as they began to throw themselves at it.

Rachel saw her rear view mirror fill with fire bright enough to sear her eyes, and felt the impact slam into the bus at roughly the same moment the immense noise of the explosion reached her, crashing into the back of the bus like traffic, lifting the rear wheels off the ground.

The steering wheel juddered in her hands, but she clenched her fingers tightly, and didn't lift her foot from the accelerator for an instant as the engine shrieked in protest. When the back wheels were once again reacquainted with the road, the bus rocketed forward, and the windscreen filled with blood as she mowed down the Infected, whose assault on the bus had been ended by the reverberating roar of the explosion as the petrol station went up.

Even as the bulk of the herd thinned, and the road cleared, Rachel ensured the windscreen continued to fill with gore and bone, making no attempt to avoid the Infected that clutched their palms to their ears and shrieked in pain, collapsing to the ground as the wall of noise hit them.

In blind fury, screaming until her voice faded into a scratchy choke, Rachel steered toward them, killing everything that stood between the bus and the open road beyond. The bus swerved wildly, the man clinging to the roof of the vehicle completely forgotten.

Only when they had been clear of the herd for twenty seconds and more did Rachel ease up on the accelerator. Slowing the bus was easy, but she thought quelling the urge to scream might take forever.

She heard insistent banging, and raised voices shouting her name, but it took a long time for the noises to mean anything to her. When finally they did, she brought the bus to a stop and leapt outside to see John clinging to the knives he had plunged into the roof like a rock climber hanging over an endless drop, and then she bent double and sucked in a lungful of oxygen that felt like it had been a long time coming.

John withdrew the knives and rolled from the roof, landing next to Rachel. He looked wide-eyed, and as close to terrified as Rachel could imagine him ever being.

"I think I'll drive," he said in a trembling, breathless voice, and Rachel began to giggle uncontrollably, giving in to the hysteria that had nibbled at the fringes of her mind ever since she first sat behind the wheel of the bus.

"Probably for the best," Rachel replied with a wheeze. "I never did pass my driving test."

21

It took Ed a long time to drag the comatose body of his saviour back to his home, and every second of the task was spent steeped in a cold dread at the noise he was making and the fact that he was unable to check every direction all at once. He felt hopelessly exposed.

More than once he thought about leaving the man and heading back alone to find some medication. He dismissed the idea primarily because the man surviving would mean an end to Ed's isolation.

Of course, saving the guy was the *right* thing to do, and his mother would have approved - which was rare in itself - but try as he might, Ed couldn't persuade himself that his actions were in any way noble. Not that it really mattered. There was no one left to judge him.

By the time Ed reached the door that led back into the kitchen he had only just abandoned, he was panting heavily and sweating from the exertion of hauling the heavy man, despite the weight he had already lost. The apocalypse was no place for couch potatoes. He eyed the unconscious man's bulging muscles and resolved to get fitter as soon as was practicably possible.

It was a life-long promise to himself that he had repeatedly broken, but if the whole world had turned into a vast replica of the madness on Orchard Grove, Ed realised that physical strength had once again become vital for survival.

For centuries advancement in life had been a cerebral matter: it was intelligence that promised a healthy future. Physicality only had any relevance in the schoolyard, and it quickly faded into obscurity thereafter. But now the whole world was a vicious playground, and that was a fact that made Ed exceedingly nervous. His experience at school, when hierarchy *had* been a physical matter and Ed had found his head plunged into a flushing toilet more than once, did not bode well.

There was no way Ed was going to be able to drag the huge man up the stairs to the relative safety of one of the bedrooms, so he settled for laying him on the floor in the hallway, away from all the windows, and raced upstairs to fetch a blanket and as much medication as he could carry from the bathroom cabinet.

His mother's nursing job meant she kept her medical supplies well stocked: Ed had often joked that she was turning the house into a pharmacy. His mother never engaged in conversation about it. She was, Ed thought, probably unwilling to dwell on the subject, because it would inevitably lead to questions about where the prescription-strength painkillers she kept stocking the closet with disappeared to. They both knew the answer, of course, but as long as they never discussed it, they could avoid adding Codeine to the list of Ed's addictions.

In the bathroom, he took the Codeine, as well as several bottles that sounded like antibiotics. *Just get everything that ends in 'cillin',* Ed thought, *and you won't go far wrong.*

He took some antiseptic ointment and anti-bacterial handwash to clean the man's wounds, and a roll of gauze to bandage them. It was hardly comprehensive, but it was the best Ed was going to manage. There were several other medications in the cabinet with names that bewildered him. Many he hadn't even realised were there. He saw the label *anti-depressant* on one half-empty bottle, and his heart ached.

The first task was to clean the man's skin, which was liberally caked in blood and dirt. Ed used almost the whole bottle of handwash. It was one of those no-water-required types that were now rife throughout UK hospitals as they had tried to battle the growing threat of MRSA. Ed's mother had taken that threat seriously and stocked the house with the stuff as well, washing her hands in it after she touched pretty much anything. It was, Ed thought, more of a nervous compulsion than anything else.

The bottle advised him to keep the contents away from open wounds, so he figured it would probably sting, but several of the cuts looked dark and rotten with infection. It was best not to take chances.

The man was bare-chested, and Ed was grateful that he remained unconscious as Ed treated his wounds. It was an oddly tender, intimate endeavour that made Ed squirm with embarrassment. He kept going despite his discomfort, because the idea of being left alone again was far worse than rubbing lotion on another man's body.

Finally, as Ed slathered the handwash over a long, ragged cut that started at the man's shoulder and ended almost at his waist, Ed's patient flinched, almost making him cry out in surprise.

The man's eyes were open, but unfocused. He stared blearily at Ed.

"Just trying to clean you up, big man," Ed said. "You have some nasty looking cuts here, okay? Just trying to help."

"Hurts, mum..." The guy moaned, before slipping away from consciousness again. He didn't wake as Ed smeared his body with the ointment and bandaged a couple of the larger wounds, but when Ed was done, he spoke to the man anyway, because it felt good just to have someone to speak to again, whether they heard him or not.

"You'll be alright here, big man," Ed whispered. "I'm going to get some food and then I'll be right back, okay?"

There was no trace of acknowledgement on the man's face. He was out cold.

Ed covered him with the blanket, and started for the kitchen door when suddenly the man's words came back to him.

They're after me.

Ed had no idea who might be after the injured man. He realised abruptly that he might be helping a bad guy, someone that the authorities were after, maybe. It didn't feel like that, though. And besides, Ed had a feeling the authorities were long gone; if they weren't, he would be putting in an official complaint to *someone* about being left alone on a street full of corpses and murderous self-harming psychopaths.

He stared back at the comatose man.

Whatever he is, Ed, he saved your life. Can't leave him there.

After a moment of furious thought, Ed strode past the man and opened a small door to a large storage space under the stairs, and heaved the man's solid body inside. He covered him again with the blanket, this time pulling it up over his face, and for good measure dragged a toolbox in front of the sleeping mound to obscure it a little.

If anybody searched the place thoroughly, they'd find the man, but he would pass a cursory inspection. It would have to do.

Ed closed the door to the cupboard softly, and once again stepped out onto Orchard Grove with his heart in his mouth.

The Infected girl was still trapped in Mr Wallace's house somewhere, so he discounted the idea of trying there again. He had the keys; he didn't quite have the courage. Instead he turned left, suspiciously peering at the trail of corpses that now littered the street, their lives crunched to an end by a mighty swing of the two-by-four. Again he half expected to see one of them rise up as a walking corpse and shamble toward him, but there was no movement.

He made his way cautiously toward the nearest neighbour in the other direction. The house built by the Atkinson family was the polar opposite of Mr Wallace's attempts to recreate history. The Atkinson house was all glass and sharp edges, ultra-modern and, Ed thought, kind of ugly for it. The entire front of the house was dominated by floor-to-ceiling glass. At least if there *was* an Infected creature trapped inside, he'd see it coming.

And how will you get inside?

Ed approached the house quietly, feeling like his eyes were stretched painfully wide to catch a sign of movement. All clear.

He had thought he might have to smash a window to get into the building, and the idea that he might set off a burglar alarm made his nerves sing, but as he neared the front door he saw there would be no need. The door was a single sliding piece of glass that was all but invisible, and had always struck Ed as an annoyingly pretentious method to use for an entrance to a house. It was also wide open, a gaping maw that stood out from the rest of the frontage because it didn't catch and reflect the fading light.

He slipped inside, and found himself in a large living room.

For a moment he was struck by the fact that he had never once stepped into his neighbour's house; in fact he had no idea what the interior looked like at all. Apparently it took an apocalypse to bring neighbours together. And even then only because one half was trying to steal the other's food, and one half had decided the other *was* food.

Fucked. Up.

Focus.

The living room was open-plan, arranged around a fireplace that acted as a focal point. Ed saw a heavy-looking poker sitting next to it, and snatched it up, relishing the solid weight of it in his hand.

He moved slowly through a large arch that led to a gleaming kitchen of chrome and black marble, half-expecting something to pounce from a dark corner. His grip on the poker tightened.

The kitchen was empty.

Heaving a sigh of relief, Ed scurried to the row of cupboards over the kitchen counter. In the second one, he hit the jackpot: two shelves of canned food and sachets of dried pasta and cup-a-soup that only required hot water. The thought of eating something warm made him salivate.

After a brief search, he found a plastic bag tucked in a drawer, and began to load as much of the food into the bag as possible.

He was just dropping a curry-flavour *pot noodle* into the bag and promising himself it would be the first thing he would eat when he heard a noise that made him freeze, almost dropping the bag in fright.

Footsteps.

22

Michael's mind was sick with anxiety and memories. He sat alone in the ground floor room he had made his own. It was the room in which he had spent his first night in the castle. The room in which he had gunned down an old woman who didn't understand why the man she had trusted was pointing a gun at her.

Sickening images lurched through his mind. Carl. Victor. Jason. Gwyneth. Darren. A man dragging a blade across a squealing baby's throat. A roll call of the dead that followed in his wake, trailing him like a shadow.

All Michael had wanted was to survive, to live for his daughter. He still *lived* but he was no longer certain that he had survived at all, and certainly not without taking major damage.

Who am I?

Behind all the images and the nauseating self-doubt, there was the number. Ticking steadily downward. Edging toward zero.

Twenty-three.

If John and the others didn't make it back, Michael reasoned, his time at the castle was most likely up. There were a handful of people left in Caernarfon that could handle themselves if violence erupted. He didn't count himself: if for some reason he lost the rifle, he would be worse than useless. The children would be little help, and at least half of Darren's people laboured under psychological scars that made them distant and unreliable.

Without John and Rachel; without Ray and Shirley - and even Glyn - what hope was there of making a life in the castle viable? Going outside would mean death. Staying inside would mean starvation and slow decay. He cursed himself for letting the others go, and with every second that passed he felt more and more certain they were already dead.

For a couple of hours after John had led the others out of the castle, Michael sat alone in morbid silence, letting a heavy fog of depression settle across his thoughts. Nothing he did seemed to make either himself or his daughter any safer.

"Dad?"

With an effort, Michael turned his attention outwards. He hadn't even realised Claire had entered the room. He wondered briefly how long she had been watching him; what dark secrets she might have seen written on his face.

"What should we do?" Claire asked. "Is the boat coming back?"

"Most likely," Michael said a little wearily. He had told Claire about the boat only because she had questioned him incessantly about John and Rachel's whereabouts. He had told nobody else. All those who hid in the stone towers when the boat passed didn't seem to have heard the engine, or at least they didn't feel like talking to Michael about it.

"But John thinks they might be bad guys, and we might have to keep them out."

Claire nodded, frowning.

"How?" She said.

Michael smiled despite himself.

"You know how some animals make themselves look big, to scare off other animals?"

Claire nodded slowly.

"We have to do that. We have to make them think the castle is full of people, and then they'll think twice about trying to come in."

"But I thought we wanted other people to come," Claire said uncertainly.

"We did," Michael said with a sigh. "But I'm not sure these other people are going to be friendly. The people who've made it this far, well, they are probably frightened. They've had a bad time, and that makes them dangerous. You know what I mean?"

"I think so," Claire said. "But what if they're not? I mean, you made it, and you're not dangerous."

Michael said nothing. As he stared at his daughter's trusting face, his eyes slowly filled with tears. He blinked them away.

"Tell you what," Michael said. "There's something you and Pete can do to help. It's important."

Claire brightened.

"Find every candle you can get your hands on. Or lamps, lanterns, anything you can find like that, okay?"

"Like a treasure hunt," Claire said, and her eyes shone eagerly.

"Exactly," Michael said with a smile, giving Claire's narrow shoulders a squeeze. "Once you find them, bring them to me, okay? As much as you can carry. As quick as you can."

Claire stood up straight, and delivered a salute.

"Yes, Sir!" She said, and scampered away.

Michael returned the salute with a smile, and wondered dimly where she had learned the gesture. As she scampered away dutifully, Michael lapsed back into his memories.

*

Hello, Michael, take a seat."

Susan motioned to the couch with a warm smile, and gathered her jacket tightly around herself as she sat behind her desk.

"It's a little chilly today, isn't it? Do you need me to turn the air-conditioning down?"

She smiled again. Susan smiled a lot. It was, Michael supposed, a conscious effort on her part. All part of the web of therapeutic illusion she carefully crafted. He imagined that all the counsellors out there - all the good ones, at least - smiled all the time: big plastic grins that came straight from the *Good Therapy* textbook. Still, she wore the smile well. Across the five sessions they had following Michael's murder of a member of the public, he had grown to like her. The smile, he thought, was practiced, but not fake.

He shook his head, and looked at her expectantly.

Susan flipped open a large journal.

"Last time we were talking about your father. About you growing up with his illness."

Illness. Michael's father would never have called his depression that. He never talked about it at all, of course, but Michael knew the man didn't think of depression as an illness. It was a *flaw.*

"My father's illness," - Michael couldn't keep the bitter inflection from his voice; the inherited disdain - "is nothing to do with this. Even if it were hereditary, it's not the reason I am here."

Susan nodded, her face contemplative.

"Some people believe everything is connected," Susan said breezily. "Everything we do has a root cause, and one thing leads to the next, even if we're not aware of it."

"Cause and effect?" He asked. "What does that have to do with anything?"

"You are here, Michael," Susan said kindly, "because of your response to a specific situation. You are also here to understand why you responded in that manner. Why do *you* think you responded the way you did?"

"The guy killed a baby in front of me. My response was..." He trailed off. The sentence, he realised abruptly, had no ending in his mind.

"You've been an officer for some time," Susan said. "You've been faced by violence before, and highly-charged situations. Have you ever responded emotionally?"

"No," Michael said immediately.

"So what was different this time? The crime was appalling, yes, but what else?"

Michael opened his mouth, and again his mind let him down. In none of their other sessions had Susan fired questions at him in such rapid succession. Normally she smiled and nodded and let Michael talk about whatever popped into his mind. He felt like a boxer on the ropes, hiding behind his guard and hoping to ride out the punches.

"Maybe you are right," Susan said. "Maybe it's nothing to do with your father. Anything more recent?"

Suddenly Michael saw where she was going, and relaxed a little. It was familiar ground at least, something they had already discussed.

"You think this is about my wife leaving me?" He said, and fabricated a scaffold of mock disbelief to prop the question up. "We already talked about that."

He shrugged.

"Briefly," Susan replied. "You don't seem to think the collapse of your marriage has affected you."

"It hasn't," Michael snapped.

"Everyone responds to trauma differently, Michael," Susan said with something approaching a sigh. "For some people the response is instant and unmistakeable. For others it might manifest years later, triggered by unrelated events. For some people, it can alter them permanently, unless they are able to address the underlying issues."

Susan leaned forward and fixed him with a smile, and Michael suddenly felt as though she was a different person, someone trying to forge a real connection that went beyond the professional. The smile was genuine, and there was concern in her eyes.

"You have suffered a trauma, Michael, and now you have beaten a suspect to death. Yet you present yourself as unaffected, as though you believe there is no connection at all."

"Because there isn't," Michael responded, a little too quickly. "I'm not programmed to respond in a certain way to anything. Nobody is. If that were true then everybody could have a murderer lurking inside them, just waiting for the trigger that brings them out."

"We're not here to talk about *everyone*, Michael," Susan said with a smile. "Just you."

It was the closest any of Michael's therapy sessions came to looking at something he didn't want to see. He had nodded and smiled at Susan, refusing to engage her words as anything more than homespun wisdom, and the sessions soon returned to the mundane, until finally he told Susan he was feeling fine and stable and happy, and was ready to return to work. He had, he said, come to understand that it was all to do with his father after all, and spun a tale of coming to terms with the fact he suffered from depression and would look into getting medication. He repeated it often enough that eventually Susan had little choice but to agree to end the therapy.

As Michael stared through the thick stone of Caernarfon Castle's walls, he thought about that strange barrage of questions from Susan, and the odd feeling that she was trying to cast aside the therapist/patient relationship and really *talk* to him.

And about the possibility that an intrinsic darkness lurked inside him, something inevitable and fundamental.

*

Michael was still lost in brooding silence when Linda stepped into his room, startling him.

"Sorry," she said with a grin. "I can come back if you're busy...uh...staring at the wall?"

Michael smiled wearily.

"Just thinking," he said.

"Ouch. I don't think there's a cure for that."

Michael laughed softly.

"Everything okay?"

Linda nodded.

"Everything apart from your daughter taking away all my candles."

"Ha, sorry about that. She's on a...secret mission, I guess you could call it."

Linda nodded solemnly.

"So I gathered. It's sort of why I wanted to talk to you."

"Oh?"

Linda drew in a deep breath, and Michael felt his nerves begin to prickle.

"The thing is," Linda said, "I get that you guys are all close. You and John and Rachel. And everyone is grateful for you being here, and getting rid of Darren, really. But it sort of feels like you're all keeping yourselves separate from the rest of us, you know? And I don't think it's helping the general mood in here. Everyone is confused, Michael. All of a sudden half the men in this place are gone, and you're...well, I don't know what you're doing. But I know something is going on, and I'd like to know what it is."

Linda rushed through the final few words in a single breath, like she wanted to get them out before she had a chance to reconsider.

Michael blinked.

Is she afraid of me?

He knew the answer immediately. Of *course* Linda was afraid. *Everybody* was afraid. The people in the castle had transitioned from being terrified of a man who openly intimidated them to being wary of a man who told them very little and kept a gun on show at all times. When he thought about how things must have looked to Linda - and everyone else - he felt like laughing at the absurdity of it all.

He snorted and smiled broadly.

Linda flushed angrily.

"I didn't pick you for the kind of guy who would-"

Michael held up his hands apologetically and Linda fell silent, glaring at him.

"You're right. I'm sorry, I was just laughing at, I don't know, how ridiculous this all is, I suppose. I always did spend too much time in my head. It's just that before there weren't people around me wondering if I was planning to kill them or something."

He grinned.

"I don't think anyone thinks that," Linda said cautiously. "But the fact is that everybody here had just gotten used to the way things were. No one liked it, but everyone knew where they stood. Now we've got a group of bikers in here, and they pretty much keep to themselves. We've got John telling everybody the castle isn't safe and trying to train a bunch of terrified teenage girls to use swords without telling them *why* and Rachel, uh, well, Rachel frankly scares the shit out of me. And then there's you, and you don't seem to be talking to anyone at all."

Linda shrugged.

"I just want to know what's going on. Where did John go? And why have I just lost all my candles?"

Linda smiled weakly. It wasn't much of a joke, but Michael could tell she wanted to keep things light-hearted. He appreciated it. Wished he could have answered in the same vein.

Michael sighed.

"I don't know where to begin," he said.

"Let's try the beginning," Linda replied.

Michael nodded, and thought about his sessions with the therapist, and about cause and effect, and realised he was no longer sure where the beginning actually began.

Panic crawled along Ed's nerves, turning his blood to ice and spreading a fearful, immobilising chill through his body. He stood, paralysed, in the dark kitchen, listening to the approaching footsteps. The sound was like a ticking timer. A countdown to something terrible that approached him unseen in the gloom.

The steps were slow and shuffling, but definitely coming closer. Maybe the Infected converging outside didn't know he was there. Indecision pulled his mind apart.

Run? Hide?

The footsteps got closer. Closer.

They're right outside the house.

Ed swallowed painfully, his mouth suddenly dry enough to plant the horrific notion of coughing into his mind, and he lifted the poker, eyes scanning each of the kitchen's three large windows for movement outside. If they entered the living room first, he might have a chance to smash through one of the windows and flee. If one of the things threw itself through the glass, he would sprint back the way he came, out the living room and away from the building.

If they block both exits, you'll have to fight. And die.

The footsteps stopped.

Ed clenched his teeth so tightly that his jaw ached.

What are they doing?

As if in response, Ed heard something that almost made him lose his grip on the poker.

"You sure he went in there?"

A whispered hiss in the gathering darkness.

People.

For a moment Ed felt like laughing in relief, but something held him back. Some primitive instinct; long dormant but now screaming for his attention. Maybe it was the troubling tone of the voice he heard. Or maybe it was the words of the man lying unconscious in his mother's storage cupboard: *they're after me.*

"And he definitely wasn't infected?" A second voice, deeper than the first.

"Didn't look like it. He wasn't moving the way they do." A third voice.

"Then he's probably in there right now listening to every word you idiots are saying." A fourth voice. "Which is probably going to make him more difficult to catch, right?" The fourth voice lifted until it was almost a shout, and Ed realised the speaker was now addressing him directly, and they definitely did not sound friendly.

Catch?

The word burned itself into Ed's consciousness. Burned bright. A unique choice of word; particular and sharp enough to cut a long furrow of anxiety in his mind.

"Maybe he's even got a weapon in there?"

Ed placed the bag of food down on the tiled floor gently, keeping an eye on the archway that led into the huge glass-fronted living room. They were out front, apparently hesitant to enter the property so directly, but Ed didn't think that would last long. As soon as one of them stepped into the living room they'd see him standing there frozen in place like a terrified child.

Move!

There was another door leading from the kitchen, and Ed bolted through it, finding himself in a large double garage.

There was no easy way out, unless he pressed the button he saw on the wall that would open the garage doors and which would give away his position in an instant.

His breath poured from his lungs in rapid, shallow gasps that made him feel as lightheaded as a deep bong hit. He saw one alternative, set high in the rear garage wall: a narrow window that Ed definitely wouldn't have fitted through two weeks earlier. Even with the starvation-induced weight loss, the pane looked too narrow.

Beyond the kitchen, he heard the first of the men outside entering the house. Heard them say *can't see him*, and felt his bladder loosen a little. Staring at the door to the kitchen, he took the only option available to him and slid the poker through the handle like a deadbolt. If they tried the door, the game would be up, but the improvised lock would buy him time.

Leaning close to the barred door, he listened intently. It sounded like they were all in the house now, and Ed thought he could hear faint whispering, but nothing that resolved itself into words.

His face was only inches from the door when it began to rattle as someone pulled it from the other side. Ed stumbled backwards, biting down on the urge to cry out.

"This one's locked," a voice whispered from beyond the door.

He heard a response, but it was muddy and indistinct. Moments later he heard two sets of footsteps climbing the staircase that led from the living room to the upper floor.

When they find out you're not up there, they'll be coming back to this door.

Ed's subconscious had developed a troubling habit of delivering news he didn't want to hear, but he knew it was the truth. It might take them five minutes to search the house, but once they had eliminated all the rooms they would know exactly where he was hiding. They might not be able to break into the garage, but they didn't need to. If they were determined to get Ed, they could just wait him out.

Or set fire to the house.

Ed told his subconscious to shut the *fuck* up and frantically searched the garage for some means to defend himself. Surprisingly enough, the Atkinson family didn't keep a range of weapons in their garage. Just some storage boxes, half-empty paint cans and various unhelpful stacks of old crap, alongside the small sports car that Ed had seen Mr Atkinson driving. The man had looked ridiculous: fat and middle-aged, driving ninety-grand-plus of midlife crisis with a v-8 engine and apparently no idea that he was a bloated cliché.

The door leading to the kitchen rattled again, and then shook as someone delivered a heavy kick from the other side.

Focus!

Flicking the switch to open the garage door would alert the men searching the house for him, but there was nothing else for it. The moment the garage door was a foot off the floor, Ed would be scrambling underneath it and bolting. He knew Orchard Grove well. Just had to find somewhere to hide; had to move quick. Speed had never particularly been a strong point for Ed, but he had a sudden feeling that sprinting was just a matter of motivation, and he had plenty to spare.

The door shook under another kick, but the poker held firm. They could kick it a thousand times and the improvised lock would hold.

Ed paused in front of the switch on the wall, marked *open* and *close*. Once he hit the switch, he would have a couple of seconds to wait until there was enough of a gap to squeeze through.

That wait would be the worst couple of seconds Ed could imagine anyone having to endure. He paused, scarcely able to believe what he was doing. It all seemed like a bizarre dream.

Another kick brought him back to life and he flicked the switch to the *open* position.

It responded with an apologetic click.

Ed's eyes widened.

No electricity.

Ed's mother had been right: his stupid, dope-addled brain would let him down one day, just when he needed it most.

Like now.

Trapped in the garage, wincing at the rattling of the door to his left and unable to open the door in front, Ed's mind promptly went blank, apparently choosing that very moment as a perfect time to take a brief vacation.

Shit.

Things couldn't get much worse.

Ed heard mumbling on the other side of the door. At least two of them were in the kitchen. He imagined the other two were waiting outside the garage, just in case Ed somehow found a way to open the door.

He pressed his ear to the door, trying to make out the words.

"You sure it was him?"

Ed frowned.

The response was too distant; too muffled. He couldn't make it out.

"What's the point? The dumb bastard barely understands a word anyone says anyway," The first voice said.

They think I'm him.

Another indistinct mumble from inside the kitchen.

"Fuck's sake," the first voice said loudly, and the door rattled under another heavy impact.

Ed leapt away from it, startled, and sent another furtive glance around the dark garage. There were a couple of spanners and screwdrivers he could use as weapons, and if he withdrew it quickly enough, he could still use the poker. But the image of him brandishing a poker and fighting off four men was something from a darkly comedic nightmare. Something he could easily accomplish with an *xbox* controller. Not while almost pissing himself with terror in his neighbour's garage.

His eyes fell again on the narrow window, and once more he frantically tried to judge whether his frame would fit through or whether he should just wait them out, when the voice on the other side decided for him.

"Find something to get this door down."

Ed clambered on top of a new-looking washing machine and felt along the window pane and discovered there was no latch. The window was designed only for light to get in; not for potential victims to get out.

Ed's brow furrowed in frustration. He was going to have to smash the window, but the men trying to catch him would surely hear the shattering glass and make their way outside. Motivation or not, Ed doubted he would outrun them if they were out there waiting when he emerged through the window. His only chance was getting a head start.

Need to make a noise, he thought, *need to cover the sound of the glass breaking.*

He turned, and looked down on the garage.

And on Mr Atkinson's ninety grand sports car, and Ed astonished himself with a grin. He didn't have keys, but the car would make noise without them. Noise that he had heard many times before, reverberating around the neighbourhood irritatingly.

He jumped down and pulled on the car door, and his grin widened when the deafening alarm burst into life, valiantly trying to inform its dead owner of the attempted entry. In the confined garage, the noise was ear-splitting. Still grinning, Ed leapt back onto the washing machine, and drove the spanner into the glass.

The window was too narrow. There really hadn't been much doubt in Ed's mind from the moment he first felt for a latch to open it. Even if he could somehow squeeze his shoulders through it, he imagined himself getting stuck at the waist and being left to just hang there like a drying ham until the men found him.

That was why, when the car alarm finally shut down with a final dramatic *peep* and the men waited outside the garage door patiently, expecting it to open and a car to roar through it at any moment, Ed was still inside, holding his breath on the cold concrete floor directly under the now-silent Aston Martin.

Come on, he thought, *just check the back.*

He almost jumped clear through the engine when he heard a voice at the smashed window, so loud and clear it sounded like the speaker was standing right next to him.

"Shit...guys. I think he's gone."

Ed heard footsteps making their way from the front of the garage to the back. A moment later he heard a grunt and then a beam of light lanced through the broken window, playing over the garage interior.

Ed knew he was taking a risk: if the men outside stopped to think for a moment they would surely realise the window was too narrow for anyone to climb through.

He prayed they would see the glass outside and jump to conclusions.

Ed held his breath; only released it when the light withdrew and he heard the voice he recognised as being the one he had heard earlier in the kitchen. The voice sounded weary, and irritated. No, *furious*. Dangerous.

"Spread out. Fucking find him or she'll kill us all."

Exhale.

Ed waited until he heard the footsteps recede into silence before shuffling out from under the car. He rolled clear of the vehicle before standing, fearful that even the slightest touch would unleash the alarm again and render the ruse meaningless. Careful to remain quiet, he climbed back onto the washing machine and peeked through the smashed window. He saw their flashlights immediately: a four splashes of light in the darkness. It looked like they were a few hundred yards away already, searching the road and the gardens. If they were planning to be as thorough as he feared, they might start entering the houses when they couldn't find him. The man he had left under a blanket in the cupboard would be in danger, then.

And what am I going to do about it? I'm no hero.

When Ed was certain all of the men were far enough away, he eased the poker that had barred the door to one side, and stepped once more into the dark kitchen, almost tripping over the bag of food he had dropped on the floor, and congratulating himself on his clever little plan.

He stepped over the bag and into the glass-fronted living room.

And knew immediately that he wasn't as smart as he had believed, and that four flashlights did not necessarily mean four people.

He hadn't been able to see the dark figure waiting for him in the living room. He saw the fist that arced through the gloom, though; saw it at the last second, when it was mere inches from his face, and then everything was darkness.

24

Michael told Linda everything. Once the words began to fall from his mouth, it seemed they gained a momentum of their own and he was powerless to stop them. He told her about the first morning, about Carl and his stale doughnuts and his terrifying transformation into an eyeless killer. Told her about Victor and the bunker, about his frantic flight to Aberystwyth to find his daughter. Told her about John and Project Wildfire.

He told her about the corridor of blood and bone and about killing Gwyneth; about the beginning and what he had thought was the end when he had finally secured the castle and locked the virus outside.

As he spoke, his voice cracked and lowered, and by the time he was done, tears flowed freely from his eyes, and he was surprised to find that Linda was weeping too.

"I didn't know what to do," Michael said in a choked voice. "She was infected. It was the only way to keep everyone safe."

Linda stared at him for a moment and said nothing.

"You have to tell everyone else," Michael said. "I understand. I'm a killer. And if everyone wants me to leave I will. I won't cause trouble."

Linda's eyes shimmered, and she leaned forward and wrapped her arms around Michael, hugging him tightly.

Michael blinked in surprise, and returned the hug awkwardly.

"You've done terrible things," Linda breathed in his ear, and pulled away from him, staring into his eyes. "I can't imagine there's anyone left who hasn't. Maybe you could have chosen another way. Maybe I could. Maybe Darren could. Or John. Whoever. It doesn't matter, Michael. You're here. You're still alive. Your daughter is alive. Right now she needs you, and for better or worse everybody here needs you to pull yourself together."

Michael stared at her in faint astonishment. He had expected revulsion and fury. Her unexpected response very nearly made him break down completely.

Linda smiled.

"Now, I didn't ask to hear your whole life story, Officer Evans. I asked where John had gone, and where the hell my candles have disappeared to."

Michael snorted a laugh.

"I'm afraid that isn't exactly good news either," he said.

"Why am I not surprised?"

Michael nodded grimly.

"There was a boat. Came close and then disappeared. John thinks it was a scouting mission, and I guess he would know."

"Scouting for who?"

Michael shrugged.

"No idea. But it looks like there are other people close by, and they know we are in here."

"So why wouldn't they come to the castle?"

Michael looked at her wryly.

"Oh," Linda said, and sighed. "I guess it would be too much to ask that people stopped fighting each other at a time like this."

"I don't think it's in our nature," Michael said glumly.

"So what about the candles?"

"John thinks they'll be coming back. Maybe in force. The only thing I can think to do is make it look like there are a *lot* of people in the castle, Get a light in every window, get bodies up on the battlements. Maybe if we don't look weak they'll think twice about trying to get in here."

Linda frowned.

"Maybe," she said, but her tone said she didn't quite believe it.

That makes two of us, Michael thought.

"You can't keep this stuff from everybody, Michael. We have to tell them what's coming. They have a right to know, and the uncertainty is just making everything worse. Who knows, maybe what we all need right now is something to focus our minds. You must have known you'd have to tell them eventually, unless you were just hoping everyone would feel like a stroll on the battlements and wouldn't notice a boat heading for us. I know you guys think a lot of us here in the castle are damaged and useless-"

Michael raised his hands to protest, but Linda waved his objection away.

"And you might be right," she continued. "But everyone has the right to fight for themselves if it comes to it. We might just surprise you."

Michael nodded slowly.

Before he could respond, the door opened, and Claire and Pete appeared, each carrying an armful of candles and oil lamps. Claire beamed proudly at Michael, and his face split in a smile.

"Then let's do it," he said.

*

Ed awoke on a hard, ridged mattress that felt more like the back of a flat-bed truck than a bed. He was freezing, and it almost felt like the wind had relentlessly whipped him as he slept. He frowned a little as he lurched toward consciousness.

Once or twice, in an effort to get her lazy son out of bed, Ed's mother had deliberately opened all the windows in his bedroom, allowing the coastal wind to freeze him until he woke up. Clearly, she was up to her old tricks again.

"Mum," he slurred disapprovingly.

That explains the cold. Why is your bed so hard?

Ed's eyes flared open, and he found himself staring up at sky that flitted on the fading edge of full darkness, and the memories flooded back to him.

Mum's dead. Everybody's dead.

Why am I not dead?

Ed sat upright, or at least tried to. He was able to arch his back a few degrees before he met resistance. He twisted his neck as far to the side as he could, and his eyes widened in fear.

The reason his bed had felt like the back of a truck is because that's exactly what it was. And he was tied to it. He saw a large building looming above him to his right. It was hard to tell, but Ed thought it looked a little like the hotel that served the golf course a couple of miles south of Orchard Grove.

Which means I'm tied up in the car park.

Ed's mind refused to process the notion.

"Uh...hello?" He said, and berated himself for how pathetic he sounded. Nobody, he thought, had ever woken up kidnapped and tied up, and responded so feebly.

"Kid's awake," a voice said. Ed recognised it as the voice of the man that had knocked him unconscious in Mrs Atkinson's kitchen.

"It's about time. Go get her."

"What should I say?"

"I don't fucking know. Just get her out here."

"Should I say we didn't find him?"

"Not if you want to keep your nuts attached. Let her find out herself. She'll take it out on *somebody*. Let that somebody be this guy, if you know what I mean."

Ed heard a grunt of acknowledgement, and then footsteps receded away from him. He had listened to the entire conversation in a state of increasing panic and confusion. He had no idea who the men were, nor who the woman they were talking about was, but it was obvious to him that both his captors were terrified of her. If they were terrified...

The old saying about shit rolling downhill popped into Ed's thoughts abruptly, like a rotten smell.

I'm the bottom of the hill...

He spent a few moments testing out his bonds, but they all seemed secure. His brow beaded with sweat that froze on the cold breeze, and he implored his foggy brain to come up with something - *anything* - resembling a plan to save himself from the strange group of people. His subconscious offered up numerous options that might have served Steven Seagal or Jackie Chan very well indeed, but it came up disappointingly short of ideas that might be of benefit to a slightly overweight Welsh pothead.

"Uh...are you still there?" Ed asked feebly.

He heard a grunt of acknowledgment.

"If you guys are after money, uh, I don't have any, but my mother-"

Ed couldn't see the man from his position, but the caustic laugh that interrupted him made his muscles tense up. He wanted more than anything to put on a brave front. It was somewhat dismaying to realise that he was already on the verge of sobbing.

"Who the *fuck* is that? Where's Voorhees?"

An old woman's voice, dry and rasping. The harsh tone of her words slipped under Ed's skin like a splinter. This, presumably, was the *her* that the two men had seemed so afraid of.

"Ask this guy. He saw him. Claims he doesn't know anything about it."

Ed felt outrage building inside him. He didn't remember having claimed anything of the sort. Bad enough that these bastards had kidnapped him, but now they were going to lie about him to make things even worse?

"I don't know anyone called Voorhees," he wailed. "Are you people fucking *crazy*? Is the whole world fucking *insane*? Untie me!"

He roared the last couple of words, and was mildly impressed at how determined he sounded.

"Hush, child. I'll get to you in a minute."

The woman's words were kind, but her tone sounded like the approach of something *bad.*

Ed swallowed, and did as he was told.

"Where did you find this one?"

"Orchard Grove, Ma. Pretty sure that's where Voorhees went. When we arrived we found this guy there looting. He knows something, but he won't talk."

"I don't know anything," Ed snapped. "I told you I don't know anyone called Voorhees. What kind of a stupid name is that any-"

Ed fell silent as the face of the old woman appeared above him. She stared down at him with a smile that made her manic eyes seem all the more unsettling.

"I believe you," she said softly.

Ed let out a huge breath that felt like it had been held in until it began to rot.

"After all, no reason why he would have told you his name. Not even his fake name. So forget we're looking for a man called Voorhees. How about a guy who stands about six foot six, and looks like someone has recently tried to put him through a blender? Yes? No?"

Ed tried to keep his face expressionless.

Failed.

The old woman's smile widened.

"There, now. I think we're both on the same page. Now you have a choice to make. Are you going to tell me where that man is? Or am I going to have to cut it out of you?"

25

Ed couldn't remember a time when he had ever been *brave*. It wasn't that he was a coward, not exactly. It was more the case that his life never really reached any points at which bravery or cowardice were even options. To him bravery was taking on a far more skilled player in a one-on-one on *Call of Duty*. Cowardice was backing out and shutting down the *xbox* when it was clear he was going to lose. In either case, the worst possible outcome would be a flood of insults from faceless names on the internet. Nothing that required any loss of sleep.

The fact that he was determined not to give up the man who saved his life surprised him a little. It was, he would have to admit, out of character. But then again, when had his character ever been tested before? Life had been pretty easy up until a couple of weeks earlier. It wasn't his fault he had faced little in the way of adversity.

Maybe I'm a brave type of guy after all.

When the old woman had quizzed him about the man currently laying unconscious in his mother's storage closet, Ed had let his surprise and fear give the game away. But he would be damned if he was going to give the big man's location to this weird family. After all, what were these people going to do? *Torture* him? This wasn't the movies. People didn't just *torture* other people. Not in *Wales*.

Ed changed his mind about that when the blade entered his flesh for the first time. The man who had knocked him out - whose name Ed had subsequently learned was Rhys - had spent several minutes waving the straight razor in front of Ed's face and repeating the same question over and over: *where is Voorhees?*

The questioning and gesticulating continued for long enough that Ed began to think that the man didn't want to cut Ed any more than he wanted to be cut. In fact, the man's face looked a little green around the edges at even being forced to contemplate it. Ed felt his resolve stiffen, and he began to believe that maybe he would be okay after all.

Until the old woman appeared and asked her son what progress he had made in a tone that dripped venom.

The cutting began almost immediately.

Ed screamed in horror when the man dragged the cold blade across his gut - *my stomach!* - and when Rhys Holloway withdrew the blade and held it up in front of Ed's face, he screamed even louder at the sight of the dark blood dripping from it. He wanted so much to be brave, and to repay the debt he owed to the man that had saved his life. He even thought maybe he could handle the pain; certainly when the knife ate into his flesh the first time it didn't hurt in the way Ed had expected it would. But when the blade was pulled away, the pain rushed in like the tide, and Ed knew that noble intentions were worth nothing if they meant his flesh was to be split apart.

By the time Holloway made a second cut, Ed gave Voorhees up like a bad habit. He told them he had placed the man in a cupboard in his mother's house; he hoped and prayed that would be the end of it, but he knew as soon as he saw the old woman's face that it wasn't over.

"Take us there," she said.

*

Ed walked in front, and had his hands tied behind him. The man who had cut him with the blade played several feet of rope out behind Ed, like a leash. In a strange way Ed was glad he was tied up. It at least gave him an immediate problem to focus on.

He focused on that problem like he'd never focused on anything before in his entire life, because Ed felt the dire truth of his situation crawling around the edge of his thoughts constantly. The crazy bastards he was leading to Orchard Grove were going to kill him. Nothing had ever seemed as certain. He had no idea how to escape them, but the bonds that tied his wrists together made the first step obvious, and he did the only thing he could think to do: he fell.

Repeatedly. And *loudly.*

By the fifth time Ed stumbled to the ground, his knees were battered and bloody, but more importantly Annie Holloway was pissed off, and heading inexorably toward fire-spitting all-out *fury.*

"Cut the damn ropes off him," she hissed as Ed struggled to get unsteadily to his feet following his latest manufactured tumble. "What do you think he's going to do? Run away? For God's sake."

Running away was Ed's plan in its entirety, but as Rhys cut his hands free and pushed him forwards, Ed reined in his desire to simply sprint away in panic.

Do it at the right time, he thought. *It's your only chance. Calm...*

With every few steps, Ed expected to see Infected charging at him; almost wished it would happen so that he could slip away in the ensuing chaos, but the fields they crossed remained dark and empty.

It took about twenty minutes to reach Orchard Grove, and the sight of Ed's home, familiar and alien at the same time, made his heart feel heavy.

Maybe he woke up. Maybe he's already gone.

The thought simultaneously gave Ed hope and chilled him. If the big man had awoken and wandered away, Ed thought he would feel strangely triumphant, but he didn't imagine he'd get to enjoy the tiny victory for long. The old woman's anger would most likely be fucking *biblical* and there was only one person she would direct it towards.

"It's that one," Ed said, pointing to his mother's house.

"I told you we should have searched these houses," a voice behind Ed whispered, and he couldn't help but smile.

Another voice hushed the first quickly.

Don't want mummy to hear that, do you?

Ed smirked, and his heart began to race. A vague plan had formed in his head that was just crazy enough that it might work. It required delicate timing. It wouldn't help the man in the storage closet, and Ed felt a surge of guilt that he dismissed angrily. There was no way to help the man if he couldn't even help himself.

He led the group following him to the kitchen door at the rear of the house and shuffled inside, keeping his eyes painfully wide, searching for any sign of movement.

Rough hands grabbed his shoulders and span him around.

"So where is he?" Rhys growled, and followed Ed's hand as he pointed at the cupboard door in the narrow hallway. Rhys and the two other men with him shuffled past Ed, and pulled the cupboard door open, glaring accusingly at Ed.

"Behind the toolbox, under the blanket," Ed said, taking a slow step backwards.

Rhys leaned into the cupboard.

Ed took another step, easing away from the men in his mother's house.

He felt a bony finger prodding his back.

"Stay still," the old woman hissed.

"Got him, Ma! He's here alright. Here, give me a hand…"

Rhys passed the toolbox to the man next to him.

Now or never. She's just an old woman.

As the three men in the hallway began to grunt with the effort of hauling the big man out of the cupboard, Ed finally persuaded his limbs to follow orders. Spinning around, he shoulder charged Annie Holloway to the ground and bolted through the door and into the garden.

Once he was outside, he put his head down and ran as he had never run before.

*

"Shit," Rhys cried as he leapt back out of the cupboard, slamming his head painfully into the low doorway. He emerged just as his mother pulled herself unsteadily back to her feet. Her face looked like a gathering storm.

Rhys froze.

"Shall I go after him?"

Annie squinted through the windows and saw Ed disappearing into the distance.

"The idiot's running straight back toward the hotel," she snapped. "He's not important. Bring *him.*"

She pointed her crooked finger at the inert shape the other two men were pulling from the cupboard.

*

Ed ran until his lungs felt like they were tearing themselves apart. He glanced back several times as he ran, and saw they weren't following. He hadn't expected them to. Whatever they wanted the man they called Voorhees for, it was obviously far more important to them than Ed. Given the choice, they had stayed with their primary target.

It was only stage one of Ed's grand escape plan. Stage two bordered on stupidity, but Ed didn't believe he would last long running around in the open. So far he hadn't seen any of the Infected zombies, but he didn't expect his luck to hold.

For a few seconds he put his hands on his knees and sucked in deep breaths. The oxygen burned in his chest, but there was no time to waste.

He made his way straight back to the hotel, slowing only when he saw the dark building looming ahead of him. Trotting along, Ed scanned the windows for movement.

He saw plenty.

How many of these bastards are there?

Ed gave the hotel a wide berth, skirting down toward the water's edge, and felt his nerves blaze when he saw the boat bobbing next to the narrow jetty.

It was going to work.

Ed quickened his pace, and let out a strangled yelp when he felt a strong hand clutch his collar and bring him to an abrupt halt. He crashed to the ground.

"Who the hell are you?"

Ed turned to stare at the bald man looming above him. The man was slight, with a face filled more with concern and curiosity than the sort of vindictive aggression he had observed in the group he had escaped from at Orchard Grove. Before Ed even knew what he was doing, he twisted away from the man's grasp and rose to his feet, picking up a small rock and smashing it into the bald man's temple. The man stared at him for a moment, stupefied, as though he hadn't even registered the impact, so Ed hit him again, harder, and the bald man hit the ground like a felled tree.

Ed didn't wait to see the bald man fall. Wondering in horror if he had just *killed* somebody, Ed focused on the jetty and the boat, and he dropped the rock and ran.

26

Michael counted nearly forty windows that faced the sea, and each and every one now glowed softly with the light of the candles he had told everyone to place in the rooms beyond.

Most of the twenty-three people left in the castle seemed relieved to have something to actually *do*, and Michael cursed himself for not realising sooner that leaving the people to dwell on the horrors of the recent past would do them no good. He had, he supposed, been too wrapped up in his own morbid introspection.

He wondered if maybe it was overkill, lighting up every room like that, but figured it was better to bank on a show of strength than to worry about whether whoever was out there watching the castle would call his bluff.

Every single one of the rooms contained a candle. Not one contained a person. To Michael it felt a little like going all in with a pair of threes in a high-stakes game of poker.

As the candles were lit by those for whom stairs were *not* an insurmountable obstacle, Michael busied himself with building three large fires in the courtyard, creating a glow which scorched the deepening night above the castle. From a distance, bathed in the glow of the flames, he thought the castle must have looked as though it was full of people. A closer inspection would reveal the ruse immediately, but Michael told himself that if he saw a force of people arriving by sea, he would gladly expend a few of his precious rifle rounds to dissuade them from coming any closer.

If all went to plan, it wouldn't come to that.

When the place was as ready as they could make it, all twenty-three inhabitants of Caernarfon Castle gathered in the courtyard under the stars, with nothing left to do but wait. Clammy tension descended on the group, and for a long time no one spoke, straining their ears to catch a hint of an engine approaching in the distance.

After many uneventful minutes nervous smiles broke out, and even Michael began to wonder if they had been worrying about nothing.

Eventually Michael asked Claire to gather what food she could find, and he set about cooking their last few battered cans of beans over the fires.

Whatever happens, he thought, *at least we won't have empty stomachs.*

One way or another, he knew, it would be their last supper. The beans represented the last of the food he had been trying to ration out; the final part of Darren's supply.

He ate with Linda and Claire, and for a fleeting moment allowed himself to forget the horrors that crawled around the town outside and around his memories inside. They were like a small family camping out under the stars.

Linda had stood beside him, offering much-needed moral support, as he informed the others that the castle might be in danger, and at no point had she even hinted that she might divulge the things he had told her. He felt as though he could trust Linda, and the notion was jarring and odd, until he realised that he hadn't felt like he could trust anybody in a long time; not since long before Project Wildfire reduced the world to savage barbarity.

They ate the beans and talked and laughed, and Michael listened happily as Linda told him stories of her time as a school teacher, mundane little anecdotes that reminded him how normal the world had once been.

Sometimes when she talked of the children she had taught and their exploits, he saw a hint of sadness in Linda's eyes, and wanted very much to return the hug she had given him, and to let her know that everything would be okay, whether he believed it himself or not.

"Maybe they're not coming today," Linda said finally.

Michael shrugged.

"Maybe they're not coming *at all.*"

Linda looked at him hopefully, and Michael shook his head.

"I don't know," he said. "But John was right about one thing: this castle is an open invitation to anybody left out there. I travelled all the way up the coast, and didn't see a single place that looked as safe as this. If there are people out there, they'll come eventually. It's up to us to be prepared for the ones that don't come to talk."

Linda nodded morosely.

"Maybe you've just been unlucky," she said. "You've run into bad people, but there must be good people left out there. People who just want to survive."

"I'm sure there are," Michael replied. "But it seems like it takes a certain sort of person to do more than survive. The ones who manage to organise themselves somehow...well, I'd guess they are the ruthless type."

"Like you?"

Linda smiled, and Michael realised that her words were no more than light teasing.

The noise of the outboard engine halted Michael's response before he could form it, cutting through the night like a laser and neatly severing the tentative relaxed atmosphere that had slowly blossomed during the strange picnic under the stars.

He stared at Claire, and at Linda, and saw their eyes widen. They heard it too.

"Up to the battlements," Michael cried, lifting his voice just enough so that they could all hear. He knew the noise might draw the Infected from Caernarfon, but for now, crazily, the eyeless horrors felt like a secondary threat.

Better the devil you know, he thought.

"Be as visible as possible," Michael said. "Let them know you're here."

There was movement everywhere as the campfires were abandoned, and all the people in the castle bolted for the steep steps that led to the battlements. Michael wheeled his chair to the foot of the steps and dragged himself from it, slinging his rifle over his back and lifting himself up each step on his backside one at a time until his triceps burned.

He reached the top of the steps as the whine of the engine reached its apex, and Linda helped him haul himself up to sit on the wall so he could see.

The sea looked dark and empty.

Just one boat, Michael thought. *A decoy? Was John wrong?*

He scanned the black water, trying in vain to locate the source of the noise. It sounded close, but the combination of the dark skies and the low mist that hung over the water made it impossible to spot.

For a brief moment he fantasised that there were many boats out there without engines, rowing toward him, silent and all but invisible, as if a horde of Viking warriors approached. He strained his ears, trying to catch anything that sounded like oars splashing in water, but beyond the whine of the single engine and the rolling roar of the waves, he heard nothing.

All along the battlements the people of the castle stood like watchful guardians, some holding flaming torches, others lifting pieces of wood that Michael hoped would look like weapons from a distance.

The engine drew closer.

Closer.

He slung the rifle from his shoulder and aimed it into the darkness, ready to fire a warning shot that would be the last card he had to play, and went rigid with shock when he heard the distant explosion behind him, rolling across the land like thunder.

The noise of the engine began to recede, but Michael had already turned his attention inland, to a distant plume of fire that rose up into the night.

He felt a hand on his arm and turned to see Linda looking at him, wide-eyed and quizzical.

"That'll be John," Michael said with an elated grin. "That guy *loves* blowing things up."

He pointed at the wall opposite the one on which they all currently stood.

"Go see," he said, "but stay *quiet*."

Michael watched as they all filtered along the wall to the other side. He couldn't hear the noise of the engine anymore, and began - finally - to believe they might make it.

When he saw Linda raise her arms aloft in silent victory and turn towards him beaming a huge smile, he didn't need to see Caernarfon himself to know. The plan had worked.

The Infected were leaving.

27

Ed had no idea how to control a boat. Getting the engine started was fine: he'd seen how that worked plenty of times on television. Just a case of pulling on the cord that fired the engine. The boat emitted a throaty roar and lurched away from the small jetty and Ed took a moment to give thanks that the boat had fuel in it, and to suffer through a pulse of cold dread at what might have happened to him if the tank was empty. Already he heard people emerging from the hotel behind him, and he knew it wouldn't be long before they found the man that Ed had either killed or knocked unconscious.

Even as it was, he cast furtive glances back at the shore for a good thirty seconds, half expecting to see the old woman appear with an assault rifle or a bazooka, and only when he was far out of range of all but the most unlikely of weapons did he turn his thoughts to actually *steering* the boat.

His first mistake was as obvious as it was foolish: he pulled the tiller to the left expecting that the boat would follow suit, and nearly threw himself overboard when the boat turned right instead.

Oh, right, he thought to himself feebly. *Inverted controls. Like a flight simulator.*

Once he had mastered left and right, Ed turned his thoughts to navigating the waves that reared up in front of him, but nothing he tried helped him avoid ploughing straight into them and blinding himself at regular intervals with spray. It felt like there was someone out front launching buckets of water at his face.

After a minute or two of attempting to adjust, Ed decided to just go with it and stopped flinching aside when the water hit him, figuring that seeing enough to nullify the possibility of running into rocks was far more important that getting soaked by the freezing waters of the Menai Strait.

He hadn't left the jetty with thoughts of anything beyond getting away from the crazy freakshow that was unfolding on Anglesey, and when he saw lights in the distance on the opposite shore he felt like crying with relief. From the look of it, the power cut only extended as far as Anglesey. Maybe the insanity and violence did too, though Ed could think of no reason why the mainland authorities hadn't stepped in to put a halt to the bloodshed.

Fighting against the powerful waves, he aimed the boat toward the lights.

The Menai Strait was only a little more than a half-mile wide, and it didn't take long to cross, even in an old tub with an engine that chugged and coughed like an asthmatic. He had only been on the water for five minutes when he saw that what he had assumed were the lights of Caernarfon were in fact just the lights of the castle.

He frowned into the darkness.

The castle was a tourist destination; no one actually *lived* there. The place being lit up at night seemed...*odd.* The lights that burned in every window unsettled Ed, and he searched around the castle for evidence of life in the town itself, but all he saw was darkness.

He steered the boat to the right, moving parallel to Caernarfon rather than straight at it, and after checking the water in front of him was clear of obstacles, he focused his attention on the castle.

Are there people up there?

It looked to Ed like a line of people manned the battlements, almost like they were reconstructing some ancient siege.

Are they holding weapons?

Ed's hand began to tremble on the tiller. He couldn't be sure whether that was due to the cold or fear, but if he had to put money on it, he would have picked the latter.

He squinted in frustration, desperately trying to make a lie of the truth his eyes imparted to him. When he was a few hundred feet out, he saw them clearly enough: something like thirty people lined the battlements, some holding flaming torches, others holding what looked like clubs.

What the fuck?

Before he could even begin to come up with theories about the strange people in the castle, the sound of an enormous explosion reached him, and his mouth dropped open. In the distance beyond Caernarfon, a huge plume of fire billowed up into the sky, like a small nuclear device had been detonated.

Ed was no believer in signs from God, but he was a firm believer in staying the *fuck* away from trouble. He steered the boat away from the castle, and headed down the coast as fast as the whining engine and the stubborn ocean would allow.

He didn't make it far - a mile or two maybe, Ed had no idea, no frame of reference when it came to navigating the sea - before the engine chugged and spluttered and died.

Oh shit.

Again and again he tried to rev the engine into life and was met with obstinate choking and empty rattling.

No fuel.

Ed stared at the outboard motor in seething frustration. He was so focused on it that he didn't even see the sails as the yacht moved silently alongside him.

"Engine trouble?"

The voice in the darkness nearly made Ed leap into the sea in fright. When he turned he saw a man leaning over the side of a much larger boat than his. As the vessel neared, the man leapt down onto Ed's stranded boat and grinned.

"Reckon you might need a ride, mate. Dangerous out here, you know. Sockets can swim, after all."

*

A sea of sightless corpses charged at him, shearing his flesh with their teeth, and he screamed and screamed as they tore away his body, praying that he would die, but the torment was eternal. When he shut his eyes to block out the image, another replaced it: a blood-soaked rat, crawling along inside his intestines, chewing its way toward his heart. In the darkness he writhed and twisted, trying to turn away from the horrors that loomed all around him, and found that there was no escape. The terror wasn't something he could outrun: it followed relentlessly; attached itself to him like a diseased shadow.

He wanted to scream, but found that when he opened his mouth, no sound came out. Just a whispered sigh that echoed, and sounded like a distant voice sneering at him. A familiar voice somehow, yet one that he could not place.

He awoke abruptly from half-remembered dreams of movement, like someone had dragged him in his sleep.

He awoke to pain.

And when he tried to speak, he awoke to find that his tongue had been removed. The stump that squirmed in his mouth felt like an alien object.

He wasn't Jason anymore, not really. Wasn't *Voorhees* either. Whatever Jason was now existed purely in the cracks that divided sanity from insanity, drowning in an endless lake of pain both real and imagined.

He was tied again, once more posed like a crucifixion. No; not tied. He tried to move his hands and shards of agony that burrowed into his palms made him moan.

Nailed.

Not *posed*. Actually crucified.

Opening his eyes was a task that seemed almost beyond him. They felt as though they were glued shut. With a force of effort, he persuaded the lids to open. They did so obstinately, in increments, feeling like they might at any moment tear themselves apart as they struggled to unblock the dried blood that glued them together.

When he finally succeeded, the light brought a whole new pain along with it. A pain that seemed to sear his retinas and jab a hot brand onto the surface of his mind.

The view seemed familiar somehow, but the images in Jason's head tumbled and shifted constantly, never staying still long enough for him to grasp. He saw a large window - smashed - that let in a stunning view of the dark ocean beyond and a wind that froze his bare torso.

Have I been here before?

He searched for memories, but all he found was pain that fizzed like an electric shock.

He looked down at his chest, and saw the rips and the tears that mirrored the carnage he felt inside. His mind was adrift on a river of poison. He trembled as much as the nails driven through him would allow. Even worse than the pain, worse than the horror, was the uncertainty and the fear at being so alone, and so helpless. He moaned again, and looked up sharply when an old woman appeared in front of him.

"There's my boy," she said with a benevolent smile. "I thought we'd lost you."

Jason's brow wrinkled. He understood the words, but they made no sense. Who was this old woman?

A gurgling moan bubbled from his dry lips.

"Oh, I'm sorry child. We had to put you there to keep you safe. You can't just go wandering off, you know. It's dangerous out there, and you're very special. We all need you here."

Special?

The old woman stepped in front of him and studied his eyes carefully, as though she was searching for a trace of something she expected to find but could not. After a moment she smiled at him again, and her expression made a hopeful warmth flicker into life deep in his ravaged heart.

"I think you're ready to come down now, my child."

She placed her hand softly on his cheek.

Are you my mother?

Jason rested his cheek on the cold, wrinkled flesh of the old woman's palm, and sighed.

Ed surrendered immediately. In truth, he would have surrendered immediately to the man who had - and there was no other way Ed could describe it - *boarded* his boat like a goddamned *pirate*, even if the man had been alone. The fact that the man had backup simply made the surrender all the easier to contemplate.

The man talking about *sockets* was terrifying enough, far bigger than Ed and covered in ominous-looking tattoos. But on the boat beside him Ed saw an even larger man - equally heavily tattooed and glaring at Ed beneath fierce, bushy eyebrows - and a woman staring down at him with sharp, penetrating eyes that made him instinctively edgy. The woman threw a rope ladder over the rail and it landed in the water with a splash next to Ed's dormant engine.

The tattooed man shoved Ed toward the rope and he climbed it with a sense of rising dread that he imagined prisoners on death row felt when they made their final walk from their cell.

Once aboard the yacht, they circled him like vultures.

"Where are the rest of your people?"

The tattooed man who had boarded Ed's boat put himself right in Ed's face and growled the question. His tone left Ed in no doubt that the wrong answer would probably get him killed.

"My...people?"

Ed hadn't expected the zombie apocalypse to include quite so many unanswerable questions. He wondered, even as he stuttered out the response, whether he was shortly going to be knocked unconscious again.

"Calm down, Ray."

Ed turned to see a man step out of the yacht's cabin, who might have been marginally less terrifying than the others if it weren't for the knives he carried, and backed up against the main mast, wondering how long it would be before he felt steel slicing through his flesh once more.

*

Ray looked to be about two questions away from gutting the quivering kid by the time John stepped in. Torture and intimidation generally provided answers in his experience, but they weren't always the right ones. The kid looked terrified. Scaring him *more* wasn't going to get anybody anywhere.

"Take it easy," John said calmly, and shot a glance at the others. "He means the people you got this boat from, that's all. Where are they?"

The kid stuttered and stammered, and twisted his neck wildly to keep an eye on the people around him. His eyes flitted from John to Shirley to Ray and back again.

John sighed, and sat cross-legged on the deck holding his arms wide, and smiled when he saw confusion dilute the fear on the kid's face.

"I'm John," he said. "The big guy is Shirley. I shit you not. That's Rachel, and you've already met Ray. Kid over there doing his best to stay invisible is Glyn. Nobody here is going to hurt you. So tell me your name."

"Uh...Ed."

"Okay, Ed. The people who own this boat checked us out a while ago, and it seemed, well, a little threatening to be honest with you. I'm guessing you're not with them, but you have their boat. Where did you get it?"

"Anglesey. A hotel," Ed mumbled, and John saw everyone else on the boat relax a little at the kid's tone. "Just across the Strait. Look, I'm not *with* them, okay? I only know a couple of their names, and I don't know anything about them checking you out, but I can tell you it probably *was* threatening because they are fucking *psychos*. Every last one of them. Anglesey is *fucked* up."

John couldn't help but grin.

"No shit," he said, and heard Shirley chuckle.

"Everywhere is fucked up, kid," the big man rumbled.

"Okay," John said abruptly, and stood, turning back toward the cabin.

"Uh, is that it?" Ed said, looking nervously from John to Shirley.

John shrugged. "I believe you," he said. "We'll talk some more. But right now we're in kind of a rush."

"So you're...kidnapping me?"

John laughed.

"I guess that would only be possible if you had somewhere else to be, right?"

He grinned, and disappeared back into the cabin. Moments later the boat adjusted course, and Ed was left to stare fearfully at the others and wonder whether he had just been saved or *taken.*

*

John expected to hear someone in the cabin almost immediately. He wasn't surprised that it was Rachel.

"You *believe* him?"

John nodded.

"Why not? The guy is practically pissing himself just being here. He doesn't strike me as a great choice to go and infiltrate the enemy, so, yeah, I believe him. He didn't find us. We found *him.* He was running. As for that stuff about people acting like psychos in Anglesey?"

He shrugged.

"That sounds about right to me. It doesn't to you? Seems like it's pretty much par for the course."

Rachel flushed angrily.

"He knows more," she said hotly.

"I don't doubt it," John said, staring through the window at the sea ahead. "But we didn't just go through all that to clear the Infected away from Caernarfon just to waste time chatting. I'm going to have enough of *that* to deal with when we get back to Michael, and I don't know how much time we have to waste. I'd prefer not to push our luck."

He glanced quickly at Rachel.

"You guys want to carry on talking to him, go ahead. I just didn't want anyone killing the guy, that's all. He's harmless. At least until he shows me otherwise."

For a moment, John thought Rachel was going to argue on, but she flicked her gaze to the window and the dark landscape beyond.

"He's scared shitless of *you*, that's for sure," John said with a wry grin. "You see the way he looks at you? I've seen guys with that look on their faces before. Usually right after someone shouts *incoming*."

Rachel snorted a laugh.

"One scary lady," John muttered with a chuckle, and winced as Rachel landed a punch on his arm.

Outside the boat, the castle hovered into view in the distance, spilling dozens of flickering lights into the darkness that looked like a cloud of tiny fireflies. John's fingers tightened around the wheel. Something had happened at the castle, and whatever it was, John suspected it was going to slow him up. If he was right about Sullivan and the navy, they had to leave the castle as soon as possible, and he was going to have to persuade Michael to leave the place he had believed his story was going to end.

He grimaced.

"How many people?"

John had to give Michael credit; the guy knew which questions to ask when John pushed Ed in front of the man's wheelchair. That first one was the most important of all.

It had taken almost an hour for John to wrestle the boat back up the coast. The wind was against him, and every yard gained felt like pulling teeth. The castle hovered in the distance for a long time, without ever really seeming to get any closer. It gave him plenty of time to wonder why the place was lit up like a Christmas tree. None of the possible answers he came up with settled his nerves.

The boat had a small anchor attached to a winch, and John deployed it in a calm spot as close to the mouth of the river that flowed past the castle as possible. He wasn't sure if he would need the boat again, despite how crucial he felt it was to persuade Michael to leave. The simple fact was that even if Michael agreed, not everyone at the castle would fit onto the small yacht. They would need something far larger.

Once he was certain the boat wasn't going to drift away, John paused on the deck to survey Caernarfon's small waterfront. The ancient, twisting buildings, huddling together as though trying to keep warm in the endless onslaught of the coastal wind, gave up no sign of movement. Most of the Infected would have trundled off toward the noise of the explosion, but John knew better than to assume Caernarfon was safe. Any one of the buildings might have one of the creatures trapped inside, frantically trying to figure out how to get through the doors that prevented it from tracking down the source of the distant explosion.

Still, the streets seemed clear. It was a start.

While the others waited, dividing their expectant stares between John and the castle, he rooted around in the various storage lockers on the boat until he found what he was looking for: a length of sturdy rope, long enough to span the river.

Rachel looked at him quizzically.

"We'll need to be able to cross the river fast," John explained. "And to transport back whatever we take from the town. I'll tie this across the river, and we can pull ourselves across on a raft. Not great, but..."

He shrugged.

"Better than swimming," Rachel said, her eyes darkening at the memory of her last dip in the cold water.

"Right," John said. "You guys stay here. If the castle isn't safe - if I don't come back - pull up that anchor and get the hell away. Okay?"

John glared at Rachel as she looked at him dubiously.

"I mean it, Rachel. If things have gone bad, there will be nothing you can do. Just stay safe until I come back."

He didn't give her time to respond. Looping the rope around his shoulders, he dived into the water and swam towards Caernarfon.

Rachel watched as he tied the rope off around a post near the river bank, and dived back in, swimming toward the castle until he moved out of her sight, pulling the rope taut behind him.

The wait felt like an eternity; until Rachel began to wonder how she would even know if John had run into trouble.

Maybe he's already dead, and I'm waiting here for a ghost.

Almost as soon as the thought formed in her mind she heard splashing in the water, and saw John heading back toward the boat. He grinned and gave her a thumbs-up.

"All clear," he said, lifting his voice a fraction above the murmuring of the river. "Time to get your feet wet."

He beckoned the others to follow, and turned to swim back upstream toward the castle's main entrance. Once they were all inside and the main gate had been shut behind them, John finally let himself breathe a little easier.

Michael began questioning Ed immediately. All John wanted to do was find a room with a door that locked and sleep, but his own words rang in his head. There was no time to waste. He pushed away his exhaustion, wondering idly if he would ever again get to drink coffee.

When Michael started firing questions at Ed, John leaned against the wall of Michael's room, which had somehow developed the feel of a sort of state area, like the steps at *10 Downing Street* or the *Oval Office*, and listened quietly.

Ed shook his head. "I'm not sure how many there are," he said. "I only saw a few. Ten at most, maybe less. I didn't spend much time counting. But I think there were others. They're in a hotel on the shore."

"Who's in charge there?"

"I think it's an old woman called Annie. All the ones I saw were terrified of her, anyway."

"They know about the castle?"

Ed nodded at John. "Like I told *him*, I don't know anything about it. They were after some guy, they found me instead. I was only with them a few hours. I got the chance to run, and I took it."

Michael nodded.

"What guy?"

Ed shook his head.

"I don't know, just some guy, man. He got away from them or something, I don't know. He was crazy, they were crazy. I didn't ask many questions, you know? My experience with them was pretty similar to what's happening right now. Only difference is you haven't started cutting me up. Yet."

Ed lifted his jaw in an attempt at defiance, but the gesture was undermined by the fearful widening of his eyes, as if he couldn't believe the words had fallen from his own mouth.

Michael ignored Ed's attempt at attitude, catching John's eye and shooting him an inquisitive look.

"Maybe they aren't interested in the castle after all?"

John held his hands up.

"I don't know, Michael. Maybe. It really doesn't matter right now. The castle isn't safe regardless."

Michael sighed.

"We've been through this, John. You said you wanted a place you could defend. Where better than here? Where is safer?"

"Not just the castle, Michael," John muttered in a low, frustrated tone. "The whole country."

Michael blinked.

"Listen, the guys behind all this, I think they have control of the navy. Nuclear capabilities. Every day that passes tells me they can't get this situation under control. They *will* take the nuclear option. We need to get a boat. A big fucking boat, and we need to get away from here fucking *pronto*."

Michael stared at him blankly.

"Where are we going to go on this boat?"

"Anywhere," John said flatly. "Just being at sea will be a hundred per cent safer than being here."

"This *just* occurred to you?"

John shrugged.

"I've had a lot on my mind."

Michael stared at him, lost in thought.

"Uh...nuclear?" Ed broke the heavy silence in an apologetic tone, though his eavesdropping had been all but unavoidable. "You mean Wylfa?"

John and Michael both turned to stare at him.

"What's Wylfa?" John asked in a low voice.

"Wylfa Power Station?" Ed said in a tone that increased in pitch despite his efforts to keep it under control. "You said nuclear, right? You meant Wylfa?"

The sinking sensation in John's gut told him the answer before his lips had even had time to frame the question.

"Where's Wylfa?" He asked.

"On Anglesey," Ed said in an *oh-you-guys-didn't-know-that* tone.

John choked out an involuntary chuckle. Michael squeezed his eyes shut and lifted his face to the ceiling. He looked very much like he wanted to scream in frustration.

"Whole country's falling apart," John said. "*'Time bombs all around us'*. And we set up camp outside a nuclear power station. At least that settles it. We can't stay here. Doesn't matter whether Sullivan nukes the country or not. This place is going up in smoke either way."

Once more silence fell on the group. All faces turned toward Michael. John braced himself for an argument as Michael's brow furrowed.

"Agreed," Michael said abruptly, and John's mouth dropped open in astonishment at the immediate acceptance. "We get what we need from Caernarfon, and then we figure out getting away from here as quick as we can."

"And go where?" John said.

Michael shrugged. "Liverpool? We need a *big fucking boat*, right? So we head to the nearest large port. Stay on the coast. Maybe we'll get lucky and find something on the way. We know there's nothing south."

John nodded.

Rachel snorted a bitter laugh.

"Running again," she said. "At least we won't have to fight your weird friends across the strait," she said, drilling her gaze into Ed. He let out a nervy chuckle.

"I'd say they are busy with that guy Voorhees anyway," he said almost absent-mindedly, and took a step backwards in surprise when Rachel's eyes blazed at him.

"With *who*?"

*

The old woman put a rope around his neck, and clutched the other end in her bony fingers. The rope, she said, would keep him safe, and would mean that he would never get lost again.

He smiled happily, riding on a cushion of heavy, comfortable air that built up around him when the old woman - who was surely his mother - made him swallow the multi-coloured tablets that took away all his pain.

She took him outside, into the fresh air, walking him like a dog, but he didn't mind. He wasn't sure he had ever felt so safe, or so at home. The old woman muttered softly at him as he walked, dazed, ahead of her, and her crooning voice comforted him.

When she found the body of the man near the water, his head caked in dry blood and his eyes fixed on the sea, and discovered that the small boat which had been moored to the jetty was gone, her grip on the rope around his neck tightened, but it was the change in her that lit a fire in his nerves.

She raged and spat, and stared furiously at the building that poured light into the night in the distance across the water, and the change in her made him feel sick and anxious, and tears rolled down his cheeks as he tried to understand her anger, and could not.

*

Ed's words shook Rachel like an earthquake, rattling her to the core.

Voorhees? It couldn't be...

Voorhees was the nickname the cruel children at school had used to mercilessly tease her giant brother. She remembered they used to play a game, pretending he was the monster from the horror films, and they would all run away from him on the schoolyard. Jason had even thought it was funny for a while and had played along. Until one day he grew old enough to understand the meaning of the word *outcast*, and realised just how it applied to him. *Voorhees.* It had to be coincidence. *Had to.*

"What did he look like?" Rachel mumbled softly, almost as though she was afraid to hear the answer.

"I don't know. Massive. Guy looked like he was on a steady diet of about twenty thousand calories a day. Brown hair."

Ed shrugged.

Tears stung Rachel's eyes as she remembered Jason muttering an apology to her before the Infected blocked him from her sight in Aberystwyth. It was the last time she had seen her brother. The last time she thought she ever *would* see him.

Sorry, Rach.

A fat, warm tear spilled down her cheek, and she dropped her gaze to the floor.

"Rachel?" John said. "What is it?"

Rachel blinked rapidly.

"It's Jason."

John stared at her blankly.

"How? Jason's dead." He cringed a little as he said it and saw her stricken face, and moved on quickly. "What do you mean?"

Rachel shook her head at John impatiently, and turned to Ed.

"What was he doing? Voorhees. You said they were *after* him?"

Ed nodded.

"I had the...uh...zombies after me." He flushed a little, as though the word embarrassed him. "He saved me. But he was injured. The only thing he said to me was 'they're after me'. After that he passed out."

He lifted his hands in a gesture of surrender when he saw Rachel's eyes widen.

"I helped him, patched him up, but the old woman's people found us. That's when I met her. But she didn't care about me."

Ed lowered his hands, apparently concluding that despite appearances Rachel was not about to attack him.

"He meant the old woman was after him, I think. When I first saw her all she cared about was where *he* was."

Ed shuffled uneasily, as though he had just realised he had said too much.

Rachel's eyes narrowed.

"You told her."

Ed began to shake, staring around the room as if expecting everyone to jump him. His pleading gaze settled on John, but John was oblivious, focused only on staring at Rachel.

"Look, she was *torturing* me, okay? She had her son fucking *cutting me open*. What was I supposed to do? I don't even know what the *fuck* is going on."

Ed seemed surprised at the ferocity in his tone. He spat the words out like darts.

"Rachel," John said evenly, cutting through the thickening atmosphere. "We saw Jason die. We all saw it."

"I didn't," Rachel snapped. "I saw him get overrun by the Infected. That's all. I didn't see him *die*. Did you? Actually *see* it?"

John replayed the scene in his mind. Saw Jason swinging as the Infected swarmed past him. Saw the big man knocked to the ground, disappearing under the herd as it converged on the boat they had used to escape from Aberystwyth. Didn't see anything else. He snapped his mouth shut.

"I assumed he was dead because the Infected *kill* people, because that's *all* I thought they did," Rachel said. "But now I know they don't kill everything. They didn't kill the girl Darren had tied up outside."

"But she was infected..." Michael said, and his gaze flitted from Rachel to John, his eyes widening as understanding crept across his mind. "The rat..."

The truth of what had happened in the small farmhouse outside St. Davids hung in the air between the three of them. Jason had been bitten, and he hadn't turned. At the time, none of them had known what it meant.

Ed opened his mouth to say something, but seeing the stunned look on their faces, he thought better of it.

"The rat." Rachel said, nodding her head vigorously.

John knew what was coming even before Rachel opened her mouth to speak again, and he felt a crushing weight land on him. They were supposed to be running *away*. For all they knew, the power station on Anglesey was already beginning to melt down. John had no idea how long such a facility would last without electricity; he did *not* want to find out.

"I have to go get him," Rachel said, and John's head dropped.

30

Persuading Rachel not to drop everything and sprint for the boat immediately wasn't easy, and John was grateful that for once he found Michael in full agreement with him. They needed supplies, John argued; needed to secure Caernarfon before they launched any kind of an attack on what John suspected was a larger force that had taken up a secure position and were most likely expecting company.

In the end, John was able to penetrate Rachel's seething anger and determination by grabbing her shoulders and staring into her eyes and *promising* her that if Jason was alive, he would bring him back to the castle.

Have I let you down? John had finally snapped, drilling his gaze into her until she shook her head. The tears in her eyes made John's heart ache, but her pain was necessary. Charging off to Anglesey half-cocked would be a disaster. A full frontal attack - even if they were ultimately successful - would mean people dying. *Lots* of people. John could only think of one way to avoid the carnage, just one crazy way, and if he told Rachel what he was planning, it would fall apart before it began.

You must be insane, John, he thought as the plan formed in his mind, and the notion struck him as almost funny. It seemed the only way to survive now was by being crazy.

Only when John said that every minute they wasted arguing was another minute Jason was being held by a psychopath did Rachel agree to raiding Caernarfon first. John felt bad for pushing her buttons, knowing full well what the word *psychopath* would do to her, but the end justified the means. If the vague plan he was working on bore fruit, there was a chance he could get Jason - if indeed it *was* Jason - without bloodshed.

When Rachel had a moment to think about her brother potentially being held by someone like Darren - or worse, Victor - she agreed to follow John's lead.

John hurriedly outlined a plan to get everyone that could walk into Caernarfon, grabbing everything they might possibly need - food, fuel, batteries. Anything that looked like it might make a noise that might damage the Infected. Weapons. Blades. John didn't think they would be able to find any firearms in Caernarfon, but he told them to find the police station as quickly as possible and raid it. Riot gear, nightsticks, tasers, pepper spray. If they were really lucky, the police might even have a gun or two. Caernarfon had a moderately large population, maybe enough for the police to require firepower. Failing that, he said, everybody was to keep their eyes peeled for *anything* that could be used as a ranged weapon.

He drew up a shopping list using a pen from the castle's tiny gift shop - which had long ago been cleared of traditional Welsh fudge and cookies, and passed out copies. Michael, Ray and Shirley looked over it carefully, and added items of their own.

Once the castle was stocked with everything that looked like it might be useful, John proposed to lead a team to Anglesey, while those he left behind would prepare as best they could for journeying north to find a boat large enough to get them all away from the UK.

If his assumptions about Fred Sullivan were correct, John believed there would be a country out there that remained untouched by Project Wildfire, and John was willing to bet that country was Australia; remote enough to be safe as the world burned, with an advanced infrastructure and plenty of space to rebuild.

Australia was virtually self-sustaining: very little of its food was imported, and the country had always maintained ultra-strict immigration controls. It was exactly where John would go if he was in Sullivan's shoes, even if it meant turning up in Sydney harbour with a fleet of battleships and declaring war.

Getting to the other side of the planet for the people living in Caernarfon Castle was most likely all but impossible, but John didn't care about that. For now, just being at sea would mean safety. If they had to find some tiny island somewhere and live like castaways, so be it.

As John, Michael, Ray and Shirley planned, Rachel paced furiously.

"We get it," she eventually snapped. "Loot everything. Can we just go and *do it?*

John nodded.

"Ray, go gather up everyone that can walk," he said. "Get them all to the gate. Don't tell them anything yet, just tell them...uh, tell them Michael needs to speak to them, okay?"

Ray delivered a mock salute and left the room at pace. Moments later John heard him calling people to him.

Michael looked at John with a question forming in his eyes.

"They all trust you," John said with a shrug. "It's better coming from you. Don't mention Jason, though. I don't think many people will be keen to risk their lives for someone they've never met. Cross that bridge when we get to it. In the meantime, I'll find something we can use as a raft to cross the river."

*

They coalesced at the gate slowly, as though reluctantly drawn together by a weak magnetism they could not resist.

Michael wheeled himself in front of the group that Ray had gathered together with his mind racing. If Rachel and Linda were right, the people waiting for him to speak looked to him as some sort of leader. He couldn't help but wonder how many of them he would end up getting killed.

Michael counted seventeen in addition to the group that had just returned to the castle. Ray had obviously decided the rest were of little use - either too young, like Claire and Pete, or perhaps too valuable, like Linda, the closest thing they had to a medic; or simply too broken. Some of the people at the castle were lost, as Jason Roberts had been, trapped inside their heads by horrors only they could see.

They all stared at Michael silently, their faces a mixture of anxiety and anticipation. Thanks to Darren Oliver's repopulation programme the group was mostly young and female; thanks to John's training at least a handful of them looked something other than flat-out terrified.

Michael stared at the gate, wondering dimly how many times in the past people had cowered behind it, waiting to rush outside to a battle that might be their last.

Not this time, he thought. *This time we are ready. This time we survive.*

"We have a window," Michael said, lifting his voice just enough for them all to hear him clearly. "The Infected have cleared out of Caernarfon for now, but they will be back, so we have to act fast."

A nervous murmur ran through the small crowd.

"We're going to raid Caernarfon. We need food and weapons. Fuel and batteries. If you see anything that makes noise, get it. Air-horns, fireworks, *anything*. But be careful. The streets are clear but the buildings may not be. So nobody goes anywhere alone. We have four high-priority targets, so you'll be divided into four teams, one each for the police station, hardware store, grocery store and the pharmacy. Get *everything* from the pharmacy. A few of you know where these places are. If you don't, talk to someone who does. Move quick, and stay quiet. And be *smart*. If you so much as *think* a building looks dangerous, you stay *out*, okay? Look for movement inside, look for blood inside. Keep an eye out for anything that doesn't feel right. Don't risk your life. This is about getting whatever we can, and getting back in one piece."

Michael looked around the faces gathered in front of him and saw terror and desperation looming among them. Most of them hadn't set foot outside the castle since they got there. Many of them, he knew, would be replaying in their minds memories of the last time they were outside the walls, dwelling on the horrors they had witnessed when the virus originally decimated Caernarfon and forced them into the hands of a man who saw them only as an opportunity for breeding.

"Wear thick clothes," Michael continued. "Arm yourselves with whatever you can. Remember everything John has taught you all about fighting these things. If you need to, you *run.* You've got ten minutes to get ready, and then you go."

Michael fell silent. He was sure there were a hundred other things he could say, sure that the people wanted to hear another hundred things that might give them courage, but there was little point. Once they were out in the open and vulnerable, no pep talk or training would help them. He knew all too well that encountering the Infected and surviving was a matter of instinct and luck. All he could do was pray that the decoy had worked, and that the Infected weren't already circling back to the town.

The crowd stared at him expectantly, and his mind went blank.

"Go!" Rachel yelled, and they hurried away in fraught silence.

31

John was planning something. Rachel saw it in his eyes and his stiff body language; saw it in the hesitant way he spoke to her as they got ready to leave.

He had found a large slab of wood in the castle among the pieces that Darren had collected to have his people build shelters within the courtyard. The skeleton of the building Darren had visualised was still in place, but work on it had stopped the minute the man's dark heart was stilled.

The wood was sturdy, and large enough for five people at a time to clamber on board. John said it would serve just fine as a raft.

Michael had volunteered to be the one that would pull the raft back and forth across the river using the rope John had already set up. John looked as dubious as Rachel felt, but Michael insisted that as long as he left the wheelchair behind he could sit on the raft and keep hold of the rope, and he would be safe enough.

Everybody had to pull their weight, Michael said, including himself, and nobody appeared to feel there was time to debate it. If the man fell into the river, he'd have to claw his way to shore by himself, legs or not.

Once Michael was securely on the raft, he pulled the first group across. As supplies were brought back to the river, it would be Michael's job - along with Linda, Claire and Pete - to shuttle them across to the castle and come back for more.

The first group to cross included both John and Rachel. Once across, they began to scour the narrow, crooked streets as the others filtered across the river, and by the time everyone was standing nervously on the fringes of Caernarfon, John seemed satisfied that there was no immediate danger. With his voice barely rising above a whisper, he began to divide the group into smaller teams. Ray, Shirley, John and Rachel would each take care of four or five people.

Rachel watched John carefully, and couldn't help but notice that he didn't meet her eyes when he informed her they would be going their separate ways.

What are you up to?

After a quick glance around everybody to make sure they were ready, John nodded and scampered off toward the police station. Ray took his team toward the hardware store in the centre of Caernarfon. Shirley's team headed for the grocery store nearby. Rachel got the pharmacy. She had been there once before, hurriedly picking up items to patch John up after he had been attacked by a group of Darren's men and nearly beaten to death.

She watched John leading his group away at a light canter, and her eyes narrowed with suspicion.

*

The police station was small, and according to Emma it sat at the northern end of Caernarfon. As John ran, he stayed alert for movement, and kept glancing at the girl, waiting until she nodded that he was moving in the right direction before setting off again.

The ground was painted with blood and gore; John heard the whimpering of the young women who ran with him as they passed each body, and he prayed they wouldn't crack and start screaming. He had a plan that he thought might just avoid bloodshed altogether, but it relied on getting in and out of Caernarfon quickly, and avoiding Rachel.

Pursing his lips, he upped the pace.

*

Ray had the furthest to travel, and the largest group. The hardware store, which he had been assured was bigger than he might expect from a town like Caernarfon, was located deep in the maze of winding streets. He had a team of four men - including Glyn and Ed, who he kept a close eye on - and one woman. Most of the other teams were primarily female.

As John had divided up the four teams, he explained away the decision to allocate most of the men to one team with a straightforward answer: Ray's team would be doing most of the heavy lifting.

When Ray's brow had furrowed in response, John pressed a crumpled piece of paper into his hand. Several items were listed, most underlined. Ray had looked at it in confusion.

"I thought I already had a list," Ray said dubiously as he scanned the items.

"Now you have a new one," John replied curtly.

"Fertiliser? Paint thinner?" Ray had asked.

"Homemade explosives," John said, "Get as much as you can carry. Michael's talking about *air-horns and fireworks*, for Christ's sake. We're going to need something bigger. You get all this, and I'll do the rest. No more bows and arrows."

Ray ran with the paper burning a hole his pocket, and tried to focus only on committing the new shopping list to memory, but as soon as he left the wide open space of the river, and the town became claustrophobic and eerie, he found his mind turning to the possibility that the buildings he ran past were not empty.

The silence was heavy, weighed down by fear that rose with each passing step.

As he ran, Ray pulled his crossbow from his back. It was unwieldy, and made running awkward, but as the huddling buildings began to block out the faint light from the stars above, he decided there was no damn way he was going anywhere without a weapon in his hand. He loaded a bolt, and readied the firing mechanism, and tried in vain to suppress the image of the Infected pouring from the buildings around him as he ran deep into enemy territory.

When he finally saw the hardware store ahead, Ray let out an explosive gasp of relief. Just the thought of being inside a building again, surrounded by walls, helped to ease his nerves. He slowed his pace a little, mindful of the noise his increasingly frantic run was making, and almost screamed when he felt the fingers clutching at his arm.

The pharmacy was the closest of John's high-priority targets, but also the most intensive: John had stressed that he wanted *everything* from the pharmacy. Food, he had argued, was something they could obtain from almost anywhere once they left Caernarfon and headed north to find a ship on which to escape the UK. Medicine would be far harder to come by.

He painted a vivid picture of surviving the Infected and the inevitable nuclear meltdown on Anglesey only to die from a common-or-garden illness simply because they had no medical supplies. It made sense, but still Rachel had felt like she wasn't getting the whole story.

Rachel took three of Darren Oliver's former prisoners - one of whom she recognised as the young woman she had spoken to on her first morning at the castle - and sprinted back and forth along the waterfront, filling carrier bags with pills and bandages and carting them back to Michael and Linda, who shuttled them across the river and dropped them off with Claire and Pete.

She was making good time, and the pharmacy's shelves rapidly emptied. There was no sign of the Infected, and she began to relax a little. On her third trip back to the pharmacy, Rachel detoured to a small newsagent's opposite and filled a bag with cigarettes and tobacco pouches, feeling her nerves race deliriously as they anticipated the influx of nicotine that had been absent for far too long.

She thought about how Jason would nag her for smoking, as he always had before, and smiled. *Those things will kill you one day,* he had always said, *or mum will if she finds out.* At that moment, Rachel figured that if she lived long enough for smoking to kill her, she would have done pretty well.

She raced across the street to the pharmacy, and filled three more bags. The shelves were all but empty. Only nappies and baby food and beauty products remained.

"That's enough," Rachel said, bringing her team's raiding of the shelves to a halt. "Let's go."

*

Ray stared at Ed in disbelief, pulling the kid's fingers away from his arm.

"You crazy, kid?" He hissed. "I came *this* close to putting a damn bolt in your gut."

Ed pressed a finger to his lips and cocked an ear, listening intently, and Ray felt the blood draining from his face. He strained his ears, trying to pick up what Ed was hearing.

There was nothing.

"Sockets?" He breathed.

Ed shook his head and frowned.

"Something else. Listen."

Ray fell silent again. Somewhere below the thundering of his pulse, he *could* hear something.

What is that?

Somewhere to Ray's right, something sounded almost like it was *crying.*

Wide-eyed, Ray motioned to the others to stay put, and began to creep along the shop fronts until he reached a narrow alley. He peeked down it, and saw a parked car and a few overturned bins. It sounded like the noise was coming from them.

He advanced cautiously, keeping his finger crooked around the trigger of the crossbow. Sweat began to run down his temples.

It sounds like...it can't be...

Ray passed the car and saw dark blood smeared across the radiator grille, and rounded the toppled bins at exactly the same moment as his mind put together the sound he was hearing. By then it was too late. By then he was standing right next to the overturned pram, and his thoughts leaked away like a plug had been pulled in his mind.

A baby.

He stood, paralysed, the crossbow dangling from useless fingers, and stared at the filthy baby in horror, stared deep into its empty eye sockets and didn't move a muscle when it latched onto his calf muscle and clamped toothless gums on his flesh.

A wave of revulsion washed through Ray and he staggered backwards, frantically trying to shake the creature from his calf. Focusing entirely on the horror that tried in vain to chew through his leg, Ray didn't even see the empty soda bottle on the ground behind him, and when his foot tried to find purchase on it, he toppled backwards into the pile of bins with a crash that sounded like drums pounding in Hell.

The sickening stench of rotting waste washed over him, making him gag. But there was something else too, an odour that hung beneath the stink of rotten food. The smell of blood.

Ray's eyes widened, and he twisted his neck just in time to see the woman that had been pinned underneath the pile of rubbish. The woman whose spine looked like it was trying to free itself from the fleshy confines of her body. The woman with no eyes, who clawed herself on top of him and sank her teeth into his exposed midriff.

For a fraction of a second Ray felt like screaming, but the fear departed as quickly as it had arrived, and it took his eyes with it.

*

John pushed the door to the small police station cautiously, letting it swing open fully so he could stare into the gloomy interior for a second before stepping inside.

The trip from the castle had passed without incident, but stepping inside the two-storey building felt disconcertingly similar to the times he had breached buildings in the desert, expecting them to be fortified and full of enemy combatants; expecting to get a bullet in the face at any moment. Bullets weren't a problem in

Caernarfon, though John thought he might have preferred it if they were. At least bullets were *quick*.

He held a short sword he had taken from the castle's armoury out in front of him. The blade wasn't much bigger than a hunting knife, and it was far from *sharp*; probably it hadn't been effective for centuries, but it would cut well enough if swung with enough force. If the sword let him down, he had a smaller knife attached to his belt.

He proceeded slowly, creeping forward until he was fully inside and his eyes adjusted to the dim starlight that spilled through the dusty windows.

The entrance opened out into a small waiting area which held three uncomfortable-looking plastic chairs, and a long enquiry desk. John breathed a sigh of relief when he saw the layout of the place. He'd had visions of bulletproof glass partitions and heavy duty doors that would bar any progress into the building itself, but the Caernarfon police station was a far cry from *Scotland Yard*.

He beckoned the others to follow him inside and vaulted the enquiry desk as quietly as possible.

His gaze immediately fell on a handful of large flashlights lining a shelf, and he scooped them up and passed them out, checking each to make sure the batteries worked. Once the building was bathed in the roving lights, John allowed himself to breathe a little easier.

Empty.

He saw two cells that probably housed drunks most of the time, and aimed his light through the small viewing windows. Both were unoccupied.

The size of the place made John's heart sink a little. One look around told him the chances of finding guns inside was probably zero, and he didn't hold out much hope for riot gear, either.

A few desks with now-extinct computers sitting on them comprised the bulk of the ground floor, and John saw corkboards lining the walls, onto which were pinned pictures of missing children who would never be found.

John spotted a door to the rear of the room, next to the stairs that led up to the first floor, which was marked *authorised access only*. He moved to it slowly, keeping his eyes and the beam of his flashlight trained on the stairs, and gently tried the handle. Locked.

"Search the desks for keys to this door," he whispered to Emma, who stayed close enough behind him that she was practically attached. "And wait here."

"Where are you going?" Emma said, her eyes widening.

In response, John pointed his light at the stairs again, and put his finger to his lips. Emma nodded, and her face hardened a little in determination.

John smiled. When he had first met Emma, on the day she told him that Darren Oliver was waiting to meet the castle's new arrivals, John thought he had never seen anybody look so frightened, or so damaged. The girl now standing in front of him looked like she was consciously modelling herself on Rachel, and he thought she just might make it.

He nodded at Emma and left the others to search the ground floor and climbed, thankful that the stairs were of the solid marble variety, rather than wooden and creaky.

When he reached the top he paused, and played the flashlight across a narrow corridor and two small offices that presumably belonged to whoever had been the senior police officers in Caernarfon.

There was no sign of movement. He heard desk drawers being opened stealthily below him and prayed the noise wasn't carrying too far, and scurried into the first office, racing to the desk and opening each drawer in turn. He saw nothing of any value.

In the second office, which was far more opulent and must have belonged to Caernarfon's Chief Inspector, he spotted a nightstick leaning against the wall and tucked it under his arm. One by one, he went through the drawers in the desk, and was about to give up and return to the ground floor when he found a small padlocked box hidden at the rear of the bottom drawer.

A set of keys sat on the desk, and John searched through them until he found the one that matched the padlock.

Inside the box, John saw a small handwritten note laid across a plush velvet pouch:

Congratulations on thirty years of distinguished service, no shots fired!
Enjoy taking it easy in Wales ;)

John set the note aside and unwrapped the velvet pouch. Inside he found a ceremonial revolver that looked like something John Wayne might have carried, along with six polished rounds. The gun looked like a gleaming museum piece destined to sit in a display cabinet, and clearly had been made without the intention that it would ever be fired.

Jackpot.

John loaded the rounds into the six empty chambers and tucked the gun into his belt. Intended or not, he had a feeling the gun would end up being fired sooner rather than later.

With a quick final glance around to make sure there was nothing else of interest on the first floor, John hurried downstairs to find that Emma had opened the locked door, and was handing out tasers and pepper spray. It looked like everyone had a nightstick. It was hardly the haul John had optimistically hoped for, but it would do.

"Let's head back to Michael. Quickly, now," John said, and jogged outside into the cold, grey light, making for the castle.

That's when he heard the screaming.

32

Michael felt the blood draining from his face when the scream pierced the silence that hung over Caernarfon like a veil.

His arms ached like hell from pulling the raft across the river again and again and unloading the supplies that the groups raiding the town dropped off, but on hearing the blood-curdling cry he forgot the throbbing pain completely.

The scream seemed to go on forever, rising to a nerve-ripping crescendo before winding down and fading away like the whine of a circular saw.

Michael was on the castle-side of the river, unloading what felt like an endless supply of carrier bags and boxes that Rachel and Shirley's groups dropped off as they shuttled between the river and the town. They had plenty of food already, and what looked like the entire contents of a moderately-sized pharmacy.

He had seen no sign of John or Ray. Their destinations were buried deeper in the town, and they planned only one trip, there and back.

Michael squinted across the river, trying to determine the source of the scream, and discern whether it sounded like it had originated in the voice box of someone he knew.

"Gun," he barked at Claire, and she passed him the rifle he had left on the ground beside her, terrified of dropping it into the river and losing it. Without it, he was just a guy in a wheelchair. *Helpless.*

He slipped the rifle under his dead legs, praying his weight would keep it secure, and hauled himself back across the river, hand over hand along John's improvised rope bridge.

The water flowing to the sea battled him, and drained away his energy at an alarming rate. He focused on Linda, waiting for him on the opposite bank, and registered the fear in her eyes. Doubling his efforts, he pulled on the rope until his palms burned, and grasped

Linda's hand when he reached the other side, letting her hold him steady, and readying the rifle.

A dreadful notion crawled into his mind.

What if none of them make it?

He nearly let off a shot in surprise when Linda cried out next to him and pointed toward the harbour. Michael heaved a sigh of relief when he saw Rachel's group tearing toward him, still clutching a final load plundered from the pharmacy.

"Did you hear it?" Rachel gasped when she reached him.

"Yeah," Michael said with a grimace. "Any idea who it was?"

Rachel shook her head, and drew in several deep breaths.

"Here, help me get off this thing," Michael said, and leaned on Linda and Rachel to lever himself off the raft. He sat heavily on the ground, swinging the rifle left and right along the streets. "Get the stuff over the river," Michael grunted. "I've got your back."

Rachel had almost loaded all her items onto the raft when Michael saw Shirley racing toward him. He looked scared, but unscathed.

"Dropped the bags mate, sorry," Shirley puffed as he approached with his own small group of followers. "Decided pasta is off the menu when I heard *that*."

Michael grunted and nodded.

Two down, two to go.

Another scream. It sounded closer.

No, not a scream. A shriek. Michael knew what the noise meant. He had heard it often enough. It was the sound of the Infected locking onto prey.

"Rachel, Shirley, get everyone across," Michael said, keeping his eyes focused down the barrel of the rifle. "Be ready to shut the gate. If this goes bad, you shut it, okay? And you keep Claire safe."

He tore his eyes away from the streets and glared at Rachel.

"Keep her *safe*, Rachel. *Please*."

Rachel stared at him for a moment, and nodded, and then she was gone, helping Shirley with the task of hauling on the rope and shuttling over everybody that had returned from Caernarfon and ushering them inside the castle's main gate. Michael returned his gaze to the street, and saw movement.

He rested his finger on the trigger. He had only ever successfully fired the weapon at close quarters, and he knew he was no marksman. He had five rounds in the gun, and maybe another twenty stored in his room back in the castle. Every bullet counted. He had to wait.

The movement resolved itself into a single figure, barrelling straight toward him.

Infected?

Michael couldn't be sure. The figure ran chaotically, the movements not unlike the strange, angular gait that signified infection. Stifling a curse, he squinted, letting the figure get closer. His finger began to squeeze the trigger almost by itself.

"Don't shoot!"

Michael gasped and released the trigger.

The figure galloping toward him was the kid that John and Rachel had brought back on the yacht. *Ed.*

He was alone, tearing toward Michael with a look on his face that said he wasn't running for the hell of it, and Michael's heart sank.

"Behind me," Ed shrieked as he reached Michael. He didn't wait for the raft, plunging straight into the river. Michael heard the frantic splashing as he made his way across to the castle, and he pointed the rifle at the street Ed had sprinted down, and held his breath. Ed was alone, which meant that Ray and Glyn and the others...

Don't think about it.

Michael heard Shirley pulling the raft back across the river behind him, and knew the big man was coming to transport him across to the safety of the opposite bank. Michael gritted his teeth. He would hold on until the last second.

Where are you John?

"Go!" John roared.

They had made it roughly halfway back to the castle when he saw Glyn rocketing toward him along a narrow road comprised mainly of shops that sold gifts and souvenirs, unleashing a shriek that echoed around the cobbled streets and made them all freeze.

No eyes.

Most of the others travelling with John broke into a terrified sprint immediately, but John became aware of Emma rooted to the spot next to him, her eyes wide with fright.

"Emma, go!" He screamed. "They won't get past me. You have to *go!*"

John shoved her roughly away from him, half-worried that she would stumble to the ground. He let out an explosive gasp of relief when he saw her regain her balance and tear away after the others.

Seconds later, he heard the pounding feet and ragged breath as Glyn charged at him, and John fell to one side, raising a foot into the kid's stomach and propelling him into the wall of the nearest building with an awkward approximation of a judo throw. As John rose to his feet, he saw Glyn bouncing back up, oblivious to the smashed nose his meeting with the wall had produced.

The memory of the last time the kid had been part of an attack on John surfaced unbidden. Attacking John when he had been human had terrified Glyn; had almost left him in tears. Clearly he had no such issues now. With a roar, Glyn charged.

Damn things never stay down.

John slid the nightstick he'd acquired at the police station from his belt and smashed it into the incoming creature's throat, driving it back into the wall once more. The thing that had been Glyn coughed and sputtered, sounding almost human.

John didn't hesitate. He hefted the short sword and buried it deep into the kid's belly, twisting the blade and ripping it across his abdomen. John pivoted from the hip using all the strength in his upper body to compensate for the dull blade and swept it clear of Glyn's flesh.

Glyn staggered, still grasping weakly at John, until a final shattering blow with the flat edge of the sword knocked the poor bastard sideways. Glyn's body hit the ground a half-second after his intestines spilled out onto the cobbles.

John turned away, feeling nauseous, and his eyes widened.

More movement, charging toward him, like Glyn had called for reinforcements.

Ray. All of them.

It looked like the scream he had heard had been the sound of Ray's group failing to reach the hardware store. There was no time for John to curse the fact that he wouldn't be home-brewing any explosives. He counted four figures streaking down the road toward him.

Running is my plan A, he remembered saying to Emma. The girl had looked at him like she didn't quite believe him; like John could handle himself and would fight his way out of trouble.

John flung his nightstick at Ray as the eyeless biker closed in on him, and heard the *crunch* as the baton caught the infected man across the nose and floored him, but John didn't see the impact.

He was already running.

*

Shirley had done his best to persuade Michael to get on the raft, but Michael wouldn't even acknowledge the man. He stayed focused on the rifle's iron sights, waiting for a target to appear. The road Ed had appeared on remained empty.

Maybe something drew them away from him?

The notion made a cold knot of tension form in Michael's gut. There was only one other thing that could possibly draw the Infected away from their pursuit of a human, and that was other humans. And there were only a handful of *those* in Caernarfon.

He swept his gaze north, to the street John had taken en route to the police station.

Come on, John. Come on.

When Michael saw the first of John's group appear, sprinting and terrified but still in one piece, he clenched his fist in triumph.

They're going to make it.

But something was wrong. Michael counted the figures that sprinted toward him, but he didn't need numbers to tell him the truth. The people running toward the raft were all small and slight. All female.

"On the raft," Michael roared as they approached. "Emma, where's John?"

Emma looked back in the direction she had come from, and her face contorted in confusion.

"He was behind me," she said, her eyes filling with tears. "He was fighting them, but then he ran, and he was *right behind me.*"

Michael felt himself deflating as the thought of having to proceed without John loomed in his mind. He spent a lot of time butting heads with John, but the man was invaluable; the only reason any of them were still alive.

Fuck.

Michael saw movement on the street. Something *had* been running behind Emma, but it wasn't John. It was Ray. *Had been* Ray. But Ray was gone, replaced by a walking weapon that closed on the raft with a fearsome, single-minded purpose.

Michael heard Shirley let out a grief-stricken moan behind him, and then he felt the big man's arms wrapping themselves around his torso, and suddenly Michael was on the raft, and Shirley was pulling hand over hand on the rope, dragging Michael away from Caernarfon and back to the castle, and Michael felt dark clouds gathering in his mind.

33

"John didn't make it," Michael said to nobody in particular, in a bereft tone.

They were gathered on the edge of the river, watching, stunned, as the last of the group of Infected that had been their friends were washed out to sea.

Rachel couldn't believe it. *Wouldn't* believe it. When the raft made its final voyage across the river, delivering Michael and Shirley to the castle and she saw Ray, eyeless and horrific, plunging into the fast-flowing water and being pulled away by the current, all she could think about was John.

He can't be gone.

The man had survived far worse. He was practically fucking *bulletproof.* How could he have fallen while Emma and the others made it?

"Where's John?" She snapped at Emma, grabbing the crying girl's narrow shoulders and forcing her to look into Rachel's blazing eyes.

Emma shook her head miserably.

"I...he...he was catching me up!" She moaned. "He was right behind me, and they were chasing us. I don't know."

Tears flowed freely down Emma's face, and Rachel felt a stab of sympathy for the girl. Somehow it had been easy to view the other people at the castle purely as comrades-in-arms, but when Emma began to cry, Rachel abruptly realised that the person standing in front of her was a young girl who a couple of weeks earlier had probably been busy worrying about school exams and whether that boy in her class liked her in *that* way.

Tears blurred her own eyes as Rachel realised that the effect the violence of the world was having on her was profound and irreversible. She was hardening, becoming cynical and cold.

She grabbed Emma and pulled her close, hugging her fiercely. After a moment, Emma returned the hug and sobbed into Rachel's shoulder.

"You did great, Emma," Rachel said, brushing away the girl's tears. "You did great."

Emma shook her head and choked out a sob.

"I don't know what happened," she said. "He was right behind me."

Rachel's eyes narrowed.

Ray had been a good distance behind Emma. Of course, he could have been slowed down when he stopped to tear John apart, or...

She remembered the way John had been acting before they left the castle, like he was up to something. He had avoided Rachel's gaze, almost as if he was guilty about something he didn't want her to know. She frowned.

"You didn't see him...uh...getting attacked?"

Emma shook her head and sniffed. "He killed Glyn, but then he ran. He was catching up to me."

"Didn't hear anything?"

"No, nothing." Emma looked at Rachel, and suddenly her wet eyes were filled with incomprehension. "Why?"

The truth wriggled free and danced in Rachel's mind until she acknowledged it. Her eyes widened.

John, you bastard, she thought.

She grabbed Emma's shoulders again.

"Tell Michael I'm coming back, okay? Tell him to keep a look out."

Emma stared at Rachel in confusion that deepened when Rachel turned and dived into the river, swimming frantically with the current, and disappearing toward the sea.

*

John's arms ached like a rotten tooth; his whole body burned and throbbed from yet another battle with the surging waves of the Irish Sea. He had felt bad about leaving Emma and the others, but they had been close enough to the castle for him to trust they would be okay.

As soon as he saw the river, John had thrown himself into it, crossing in a few powerful strokes and emerging on the steep, jagged rocks behind the castle. Glancing back at the town, he saw Ray tearing after Emma, and paused until he was sure she had made it back to the raft safely. Michael would know how to deal with Ray. If all else failed, he had the rifle.

John turned his attention to the rocks, which were sharp and forbidding. He had done a little climbing in a past life, and he navigated them without too much trouble, clambering carefully across the unforgiving terrain until he finally reached a vertical drop that fell away into the sea around forty feet below.

After taking a moment to check that he wasn't going to land on rocks, John dived.

The current was against him, and it took John an eternity to reach the boat. He spent most of the swim praying that Rachel hadn't pulled up the rope ladder he had left dangling over the side, and feeling guilty that he hadn't filled her in on his intention to go to Anglesey alone. Right now, Rachel - all of them - probably thought John was dead.

There had been no other way. Rachel would have insisted on going with him to find Jason, and that would doubtless have spiralled into going in force. Bloodshed would inevitably follow. Far better for John to go alone. Without the others to look after, he could find the people that had tortured Ed, find Jason and get the hell out.

If it all worked perfectly, no one would even know John had been there. If it didn't, well, he had the gun. He doubted anyone on Anglesey had a gun, but even if they did, John would back himself if matters devolved to the point where shooting became inevitable. He had six shots, and he had his knife. More importantly he would have the element of surprise.

Finally, when the build-up of lactic acid in his muscles felt like it was close to paralysing him, he reached the boat, and gave silent thanks when he saw the rope ladder still hanging over the side.

He pulled himself up and crashed onto his back on the deck, breathing heavily, waiting for the burning in his limbs to fade.

After taking a minute to catch his breath he twisted the lever that would raise the yacht's small anchor from the depths. The boat began to bob away from the castle, and John pulled on the rope that released the main sail, grateful that he finally had a vague idea how to operate the boat. The wind had died a little, but the sail slowly billowed out and the boat began to move smoothly away from Caernarfon.

He secured the sail and stepped into the cabin to steer toward the distant Anglesey shore.

"Bastard."

John squeezed his eyes shut in frustration.

"Hi, Rachel," he said through gritted teeth.

"What the hell are you doing, John?"

John sighed. Somehow, while he had been congratulating himself on successfully carrying out his clever plan, he had overlooked just how damn *sharp* Rachel could be.

She stood in the cabin, dripping water and breathing heavily. It looked like she had arrived not long before him. Her face told a tale of righteous fury.

"I'm trying to avoid a damn war, Rachel. What the hell are *you* doing here?"

"He's my brother," Rachel said in a flat tone that barely disguised her anger. "Where else would I be?"

"Back in the castle. *Safe,*" John snapped. "I can get him, and nobody needs to get killed. We don't need to start a fight with whoever these lunatics are. Haven't we got enough problems already?"

Rachel snorted.

"So, what, you're going to sneak in like James bloody Bond and just whisk him away without them even noticing, is that it?"

"Something like that," John said glumly. Rachel had a way of making it sound ridiculous, and for a moment, John considered telling her that this wouldn't be his first rodeo, but he shook the idea away. She would inevitably ask questions, and there was too much history that he didn't want to relive.

"Well, now you've got help. How about that?"

John glared at Rachel and she glared right back, setting her mouth in a firm grimace that dared him to object. For a moment John searched his mind for some response; some way to put a plan that had unravelled spectacularly back together.

He heaved a weary sigh.

"Then let's go," he said finally.

34

According to what Ed had told them of Anglesey, the hotel that the old woman was using as a base of operations was a little way south of a huge area of sand dunes.

John dropped the anchor about fifty feet away from the sand and figured all he had to do once he was on dry land was follow the coast until he found his target.

Ed had told them all that there *were* Infected on Anglesey, but there didn't appear to be many. It made sense: the island had a small population and the only link to the mainland was a pair of long suspension bridges. It didn't seem likely the Infected would cross them unless they were pursuing something. And besides, most of the Infected in the northern part of Wales had already been drawn to Caernarfon.

Anglesey, once it had finished tearing itself apart, would comprise a few survivors, a few Infected, and a whole lot of dead bodies. When the power station inevitably decimated the island, it would become a wasteland.

The place made John's nerves complain loudly.

John and Rachel moved slowly along the sand, keeping low, and searching for signs of movement. Finally the sand gave way to grass that seemed to John to be strangely manicured, until he realised he was standing on a fairway. The hotel's golf course.

"We're close," John hissed at Rachel. "Stay low. If they've got any sense they'll have posted lookouts. Make sure we see them before they see us."

Rachel nodded and followed John off the fairway. The area that comprised *the rough*, into which presumably thousands of golf balls had been sent to a chorus of muttered curses, was mainly low bushes and the odd tree that rustled softly in the slight wind.

John crouched low in the bushes and made his way forward by inches, ignoring the impatience that radiated from Rachel next to him. If she was determined to tag along, she would do it *his* way, he thought, and that meant going slow, and not getting spotted.

Eventually, John was close enough to see the hotel, and he put a hand on Rachel's shoulder to stop her. Together, they laid prone in the bushes, crawling forward until John could part the branches that jabbed painfully into his torso and get a clear view.

The hotel was large, and grand. Ed had mentioned a jetty, and John saw it to his right. To his left he saw an open-air eating area with wooden picnic benches. Beyond that a bar area lurked behind floor-to-ceiling glass. The place had four floors, and he saw movement in several of the windows. The window that led to the bar had been smashed, and Rachel pointed at it and looked at John inquiringly.

He frowned. It was a way in, but it all seemed a little *too* easy. The bar beyond was dark, but it looked empty. *Are they so complacent?*

John couldn't imagine anyone being so relaxed about maintaining a watch on their surroundings. Maybe Ed had been right, and the small number of Infected on Anglesey meant the people at the hotel weren't fully aware of just how the world worked now. Or maybe they were simply arrogant enough that they believed themselves to be safe. If that was the case, John thought, there was a chance they had gotten their hands on some weapon that he had not anticipated; something that gave them confidence that they could deal with the Infected easily.

He shook his head firmly at Rachel.

"Wait," he breathed. "Watch for however long it takes. We don't even know if Jason is really in there, but even if he is we don't go charging in. If somebody leaves a door open, it's because they *want* you to use it."

Rachel nodded, and settled down to wait.

An hour or more had passed by the time John saw movement in the bar. An old woman walking alongside a tall, thin man, talking animatedly.

That must be her, John thought. *Ed's crazy old psycho.*

To John, she looked no more threatening than the average grandmother. Short and plump, grey-haired and waddling. He reminded himself that Gwyneth had looked like an average old woman too, and had been anything but. If the woman led a large group of people loyal enough or afraid enough to overlook her apparent lunacy, underestimating her would be dangerous.

The woman and the man disappeared from John's sight. Moments later, they returned, walking back the way they had come. But this time another figure trailed behind them, and as soon as John's eyes brought the figure into focus, his mouth dropped open and his heart sank. The former because Rachel had been right: Jason was alive and no more than fifty yards away. The latter because the old woman was leading Jason by a rope tied around his neck, like a dog on a leash, and even from this distance John could see the scars that laced the man's bare torso.

Jason looked like he had suffered extensive torture.

Rachel won't be able to help herself, she will -

He reached out to grab Rachel, but too late. She was already leaping to her feet, already screaming her brother's name and rushing forward.

Things began to move quickly, and all John's careful preparation collapsed like a house of cards.

John leapt to his feet, charging past Rachel as the old woman and her companion turned to face him, their mouths slackening with surprise.

"Rachel, wait," John snarled as he passed her, grabbing her arm to halt her forward momentum.

Without looking back, he raced toward the broken window, and the old woman, pulling the revolver from his belt and pointing it at her face.

"You let him go, you live," John growled, his gaze flitting between the old woman's wrinkled, tiny eyes and Jason's familiar, vacant stare.

"You must be from the castle," the old woman said with a devious smile. She looked over John's shoulder at Rachel. "He talked about *you*," she said with a smirk. "Back when he could talk."

Her eyes glittered with malice.

"Let him go," John said again. "I've been killing people since long before all *this* started. I *will* shoot you if I have to."

The old woman shrugged and dropped the leash that connected her to Jason. She turned to face him and pointed a bony finger at John. "He wants to hurt your mother, dear child," she said softly, and ran her hand down Jason's cheek.

John's brow furrowed as he watched Jason sigh and nuzzle her palm like a loving pet.

What the fuck?

Jason lumbered through the smashed window, and Rachel burst past John. When she threw her arms around her brother and Jason didn't even acknowledge her, peeling her away from him like burnt skin and pushing her aside, John realised that the rescue mission had been doomed from the beginning. There was no rescuing a man that didn't want to be rescued. No helping a man whose mind was as broken as Jason's clearly was.

As John looked into the big man's eyes, he saw no flicker of emotion or recognition. Whatever the old woman had done to him had caused grievous, catastrophic damage.

"Jason, stop," John said firmly, bringing the gun around and pointing it at him.

Jason didn't stop, and when John heard Rachel shrieking in horror he knew that there was no way he could shoot him.

Fuck.

He began to crouch even as Jason swung his massive arm in a punch that would have pulverized John's face if it had connected.

John ran to his default response, dropping low instinctively and sweeping Jason's leg. It was like sweeping a solid oak tree. John felt a little give in the big man's knee, but not enough. Before he had time to think that getting Jason to the floor was imperative and perhaps impossible, a fist like a sledgehammer crunched into John's cheek with the force of a locomotive, and his head rang like a bell.

The world tilted dangerously.

Move.

John rolled away from a second punch that whistled harmlessly past his face and lurched to his feet already spinning, delivering a solid kick into Jason's ribs.

He heard the breath exploding from the big man's lungs and followed up the kick with a blur of punches to Jason's torso. Jason staggered backwards in surprise and pain, and John lined up a kick that would land on Jason's square jaw and put an end to it.

"John, stop!"

Rachel, screaming. Crying.

John hesitated, and his gaze flicked to her for just an instant.

It was long enough.

He didn't see the punch coming; barely even realised that he had been struck before he was lying on the ground blinking up at the clouds that meandered across the dark sky.

On auto-pilot, John rolled to one side as Jason threw an enormous punch down at him, springing onto his haunches and shoulder-charging Jason's knee, desperate to bring him to the deck.

This time Jason's leg *did* snap backwards, but still the big man remained upright, and John felt huge arms wrapping around his ribs like a vice, lifting him away from the ground and smashing him back down. A searing jolt of pain travelled up John's spine and he gasped. His vision began to fray around the edges.

"Jason, wait," John tried to say feebly, but the words were lost in the crunching impact as Jason brought his fist down from the heavens and smashed John's head into the ground.

As the darkness claimed John, he heard Rachel crying and an old woman laughing, chuckling appreciatively, as if someone had just told her a vaguely amusing anecdote.

35

John woke to a feeling of insistent nausea, almost as if he were being carried along by choppy seas. He blinked, staring up at clouds, dimly aware that it was daylight now, and hadn't been when he had been smashed into unconsciousness by Jason. His heart pounded out a concerned rhythm.

At least opening his eyes explained the rolling nausea: one-part concussion, two-parts the fact that he actually *was* on the sea, on his own boat in fact, though this was the first time he'd travelled on it while being tied down to the deck.

He craned his neck to see who else was aboard, groaning inwardly at the pain even that slight motion caused.

He saw Rachel immediately, tied to the boat's low handrail, staring vacantly at the deck. Her blank expression told John all he needed to know: she hadn't been able to get through to Jason, not even after the big man had finished rearranging John's face.

John heard muttered curses: there were a handful of men on the boat, struggling to comprehend the operation of the sails, apparently unaware that they could move the boom to switch the sail from left to right to catch the wind. John heard the old woman's voice muttering something he couldn't quite make out. After a brief moment of struggle, John discovered that he had been tied by someone that knew their way around a knot, and wouldn't be freeing himself any time soon. He closed his eyes, and let his pounding head fall back to the deck.

When he opened his eyes again, the boat was anchored near the mouth of the river, and he saw the stone towers of Caernarfon Castle looming above him, and he felt a sickly anxiety rising in his gut.

*

"There, Dad!"

Michael focused on the ocean in the distance, following the direction Claire pointed out. After a moment, he was able to pick out the rippling white smear of the sail against the grey waves.

When Emma had told him about the strange conversation she'd had with Rachel, and the way Rachel had subsequently disappeared, taking the yacht with her, he had spent a long time putting the pieces together. Rachel had gone after Jason, that much was obvious, what Michael couldn't work out was *why*. Why *then*, rather than waiting to plan out a proper attack?

The answer, of course, had to be John, who had a track record of disappearing on missions of his own whenever he felt like it. As the night had worn on, Michael felt bitter anger flowing freely through him at John's selfishness, mixed with desperate hope that the man was still alive.

Hour after hour, he waited for the boat to return, and finally as dawn began to break over the horizon, he resigned himself to the fact that whatever had happened on Anglesey - whether Rachel had been right about Jason or not - they weren't coming back.

The anger Michael felt was, he realised eventually, as much to do with his own helplessness as his grief at two more people dying. John and Rachel had become almost like family, despite how briefly he had known them. They bickered, and Michael was pretty sure John couldn't stand him, but they worked well together, and they had each other's backs. Without them, the idea of travelling north and getting away from Wales seemed overwhelming.

Finally he gave up on watching the featureless ocean and slept, only to be woken a couple of hours later by Pete and Claire, excitedly telling him that the boat was coming back.

He rubbed away the fog of sleep in his eyes and shivered at the cold that felt like it had invaded his bones.

The boat looked to be a few minutes out, approaching the castle in a wide arc that made seeing who was aboard impossible. Something about that angle of approach made him nervous, and Michael told everyone to wait at the gate. He waited with them, and he kept the rifle clutched tightly in his hands.

He laughed in relief when he heard Rachel's voice shouting to open the gate, and moved to the portcullis mechanism without thinking; without recognising the strange, clipped tone of her voice.

The portcullis rose with a screech, and Michael nodded to Shirley to push the huge door open. Shirley heaved against the heavy wood with a wide, welcoming smile on his face and light flooded into the courtyard.

The smile fell away immediately.

*

Annie blinked in surprise when she saw the large, tattooed man standing in front of her as the gate opened. She hadn't known what to expect: Rachel had refused to say anything about the occupants of the castle or the man Voorhees had beaten to a pulp.

Annie knew his name - John - and nothing more, but she had seen him fight, and it had been impossible to miss the steely resolve in his eyes as he had pointed the pistol at her. *I've been killing people since long before all this started,* he had said, and it had not struck Annie as an empty bluff.

The threat made him either military, police or some sort of serial killer. The way he had so efficiently taken Voorhees apart before the girl's *unfortunate* intervention narrowed that short list down even further.

The girl had spark, Annie thought, and a dangerous, mutinous look in her eyes. Annie would have killed them both instantly, if it weren't for Voorhees. The big man was broken, perhaps irreparably, but there was no sense in risking losing her grip on him by executing Rachel.

So she had settled for killing John, but had been stopped at the last minute by Gareth Hughes' ever-logical advice.

We can use them to get inside the castle, Annie. Nowhere will be safer than there, Hughes had said.

He was right, but that didn't make Annie feel any better about essentially being overruled in front of her sons and the rest of what remained of Newborough. Hughes had to be re-educated about his position, Annie decided, and filed his insolence away, determined to revisit it at the appropriate time.

Annie finally got Rachel to speak for the first time when they reached the castle gate after an irritating swim that Annie thought was no dignified way for a woman of her age and standing to be travelling.

Rachel had refused for a moment, glaring stubbornly at Annie, and had only relented when Annie pushed the barrel of the pistol into John's forehead.

Her voice was like a key to the huge wooden door.

Annie surveyed the small group of people that stood behind the tattooed man that had opened the door. To her surprise the majority of them were young girls. Annie had feared a force of people like John, but the most dangerous of all of them looked to be a man that sat in a wheelchair cradling a rifle.

Annie had just five people with her, alongside the two prisoners, but all were large men, and all except one were armed with golf clubs. Annie knew Rhys and Bryn would not hesitate to use the weapons if she told them to. Both her sons had come a long way, and shared traits with their dead brother that were blossoming in the new world. They were finally making her proud.

As for the others...well, the fear of the gun would work just as well on them if they fell out of line. The final man in her group was unarmed, but the sheer size of him would intimidate most people, and Annie did not think Voorhees would betray her, not now that the damaged giant had somehow concluded that she was his mother.

"Hand over your rifle," Annie said pleasantly to the man in the wheelchair. She jabbed the pistol further into John's temple.

"Don't, Michael," John mumbled. He appeared to be having trouble staying conscious. Annie smirked at him, and fixed the man in the wheelchair with a penetrating stare.

"I'll kill them both," she said with a shrug. "Your choice."

*

Michael barely heard John's plea. As he stared at the group that stood outside the castle gate, his mind flitted between the present and a past filled with blood and the sound of a baby screaming, and a choice that had led to violence and death.

He tightened his grip on the rifle, measuring the distance between himself and the old woman, wondering whether he was a good enough shot. A dark, insistent urge to shoot pulsed in his mind, and he fought to control it, focusing on Claire, standing beside him. Everything he had done had been with one goal in mind: keeping her safe. Staring at the old woman's cold, calculating eyes, he didn't think for a second that she would hesitate to kill a child.

But if Michael started shooting...

Darren Oliver's words came back to him abruptly.

We do what we have to do, don't we Michael?

Michael's shoulders slumped, and he let the rifle fall to the ground.

"This castle is under new management," Annie said, beaming as she picked up the rifle and passed it to the man that held John's collar. "You'll all have a chance to prove your loyalty. Until then, I'm afraid you'll have to be locked up for a little while. It's for your own good."

She grinned savagely at Michael.

"But first, an example must be set," she sneered.

*

Kneeling, with his hands tied firmly behind his back, John watched numbly as the old woman and the man who now held Michael's beloved rifle herded the occupants of the castle up against the wall, and told them that if anybody moved, they would die.

It almost made him smile. Even after everything that had happened; even with their very race on the brink of extinction, it seemed people hadn't changed one bit. Maybe they *couldn't*. If he closed his eyes, John could almost imagine that he was back in the desert. Only the names had changed.

It's no wonder we've ended up destroying ourselves, he thought. *It's in our nature.*

Rhys and Bryn grabbed John's armpits and hauled him to his feet. As they dragged him past Michael, he forced a stumble and fell onto the crippled man's lap.

"Get to Australia, Mike," he growled. "They haven't touched Aus-"

Rhys hauled John upright and pulled him away, but when John looked back over his shoulder he saw recognition in Michael's eyes and knew the message had been understood. It was all he could do.

When they reached the centre of the courtyard, the two men forced John back down onto his knees, and for a moment they paused, looking to their mother for final confirmation. John felt the crushing weight of everybody's eyes on him, and heard a woman's voice cry out a wordless grief-stricken moan, and his heart broke.

Annie nodded, and John felt the cold steel of a knife against his neck.

"You can do this, Rachel," John said, staring numbly at the floor.

When he lifted his gaze, a crippling, overwhelming sadness consumed him as he forced himself to look at her, and saw the tears in her eyes.

Should have kissed her when you had the chance, John. You always were an idio-

The thought dissolved in an acid bath of blinding pain as the knife bit deep into John's throat and began its ragged journey through muscle and cartilage, and then with a strangely euphoric rush the blade was pulled free. John had a terrible, eternal moment to feel his life ebbing from the catastrophic hole that had been torn in him, and then finally, after a life soaked in unrelenting violence, he found peace.

There was, Annie decreed, no need to lock up the cripple or the children. After all, she informed Michael with a sly grin, she wasn't a *monster*.

All the others - including Rachel - Annie told her people to lock into the cramped cells that lined the interior of the wall, leaving the castle almost empty while she sent one of her sons back to the boat to begin the task of shuttling over all her people from Anglesey.

When she was satisfied the others posed no threat, she said, they would be welcome to join what she called *my family*. At least *some* of them, she had told Michael with a knowing smile, would be set free.

He hadn't missed the implication of her words. Some of the people now imprisoned would never get out alive. Maybe all of them would be left to rot. The castle was now in the possession of a cult, led by a maniac, and those that didn't conform would be killed.

But the castle would kill them all. John had been right about that from day one, and Michael wished he had listened.

He sat once more on the battlements, staring out to sea and watching the yacht as it made the first of many trips across the Menai Strait.

It was a clear day, and in the distance he thought he saw a thin plume of grey smoke rising into the sky. Trouble was brewing on Anglesey, uranium-tipped and deadly.

We have to get out.

I have to get them out.

Michael dropped his gaze to his feet, and strained every muscle, willing them to move, gritting his teeth with the effort of trying to shift his legs, just an inch.

His eyes widened.

Epilogue

Phil Sanderson had asked to meet Fred Sullivan at 3pm, So Fred left his office at one, and made his way directly to the research deck.

The journey was irritating: everything on the ship was narrow, and the chopping waves of the North Sea challenged his balance with every step. Walking anywhere was a matter of squeezing through gaps and clumsily navigating the other people he met in the thin metallic veins of the vessel, and of grabbing handholds to prevent stumbling.

Irritating, but worth it. Fred had long ago learned the virtue of dropping in on his staff unannounced. Arriving early was the quickest route through the bullshit.

When Fred stepped into the large space that Sanderson and his team inhabited he was struck by how messy and chaotic it appeared, and by the *cornered* look on Sanderson's infuriatingly round face.

The journey had been essential: Fred could tell from the man's slack expression that the scientists Fred paid so handsomely were making no progress. Shaving off all the bullshit Sanderson would doubtless have embalmed his report in was a time saver in Fred's case, and possible a life-saver in Sanderson's. Fred desperately wanted to kill the man. The big brain concealed beneath his expansive, sweaty forehead kept the scientist alive, but Fred's patience was being severely tested.

While Sanderson stammered and the atmosphere in the room began to thicken with anxiety, Fred said nothing. He marched to a bank of monitors that relayed images of the mutation's brain. The visual was, Fred thought, quite beautiful. Like a miniature universe, an array of pulsing lights like stars.

"Mr Sanderson," Fred said without looking at the man. "Bad news is beginning to irritate me." His tone was like a loaded gun, and he knew the scientist wouldn't miss the implication of his words.

Fred turned and looked at the man expectantly. Sanderson clutched at a handful of papers like a security blanket. He looked like he was having trouble choking back the urge to vomit.

"Uh, Sir, it's not *bad* news exactly but, uh, well. You see the activity in his brain?" He pointed at the screen Fred had been watching, and cleared his throat, his eyes rolling up to the ceiling, as though trying to recall the best way to begin a rehearsed speech.

"All humans have-"

"Mr Sanderson," Fred hissed. "Get to the point. *Now.*"

Phil Sanderson swallowed visibly and nodded.

"We need McIntosh awake, Sir."

Fred's bushy grey eyebrows lowered.

*

At first in the underground base in Northumberland, and then on the ship that held position among a small fleet in the North Sea, they had tested the small vial of blood, hoping to reverse engineer the extraordinary mutation that had transformed Jake McIntosh from a schizoid serial killer into a more physical sort of monster, with some *fascinating* talents.

The first experiment had been a disaster. Of course, to Fred, the fact they were once more using words like *experiment* was a disaster in and of itself. The time for experimenting was meant to have been over. Decades had been spent on tests and trial runs. Fred had spent countless hours staring at flipboards, his eyes gradually glazing over, as he listened to scientists and researchers prattling on about this breakthrough or that advance.

He hadn't cared about any of it. The minutiae were for the people he paid to work out; the very reason he had sunk billions into Project Wildfire was so he wouldn't have to worry about *how* it would work, just that it did.

In many ways, that was all money wasted. Project Wildfire had collapsed. One tiny alteration by one insignificant programmer had corrupted the entire process. What was left was not the sort of precision strike that Fred had wanted. It was more like a cluster bomb dropped blindly.

The damage was enormous, but it was also uncontrolled; messy. It threw all their plans for clearing up the aftermath into chaos. Hell, more than *chaos*: increasingly it appeared that the straightforward cleanup Fred had anticipated was going to look more like a war. Money wasted.

Fred hated wasting money, but wasting *time* was an unforgivable crime. He had plenty of money; as he approached his mid-seventies, it was time that was valuable.

They had conducted the first experiment at the underground base in Northumberland, at Sanderson's request.

Sanderson had argued that they would need to establish a baseline for their results. He waffled about control groups and comparison studies until Fred's vision blurred with the tedium of it and his mind ran to blowing the man's head off with a large-calibre weapon.

When he finally reached the point, that they needed to test McIntosh's blood on the various blood types to determine the effects, Fred acquiesced without a blink, and was irritated that the head of research had even brought the matter to him. Sanderson, it appeared, still had some sort of conscience when faced with the prospect of killing a human being in the name of science. Clearly, Fred had thought, the man hadn't been paying attention.

The first round of tests made the group of subjects' blood boil in their bodies, slowly cooking their organs. It was, Fred supposed, an excruciating way to die. More importantly it was a colossal waste of time. Only those with AB Negative - the rarest of the blood types - were important.

Sanderson had wasted time on rediscovering what they already knew, but he also wasted the blood. They had started with around 100ml of McIntosh's blood which was, Fred reckoned, by a distance the most valuable substance on earth. Already half of it had been wasted on the first experiments.

When Sanderson had finally tested one of the small number of *volunteers* that had the correct blood type, the outcome had been different but the ultimate result the same.

The unfortunate recipient of the blood had changed alright, but the change had been nothing like the incredible transformation Jake McIntosh himself had undergone. No, this time the blood turned the subject into a vast boil, swelling remorselessly until his body *burst* and left a mess that would take days to clear.

There had been no superhuman strength or speed. Even worse, the subject's mind had been the first thing to go: as his body had inflated, skin stretching and tearing, the man had been reduced to unintelligible screams and grunts. If they couldn't keep the mind intact, as McIntosh had, there was no point at all. Fred had tried creating brainless monsters once, and that had turned out pretty badly.

When Sanderson had come to the panic room that Fred had made his office to report that he needed more of McIntosh's blood, Fred had come perilously close to killing the trembling man on the spot.

McIntosh had already decimated the Northumberland base, and left it vulnerable and exposed, carving open a path from the subterranean guts up into the open air that left a trail of destruction and bodies. Ordinarily, Fred wouldn't have cared about the bodies, but the troubling fact was that he didn't have that many to spare. Most of the people that had bought their way into the base were worse than useless, and many of the soldiers that *would* have been of use had been ripped to pieces during McIntosh's escape.

The ultimate goal of Wildfire: the cleansing of the planet; the population reduction that would allow the select few involved to take unassailable control, was further away than ever. Fred had known when he found his head of security's body - *the parts of his body* - that the utopia he had striven for was not going to transpire. So the people at the base, the ones with lots of money and no real use, were just dead weight.

Fred forcibly took the ones that were AB Negative, and executed the rest.

Half a century in the cutthroat world of business had taught him to move swiftly with the markets. Goals and strategies needed to be fluid and adaptable.

Cutting the base loose just made good sense. Besides, there were other bases. And what McIntosh's miraculous transformation offered was not just a seat at the table when the other leaders around the world emerged from their cocoons to take control once more, but a throne to rule them all. There would be other mutations out there, other variations on the Jake McIntosh theme, but Fred thought that for the most part, the other bases might not even know what was happening. Fred had the competitive edge, as long as he had the blood and the scientists to tame it into a form that could be controlled and exploited.

Tracking McIntosh down after his escape from Northumberland had been easy, even without the help of satellites. Just a matter of following the absurd trail of death. Given godlike power, McIntosh had simply sought to carry on the life he had lived before: mindless killing and slavering insanity.

The man - hyperevolved or not - was doomed to think *small.*

Capturing the abomination had been a thing of beauty; a rare instance of a plan carried out to perfection, like a musician delivering a perfect rendition of a complicated overture. Fred had even had the chance to talk to McIntosh before they took him, and to see the pain and the outrage at the humbling defeat contort the monster's misshapen face. *Delicious.*

It was as the helicopters had flown to intercept McIntosh that Fred got to actually see what Project Wildfire had done to the country. They flew over ruined towns and burning cities, over great herds of the Infected that were supposed to have died as per their programming, but which instead roamed the lands like flocking birds, hunting down the surviving members of the human race and converting them. There would be other mutations down there too, Sanderson had promised

Fred, though he hypothesised that each could be unique. The virus, he said, would react differently depending on the host. Wildfire had taken human evolution and poured rocketfuel into its engine. The results were likely to be...unpredictable.

What was certain was that the UK was lost. It would be just a matter of time before one of the herds found their way to the installation in Northumberland, and the people within would not be able to hide. McIntosh had left the front door wide open.

So Fred was forced to cede the country for the time being, retreating to the fleet of ships that sat off the coast of Scotland. Again he was to be surrounded by the wealthy, by the paying tourists, but they no longer mattered in the slightest. There was a greater military presence within the fleet, and far greater weaponry. If the mystery of McIntosh's blood couldn't be unravelled, Fred would be forced to the last resort.

The idea of nuking his own country didn't appal Fred; he couldn't have cared less. But the notion that after all he had gone through, across decades and billions, he would wind up having accomplished nothing, well, that bothered him greatly.

It was time to conduct a second experiment. And this time, they could use as much blood as they needed. McIntosh was secure. Wildfire was far from done.

Yet now, after all that Fred had gone through, when the ongoing clusterfuck appeared to have finally been brought under control, Sanderson was standing in front of Fred and telling him that they needed Jake McIntosh *awake.*

Fred punched the man squarely in the nose, almost sighing with satisfaction as his bony knuckles impacted on the man's sweaty flesh. Fred had been a boxer in his youth. As his years advanced he fought against aging with the same energetic vigour he had utilised in the ring, battling it with a strict exercise regime. It was a punch from a pensioner in name only.

Sanderson crumpled to the floor with a whimper, and Fred drew himself up to his full height and drew in a deep breath, closing his eyes and searching for calm. Only when he was certain he wasn't going to beat Sanderson to death did he reopen them.

"Why?" Fred asked in a low voice that oozed menace.

Sanderson wiped blood away from his broken nose and blinked rapidly to clear the tears from his eyes.

"When we keep him comatose," Sanderson replied with a sniff, "Only a certain part of his brain is active. It's not the same pattern we see in humans. The pattern is steady, and in his current state his blood has different properties. You see," Sanderson said, climbing upright with a wary look on his face, like he expected to be knocked straight back down, "on the screen, the dark areas?"

He pointed.

"In a normal human brain, we would see activity here, but in McIntosh there is none. It would take years of tests to understand that activity."

He held his hands up protectively as Fred glowered.

"B-but I think if he is awake, we'll see activity in *this* part of the brain, the dormant part, and there will be an effect on his blood. If we're trying to recreate Jake's condition, we need something to recreate."

"When did you start calling him Jake?"

The question seemed to throw Phil Sanderson, and he stammered and mumbled while Fred's mind raced. He had already seen what McIntosh could do, but they were prepared for it now. McIntosh could be restrained. Immobilised. But getting blood from his body while he was awake wasn't a job Fred imagined anybody would be volunteering for.

"Fine," Fred said, cleaving the legs from Sanderson's mumbling response. "Security will be provided. Once everything is in order you can wake him, Sanderson."

Fred turned to leave as Sanderson nodded profuse, sweaty thanks. As he slipped through the narrow doorway he spoke again without looking back.

"Get ready to leave," Fred said. "You'll be extracting the blood yourself."

Fred strode away without waiting to hear Phil's protest, and chuckled when he thought he could almost *hear* the colour draining from Sanderson's face.

*

When Fred departed, and the shadow he had cast over Phil Sanderson finally began to clear, Phil walked from the lab on weak, trembling legs. The decision had been made to keep McIntosh isolated on one of the smaller ships in the fleet. No one who had been present in Northumberland disagreed. The notion of McIntosh somehow breaking free and being trapped on a fucking *boat* with the monster was too terrible for anyone to contemplate.

Phil headed for the helipad, and the chopper which would take him on the short journey to the ship that terrified him, but he would be damned if he would go alone. As he moved through the narrow steel arteries of the ship, he searched for anyone that would provide him with some sort of personal security.

Or someone you can blame when this goes wrong.

Phil blinked the thought away and wiped his sweaty brow.

The ship seemed suddenly deserted, as though all the crew had realised that Phil was a marked man; a plague-carrier that they should avoid at all costs. He was nearly at the helipad when he heard voices talking in a hushed whisper nearby.

He took a detour and headed toward the noise, stumbling upon two men sitting in a cabin. Phil didn't know the men, nor did he feel much reassurance when he looked at them. Both wore loose-fitting security uniforms, and neither boasted the sort of blank, psychotic stares that most of the security detail did. They didn't give the impression they were experienced enough to keep Phil safe, but there were no alternatives.

Phil clenched his teeth. They would have to do.

"Sullivan's orders," Phil said in as forceful a tone as he could muster. "You two are to escort me to the McIntosh ship."

The two young men stared at him for a moment, confused. Their facial features were similar enough that he thought that had to be related. Brothers, maybe.

"Quickly, now," Phil barked, and the two men stood and fell into line behind him.

"You two are to stay alert at all times, okay? This should be routine, but...er...just stay frosty, right?"

Stay frosty. The words sounded ridiculous as they spilled from Phil's lips. The kind of nonsense overly-muscled stars spouted in cheesy action films. He had no idea why he'd said it. Phil kept his eyes pointed forward so the two men wouldn't see the embarrassment squirming across his face.

"Uh...yes, Sir," one of the men replied.

"Good, good. What are your names?"

"I'm Kyle, Sir, and this is Tom."

"Good. Kyle, Tom, this is extremely important, you understand? Everything we've worked for depends on us getting this right, so no fuckups, okay?"

"Absolutely, Sir," the one called Tom replied, and Phil could have sworn from the man's tone that he was *smirking.*

Reaction

Prologue

The world ended not with a bang, but with a steady dissolve like the final shot of a movie fading to black as the credits prepared to roll. It had begun suddenly and without warning, but the end of all things was ongoing; a process of steady decay that advanced and corrupted, growing like a malignant tumour.

All across the UK, as the new species created by Project Wildfire's disastrous genetic interference scoured the land, the resistance of humans was fractured and fragmented; weak and isolated as dead pixels on a vast screen.

There were a number of places that humanity could, if not *thrive*, then perhaps at least *survive*, but survival had become something of an abstract concept, and humanity even more so.

The new world had been born in fire and savagery, and the response of the few that had lived through the collapse of civilization was like a reflection in a cracked mirror. Violence and brutality came easily; for those that remained it made more sense than any other approach. Wildfire had created one species and driven another back to its primal roots, until a casual observer might struggle to distinguish one from the other, though of course there were no observers, casual or otherwise.

To Charlotte Elleray 'civilization' wasn't even a memory. In fact there were no memories.

Just the hunt.

Just the constant, insatiable need to locate and track; to eradicate the human stain from the land.

She had no more idea *why* she hunted now than she did when she had killed her first—her husband, who died in a frenzy of teeth and blood and bewilderment—or the many since. Tearing apart her own two young children had meant nothing to Charlotte, nothing beyond the fact that their presence buzzed with a peculiar intensity and filled her with a primordial rage. Their removal had been as necessary as amputating rotten flesh, as natural as breathing.

Charlotte had no idea *why*. The *why* didn't matter, and that fact gave her a freedom she didn't have the resources to understand.

Killing the children had been an act of shrieking fury and orgasmic release, but the event had faded from her mind, running like fresh paint in a rainstorm; draining away until there was nothing left.

Just the vacuum.

Just the hunt.

The creature that had once been Charlotte stalked the countryside, naked and barefoot, sometimes circling aimlessly like a bird of prey searching for its next meal and sometimes swooping forward and tearing at the humans she stumbled across, forever silencing the terrible noise of their presence. The noise that made her head feel like it was burning.

For weeks she wandered, and in the beginning the hunt was frantic and plentiful, and she was able to launch herself from one victim to the next without pause. Some fell and became like her: new siblings that comforted her and helped in her quest to silence the noise that seemed to be everywhere and everything.

Gradually the world began to fall silent, and increasingly the time between Charlotte's kills began to stretch out. Sometimes she could go several days without locking onto prey. The emptiness of the land underlined just how successful her hunt had been and might have satisfied her, but satisfaction was a human trait that she had left behind the moment her blood boiled in her veins.

She felt nothing other than the insistent need to press ahead, but the success of the hunt and the scarcity of humans did have one consequence: even with an altered metabolism which allowed her to function without eating for long periods, hunger eventually began to gnaw at Charlotte, and her movements began to slow and weaken.

The people she had killed outright had provided a few morsels of meat; scant drops of energy that sustained her for a time, but after that first glorious orgy of killing was over, she began to find that when she attacked she no longer had the strength or the speed to kill, merely to convert.

More hungry mouths meant less food, and slowly Charlotte began to die, a process as long and slow and catastrophic as the collapse of the world itself.

After an age of solitary wandering, Charlotte happened across a small herd, and discovered a sibling that was different to the others. It hummed, and she followed it in surprise, humming her own answer to a question she did not understand.

The leader of the herd taught her that she was able to eat beyond the meat her kills provided, and its humming both soothed and energised her. It showed her how to find fruits and berries on the trees, how to focus her attention on tracking animals that provided precious fuel.

Their meat was different, but it sustained her, and Charlotte felt her body growing strong once more.

In the increasingly infrequent encounters with the humans, the leader hummed constantly, orchestrating its brethren as best it could throughout the ensuing battles. The humans were cunning and dangerous, but with each encounter, marshalled by the humming of the leader, the herd swelled and life became easier.

For a time, when the number of humans nearby had dwindled to zero, the herd circled just as Charlotte had when she had been alone, pouring across the countryside like a toxic spill, rolling and searching.

Until the noise.

The roaring of an engine.

The shattering, violent cacophony of humans. A sound so loud in the endless silence that it seemed to shake Charlotte to her very bones, and the herd knew as one that the hunt had been renewed.

Driven by hunger and gene-deep necessity; directed by the insistent humming of its leader, the herd charged toward the source of the noise, and was engulfed in fire and another noise, far louder and more terrible than anything Charlotte's mind could comprehend. A shockwave ripped through her consciousness a fraction of a second before a concussive blast hammered into her body, and both did terrible damage.

For a time she rested on the cold ground, broken and burned and slowly dying, until her ears caught a sound in the distance, faint; barely-there. She dragged herself toward it through the agony, across rocks and rough ground that scraped and bit at her charred flesh until she suddenly felt smooth stone beneath her.

The noise was impossible to miss, now: an insistent clanging of metal on metal, ringing out rhythmically, like the beat of a drum.

A human sound; a sound that *wanted* to be heard.

A sound that beckoned her forward.

Summoning up the last vestiges of her energy, oblivious to the pain in her shattered body, Charlotte crawled in the direction of the noise, powerless to resist the magnetic draw of the creatures she was hardwired to kill, yet when the metallic clatter ceased it was like sight had been ripped away from her once more. There was no human. There was nothing but silence and the vacuum.

Charlotte moaned in despair and incomprehension, low and guttural. It was the sound of an animal in pain.

*

Jason Roberts stared down at the creature that had stopped a few feet away from him. It appeared to be *crying*. Somewhere deep in his broken mind, a spark of empathy tried to light the fractured darkness, but flickered away to nothing until all that was left was an incessant itch and a burning need.

He watched impassively for a moment, and then took a single step forward and swung the lead pipe. The blunt weapon lodged into the creature's head with a dull, wet *thud*, driving fragments of bone deep into its brain and ending its pitiful torment.

With a grunt, Jason heaved the pipe clear of the twitching mess and straightened. There was no victory in his eyes, no sense of satisfaction.

Just emptiness.

Just the hunt.

After a moment he extended the hand that clutched the gore-drenched pipe and began to tap out the rhythm on the dumpster once more, drawing the next one toward him.

Clang.

Clang.

Clang...

1

You'll all have a chance to demonstrate your loyalty.

The old woman's words had provided at least a crumb of comfort to Michael Evans: she wasn't going to have them all executed on the spot.

Just John.

When she had finished bringing her people to the castle—Michael estimated there were around sixty in total—the woman had introduced herself to him as Annie Holloway. It was a pleasant introduction, delivered with a warm smile and a sympathetic glance at Michael's useless legs. Watching her act like a kindly grandmother making polite conversation, Michael thought it was almost possible to overlook the fact that she was a psychopath.

Almost. The old woman's normality was a fleeting notion, evaporating like morning dew as soon as she turned her attention to other matters.

Immediately after the cordial introduction she had told her two sons to nail John's corpse to a cross in the centre of the courtyard, and told Michael that he would watch, and that he would hold the wood and the nails for them while they worked.

If he wanted to get along, Michael would have to *make himself useful*, she said brightly, as though she were demanding nothing more unusual than that he boil a kettle and make a pot of tea for everybody to enjoy.

Then she turned to a middle aged-man who hovered at her side like an advisor, and informed him that he was to have the boat that they had all arrived in sunk so that nobody would get any 'funny ideas'.

Crucifixion and wilfully destroying the only legitimate means of getting away from the castle, Michael thought grimly. *And that's just day one.*

There was no mistaking the dark chasms in her sanity then.

Michael sat in the courtyard of Caernarfon Castle, locked into place in the wheelchair, watching with grim fascination as the two men strapped together two enormous wooden beams to make the cross and began to strip John Francis' body of its clothes.

The Holloway boys—Rhys and Bryn—looked to Michael like the sort of men that made a hobby of beating the shit out of people who accidentally bumped into them in pubs. Small town bullies; all sneering ignorance and low-level menace, suddenly vaulted into a position of power that they were clearly unequipped to handle.

They might be even more crazy than their mother, he thought, as he watched the two men pointing and laughing at John's exposed genitals.

Things can't get much worse.

He dropped his gaze to his paralysed legs for a moment, urging them to tremble; to move even a fraction of an inch as he was so certain they had earlier, but there was no response.

Frustrated, he lifted his gaze once more to see Rhys Holloway driving a handful of huge nails into the wooden cross to shore it up, and then the two men lifted the enormous structure upright, driving the base down into the soft earth of one of the castle's once-pretty flowerbeds to hold it steady.

Michael wondered for a moment why Annie felt the need to have the grisly monument erected in her new home: all the people that had been at the castle—the people she presumably thought of as her enemies—had seen her execute what the old woman assumed had been their leader, and all but Michael and the children had already been locked up.

If spreading fear was the old woman's objective, she had already accomplished it. It seemed like there was nothing further to be gained by decorating the courtyard in such an horrific manner. Certainly there seemed little point in putting on such a show for two young children and a man confined to a wheelchair.

Unless, Michael realised abruptly, the crucified corpse wasn't meant for them, but was instead a grisly message for the old woman's own people.

He thought back to the faces of the men and women that he had watched as they were being ferried across to the castle from the nearby island of Anglesey. Stilted, barely-controlled masks of stoicism that reminded him of Rachel's face as she had stood, helpless, in an underground bunker with a psychopath's arm around her waist like a lover's embrace.

To Michael, they had been the expressions of people that were fully engaged in trying to prevent a scream from escaping their lips.

Holloway's small army of followers outnumbered Michael's people by roughly three-to-one, but he couldn't shake the feeling that most of them followed her in a state of numb terror. Ruled by fear.

This wasn't some marauding army, but a desperate battalion of the lost and the wounded, driven ahead of the Holloway family like cattle fleeing the sharp crack of a bullwhip.

The fear Annie wanted to create was designed for *them*.

Michael swept his gaze around the courtyard.

It certainly didn't look like the castle held dozens of people now: all of Holloway's people, other than those few that Michael thought of as her inner circle, had retreated to the castle's eight huge towers, hibernating and hoping that the storm of violence outside would pass while they remained hidden.

That gave Michael some hope. His first impression of Holloway had been that she was the leader of a large cult of demented and loyal followers, but it no longer looked like that was true. At least, not yet.

He stared at the cross in growing horror as Rhys Holloway drove the first of the nails through John's wrist.

That's clearly her endgame, though. Terror, intimidation and unassailable control. Leadership of an army of maniacs.

Michael guessed, from the way the people of Anglesey acted, that Annie had no more than seven or eight followers who were actually insane enough to follow her voluntarily. Not many, but in the new world, with survivors scattered and broken, even seven people could represent a powerful force.

All it took to secure the castle was a tiny group of people loyal to her and threatening enough to subdue any notions anybody might have of offering resistance. A couple of guns; probably with no more than thirty bullets between them. In the world that existed now, that was all it took to found an empire. Many of the old woman's people had a haunted not-quite-there look in their eyes that reminded Michael of his first meeting with Jason Roberts.

People with broken minds, he thought, could more easily be persuaded to follow.

Jason.

The big man, it turned out, was still alive, but also not.

The vacant misery in Jason's eyes had given way to something else: a fractured, opaque darkness. Holloway's two sons were snarling guard dogs, but Jason was a different weapon altogether: strangely separate from all the others, and apparently only able or willing to interact directly with the old woman.

Jason gave Annie Holloway power in a way Michael didn't understand. At least, not as clearly as he understood the hold she had over the big man: a firm grip that stemmed from the drugs she poured into his system constantly and the catastrophic fracture in his mind.

Michael remembered the way Jason had slowly faded away as the group of survivors entered Aberystwyth; remembered the big man calling Michael *mum*, like he was trapped in some parallel dimension in which he hadn't been forced to kill his own mother with a fragment of roofing tile.

Jason had been damaged then. In the period that had followed that devastating event, it seemed clear that the trauma he had suffered had only been exacerbated further. Michael saw the way Jason looked at Annie Holloway; watched in disbelief as the man nuzzled at her palm like a faithful pet, and he felt certain that on some level, Jason actually believed she *was* his mother.

Michael had heard of *Stockholm Syndrome*, and had always thought it sounded bizarre and far-fetched. The notion that somebody could grow to love the very person that imprisoned and tortured them; it sounded impossible.

Yet it was the only theory Michael had when it came to explaining the big man's behaviour. Holloway tortured him until there was nothing left for him to do but love her.

Jason's body was ravaged by scars. His tongue had been cut out. The old woman poured a cocktail of prescription drugs down his throat at every opportunity, sealing him off from the world in a haze.

Despite all that torment, the only time Michael ever saw a flicker of emotion in Jason's eyes was when he looked at the old woman who led him around the castle on a leash like a mutt: a sickly sort of adoration. No, more than that: Jason appeared to *worship* Annie Holloway.

As baffling as Jason's attachment to Annie was, his survival bewildered Michael even more. He should have died in Aberystwyth, torn to pieces by a herd of Infected, and Michael clung stubbornly to that belief right up until he saw Jason shuffling into the castle, led like a dog by the old woman.

An explanation of sorts presented itself as soon as Annie sent Jason out through the castle's huge wooden gate and into the town of Caernarfon beyond the river with no more than a lead pipe for company for the first time, and the air filled with the distant sound of Infected shrieks.

She had sent him out there to take on the Infected. Alone.

What would have been a death sentence for any normal human being proved to be something else entirely for Jason.

A couple of hours later Michael was sitting in his chair, holding the tools for the two lunatics building a giant cross, when Jason returned, led by Annie's bald advisor. The man pulled Jason into the castle, clutching the leash tied around the big man's thick neck in white-knuckled fists.

Michael stared in astonishment. Jason was soaked in the blood of what looked like a lot of people. A lot of *Infected*.

Aberystwyth hadn't been a death sentence for Jason because the words *normal human being* did not apply to him. The big man was infected. Mutated, just as Gwyneth had been. The only question was *how* the virus had affected him.

Michael watched as Jason moved through the castle like a ghost in a dream, apparently unaware of his surroundings, until the bald man led him into the main tower and they both disappeared from sight.

What are you, Jason?

"Cripple. The nails."

Michael blinked the thoughts of Jason away, and stared at Rhys Holloway. The man who had sliced John's neck open, and who had driven nails through his wrists.

"Wake up, Cripple. I said I need nails for his feet."

Michael suppressed a shudder, and swallowed back the urge to strike out at the man; to clutch the nails tightly in a fist and see how far he could drive them into Rhys' pale, hateful flesh.

It would solve nothing, Mike, he thought. *Not yet. Do what you have to do. Watch. Learn. Gain their trust.*

Michael forced himself to nod meekly, and held out an outstretched palm. Two nails left: huge six-inch monsters that looked more like weapons than tools.

"Good boy," Rhys said with a sickening grin, reaching for the nails.

He paused.

"Tell you what, Cripple," he said. "I'll let you do the feet. This was your glorious leader, after all. So it's only right that you should do the honours."

Rhys handed Michael the ancient mace he had been using as a hammer, and his eyes glittered with menace as Michael took the weapon silently.

A test, then, Michael thought. *A chance to prove my loyalty. Or how far I'm willing to lower myself in order to survive.*

Michael stared at Rhys for a moment, and saw the challenge in the man's gaze as Michael's fingers curled around the handle of the mace. He could well imagine what was running through Rhys Holloway's mind.

Go ahead, Cripple. I dare you. Try it.

Michael swallowed painfully, and felt bile rising in his throat. John had been right, and Michael hadn't listened. The castle was dangerous. *People* were dangerous, and Michael had stopped running too soon, and might never get the chance to run again.

Sorry, John, Michael thought.

And then he leaned forward as far as his damaged back would allow and drove the nails through John's dead flesh.

*

By the time Michael was allowed to return to the tower to see his daughter and get some sleep, he had a pretty good idea of just how he would be expected to demonstrate his loyalty to Annie Holloway.

After he was done with the grisly task of crucifying John's corpse, the old woman informed him that she was looking forward to having a conversation with him about 'circumstances in the castle', and that in the meantime he was to take bread and water to the prisoners in the cells, and to ensure that each cell had a slop bucket.

Which it would be his task to empty, of course.

Holloway didn't just want loyalty. She wanted *fealty*. She wanted willing slaves. Michael imagined she would let the others out of their cells one at a time, giving them the opportunity to integrate and adjust to their new reality. Time to indoctrinate and dehumanise them.

She wasn't a cult leader. She was an *aspiring* cult leader. Somehow, that prospect seemed even more terrifying.

He had seen the scars that laced almost every inch of Jason Roberts' flesh. It didn't take a genius to work out how Annie felt persuasion was most easily accomplished, and how true obedience was obtained.

So I'm the test subject, he thought. *I'm the one she will break first. Because I'm in a wheelchair and I'm the least threatening.*

He carried dry bread from the stockpile of food that Shirley and the others had gathered during the raid on Caernarfon, and took it to the cells, accompanied by Rhys, who hadn't left his side for a moment. The man smirked and whistled cheerily as he opened the doors for the wheelchair to slip through, but Michael was under no illusions: Rhys gave the impression of being relaxed; *bored* even, but he watched like a hawk.

There were six cells in total, each crammed with anything up to six people. They weren't separated by gender, and Michael hadn't expected them to be: bullies operated on intimidation and humiliation, and the Holloway family conformed to the letter.

Forcing the prisoners to humiliate themselves in front of the opposite sex was probably on page one of the *torturer's handbook*.

He wheeled himself into each cell in silence, avoiding eye contact wherever possible as he handed out the food and the buckets. Only in the final cell—the one that held Linda and Rachel and Ed, the kid whose appearance had coincided with everything falling apart—did Michael's resolve weaken.

He looked at Rachel; at the impotent fury written on her face, and felt his heart break a little. It was clear from the fire in her eyes that she had watched through the bars set in the door as Michael had helped to crucify John's body.

Clear also that her confusion was matched only by her anger.

Michael gave a barely-discernible shake of his head and grimaced as he passed the bread and water to Linda. He desperately wanted to speak to Rachel, to reassure her that the trust she had built in him during the horror of the previous weeks hadn't been misplaced.

He didn't dare. With the eyes of Annie Holloway's son burning into the back of his skull, Michael took the bucket he had placed on his lap and set it on the floor apologetically.

Rhys wheeled the chair back outside and locked the cell door behind him, and Michael watched from the corner of his eye as he attached the key ring securely to his belt.

The only way to get those keys, Michael decided, would be if the man was dead.

So be it.

2

When Michael's horrific work was finally done, Rhys wheeled him to the tower that had become Michael's home.

"You get to take the rest of the night off," Rhys said amiably, as though he was the manager of a shop telling a cashier they could knock off fifteen minutes early. For his part, Rhys seemed to find it hilarious.

Michael felt his fingers clench involuntarily at his sides. Almost got away with it, too, but Rhys had razor-sharp eyes. He leaned in close.

"There it is, *Cripple*. Not as meek as you've been making out, huh? Something you'd like to do?"

Michael stared at Rhys for a moment, searching for an answer and a tone that wouldn't guarantee the conversation would head to a bad place.

Before he could say anything, Rhys whipped a knife from his belt and aimed it between Michael's eyes.

Michael found himself transfixed as he watch the blade dancing in front of his face, cleaving the air as the atmosphere thickened around it and became heavy with menace.

After a moment he lowered his head in surrender.

And saw the tip of the blade eat into his thigh.

Michael's eyes widened in shock.

Rhys snorted. It sounded to Michael oddly like rueful disappointment, as if the man had just lost a friendly bet.

"Not even a twitch. So you actually *are* a cripple."

Rhys shook his head and chuckled as he wiped the tip of the knife on his shirt and slid it into his belt.

"How the fuck did someone like you survive all this?"

Michael stared at the man, wondering if he expected an answer. Apparently not.

"Get inside," Rhys growled, and Michael turned the chair and entered the tower without a word. Only when he heard the lock engage loudly and the sound of Rhys' footsteps dissolved into deafening silence did he realise that he had been holding his breath for an eternity and allow his lungs to fill with air once more.

He let it out in a long trembling breath and stared down in wonder, focused on the dark bead of blood and the shallow wound in the middle of his thigh.

And the wondrous agony that blossomed from it, like petals opening to receive the rays of a long-absent sun.

The room was illuminated only by failing light that crept apologetically through a window that was no more than a scratch in the castle's stone flesh. When he was finally able to tear his gaze away from the cut on his leg, Michael squinted into the gloom, and felt his heart race. The tower looked empty.

"Claire?"

For a heart-stopping moment the silence and the darkness prevailed, and Michael let out a soft, trembling laugh of relief when he heard footsteps tumbling down the stairs from the level above.

His daughter appeared like a speeding train and braked only a little when she reached him, throwing her arms around his neck and hugging him fiercely.

He let her sob awhile, and found her outpouring of emotion infectious. Before long, tears ran freely down his own face and dissolved into her hair for several minutes, until Claire's sobs became coughs and, finally, weary silence.

All I wanted was to protect her, he thought.

You kept her alive; no more than that. You protected *her from nothing.*

Michael blinked in surprise at the response he heard in his head: at the reproachful voice of his dead wife, twisted until he almost couldn't recognise it; sagging under the weight of aching loss and sadness.

He pushed her words away, banishing the eager darkness that lurked between each syllable, beckoning him forward.

The depression Michael had inherited from his father had crushed the life out of his marriage, and Elise had hated the way her husband had slowly begun to focus inward, yet even as Michael had turned on himself she had never once joined in. He couldn't remember a single time at which it felt like Elise Evans hated Michael as much as he himself did.

Which meant it wasn't her voice he was hearing at all, but his own; camouflaged and insidious and familiar and terrible. The voice of the yawning dark chasm.

Stop that.

He pulled Claire away from him gently and looked into her eyes.

"Are you okay?"

She nodded.

"And Pete?"

She shook her head sadly.

"The old lady took him away. She said it wasn't proper for us to be 'sharing a room'."

Claire stared at Michael, puzzled, and her lack of years hit him like an invisible juggernaut. There were some things his daughter had no knowledge of; not yet. Ordinary, everyday things like why a boy and a girl approaching their teens shouldn't share a room.

Yet she knew death. Intimately. Childhood innocence was a thing of the past for Claire. Maybe for everybody.

"Do you know where she took him?"

Claire shook her head again, and Michael wiped a fat tear from her cheek.

"It's okay," he said. "I'm sure Pete's fine. She told me she wouldn't hurt the children, and I believed her. You believe me?"

Claire looked at him for a moment, and nodded.

"Good. And I'm going to get us out of here. You believe that too?"

Claire grinned through the tears and nodded fiercely.

"Good," he said, and held his daughter in his arms until sleep took her.

Eventually, despite him believing that it was impossible, sleep found him too.

*

"Pain is a construct, Mr Evans," the doctor said with a warm smile. "Think of it as nothing more than information. It's just some part of your body sending an email to your brain which reads *Hey! Pay attention to this!*"

Michael looked at the doctor dubiously. The miniature apocalypse that seemed to have been unleashed on the lower part of his spine didn't feel much like a *construct*. It felt more like someone had buried a serrated blade into his back, and every time he tried to move, they decided to twist it.

"Pain is a relic of an outdated phase of human evolution. It existed so that you would examine its source to determine whether it was likely to be life-threatening and requiring of immediate treatment. Well, now you have doctors to do that for you."

The doctor smiled again, almost eagerly, as if he'd said something particularly funny.

Ah, that was a joke, Michael thought. *Good one, Doc.*

The doctor's face fell a little when Michael didn't return the smile.

In truth, Michael *couldn't* smile: ever since he'd wrenched his back even that bare minimum of movement felt like it was yanking a cord in his jaw that connected all the way down to his vertebrae, where it wrapped like razor wire around bundles of tender nerves and squeezed mercilessly.

So far the injury had kept him away from work for almost two weeks, and he was beginning to feel a little stir crazy.

"You've seen people walking on hot coals, right?"

Michael gave a hint of a nod, and immediately regretted the movement as a surge of *information* shot up his spine and detonated at the base of his neck.

"Same thing," the doctor said. "Those people are simply able to disconnect their conscious mind from the concept of pain. I've heard about people involved in accidents that suffered horrendous trauma which they weren't even aware of until they were able to see it; until it became real in their minds. Only then did they feel the pain that accompanied their injuries. Pain exists only in the mind. Am I making any sense?"

"I guess," Michael said. "But how does that help me? Because I *am* feeling the pain."

"Your muscles need to move, Mr Evans. I realise that might seem illogical, but the swelling in your back isn't helped by remaining immobile. When you keep yourself tense because you anticipate pain, or avoid movement or use incorrect posture, what you are actually doing is creating multiple other sources of pain that feed into the primary cause and slow down the healing process."

"Huh," Michael said dubiously. He had hoped visiting the medical centre would result in a pocket full of heavy-duty painkillers, not a lecture.

The doctor reclined in his leather chair and ran a hand absently across his expansive desk like a spider.

"The human brain is powerful beyond our understanding, Mr Evans. Nobody can fully explain the placebo effect, for example. Nobody can really explain those feats of strength you see from entertainers, like those strongmen who pull along trucks with their teeth. But those people would tell you that they are aware of the pain; they can simply choose to ignore it."

The doctor delivered the words with a sort of practised sincerity that made Michael feel like they were well-rehearsed.

That was, he thought, probably true: humanity's evolution seemed to be heading inexorably toward a state of blissful catatonia. Technological innovation almost seemed to be built on achieving an ideal of laziness:

everything humans needed or desired was slowly being made more convenient, smaller; *easier*. Long periods of sitting, and letting the physicality of life fall by the wayside were an inevitable side-effect.

Hell, Michael thought, *even* my *job mostly entails sitting down, now. And eating Carl's doughnuts. And my job description is basically* patrol*, for Christ's sake.*

He imagined that Doctor Curtis had to give the same speech to several patients a week. Maybe more.

Virtually everyone Michael knew seemed to have a bad back, although that particular piece of data wasn't entirely unbiased: Michael would readily concede that the majority of the people he knew in St Davids were 'advancing' in years.

A recurring topic of wry conversation among the inhabitants of the tiny city was the ongoing comparison of their various ailments. They treated it almost like a sport. A league table that ranked the likes of arthritis and heart disease and cancer in a way that was darkly funny.

Maybe that's the point, Michael thought. *When faced by the dawning realisation that you were destined to lose the lifelong battle with your body, what else was there to do but laugh?*

All mildly interesting, sure, but not as important to Michael as a fistful of Codeine would have been.

"So what should I do, then, Doctor?" Michael asked a little apprehensively, as it dawned on him that he wasn't going to get the pharmaceutical relief he hoped for.

"You need to be *active*, Mr Evans. You need to push through the pain. You need to move."

You need to move.

Michael's eyes flared open, and he saw grey stone walls and smelled damp and age. He had slept in the chair, of course, and had woken with the usual aching neck after his chin spent the night getting acquainted with his chest.

He didn't feel the ache in his neck though, because his eyes suddenly fixed on something that took all his attention: a faint trembling in his left foot. He blinked away the fog of sleep and focused on the moment until he was sure that he wasn't still dreaming.

For a second there, he had seen definite movement.

Cold sunlight slipped into the stone room. At some point in the night Claire had extricated herself from his arms and had curled up on the floor next to his wheelchair underneath an ornate blanket.

He smiled at her sleeping face for only a moment before the dull click of the lock disengaging tore his eyes reluctantly to the door and the smile fell away.

"Morning, Cripple. Busy day ahead."

3

For Ed Cartwright, the night in the cell had been spent in a state of constant terror and morning arrived like a thinly-veiled threat.

Every dreadful minute that passed had increased his certainty that either the old woman or one of her sons would recognise him and he would meet the kind of grisly end that the NPCs in his favourite videogames routinely endured.

After Annie had taken control of the castle, Ed had managed to fade into the crowd, keeping his head down and letting his tangled hair fall over his face as much as possible. When the Holloway boys—each now brandishing a gun along with the ever-present knives—began to herd people toward the cells, Ed moved eagerly; diving into a cell without complaint and installing himself in the thick shadows that clung to the corner furthest from the door.

But the morning brought light, and an insistent feeling of urgency in Ed's mind like a timer ticking down towards a terrible and significant *zero*.

It was just a matter of time before one of them realised that the guy huddled at the back of the cell was the same guy that had beaten one of their friends over the head with a rock and stolen their boat.

Ed thought there was a good chance that he had killed the man with the rock; certainly the way he had dropped to the ground said *sack of meat* as much as it said *stunned human*. Still, he couldn't shake the certainty that he had committed an even worse crime: knocking the old woman to the floor in his mother's kitchen before fleeing.

Everything about Annie Holloway's demeanour suggested to Ed that such a personal slight would be met by severe recrimination.

Please just let them keep us locked in the cells. Please...

Ed's cell held four people. Alongside himself there was a woman who introduced herself with a kindly smile as

Linda, and a frightened young girl by the name of Emma, who seemed to have taken John's death particularly hard, and had sobbed softly until sleep finally silenced her. And in the corner opposite the one he had made his home sat the woman whose fierce eyes and burning intensity made him wonder if he might be better off with Annie Holloway after all.

Rachel.

When he had first met her, Rachel had seemed intimidating to Ed. Following her imprisonment, she became something more. She sat, hugging her knees and staring at the filthy stone floor, and rage seemed to leak from her incessantly until the atmosphere in the tiny cell felt thick and heavy with tension. To Ed it felt like being caged up with a rabid dog.

Or a time bomb.

Rachel hadn't spoken a word all night, and hadn't responded to Linda's attempts to engage her.

Ed didn't know the full story, but he knew the big man that Annie Holloway had turned into a dog and kept on a leash was Rachel's brother, and he knew that John, who had seemed like the most confident guy Ed had ever met, had returned from the rescue mission with his hands tied and his throat waiting to be cut.

Understanding only half of whatever-the-hell was going on was par for the course in the new world, and Ed cursed himself for ever leaving the safety of his mother's house. Isolation and starvation had frightened him, but after a night spent in the cramped cell chewing on dry bread and terror, he would have happily accepted being alone and hungry once more.

Because if guys like John and Rachel's enormous brother could end up so comprehensively fucked-over, Ed put his chances of remaining unscathed somewhere near the wrong side of *none*.

The cell door unlocked suddenly with a loud *clunk*, and the door swung open, bathing the cell in cold morning sunlight.

Ed's heart dropped.

The smaller of Annie Holloway's two sons.

Looking directly at him.

"You," Bryn Holloway rasped with a sneer as he pointed a dirty finger straight at Ed.

"Out."

*

The throne room.

By the standards of most castles, it was probably a little underwhelming. The seat itself was no more than a wooden chair with a high back: ornately carved, sure, but a far cry from the sort of solid-gold-and-jewel-encrusted affairs that Michael typically might picture on hearing the word *throne*.

The room was large—the largest in the castle—serving as what would once have been a general meeting chamber perhaps, or even a place of prayer: long, low wooden benches occupied the bulk of the floor space, lending the place the feel of a small cathedral.

For Michael, it was simply the room in which he had first been able to see threat lurking in Darren Oliver's eyes; burgeoning realisation that the man would do whatever it took to maintain his grip on the castle.

It came as no surprise to Michael that the latest psychopath to take charge in the castle was to be found in the throne room: it seemed the ancient space exerted a gravitational pull over those who wanted to assert dominance over their peers. Maybe it had always been that way; maybe it was something inherent in the design of the room or, more likely, the people who inhabited it.

Darren Oliver had at least had the humility—or perhaps just the foresight—not to position himself on the throne itself; not to broadcast his intentions so clearly. Yet when Michael wheeled his chair into the room, he found that Annie Holloway had no such reservations.

She was to be the second maniac Michael would have a conversation with while entombed in the ancient wood and stone of Caernarfon Castle. One way or another, he decided when he saw her perched regally on the ancient seat, she would be the last.

The old woman's small, dark eyes didn't leave Michael for a second as he wheeled himself toward her. Only when he came to a stop before the elevated throne that she sat on without a trace of irony did she look at her son, who followed a few paces behind the wheelchair.

"That will be all, Rhys," she said. "Wait outside."

Her voice was thin and almost tremulous; wrinkled and coarsened by age, but her sharp tone left no room for debate.

Michael watched Annie carefully. Being left alone with a man whose friends she had just either taken hostage or had executed didn't seem to bother her in the slightest.

Michael expected that Rhys would argue that he should stay put, to protect his mother perhaps, but there was no response beyond an acquiescent grunt and footsteps that receded until the door closed with a soft *thump*. The man's entire demeanour had changed as soon as he entered the room and saw his mother there. All the bristling confidence that exuded from him had suddenly evaporated.

Michael got the sense that leaving Annie's presence was a source of relief for Rhys, and he felt his nerves tighten a little. Even the woman's own sons—lunatics in their own right—were terrified of her.

Michael couldn't shake the feeling that Annie Holloway had been insane long before the world twisted to mirror her.

"Michael, isn't it?"

Michael nodded.

"I presume the others looked up to you."

Michael blinked in surprise.

"You had the gun, after all," Annie continued, when it became clear that Michael had no response to her words. "Interesting that they would let a man in a wheelchair have a gun, don't you think?"

Michael shrugged.

"I assume I was allowed to have it because I was no threat to anybody. Even if I *had* decided I wanted to shoot someone, it's not like I could just run away. I guess I was the one person that wouldn't use the gun. Letting anyone else have it would have been more of a risk."

Annie pondered that for a moment.

"How did you end up in a wheelchair?"

"Car accident," Michael said flatly. The old woman's eyes drilled into Michael, searching for lies in his answer. He met her gaze evenly. Apparently satisfied, Annie nodded.

"I suppose that's one silver lining to come out of all this. No more people dying tragically in car accidents. Such a waste of young lives."

She shook her head sadly.

"In my experience, people tend to find ways to kill each other somehow," Michael said. "If not with cars, they just get a little more...creative."

"And just what *is* your experience, Michael?"

Michael forced a non-committal shrug.

"I doubt it's that dissimilar to yours. I was in South Wales when all this began, and then Aberystwyth, and now I'm here. The towns are different; the faces are different, but the people have remained the same. All killing each other instead of working together."

"And yet none of them have killed you."

Michael said nothing.

"Despite your being something of an easy target."

Aware that the old woman expected an answer to the question she hadn't quite asked, Michael felt his mind begin to race.

"I suppose it takes a certain kind of person to kill a paralysed man," he said finally. "Maybe I just haven't met that kind of person yet."

He tried to keep his voice parked in neutral; tried to avoid pressing the accelerator on that final syllable.

Judging by the flicker of understanding that flashed across Annie's eyes, he didn't quite make it.

"Maybe not," Annie said with a smirk. "You're probably wondering why you're not in a cell with all the others."

Michael nodded slowly.

"You could say that."

"The thing is, Michael, that I meant exactly what I said. I'm not a monster. I have no wish to kill for the sake of killing; not at all. Your friend in the courtyard—the man who was leading this group, I presume?"

Michael met Annie's penetrating stare coolly and forced himself not to respond.

"Well," Annie continued. "I'm afraid he was dangerous. No doubt you liked him, and no doubt he was good to all you people. Still, he turned up on my doorstep waving a gun. Threatened to kill me. Did his best to kill the poor soul who was protecting us. Letting him live was not an option. You understand?"

Michael shrugged.

"Believe it or not I actually *do* understand that," he said. "What I don't understand is why you don't just let us all go. You wanted the castle and you have it. However John offended you—and I'm sure he did; he could be...*abrasive*—well, you've dealt with that. Why keep us here?"

For a moment a look of genuine confusion passed across Annie's wrinkled features, as though Michael was a child asking a question with an obvious answer, something she hadn't even thought it would occur to anybody to ask.

"Despite what you or some of the people I'm with might assume, Michael, this castle isn't of huge significance to me. I *had* a good place. It might not have had these walls, but it was secure enough. At least, it was safe from the Infected people. I took the castle—once your friend John had so kindly alerted me to its presence—because of what was *inside* the walls."

It was Michael's turn to look confused. Annie smiled benevolently.

"I'm no businesswoman," she said, "but I do understand the principle of supply and demand. I'm sure a smart fellow like you does, too, though you may not have given much thought to it in light of the way things have changed recently. The less there is of something— oil, gold, whatever—the more valuable it becomes. You know what occurred to me as I watched my friends and neighbours tear each other apart Michael?"

Michael shook his head, though a faint outline of an answer to her question had already begun to emerge in his mind.

"*People*, Michael. All of a sudden, they're in quite short supply, wouldn't you say? I didn't want the castle for its walls. I wanted it for the people hiding behind them."

4

"Wh-where are you taking me?"

Ed knew he shouldn't have asked, but sheer panic ripped the question from his throat. His answer, of course, was an open-palmed blow on the side of his head that made his eyes water and his ears ring.

Bryn had tied Ed's hands together as soon as he had pulled him from the cell. He tied the knot expertly, tightly enough that it dug painfully into Ed's wrist and felt like it cut off the blood supply to his fingers. The man didn't even look down as he worked the rope; his eyes never left Ed's. Something about his stare felt worse than the rope biting into Ed's flesh.

Bryn shoved him forwards, and Ed fell to the ground. He heard the man chuckling and knew what the sound meant. Ed had pulled the same stunt once before, and it had ultimately resulted in his freedom. Bryn apparently hadn't forgotten being made a fool of.

This time, when Ed stumbled to the ground, he wasn't hauled back to his feet to have his bonds cut away. Instead, a hefty kick to the ribs persuaded him that he should get up of his own accord.

Ed's teachers had never described him as a *fast learner*; no one had. Turned out that learning was just a matter of motivation.

He was learning quickly now. Information had a way of sticking in even his dope-addled mind when knowing something might just mean the difference between living and dying.

He pushed himself upright, coughing out the dust he had inhaled after Bryn's boot had driven the air from his lungs. When Bryn prodded him forward once more, Ed watched his step carefully.

Bryn guided him to the rear of the castle's main tower, and an unobtrusive door set deep into the wall that Ed hadn't even noticed before.

When the man heaved the door open, and Ed saw steep, narrow steps leading down into thick darkness, and smelled damp air that felt like it had been trapped underground for many years, a dim flicker of understanding began to fire in Ed's mind, but he found himself unable to focus on it. Unable to focus on anything apart from one all-consuming word.

Dungeon.

*

People.

It was as simple as that. In the end the old woman differed to Darren Oliver only in the scope of her ambitions. Where he had wanted to draw people to the castle and keep only the ones that suited his needs, Annie Holloway was prepared to go out and *get* people. The only difference was the degree of power they sought. Darren wanted enough to preserve a life of authority and comfort for himself. Annie wanted it *all*.

"Do you plan on staying here?" Michael asked.

"I see no reason not to. Presumably the reason you had a signal fire on the tower was to bring people to you, and it worked, didn't it?"

Annie's leathery face split in a wry grin.

Michael grunted his acknowledgment.

"So it will work just as well for me, I think. The more people I can gather, the better, if we are to have any chance of surviving the way the world is now. Someone has to be in charge, and though you might not like it, or any of the people in the cells for that matter, I think I would prefer that person to be me."

For a moment Michael considered telling the old woman what Ed had said about Wylfa Power Station, but the satisfaction he would have found in bursting her little bubble would have been short-lived. The castle would soon enough see fire rain down on it; would see the air itself become toxic. If Michael failed in getting out of the place, he would die content in the knowledge that Annie and all her people would follow him from one Hell to the next in short order.

"We're in agreement about one thing at least," Michael said. "Survival *is* all that matters. I tried telling that to John, but he wasn't exactly what you'd call a *people person*. He had no interest in gathering people together; in strength in numbers. I don't much care *who* is in charge, as long as my daughter is safe. It's not like I can protect her beyond these walls by myself."

He fixed Annie with an earnest stare.

"You'll have my cooperation, and I'll do my best to get everybody else to fall in line if and when you let them out. I ask only one thing in return."

Annie seemed highly amused by the idea of Michael making demands.

"Go on," she said.

"There's a woman in the cells I'd like you to free. It will benefit you as much as me."

"Oh?"

"Her name is Linda. She's a doctor. I'm guessing you don't have one because the big guy you've got out there killing the Infected looks like he's got a lot of untreated wounds, and I'd say it won't be long before his own infections get to be too much for him. We have plenty of medication here, but unless you have a doctor that knows how to use it..."

Michael shrugged.

"We *did* have a doctor," Annie said thoughtfully, "but I'm afraid his attitude left a little to be desired and he is...no longer with us. In retrospect, that was, perhaps, a rash move on my part."

It didn't take much for Michael to picture what Annie Holloway's version of an *attitude adjustment* might be.

"Well, you do still have a doctor in the cells," Michael said carefully. "As far as I'm aware she had no particular allegiance to John, but of course, what you do with her is up to you."

Annie stared at Michael for a long, heavy moment.

"I'll consider letting your friend the doctor out next, though how soon that might be will depend on you. I must say, you are being *very* reasonable, Michael. Considering."

Annie's eyes glittered darkly.

"But of course I am far too long in the tooth to take a man at his word. Especially a man who seems able to switch allegiances without batting an eyelid. I said you'd be given a chance to prove your loyalty, and you will. Right now."

Michael's jaw dropped a little.

"I thought-"

"You thought that putting a nail through a dead man's foot and passing out some bread might do it?"

Annie laughed. It was a mirthless, unsettling sound that set Michael's teeth on edge.

"Afraid not. There's no loyalty without sacrifice, I think. And no sacrifice without pain."

Annie sucked in a deep breath and yelled with as much power as her old lungs would allow.

"Rhys?"

Michael heard the door behind him opening and footsteps stalked toward his wheelchair.

"Michael here is going to be our first volunteer. Isn't that nice? Soon he will be like a part of the family."

Annie beamed at Michael, and he felt his gut begin to squirm.

5

Dad must be on the battlements again.

In Claire Evans' brief time at the castle, whenever she hadn't been able to locate her father immediately, she had eventually found him up on the wall, usually staring blankly into space. Claire didn't like the look on his face when she found him up there; it looked to her like he was staring at things that she could not see.

When she had awoken on the cold stone floor to find the room empty, she had spent a few minutes assuming that she was locked inside the tower once more. Just like a princess in a fairytale, aside from the blood and the death and the constant terror.

Yet when she finally worked up the courage to try the door she discovered that it swung open easily, and she peered out into the courtyard, hoping that nobody would spot her. What she saw outside surprised her.

There were dozens of people in the castle now—Claire had watched them with wide eyes as they arrived in groups of eight or nine at a time—but the place actually looked *more* empty than it had previously. Of course a lot of people had been locked in the cells; all the people that Claire knew, in fact, but she found it strange that all the new people seemed content to hide in their rooms in the towers.

Maybe they're locked in, too.

Claire frowned, and stared up at the battlements. She couldn't see the wheelchair anywhere - usually if Dad made his way up to the wall alone, heaving himself up one step at a time, he left the chair at the base of the steps so he could easily return to it.

Maybe he left it somewhere else.

Yet when Claire ascended the steep steps she found the battlements deserted. The wall encircled the entire castle, and it was possible to walk all the way around it, passing through arches carved into each of the eight towers. She began to walk the perimeter, hoping to spot her father somewhere below.

Glancing down, Claire thought she understood why there was nobody to be seen: no one wanted to look at the grisly horror in the centre of the castle's wide courtyard. A splash of terrible colour against the castle's dull grey interior; a dark, queasy red stain that made her feel like she might be sick.

Claire had an idea that things were happening that were beyond her understanding, much like the vague memories she had of her parents splitting up. Conversations just beyond her earshot; pointed looks loaded with meaning that she was not supposed to see. She was a natural at puzzles, but the weirdness between her parents didn't seem like a puzzle to Claire: it did not appear to be something that could be put back together.

She had given up trying to figure that problem out, and she figured the best course of action was to give up trying to work out what was happening at the castle, too. The new people were terrifying; understanding *why* didn't seem to matter.

All that mattered to Claire Evans was that she was hungry, and cold, and scared. And that she missed her mother. Every time she thought about her, Claire's heart ached in a way it never had before in her brief life. Eight—very nearly nine, her birthday was just a couple of months away—years of childhood innocence and happiness had been obliterated the moment her mother came for her, the ripped flesh of one of their neighbour's cheeks hanging from her bloody teeth, her pretty face mutilated and twisted into a mask of rage and dark hunger.

The fear Claire had felt then had abated a little, but in some way she struggled to grasp, the constant sense of panic that had typified her time spent alone on the blood-soaked streets of Aberystwyth had been better than drifting aimlessly around the castle.

At first the castle had been source of endless delight. It was like living in a history book: every surface, every object older than Claire could imagine. Every item seemed to have a story to tell. She loved the ancient weapons and faded art and ornate furniture, and imagined herself to be like a princess in a fairytale, waiting in the castle for Prince Charming to rescue her and whisk her away on a white stallion. Now the castle was a place of pain: a place that gave her a whole lot of time to think, and inevitably that meant thinking about her mother.

Claire didn't have a word for the way the loss of her mother felt, but she had become used to the sensation of terror, and she didn't think it was that which she felt in the castle. She had experienced genuine terror in Aberystwyth, on more than one occasion. She doubted that she would forget the way it had felt if she lived to be a hundred years old.

This was more like *dread*.

Claire had never understood the difference before. She thought she did now.

Terror had shoved her in the back and screamed in her ear, but it passed quickly. Dread seemed to harden in the pit of her stomach until she felt sick all the time, and it didn't appear to be going anywhere.

Claire wasn't sure which she preferred. Hard to choose when either emotion was tied so closely to watching people die horribly right in front of her.

She turned left on the battlements and began to walk along the wall, keeping an eye out for her father below, but trying not to look too closely. Trying not to see what was in the middle.

In Aberystwyth Claire had kept a count of the people she saw killed, totting up the numbers like jellybeans. It made the inexplicable chaos that unfolded around her seem almost like a game played on her mother's tablet, as if she could somehow distance herself from the reality of it by avoiding thinking about it head-on. She definitely didn't want to think about it head-on.

She finally stopped counting at number one-hundred-and-seven.

John would have been one-hundred-and-eight.

She saw the knife being dragged across his throat every time she closed her eyes; saw the obscene chasm in his neck as he began to fall backwards and the jet of dark blood that spurted across the stone floor. Now it seemed like head-on was the only way she *could* think.

When Claire reached the sharp left turn that would take the sea out of her sight and replace it with the town, she couldn't help but glance down to the centre of the courtyard, as though her eyes moved of their own accord.

The body of John Francis.

Naked.

Nailed, upright, to a huge cross made of wood. At this distance, in the grey morning light, the dark blood that dried on his chest made it look like he was wearing an apron. *You could almost believe he is alive*, Claire thought. *Apart from his neck.*

Nausea tumbled in her stomach. John's neck had been cut so deeply that bone was visible. His head hung at an impossible angle, as though it might topple off his body at any moment.

Claire looked away and took a deep breath.

Dread, Claire decided, was definitely far worse than terror. With dread, you knew what was coming and just had to wait for it to happen. You couldn't miss it: dread was nailed up like a sculpture for everyone to see. To constantly remind them. Dread lingered in the shadows of every thought, infecting them and corrupting them until *everything* became frightening.

"Hello, girl."

Claire jumped, and nearly let out a scream. She had been so engaged in her own thoughts that she hadn't seen Bryn Holloway ascending to the battlements. She had a sudden, overwhelming feeling that he had been up there all along, walking along silently behind her like a ghost. Closing in.

Of all the new people she had seen in the castle, Bryn scared Claire the most. He was slight, and quiet, and he hadn't killed anybody. But there was something in his eyes, a sort of hunger that got under her skin and made her small hands shake a little.

"My mother would like to see you," Bryn said, with a smirk that Claire didn't understand.

When Bryn put his hand on the small of her back and began to guide her toward the stairs that led down to the courtyard, and let his fingers linger there, Claire felt the oddly tender caress and had a sudden intuition that the memory of the man's smirking grin would linger as long as the image of the terrifying hole that had been torn in John's neck.

6

"I won't do it. I can't."

Rhys had carried Michael down the narrow steps into the gloomy dungeon. It was an oddly intimate and profoundly unsettling experience, yet when the steps reached an end it was clear the uncomfortable descent was just an *aperitif*. The main course trembled and whimpered in front of Michael, tied and gagged and terrified in the damp and the dark.

Ed Cartwright wasn't just shaking with fear. He was practically *vibrating*.

Even in the barely-lit dungeon, an almost tangible darkness sat between Michael and Ed. A shared understanding that Ed was meat just waiting to be carved, and Michael was the one holding the knife.

The weapon felt heavy and terrible in Michael's hand; warm and clammy where Annie Holloway had gripped the handle before passing it to him with an expression of unsettling eagerness on her face.

She stared at him expectantly, and her eyes danced with amusement, as if she had just recalled a hilarious joke long-forgotten.

"I thought you might say that," she said serenely. "Lucky for you I'm not like those quiz show hosts. I don't have to accept your first answer. In fact, down here, I don't think I'll be accepting *anyone's* first answer, if you know what I mean?"

Michael felt his stomach attempt a somersault, and it botched the landing. Bile rose at the back of his throat.

He stared at Ed's wide, pleading eyes.

I can't do this.

"Why?" He asked in a thick voice.

Annie's face split in a devilish grin.

"There are two answers to that. If you mean why *him*, well, let's just say Mr Cartwright here and I have a little history. He hasn't been a very good boy, have you, Mr Cartwright?"

Ed whimpered through the gag. Muffled. It might have been a word; might have been *please*, but Michael suspected that begging would amount to nothing in the dungeon. Down there, away from any set of eyes that might judge her, Annie's power and insanity seemed to ramp up to dizzying levels.

"If you mean *why* in a more general sense," Annie continued, "I think you already know the answer. I expect loyalty. Obedience. Not an easy thing to guarantee from people who have just been part of a...hostile takeover."

She grinned, as if the analogy were the funniest thing she'd ever imagined.

"I've wracked my brain trying to think up a way to get all of you on side, and I find myself having serious doubts that it's even possible. But I would like to try, and believe me, it's better for you and your friends if I *try*. The alternative would be much quicker and easier, but a little disappointing, too. This seems like the best solution to me."

Ed whimpered again.

"To *me*," Annie repeated. "I understand others will have their own view, but as I told you, it's me in charge here. *Only* me."

Michael shook his head, trying to clear it of the lunacy that threatened to enter by osmosis.

"Don't worry, Michael. You're the first, but everybody will have their chance to cut something off Mr Cartwright in due course. Your friend the doctor will be up next. Call it a rite of passage."

"And if I refuse?"

Annie eyes glittered in the half-light emanating from a single flickering torch attached to the wall. In the dancing illumination she looked less like a person to Michael and more like a demon.

"Then you will take your place alongside our friend here, and everyone else will be required to cut something off each of you. If I end up with every single one of you down here refusing to follow my instructions..."

Annie shrugged, apparently deciding that statement didn't require completion.

"The children can go last," Annie said brightly, as if the notion had just occurred to her.

She is utterly insane, Michael thought.

He had noticed the old woman's hands trembling involuntarily, and the way she tried to disguise the movement, and had filed it away in a mental notebook, wondering when the information might become useful. Maybe never.

Annie was old, and could well be suffering from Parkinson's disease; maybe Alzheimer's or some sort of dementia. None of it mattered. None of it was useful. Just terrifying. Annie wasn't going to give him time to strategise and figure anything out. Instead she was going to plunge him straight into the deep end and let *him* decide whether he would drown or not.

He thought back to Darren Oliver. The man had run the castle in a brutal manner, but Michael didn't ever get the impression he had been full-bore crazy. Oliver had followed a twisted sort of logic, and in some ways Michael was convinced the man believed he was doing the Right Thing.

Annie *was* crazy though; demented as a return ticket to Hell, and maybe it was nothing to do with age or disease. Quite possibly, Michael thought, she had been born wrong and raised worse. Certainly the genes she had passed on to her sons had...issues.

He saw no way out.

Saw Claire in the dungeon, a knife clutched in her small fingers, being ordered to slice away her father's flesh. It couldn't be allowed.

"I'm sorry, Ed," Michael said abruptly, and Ed thrashed wildly against his bonds.

"Take the gag off him, Rhys," Annie said smugly. "I think it would benefit everybody to hear Mr Cartwright screaming."

Michael choked back the vomit that desperately wanted to evacuate his stomach and reached out, taking hold of one of Ed's fingers.

"Predictable," Annie said, with a little disappointment in her voice. "The fingers. I suppose they seem like the part that Mr Cartwright will miss the least, but don't worry, Michael, sooner or later someone will have to cut off something a little more...vital."

Annie made for the stairs, and paused.

"In fact, let's make it sooner," she said. "You can go for the fingers if you wish, but I expect to see at least five of them gone when I come back. I don't like the thought that ten of you will take a finger each. That's no fun at all."

She nodded at her son.

"Stay until he is done, Rhys," she said. "And then let Michael stay awhile down here. Give it all time to sink in."

She chuckled as she ascended the steps, leaving Michael alone with Rhys and Ed.

Rhys glowered at him.

For a moment crazy thoughts ran through Michael's mind, dark visions of driving the knife into Rhys' belly and cutting Ed free, but they were no more than fantasies. If he was going to get Claire and the others—Ed included—out of the castle, it wasn't going to be like that.

Darren Oliver's words came back to him.

I've had to do terrible things, because someone *has to do terrible things, or we'll all end up dead.*

Michael dropped his eyes to the knife.

And the fingers.

Gritting his teeth and trying his best to block out Ed's nerve-shredding screams, Michael began to cut.

*

Annie listened to the muffled explosion of screams as she made her way back to the main tower's front entrance with a savage smile and glazed eyes.

When she stepped into the throne room, she found Bryn waiting for her; his hand on the shoulder of Michael's young daughter. Gareth Hughes stood as far away from Bryn as was possible without the distance becoming an obvious snub; his face contorted by concern.

Annie ignored Gareth. His advice had been invaluable over the years, but increasingly she was beginning to believe that he didn't have the *stomach* for the way things were now. Never would Annie have expected a situation to arise in which her slow-witted sons were more useful to her than a man of Gareth's intellect, yet that time had now come. What Annie required now was not *counsel* but *obedience*, and her sons had a lifetime of practice as far as that was concerned.

She focused her gaze on Michael's daughter.

The crippled man was clever, but Annie had been around long enough to spot a liar at a hundred paces. No one simply *let* a cripple have a gun because they didn't think he would be a threat. If you wanted to feel safe, you kept the gun for yourself. Simple logic. Giving such a weapon to anybody—regardless of the status of their legs—*made* them a threat.

Annie felt the weight of the revolver she had taken from John in the pocket of her skirt. She couldn't imagine giving it to anybody voluntarily. Nobody would do such a thing.

That meant the man in the wheelchair was a little more important to the group than he was letting on. Annie supposed she should have felt irked that she hadn't killed the man outright; that he had fooled her, for a while at least, into believing that he was harmless, but in a way she was glad. If the others looked up to the paralysed man then it followed naturally that breaking him completely would break their spirits too.

Annie felt pleased with the way things were working out. Efficiency was always to be applauded, yet she reminded herself sternly that Michael wasn't broken *yet.*

Having Michael torture Cartwright was a step in the right direction, but the wheelchair-bound man was slippery; he seemed to adjust to each new demand easily. Too easily. What Annie needed was a threat that she could hang over Michael's head. Something that would disrupt his helpful butter-wouldn't-melt demeanour and reveal his true colours.

The next step was obvious. Nothing could sway a person more than the wellbeing of their child. Annie knew that only too well, despite the fact that her own children had been crushing disappointments.

Blood, after all, was blood.

*

Claire watched the old woman nervously as she stalked into the throne room. Somewhere in the distance she could hear a man screaming. It didn't sound like Dad, but Claire couldn't be sure, and she felt her bladder loosen a little in apprehension.

She clamped her lips together as the old woman approached, reminding herself sternly that she hadn't wet herself when her eyeless mother had tried to eat her in Aberystwyth, and so there would be no way she would start now.

Annie stepped forward, crouching down to Claire's eye-level as much as her old knees would allow.

"I always wanted a girl," Annie said, beaming. "And a grandchild, though there never seemed to be much chance of *that.*"

She spat the last word out venomously, and for a moment her eyes became a little unfocused, as if she was staring straight through Claire and into the wall behind her.

Bryn coughed uncomfortably.

"At least, not until now," Annie continued. "*Now* I think my boys will have their pick of the women. God knows, when it was the women doing the choosing, there was little chance of them ever having children. Isn't that right, Bryn?"

Bryn did not respond.

Annie turned her attention back to Claire.

"You wouldn't know about all of that though, of course. Too young."

Claire saw a sort of unhinged craziness in the old woman's eyes, and decided that since it hadn't been a question and she had no idea how to respond, it would be best to keep quiet. After a moment Annie blinked and seemed to return to the present, and the warm smile reappeared on her lips.

It didn't reach her eyes.

"Did you know your grandparents?"

Claire frowned. Her father's parents had died before she was born, but her mother's parents had lived not far from Aberystwyth. She hadn't even thought about them. And now they were gone, and she would never see them again. Her eyes shimmered.

Annie's face dropped.

"You did. Poor child. It's a terrible world out there."

Annie grabbed Claire and pulled her into an awkward hug. Claire stiffened.

"I need to talk to you about your father," Annie whispered, stroking Claire's hair.

Claire's eyes widened, and finally she was scared enough to speak in a thin, trembling voice.

"Is that...*him*?"

For a moment Annie seemed puzzled.

"Oh, the screaming? Well, yes and no."

A fat tear escaped from Claire's right eye and rolled down her cheek.

"Don't worry, child, he is perfectly fine, but I do need to ask you about him. You want to keep him safe, don't you?"

Claire nodded slowly.

"Then I just need you to answer a couple of questions, and no lying to me, right? I'll know if you lie, and if you do I will be forced to hurt your dad."

Claire stared at Annie in horror, and nodded again.

"Your father was important around here, wasn't he? That's why he had the gun."

Annie pulled back and gripped Claire's narrow shoulders, drilling a piercing, unnerving gaze into her. After a moment, Claire nodded.

"Was he in the army, too? Like John?"

Claire shook her head and sniffed, pulling away from Annie. Once she was free of the old woman's grasping, bony fingers, she wiped her eyes and stared at Annie defiantly, pursing her lips.

Annie laughed.

"Raised himself a tough cookie, did he? It doesn't matter what your father was before. I know exactly what he is *now*."

She stared at Claire, and her face hardened, all the maternal pretence slipping from it.

"I have a message I'd like you to pass on to your dad. Just a little something for him to think about, okay? Will you do that for me?"

Claire decided that passing on a message didn't sound so bad, and if it got her away from the old woman and her strange son, she'd gladly do it. She nodded.

"Good girl. Tell your father that if I feel like I'm not getting his full cooperation, that I'm thinking of letting Bryn here have his way with you. Do you know what that phrase means?"

Claire furrowed her brow and shook her head a little.

Annie clapped her hands together and grinned.

"Perfect," she said brightly, and nodded curtly at Bryn before returning her glittering eyes to Claire. "Your father will."

Moments later, Claire shuddered as she felt Bryn's hands on her back once more, touching her almost tenderly, and she allowed herself to be guided back out into the courtyard.

As soon as she felt the crisp air on her skin, Claire wriggled free of the man's touch and ran without looking back, straight to the tower that had become her home, and wished she had been locked in after all.

*

"Do you think that was wise, Annabel?"

Annie's eyes narrowed dangerously. She hated anyone using her full name, and hated the thought that she was being *questioned* even more.

Gareth Hughes had always been a trusted advisor to her, and on the surface the question was no different to many others that he had asked across two decades as he helped her navigate the quagmire of small town politics. Yet under the surface, Annie detected something different in the man's tone; something that had appeared only since the world fell apart. Something that bubbled up and seeped out until she felt like she was standing ankle deep in it.

Reproach?

Challenge?

"Our friend Michael," she said in a low tone. "Would make an excellent poker player, I think. A man who would cut off pieces of a person when told to is either completely broken or very dangerous indeed. I don't get the impression that Michael is *broken*, do you?"

Annie watched Gareth's face closely as he pondered the question, searching for some visible clue as to what was going on in the man's head.

"I...suppose not," Gareth said finally. "Not exactly. But threatening a man's child with...you wouldn't actually let that happen, would you?"

Annie felt her jaw clench involuntarily.

Gareth Hughes was getting ideas way above his station.

She shuffled forward, closing the gap between herself and Hughes with speed that slackened his face in surprise. Hughes stood several inches taller than Annie, and she lifted her chin and stared up at him.

"Nobody has *chastised* me since I put my father in the ground," she whispered. "Are you *chastising* me, Gareth?"

The expression of blank confusion on Gareth's face resolved itself into something approaching understanding, and Annie felt a smirk building inside as fear and comprehension appeared to reach him simultaneously. The tone of the conversation had been radically altered, and apparently Gareth hadn't been aware it was happening until it punched him in the gut.

"If I decide a threat needs to be carried out, then I *will* carry it out, Gareth. Do you understand?"

Gareth nodded hurriedly.

"Of course, Annab-"

Annie's eyes narrowed.

"Uh...Annie," he stammered.

"Michael *is* broken though, Ma."

Annie turned to face Bryn and stifled a sigh. The boy generally took in conversations like a time-lapse camera. As usual, he was taking a while to catch up.

"His back, I mean. Rhys stabbed him, and he's definitely a cripple. I mean, even if this scares the shit out of him, what's he gonna do?"

Annie frowned at *shit,* and Bryn stammered to a halt.

"You can tell a lot about a person by how they respond when their child is threatened, Bryn," she said finally. "It's very hard to conceal emotions behind a poker face when the stakes are that high, no matter how good a liar you might be. Michael's reaction will be probably the only genuine thing that man ever does."

Annie slumped down onto the uncomfortable throne.

"And it will help me to decide whether or not he has to die."

7

Precautions had been taken, but there was no way for Fred Sullivan to be certain that they would mean anything. After all, the mutation that Fred's research team assured him could be valuable beyond measure was an aberration that hadn't even existed until a few short days earlier.

It was impossible to ensure safety or to guarantee results when nobody truly knew what the thing was capable of.

Fred wondered idly how many of humanity's scientific advances over the centuries had felt like this. Was there someone standing in the shadows behind every leap forward, wondering if their experiment was going to eviscerate them and devour their innards?

Fred leaned against the handrail that overlooked the expansive deck of the aircraft carrier that now represented the UK headquarters—or perhaps more accurately the *last refuge*—of Project Wildfire and its creators.

High on the superstructure that loomed above the deck, buffeted by the icy wind that blasted across the North Sea, he watched as the far-away helicopter's blades began to slice through the misty air. The sound of the engine barely reached him; what was a thunderous roar up close was a faint whine at this distance.

Fred watched keenly for several seconds, until he saw Phil Sanderson appear below him. Wildfire's head of research scurried toward the vehicle that would carry him on a short journey across churning gunmetal waves, pausing every few yards as if waiting for someone to catch up.

Fred gave Sanderson a fifty-fifty chance of ever coming back, and in truth Fred had expected the man to attempt to flee or to pass the task on to one of his subordinates. That was exactly why Fred was wasting time leaning on a rail and taking in the view.

If he hadn't seen Sanderson making his way to the chopper, Fred would have gleefully hunted the man down and ventilated his skull with a .38 round from the antique revolver he always carried beneath his silver jacket.

He nodded in satisfaction when he saw Sanderson. The mutation was a scary prospect. Not, it turned out, as scary as the thought of disobeying a direct order.

Sending the scientist to take a sample of the mutation's blood, and witnessing the frozen look of terror on his irritating face as Sanderson processed the order had been enormously satisfying, but Fred had to concede it was a little impetuous.

He'd been called *impetuous* frequently in his juvenile years, and hated the label. Loathed it for its vague hint of truth and for the way it implied weakness. The notion that anybody considered themselves sufficiently superior to him to offer such a withering analysis of his character had always made his blood boil in his veins.

The last person to label Fred *impetuous* to his face, when he had been no more than seventeen years old, had received a right hook which offered up a creative new look for his nose. If you were going to condescend to someone, Fred's youthful self had decided, you'd better be able to back your superiority over them. Better be able to *show* it.

That man hadn't been able to. Nor anyone since. Power, Fred discovered, wasn't bestowed on anyone. If you wanted it, you took it. And if no one took it back, then you took more. Darwinism at its purest; simple and elegant and brutal.

Fred had built his entire life—and his enormous wealth—on that one basic foundation: *take more.*

And just when taking more had seemed impossible; when it appeared there was nothing left to take, Jake McIntosh had turned up.

And everything had changed.

Wildfire was finished. The project had failed, or at least had evolved into something that was beyond Fred's control. Yet within the collapse of a project that had been decades in the planning, an opportunity had arisen, and like any good businessman, he was determined to seize opportunity wherever he found it.

Fred stared thoughtfully across at the huge deck that sprawled out below him.

The helicopter was far enough away that by the time Phil Sanderson reached it, he was no more than a tiny stick figure to Fred. Sanderson had paused next to the helicopter, apparently waiting for two men wearing security uniforms to join him. Presumably they were Sanderson's own personal insurance policy, for all the good it would do him.

Fred felt a vague twinge of irritation. He had been clear that Sanderson was to proceed alone, but he could hardly blame the scientist for at least trying to manufacture the illusion of safety. It was almost enough to persuade Fred that somewhere within Phil Sanderson's wobbling mass there resided some sort of backbone.

Let him have his bodyguards.

A security team of Fred's own choosing waited for Sanderson in the fat belly of the chopper: five weathered, battle-hardened soldiers that were under clear instructions that they were to escort the scientist to and from the ship and no more. If the pudgy bastard managed to fuck the situation up he was going to end up dead one way or another. Fred just hoped it would be him that got to pull the trigger if it came to it.

In any case, there was nothing left to be done about Sanderson and the mutation but wait.

In the meantime there were other things to take into consideration beyond the advancement of science or how Phil Sanderson might look with a large entry wound in the centre of his expansive forehead. Equally important things, like a small army of people floating on ships off the coast of northern Scotland, and the fact that most of them were hired grunts who hadn't even been informed that the world they had known was going to be destroyed.

Some of them weren't taking the news so well, and all of them had guns.

Yet another consequence of the interference that had doomed Project Wildfire before it began: the fleet—and the mercenaries that populated it—was meant purely for cleanup and peacekeeping after the virus burned itself out. The ships were the white horse that Fred would ride in on to clear up the aftermath of the disaster. It certainly wasn't meant to be a place for Fred Sullivan to take up permanent residence.

The collapse of the world had made everyone who hadn't been included in the plan until it had been set in motion jittery, and jittery people whose fingers were curled around triggers were, to Fred's mind, not good company.

With every passing hour that the ships spent holding their position, they began to feel more and more like floating pressure cookers. With nothing to do, and nowhere to direct their rage at the devastation wrought on their species, it was only a matter of time before the troops on the ships began to search inwardly for a target, and Fred had a suspicion they wouldn't look far.

If Sanderson couldn't make a breakthrough quickly, Fred would be left with no option but to destroy the creature and flee to the rally point, quite possibly abandoning the bulk of the increasingly mutinous fleet in the process. It would be a catastrophic failure, and worse, it would be the only path he could take.

Fred detested being stuck with no choice. A lack of choice was a lack of power, and he had spent his entire life building influence and accruing wealth in the billions to ensure that the one thing he would never be was *powerless*.

A mutiny within the fleet was something that Fred could handle. He had prepared for every outcome. What he could not handle was the prospect of running to Australia and finding himself with no more influence than the average pensioner.

Everything now hinged on McIntosh; on a creature of immense unpredictability with a predilection for savage violence toward humans in general and Fred in particular.

It was the things you left to chance, Fred thought, *that would undo you in the end.*

Fate, in his experience, could be controlled and tamed, its impact minimised almost entirely, as long as you had enough money. Yet there was always that sliver of light, that crack in the door through which luck could force an entry. To fail to acknowledge it was folly, and *failure to prepare* was, as one of the slightly nauseating slogans peppered around the gleaming London HQ of Chrysalis Systems would have it, *to prepare to fail.*

Those sort of trite clichés generally made Fred's teeth grind noisily, but that one contained more than a modicum of truth.

Far below him on the deck, the chopper's blades had reached full speed.

There was nothing else to be done about the McIntosh problem now. Luck and chance had been eliminated as far as was possible, and even Phil Sanderson couldn't possibly fuck things up, but Fred didn't hold out much hope of the man being able to unlock the secrets of the mutation's blood *quickly.*

Which meant that Fred was going to have to deal with the growing dissatisfaction of the people aboard the ships himself, in the only way that he and they would understand.

As the helicopter lifted from the deck, Fred turned away, and made his way back into the ship.

He had a meeting to attend.

8

The chopper speared up through the mist that clung low to the North Sea, and the all-consuming roar of the engine made it difficult for Kyle Robinson to think clearly.

That seemed to be becoming a recurring theme.

Only minutes earlier he had been engaged in the same argument he'd been having with his brother over and over, ever since they had first sneaked aboard the ship. Well, almost. Right up until Project Wildfire actually went ahead, the argument had been about how to *stop* it, but it turned out that knowing about Wildfire was one thing, while throwing a spanner into the works of the vast machinery that Fred Sullivan had created was another entirely.

Tom had fantasized ever-more bizarre and unlikely ways to stop Sullivan, including blowing up the entire fleet with no working knowledge of explosives whatsoever, or infiltrating Fred's personal security and assassinating the man like *James Bond*, until his desperation and impotence became obvious even to him.

It became abundantly clear that stopping the apocalypse was the stuff of fantasy when Sullivan's satellites spat the Wildfire virus down onto the surface of the Earth, and humans everywhere began to tear each other apart. At that point Kyle and Tom's recurring disagreement evolved to focus more on just what the hell they were supposed to do *next*.

Kyle shifted his gaze to Phil Sanderson, who sat in the chopper with an anxious expression on his face and a stack of papers clutched in his sweaty palms.

The balding scientist had interrupted the brothers' latest heated discussion, and had seemingly removed the decision of what they should do next from their hands entirely. For weeks they had pretended to be soldiers, replete in dead men's uniforms, and that had been fine. Heart-stopping occasionally, but fine.

Thanks to Sanderson, now Kyle and Tom would have to do some actual soldiering.

This will not end well.

Kyle scanned the rest of the helicopter's interior furtively.

There were a grand total of eight men in the chopper. Alongside Kyle, Tom and Sanderson, sat five men who clearly *did* know something about being in the military, and who for the most part stared at Kyle with barely-disguised disdain.

I must look like a rookie to them, Kyle thought. *If only they knew. I'm not even that.*

Kyle might have no experience of being in the armed forces, but he *did* have recent experience of killing. Experience that had been forced upon him by his brother, and which had left a dark shadow in his mind.

Following the failed attempt to kidnap Fred Sullivan's daughter, the brothers had fled London, heading north as far as the land would take them. There, they found a town that wasn't supposed to exist, hidden among the craggy cliffs and barren, sporadic islands that comprised Scotland's harsh northern coastline.

That was when Kyle saw the fleet for the first time.

Seventeen huge ships pockmarked the choppy waters, and a dozen smaller vessels clung to them like parasites, shuttling troops across from the coast. Among container ships and civilian ferries, Kyle saw a half-dozen battleships of varying sizes and one honest-to-God *aircraft carrier.*

And people. A *lot* of people. Most of them military in appearance, all of them looking like they were preparing for something big to go down.

For a town that didn't appear on any map, the place sure was fucking *busy.*

Kyle had half-expected that they would find nothing when they travelled north; had hoped as much, though discovering a lack of evidence would have been a shattering blow to his brother's precarious mental stability. But the existence of the town further reinforced Tom's delusion, until Kyle was pretty sure that it wasn't actually a delusion at all.

The 'town' was really no more than a tent city that had sprung up around a handful of ancient stone buildings that looked like they had been abandoned many years before and only recently refurbished.

It appeared to serve only as a way-station for the huge numbers of troops that waited to be shuttled across to the fleet, and Kyle imagined that when everyone had finally made it over to their new posts, the town would cease to exist. Maybe it would look like it had never been there in the first place.

Kyle and Tom had spent a couple of days camped out on the hill that overlooked the town, watching from the cover of trees, searching for an opportunity to somehow blend in.

In the end, opportunity came to them: a couple of soldiers in the now-familiar black uniforms that bore no insignia stumbled drunkenly towards them in the dark, laughing raucously.

We have to kill them, Tom had hissed at Kyle and, before Kyle had even had a chance to respond, he found himself watching in mute horror as Tom hurtled down the hill toward the men, pulling a flick knife from his pocket.

With a stifled curse, Kyle had taken the only option he had left, and chased after his brother.

By the time Kyle reached the bottom of the slope, Tom had already buried his knife in one of the men, and was struggling with the second.

And losing.

Even with the element of surprise on his side, Tom was no fighter, and his knees began to crumple as the stunned soldier wrapped his hands around the neck of the man who had appeared out of nowhere with a sharp knife and a set of bad intentions.

Kyle had no choice. He withdrew his own knife and charged forward, planting it to the hilt in the neck of the man trying to choke his brother.

He saw a dark spray of blood arcing into the night air, and a look of stupid surprise on the face of the stricken man as Tom stumbled away.

Kyle felt a light slap on his wrist that confused him, until he realised it wasn't a slap at all; it was a *splash*, warm and sticky and terrifying.

An obscene torrent of blood pumped from the ragged tear in the soldier's neck, dousing Kyle's forearm up to the elbow.

Kyle's eyes widened in horror, and for a moment he felt oddly connected with the face that loomed in front of him, linked together invisibly by a shared sense of shock.

The dying man opened his mouth, though strangely it didn't look like he was about to scream in pain or horror or fury. He looked more like he was going to ask a question. Just some dopey question.

Kyle saw his brother reappear with his own knife, watched him plunging it into the man's back. The dying soldier fell away and the dopey question became nothing more than a sad gurgle.

"Quickly," Tom hissed, breaking the paralysing spell that had fallen over Kyle. "Their uniforms. You get that one."

Kyle blinked at his brother. Tom's face was covered in blood. It made him look like a monster from a horror movie; like a cleverly constructed special effect.

"Kyle," Tom said sharply as he hauled up one of the leaking bodies at his feet. "It's done. It had to be done. They are just a means to an end, that's all. We have to move."

A means to an end.

Kyle rubbed at the blood that covered his forearm, watching as it dripped to the ground, and couldn't help but wonder if Fred Sullivan told himself the same thing to help him sleep at night.

Maybe not, he thought. *Maybe when you plan to kill in the millions, death just becomes a statistic, like points on a scoreboard. Maybe it feels different when your arm is soaked in warm blood and you can see the light in the dying man's eyes as it flicks off forever.*

After they dumped the bodies in the woods a few miles south of the coast, the two brothers washed the uniforms clean of the blood as best they could in a stream, and put them on. They were ill-fitting, and to Kyle they looked ridiculous, but he had little doubt they would serve their purpose. There were hundreds, maybe thousands of identically-clad men and women in the tent city. The black uniforms would render Kyle and Tom all-but invisible in the crowd.

Wearing the uniforms and doing their best to wear a military attitude to match; and with credit-card style identity cards issued by Chrysalis Systems in their pockets, Kyle and Tom had made their way to the tent city, and ultimately to the fleet, and Kyle had spent his time ever since trying to remind himself that he and Tom were supposed to be the good guys.

Serial killers.

Good guys.

The world had become a fucked-up place weeks before Project Wildfire destroyed it.

And now, as Kyle sat in the chopper, surrounded by men for whom the military attitude he had tried to fabricate came naturally; drafted into a mission he did not understand, he thought once more about Tom's words on the hill, and wondered if they would ever stop feeling so relevant.

We have to kill them.

The chopper lurched as turbulence buffeted it. Or maybe that was just Kyle's stomach, doing its best to warn him that things were careering out of control now, just as they had been when Tom charged down the hill in the dark with a knife in his hand.

Kyle couldn't help but wonder if he was charging down a hill after his brother once more, and death was waiting at the bottom.

9

Fred Sullivan drummed his fingers on the polished table and idly daydreamed about the days when ship's captains were able to make the irritants they had aboard their vessels walk the plank.

He wasn't the ship's captain, of course, but the man who was in charge of the boat understood the concept of hierarchy well enough, and had the good sense to appear terrified whenever Fred's piercing eyes drilled into him.

Sitting in the makeshift boardroom, in what would be his last ever *senior management meeting*, Fred cast a glance around the seven familiar faces seated around the huge table and felt a twinge of regret that his revolver held just six bullets. Meetings had always been an infuriating time-sink, and he had often dwelled on fantasies of ending them in bloodshed.

You may never get another chance...

Fred shook the thought away. The people that sat around him had all been pivotal in the smooth running of Project Wildfire, and none of them was technically to blame for the way it ended.

Technically.

They had been the engine that had helped him to drive Chrysalis Systems toward its ultimate goal. Each of them had performed admirably in the past—which was why they were still breathing—but none of them seemed to be taking the spectacular failure of the project personally, and Fred wasn't sure they even realised how lucky they were to be alive and sitting on the boat.

'Boat' was, of course, a singularly underwhelming way to describe the ship that Fred had made his floating HQ after abandoning the underground base in Northumberland. The newly-renamed *Conqueror* had been one of the jewels of the French navy before Fred's bank balance persuaded the government of the time that they needed to decommission it and begin work on a newer model.

The carrier was a shade under one thousand feet long. In its previous life it had been home to sixty fighter jets and fifteen attack helicopters, and had been the first vessel built outside the USA to allow for catapult-assisted take-off. Now 'decommissioned', it was able to comfortably act as a base of operations for the twenty-five Harrier jets and seven attack helicopters Fred's company had procured. With around four thousand troops on board, the nuclear-powered ship was technically under-populated, yet Fred felt claustrophobic on his floating HQ. Trapped.

The *Conqueror*'s static weapons fell a little short in Fred's opinion, but carriers had never been designed as fast-attack vessels. Instead, they sat back while destroyers got up close and personal, and utilised their long-range aircraft to rain death from the skies.

Still, even without satisfactory on-board artillery, the *Conqueror* was a floating fortress, and quite possibly the most powerful man-made object still active on planet Earth.

Only the American fleet boasted vessels that exceeded the power of the *Conqueror*, and, of course, contact with America had been plunged back into the pre-Columbus era. The sheer distance between Fred and whatever was left of the United States meant their power was worth little more to him than a whispered promise.

Sometimes Fred indulged himself in imagining how Wildfire might have gone down in America; a country with a vast and well-armed population. Messily, he suspected.

In all likelihood, he would never know. The New World might be nothing more than a continent of decaying corpses by now; a gargantuan graveyard spanning more than three thousand miles. Wildfire hadn't *trimmed* humanity as originally intended. Instead, Victor Chamberlain's global-level interference with the delivery system had rebranded the project as an extinction-level event.

That didn't bother Fred in the slightest. Most of the human race had been no more than worthless vermin, scrabbling around ineffectually in the cages of their unremarkable lives. For most, Fred would not even accept that what he had done to them was a crime. No, it was a mercy. Given another fifty years of the feverish expansion of the human race and the fucking cretins would have gladly eaten each other without any prompting from Fred.

No, what mattered to Fred now was what was left in the ashes of Project Wildfire. A vacuum. Power just waiting to be claimed. If Phil Sanderson was correct, Jake McIntosh offered him the opportunity to control humanity at a species-level. Even if the Americans did make it to the rally point before him, he felt certain they wouldn't have leverage over him. Fuck their big ships. The mutation's blood was all that mattered now, and Fred was the one that had it.

"Fred?"

Fred blinked. For a moment there, lost in dreams of death and power, he had completely forgotten that he was in the middle of a meeting.

He glared at the woman that had interrupted his thoughts. Sandra Adkins, a prissy bitch with a nasal voice and almost comically ratty features. Adkins had been Director of Human Resources at Chrysalis, and her job title now seemed a little ironic to Fred. He fixed her with a stare that he hoped conveyed contemptuous disinterest.

"Uh, Fred, I was just asking what sort of measures are in place to protect the safety of the staff once you wake the monster up?"

Fred twisted his wrinkled face into a snarl. No missing the contempt. Not now.

The staff? For a fraction of a second, Fred wondered if Adkins was joking, but the businesslike expression on her face said otherwise.

"I have taken the measure of purchasing seventeen ships and putting *my staff* aboard them, Ms Adkins. I'd say the only thing threatening any of *my staff* is a proclivity for asking stupid fucking questions."

Adkins stared at him in shock for a moment but gathered herself quickly.

"It seems that the only questions left to ask are the fucking stupid ones, Fred," she said curtly.

Fred chuckled. So few ever dared to spar with him.

"You don't give any more of a shit about the staff than I do, Adkins. You want to know why your own bony arse is in danger, and just how much, isn't that right? Come on, now, the time for boardroom bullshit is over, wouldn't you say?"

Adkins flushed.

Fred stood. Age had done nothing to curve his spine, and when he drew himself up to his full height, he towered over the rest of them.

"You all want answers. Fine. Here are some truths for you."

He turned to his left, fixing his gaze on Charles Ennis. A company man for twenty-five years, and a bona fide genius when it came to adding zeroes onto spreadsheets.

"Ennis, I haven't liked your face for twenty-five years, and now I find that your skills are of little use to me."

Charles Ennis' mouth formed a perfect 'o' that matched his round features as Fred smoothly withdrew the revolver from its holster under his jacket and painted the wall with the man's brains.

Fred let out a satisfied sigh as the roar of the gun echoed around the enclosed space. *Damn,* he thought, *I do love firing that weapon.*

"Let's be clear about something," Fred said finally, breaking the silence that had settled over the room like radioactive dust. "Chrysalis Systems no longer exists. Your jobs no longer exist. This is to be the last of these meetings that I will suffer through. If you all wish to continue prattling away without my input, feel free, but I don't want you to toil away under any illusions. None of you matter, not in the slightest. Your continued presence on this boat is a mild irritant, but I am willing to endure that much because the work you once did for me was useful."

Fred paused for a response. As he expected, there was none. Nothing underlined authority in a meeting quite like killing the attendees. He wished he had done it many, many years earlier.

"This is no longer a corporation. It certainly is no longer anything resembling a *democracy*. You'd be wise to proceed under the impression that this is in fact a dictatorship, and not a benign one. So here is what will happen: we will hold this position until the scientists give me something I can work with. If that does not transpire I will have all the various parts of this fleet that I consider to be *redundant* destroyed. Then I will give the order to move to Australia. Not before."

Fred saw Sandra Adkins' face contorting, as if she was trying desperately to hold something in. Eventually she failed.

"And what if we don't have that long to wait?" She said cautiously, eyeing the smouldering corpse that sat to her right. "People are getting...anxious Fred. Most of the troops don't even know what happened. They're becoming...difficult to control. Unpredictable."

"I am fully aware of the mutinous atmosphere on this ship," Fred barked. "And it shall be taken care of. That is the end of the matter."

Fred slipped the revolver back into its holster. It felt warm against his ribs.

"I hope I've made myself clear."

Fred turned and strode out of the thunderous silence of the boardroom, and couldn't help but feel a little disappointed. At one time he had believed his senior management team to be brilliant people; the best and the brightest. Yet it appeared they were only just now concluding that an army of hired thugs who were slowly waking up to the fact that their payment was meaningless might prove to be trouble.

So slow, he thought. *So reactionary.*

The plan was never meant to involve them ending up on ships staffed with mercenaries, travelling to the other side of the planet. If the people that had once been his staff could not adapt to their new reality, they truly had outlived their usefulness.

Fred grimaced, leaving the boardroom behind him and stalked through the narrow steel corridors, making his way to the quarters of one of the very few people on board the ship that *did* matter.

10

Rachel Roberts sat with her back against the cold stone wall, her eyes fixed straight ahead; seeing nothing.

She had been locked in a cell with three other people, including two that she knew at least moderately well—Linda and Emma—but their attempts to engage her had been like seeds dropped on concrete.

Lost in her thoughts, locked in memories both recent and long-passed, Rachel's mind bubbled and spat like an active volcano. Her rage sought an outlet, trying to break free of her and inhabit the world like a living entity. Only by erecting isolating walls in her thoughts to keep her away from the people around her could she guarantee their safety.

The impulse to do harm—to lash out at the nearest person in the most violent way possible—was almost overpowering.

Finding the brother she had been certain was dead had been her one shot at clinging to some sort of hope; some faint semblance of an idea that the world had not sunk into a bottomless abyss of pain and horror.

The darkening of her soul that she had felt ever since the disastrous escape from Aberystwyth had not been lessened by finding Jason alive: instead it had hardened like cooling steel, until it felt like a part of her that she would never be able to remove.

Jason was alive, but Jason was also dead. Lost to her, corrupted by the old woman's torture; broken in mind and spirit until he hadn't even recognised his own sister.

It was Jason that had killed John, though he hadn't been the one to slice his throat open. Yet it was Rachel who felt responsible. For forcing John to go to Anglesey on a hopeless rescue mission and bringing the psychotic old bitch and her people to the castle. For leaving Jason alone in Aberystwyth in the first place.

For giving up on her little brother when he had needed her most.

Rachel's cellmates gave her as wide a berth as was possible in the tiny cell, and soon gave up trying to talk to her.

Rachel's gaze was pointed at the stone wall, but what she saw was the emptiness in Jason's eyes when she had run toward him in Anglesey. Not the same sad emptiness that had been there after he had been forced to kill their mother, but something darker. Something almost inhuman.

She closed her eyes and drew in a deep breath. The cell stank of damp and sweat and cloying fear. Worse, it smelled to Rachel of inevitability. She would never be freed, not unless the old woman decided to kill her. Rachel thought she'd be dead already if Annie Holloway was convinced that the grip she had over Jason was unbreakable.

It was just a matter of time before Annie *was* certain of Jason's loyalty, or of the totality of her destruction of him. Rachel was on death row. Maybe they all were.

You can do this, Rach.

John's final words haunted her.

Do what? There's nothing I can do.

Only when someone came to take Ed from the cell did Rachel's attention flicker back to the present. From the corner of her eye she watched the man as he bundled Ed out of the door. He was slight, balding.

And he carried the shotgun she had taken from Darren Oliver's men. The one she had used to save John's life.

She knew all too well that the gun had just one round in it. She had searched the castle for more shells and found none. If Darren had more ammunition he had hidden it well.

One shot.

She wondered if the man had checked the ammunition himself, and just how good a shot he might be. Not that it particularly mattered with a shotgun; not unless you were trying to use it at range. She had seen what the weapon did at close quarters. It ripped flesh apart like an explosive charge.

She lapsed back into dark thoughts for a time, and her mood only darkened further when she heard distant, muffled screaming. A man's voice. She couldn't tell whether it belonged to Ed or Michael.

Michael's desecration of John's corpse had shaken Rachel to her core, and she spent a good deal of time wondering if the police officer might just have joined up with the people now running the castle.

She wouldn't believe it.

Couldn't.

As vulnerable as the wheelchair left Michael, and as important as keeping his daughter safe was to him, Rachel didn't think the man who had helped her in St. Davids, and who owed her at least as much as she owed him, could be a turncoat. Not even if the crazy old woman offered safety for himself and for Claire.

Yet if Michael had a plan, Rachel could not see it; could not imagine how a paralysed man with no weapons could do anything against the forces that now held them all prisoner.

Despair began to creep into her thoughts; bleak and unending. Jason was lost to her. John: dead. Michael in no position to do anything.

And herself.

Blindsided by finding Jason alive, she had lost all her caution, had thrown it to the wind like confetti, and had ended up once more in the clutches of a psychopath. She wondered how long it would be before the men that followed the old woman decided they liked the look of the young women that were locked in the cells; questioned whether the old woman would stop them when it came to it. If she even *could*.

No one will touch me again, not like Victor did. If it comes to that, I'll make them kill me.

Lost in the dark country that her thoughts had become, Rachel barely noticed when the cell door opened and Michael was ushered in, carrying another load of stale bread and water. She didn't see the haunted look on his face, or the blood on his shirt.

But she heard him.

Heard the words whispered furtively, just quiet enough that the man who stood outside the cell watching Michael would miss them.

Listen to Claire.

Just three words, and Rachel could not piece together their meaning, but she read the intent in them. Michael was going to try something.

And she would be ready.

*

"Listen to Claire," Michael hissed.

It was all he could manage. Rhys Holloway had become a shadow that clung to Michael, a shadow that stank of sweat and intimidation.

Michael kept his voice low; hoped it wouldn't carry beyond the cell. He clattered the fresh slop bucket down onto the stone floor, masking the noise of his words as much as possible.

When he lifted his eyes, he saw that the message had been heard as he intended.

Linda stared at him quizzically, and when she gave a faint hint of a nod, he sighed in relief.

Nobody was going to let Michael talk to the prisoners; that much was obvious, but the old woman and her sons were so focused on observing him that they seemed to have forgotten all about Claire.

After all, what danger could a helpless little girl possibly pose to them?

Asking Claire to pass on a message for him was dangerous enough that Michael almost abandoned the idea, but he could see no other way. A vague notion of how he might be able to get everybody out of the castle was forming in his mind. It was a plan so insane that Michael was sure John would have approved, but it would all fall apart without Linda, and to get her to agree to her part in it would mean using Claire.

Michael wheeled himself away from the cell as Rhys locked the door behind him, and waited until he was told he could leave.

With a nod, Michael turned the chair away from Rhys and made his way back toward the tower that had become his home and his prison, and which he thought might yet become his tomb.

11

The throne was hard and uncomfortable. Doubtless, Annie thought, pampered arses had once demanded that plush cushions be placed upon it, but the discomfort didn't bother her unduly. Her entire life had been hard and uncomfortable. That was simply the cost of prevailing.

She wouldn't dream of bleating about an uncomfortable chair, especially not a chair that conferred the status that the throne did. Appearances needed to be maintained, and an aching posterior was a small price to pay.

She stared at her son, who stood awkwardly in front of her, practically squirming as he had when he had been just a little boy trying to find the right words to confess that he had wet the bed.

"What is it, Rhys?"

"I don't understand why you don't just kill him, Ma."

Annie rolled her eyes and sighed softly. If she counted up the number of things her eldest son didn't understand, she couldn't help but wonder if she would run out of numbers or patience first.

He did have a point on this occasion, though, and Annie *had* thought about killing the man in the wheelchair; had given it serious consideration the moment she saw the cogs whirring behind his lying eyes.

"We need people, Rhys. Strength in numbers. It's the only way we'll survive this madness. If we just kill everyone we meet, we won't last long. Not even in this castle."

Rhys nodded sombrely, but Annie could tell he had failed to grasp the concept.

"We've already killed the man who was in charge here," Annie said. "And that leaves us with an uphill battle with these folks. Kill Michael, and we might as well kill them all. He was important to them, and if they will listen to him then maybe they will come around to our way of thinking."

"Will *he*?"

Annie stared at her boy thoughtfully. It was a rare and insightful question.

The truth was that she had no idea if Michael could be persuaded to follow her—whether willingly or grudgingly—but the mere fact that he'd had possession of the gun meant the others had placed stock in him. His words must have carried sway within the group. If he led, they would surely follow.

She could break him, there was no doubt in her mind about that. A crippled man in a wheelchair, alone and vulnerable, with a young daughter to be used as leverage against him if necessary. Annie knew she could subdue the man, just as she had subdued the giant who called himself Voorhees. But a broken Michael wouldn't be a great deal of use to her.

Not unless she was prepared to break them all, and Annie already had more than her share of damaged people to look after.

"We've got another, problem, Ma," Rhys said hesitantly.

Annie stared at him, her eyes narrowing.

"It's Voorhees. I think he's sick."

Annie grimaced. She had seen the dark wounds festering on the big man's skin; had smelled the sweet fragrance of his slowly rotting flesh.

She doubted that Voorhees felt anything himself: whatever awareness was left in his fractured mind *might* be able to feel pain, but she continued to dose him with numerous painkillers to keep him pliant. Eventually she hoped she wouldn't need them, and that obedience would come as naturally to Voorhees as breathing, but that depended on him surviving.

The painkillers would do nothing to stem the infection that crept through his body. He needed proper treatment. A doctor.

How convenient, Annie thought, *that Michael has just dropped one of those into my lap.*

The man in the wheelchair was chasing a scheme that she could not see or understand; at least not yet. What she was certain of was that if Michael wanted the doctor—*Linda?*—freed, it was to satisfy some part of his own agenda.

Michael was trying to manipulate her, and that had never ended well for anybody other than Annie herself.

"We'll let this doctor Michael mentioned out soon," Annie said. "And I want your eyes on her the entire time she is out of that cell. When she's done tending to Voorhees, we'll put her right back. If she and Michael so much as look at each other, they'll both be joining our friend Mr Cartwright in the dungeon."

Rhys nodded and smiled happily.

12

"We're going to have to get out of here, Kiddo."

Claire frowned, and with good reason. Michael couldn't remember ever calling her *Kiddo* in his life.

He stifled a sigh. Trying to make the conversation he was about to have with his daughter seem normal suddenly looked like a ridiculous proposition. It probably had been all along.

For a moment he was jarred by how much he had missed of her growing, and how quickly she had changed. It had only been a couple of years since Elise left, taking their daughter with her. Just a couple of years.

A quarter of her life.

When did she become so sharp?

"Sorry," Michael said with an embarrassed grin. "I guess that was me still thinking you are six years old."

Claire's frown deepened and she folded her arms across her chest.

"What's going on?"

Michael wheeled himself to the door, and listened intently. There was no reason to think Rhys or anybody else was standing out there in the silence, straining to catch his words. Still, he had been caught out once before, and had ended up shooting two people dead. One of them just a kindly old lady who had died with a look of sad confusion plastered across her face that he did not think he would ever be able to forget.

It didn't do any harm to make sure.

Outside the tower, he heard only silence.

After a few seconds he wheeled himself back to Claire. He kept his voice low.

"These people are very dangerous. I have to get us—all of us—out of here as quickly as possible. You understand?"

Claire nodded sombrely.

"I can't do it without your help," Michael said.

For a moment the frown clung to Claire's brow, and then she straightened suddenly, as if standing to attention.

"You can count on me."

Michael smiled. One thing he had known about Claire when she was six hadn't changed at all in the intervening years. In fact it had only become more apparent. She liked a challenge.

She'll do great things when she grows up, he thought.

If.

Michael's expression darkened. He had studiously tried to avoid thinking long-term; to push aside dark fantasies of what life might be like if they survived a year. Five. Twenty.

Yet the future stood right in front of him with an eager, determined expression on its face. Avoiding it was like trying to stay dry by walking between raindrops.

Claire wouldn't live to see another birthday in the castle. That much was certain to him. His resolve stiffened. Despite what Holloway might think, Claire wasn't a helpless little girl. She had survived the destruction of Aberystwyth alone for days, and seemed to take each new horror in her stride.

She will be okay.

"I'm going to distract them," Michael said. "And while I'm doing that, I need you to go and talk to Linda, okay? I need you to tell her exactly what I tell you to. Exactly. Word-for-word. Without getting seen. Will you be able to do that?"

Claire pondered the question for a moment, and nodded firmly.

"I'll have my way with Linda," Claire said.

Michael arched an eyebrow in surprise at the odd phrase. Like something Claire had heard somebody say and repeated it without fully understanding.

"What do you mean?"

Claire flushed, as if suddenly aware that she had said something wrong.

"Where did you hear that saying?" Michael asked, but the dark clouds gathering in his mind told him he already knew.

"The old lady's son," Claire said. "The little one. She said she would let him have his way with me."

Claire bit her lip and her eyes widened, and Michael realised that the expression on his face must have twisted to match the fury coiling around his gut. He took a deep breath and calmed himself.

"She told you to say that to me," he said softly. It wasn't a question, but a realisation.

Claire nodded.

For a brief moment Michael flirted with the idea of telling Claire to forget he'd said anything; of following the deranged old woman meekly. Anything to keep his daughter safe.

Then he thought of Rachel, alone at the mercy of a psychopath and still finding time to tend to Michael's damaged body while he lay unconscious. He was alive because of Rachel. Victor would have killed him without a second thought, and it was her intervention that had allowed him to survive. Without Rachel, Claire too would surely be dead already.

And what of John? He had saved them all more than once, and now John was dead and Michael had helped to crucify his corpse.

I owe these people.

He remembered once before mulling over whether to take the easy choice: when he was sitting on a pathetic scooter outside of St. Davids just as the town's population began to explode into violence. He had taken the hard option then. He could have run, and for a while he thought he *should* have run, but he hadn't. Instead he had done what was *right*.

Maybe that, more than anything, was what had kept him alive until now. If he turned his back on Rachel and the others after all they had done for him, he really would be no different to Darren, or even to Annie. He would no longer be able to tell himself that he had gunned down a scared old woman because he had to, but would know he had done it because it was the easy option.

He had to use Claire. Because it was the difficult choice, and because it was the only choice that might ultimately keep her safe.

Have his way with my daughter.

A fire began to burn in Michael's mind, and it consumed the self-doubt that had plagued him for what felt like an eternity. It spread from his thoughts, enveloping him, raging through his torso.

Into his legs.

Michael's face contorted in fury and pain, twisting with the effort as his mind screamed silently at his obstinate legs.

Pain is just a message. Just an email sent to the brain.

Michael received the message; got it loud and clear.

He sent one back.

You have to move.

And with gritted teeth and muscles that burned like they had been dipped in acid; like they were being used for the very first time, Michael pushed himself up from the chair, and stood before his shocked daughter, swaying slightly on legs that felt like they didn't quite belong to him; euphoria coursing through his veins like a powerful drug.

Claire's mouth dropped open and she stared at her father in astonishment.

For a moment Michael thought he would fall, and he put a hand against the wall to steady himself. The pain was enormous, but he embraced it like a long-lost friend.

When the agony finally abated a little and his vision began to clear, Michael looked down at his daughter's beautiful face; at the eyes that had already lost too much of their innocence.

"We're leaving," he said.

13

"It's fine, Mr Sullivan, uh, Sir. Nathan can be trusted."

Nathan Colston gritted his teeth and bit down on his desire to voice his disagreement.

No, Sir, I can't be trusted. Best all round if I fuck off somewhere else while you two have this conversation.

Nathan had served as part of Fred Sullivan's security forces in the Northumberland base, and had held a position of slight authority and relative anonymity that had suited him perfectly. Near-invisibility was, Nathan believed, crucial to his chances of surviving any longer than the average British summer.

He had headed up a small team that reported ultimately to Simon Ripley, the head of security at the base. Ripley had been one-part dedicated soldier and at least four-parts raving lunatic, and Nathan had avoided him as much as it was possible to avoid a man who was technically your boss and who you were actually trapped in a hole with.

Insanity, Nathan figured, probably came with the job title. Head of Security, as it turned out, was just a polite euphemism for *enforcer*.

Or *executioner*.

Nathan didn't envy Ripley his position at all, and had no ambitions toward getting himself promoted, and so it was unfortunate that Jake McIntosh's massacre at the base had propelled Nathan so far up the ladder.

As the second highest-ranking officer left alive when McIntosh exited the underground base, leaving a trail of bodies in his wake, Nathan's resulting close proximity to the position of Head of Security had been inevitable. It wasn't something Nathan had *earned*—just a matter of his surviving; impossible to avoid, like defective genes or the onset of old age.

Pure, dumb, bad luck.

One more stroke of which could strike at any moment, and Nathan was painfully aware that he was only two promotions away from taking up a permanent position at the Pearly Gates.

Or the other place. After you became Head of Security for Chrysalis Systems, it seemed like the only way left to go was down.

The man who currently held the position that stood between Nathan and an all-too-early death was Richard Skinner. He had probably been a dependable soldier before he became a mercenary, Nathan thought, but he was a piss-poor hired gun.

Skinner still believed in the chain of command and studious deference in the presence of what he called 'my superiors', and he seemed to have a genuine problem when it came to forming his own opinion on anything.

There was a reason all the other men shortened his name to *Dick*, and it had nothing to do with affection.

And now Dick had shoved Nathan in front of the old bastard that had fucked the whole world up, and told him that this was a man Fred Sullivan could trust. It didn't feel so much like getting thrown under the bus as being tied to the ground in front of its wheels and made to wait.

Nice one.

Dick.

Nathan withered under the old man's gaze, and did his best to make himself look forgettable.

After a moment, Fred shrugged.

"If you say so, Skinner," he growled. "I'll have to take your word for it. That is why I'm here, after all."

Old fucker loves being cryptic, Nathan thought, but he saw through the veneer of bullshit. Fred Sullivan was consulting with Dick Skinner—a blustering cretin that the old man wouldn't have trusted to shine his boots a few short weeks earlier—because he was desperate, plain and simple. Because the mercenaries that Sullivan had bought and paid for were starting to wonder just why the hell they should give a damn about money when all the shops were full of demented eyeless cannibals.

Dick Skinner had been the head of security for all of five bewildering minutes when Fred Sullivan abandoned the base and fled to the fleet. Compared to Ripley's command, the ship should have been a breeze.

Judging by Skinner's hopeless attempts to corral the men on the ship, it was proving to be anything but.

Tension was rising inexorably aboard the *Conqueror*, and the limited radio contact with the other ships in the fleet revealed a similar, and in some cases, even more precarious situation. Most of the troops Sullivan had hired to staff the vessels had known only as much as they needed to, which of course was the square root of fuck all. The majority had no idea what Chrysalis Systems had been planning, and that they were only ever meant to be a contingency plan.

A glorified clean-up crew.

Whatever Nathan or anybody else thought about Fred Sullivan, there was no denying that the old bastard was cunning, and seventy-plus years of money and power had only served to hone that intelligence until it was razor-sharp. The old man knew which way the wind was blowing, which was exactly why he had tasked Dick Skinner with tallying up how many men could be counted on for their loyalty *if matters on the fleet should come to a head.*

Sullivan loved his euphemisms.

Coming to a head, in this instance, was a vague way of accepting that violent bloodshed was brewing on the *Conqueror*—and almost certainly on every other ship in the fleet—and that Fred Sullivan wasn't prepared to let anyone else get the jump on him when it came to killing.

Skinner, after a typical period of dithering, had sought out Nathan's help. Together they had drawn up a list of around five hundred names that Sullivan would be able to count on when civil war broke out on the North Sea.

Just five hundred, most of whom had been present at the Northumberland base.

The *Conqueror* alone held close to four thousand troops. If it came down to a straight fight, those loyal to Sullivan's cause would be heavily outnumbered and outgunned.

The ship that had felt secure, detached from the violent chaos spreading across the UK, suddenly felt very dangerous indeed, and every bit as claustrophobic as the underground base had been.

Nathan's combat experience was limited, but not so much that he didn't recognise a deadly situation when it knocked at his door and waved a weapon in his face.

Like most of the people serving as a private army for Chrysalis, Nathan had been former military, before the world collapsed and everything became 'former' in one way or another. He had served a couple of tours in the Middle East, mostly as a peacekeeper in already-secured provinces rather than being involved in any actual front-line combat.

Some of the men and women headhunted by Sullivan were disgraced, discharged from the military under a cloud. By contrast Nathan hadn't ever put a foot wrong during his time in the desert and his tour ended only when doctors discovered a congenital heart defect during a routine medical checkup.

He felt—still felt—as strong as an ox, but according to various charts and diagrams that Nathan couldn't decipher, his heart was liable to stop pumping at any given minute. It was, for the army, too much of a risk to take.

He received a medical discharge and a full pension, but at the age of thirty-six, *retirement* seemed painfully ludicrous, and the thought of finding menial work in an office somewhere, tapping his life away at a keyboard, seemed far worse than the prospect of his heart giving out.

When Sullivan's people had found him, Nathan had jumped at the chance to see action again.

No one ever told him just what sort of 'action' it would be. Not until he was holed up underground while civilization collapsed above him. Even then he only got the full story when a damned *monster* tore through the base, massacring scores of people.

He hadn't felt sick at all before. But now, after it was done and there was no way back, Nathan Colston could detect the sickness in his chest; could feel it every time he drew in a breath.

This sickness didn't feel congenital, though. It felt like Sullivan's doing: as if the old man's gnarled fingers had penetrated Nathan's chest and were curling around his heart and beginning to squeeze...

"We believe we can count on around five hundred, Sir," Skinner said, and had the good sense to look mortified at the number as it spilled from his lips.

Sullivan's eyebrows lowered, almost obscuring eyes that flashed dangerously.

"Five hundred," he repeated flatly.

"Uh, it's difficult for us to ascertain a definite number, Sir. It's not as if we can just *ask* the men if they will help, and..."

Skinner trailed off, apparently aware that the tone he had employed might lead to him shortly having his forehead decorated with a bullet.

Nathan was mildly impressed.

At least Skinner hadn't bullshitted a number to make the old man happy. Surely now, Nathan thought, Sullivan would see the folly in trying to rid the *Conqueror* of dissidents through violence. Hell, maybe he would even finally give the order for the fleet to move. No one understood why they were holding position a few miles off shore while the apocalypse tore the UK apart. Some believed Sullivan was going to stage a land invasion and take the country back. Others whispered about a plan to flee to Australia, and according to the rumours, the virus *hadn't* reached the land down under.

Most of the increasing hostility on the *Conqueror* would have been assuaged by the simple knowledge that they were doing *something*. If that something happened to be fleeing to safety and endless golden beaches under a sizzling sun, so much the better.

What nobody seemed to understand was just why the hell they were sitting there doing *nothing*.

"Then we'll have to act fast," Fred said through gritted teeth.

"Uh...Sir?" Skinner mumbled.

"Speak to everybody you know to be loyal. Tell them to be armed and ready. By tonight I want every person on this ship to be either loyal to this enterprise, or dead."

Nathan snorted.

Couldn't help himself.

If the old man thought five hundred men could take the *Conqueror* by force, he really was as insane as the whispered voices in the corridors of the ship suggested.

"You," Fred said, pointing a bony finger like a gun barrel at Nathan.

"Come with me."

14

"We'll be at the McIntosh ship in three minutes."

The pilot's voice, crackling over the intercom.

The McIntosh ship?

The words meant nothing to Kyle. Once again he was being dragged into the unknown. It was starting to feel like whenever that happened, people ended up dying. It was a noticeable sort of trend; the kind that leapt around at the front of a person's mind, waving its arms and yelling.

He took a deep breath and stared out of the small window to his right, trying to figure out why one of Fred Sullivan's ships was floating so far away from the rest; ostracised from the party like an aggressive drunk. No theories presented themselves, but it sounded like he only had three minutes to wait before he found out the truth.

He felt a sudden, lurching drop as the chopper began its descent toward the helipad on the deck of the McIntosh ship.

His heart sank at a different, more troubling pace.

*

Kyle ducked instinctively as he disembarked the helicopter, and realised immediately that he needn't have bothered: the chopper was enormous, a far cry from the police helicopters he had occasionally seen buzzing over the London skyline, and the blades span far above his head.

Like all of the aircraft that ferried people between the ships that comprised the fleet, the chopper was huge and lethal-looking with forward-pointing 50-cal machine guns and rocket arrays that gave the front of the vehicle an aggressive appearance, like a snarling animal.

He watched as the silent security team dropped out of the chopper and moved away, remaining alert and watchful. None of them had uttered a word during the short trip between the ships, and it didn't look like they were about to start talking now. They clutched assault rifles, and the hard emptiness in their eyes made Kyle feel like they were itching to get a chance to use them.

As the security team lined up alongside the chopper, all resolute faces and well-practised *don't-fuck-with-us* attitude, Kyle began to understand that they had no intention of leaving the vehicle, and muttered at Sanderson as the scientist climbed down onto the deck.

"What's the deal with your security, uh, Sir?"

Sanderson blinked and snorted.

"*You* are my security," he said with a wry grimace. "Mr Sullivan made it abundantly clear that I am to do this alone. Those men...well, I imagine they are here mainly to ensure that I do not abscond."

Kyle arched an eyebrow.

"So if you're meant to do this alone, what—"

"...Are you two doing here," Sanderson finished. "That is my call. Mr Sullivan has no idea you two are here. None whatsoever."

No kidding, Kyle thought, but he remained silent. As he moved clear of the chopper, his questions about the security team's motivations evaporated, replaced by something altogether more difficult to understand.

The ship was one of the smaller in the fleet, and of all seventeen vessels, it looked to Kyle to be the least military in appearance; and the least threatening. Yet as Kyle began to cross the deck toward the superstructure, he felt a strange dread growing in the pit of his stomach. Maybe it was something to do with being so close to whatever Phil Sanderson had claimed was vital to the success of Project Wildfire, and wondering if Tom was going to hold it together. Or maybe something else.

Something Kyle could not identify.

Far ahead, he saw a small group of people emerging from the ship. They were as military in appearance as the security team that Kyle had just travelled with, yet even at a distance he noticed that something about them seemed...different somehow. Something in the way they carried themselves.

A welcome committee, he thought. *But they don't look very welcoming.*

He scanned the faces of the new group as they approached the chopper, and realised what was different about them. The churning he felt in his own gut was replicated on the faces of the handful of men and women that moved to greet the chopper. All of them looked...scared?

What the hell has Sullivan got on this boat?

"Looks like we have a welcome committee," Kyle said, nodding at the group moving toward them.

Sanderson nodded, cold sunlight reflecting off his expansive brow.

"The ship has a skeleton staff. That's probably most of them right there."

Kyle glanced at his brother in surprise and saw his own confusion mirrored on Tom's furrowed brow.

"On a ship this size?" Tom asked hesitantly. "Why?"

Sanderson shrugged, and paused on the deck, as though the emphasis his words required was impossible to manufacture while walking.

"There's only one thing on this ship," he replied. "Not much work for more than a handful of people. And besides, who the hell would volunteer for this job?"

Kyle felt the dread knotting his stomach tighten.

"What job? What's on this ship...uh, Sir?"

Sanderson blinked.

"You don't know?"

Kyle and Tom shook their heads in unison and Sanderson chuckled. To Kyle's ears it was a nasty, sneering sort of noise, brimming with mockery and disdain. It sounded like Sanderson didn't get a chance to lord his superiority over people that often, and he was relishing every second of their bewilderment.

"Then you're in for a treat," Sanderson said with a smirk, and turned to meet the welcome committee.

Four men, two women. Kyle thought they all looked hard-bitten, like they had seen more than their fair share of combat in a previous life. None of them wore the masks of fear well.

What would scare these sort of people so much?

"If you're here to relieve us, I hope there's another chopper-full of you on the way."

The man leading the welcome committee didn't sound like he respected Sanderson's position in the slightest. He sounded tired, and pissed off.

And frightened.

"You haven't had contact from Mr Sullivan?"

Kyle watched Sanderson closely as he spoke, and thought he saw a flash of genuine surprise pass across the man's jowly face.

He's almost as clueless as we are, Kyle thought abruptly. *Dropped into something he wasn't expecting.*

Kyle's jaw clenched involuntarily. With every passing moment on the ship, things were beginning to feel more and more *wrong* somehow. He felt an almost overpowering urge to leap back onto the chopper, and to refuse to disembark until it left.

"We've had no contact from Mr Sullivan since we were sent here," the man replied, and his thick eyebrows lowered. "You're not here to relieve us," he said flatly. It wasn't a question.

"I'm afraid not, Mr..?"

"Sykes," the man said with a weary sigh. "Just Sykes will do. I haven't been a *Mr* for a long time, and it sure as shit doesn't feel like I'm a corporal anymore."

Sanderson nodded absent-mindedly. "Phil Sanderson," he said, extending his hand for a moment before dropping it when it became clear Sykes wasn't in a hand-shaking sort of mood. "Head of research," Sanderson continued, "and this is my private security detail."

He waved a hand in the general direction of Kyle and Tom. Sykes looked them over with cold mirth in his eyes that made Kyle feel uneasy.

"You ever see that episode of *Road Runner*, where *Wile E Coyote* has about two hundred boulders falling on his head, and he lifts up a little umbrella to protect himself before he gets squashed?" Sykes asked with a watery grin.

Sanderson stared at him, his mouth half-open, and said nothing.

"If there comes a time you need *security* on this boat," Sykes said. "Then these two greenhorns are gonna be your umbrella, Mr Sanderson." Sykes chuckled. "If you wanted *security*, you'd have been best off staying over there."

He pointed in the direction of the fleet, but when Kyle followed the gesture he saw nothing but the flat horizon.

Somewhere at the back of Kyle's mind a faint alarm began to sound, and a question repeated itself, as if his mind was trying to underline it so he would pay it the proper amount of attention.

Why is this ship on its own, all the way out here?

Sanderson nodded at Sykes.

"Agreed. And believe me, I *would* have stayed over there if I could, but Sullivan has pressing business on this ship."

Sykes arched an inquisitive eyebrow, and Sanderson cleared his throat, seeming more than a little nervous.

"I'm here to wake McIntosh up," Sanderson said, and this time, it was Sykes' mouth that Kyle saw drop open in mute astonishment.

15

"Walk with me, Mr Colston."

Nathan opened his mouth to answer, and shut it again when he realised no response was required. Fred Sullivan had already turned on his heel and marched away at a brisk pace, with all the arrogance that stemmed from a lifetime of having his orders followed without question.

"I detest these metal boxes we are forced to live in, don't you?" Fred said as Nathan scurried to catch up to the old man's leggy stride.

"It's not the luxuries I miss," Fred continued. "And God knows I had plenty of those before all this. No, it's the *space*. All of us living on top of each other, breathing in each other's stink, bumping into each other in the corridors. Sort of makes a mockery of depopulating the planet, wouldn't you say?"

Fred shot a glance at Nathan and seemed amused at the confused look he received in return.

"That was a joke. Lighten up, Mr Colston. As yet, you haven't given me any reason to become irritated with you. I'm not a monster or some deranged psychopath, despite what you might have heard to the contrary. What I am is a businessman who doesn't like his time being wasted."

Those last few syllables seemed dangerous to Nathan, like Sullivan had spent decades sparring with barbed words and knew exactly when to employ a jab for maximum effect.

Here comes the point, Nathan thought.

Fred stooped to pass through a small doorway that led out onto the huge flight deck, and breathed in a deep lungful of fresh air.

In the distance, Nathan saw a team of mechanics tinkering with a harrier. The rest of the deck was largely empty. Not for the first time Nathan marvelled at the fact that the ship was so large that he felt no sensation of rocking as the harsh waves of the North Sea battered the hull.

After a few paces, Sullivan stopped and arched his back with a satisfied sigh, like a cat that had just been released after many hours trapped in a basket.

"You don't agree with what we're doing—or should I say: what we've *done*," Fred said finally.

"No, Sir, It's not that-"

Fred snorted.

"It's fine, Mr Colston. I understand perfectly. I've killed a lot of people. I certainly expect nothing other than vilification. I don't expect you to agree, nor even to understand, really. Somebody had to initiate Project Wildfire, or something very like it. There were several arms manufacturers close to producing a weapon as powerful as mine. It was only a matter of time."

He shrugged.

Nathan frowned dubiously.

"Permission to speak freely, Sir?"

Fred's eyes twinkled with amusement.

"I'm not a military officer, Mr Colston, but...permission granted," he said.

"What about the people?" Nathan said, surprising himself a little with the bitterness in his tone. "Even if I buy the idea that the planet was overcrowded, that the people needed...pruning somehow, it doesn't change the fact that you—we, I guess—acted outside the law. No government would allow—"

"Oh, *please*," Fred interrupted with weary sarcasm. "Governments? Is that where you think power resided before all this? I thought of our government as a mildly diverting puppet show. I suppose perception really is everything."

Fred began to stroll forward.

"Chrysalis had been retained by the governments of the world for decades to develop better and better weapons, and not one of them had the foresight to understand that letting others create weapons for you is a route to certain disaster. The governments of the world were more than happy for me to hold enormous power because I promised them that my work would be cheap, and would not be paraded in front of the media. What sort of businessman would I be if I didn't leverage that power to secure the best outcome for my company? For myself?"

He stopped and looked Nathan in the eye.

"Do you know that Oppenheimer is said to have regretted creating the atomic bomb?"

Nathan shook his head. In truth he had heard something similar a long time ago, but he had a feeling the question was rhetorical.

"So they say," Fred said thoughtfully, staring out to sea. "For myself, I think that is probably bullshit. Can you imagine giving birth to such power and wishing you had not? Can you imagine anything more pointless?"

The old man's gaze flicked sharply back to Nathan, like a viper striking.

"What happens when somebody develops a weapon that is too dangerous to sell? The only thing left then is to *use* the damn thing, or destroy it and render the entire endeavour a pointless charade. Well, I don't like charades. And I like pointlessness even less."

Nathan cleared his throat awkwardly. Increasingly as Fred spoke, he as beginning to get the impression that the old man was talking primarily to himself.

"I became attached to this projects in the 1970s. *Forty years ago.* Hard to believe, isn't it? I've handed over my entire life to Project Wildfire, but it goes back further than that. A long way back, way before I was even born."

When Fred paused for effect, Nathan decided the best course of action was silence, and he took it.

"Mostly prior to my involvement it was just idle dreaming by fat men with a great deal of money and an even greater deal of time on their hands. Their dreams were small and messy, and seemed to inevitably gravitate toward starting petty wars with little thought of controlling the outcome. Such imprecise ways of achieving their goals."

He's not a psychopath, Nathan thought. *What the hell is he?*

"Most of them were too concerned with the aftermath, you see. Preoccupied with keeping their presence a secret; all of them worried that *the masses* would discover who really ran things, and would rise up to oust them. Thinking small. No *vision*."

Fred's hands were clenched into fists. Nathan edged away from the old man a little.

"*My* plan was perfect. Or, at least, it should have been perfect. But when you are forced to rely on other people..."

Nathan thought he detected a slight wistfulness in Fred's tone as he trailed off; regret that the old man had tried to bury deeply but hadn't quite succeeded.

At no point did Nathan hear even a hint of remorse about the genocide—or worse, the *transformation*—of billions. The only thing that seemed to matter to Fred Sullivan was that his immaculately-prepared scheme hadn't been quite so immaculate after all.

Nathan shuddered involuntarily. The conversation had not gone as he had expected it would. Fred's reputation for threats and intimidation preceded the old man by a long distance, but to Nathan it felt more like the man simply wanted somebody to hear his thoughts. Almost as if the old bastard somehow believed the end was near, and that somebody at least should know *why* he had done it.

"You can choose to think of me as a monster if you wish, Mr Colston. I don't care. The only thing I care about at this point is your loyalty. I need to know that despite whatever...*reservations* you might have about all of this, that you can be trusted to carry out orders."

Nathan nodded.

"Of course. It's not like there's anything else out there anyway, right?"

Fred chuckled and clapped Nathan on the shoulder.

"Quite so, my boy. And I'm glad to hear it, because we have reached a crossroads, and I have to make a decision. Your input would be appreciated."

Nathan lifted an eyebrow in surprise.

"I'm not much of a tactician, Sir. I-"

Fred waved a dismissive hand.

"Phil Sanderson believes he can pull a rabbit out of the proverbial hat and turn this clusterfuck into something I can make use of. As useless as he is in most aspects, Sanderson knows his way around research."

Fred spat the last word out; laced it with contempt and poisoned the air with it.

"And so he may very well be right. However, given Sanderson's recent track record, it would be prudent to assume otherwise and to plan accordingly. So what I need from you is an answer on one simple question."

Nathan stared at Fred expectantly.

"How many people on this boat remain loyal to our cause? To *my* cause, if you prefer to think in those terms."

"Sir, I'm not sure I understand-"

"We've been getting along so well, Mr Colston. Don't throw it all away now. I know very well that there are...agitators on this ship. The only reason I can see for you to deny that would be that you are one of them. Is that the case?"

"No, Sir."

"Good," Fred said. "This is a numbers game now, Mr Colston, and I need to *know* how many I have. I believe implicitly in our friend Mr Skinner's loyalty, but I have considerably less confidence that he has his finger on the pulse. The fact that he insisted on your joining our little meeting confirms that pretty clearly, I'd say, wouldn't you?"

Nathan frowned.

"It's just as Skinner said, Mr Sullivan. I'd estimate three to four hundred, but it could be less. Mostly those that came with us from Northumberland. But, Sir, even many of them are having doubts. If this turns violent I am honestly not sure how many people you could count on to back you."

Fred nodded, as if the news was not unexpected.

"If your estimate is correct we would be outnumbered by roughly six-to-one, at least."

"Outnumbered, Sir?"

Fred levelled his gaze at Nathan.

"The situation on this boat is going to escalate, Mr Colston. Accepting that truth as inevitable leaves me with a simple decision to make. And that is who gets to turn up the temperature: them or *me.*"

Nathan nodded, and felt anxiety begin to unravel in his stomach. All Fred's reminiscing suddenly seemed to have little to do with the past. Instead Nathan felt like it had been designed to test how he might react to the future that Fred was planning.

"Find the people that are loyal to me," Fred said. "Gather them together, and get them ready."

"Ready, Sir?"

Fred levelled his gaze at Nathan, and for a brief moment the legendary menace was more than evident in the old man's eyes.

"For escalation."

16

"You're here to *wake him up*?"

Kyle didn't think he had ever heard six words uttered in such a way; six little words that carried a slew of emotions on their back, spoken with an intensity that made the hairs on the back of Kyle's neck stand to attention.

"It," Sanderson said, somewhat irritably. "Not *him.*"

Sykes looked around at the rest of the welcome committee, and his stupefied gaze was met by four haunted stares and one nervous snort. When he finally returned his eyes to the scientist, the expression on the soldier's face was how Kyle imagined somebody might look if they were told that they had just stepped on a landmine and they should *not* move.

"Are you insane? You *do* know what's on this boat, right?"

Sanderson nodded impatiently and began to walk to the door that led from the landing deck into the ship itself. He waved at Kyle and Tom to follow. Kyle shot a questioning glance at his brother, and gritted his teeth at the noncommittal shrug he got in return. If Tom had picked up on the strained atmosphere, he wasn't showing it.

Kyle fell into step behind Sanderson, listening intently.

"I know exactly what's on the boat, Sykes," Sanderson said. "And I *have* to wake it up. I didn't say I was going to *free* it. There is no need to be alarmed. Inventory the security protocols, please."

They entered the ship, and Sykes' bewildered spluttering gave way to uneasy silence.

Inside, the vessel was sparse; echoing with emptiness. Functional steel corridors ran through the body of the ship like bones, and everywhere appeared to be deserted, giving the interior a funereal feel.

To Kyle's untrained eye the ship almost looked like a work-in-progress: exposed cables and ducting seemed to run everywhere, as though whoever had been building the ship had fallen at the final hurdle. It had been the same on the *Conqueror*, he realised abruptly, but had been less noticeable there because the ship had been full of people.

This one appeared like it had been abandoned.

Sanderson's description of the McIntosh ship having a s*keleton crew* started to look to Kyle like an understatement. The realisation that the 'welcome committee' might in fact be the entire crew ran through his mind, and left nagging doubt in its wake.

Sykes moved alongside Sanderson, and Kyle noticed that the soldier's posture appeared to have changed as soon as he entered the ship. On the deck Sykes had projected an air of authority, but with each step into the interior his spine appeared to bend a fraction and his shoulders drooped. Sanderson and Sykes began to speak in low, almost hushed tones and Kyle couldn't hear what they were saying, but if he had to guess from observing their body language he would have said that the soldier who had been so bullish at first was now pleading. *Begging.*

Kyle felt the flesh on his arms begin to crawl, and he quickened his pace a little to catch their conversation.

"The subject is shackled and caged. It has been kept in a medically-induced coma since it arrived. We have low frequency emitters surrounding him...*it*," Sykes said. "Linked to motion sensors. Any movement more significant than a heartbeat will trigger a sonic pulse that should knock it back into a coma."

"It sounds secure," Sanderson said.

"It doesn't feel secure."

Kyle couldn't see Sykes' face as he said the words, but it sounded like the man was pouting.

Sanderson nodded. "Yes. The creature continues to surprise. The defense mechanism the mutation is employing while catatonic is a little...unexpected. And I do appreciate how difficult it makes life on this boat," he said. "Once I'm done here, I will personally make sure you are all relieved. Please, show me the medication you have administered today."

Sykes waved an arm at a young woman who walked behind him.

"Patricia can talk you through all that stuff. I'm only here to point a gun if the need arises."

While the rest of the crew was dressed in unmarked uniforms identical to the one Kyle himself wore, the young woman who Sykes gestured at to join him and Sanderson was dressed in a white lab coat like a doctor.

Kyle would have placed her in her late twenties, but pallid skin and shadows cast on her face by obvious fear made her look older.

Sanderson motioned to an office, and followed the young woman inside, pulling the door almost closed behind him. When Kyle heard them begin to murmur, but found the words too faint to make out, he pulled Tom away from the rest of the crew firmly.

"There's something wrong here, Tom," Kyle whispered quietly. "You feel it?"

Tom shook his head and stared at Kyle's hand until the grip on his arm was released.

"Whatever Sullivan has got on this boat, it's important," Tom hissed. "Maybe the key to stopping all this."

"It's too *late* to stop this, Tom," Kyle growled, grabbing his brother's arm once more. "It's already happened. Wildfire has happened. What's left to stop?"

"Sullivan," Tom responded in a surprised tone. "He's not done."

Tom shrugged off Kyle's grip and stepped away, moving a little closer to the half-closed office door, tilting his head a little to listen.

Kyle gritted his teeth in frustration.

There it was again, that feeling. Drifting. Being pulled helplessly toward something terrible. Something that Kyle did not understand and could not stop. It felt like a pressure was building inside him, growing like a tumour.

Enough.

"Sykes," he said abruptly. The word tore itself from his mouth almost before he had given it permission to leave. He spoke loudly enough that everyone—even Sanderson and the doctor in the adjoining room—looked at him sharply.

"I've had more than enough of being kept in the fucking dark, and I'm tired of riddles. What's on this ship?"

Kyle felt Sanderson's gaze on him from the adjoining room, and he flicked his gaze at the balding man defiantly for a moment. Sanderson, apparently, decided that the conversation wasn't worth his time, and returned to the clipboard the doctor held before him.

Kyle turned his attention back to Sykes.

"The mutation," Sykes said at last. "Something that was changed by the virus. It's more monster than human. They say it moves so fast that it's invisible to the naked eye. Powerful. Really powerful. It can't be killed."

Kyle heard a loud snort from the next room, and his nerves began to dance on a razor's edge of irritation.

"Something to add…Sir?"

Sanderson stepped back into the room.

"It is stronger than anything I've seen," he said, "and it's true that the creature's movement is extraordinary, but it can be killed. Everything can be killed. I could kill it right now simply by altering the drugs we're pumping into it."

"So why don't you?"

"Because it is not my call," Sanderson said with a trace of bitterness. "And because the creature represents an opportunity for a scientific leap that we may never see again. The information locked in the mutation's genes could offer humanity the chance to make huge strides forward."

Sanderson waved an arm around the room. His voice began to rise in pitch.

"Let's not lose sight of what can be accomplished. I know what you are feeling, but everybody here is safe. The creature is something that nobody has encountered before, because it did not exist until *we* gave birth to it. I believe it is connected to the Infected as much to us. It is an incipient species."

From the corner of his eye, Kyle noticed his brother's head whip up sharply when Sanderson mentioned the Infected. He ignored him.

"And, what?" Kyle snorted. "This creature of yours has *superpowers?*"

Sanderson sighed wearily.

"Do you know what an *area of effect* is, soldier?"

Kyle searched his memory banks. The phrase seemed familiar, but he couldn't place it.

"I do, Sir." Tom said suddenly.

Kyle looked at him in surprise. In general, Tom didn't talk much to people. Couldn't. Kyle could not remember the last time he had seen his brother voluntarily address a group of strangers with such confidence.

"It's a videogame term," Tom continued. "Weapons, magic spells, special powers. They only effect a certain radius around the character in the game."

Sanderson blinked.

"Exactly," he said, sounding more than a little surprised. "I believe the mutation has the power to affect the molecules around it in ways we do not yet understand. It has an *area of effect*. This allows it to move at incredible speed; to display incredible strength. It is not operating under the same rules of physics that we do. Maybe gravity affects it in a different way; we don't know for sure. Yet."

Sanderson shrugged, as if that alone was enough reason for not killing the creature, no matter how dangerous it might be.

The dismissive gesture made Kyle's jaw clench involuntarily, and for a moment he found himself wondering just how to operate the assault rifle he was carrying.

"What we *do* know," Sanderson continued, "is that when it is unconscious—as it is right now—it exhibits a defense mechanism across this area of effect.

"To us it feels like the atmosphere in the creature's vicinity has been poisoned by...I suppose you'd say by fear. Very possibly it is emitting a pheromone that we have not encountered, something that triggers a flight response in would-be predators. A natural defense mechanism, like a hedgehog curling up behind its spines, or a toad that secretes poison on its skin."

Sanderson paused, as though he was used to having to wait for people to catch up with his thoughts.

"Those near to the mutation feel overwhelming dread, designed to convey one message: stay away. It is...unsettling, but we are in no danger. Not now. All of that might sound strange or supernatural somehow, but it is not. The properties the creature exhibits are found elsewhere in nature. Only the fact that those properties are inherent in something that used to be human makes it of interest."

Kyle shook his head, and almost snorted. *Might sound strange?*

"What you're saying sounds like science fiction," he said.

Sanderson smiled.

"A lot of science does, right before it becomes science fact."

"So how is any of that even possible?"

Sanderson paused, apparently searching for the simplest way to put his answer in layman's terms.

"How does a bee fly? How does a chameleon change the colour of its skin? How does an ant carry a leaf many times heavier than its body? Or a hummingbird beat its wings so fast that the human eye can barely perceive them? There are miracles all around us in nature. What we have become exceedingly good at is tapping into those miracles, and turning them into resources that we can exploit. That's *our* miracle."

Kyle rubbed his temples. Either the *area of effect* was giving him a headache, or talking to Sanderson was.

Probably both, he thought.

"But you said this was a man who was infected. No human can do those sort of things."

Sanderson blinked.

"I don't believe it is human; not any more, at least. It is something else altogether. If the Infected are a leap backwards on the evolutionary scale, the mutation is like a giant leap forward. Or perhaps *sideways* might be more accurate. I'd say the only thing it has in common with humans is its ability to think; its emotions."

"And doesn't that make it human?"

Sanderson rolled his eyes, as though matters of philosophy were not worth spending much time thinking about.

"That makes it dangerous."

Kyle sighed. The conversation appeared to be meandering in circles, and getting straight answers out of Sanderson about anything looked unlikely. He let it drop.

Just get the job done, he thought, *whatever the hell the job is—and get off this ship*.

"What do you need us to do, Sir?"

Sanderson seemed to respond well to being addressed so formally. Kyle figured if he was going to get any simple answers from the head of research, it would be by deferring to him.

Sanderson took a final look at the clipboard and passed it back to the ashen-faced woman dressed like a doctor.

"You're here for protection. Specifically, of me. We need a sample of the mutation's blood. And unfortunately, chemical changes induced by its unconsciousness mean we need the blood when it is awake. And quite possibly when it is enraged. Though I don't think *that* part will be a problem."

He glanced at the young doctor.

"Start reducing the dose, but do it slowly. I'd rather it wakes gradually."

The doctor nodded and left the room, her face stricken.

"Sykes," Sanderson said. "Check the emitters. Low frequency noise is the only thing we've found that slows the mutation down. I'd rather they were up and running at a low level before it wakes, just loud enough to keep it...friendly. I wouldn't trust a motion detector to catch this thing if it gets free, and when it wakes up it's going to be pissed."

"And what do we do in the meantime?" Kyle said.

"We wait. And make sure we have every weapon we can get our hands on pointed at the mutation until this is over."

17

Like sand trickling through an hourglass, the inhabitants of Caernarfon Castle had finally begun to filter from the segregated safety of the towers. Slowly at first, in faltering twos and threes, the people formerly of the quiet town of Newborough crept into the courtyard and sought the comfort of the herd.

Michael's door was unlocked, which he presumed was either his reward for engaging in the torture of a terrified kid or another test to see what he would do once free.

He cracked the door cautiously and watched for a long time as people began to enter the courtyard. It was like a dam cracking. As soon as those watching from the towers saw someone outside who didn't terrify them, they added themselves to the trickle until it became a flow.

When there were around twenty people out there, he turned to Claire.

"Are you ready?"

Claire nodded.

Michael's instinct had been to wait before trying anything. To bide his time and look for the right opportunity. But caution had so far got him nowhere.

The element of surprise. John had been all about that. Attack before the enemy can settle. End the fight before they know it's happening.

Michael couldn't fight Holloway's people. Not directly. But he could surprise them.

It had to be done immediately. There was no telling how long he had before Linda was taken from the cells. And a darker reason for acting promptly lurked in Michael's mind: every moment he delayed was a moment during which he might get to know the people standing in the courtyard talking in hushed whispers. A chance to discover that they were lost and terrified; no different to himself.

That would make it much harder to do what he had to do. Maybe even impossible.

It's now or never.

He checked the cells. Rhys and Bryn Holloway, along with an older man that Michael had seen hovering around Annie like an advisor, rotated guard duty between them. After a moment he picked out Rhys, leaning against a distant wall and keeping a bored eye on the people in the courtyard, occasionally glancing toward the cells.

"Okay," Michael said, pointing at Rhys, "Watch him. When he leaves that spot, you go talk to Linda. The cell on the far left. If he doesn't leave, you stay here, right?"

Claire rolled her eyes.

"Got it, Dad."

Michael winked at her, and threw the door open. He pulled it nearly shut behind him, leaving just a crack for Claire to watch through, and wheeled the chair away from the tower without looking back.

Distracting the Holloway brothers was a course of action that had the potential for any number of poor outcomes. They seemed slow-witted, but they were suspicious. Any obvious effort Michael made to interact with them would be reported back to their mother. From there, anything could happen.

The best option was to play on their ignorance and their arrogance. Make them come to him.

He wheeled himself to the nearest set of the steps that led up to the battlements. Knew that Rhys' eyes were on him as soon as he appeared, but didn't acknowledge the man. When he reached the base of the steps, Michael placed his palms on a low wall and hauled himself from the wheelchair. He slipped and crashed to the ground.

And heard a snorted laugh.

Perfect.

He pulled himself onto his backside and dragged himself to the steps, heaving himself up them one by one, feeling a fire beginning to build in his triceps. After four steps, he made a show of slipping again, and threw himself back to the ground.

For a moment he remained on his back, staring up at the grey sky, and hoped he wouldn't need to do it all over again.

"Told you that you had to see this."

Rhys' voice.

A giggle.

"What is he doing?"

Bryn's voice.

Moments later, the faces of the two Holloway brothers loomed above him, blotting out the sky. Both wore a mask of sneering mirth.

"What the fuck are you trying to do, Cripple?"

*

Linda had stretched out across the cell and shut her eyes hours earlier, desperately trying to persuade her mind to retreat to a better place and failing miserably. Lying on her back, she was almost able to touch both walls of the cell that she had spent two freezing nights in. It turned out that it was difficult to go to your *happy place* when your *current* place was little bigger than a coffin.

She was starving, and frequently found herself daydreaming of chocolate, and she had been forced to defecate into a bucket in front of two complete strangers. Until a couple of weeks earlier her idea of a bad day had involved walking into a classroom full of unsupervised children. It was amazing how quickly things could change.

So far, the tiny cell and the bucket didn't even represent her worst day since days officially ended. Technically, this had actually been one of the *better* days.

The worst one had been the day of the amputations. The cutting up of the meat that would feed the horror that Darren Oliver kept chained up outside the castle.

No ordinary life would ever involve a day as bad as that. Linda couldn't help wondering how long that day would remain the worst in her memory. She had a nagging feeling it might be surpassed soon.

"Linda?"

Linda's eyes flared open and she sat bolt upright. She stared at Emma and Rachel. Both looked to be asleep.

"Dad told me to give you a message," Claire whispered through the bars set into the centre of the door.

Linda nodded.

"They're going to let you out next, and they are going to ask you to do something horrible and you must do it. Tell them you're a doctor, and they'll ask you to treat the big man. When you do, you have to get something, and give it to Claire."

Claire flushed.

"Uh, to me," she corrected.

Linda stared at the little girl.

"Get what?"

*

There was nothing to do but wait. Eventually Bryn and Rhys had grown tired of watching gleefully as Michael struggled to ascend to the battlements. They had laughed in particular when he told them that he just wanted to *see the sights*, but finally the joke had worn thin, and they had roughly bundled him back into the wheelchair and told him to fuck off in a tone that left no room for doubt that the fun was over.

Michael nodded and tried to look broken and humiliated. Inside his nerves hummed like a herd of Infected, and he focused all his efforts on keeping the anxiety he felt from reaching his face.

When he returned to the tower and saw Claire waiting for him he knew immediately from the look of eager pride on her face that she had done as he had asked.

And so they waited.

After an hour Michael watched as Bryn hauled Linda from the cells and followed her toward the dungeon, prodding her in the small of her back with a shotgun. It was another thirty minutes or so before he heard the screams, and guilt surged within Michael when he realised he was glad it was Ed's voice he heard, and not Linda's.

He didn't see Linda for a couple of hours after that.

18

Linda stood at the door to the cell, trying not to give away the fact that she was *waiting*. She saw one of the old woman's sons approaching soon enough, walking alongside a middle-aged man who wore a troubled look on his face that didn't quite negate the importance of the knife that hung from his belt.

The younger one, who Linda was fairly sure was called Rhys, carried a rifle slung across his shoulder. Michael's rifle.

Linda trusted Michael. If pushed she would have been hard-pressed to say *why* exactly. The man had darkness in his past that she thought reached his eyes a little too often, but there was a genuine tone to his words. The things he had confessed to her had been ripped from him, and even as he spoke Linda had the impression that he was trying to claw back the words, as if he wanted to force them back where they came from. It hadn't been an act. No one could be such a good actor.

Still, as she watched the men approaching the cell, and knew from the businesslike look on Rhys' face that they were coming for her, just as Claire—as *Michael*—had predicted they would, she could not help but feel some doubt.

The expression on Rhys' face chilled Linda, but it was the other one's look of concern that troubled her most. The older one.

His was the expression of a man who knew he was about to do something that he wanted no part of.

Linda shrank away from the cell door as it opened, and when Rhys said *you're the doctor, right?* Linda thought for a moment about denying it.

Only for a moment.

They led her silently to one of the castle's huge towers, and up to a room on the second floor.

To Jason's room.

*

Jason was unconscious on a four-poster bed that looked like something from a *Disney* fantasy, and a rope leash around his neck was tied off around one of the bed's ornate pillars. To Linda, he looked like someone's dog, chained up outside a store and waiting patiently for its master to return.

"What has he been given?" She asked Rhys, aiming for an authoritative tone and painfully aware that if Rhys started throwing the names of various medicines at her, she probably would not have a clue what they actually were.

"Uh..." Rhys stared at her blankly.

"Just painkillers," the middle-aged man said. "A *lot* of painkillers. Some sleeping tablets too, I think. *Zopiclone*, I think they're called."

Linda nodded thoughtfully.

Never heard of it.

"Is this all of your medical supplies?"

She pointed at carrier bags full of bottles and packets, knowing full well that there was more. Everything in the castle had come from the nearby pharmacy, and Rachel had all-but cleaned the place out.

"I think so," the middle-aged man said.

Linda suppressed a knowing smirk, and moved to the bags, searching through them and making a show of examining various bottles, scrutinising labels that meant nothing to her and tossing them aside.

Jason had wounds—a *lot* of wounds—that looked to have become infected by the filth that covered much of the man's huge body. That much was obvious, and might explain his sickly appearance (and the *smell*), but whatever caused his bizarre, detached behaviour was beyond solving for her. Maybe for anyone.

Oddly, it looked to Linda like someone *had* tried to treat some of the wounds. A few appeared to be cleaner than the others and healing nicely, but the rest...

Jesus Christ...

Jason's body was a roadmap of cuts: some thin and precise, as if somebody had attacked him with a scalpel. Others were long, ragged tears that glistened and oozed a noxious yellow pus.

Linda had no idea what sort of treatment the man might truly require, but it was obvious even to her that Jason needed antibiotics at the very least, and she knew the names of some of those. A teacher generally picked up tidbits like that, gleaned from the various ailments the kids brought into the classroom with them, and, in the case of the boys at least, took great delight in showing off.

Mostly though, Linda had seen or heard of antibiotics only in tablet form, and if that was all the bags contained, Michael's plan, whatever it was, would fall at the first hurdle.

She almost yelled out in relief when she pulled a bottle of clear liquid from a bag and read the label.

Amoxicillin.

Perfect.

Linda stood, turning to face the two men who watched her like hawks.

I'm going to need to bathe him and dress his wounds properly," she said. "And then I'll have to give him a shot of this."

She held up the bottle.

"Uh...I don't know about that," Rhys said dubiously. "I think I should tell Ma if you're gonna stick him with something. Right, Gareth?"

He glanced at the middle-aged man.

Gareth held out his hand for the bottle, and Linda passed it to him.

After a moment of reading the label, Gareth handed it back to her.

"No need," he said. "It's just antibiotics. I never heard of that hurting anyone. Let's just get this over with, shall we?"

Linda got the distinct impression that the man called Gareth wanted to stay as far away from Rhys' mother as possible.

That makes two of us, she thought, breathing a soft sigh of relief.

Linda took a long time cleaning Jason up. Long enough that the two men watching her began to shift their feet in boredom. Neither paid much attention when she fished a syringe from one of the bags of medical supplies and tore it from its packet, before plunging it into the bottle and extracting a large dose of the antibiotic.

Neither noticed that once she was done injecting the medicine into Jason, she paused for a second before carefully withdrawing a measure of blood and dropping the needle quietly into her pocket.

"All done," she said brightly. "He will improve in a day or so. Be fine in a week."

Rhys snorted his disinterest.

"Uh...so, what now?" Linda asked.

"You're not done, Doc," Rhys said, and the bored expression on his face dissolved and became something else, a dark and intangible something that made Linda's pulse race.

"Now it's time for *surgery*," Rhys said, and laughed as though he had been waiting an age to say the line, and he thought those might just be the funniest five words in the English language.

*

Michael's heart sank when he saw Linda being led back toward the cells. The sense of crushing disappointment he felt wasn't just that he had hoped she would be freed from the cells once she had treated Jason;

it was the look on her face. The blood splashed across her coat.

They *had* taken her to Jason. And then they had taken her straight to the dungeon. To Ed, and to knives that gleamed dully in the half-light and to the sickening stench of blood and terror.

Fury welled up in Michael; a cold rage that had lurked inside ever since he had looked into Ed's fearful eyes as he began to methodically slice off the fingers on the man's left hand.

Michael had managed to block out the emotion during the cutting itself—he had focused exclusively on wondering whether or not the man was left-handed and if he played any musical instruments; mundane bullshit to occupy his thoughts while his hands did something terrible.

Still, the mere act of forcing himself to ignore Ed's screams felt like it had twisted something out of shape inside Michael. The look on Linda's face—shock, maybe, but disgust and self-loathing, too—reminded Michael of the squirming in his own gut.

He forced himself to focus.

If Linda had done as he had asked, she would be carrying the syringe on her person right now, and the question that really needed answering was *how am I going to get it?*

Linda was not being set free; she was being returned to the cells. That presented a huge problem.

Michael dropped his gaze from the window to the stone floor, lost in thought.

"I can go get it, Dad."

Michael stared at Claire in surprise. She had apparently read his mind.

"You keep that up and I'll have to start calling you Claire-voyant," Michael said with a grin.

Claire stared at him, puzzled.

"I don't—"

"Just a joke," Michael said, holding an apologetic hand up. "A bad one. They call those Dad-jokes. Better get used to them."

Claire nodded, but it was clear from the expression on her face that she was half-wondering if her father had lost the plot.

"They'll see you," Michael said.

"They might not. I can run fast. I know what you're going to do."

"You do?" Michael said, surprised.

Claire nodded proudly.

"It wasn't that hard to figure out."

"And you're okay with it?"

Claire shrugged.

"I don't like these people," she said simply, and Michael surprised himself with a laugh.

"Me neither," he said. "Okay, if you think you can get to Linda and get back without getting spotted."

Claire nodded eagerly.

"I'll be quick."

She stared at Michael solemnly.

"Okay, then," Michael said. "Do it, before I have a chance to think about what a bad idea this is. Just get back here quick. If they see you, get back here no matter what. Deal?"

Claire nodded and bolted from the room before Michael could say another word.

*

Claire slipped through the door and out into the wide courtyard, and for a moment she stood still, scanning the area for a sign that she had been spotted. Increasingly the courtyard was filling up, and most of the people there—none of whom she recognised—seemed to be busy conversing with each other in hushed tones. Nobody appeared to notice the little girl watching them.

When she was satisfied that she wasn't being watched, she slipped away from the door, leaving it open a crack, and moved toward the row of cells to the right of the tower.

It wasn't a long journey, but she forced herself to take it slowly, trying to appear as casual as possible. She hadn't seen either of the old woman's sons; nor the bald man who often seemed to be by Annie Holloway's side, but Claire knew they were out there somewhere. Probably watching over the people who filtered slowly into the courtyard. Instinct told Claire to run, but running would be more likely to draw attention, so she bit her lip in concentration and walked slowly.

She didn't take her eyes off the cells, as if she were hiding under a blanket, terrified of the monster that lived in her closet; certain that if she couldn't see it, it couldn't see her.

You're not a baby anymore, Claire.

Her mother's voice in her head, soothing and full of laughter. She could almost picture her eyes twinkling as she said the words, and she let the memory give her strength, trying desperately not to throw light on the thought that lurked in the shadows at the corners of her mind.

Mum's eyes don't twinkle anymore.

Mum's eyes are gone.

Claire was grateful when she reached the cell unimpeded, mainly because reaching the cell meant breaking a train of thought that seemed like it was headed in a bad direction.

"Linda, did you get it?"

Claire whispered the words, and felt a little odd addressing the woman by her first name. Not so long ago all adults who weren't her parents had been Mr-this or Mrs-that.

She heard a soft exclamation through the small viewing window.

"What the fuck?"

Rachel's voice. Claire was glad to hear it. Rachel was scary, but in a good way. Scary the way her mother had been that time when Claire almost wandered out onto the road in front of a speeding bus.

"What does she mean?" Rachel asked. "Get what?"

"I'll explain."

Linda's voice.

Claire frowned and shot a worried glance behind her. This didn't seem like a good time for Linda and Rachel to start having a conversation.

"Do you have it?" Claire whispered again, a little impatiently, rising onto her tiptoes to peer into the dark cell.

Linda looked startled to see Claire's face appear right in front of her, and she opened her mouth to speak.

But the noise Claire heard didn't come from Linda's mouth. It was a man's voice. Behind her.

"Hey, what are you doing over there?"

Claire felt the blood draining from her face.

"No time!" Claire yelled, thrusting her hand through the bars. "I need it now!"

She heard footsteps behind her, rattling across the stone courtyard like machine gun fire. Closing fast.

A small cylindrical object slipped into her palm.

"Be careful with th—" Claire heard Linda begin to say, but her words were drowned out by the deeper voice that spoke behind her.

"What have you got there, girl?"

Claire turned and saw Bryn Holloway standing a few feet away, staring fiercely at her; a hungry grin twisting his face into a frightening mask. She stood and stared at him, wide-eyed and unresponsive.

He took a menacing step toward her.

"I *said* what have you got there, girl?"

She held the syringe behind her back.

"Better hand it over, unless you want to get hurt."

He took another step toward her. One more, she thought, and he would be able to grab her, and it would be over. She would let her father down.

Claire nodded, reached out a hand toward Bryn...and bolted past him.

She felt fingers clutching at her sweater, and for a moment thought that Bryn had enough of a grip to halt her in her tracks, but then with a jolt she was free, and running like she was back in Aberystwyth; like her mother was chasing her and death was coming at her from all angles.

*

Michael sat alone in the tower and cursed himself for letting his daughter go. In a lifetime of bad decisions, with every second that passed he became more certain that this was the worst of all.

Stupid.

Selfish.

There was no other way.

Sitting in the gloomy half-light, every second felt like an hour.

Until he heard the commotion outside; the hammering of footsteps. More than one set of feet was headed in his direction. All hopes of being able to plan his next move evaporated instantly, and he knew as the thumping feet approached that he was going to have to wing it.

For a fraction of a second he thought about John, and about how much he missed the man. John's ability to fight had always been there; a stable foundation that ran underneath every action Michael took. He had always been able to rely on John if things turned physical.

But John was dead.

Michael's heart began to keep pace with the approaching footsteps.

And then the door burst open and Claire hurtled inside, half-gasping for air and half-screaming.

She was just a few steps ahead of Bryn Holloway. Claire ran past Michael's wheelchair, cowering behind him as Bryn came to a stop in front of them, panting heavily.

He stared accusingly at Michael, and for a moment time seemed to stand still.

Do it.

"Good," Michael said almost amiably. "Don't get me wrong, the other one's a prick, too, but I sort of hoped it would be you."

Bryn's mouth dropped open.

"What the fuck did you say, Crip—"

Bryn was halfway through the word and reaching for the shotgun that hung at his hip when Michael sprang from the chair, praying with all his heart that his weak legs would not collapse underneath him, and slammed his knuckles into the man's teeth.

Before the awareness of pain had even reached Bryn's eyes, Michael gave in to the rage and the darkness and threw a flurry of punches from the past, all the way from the corridor of blood and bone into Bryn's stunned face, raining his fists down onto the man before he had a chance to react.

Bryn slumped to the floor, and Michael fell on top of him spitting out jabs like a machine, slamming the man's head into the stone, barely even aware that the cracking noise he heard was Bryn's skull.

He only stopped when Claire's voice penetrated the gathering fog in his mind.

"Stop, Dad, you'll kill him!"

She sounded scared.

Of me?

Michael paused, his bloodied right fist raised, and looked down at Bryn.

A bubble of blood and saliva burst on the man's ruined lips. He groaned softly.

"You're right," Michael said in a trembling voice. "He's no good to us dead."

Claire nodded, her eyes wide and fearful, and she held out a shaking hand.

"They're not zombies, Dad. They're people. It won't bring them *back*." Claire said.

Michael blinked.

She hadn't been scared of him. Just that he might lose control and ruin his one chance.

She really does know what I plan to do.

He reached out and took the object that Claire held out to him, lifting it up to catch the failing light. A syringe filled with the blood of Linda's patient. Annie had taken the bait, as Michael had known she must. If Jason was sick; if she let him die of some common-or-garden infection, she would lose the most powerful weapon she had, the one thing that elevated her far beyond the people she controlled.

Michael did not doubt for a second that Annie had been suspicious about his suggestion that she release Linda, but he knew that sometimes suggestion had an allure that rendered people powerless to resist. Annie had released Linda because she *had* to demonstrate her control over Michael. She was compelled to take his own scheming and shove it back down his throat.

Michael had often got the impression that John Francis had thought him manipulative, and maybe he was. What else could a man without working legs in a world of relentless violence be?

Linda had come through for him. He didn't want to think about what she had been forced to do to Ed; about what effect it might have on her. In time she might come to hate him for including her in his plan, but there was no time for Michael to think about that. All that mattered was that now he had a weapon too, one that had been concealed inside Annie's own, like opening up one of those multi-layered Russian dolls to find a hand grenade hidden inside.

Jason's blood.

Michael studied it.

In the gloom it looked almost black. Toxic. Like poison.

19

It felt like waiting for the executioner's blade to fall.

Kyle had been aboard the McIntosh ship for three hours in total, and around two hours since Sanderson and Patricia had begun to reduce the dose of drugs being administered to the mutation in tiny increments, and with each passing minute the pervasive feeling of dread began to increase.

Sanderson had theorised that as the mutation neared consciousness the pheromones being emitted would actually decrease in potency, and the feeling of creeping anxiety would naturally dissipate, but Kyle's churning gut informed him that the scientist's theory was bullshit.

He couldn't shake the notion that *everything* Sanderson had said was bullshit. Far-fetched nonsense designed to conceal what was really going on. That would fit with Chrysalis Systems' *modus operandi* perfectly.

It didn't really explain the dread he felt on the ship, though. Nothing did. The only feeling that ever came close for Kyle was a one-off experiment with psychotropic drugs not long after high school had finished. Magic mushrooms, he had been told, were harmless and fun, but to him the experience had been one of out-of-control terror, like he was stuck aboard a driverless train travelling at full speed toward the end of the line.

Maybe I've been drugged, he thought.

Or maybe the dread he felt now stemmed more from common sense than drugs or Sanderson's invisible *area of effect*. Common sense that raged inside him like an inferno; just his body's way of trying to communicate to his mind that being aboard the ship—and by extension the entire fleet—was dangerous in the extreme, and that if at all possible he should investigate his options for getting the fuck away *pronto*.

For a while, upon deciding that the best course of action to quiet his racing nerves was to distract himself,

Kyle tried to engage the tiny crew of the McIntosh ship in conversation, but was met with staccato answers and haunted stares that just made the tension knotting his stomach all the worse.

He discovered that there was a further crew member he hadn't yet seen. That member—Rick—was currently on 'watch duty', which apparently consisted of sitting in a room adjoining the one that contained the mutation and scrutinising a bank of monitors and machines connected to the apparatus that held the creature in stasis.

It didn't sound like a bad job to Kyle, but the hushed tones and furtive glances of the soldier who described the detail to him suggested otherwise.

Whether or not Sanderson's farfetched story about some supernaturally powerful creature was true or not, it was clear that the crew on the ship believed it wholeheartedly.

Beyond hearing about Rick's lonely, and apparently terrible duty, information was sparse, and had to be dragged from the crew word-by-reluctant-word.

The mutation, they said, had been brought in by chopper and its cage set up by a team that had since departed.

Sykes' team had been flown in from the *Conqueror* and stationed on the McIntosh ship for 'a few days'. They made it sound like a lifetime. They told him the bare minimum about the layout of the ship: mutation in a cargo hold at the front, living quarters in the middle, engine to the rear.

The few who answered his questions—mostly Sykes and Williams, a man that Kyle quickly came to regard as Sykes' second-in-command—seemed happiest talking about the mundane. About the ship. Where they came from. The past. Anything that took their minds to some other place.

Just when they had begun to open up to him a little, a question popped into Kyle's mind that seemed harmless enough; just one of those things that, once answered, prompted a nod and immediate storage in the part of the mind where forgotten memories go.

"What does *McIntosh* mean?"

Sykes fixed a horrified gaze on Kyle, and the atmosphere that had been slowly defrosting dropped back to somewhere near absolute zero.

"You don't know? Who it is? Was?"

Kyle shook his head and Sykes let out a rueful chuckle.

"Fucking bastards. That's how they operate, you know, the fuckers at the top. The ones that did all this and left us with the wreckage. Nobody gets to know the whole story. Everyone has their own little job to keep them busy. Just enough facts to get by. It's not a secret when everyone involved knows a tiny piece of the story. Then it doesn't exist at all. Compartmentalised, see?"

Kyle was surprised at the man's sudden philosophising, but he didn't let it show. He nodded encouragement at Sykes to continue. Despite the uncomfortable nature of the conversation, he had a feeling that he was finally getting the truth, or at least some part of it.

"You came from the *Conqueror*. I did too. Most of the people over there, the grunts like me and you anyway, know fuck all about anything. Just that the world's gone to shit and we're what's left. Those who *do* know, well, they ain't saying shit. But *we* did this. Sullivan and his people. This was all planned. Only when you run across people with information you weren't allowed to have can you start to put it all together. This isn't some terrible disease. Not even an accident. There are people on these ships that will tell you this is like that test they did a few years back, remember? Smashing atoms together or some shit and there was a chance they might destroy the planet?"

Sykes fixed his gaze on Kyle, and for the first time since they had entered the ship Kyle saw a flicker of something other than fear in the soldier's eyes.

Sykes shook his head grimly.

"It's *nothing* like that. Not some side effect. This was all planned. By the few fuckers that *do* know everything. And you know what that means?"

Kyle shook his head slowly.

"We're not *survivors*. We're the fucking *bad guys*," Sykes spat bitterly. "The proof of that is caged up on this ship. McIntosh is—was—*Jake* McIntosh."

Sykes studied Kyle's eyes, apparently expecting to see recognition staring back at him.

"The *Painkiller*," he said plaintively when Kyle did not respond.

"The fucking serial killer from a couple of years back, remember? Papers were full of that bastard for an entire year. What they've got locked up here isn't just some unfortunate bastard who happened to get infected. It's the sickest fucker to ever walk the face of the Earth. *That's* who we're guarding. Now, you tell me: if we're the good guys in all this; if we're the plucky survivors, then what the fuck are we doing with a guy like that?"

Kyle lowered his eyes, searching his memory.

He had a vague recollection of the whole *Painkiller* thing in the press, partly because the name had always struck him as ridiculous, like the tabloid writers that revelled in conjuring up such stuff couldn't even be bothered to *try* anymore.

He remembered a few lurid headlines that gleefully reported some of the sickest crimes Kyle could imagine. He hadn't paid much attention at the time: the news was always full of the worst aspects of humanity, and with each year either humanity got worse or the news got more desperate and hysterical; in some ways it didn't matter which. Either possibility just made him feel glum about the world.

In any case, Kyle hadn't followed the story closely. He'd been too busy dealing with his little brother's slow crawl toward a sheer cliff of paranoid mania, hoping he could claw Tom back from the precipice and ultimately following him over it.

And finding that the drop led to the truth.

Tom was right about everything, paranoid or not.

It's not paranoia if they're really out to get you. The phrase had once been a cliché, back before everything had fallen apart. Now it felt to Kyle more like a rock-solid, inescapable truth.

If there remained any chance of him doubting his strange little brother, Sykes' earnest testimony put paid to it. The more Kyle learned about the ship and McIntosh and Project Wildfire, the less he felt he understood.

Tom did understand, though. He always had.

Kyle had a sudden intuition that Tom had abandoned all hope of stopping Project Wildfire the moment he had driven a tyre iron deep into Russian skull and brains in an underground car park. Maybe even before then. Perhaps Tom had always known that the chances of two brothers from South London affecting machinery as gargantuan as Wildfire were near-zero.

Kyle nodded at Sykes absent-mindedly, and stared thoughtfully at Tom.

As always, Tom sat alone, as far away from the nearest humans as possible. Kyle had serious doubts that, before the disastrous encounter with a Russian thug named Volkov, Tom had physically interacted with anyone other than his older brother in years.

Riddled with guilt that he had abandoned his little brother to deal with their parents alone, Kyle had been forced to care for Tom after their parents had died in a car crash.

If his mother and father had died at home, Kyle would have suspected that Tom had killed them, and he wouldn't have blamed him for that one bit. Their parents were what some would once have described as stern or authoritative. As society had begun to focus more on— and better understand—child abuse, the Robinsons would have been bestowed with far less complimentary labels.

Except, of course, for the fact that *society* give a shit about what went on in the Robinson house when the front door was locked at night.

But Tom hadn't killed them. By the time Kyle's parents wound up decorating the radiator grille of a speeding truck, Tom was already a shut-in. Kyle moving home to help his brother was inevitable.

Tom picked nervously at his nails, staring at the floor and apparently unaware of Kyle's gaze.

Maybe me getting involved in all this was inevitable too, Kyle thought.

A fresh surge of guilt washed through him. Ever since Volkov, Kyle had erected an invisible barrier between himself and his brother, and that barrier had merely grown larger as the world became progressively more bizarre and dangerous. Kyle had been so wrapped up in his own thoughts that he hadn't stopped to see things from Tom's point of view.

The kid was like a walking *Wikipedia* page dedicated to explaining neuroses and anxiety; he always had been. He probably didn't feel dread on the McIntosh ship because he felt it all the damn time.

And he was *right*.

About *everything*.

Kyle stood up and nodded a silent *thanks* at Sykes, who was intently focused on his own boots once more, and moved over to Tom, sitting heavily on a chair next to him.

Tom looked at him inquisitively.

"Okay," Kyle said quietly in a tone that suggested a continuation of a debate that had been on pause for a long time. "Everything's fucked, and we're here. So what now?"

Tom studied Kyle's face for a moment and broke into a rare grin.

"Now we do the only thing we *can* do," he said.

"Which is?"

"We bring the whole fucking thing down on their heads."

20

This is insane.

The words had been rolling around in Nathan's head for several long minutes.

Ever since Dick Skinner had passed him the gas mask.

Some part of Nathan had held out hope that Fred Sullivan would see the folly in his plan to rid the ship of all dissenting voices. Even a civilian would surely understand that a force numbering no more than five hundred had no chance of defeating a force at least six times its size in a battle.

Only when Nathan saw the crate of masks did he realize that Fred Sullivan was no ordinary civilian. In fact, he thought, the old man could very well be Satan himself.

Hell, if Satan actually exists, he's probably watching Sullivan and taking fucking notes on how to most efficiently kill an entire species.

There would be no battle. Fred Sullivan was not the kind of man who engaged in simple fighting, fair or otherwise. He was a man that focused on outcomes, and how best to attain the ones that benefited only himself.

Nathan stared around the deck. All five hundred of the names that he and Skinner had decided would be loyal to the cause had been alerted that they were required on the flight deck for 'a drill'. There were a few dozen others who happened to be on deck too, including a couple that Nathan knew were very definitely *not* loyal; men who had muttered in dark corners that money was worthless, and that all that mattered now was power and those who had the balls to take it.

Nathan pointed them out to Skinner, and had received a shrug in return.

"By the time this is over, they will be the ones that are outnumbered," Skinner replied.

"And you think they'll just take this on the chin?"

Skinner looked at Nathan thoughtfully.

"They will if they want to live."

Fuck me. Spend a little time with Sullivan and even a hopeless case like Skinner turns into a ruthless bastard.

"Better put the mask on, Nathan. The...uh, drill starts in sixty seconds."

Nathan slid the mask over his face and tightened the straps at the back of his head. The world became suddenly muffled, distant and muddy as white noise.

He felt numb.

Sullivan had contingency built on contingency. The *Conqueror* was rigged: the air conditioning vents had been loaded with a deadly nerve agent ready to fill the lower decks with gasping, rattling death at a moment's notice.

Sullivan had planned for the eventuality of killing the entire crew before any of them had even set foot on the ship.

He wasn't a psychopath. He was a monster, every bit as bad as the one locked up on the ship that sat miles to the west.

The old man hadn't wanted a list of loyalists because he wanted an army to fight for him. He just wanted to know how many would be left when he was done with the killing.

What if it hadn't been enough to crew the ship?

It wasn't a question Nathan wanted to dwell on. He felt a strange, lurking certainty that if that had been the case, Fred Sullivan would have killed them all anyway. Better to die than to admit defeat.

In the distance, across the ominous sea of gas masks, Nathan heard a muffled voice counting down.

Ten.

Nine.

A couple of the soldiers on the deck shuffled awkwardly on the spot; doubtless they were the ones who had some idea of what was actually happening. Maybe they were picturing the clean-up they would be required to undertake over the next few hours, tossing the corpses of their friends overboard until their arms ached.

Eight.

Seven.

Six.

We're all utterly disposable to him. Every last one of us. No more than cattle.

Five.

Four.

Three.

Two.

I've got to get the hell off this boat.

One.

Below deck, air vents sighed poison into the narrow steel corridors; into the mess rooms and the sleeping quarters, filling every corner of the ship with a killer every bit as invisible as the one that Fred Sullivan's satellites had dropped onto the surface of the planet weeks earlier.

This was no sophisticated scientific apocalypse, though. There was no reshuffling of the genes; no extraordinary side-effects.

Just death.

Unlike Wildfire, the release of the gas proceeded without a hitch: humans had long ago perfected the art of simple killing.

Far above the deck, Fred stood on the viewing platform, breathing filtered air through a gas mask. There was very little danger of the toxin making its way to the deck, and even less likelihood of it proving deadly when the harsh North Sea wind dispersed it. There was virtually no chance of the poisonous cloud reaching Fred's position.

But only a fool would fail to prepare for the worst possible outcome.

21

At first glance, the mutation didn't appear to be much of anything, but when Kyle stepped into the cargo bay that had been retrofitted to become a very specific kind of prison, he felt the hairs on his neck stand up nonetheless.

The hold was a vast space, and for a moment Kyle was reminded of *King Kong* being shut in a similar cell while he was transported toward his inevitable Hollywood death.

Most of the huge space that greeted Kyle, though, was empty; a place of shadows that claimed all the corners, making the place feel dislocated and surreal as a bad dream. There was no giant monster.

In the centre of that empty space, lit by harsh floodlights that kept the gathering shadows at bay, stood an array of machinery that looked to Kyle like a blend of a high-tech hospital and an engineering bay. Blinking lights danced across metallic surfaces. He saw something that looked like a pulse monitor, and other displays that he didn't recognise.

Tangled tubes and wires snaked from the equipment, all making the same short pilgrimage to the large table onto which Jake McIntosh had been placed.

From where Kyle stood, wreathed in the shadows, very little of the creature was visible. Enormous steel manacles covered the thing's limbs almost entirely, and were reinforced by heavy chains. The creature looked roughly human-sized, if on the big side. A far cry from a fifty-foot tall gorilla.

Beyond the table, Kyle saw what looked like four banks of audio speakers, as though a rock band had set up their equipment in preparation for an ear-shattering performance to come. *That must be the low frequency sound equipment Sanderson mentioned*, Kyle guessed, though he could not fathom why such a setup might be required.

For good measure, the entire construction was locked inside a huge steel cage. Six-inch thick bars prevented Kyle from getting any closer than fifty feet or so away from the table that held the key to whatever the hell Project Wildfire was all about.

He stood a few feet back from the bars, peering through the gaps and trying to make out some part of the terrifying creature the crew and Sanderson had described to him, but could see nothing.

He took a half-step closer.

"Don't," Tom whispered at his side, and pointed at a discreet CCTV camera mounted on a nearby wall. "We're not supposed to be down here. Stay in the shadows."

Phil Sanderson was still locked in debate with the young female doctor, and the rest of the crew were apparently still locked in debates that were entirely more internal in nature.

Whatever happened on the ship, Kyle didn't give the crew much chance of lasting long if Sanderson reneged on his promise to have them relieved. Somewhere below the general air of dread on the ship, Kyle could feel an undercurrent of something else. Despair, maybe. Crawling insanity. Something dark was written in the eyes of the crew members. Something permanent.

One way or another, things on the ship were going bad, rotting like a corpse in the sun.

When the brothers were finally alone, Tom finally seemed to relax a little.

"What do you think?" Kyle asked.

Tom stared thoughtfully at Kyle for a moment before responding.

"I think they're feeding us bullshit and trying to persuade us it's chocolate. It's like Sykes said, nobody gets to know the whole truth. That's how Sullivan operates. It always has been. This whole thing was built on the work of tens of thousands of people, most of whom didn't know a thing about it until it all kicked off. So all this stuff?"

Tom waved a hand around the cargo hold.

"I'd say that whatever this is, it's definitely *not* what they have told us. Or what they've told Sykes, for that matter."

Kyle nodded. It made sense, or at least as much sense as anything seemed to make these days.

"You think Sanderson knows what's going on?"

"Maybe. He probably knows more than anyone else here, sure, but come on, Kyle. Some kind of hyper-evolved monster? Incredible speed and strength? Something that doesn't operate according to the laws of physics as we know them? Doesn't it all sound like the kind of fairytale you'd tell a child to keep them away from something you don't want them to go near?"

"Yeah, could be," Kyle admitted.

"I wouldn't be surprised if whatever this sensation everybody is feeling on this ship turns out to be man-made either. Gas, maybe. And just look at all this security. Rather than being designed to keep something in, doesn't it seem more like it's here to keep people from getting too close? It's like the lion enclosure at the zoo. We can look, but only from a distance. Sanderson says he is here to extract the thing's blood. But maybe he is here to *inject* it with something."

Kyle rubbed his forehead as he tried to digest his brother's words. It felt like his headache had decided to take up permanent residence.

"So what else could all this be about?" He asked finally.

"It looks to me more like a life support system," Tom said. "I have no idea why, but if keeping this thing alive is so important to Fred Sullivan, I think we have to take it away from him. It's the chance we've been waiting for."

"Take it away how?"

For a long moment Kyle wasn't sure his brother had heard him. When Tom finally answered, his tone was a little hesitant, as though he was still working through it in his mind.

"Everything here runs on electricity, right?"

"I guess."

"So let's cut the power."

22

Michael patted Bryn down and felt a surge of frustration when he discovered the man wasn't carrying a set of keys. As satisfying as it had been to rearrange the face of the man who had stared at his daughter in such an unsettling way, he found himself wishing it had been Rhys that had followed Claire instead.

Bryn chuckled through the blood filling his mouth, his humour dissolving into a hacking cough. He spat a gob of blood and saliva onto the floor.

"Ma will kill you for this," he mumbled thickly. Michael stared down at the man's grinning face, and saw broken, bloodied teeth. For a second he balled up his fist again and fought to suppress the urge to finish what he had started. Beating a man to death was easy; it was just a case of forgetting to stop. Michael knew that only too well.

"Thought you'd free your friends and run, is that it, Cripple? Heh...I guess I shouldn't call you that now though, right?"

Michael swayed a little on unsteady legs. He still felt mostly numb below the waist, and standing unaided was like trying to balance on a narrow beam that stubbornly refused to remain still.

"I need you alive, Holloway. I *don't* need you talking."

Michael let his legs tumble beneath him, and used his momentum to connect a final solid punch on Bryn Holloway's jaw. The back of the man's skull connected with the floor with a dull thud, and the light in his eyes flickered.

More importantly, he shut up.

Bryn still had Darren Oliver's shotgun tied to a makeshift holster around his waist. Michael retrieved it and popped it open. As Rachel had informed him several days earlier, the gun held a single shell.

I definitely won't be shooting my way out of here.

"Dad, what are you going to do?"

With his pulse thundering in his ears, Michael had momentarily forgotten that Claire was standing behind him. He frowned.

"Don't worry, Claire. The gun's not for him."

He cracked the door open and scanned the courtyard. It had filled up considerably since the last time he looked. He didn't see Rhys or Annie, but it looked like most of her people had now emerged from the towers. He saw a fire had been lit, and smelled the aroma of roasting chicken and his mouth began to water.

It seemed like only moments earlier that he had been sitting next to that fire himself, cooking up canned beans to serve as a celebratory feast. Sitting with Claire and Pete and Linda, and feeling almost like a family. Almost normal.

They're just people, he thought. *No different to us. Sitting out there, terrified and hungry, wondering if the castle will keep them safe from the horrors outside the walls. Afraid of the horrors that might be lurking inside.*

Just people.

Michael felt a surge of guilt and hesitated.

Can I do this?

He heard a faint moan. Bryn. Beating the man to a pulp had been the point of no return. Turning back now meant death. For Michael. For Claire. For everybody.

I have to do this.

"We have to hide, Claire, and we have to stay quiet. Just like in Aberystwyth, okay?"

Claire nodded, her eyes wide.

"Do it, Dad."

Michael pulled himself back to his feet a little shakily, marvelling at the legs that he couldn't quite feel, but which seemed to be gradually growing stronger. The pain in his back was a raging inferno, but he welcomed it with open arms.

With a grunt he bent and hauled Bryn to his feet. The man was punch drunk. Michael propped him against the wall, leaning his hip into Bryn to keep him from falling, and threw the tower door open wide.

Nobody in the courtyard seemed to notice. None of them would see it coming.

Michael grabbed Bryn's collar, and leaned in close.

"Say hi to the family for me, Bryn," he said.

And then he stuck the needle deep into Bryn's arm and filled his veins with Jason's blood. He pushed Bryn outside and closed the door, turning to Claire and pointing at the stairs."

"Up," he hissed.

Moments later, muffled by the heavy wood, Michael heard a noise that filled him with euphoria and remorse and familiar terror.

Shrieking.

*

The shriek snapped Rachel out of the fog of shock that had clawed at her ever since John had died, dragging her forcefully back into the present.

In the cell, the noise reverberated around the walls and chilled her. It almost sounded like it was *multiplying.*

Because it was.

Rachel bolted to her feet and stared through the narrow viewing window in the door. In the courtyard she saw a familiar and terrible sight: one eyeless monster giving birth to two more. And then to five.

Death swirled around the enclosed space; a vortex of blood and teeth.

Linda had told Rachel that Michael had asked her to take some of Jason's blood, and only now did she truly understand why. Stripped of all weapons, Michael had engineered a way of getting his hands on the most powerful weapon of all; the one that had destroyed the whole world.

It was a manoeuvre so reckless, so rash, that Rachel could only stare for a moment in stunned silence, wondering if could possibly have come from Michael.

And then she grinned.

Michael had been resisting taking direct action ever since Victor's bunker. Even as the knowledge that her brother's blood was poison reverberated darkly around the corners of her mind, Rachel couldn't help but feel that Michael—the Michael she had first met in St. Davids; the man that had been determined to stop the carnage—had finally returned.

Rachel was surprised to find tears stinging her eyes. Only now, as an extraordinary symphony of violence raged beyond the safety provided by the sturdy locked door, did she realise how totally she had abandoned all hope. Its unexpected return cracked open a door in her mind and allowed an emotion other than rage and hate to have its day.

She blinked the tears away angrily and scanned the crowd outside, ignoring the screams and the shrieks and the arterial spray that pumped into the air, like a dozen grisly garden sprinklers had been set off in succession.

She saw no sign of Michael, and hoped he was locked in somewhere safely, as she herself was.

When Rachel felt Emma's hand land softly on her shoulder, she turned and choked out a half-laugh, half-sob at the sight of the girl's wide, frightened eyes.

"Michael," Rachel said by way of explanation. Emma's confused expression informed Rachel that she hadn't quite put it all together.

"We might get out of this, yet," Rachel said, and returned her gaze to the massacre unfolding beyond the door.

Reckless and rash, and so flat-out crazy that it might just have a chance of working.

John would have been proud.

By the time Annie had hoisted her old bones from the throne, one shriek had become many, and the blood had drained from her face.

She stared at Gareth Hughes for a moment in stunned shock, and he stared right back at her, his eyes wide.

"The door!" Annie hissed.

She was already moving, but Gareth's younger legs beat her to it by a distance. He cracked open the heavy door and looked outside, and Annie knew the truth of the situation from his trembling gasp.

"Shut it," she said, and tossed him the keys. "Lock it."

Gareth fumbled the keys, and nearly let out a pathetic scream when they tumbled to the stone floor with a clatter.

As he stooped to retrieve them, he watched the door warily, expecting that at any moment one of the creatures he had seen running amok in the courtyard would target the noise and smash its way into the tower.

After a second that felt like a lifetime, he slid the old iron key into the lock, panting in relief when it engaged with a dull *click*. For good measure, he threw the heavy deadbolt into place.

The door was sturdy and old, designed to protect against men with weapons. It would surely stand against the tide of inhuman fingers that would attack it in moments.

"I think we're okay," he breathed.

"Okay?" Annie's voice was high-pitched with either astonishment or contempt; Gareth wasn't sure. Maybe both.

"They are inside the castle? How the fuck did they get inside the castle?"

Gareth flinched. Annie Holloway cursing was in some ways just as terrifying as the bloodbath that was unfolding just a few inches of wood away from him. He had only heard her swear a couple of times in three decades. It had never been a good omen.

"I...I have no idea. Maybe it is airborne after all?"

Annie's eyes narrowed dangerously.

"It is *not* airborne. If it were, we'd all be dead already. It's *him*."

Gareth opened his mouth to ask who, but shut it again promptly. He had a feeling that the less input he had in the conversation, the better it might go for him. Neither of Annie's thuggish sons was in the tower, but she still had the revolver she had taken from the crucified man.

Gareth couldn't picture Annie Holloway firing a gun—it seemed like a ridiculous image from a movie to him—but his imagination failing to conjure up something was no reason to suppose it couldn't happen.

It is an extraordinary situation, Gareth thought. *Has been for days. And Annie's response to the extraordinary has been to sink into malevolent insanity.*

Suddenly he *could* picture Annie firing the gun; could see it all too clearly, like he had been briefly granted the power to see the future.

"The cripple," Annie hissed. "I don't know how, but he did this."

Gareth swallowed painfully as Annie pulled the revolver from her skirt pocket and clutched it between her trembling hands. He had noticed the trembling before: Gareth was one of the few people that Annie ever let her guard down around.

He had never brought it up, of course. To do so would have been to imply that Annie was weakening, letting age get the better of her.

The gun twitched wildly, but remained pointed at the floor. For a moment Annie's eyes looked foggy, as though she had no idea what to do next. She stared down at the gun, and then back to Gareth.

"Where is Voorhees?"

Oh shit.

If you throw your lot in with a temperamental maniac, Gareth thought, *there are likely to be times when even doing exactly as they ask might provoke a catastrophic fury.*

He had always been aware of Annie's...volatility. In the past the worst outcome to disappointing her had been a snarling, ear-shredding rebuke.

Gareth felt his eyes glued to the gun. Felt his nerves jangling and his blood thundering through his veins.

Times had changed.

Annie had left Gareth in charge of Voorhees. It was Gareth that ferried the frightening man across the river on the raft to the town. Gareth that brought him back. Gareth that administered the drugs that Annie believed kept the big man docile.

Gareth had done exactly as he was supposed to: Voorhees was locked inside one of the upper rooms in a nearby tower, recovering from the treatment the doctor had administered.

The big man was comatose, drugged to the eyeballs on exactly the cocktail of drugs that Annie had ordered he be given.

The one weapon we have against the Infected, he thought, *and she has blunted it to the point of uselessness.*

Annie wouldn't see it that way.

"He's...uh...in his room."

The statement sounded ridiculous as it fell from his lips. Like he was telling a mother where she could find her sullen teenage son after an argument.

"He's, uh, out of it."

They both knew that was Annie's doing; her insistence on continually pumping Voorhees full of painkillers and sedatives. Gareth saw a flicker of recognition pass over her eyes; felt the unspoken agreement crackling in the air like electricity. It didn't matter. Annie wouldn't blame herself. She never did; never had.

Annie raised the gun, her bony old fingers trembling wildly.

And pointed it at Gareth.

"Then you are going to go and wake him up," she hissed.

*

Where the hell is Jason?

Michael cowered in one of the stately bedrooms with Claire, barely daring to breathe, and stared through the narrow window at the courtyard below.

Once again the place was painted with grisly bodies. Pieces of human flesh—some recognizable and some terrifyingly *not*—littered the enclosed space.

He had thought the old woman's response to an outbreak in the castle would be to send Jason out to put an end to it. Hell, his entire plan had been built on the Infected decimating the old woman's people and leaving him with a chance to end her with a gun taken from whichever of her sons he was able to launch his surprise attack on.

But Jason was nowhere to be seen.

Of the forty-or-so people that had been milling around the courtyard when Michael threw a man-shaped grenade into their midst, Michael estimated something like twenty had been dealt lethal blows in the violent storm that had Bryn Holloway at its epicentre.

That left roughly another twenty. The ones that had not been killed, but had instead been transformed and who were now pulsing around the courtyard like flocking birds.

Like caged predators.

Shit.

Michael scanned the human and once-human wreckage below him, and found his eye drawn to the most extreme example of carnage in his line of sight.

Rhys Holloway.

It looked like the man had been dragged through a gigantic shredder. Where others had succumbed to tears in their necks or their bellies, Rhys had been torn limb from limb. Ripped up and tossed aside like a bad lottery ticket.

Michael remembered Rachel describing to him the bloody mess she had seen in the farmhouse outside St. Davids. And hadn't Jason said something about his mother targeting her children specifically? Like somehow the family connection made the need to kill stronger?

That explained why Bryn Holloway was the only member of the Infected *not* circling aimlessly. The man that had started the carnage stood in front of the castle's main tower, pointing his empty eye-sockets at the door intently. He looked like he was trying to work out a particularly difficult puzzle.

Hope you get a chance to have a nice family reunion, pal.

Michael returned his gaze to Rhys' ruined corpse and felt frustration rising inside. In the centre of the smeared stain that the man's body had become, Michael saw his rifle. There would be a set of keys among the gore somewhere, too, but they might as well have been on the surface of the Moon for all the good they would do him now.

Annie's people had retrieved the antique weapons from the tower Michael occupied, but there was still an ancient suit of plate armour on display. For a moment he toyed with the idea of seeing if he could slip into it, and march outside to get the gun and the keys, wrapped in the safety of the iron. Like a tank.

Ridiculous.

Even if the armour protected him from the teeth and clawing fingers, the Infected would bring him to the ground through sheer weight of numbers.

There was no way out.

The people in the cells were safe. Michael was safe. But it wouldn't matter. They were all trapped, and once more

Michael was faced with the prospect of the castle keeping him protected from the virus while he slowly starved to death inside it.

Frustration rolled around his gut.

What have I done?

A flicker of movement outside caught his eye, noticeable only because it was located so far above the whirling vortex of horror at ground level.

Michael squinted.

It was the man he thought of as Annie Holloway's advisor, exiting the door at the top of the main tower and moving out onto the battlements, creeping along as slow as evolution and clearly terrified.

Michael frowned as he watched the man's progress along the wall.

Now where the hell are you going?

24

Getting out of the tower and onto the wall that ran around the castle felt bizarrely like a relief to Gareth, despite his sudden proximity to the horrors below.

Annie prowled around the inside of the tower like an angry scorpion. The Infected that circled in the courtyard far below somehow felt less threatening.

Until he stopped and actually *looked* at them.

The destruction of Newborough had mostly happened around Gareth, like movement caught only in the corner of his eye. He had been safely tucked away inside the town hall while hell was being unleashed on the streets outside.

He saw the obscene aftermath, of course; the decimated bodies and the stink of blood and death that accompanied the sight. But other than a snatched glimpse from an upstairs window, he had not seen the Infected up close.

The folly of his loyalty to Annie Holloway became apparent immediately.

Focused on killing and subduing each other, when creatures like this *are out there,* he thought. *So short sighted. So human.*

Gareth knew the creatures had extraordinary hearing, yet still he underestimated them. At first he shuffled quickly from the door onto the wall, aiming to get to the next tower as fast as possible. Within three steps he stopped dead as several eyeless faces whipped in his direction, and he realised that even the soft rustling of his shoes on the flat stone drew their hideous attention.

He held his breath, afraid that the sound of the air moving in his lungs would get him killed, and only allowed himself to breathe again when the creatures below returned to their aimless wandering.

All except for one.

Bryn Holloway.

Oh shit.

Staring at Annie Holloway's eyeless, blood-soaked son was like hearing the word of God. A revelation. When Annie discovered that her boy—possibly *both* her boys—had succumbed to the virus, her fury would be biblical.

She'll kill us all.

Gareth's mind raced even as he fought to keep his movements slow and measured. Getting Voorhees to wake up and dispatch the Infected was paramount, he decided. But returning to Annie was definitely *not*.

If he could get the big man out into the courtyard, and let him do...what he did, Gareth made up his mind that he would flee the castle the moment the last Infected body hit the ground.

The outside world frightened him terribly, but at least he would stand a chance out there. Inside the castle there would be an armed woman looking for brutal retribution, and Gareth would be her first, and maybe *only* target.

Gareth kept one sweaty hand at his hip, clutching the set of keys in his pocket tightly to keep them from jangling, and made his way inch by inch across the wall.

He had to travel around sixty feet to reach the tower that held Voorhees and the little boy that Annie had taken as her own.

Thinking about the boy, Gareth felt a pang of guilt. Leaving him there felt cruel, but Gareth knew he would not be able to protect him beyond the castle's gate. He had grave doubts about his ability to protect himself.

Will she kill the boy?

Gareth doubted it. Most likely, he thought, Annie would simply replace her own dead sons with the little boy. She had already practically adopted him, cooing over him and stroking his hair with a faraway look in her eyes.

In some ways, he thought, *that might be worse for him than death.*

Thinking about the little boy, and how he was going to abandon the poor little bastard to endure Annie's wrath alone was making Gareth edgy. Making him sloppy.

Once more he felt the eyeless faces pointed in his direction, and he dismissed all thoughts of everything else and focused only on the path ahead, and on negotiating it without making any more noise than the frantic pounding of his heart.

Only when he reached the tower that held Voorhees did he allow himself to relax a little. He knew exactly which key opened the door, and managed to slide the bunch of keys from his pocket and select it without making any further sound. Disengaging the lock might attract some attention, but by then it would be too late for the Infected, and he would be safely inside. The next person to exit the tower would be Voorhees, even if it took several hours for Gareth to rouse him from his narcotic slumber.

When he finally closed the door behind him and stood on the dark, winding stone steps that led down into the tower, he let out an explosive gasp of relief. The air he sucked into his lungs felt like razors, and the sudden intake of oxygen that his terrified journey had denied him made him feel dizzy.

Made it, he thought triumphantly, and he scurried down the steps.

The boy was locked into the tower's top room. He had been there for several hours as punishment for calling Annie a *crazy old bitch*. Gareth had the impression that the kid had idolized the man whose throat Annie had ordered to be cut. He seemed like a pretty spirited lad, and Gareth imagined it would take Annie a while to break him.

He suppressed a shudder and continued down the steps, reminding himself that he was not there for the boy.

Voorhees occupied a room on the next level down. He was locked in, though Gareth and Annie had discussed the probability that the big man no longer needed securing. Each time Annie sent him out into the town to 'cure' the Infected, he came back willingly enough.

Still, Annie insisted on continuing with the regime of imprisoning and drugging him.

Gareth unlocked the door and stepped into the room. Voorhees was out cold, unmoving as his system worked its way through the handful of powerful painkillers Gareth had dosed him with only a couple of hours earlier.

Gareth tried shaking him gently, and got no response.

It was as he was debating whether slapping the man might result in both waking him and enraging him that Gareth heard the noise behind him. The sound of the door to the room being pushed open gently.

Not Infected, he thought as he turned, *they would rush straight in.*

His mouth dropped open, and he realised that in his eagerness to get to Voorhees, he had not locked the door to the battlements behind him.

And now he was not alone.

The cripple. Not crippled at all, but standing upright with a malevolent grin on his face.

And a shotgun in his hands.

Gareth raised his arms aloft in feeble surrender, frantically trying to think of the words that might mollify the man. It was all wasted effort.

Before he could even open his mouth, Gareth's vision was filled by the butt of the gun, and he had time to hear the crunch as it impacted with his jaw before the world became brief pain and long, slow darkness.

*

Annie felt like her mind was being stretched; being slowly extended to its limits. To the point of snapping.

She stood alone in the throne room, confronted suddenly by the very real possibility that everybody else could already be dead, and that she was just one old woman with hands that shook wildly and a gun that she had no idea how to use.

Years of building influence slowly. Decades of work. Surely it could not come down to this? Surely she had not been solely reliant on the brawn of her idiot sons?

She stared at the gun, lost in dark thoughts, and found relief washing through her when she heard Gareth returning.

She turned to the base of the winding staircase, and hoped the paralysing fear she had felt only a moment earlier was not written clearly on her face. A show of weakness would be seized upon, and a strong appearance might be all she had left.

When she saw who the footsteps belonged to, the fear returned.

Michael.

Not crippled at all, but standing in front of her as large as life, with Bryn's shotgun levelled at her.

"Drop the gun," Michael said evenly.

Annie didn't hear him.

All her thoughts had coalesced into one single terrible whole.

He has Bryn's gun.

My boy...

The revolver dropped from Annie's nerveless fingers and a pitiful sob escaped from her quivering lips. Somewhere deep inside, hatred at the display of weakness flared.

She felt a single tear rolling down her wrinkled cheek, and found that she could not rip her gaze away from the shotgun. From what she knew in her heart that it represented.

"Is he dead?"

There was no strength in her voice, no sign of the fortitude that had helped her to dominate the town of Newborough for decades.

"In a manner of speaking," Michael said grimly. "The other one, though. Well, he's *definitely* dead."

Annie collapsed to her knees, ignoring the fiery complaints of her ancient joints as they struck the hard floor. Finally she tore her gaze from the gun, and focused it on Michael's smug eyes, and felt an overpowering surge of hatred for the man.

"And now I suppose you think you've won," she spat.

"Won?" Michael's voice was filled with wonder. "I think we've all lost."

"And now what?" Annie snarled bitterly. "You murder me? Somebody had to take control, to give the people direction. People need organisation, Michael, don't you understand? People need leadership. Who cares if you don't like the way I do things? What chance would we have had to survive all this without clear leadership?"

Michael shrugged.

"Maybe none. I guess you'll never know."

Annie snorted.

"You think you have it in you to kill a defenceless old woman?"

Michael let out a mirthless chuckle.

"You'd be surprised," he said, and then he squeezed the trigger.

At close range the shotgun blew the top half of the old woman's body to pieces, and the blast ricocheted off the stone walls like a violent thunderstorm.

25

When Michael returned to the room in which Jason slept, he found the man he had knocked unconscious coming to with a low, animal groan.

"You might be the last one left, pal."

"Gareth. My name is Gareth. You killed Annie?"

Michael nodded, and was surprised when Gareth let out a sigh of what appeared to be genuine relief.

"There might still be others hiding in the towers," Gareth said. "Not everybody was ready to come out. Too scared, even before...are you going to kill us all?"

He stared pointedly at the revolver that Michael had retrieved from the floor beside Annie Holloway's ruined corpse.

Michael felt an unexpected surge of anger welling up inside him.

"Of course I'm not," he snarled. "I take no pleasure in what I've done. I've had to do things I didn't want to in order to survive."

I sound just like Darren Oliver.

"Annie would have said the same," Gareth said morosely.

"Then Annie was fucking full of shit as well as insane," Michael snapped. "I told her I understood her killing John and I meant it. She thought he was a threat to her, and I get that, no matter how wrong I know she was. But that kid in the dungeon? Torture? Crucifixion? Threatening me with letting her sons rape my fucking daughter?"

Gareth's eyes widened, and he lifted his palms in surrender.

Michael fought to bring his anger under control.

"We live in a world where killing might be necessary now," Michael said eventually. "But for some people this is all just a license to act exactly how they always wanted to act. What about you, Gareth? Do I have to worry about you turning into a psychopath? Because if there's even a one per cent chance, I think I can do us both a favour right now."

He lifted the gun slightly.

Gareth shook his head firmly.

"I was about to run," he said. "I wanted no part of all this. Annie would have killed us all. I wanted to run."

Michael stared keenly at the man, and saw tears welling in his eyes.

After a long moment, he tucked the revolver into his waistband.

"Then I guess you'd better tell me what's going on with Jason. We need him awake. Or none of us are getting out of here."

*

Rachel had been watching through the bars set into the cell door for what felt like a couple of hours; maybe more. In that time she had heard a single gunshot, and she hadn't yet been able to tear her eyes away from the Infected that flocked around the courtyard.

Nor had she been able to tear her thoughts away from the certainty that everyone else was dead already. They had to be. She could see no reason why Michael hadn't yet appeared. And if the old woman was still alive, she surely would have sent Jason out to deal with the Infected that milled around the castle's grisly interior.

We're going to starve to death after all, she thought. It was almost funny. It felt like Rachel had been faced by a hundred different exotic ways to meet her maker, and in the end it would be an empty belly that claimed her. No different to billions of other humans that had died across the centuries. A mundane end.

Linda and Emma had given up trying to glimpse anything through the bars and were now slumped against the wall behind Rachel, locked behind invisible bars of despair.

When she saw a sudden flurry of movement outside, Rachel's heart leapt and sank simultaneously.

One of the tower doors opened and Jason charged out among the Infected like a bull, moving among the creatures that seemed unable to locate his presence and ending them. Jason had no weapon. There was no bloodlust on his battered face, and no sound escaped the lips that were no longer able to form words. The execution was almost serene; an act of nature.

One by one Rachel's brother snapped the necks of the Infected, and as she watched the slaughter Rachel knew that Annie Holloway had lived, and the nightmare would not end. Not until Rachel was dead.

She remembered telling Michael that she would throw herself over a cliff before she let the virus take her. It seemed now like the virus was humanity itself; it was Annie Holloway and her mania. It was Darren and Victor and who-knew how many other people who had responded to the loss of civilization with the destruction of their own kind.

Rachel wished fervently that there was a cliff available to her now. Even the single shell in the shotgun would be preferable to a slow, agonising death in a cage.

Just as she felt like she was falling into an endless abyss of despair, a miracle happened right in front of her eyes.

A miracle that wore a weary grin and carried a set of keys. A miracle that *walked*.

"Better step back if you want me to open this door, Rachel," Michael said.

And his grin widened.

*

"Since when can you fucking walk?"

Rachel's tone was half-accusation and half-joyous disbelief.

Michael smiled.

"I don't know when it started for sure. A few days ago, I think. I started to see movement...feeling came back yesterday."

He shrugged.

"Temporary paralysis?" He looked at Linda, who stood next to Rachel staring at Michael with an identical expression of disbelief. "That's a thing, right?"

Linda rolled her eyes.

"Not a doctor, remember?"

Michael laughed.

"Right. Sorry."

They stood in the courtyard, carefully avoiding stepping on the gore that was smeared across the stone, as if each chunk of torn flesh was a landmine with the potential to do terrible damage.

To their right, Jason stood, swaying slightly and staring around in confusion. With the Infected dead, Jason seemed to have no idea what to do next. He looked to Michael like a man trying to remember where he had left his keys. Or a machine awaiting the input of its next directive.

Michael caught the dark look in Rachel's eyes as she glanced at her brother, and knew exactly what she was thinking.

He's looking for Annie.

Michael could almost *see* Rachel's heart breaking; could see the devastating emotion that tried to crack her stoic face.

He was glad of the distraction when Gareth Hughes appeared in the courtyard. Glad that it took Rachel's mind off her brother, too. He saw her face darken with hostility.

"He's one of them," she spat.

"Not anymore," Michael said. "I think there might be a few of Annie's people left here, hiding out in the towers, but I'm not willing to punish them all for what she did. I think it's about time we stopped thinking in terms of *us* and *them*. We need to get the hell out of here, and the more people we have, the more chance there is that we might actually make it."

Rachel and Linda both seemed startled at Michael's tone, and he almost laughed. At one time or another, both of them had pleaded with him that he should cease the gloomy introspection that came to him so naturally and lead the people who were looking to him. Judging by the expression on their faces, neither of them had truly believed it would actually happen.

"How do we know we can trust him?" Rachel said finally.

"Can't trust anybody, remember?" Michael said with a sad smile. "We'll keep an eye on him. On all of them. And while we're on that subject..."

Michael strode away without finishing the sentence, and felt Linda and Rachel's eyes burning into him. He picked his way through the obscene mess on the floor until he found the rifle among the collection of parts that used to be Rhys Holloway. He bent down, feeling a twinge of protest in his damaged back, and scooped the weapon up.

Clutching the weapon once more felt like hugging an old friend.

When he returned to the two women, he pulled the revolver out of his waistband and passed it to Rachel.

"For me?" She said sardonically. "You shouldn't have."

"I shouldn't have done a lot of things," Michael said glumly. "But there's one thing I regret more than anything now, and that's lying to you."

Rachel froze, and her eyes narrowed.

"Full disclosure," Michael said. "I figure if we're going to get anywhere in this world, it might just be because we're honest with each other. I killed Gwyneth."

"What?" Rachel said. "I already know—"

"No. I *killed* her. Not an accident. The gun didn't just go off. I pointed it at her and I killed her, and she saw it coming."

Rachel's mouth dropped open.

"I did it because she was infected, Rachel. Not in the same way as these poor bastards were, but infected nonetheless. As long as she lived, and as long as she was in this castle with us, there was a danger that all this,"— he waved a hand at the once-human mess on the ground—"could have happened at any time."

Rachel stared at him, and Michael felt the bristling anger radiating from her.

"So John was right," she said. "He thought there was something off about Gwyneth dying."

Michael nodded.

"I guessed as much. He didn't exactly try to hide it."

"So why tell me now?"

Michael stared at her thoughtfully. There was, he realised, no point in trying to dress up the point he had to make.

"John thought Australia was clear of the virus. He told me to get there if I could. And I will," Michael said.

"And when I do, I won't be taking the virus with me."

Rachel stared at Michael blankly for a moment, and then he saw terrible understanding dawning in her eyes.

"Jason," she said softly.

"He's infected," Michael said. "I don't plan to do anything about that. That's down to you. But he can't come, Rachel. You can. Your choice. Or if you're furious about Gwyneth you can point that gun at me right now and make all this go away. I won't try to stop you."

Michael saw tears seething in Rachel's eyes. The proud, strong eyes that had dazzled him in St. Davids, and which had remained steely throughout everything. Through every terrible ordeal the world had thrown at the poor woman.

It was the closest he had seen Rachel come to genuinely breaking, and he hated himself for putting her through it.

Rachel stared at her brother. He was a barren island amid the growing sea of activity in the courtyard. As people emerged from the cells and the towers, gathering together to find out what was going to happen next, Jason seemed unaware of their presence. Seemed unaware of anything.

For reasons she could not explain, John's final words came back to her.

You can do this, Rach.

As she stared at her little brother, damaged beyond all repair, destroyed and poisoned by a world that he had struggled with long before it turned savage, Rachel found she could hold back the tears no longer.

"I need time," she sobbed.

"You don't have much. I'm burying John, he deserves that, but then we have to move. As fast as possible."

He pointed at the clouds that gathered over the battlements to the west.

At the column of smoke that rose in the distance. A column that had been faint — almost invisible — days earlier, but which was unmistakable now, like the tentacle of some great monster reaching up to attack the heavens.

Wylfa Power Station was burning.

"Our time is running out," he said.

26

In his clearer moments, Ed Cartwright thought about how quickly civilization had been stripped away. Not just the civilization you could actually *see*; not the buses and the takeaway pizzas and the endless television channels. All of that was gone too, of course, but it wasn't the sudden lack of life's little conveniences that dominated his mind. It was the things that *weren't* visible.

Like safety.

It hadn't taken generations of hardship for humanity to revert to savagery. It had taken *days*. Civilization, it turned out, had been a collective fairytale that humans blithely told each other and chose to believe. An overwrought story of a world that didn't really exist; just a way to make people feel grateful for the dull light of reality.

Now the need to tell fairytales had crumbled away and all that was left was monsters and darkness.

It had happened so *fast*. One moment he had been sitting in his bedroom, thinking about the fact that he was running out of weed and cursing the certainty that his dealer was ripping him off; selling him under weight, just a little, every single time.

The next moment, he was running and there was death everywhere, and somehow he had ended up locked in a fucking *dungeon* waiting for people to cut parts of his body away like they were trimming the fat from a side of beef.

Those were his clearer moments, and they were brief, as fleeting as summer rain. The rest of the time—the *majority* of the time—he spent screaming.

He felt another scream building in his throat when he heard the dungeon door opening above him; heard it through the one ear he had left after Linda had sliced away the other, while the taller of Annie Holloway's sons had cackled deliriously.

Linda hadn't wanted to do it, he could tell. The expression on her face spoke of remorse and pity, but that mattered little to Ed.

She'd cut him anyway. Just as Michael had.

As would they all.

Their reluctance and their pity meant nothing when you were the one watching pieces of your body being taken. All the prisoners would be given the same choice the man in the wheelchair had been given—torture or be tortured—and all would eventually pick up the knife.

Ed ran through the number of prisoners in his mind constantly like repeating a prayer, doing the terrible arithmetic again and again, and wondering which piece of his body the tenth of them would take. The fourteenth. The eighteenth. His fingers would be long gone by then, and probably his toes and his genitals, too. By the time the old bitch brought the tenth lucky contestant down the steps into the dark room, he imagined that even his limbs might be gone. After that where was there to go? Eyes? Organs?

Would number nineteen finally scoop out his brain and end it?

Ed wished fervently that he could just die; that he could persuade his heart that it would be in both of their interests if it just agreed to stop beating.

Faint light lanced apart the darkness, and Ed lifted his head as footsteps descended the stairs to the dungeon. The figure stood for a moment, silhouetted by the light from above and difficult to distinguish.

When Ed finally did recognise the person standing in front of him he felt his blood run cold. The young woman with the frightening, intense eyes stood in front of him. Rachel. She had scared the shit out of Ed long before he had been offered up to her like a blood sacrifice.

She has a gun.

Maybe this is the end.

Please, make it quick. Please.

Ed struggled to speak, but could not. Thirst raged in his mouth. No water for days. He found his cracked lips glued together; his dry, swollen tongue unwilling to comply with his request that it help him to start begging for her to end him quickly and mercifully.

It won't matter.

Begging hasn't helped so far.

Ed let his head drop, and tried to distance himself from the horror he knew was about to be done to him.

From the corner of his eye, he saw Rachel pick up a knife from a table that held a range of edged weapons, all of which Ed suspected he would get to experience.

He tried to sob, but it seemed there were no tears left.

And then suddenly his hands were free, and he was falling to the floor, and she was catching him.

"Come on, Ed. It's time for us to go," Rachel said softly.

The tears came then.

*

Ed stumbled out into the courtyard, squinting as the bright daylight lanced painfully into his eyes.

It looked like someone had set off a bomb in a butcher's shop. Blood and bodies everywhere. Ripped and torn, broken and twisted and smashed.

His feet slid on something slippery and he fought to control his balance, desperate not to end up on the ground among the dead things.

He felt Rachel's steadying arm on his shoulder, and he let her lead him to the stockpile of supplies he had helped to gather from Caernarfon. It felt like a lifetime ago. When she passed him a bottle of mineral water, Ed slurped it down greedily. It was the best thing he had ever tasted.

"Hope you don't hold a grudge, mate," Rachel said. Ed looked at her, puzzled. She nodded over his shoulder, and he turned to see Linda walking toward him.

"So do I," Linda said as she approached. "I'm sorry. About your ear."

Ed stared at the woman. He wanted to come up with a retort, but no part of his life had prepared him for how best to respond to a heartfelt apology from somebody that had recently mutilated him.

He stared at her dumbly, and nodded.

"Got to patch you up," Linda said. "Is that okay with you? Despite what you might have heard, I'm no doctor, but I guess I'm all you've got."

Ed nodded again, and let Linda take his left hand. All his fingers were gone, and the stumps oozed yellow liquid that he knew meant infection. A gift from Annie Holloway's son Rhys, who had defecated into his own hand and wiped the horrific result across Ed's weeping stumps, smearing it into the wounds like a dreadful ointment.

The man had laughed like he had just heard the greatest joke ever told. The memory of the humiliation made Ed's cheeks burn.

"This will sting," Linda said, searching through the supplies and producing a bottle of antiseptic.

"Trust me," Ed said. "I've had worse."

Linda smiled.

Ed turned his gaze back to Rachel.

"What happened?"

"The Infected happened. Thanks to Michael," she said. "You don't need to worry. They're all dead. And we're getting out of here. Very soon."

"We are? But what about the Infected out there? Isn't it safer here?"

Rachel shook her head.

"You told us about Wylfa, remember? It's in that direction, right?"

Rachel pointed at the column of smoke drifting up toward the clouds.

Ed paled. He nodded.

"Our world is built on electricity, and electricity is gone," Rachel said. "Things are breaking down. There are some things we want to be a long way away from when that happens."

Ed gulped.

"So where are we going?"

"The plan is the same as it was before the old woman got in the way," Rachel said. "We get to the docks in Liverpool. Get a boat big enough to take us all, and we don't look back."

"Get to Liverpool how?"

"On foot."

"But what about the Infected? This is crazy, do you know how far away Liverpool *is*?"

Rachel frowned.

"Not exactly."

"It's...like...seventy-five miles away. It will take *days* on foot. And even if we get there...it's a big city. It will be overrun."

Rachel shrugged.

"I never said it was a *great* plan."

27

"What do you think will happen?"

Kyle stood next to his brother, staring at the junction box. Neither of them had any idea how they might cut power to the entire ship, but Tom had suggested a more localised solution, and it seemed like it might work. They followed electrical cabling from the cargo hold until they found the junction box set near the roof about thirty yards down the adjacent corridor.

"I'm not sure. Maybe Sanderson wasn't kidding about the creature being telepathically linked to the Infected somehow. Maybe this is how Sullivan is controlling the Infected."

Kyle looked at him dubiously.

"I'm not sure *anything* is controlling the Infected."

Tom shrugged.

"You want to turn back?"

Kyle frowned in frustration.

"Look," Tom said. "The thing is locked up. If I'm wrong and it's not a life support system the worst that will happen is that it will be able to move about. It's still locked in a cage. Worst case scenario is that it kills Sanderson. I don't know about you, but I think that pompous prick could stand to do a little dying."

Kyle dropped his gaze to the floor. Increasingly it felt like his brother's agenda was simple revenge. He had a feeling Tom would kill every last person on this ship and every other if he could.

"Fine," he said at last. "Any sign of trouble and I'm getting to the chopper, and getting the fuck out of here. Are you with me?"

"Of course," Tom said.

"How will you cut the power?"

Tom dropped his gaze from the tangle of cables in the junction box to the assault rifle that looked so ridiculous clasped in his hands.

He shrugged almost apologetically.

"Oh," Kyle said. "I guess we're not keeping this quiet, then."

"I guess not."

Kyle sighed.

"Sanderson will be looking for us. I'll go find him. Once we're inside—"

"I know what to do," Tom interrupted. "It'll be fine, Kyle."

Kyle had a lurking suspicion that it would not be fine; that nothing would ever again be *fine*. He grabbed his little brother and pulled him into an awkward hug. It was, Kyle thought, quite possibly the first time they had ever had such intimate contact. He felt Tom stiffen and pulled away.

"If it goes wrong, Tom-"

"The chopper. I'll be there."

Kyle turned and left his brother in front of the junction box, making his way back toward the rest of the crew.

He couldn't help but wonder if he'd ever see him again.

*

"There you are. Where is the other one?"

Phil Sanderson was stressed. Hell, *stressed* didn't even come close. The thick soup of fear-inducing pheromones that the mutation emitted had finally dissipated a little, but when the manufactured fear departed, Phil discovered that it left a vacuum into which a more recognisable and natural sort of terror flooded.

He had seen the mutation in action; had seen it up close and personal as it smashed through a thick concrete wall. The thought of being in a room with the thing—even with all the safety precautions in place—was making him feel nauseous.

The fact that only one of the two men that he had recruited to act as his personal security team had appeared did not help the troubled writhing of nerves in his stomach.

The soldier—*Kyle?* Sanderson spent a moment trying to recall the man's name before realising it didn't matter in the slightest— shook his head and shrugged.

"No idea, Sir. I guess the, uh, pheromones got to him."

Phil bit back on his desire to rage uncontrollably at the news. When all this was over, he would find the deserter and have Fred Sullivan deal with him. For now, there was nothing to be done. *At least*, he thought, *I've still got the one who actually looks like he might be able to fire a gun.*

"It's almost time," Phil said, pointing at a readout on a monitor and overlooking the fact that Kyle clearly didn't have the first idea what any of it meant.

"Follow me."

*

When Sanderson led Kyle to the cargo hold, Kyle sneaked a quick glance down the corridor that held the junction box which supplied the power to the strange prison. There was no sign of Tom, but Kyle thought he could feel his brother's eyes on him, watching from the shadows.

He gave a slight nod of encouragement at the darkness as he left the corridor, and his nerves began to race. For a moment he was back in the van on a busy London street, sitting next to a psychotic Russian criminal, certain that the situation was spiralling beyond his control.

He shook the unhelpful memories away. Sanderson was prattling on about the mutation being almost ready for 'the extraction', muttering almost to himself while he opened a small case and withdrew a large, wicked-looking hypodermic syringe.

Kyle stared at it, fascinated. The needle looked to be a good six inches long. It looked more like a weapon than a medical instrument.

"Hey. Hey!"

Kyle blinked, and realised that Sanderson was now addressing him directly.

"Sir?"

"I want you right by my side, okay? And you keep that weapon pointed directly at the creature's face. If I say so, you execute it without hesitation, understand?"

"Yes, Sir."

Kyle wondered dimly if the assault rifle had a safety. Guns in movies had safety switches, didn't they? If it did, he hadn't disengaged it, and would not have the first idea how to.

You'd better be right about this, Tom, he thought. If Tom's hunch was correct, he would cut the power and the creature would simply die, leaving Sanderson and Fred Sullivan's bizarre experiment in tatters.

If Tom was wrong...

He hasn't been wrong so far. About any of this.

So why is Sanderson so scared?

Kyle stared around the cargo hold. Sykes and his team stood like scarecrows, unmoving and pointing their weapons a little shakily at the cage. Judging by the looks on their faces, they were all terrified. Glassy-eyed and somehow vacant, as though they were busy watching their lives flashing before their eyes.

A nagging sensation that these people hadn't been feeding him lies erupted in Kyle's mind.

What if they were all telling the truth?

It couldn't be. A super-powered monster. Impossible speed and strength. *Area of effect.* It had to be lies; had to be Sullivan's way of ensuring that the people aboard the McIntosh ship followed orders.

Phil Sanderson waved a hand at the one-way glass that separated the hold from the small monitoring room, and moments later the gate to the enormous steel cell opened with a *beep*.

Sanderson stared pointedly, and, with some effort, Kyle persuaded his feet to move, following the scientist to the entrance of the huge cell.

Kyle stepped inside, and felt cold sweat begin to trickle down to the small of his back.

*

Phil Sanderson hadn't ever been considered brave; not by himself, and certainly not by anybody else. Even his academic peers had sneered at him, because despite the fact that Phil's intellect outstripped them all and they all knew it, he contented himself with mundane research, often doing no more than confirming the pioneering work of scientists who understood less than him, but were prepared to take some actual risks.

He had been working diligently on refining the process of genetically altering corn to produce bumper harvests— a field of study not so much well-trodden as thoroughly ploughed long before he got to it—when Fred Sullivan found him.

Phil never knew how he had come to Fred's attention. All that mattered was what Fred offered: a lab and equipment that left the phrase *state of the art* in its rear view mirror and wealth that would have made the Pope blush.

All Phil had to do, Sullivan had promised, was to continue conducting his work in genetics.

That had been decades ago. And Sullivan had been good to his word: Phil never had to do anything other than interfere with natural DNA. Of course, at some point the lines had become blurred and Phil's work became less about crops and more about humans. A different sort of harvest altogether.

By then it didn't matter. By then Fred had established utter dominance over Phil, and the work he undertook had nothing to do with salary or even with scientific recognition, and everything to do with being allowed to continue breathing.

Sometimes Phil thought that Sullivan had recruited him not for his knowledge or his expertise, but for his cowardice.

He tried to manufacture bravery as he approached the mutation, but with each step a life spent cowering in fear weighed him down like an anvil around his neck. Not for the first time he wondered if he could persuade someone else to extract blood from Jake McIntosh in his stead. He dismissed the idea, as always, because word would get back to Fred, and because Phil hadn't yet encountered anything that scared him more than the old man.

Not even the mutation.

Phil had ordered that the emitters should be turned on before he even stepped into the cage. They would pump out a low frequency sound that would enrage the mutation as soon as it opened its eyes, but the noise would also paralyse the creature.

Phil had stipulated that the soldier in the monitoring booth should keep his eyes on the creature at all times, and if he felt the need, he should turn the volume all the way up to eleven.

As he made his way to the apparatus that surrounded McIntosh, Phil thought he could feel the pulsing sound himself, though he knew that was logically impossible. The trembling he felt in his muscles had nothing to do with the emitters, and everything to do with his fear.

Don't look at it.

He couldn't help it. His eyes were drawn to the horrific face as if a powerful magnet pulled at them, leaving him powerless to resist. The creature was conscious, all the readouts had confirmed it, but its eyes remained closed.

Thank God.

Phil let out a breath that trembled like an earthquake had hit it, and forced himself to focus only on an exposed patch of flesh on the creature's arm, a tiny section of its hideous body that had not been draped in restrictive steel.

He aimed the huge needle at the flesh, and it took all his strength to penetrate the skin that seemed to have the texture of thick leather. Slowly, agonisingly, the blood began to fill the syringe. Darker than ordinary human blood; thicker. Like a primordial sludge.

Phil's eyes flicked up once more and he froze in terror.

The mutation's furious eyes were wide open and pointed straight at him. It felt like the creature's livid gaze was boring deep into his mind, drilling wildly into nerves that shrieked in protest. Phil felt his mind begin to swim as he pulled the needle clear of the creature; felt the humiliating warmth spreading from his crotch.

It's done, he thought, *now get the fuck out of here and never come back.*

Phil had taken two faltering steps backwards, unable to tear his gaze from the mutation's horrific eyes when he heard the sound of distant gunfire and the lights went out.

*

Tom is *wrong.*

Kyle knew it as he watched the scientist approaching the creature. Sanderson had done well to hide his fear during the hours he had spent on the ship, but now it poured off him in waves, so powerful and unmistakable that Kyle half-wondered if the man was emitting pheromones just like those he had described earlier.

Thoughts popped into Kyle's mind like staccato gunfire.

He's terrified.

This is no life support system.

Sanderson was telling the truth about everything.

Kyle took a few steps backwards, and turned to run, praying that he would get to Tom before he cut the power.

He made it as far as the door of the cell before gunfire ripped the clammy silence in two and everything went dark.

He hadn't even had time to adjust his thoughts to the pitch-blackness that now wrapped around him like a shroud when he heard a sound that was utterly alien to him; a sound that he could only imagine was steel being *torn*.

A clattering in the darkness.

Heavy chains falling to the floor.

Kyle's breath caught in his throat.

Emergency floor lighting clicked on, bathing the room in a faint crimson glow and giving it a nightmarish quality.

Kyle couldn't help himself. He implored his muscles to keep running, but found himself locked in place by grim curiosity. He turned to see the mutation standing upright, seven foot tall; naked and wrapped in twisted, heavily-packed muscle, like an artistic impression of the human body painted by a slavering maniac in Hell.

The creature knocked Phil Sanderson to the floor with a dismissive flick of its wrist, like a lazy attempt to swat a fly.

It stared at Kyle.

Grinned.

Without thinking, Kyle lifted the assault rifle, all thoughts of whether the safety might be on long-forgotten, and squeezed the trigger, sending sixty bullets hurtling toward the creature in a matter of seconds. A fraction of a second after he began firing, Sykes' entire team followed suit, emptying their weapons at the creature, and the vast dark space echoed to the roar of automatic gunfire.

The air around the creature seemed to shimmer like a heat haze.

Kyle didn't see the thing move.

All he knew was that the bullets had hit nothing. As if the creature had somehow skipped out of their way, faster than Kyle's eyes could follow it.

Impossible.

The mutation chuckled, a low and sickly sound that made Kyle's heart feel like it was about to explode from his chest.

It switched its attention to Sanderson, who was pathetically engaged in an attempt to shuffle away from the monster on his belly. He didn't make it more than a few inches. Kyle watched as the creature placed a foot on the man's back, pressing him into the floor, like a bird pinning a worm with its talons before devouring it.

Finally Kyle's subconscious mind took over, apparently deciding that it had seen more than enough, and suddenly he was running, sprinting from the cargo hold; baffled by the fearful whimpering sound he heard until it became terrifyingly clear that the noise was spilling from his own throat.

And then he heard a different sound. One that was easy to identify. A noise that made his blood turn to ice in his veins.

Screaming.

28

Memories poured into Jake McIntosh's mind like acid, devouring and destroying everything in their path. The last thing he remembered was the old man and the noise that felt like it was tearing him apart cell by cell.

He heard the same noise now, and felt the same pain, though it was greatly reduced. He was pinned down to a flat surface, weighed down by metal that seemed to cover every inch of his deformed body.

And he was weak.

So weak.

The fatigue he felt reminded him of days back at Moorcroft; days when he had awoken after an indeterminate amount of time spent drugged and comatose. And it reminded him of waking for the first time after he had escaped the underground base, when starvation had attacked while he slept, debilitating even his extraordinary body.

Blood.

I need blood.

There was blood nearby. Jake could smell it. Warm blood, ripe with the stench of fear. Approaching him slowly.

He opened his eyes and found a spotlight burning into them painfully. It took a moment to adjust, and by then the other sense had kicked in. The new one that had been gifted to him by the blood of an Infected creature. He saw not with his eyes, but with his mind. Saw that he was in a vast space, and there were a handful of humans dotted around him, far away and indistinct.

And one that was standing right next to him.

Jake could not lift his head, couldn't move a muscle as the infernal sound poisoned him, but he was able to point his eyes towards the trembling scientist who stood inches away, holding a large needle that was buried deeply into Jake's arm.

The one that drugged me, Jake thought. The last person who had drugged him had their neck ripped open and their still-warm corpse desecrated. That had been when he had been human; back when he had been plain old Jake McIntosh, version 1.0. He dearly wanted to do much, much worse to the man who trembled alongside him now, but the wall of noise prevented it.

A bright star of fury went supernova in Jake's mind when he felt the blood being pulled from his arm, and he stared at the human, wishing with every corner of his dark soul that his hatred could kill.

And then he heard something else. Something that rode above the painful low noise that held him in agonising stasis. The clattering of gunfire.

And suddenly the world was dark, and the terrible noise had ceased.

Freedom.

For a fraction of a second Jake wondered if he might be too weak to escape the metal prison that pinned him down, but fury fuelled him, and he tore the steel manacles and chains that had pinned him apart, tossing them like aside like confetti.

He knocked the scientist to the floor before the man's face had even registered surprise, and paused for a moment as dim red lights flicked on, illuminating the group of human soldiers who surrounded his prison, pointing their pathetic weapons at him.

Jake laughed in delight as he saw the bullets floating toward him, drifting in his direction like feathers carried on a soft breeze. Avoiding them—even in his weakened state—was no more challenging than blinking or drawing in his next breath.

When the roar of the weapons gave way to confused, delectable whimpering and the frantic click of pointless reloading, Jake pinned the scientist to the floor, and felt the human's heart beat once—a single glorious, deliciously terrified pulse—before Jake tore away the man's right leg and consumed it.

Energy flowed through his deformed veins, lighting him up like a city at night.

The man's screams were almost as delicious as his blood.

Jake heard retreating, scrambling footsteps as the soldiers beyond the cage took the only option left to them and ran.

Heard a human voice screaming *lock it*!

Another voice responding that it was impossible; that there was no power.

He smiled. No lock could hold him in any case. Not now that he had fed. And now that he understood the weapon they had used against him, no human would get another chance to use it again. *Ever.*

The human beneath his foot writhed and screamed as his body's precious fuel pumped out of the torn stump that had been his right leg seconds earlier.

Jake allowed himself a moment to drink it in; savouring the man's agony like it was his first kill all over again, the one that had confirmed to him that he was different to everybody else. The one that told him he was something better, long before his body evolved and transformed belief into undeniable fact.

He stooped, until his face was inches away from the screaming man's pudgy mask of unhinged panic, and took a wrist in each of his huge hands. When he extended the man's arms fully, he saw horrified awareness replace the fear and pain that twisted his pitiful face.

"The old man," Jake rumbled. "Where is the old man?"

"On another ship," the scientist wailed.

"We're on a ship?"

"Yes, yes! Sullivan is with the main fleet."

Jake leaned even closer, until his face was almost touching the scientist's. He licked his deformed lips slowly before speaking.

"Where?"

"F-f-five miles east of here. Please, I-"

Jake ripped the man's arms away, taking an enormous bite from one and shuddering in ecstasy at the power the warm meat sent coursing through him.

There was more meat nearby. No need to gorge himself on this one.

He looked at the scientist's other arm for a moment; dangled it in front of the man's horrified face so he could see what had been done to him, and cackled when he saw the broken insanity boiling in the man's eyes.

So much fun.

Slowly and deliberately, Jake inserted the scientist's dismembered limb into his own mouth, forcing it down into his throat so that he too might understand just how delicious his flesh tasted.

As he filled the man's throat with his own arm, Jake doubted very much that the man understood.

But he did stop screaming.

Kyle erupted into the corridor adjacent to the cargo hold, frantically searching for his brother and seeing nothing, when he heard Phil Sanderson's bloodcurdling scream cut off abruptly.

Sykes' team followed Kyle out of the hold, and judging from the looks on their faces, all of their combat training had left them just as unprepared for what was happening as Kyle himself was. They bolted in all directions, scattering chaotically like someone had just called in a bomb threat in their vicinity.

Seconds later Kyle heard glass breaking, and knew that the mutation had smashed its way into the adjacent monitoring room.

There was no sign of Tom. Kyle hoped to God that his brother had already realised how wrong he had been, and had made for the chopper.

More screaming. It sounded like the soldier who had been monitoring the mutation had had his shift ended, though not in the way he hoped.

There was no time to think about Tom; about what might happen next. Kyle put his head down and pumped his legs, rocketing along the narrow corridor and hurtling up a set of grated steel steps to the next deck.

He heard a crash behind him.

It sounded like the creature was done in the monitoring room, and had decided that rather than exit through a door, it would simply smash through the steel wall.

Somewhere behind him, Kyle heard more screaming. And then more. At least three of Sykes' team sounded like they had been put down in ways so painful that Kyle's mind couldn't even conceive what might have happened to them. Half the damn crew had already gone and Kyle himself hadn't even travelled more than about forty yards.

The speed of the creature wasn't just bewildering. It was *impossible.*

He tried desperately to increase his pace, urging his muscles to match the speed of his terrified thoughts. His breath began to feel like acid spewing from his throat and dark spots flashed across his vision as he pushed his muscles beyond their limits, straining every sinew to squeeze every possible ounce of speed out of his legs.

What the fuck is it?

The question burned his mind as the oxygen burned in his lungs, but on some level he knew it didn't matter what it was. All that mattered was getting as far away from it as possible.

Another scream that ended in something that sounded horrifically like a wet *tearing.*

It's too fast. You have to slow it down.

Kyle's eyes swivelled frantically as he ran. He thought about toppling things in his wake: that's what people did when they were being chased in the movies, and it tended to work for them.

Not if they're getting chased by something that breaks through solid steel like it's warm butter.

Kyle heard another crash behind him.

Much closer.

Oh fuck oh fuck oh fuck oh—

PULL IN CASE OF EMERGENCY

The sign loomed in front of Kyle's eyes and he felt his heart leap.

Noise damaged the mutation; hurt it in a way that Kyle didn't understand. Sanderson had talked about low frequency noise, and a fire alarm wouldn't produce anything like that, but it was all Kyle had. The creature would be on him in a matter of seconds.

Kyle drove his fist into the safety glass and yanked the alarm lever down.

A half-second later an ear-splitting wail began to reverberate around the ship. Kyle didn't stop to see if pulling the lever had worked; didn't dare even to look back for fear that he would see the monster hurtling towards him.

As he ran, he thought he heard another noise mingled with the wail of the siren. A shriek that didn't sound like pain to Kyle's ears.

More like frustration.

*

The noise blinded Jake. It didn't have the same catastrophic effect as the booming, poisonous sound that the old man had introduced him to with a sneer, but it effectively blurred his vision and made bright sparks of rage burst chaotically across his mind. Where before he had been able to target the retreating human's footsteps as easily as tracing powerful spotlights on a dark night, he now found they were dissolved in an ocean of unrelenting sound; impossible to pinpoint.

Jake clapped his hands to his ears, trying to muffle the noise, trying to hear the sound of the human that he knew existed somewhere beneath the shriek of the siren, but he saw nothing. Everything was noise and light.

He howled in frustration.

It took several seconds for the rage that gripped him to ease up enough for Jake to think.

You have other senses. Use them.

He sucked in a deep breath through his deformed nose, and caught the scent. Faint, but unmistakeable.

Fear.

Following the trail by smell would force him to move much slower, but in some ways that didn't matter. In fact, he thought, *hunting* might be fun.

Grinning widely, Jake did his best to block out the shrieking noise of the siren, and followed his nose.

*

The problem with conspiracies, Nathan Colston had decided, was that nobody involved could trust anybody else, and everybody knew it.

Following Sullivan's gassing of more than three thousand men and women, Nathan's indecision about how best to proceed with his future had been cleared up nicely. He was going to get as far away from Sullivan as possible. As far away from the madness of the fleet and Project Wildfire and whatever the hell the old man was trying to accomplish with the horror on the McIntosh ship as he could.

The only possible way he could see to achieve that goal that was to take a chopper, and that meant finding a pilot.

Which was where the lack of trust came in.

Until a few hours earlier, Nathan could reliably have called on any number of potential pilots and been safe in the knowledge that word of his imminent desertion would not get back to Fred Sullivan until he was long gone.

Unfortunately those pilots were all dead, and in the process of being tossed overboard like chum before their corpses began to stink up the place.

He had an idea that the beaches along the northern coastline of Scotland would soon be awash with bodies, though it was unlikely anybody would be around to notice.

Maybe in the far future the sheer scale of the bodies entombed in the rocky sand would baffle archaeologists, though Nathan doubted that too: the blow that had been dealt to humanity by Fred Sullivan and Chrysalis Systems meant that even if humans managed to live through Sullivan's apocalypse, it could well be millennia before people ever occupied themselves with frivolous pursuits like archaeology once more.

They'd be too busy trying to eke out a living. Trying to survive.

Nathan dismissed the line of thought as unhelpful and returned to more pressing matters. Thanks to himself, the people remaining aboard the *Conqueror* were all loyal to Sullivan, and Nathan didn't trust any of them not to squeal if he started asking questions about getting the hell away from the ship.

He considered the boats.

There were plenty aboard the carrier; lifeboats mainly, but most had engines and he would at least be able to control one all by himself if necessary. He could slip away quietly, make for one of the other ships, perhaps. He had a good idea that at least a couple of them were on the brink of all-out revolution and would gladly seize on an excuse to flee.

Informing them that Sullivan had just murdered thousands in cold blood would probably do the trick.

The trouble was that a boat would be slow. The chance of his departure being noticed was high, and the chance of Fred ordering someone to fire on him even higher.

Too risky.

"I think they could use your help, Mr Colston."

Nathan flinched and turned to see Fred Sullivan standing behind him on the deck. The old man's eyes glittered, and Nathan had the uncomfortable impression that his thoughts were emblazoned above his head like a speech bubble floating over a character in a comic book.

He flushed guiltily as Fred Sullivan pointed beyond him, across the deck.

When he followed the direction of the old man's finger, he saw a group of soldiers hauling the bodies of the men and women who had been their comrades only hours earlier up to the deck and tossing them over the side into the freezing water.

"Uh, yes, Sir," Nathan said.

As he walked toward a grisly duty that made his stomach do nausea-inducing back flips, Nathan resolved that he would take a boat as soon as it was dark enough for him to slip away. He had a feeling it would take a miracle for him to escape Sullivan's clutches, and miracles no longer existed, if they ever had.

Only suffering existed now.

A boat might end up getting him killed, but Nathan had a strong feeling that his days were numbered in any case, and the number wasn't that high.

He would give it until nightfall, and then he would take his chances.

Fred Sullivan watched Nathan heading across the deck toward the pile of corpses for a moment with an intrigued expression on his face, and then made his way back into the superstructure that loomed over the deck, making for the bridge.

Kyle rocketed through the room that he had waited in earlier with Sykes and his team. He didn't slow his pace for a second, tearing through the room toward the door that led to the deck.

He burst into the crisp air like a bullet fired from a high-powered rifle, travelling at a velocity that he hadn't believed his legs to be capable of.

Sullivan's security team—as utterly useless as they were surly—were still clustered around the chopper, waiting nonchalantly for the scientist to return with the precious cargo they had been told to escort back to the *Conqueror*. Judging from the expressions on their faces, they felt very little of the fear that had gripped the people inside the ship. If anything, Kyle thought, they looked *bored.* The realisation made him feel strangely furious.

Kyle closed the distance between himself and the chopper in what felt like a few enormous strides, and saw the stoic masks on the soldiers' faces crack, just a little. Presumably the terror that pulsed in his mind was written clearly enough on his face to unnerve even them.

"We have to go," he gasped as he neared them.

A large hand materialised in front of his chest and put a sudden halt to his momentum.

"Hold up, Sport. Go where? Where's Sanderson?"

Kyle shook his head, struggling to draw in the breath required to provide an answer.

"It's free," he panted. "It's out. We have to go."

"The fuck are you jabbering about, boy?"

"It's free!" Kyle screamed. "Don't you understand? Do you even know what's on this fucking ship?"

Kyle saw a sliver of doubt pierce the soldier's confident gaze, and understanding hit him so hard that he found all he could do was laugh. He was bordering on hysteria, but it felt like the only sane response.

Sullivan hadn't told them anything either. Project Wildfire wasn't just built on lies and secrets. It was built on a rock-solid foundation of omitted facts and diligent ignorance. It was no wonder the world at large hadn't had a clue what Chrysalis Systems was planning: even the people involved knew nothing.

Before he could begin to frame words that he hoped might persuade the security team that a goddamned *monster* was coming for them, the crackle of gunfire ripped through the misty air and did the job for him.

He saw the soldier's gaze flick across the deck in surprise. The entire team hoisted their weapons as one, pressing them into their collarbones and staring down the sights. It was a smoothly-practised manoeuvre that at any other time might just have engendered a feeling of safety in Kyle; a sense that these were trained guys who could handle any situation thrown at them.

The trouble was that Kyle knew what was coming and knew that bullets might as well be balloons for all the damage they did to the creature. The soldiers readying themselves like characters in some dumb action movie simply looked ridiculous to him.

You're all going to die.

"Stay here," the soldier growled, and motioned at the others to follow him. They crept forward as one, heading for the ship's small superstructure, their weapons trained on the door in front of them.

Kyle watched them go in stunned disbelief.

He turned to face the chopper and hauled open the door to the cockpit, staring pleadingly at the pilot. He received a grimace and a shake of the head in return.

"Not moving without orders, mate," the pilot said.

Kyle seethed in frustration and despair.

Behind him, he heard one of the soldiers cry out in surprise and span on his heel to see Tom sprinting from the door, making for the chopper at top speed. Somewhere behind Tom, Kyle heard another eruption of gunfire. Another scream.

How many is that now?

Kyle had lost count, but he had a feeling that Sykes' entire team was gone.

Which meant the mutation had only one place left to go. One person left to follow.

Tom.

Kyle couldn't understand what had taken Tom so long. He should have reached the chopper long before Kyle did.

"Run!" Kyle screamed, aware even as he did so that Tom didn't need encouragement. His brother's eyes were wide with terror, and he clutched the assault rifle like a security blanket as he ran.

When Tom was close enough that Kyle could hear him whimpering in fear—a sound that reminded him starkly of being back in the van with Volkov—Kyle ripped the gun from his brother's hands and pushed Tom into the belly of the chopper.

Once Tom was inside, Kyle leapt into the cockpit next to the pilot and jammed the barrel of the assault rifle into his neck.

"Now you've got your orders," he snarled.

*

Jake burst onto the deck just as the chopper lifted into the sky. He saw a group of humans dashing toward it, screaming for it to come back and laughed.

Some of the humans would get away, but it mattered little. The helicopter headed east as it moved away from the ship, and thanks to the dead scientist, Jake knew exactly what lay to the east. He had a feeling he would see the chopper again.

The group of soldiers turned to face him, putting all their faith in the weapons they clutched in trembling fingers.

Jake plucked the guns from their grasp before they could begin to squeeze the triggers, and he tore their soft bodies apart with ruthless efficiency. The ship was deserted now, and out on the deck, away from the hollering of the siren, he found himself able to think clearly at last.

Only one thought ran through his mind; burning brightly.

Sullivan.

Before the ruined bodies of the soldiers had even finished tumbling to the deck, Jake launched himself into the sea, clawing his way through the water, moving like a torpedo.

Heading east.

31

This time, Michael thought, *we do it right. No more panic. No more blind running.*

He stood in front of the group in the courtyard, preparing to address them as he had once before. There were a few differences this time, though. This time there would be no splitting up; no underestimating the threat posed by the Infected.

Almost everybody present had dealt with the Infected at least once; they all knew exactly what to expect. Michael was confident that they would be able to hold their shit together.

Michael's back ached like someone had driven a hammer into it repeatedly. Already the pain that he had been so grateful to see return was outstaying its welcome, and he couldn't wait to be rid of it.

Funny how quickly that happened.

He had insisted on helping to dig a grave for John despite the growing fire in his spine. Adrenaline must have dampened the pain until the immediate danger had passed, but with safety came the realisation that his back wasn't healed. Maybe it *was* healing, but it seemed determined to do so only by forcing him to push through a monumental wall of agony.

He tried to focus on the doctor's words, all those months earlier. Distant words spoken in another life, to another person.

Pain is a construct Mr Evans. You have to push through the pain.

He pushed through it for John, and would maybe even have admitted that he relished the pain he felt as he dug a hole to lay John to rest. Relished it because it felt appropriate.

No, more than appropriate. Necessary.

John's death was one among many, but it hung over Michael like a low cloud. It could have been prevented. If

Michael hadn't been so...lost, would John have felt he had to rush off on a rescue mission all by himself? Would Rachel have been compelled to go after him?

In the end several pairs of hands weighed in to help with the gravedigging, and Michael was grateful for that. Not just because it eased the burden on his damaged back, and the growing burden of guilt on his mind, but because it would speed the process along.

It might have been his imagination, but Michael could swear the column of smoke rising from the island of Anglesey was thickening by the hour.

He had no idea what a fire at a nuclear power station might do, but he was pretty sure that a lack of electricity would mean any safety protocols that had been in place would be effectively useless. Maybe the core—or the reactor, or whatever—could survive a fire, but it definitely did not strike him as the kind of thing anybody should try to confirm by living through it.

John was buried and Anglesey was burning.

Time to go.

The crowd stared at him expectantly as he straightened, rubbing his lower back and wincing. Forty-one people in total. A motley assortment of damaged individuals drawn together from the ruins of St. Davids and Aberystwyth and Caernarfon and Newborough.

A family.

Each and every person carried whatever supplies they could manage on their backs, strapped up with ropes and torn scraps of expensive bed linen taken from the towers to make improvised rucksacks. Some had flashlights and most had weapons of one sort or another: mainly knives, but Michael saw the occasional ancient sword or mace as well.

Scanning the group, Michael felt his spirits darken a little. At the rear of the crowd, towering above everybody else, he saw a scarred face and vacant eyes. Rachel hadn't yet solved the problem of her brother, and had persuaded Michael that there would be no need yet; not until they reached Liverpool. He might even prove to be useful, Rachel had argued, and Michael hadn't been able to disagree with that. A man who could move among the Infected unseen and execute them without endangering himself was a powerful weapon indeed. Annie Holloway had more than proved that.

Still, the big man's presence made Michael uncomfortable. Not just because of his infected blood, or even because of the awkward emptiness that radiated off him, like he had ceased to be human altogether. No, it was the potential for damage to Rachel that Michael feared most. When the time came, he wondered if Rachel would be able to let go of her giant little brother. She was strong, Michael had no doubt about that. He wondered, though, if she was ruthless enough to cut Jason loose when she had to.

Not for the first time, he found himself wishing that John wasn't lying cold and dead beneath one of the small gardens in the courtyard. John had always had a way of getting Rachel to listen to him; at least as much as anyone could.

Michael sighed.

Could really use your help now, John.

Somebody coughed awkwardly, and Michael realised he had been standing there, lost in thought, for far too long. Virtually every face in front of him looked pensive, if not completely terrified.

Good job inspiring the troops, Mike.

"Okay," he said. "We all know what's out there. The best way for us to survive this is not to lose our heads. We want to move quickly, but most importantly we have to move quietly. If that means we go slow, so be it. Nothing is more important than remaining undetected. I'm going to tell you right now that we will come across the Infected, so best prepare yourself for it. The thing to remember is that if you don't make a noise they can't see you. Not unless they are right on top of you, and we'll all be keeping an eye out to make sure that doesn't happen, right?"

A faint murmur of agreement.

"I can't stress this enough," Michael said. "The biggest threat to your survival now is panic. As long as you don't panic, you've got a chance. More than a chance. If we all hold it together, we'll get to Liverpool and we'll get the hell away from this nightmare, okay?"

A slightly louder murmur.

"You have my word," Michael said.

"We'll move single file. I want everybody within touching distance of the person in front of them. If you see anything; if you need anything, you touch the person in front. If you feel a hand on your shoulder, you touch the person in front. If we have a problem, no matter how small it is, we all stop."

Michael paused.

"We ALL stop," he repeated. "Most of us don't know each other, and not too long ago some of us considered each other enemies, but listen to this. *Listen to this.* There are no enemies here, okay? There are not many of us left, and if any of you hope to survive, you'd better believe you'll only make it if the people standing next to you do as well."

Michael saw some enthusiastic nodding, along with what looked like grudging acceptance.

He wished he could find the words to make them all believe, to ensure that they would hold it together out there.

Maybe nobody could. Maybe those words did not exist.

Michael felt a powerful sense of deja vu.

"First step is getting across the river," he said. "We'll go in groups on the raft. Those who get to the other side first, *wait*. Stay quiet and stay alert. The town looks clear at the moment, but if you see anything, you get back to the castle immediately, okay?"

They stared at Michael silently.

"Uh, move out," he said. The group began to file toward the castle gate.

All aside from Rachel, who Michael saw working her way through the cluster of bodies toward him.

"You think this will work?"

Michael grimaced.

"Honestly, no. I can't see us all making it to Liverpool. Not like this, but what else have we got?"

"Some could take the boat," Rachel suggested.

"Annie had it sunk," Michael said. "But even if she hadn't, I would have been reluctant. Who would have got to decide which people took the boat? Me?"

He shuddered.

"Some people love the idea of getting to choose who lives and who dies. I can't think of anything worse. Better that we all go into this equally."

Rachel nodded thoughtfully.

"It's seventy-five miles, according to Ed," she said.

Michael nodded glumly.

"That sounds about right."

"Remember how long it took us to get to Aberystwyth from St. Davids? That was a lot less than seventy-five miles."

Michael sighed.

"I don't know what else to do, Rachel. If we stay, we definitely die, if we go, we maybe die. *Maybe* sounds like a better deal than *definitely* to me. At least there's a chance the number of Infected along the northern coastline is reduced. According to Shirley, anyway. He said the area had almost emptied, right?"

"Sure, days ago."

Michael gritted his teeth.

"What's on your mind, Rachel?"

"Didn't Darren say he got here by bus? Just kept on driving straight through them? The bus he used is still out there somewhere, outside the town, right? So why not try to use it? At least to get some of the way. As far as we can."

"It'll be noisy," Michael said.

"Yeah. But it's like John said: we move fast, we run into them. We move slow, we run into them. So fuck moving slow, right? We've got weapons. If a group of Infected stops the bus I think we can fight them off. And we do have Jason."

"And if we run into a herd?"

"Then we're fucked either way."

Michael stared through Rachel for several long moments. She had a point.

"Okay," he said finally. "We go and find Darren's bus. If we can use it, we will. But if not we keep moving."

Rachel nodded, and shrugged into a large pack that held as much food and medicine as she could carry without collapsing. She turned toward the gate and stopped, her eyes widening in amazement as she caught sight of the stash of supplies they were forced to leave behind.

"I don't believe it," she said.

"What?" Michael shot a glance around, as if he expected to see something terrible heading straight for him.

Rachel laughed, and scampered unsteadily over to the mound of supplies, stooping to retrieve something.

Moments later Michael heard a match striking and he saw Rachel inhaling deeply on a cigarette. A warm glow spread across her cheeks and her eyes glazed over a little.

Michael chuckled.

"You reckon you'll be able to carry all that as well?"

He pointed at the small pile of cigarette cartons and packets of rolling tobacco.

Rachel shook her head and sucked in another huge lungful of smoke, letting it seep slowly from her lips with a satisfied sigh.

She dropped the half-smoked cigarette and crushed it out under her heel.

"Nah," she said, blowing out the last of the smoke.

"I quit."

Michael winced as the portcullis rose with its customary whine of metal on stone, but the town that clung to the opposite bank of the river remained deserted. Most likely, he figured, Jason had all but eradicated the Infected that shuffled aimlessly through the town when Annie had sent him out there, like a dog charged with tracking down foxes.

It would not remain deserted for long, though, he was sure of that. Already he imagined that there were some of the creatures nearby, drifting toward the outskirts of Caernarfon. Silence was paramount. It had become more than important; it was a way of life now.

He waited with Claire and Pete, watching as the people shuttled across the river in small groups.

So far, so good.

He hadn't mentioned Rachel's idea of finding the bus that Darren claimed to have left just outside the town to anybody. Not yet. Better if they thought they still had a long and arduous trek in front of them. The more cautious they remained, the better.

He glanced down at Pete, who appeared to be doing his best to make himself invisible. He hadn't said a word since Michael had found him locked in the room above Jason's in the tower. He looked fine, at least externally, but the expression on the boy's normally excitable face spoke volumes. Michael hadn't asked yet what Annie had put Pete through. Maybe he never would. There were some things better left buried in the past. Michael knew that all too well, though his heart ached to think that someone so young might also be preoccupied with trying to forget.

When everybody was safely on the opposite bank, Shirley pulled the raft back across for Michael and the kids.

It felt strange to be leaving the castle. Inexplicably, Michael found himself feeling that he would miss the place. He put it down to fear of the unknown road that lay ahead of him. For a while the castle had seemed like everything; had been like the ultimate prize.

Yet now here he was, heading back out into the open.

Vulnerable.

He shook the dark thoughts that tried to grip him away.

Things were different now. The world had no surprises left to throw at him. He knew the Infected, and knew how to deal with them. He tried to focus on the fact that he would be travelling with a large group of people, all of them armed in one way or another, and on the fact that his legs worked now. No longer would he be faced with the prospect of being carried, abandoned to the mercy and goodwill of those around him. If things went sour, he would be able to react. Protecting Claire was no longer a hopeless fantasy.

He glanced at his daughter, trailing her hand in the river as the raft bobbed across it, and felt a sad ache in his heart. In another world, in a parallel universe, maybe, Claire was drifting in a pedal boat under a warn, comforting sun, trailing her hand in the water and daydreaming. Safe.

For the longest time, Michael had struggled with the notion that he was a murderer, and that there was a rotten core to his soul; dark and poisonous. In a strange way, putting forty-odd people to their deaths had finally cured him of that misapprehension.

Not a murderer.

A father.

Just another of Earth's creatures protecting its young.

When the raft reached the other bank, Michael scanned the people that waited patiently for him. Everybody remained silent as the grave, clustered together, waiting for direction. Michael was struck by the sudden similarity to the Infected he had seen flocking around the countryside.

This is a herd, too. Just like them.

We might just make this, he thought.

He pointed to the north, using the simple hand gestures that John had taught everybody. Everyone knew *stop* and *go* and *wait here* and *get down*. Maybe in time humans would have to evolve an entire gesture-based language.

Evolution had been tampered with, but Michael had an idea that tampering with a process like evolution was like throwing a stick into a river and expecting the water to change course. The introduction of Project Wildfire into the stream of human progression was violent only for those doomed to live through the ripples. Evolution would scoop everything up and mould it. The fittest would survive. Maybe that would be the Infected.

But Michael would be damned if he was going to go quietly. No, he would get to Australia somehow, and if it was free of the virus, he would expend every breath rallying the people of Australia to ready themselves; to prepare for the battle ahead. The battle to take the planet back.

Focus, Mike. One step at a time. You'd think a cripple would be able to grasp the concept.

Michael felt a wry smile creeping at the corners of his mouth.

But as he turned to leave, the smile fell away. Something was nagging away at the corner of Michael's mind, and he held up a closed fist, halting the group's progress before it had even begun.

What is it?

He turned and scanned the group again. Something was missing. No, not something.

Somebody.

Michael's gut seemed to know what was happening before his mind did. But when realisation caught up with instinct, he knew that they wouldn't be making their way to Liverpool unscathed, let alone Australia. They were not even going to make it out of Caernarfon without trouble.

No Jason.

The big man had slipped away unnoticed. That hardly surprised Michael: it was difficult to miss a man who was in effect absent even when he stood right next to you.

Clang.

Clang.

Clang.

The sound of a lead pipe hitting metal.

Jason had returned to his duty, still following the orders of a dead old woman. Still listening to voices nobody else could hear. Calling the Infected toward him. Toward all of them.

Michael's heart dropped.

And the sky filled with distant shrieking.

32

"Incoming."

The word cut through the atmosphere in the control room like a scalpel.

Fred liked the bridge of the *Conqueror*. Liked the efficiency of it. Everyone performing their specific function with machine-like precision.

Giles Filborn's function was to monitor the radar. Boiled down to its essence, his entire duty was to say that one word when the situation required it. *Incoming*. As far as military careers went, Fred thought, there were plenty of other, far worse jobs. Most of the time.

Incoming, he thought. *Maybe nothing is worse when that word actually needs to be said, though.*

"Is it the chopper?"

Fred burned his piercing gaze into Giles.

"Uh...I don't think so, Sir. It's coming too fast."

Fred's heavy brows lifted.

"Too *fast,*" he repeated, ladling on the emphasis. The two simple words became a complicated question. One to which an answer lurked somewhere in Fred's mind already, hiding in the shadows. An answer he didn't want to shine a light on.

He stepped closer to the radar display.

At the centre of the pulsing screen he saw a cluster of large dots that represented the fleet, and a smaller dot to the west, way off at the edge of the screen. Isolated.

And a tiny speck that arced between the two, heading unerringly straight for the fleet.

No. Two dots.

Fred stared at the screen, puzzled, and then back at Giles.

"*That's* the helicopter, Sir," Giles said, pointing. *This* one just overtook it."

"How big?"

"It's small, Sir. Very small. I think we're only picking it up because of the speed it's travelling at."

Giles frowned.

"Nothing natural moves that fast, Sir."

"How long do we have?"

"I'd guess it's going to make contact with the fleet in less than thirty seconds."

Fred sighed.

Wearily.

It was a sigh that felt like it had been building for decades, prompted to finally escape his lips by the sudden understanding that the plan had been deeply flawed from the beginning. Project Wildfire never had a chance of succeeding. Not as long as humans were involved in the process.

The entire debacle would end in panic. Survival was going to be a roll of the dice, despite everything he had done to ensure that luck played no part.

The people aboard the *Conqueror* were going to have to fight for their lives. Gassing the majority of the crew suddenly looked like a terrible idea.

Impetuous.

"Battle stations!" Fred snarled.

Giles stared at Fred and blinked slowly.

"Uh...Sir?"

Fred glared at Giles.

"What are we fighting?"

*

Tim Flynn hadn't expected the end of the world to be so *boring*. Life had never been boring before: there had always been the prospect of a roadside device livening the day up, or of stumbling blindly into a fire fight in what was supposed to be a family home. Hell, even if you were surrounded by kids, there was always the chance one of them would produce a battered *AK* from nowhere and begin rattling bullets at your head. Hard to be bored in that sort of environment.

Some thought it was terrifying, some wallowed in philosophical observations about how fucked the human race was if nine-year-olds were carrying guns and killing in the name of well, anything really. Tim was just grateful for the excitement.

It was why he'd signed up for the army in the first place. Because everything else was just so damned *mundane.*

He always hoped he would advance through the ranks, but never so far that he would be taken away from the action. He didn't want the stifling boredom of command. Spec Ops would have been ideal; Black Ops was the fevered fantasy that teased him in his dreams.

What Chrysalis Systems had offered him sounded like the greatest under-the-radar mission ever undertaken. Accepting the challenge once his army career was done hadn't even been a decision at all. At that point, faced with the prospect of finding work in private security somewhere—or worse, *civilian* work—Tim would probably have gladly signed up with the fucking mafia just to keep the adrenaline pumping.

Chrysalis Systems, Tim had been promised, would be like adrenaline injected right into his heart.

And it was *boring.*

Exciting at first; heady and intoxicating when it became clear that Chrysalis meant to survive the end of the world. But after that? Day after day of sitting on a goddamned boat going nowhere, hiding in the shadows while the real excitement went down just a few miles away, on the land. Enemies everywhere, a constantly-evolving theatre of war. No holding back. The entire world was now the textbook definition of *fire at will.* And Tim was doomed to sit around and daydream about getting involved, cooped up on a floating prison with hundreds of other bored bastards, none of whom even had the decency to be interesting.

Even the ship itself was an insult: the core of the fleet was all aircraft carriers and destroyers; at least if he had been aboard one of those ships he might have been able to maintain an illusion that he *might* see action at any moment. At least those ships had fucking *guns*.

On the former container ship *Sea Star* even delusion was out of reach. The ship was built for transporting cargo. Not a single weapon on board, other than the ones carried by the soldiers themselves. It was one of several ships within the fleet that had been designated for transporting supplies. Food, fuel, medicine. And, most ridiculously of all: at least half the ship was given over to transporting luxury items for the rich bastards who had tagged along for the ride. Tim had been down to the vast cargo decks, and had seen it all with his own eyes: supercars, works of art that he presumed were priceless, a huge library of old books.

The Sea Star was a *Noah's Ark* dedicated not to preserving animal life, but pointless bullshit.

Tim had made his feelings on the matter known by pissing all over a large painting that he recognised vaguely. One by the guy who drew faces of people at ridiculous angles. To Tim the art didn't look impressive; it looked like a half-wit had gone berserk with a set of crayons. The addition of his piss, he suspected, had probably improved the piece.

That had been the most exciting thing to happen on the *Sea Star* in days.

Until the strange explosion.

Tim was sitting in the cafeteria when it happened, chewing through a hunk of badly-cooked beef that he knew came from a can, but seriously doubted had ever been a part of an actual cow.

He stopped mid-chew when he heard the odd *bang*. It didn't really sound like an explosion; didn't have that rumbling quality that he associated with heavy ordnance.

Instead it sounded more like a plain-old impact, like some giant had smashed a fist into the hull.

Everyone in the dining area entered a comical sort of *freeze frame* state: cups held against lips, forks paused on their journey from plate to mouth.

For a second, everybody stared at each other in confusion.

"Did we just run aground?" A voice to Tim's left said.

The answer was automatic gunfire, muffled but clearly audible, rising from one of the lower decks.

A *lot* of automatic gunfire.

Tim swallowed the half-chewed beef and leapt to his feet.

Moments later a siren sounded; a long, almost mournful howl, and the ship finally became interesting.

Tim rocketed from the cafeteria, making his way back toward the dorm and the footlocker that held his until-now-pointless assault rifle. A tide of soldiers moved around him, and Tim felt the dizzying electricity in the air, the static charge that built up in men who knew they were about to engage.

His nerves raced frantically to keep up with him.

Once in the dorm, the clicking of footlockers being unlocked sounded almost insectile, a chattering cacophony, like a small army of crickets had descended on the room.

Outside the dorm, a fresh burst of gunfire shattered the silence. The sound mixed with a chorus of terrified screams.

Right outside the dorm.

Even Tim paused, his anxiety to engage whatever enemy had breached the ship stifled momentarily by the sheer horror evident in the screams that ripped through the corridor outside.

More gunfire. Further away. Receding.

Tim raced to the dorm's main door and threw it open. He stared, stunned, at the scene that greeted him.

In the corridor outside the dorm it was raining blood; thick rivulets dripping from a ceiling drenched in the stuff.

He saw dismembered limbs everywhere.

Saw a hand sliding slowly down the wall opposite him, partially-glued to the surface by blood and gristle, before it finally fell to the floor with a wet *splat.*

Something had passed through the corridor. Something that had chewed up everything in its path like a lawnmower.

What was left no longer looked like a corridor on a ship. It didn't look man-made at all; spray-painted with organic matter, the path that stretched out ahead of Tim now looked like a gigantic artery clogged with globs of glistening fat. Stepping out of the dorm felt like stepping out of sanity and entering a place of tortured madness.

For a second the shock locked Tim in place, and beneath his excitement he felt another message pulsing in his mind, desperately trying to be heard.

Run away you fucking idiot. Hide.

Only for a second, though. When his years of training and conditioning for combat came back online, he yelled out hoarsely.

"This way!"

Tim charged forward, oblivious to the fact that only a handful of people were stupid enough or dedicated enough to follow him from the dorm, and he followed the trail of blood and broken bodies, all the way back to the cafeteria.

When he kicked open the door, the sight that greeted him caused a fracture in his mind, like the first indication that an earthquake was imminent. Standing in the centre of the canteen, drenched in gore, Tim saw a creature born in nightmares, clutching a severed head and biting into it like it was an apple.

Tim looked at the creature.

The creature looked at Tim.

The assault rifle in Tim's hand only had time to move a fraction of an inch. His mind was still conveying the order to his arm to lift the weapon when something inexplicably powerful gripped the top his head.

And began to twist.

*

Fred stood in the control room and watched through powerful binoculars as the *Sea Star* began to sink into the waves. McIntosh had punctured the hull below the waterline like a fleshy torpedo, and Fred could only guess at the havoc that had been wreaked on the ship. It would take a long time to sink; the container ship was gigantic, and was taking on water slowly. Far too slowly. If McIntosh had made it all the way to the fleet, hopping from ship to ship until he tracked Fred down would present no problem whatsoever.

"Fire on that vessel," Fred barked.

The confused stares he got in response made Fred think seriously about pulling out his revolver and executing everyone in his immediate vicinity. Only the fact that there would be no one left to control the ship stayed his hand.

He gritted his teeth.

Fred heard a man's voice stuttering next to him.

Dick Skinner. Head of Security. Utterly useless, just like the rest of them. The man's lower lip trembled like he was a teenage girl about to receive her first kiss from a boy, and Fred struggled to resist the urge to begin beating the man. He succeeded in doing so only because there just wasn't *time.*

"Sir," Skinner said. "The VIPs are on that ship. "Even the Royal—

"There *are* no VIPs, Skinner," Fred snarled. "The only thing that matters on that ship is the creature that is no doubt tearing your *VIPs* to shreds as we speak. Soon that creature will come to this ship. How important do *you* feel, Skinner? Very? Or not very?"

Fred leaned in close to Skinner and spoke in a low, dangerous whisper.

"Give the order to sink that ship, Skinner. Sink it. *Now.*"

*

The old man wasn't on the ship. Jake hadn't killed everyone on board; not yet anyway, but it was already clear to him that the vessel was full of the kind of people the old bastard would think of as disposable.

The ship hovered at the periphery of the fleet. In fairness, Jake thought, it would have been lucky to find Sullivan at the first attempt. Not that it was a problem: this attempt had been enormous fun, and he suspected every other would be, too.

He almost hoped that Sullivan would be on the last ship that he attacked. Something about letting the old man stew while Jake worked his way relentlessly towards him, cutting through thousands of bodies en route, made his deformed groin ache with pleasure.

Jake stood in the cafeteria and watched the latest round of corpses settling onto the floor, letting the warm blood swill around his mouth like fine wine before swallowing.

The intake of blood was overwhelming; the energy rushing through his veins felt almost dangerously out of control and his massive heart pounded rapidly.

Is it possible to overdose?

The thought struck Jake as highly comical, and for a moment he stood alone in the lake of gore and chuckled to himself.

In the distance he heard a sound that pulsed underneath the wailing of the ship's alarm like a beating drum, and his laughter died.

A thunderous roaring, followed by a whistling shriek.

Jake began to run. Not in any particular direction; there was no need for him to know the layout of the ship in order to evacuate. Thrumming with the power the blood had given him, he was confident that smashing through the tempered steel walls would be like pushing through wet paper.

The weapons the humans carried were ineffectual, and so the old man had resorted to a larger variety. The distant booming and whistling Jake heard was presumably incoming artillery fire.

With a grunt, he kicked powerfully, rocketing through walls and exploding from the hull of the ship.

By the time enormous explosions tore the vessel in two, Jake was already a hundred yards clear, powering through the water. In his former life, swimming had been beyond him; now it was as straightforward as breathing. Just a matter of reaching forward to claw at the water and pulling himself through it. Slower that his movement on land, but somehow even more fun.

Judging by the arcing trail of smoke that hung in the sky, the shots had been fired from a ship that sat near the middle of the fleet. A destroyer that heaved under enormous guns and was probably staffed by a crew of Sullivan's most highly trained and dangerous soldiers.

Jake hurtled toward it, and hoped they would offer up some sort of challenge.

33

We might have stood a chance, Michael thought. *If only everybody had stayed quiet. We could have slipped away and let Jason draw them to him.*

If only the people huddled by the river when the shrieking started had remembered not to panic.

The first sign of the Infected had drawn a scream from someone in the group. A male voice. Michael had an idea the voice belonged to Gareth Hughes, and even as he began to process the chaos that unfolded around him, some part of Michael's mind rebuked him sternly for not killing the man when he had the opportunity.

It wouldn't have mattered. Michael had prepared himself for the eventuality that they would run into the Infected sooner or later, and that someone wouldn't be able to swallow back their terror.

He had just hoped it would be *later.* Not while they were still standing within spitting distance of the castle.

Michael saw Jason in the distance, along the harbour front, putting an end to one Infected creature and blissfully unaware of the other two that streaked behind him.

There's only a couple of them. We might be able to make it.

"Get back to the castle!" He roared, but his words were lost in a chorus of screams.

The group scattered, as though a live grenade had landed in their midst; rushing away in all directions.

Blind panic.

And then the Infected arrived.

Michael saw one of the young women that had been Darren Oliver's prisoner freed at last, her throat torn away by the teeth of a pregnant woman with empty eye-sockets, and he wondered dimly what sort of horror might be lurking in the creature's womb.

He turned away, feeling a powerful urge to vomit, and saw Rachel fall to the ground, dragged onto her backside by the grasping fingers of the other.

For a moment she scrabbled at the air helplessly like an upturned tortoise, weighted down by the heavy pack on her back, and Michael watched in mute dismay as she pulled the revolver from her waistband and blew the creature's head off in one smooth motion.

The noise of the report was deafening. Immediately the shrieking over Caernarfon seemed to multiply, and Michael could almost see the horrific figures hurtling toward them through the narrow, winding streets.

And then, in a frightening blur of motion he *could* see them.

Caernarfon wasn't clear of the Infected; far from it. All Jason's prolonged hunting of the monsters had accomplished was to draw more of them toward the town.

A small group surged along the harbour, some peeling away toward Jason.

Others making straight for the river.

There were far too many even for Jason to handle. The big man's style of execution was slow, methodical. There was no need for him to rush; they couldn't see *him*. Michael had no doubt that Jason would eventually kill them all, but *eventually* was a sharp word, loaded with deadly connotations.

For a moment Michael was paralysed once more; locked in place by an immobility that spread from his mind. His thoughts raced as chaos erupted all around him, and he struggled to process the options that would give him the best chance of survival.

Several of the group bolted into the nearest buildings, smashing their way through the windows when they found locked doors. To Michael's left, he saw Linda leaping into a tiny restaurant, dragging Pete by the hand.

Noise.

So much noise.

To his right, from the corner of his eye, Michael saw Rachel hauling herself back to her feet, loosing off another precious bullet into the oncoming horde and then abandoning the fight. She streaked away, crashing through a doorway into a small waterfront cottage and disappearing from his sight.

She was too far away. Already the creatures were moving between Michael's position and the building Rachel had taken refuge in. There was no way to reach her.

In the distance, he saw another small group of the creatures surging into sight, one of them sprinting directly into a swinging lead pipe that took most of its head off. And another. And another.

One made it past Jason. And then three. Five.

And then the time for thought was over and Michael was running on legs made of fire, heading to the left, aiming for the broken window that had swallowed Linda and Pete, grasping Claire's small hand and dragging her along with him, praying feverishly that they would make it and knowing at the same time that the building could not save them. All the walls would accomplish was to slow the Infected down, to force them into a bottleneck.

As he leapt through the shattered glass and into the dark space beyond, Michael was already spinning, losing his grip on Claire and pulling out a blunt short sword he had taken from the castle.

Driving it back through the window and into the soft flesh of an eyeless face.

The creature fell backward, and the hilt of the sword was torn from his grasp.

And then there was nothing left to do but run.

*

Rachel exploded into the tiny cottage, cursing her brother and cursing herself for firing two of the only six bullets she had.

Stupid, Rach. Bullets are wasted on the Infected. Save them for humans.

The thought was surprising, but not shocking. Rachel supposed she had finally adapted to the idea that killing people was going to be a necessary part of her future.

She stared around the room frantically, looking for a weapon larger than the knife she carried, and less valuable than the revolver. She was standing in a tiny, cramped kitchen, and her gaze immediately fell on a knife rack. She scooped up a large carving knife to add to the one she already carried, but it didn't solve her immediate problem: any battle she had with the Infected would be at close quarters if she used knives. Far too close. She longed for the baseball bat she had lost days earlier; for something she could swing in a wide arc to keep the creatures at bay.

Think, Rach.

She glanced back at the door through which she had entered. It had been unlocked, so there had been no need to smash her way in, but in the centre of the cheerfully painted wood sat a large pane of glass that would easily accommodate a standard-sized human. The cottage wouldn't keep her safe; the door would not hold, but she threw across the deadbolt anyway, and hunkered down by the exit, peering cautiously through the glass.

By the look of it, none of the Infected knew where she was. That was no great surprise: the group of survivors had bolted in all directions, pouring into the nearby buildings for refuge. For the creatures charging along the street the sudden explosion of noise must have been confusing and disorientating, but not everybody had reached safety, Rachel could tell that immediately.

She knew it by the bloodcurdling screams she heard, and the sound of snapping jaws and flesh being torn apart.

Gasping for air, certain that there must be something wrong with her lungs that prevented her from getting enough oxygen, Rachel scanned the road next to the river and tried to calm her thundering pulse. Outside, the road looked clear.

For a moment.

An Infected body shuffled into the door, stumbling against the glass, and Rachel barely managed to catch the scream of surprise in her throat before it escaped and gave her position away.

She crept backwards, holding a knife in each outstretched hand, moving away from the door slowly and silently, and nearly leapt out of her skin when she heard a whispered voice somewhere behind her, barely audible above the pounding of her heart against her ribcage.

"Rachel?"

Rachel span around to see Emma trembling in the doorway that led into the lounge beyond the kitchen. She clutched a small knife in trembling fingers, and let out an enormous sigh of relief when she saw Rachel's face.

It took Rachel a moment to realise that the terrified girl had probably assumed Rachel was infected, and that she had been just moments away from receiving a knife in her back.

Thank God you decided to check I was still me, Emma. I'm not sure I would have done the same.

She stared at Emma, wide-eyed, and put a trembling finger to her lips.

Behind her, Rachel heard another thump on the door, and she scanned the ground floor of the cottage frantically. Through the lounge she saw another exit, and wondered if she dared to leave the relative safety of the cottage and head back outside.

You have to, Rach. You've got to find Michael and the others.

She heard a thump behind her, and then a sound that made her blood freeze: the sharp crack as the glass panel in the door fractured. The creature outside had apparently decided that the door in front of it needed further exploration.

Fuck.

Ed made it about fifteen yards from the river before he felt fingers gripping his collar and pulling him off his feet. Before he could scream, a large hand clamped over his mouth and he breathed in a lungful of fear-ridden sweat that made him gag.

He twisted his head as much as he could, and saw the huge biker standing behind him, clutching Ed to his leather-clad chest in a bear hug that felt like it might well crack ribs at any moment.

"Shhh," Shirley breathed into Ed's remaining ear, and relaxed his grip when Ed made an attempt to nod.

At the entrance to the alley, Ed saw a young woman tearing past, screaming. A second after she disappeared from his sight two Infected bolted after her.

Moments later, her screams were silenced, and he heard a terrible wet *snapping* noise that he didn't want to identify. He felt his feet meet the cobbled ground as Shirley lowered him gently and released him, and he turned to face the biker, praying that the big man had some sort of a plan to survive the next few minutes.

Apparently not.

Shirley pressed his huge frame back into the wall of the building behind him in a vaguely pathetic attempt to make himself small. It didn't work. That, it appeared to Ed, was the extent of the big biker's plan.

Close by, Ed heard a fearsome shriek that made his teeth clench so hard he thought they might shatter.

We can't stay here.

After a moment spent persuading his feet that they still had the ability to move, Ed waved the hand that still had fingers, gesturing at Shirley to follow him, and pulled up short when the big man shook his head fiercely.

Why? Ed mouthed.

Shirley pointed to the pack strapped to his back, and Ed understood. The pack was makeshift: a ripped piece of bed linen tied together with some cord, and it had an enormous tear across the bottom where it had caught on the rough alley wall. Only the fact that Shirley kept pressed into the wall was preventing the canned goods inside from falling out and clattering to the ground.

Ed felt the blood draining from his face.

Go, Shirley mouthed.

Ed shook his head firmly.

No way, he thought. And then: *shit, maybe I'm brave after all.*

34

Nathan stood on the deck of the *Conqueror* and watched in stunned silence as one of the ships at the western perimeter of the fleet dissolved in a ball of flame, cracking like an egg and spilling its contents into churning water.

One of the destroyers had fired on the ship, decimating the vessel, and Nathan had watched it all happening in a bemused sort of slow motion as he carted dead bodies up from the belly of the *Conqueror* to the flight deck and tossed them overboard.

How many bodies does the old bastard want to send to the bottom of the ocean today?

Nathan stood and watched the fireworks as the container ship in the distance went up; a pulsing lightshow that hurt his eyes and defied comprehension.

What the fuck is going on?

Moments later, he saw Dick Skinner hurrying from the superstructure, hauling an assault rifle that looked ridiculous in his hands. The man had been a soldier once, Nathan reminded himself, but it always seemed more likely that he would see Skinner with a clipboard or a radio in his hands than a gun. If the man was preparing for an actual battle then matters in the control room must have taken a considerable turn for the worse.

What's worse than gassing most of the crew and tossing their bodies into the ocean? Nathan thought, but the question was quickly replaced in his mind by another, far more urgent in nature: *who is there left to fight?*

"Skinner!" He yelled, and the man stumbled to a halt, searching for the source of the shout. After a moment he focused on Nathan and smiled in relief.

"It's you," he said as he crossed the deck toward Nathan, wrinkling his nose at the pile of corpses laid out on the floor.

Nathan estimated that they had thrown roughly half of the bodies overboard, but much of the interior of the ship hadn't even been investigated yet. Thanks to Sullivan, there were rooms—hell, maybe even entire *decks*—heaving with bodies that hadn't even been discovered yet. If ever there was such a thing as a ghost ship, Nathan figured the *Conqueror* was probably it.

"Yeah, it's me," Nathan said, puzzled. "Who were you expecting?"

Dick looked flustered and shook his head.

"What's going on, Dick? Did one of the destroyers just fire on that ship?"

He pointed at the billowing plume of smoke that snaked up toward the clouds in the distance.

Dick nodded.

"Sullivan's orders," he said, as if that was all the explanation Nathan could possibly require.

"What? Why?"

The question seemed to throw Dick, and he frowned, as if questioning Sullivan's motives for anything had been beyond his remit until that moment.

"Dick, for fuck's sake. This whole enterprise is going to shit, surely you can see that? Why the fuck is Sullivan sinking his own boats? Is this just his way of putting down dissent? Because—"

"No," Dick said. "No, it's not that. It's...McIntosh. The mutation."

Memories flashed in Nathan's mind. He hadn't personally seen the creature during the attack on Northumberland...well, not really: he had seen *something*, but it hadn't been anything his mind had been willing to accept. Something that moved invisibly, like a ghost, as it ripped and chewed through bodies faster than his eye could follow it.

He definitely *did* remember the aftermath, though. The underground base had been huge, but it felt like every corner of the place had been liberally doused in gore. Even if the damage to the entrance could have been repaired, he doubted anybody would have wanted to stay: the place looked like Hell's waiting room.

The mutation?

"What about it? It's locked up miles away from here, right? It's in a coma."

Dick shook his head.

"It's loose. It was on that ship."

"So the response is to *sink the fucking ship?*" Nathan couldn't keep the disbelief from his voice. "Don't you think that's overkill?"

"Maybe," Dick said. "If it weren't for the fact that sinking the ship hasn't stopped the creature. It's here, in the fleet, Nathan. Out there, on one of those ships. Could be coming this way right now."

Nathan dropped his eyes to the assault rifle clutched in Dick's trembling hands.

"And, what, you're going to stop it with *that?* No offense meant, Dick, but if the thing just survived an artillery strike from a damn *destroyer,* I'm not sure an M27 is going to cut it, you know?"

"Oh, this isn't for the mutation," Dick said. "It's for the next pilot I see. I'm getting the fuck off this ship, Nathan, even if I have to take someone at gunpoint to do it."

Nathan gawped at Dick for a moment, stunned, and then he laughed.

"Now that's something I can get on board with, Dick," he said, peeling off the gloves that he had worn to carry corpses and tossing them to the deck.

"Fine," Dick said. "The more the merrier, right? But next time you feel like calling me 'Dick', please remember that I am carrying an assault rifle, and I'm pretty sure I've lost my mind."

Dick's got some balls after all, Nathan thought, and chuckled despite himself.

"Deal," Nathan grinned. "So where are the pilots?"

"Dead, mostly," Dick replied, and turned to scan the deck, as though hoping he might see a queue of pilots waiting to be selected from. "I hoped I'd find one on the flight deck, but—"

"All you found is me," Nathan finished.

Dick nodded.

A moment later, Nathan heard a distant engine. Faint, but unmistakable. He lifted his gaze up, scanning the sky over the western edge of the fleet.

"Not all of them are dead," he said, and pointed.

In the distance, a chopper approached, dropping smoothly down toward the deck of the *Conqueror*, framed against a backdrop of black smoke and rolling fire.

Nathan searched through the nearby pile of bodies—the latest stack of corpses that waited to be tossed overboard—and saw what he was looking for immediately: a dead man in a corporal's uniform, with a pistol in a holster attached to his hip.

With a grunt, he pushed aside a couple of the rigid bodies and retrieved the weapon.

Tucking it into his belt, he followed Skinner; racing across the deck toward the incoming chopper.

*

Kyle felt the blast rock the helicopter like a savage bout of turbulence as it approached the fleet, and the sky outside the windows darkened suddenly.

Outside, the world had been reduced to thick, rolling black smoke.

"What the fuck was that?"

The pilot shook his head and grimaced, fighting with the control lever to maintain a steady course.

"That was the *Sea Star*."

When the chopper burst from the fresh cloud that had been created over the fleet, Kyle craned his neck to see the damage below. The ship had been cracked nearly in two, and the stern was already sinking into the grey ocean.

"I don't understand," Kyle began, but the pilot cut him off.

"Join the fucking club, kid. As far as I can tell, one of the destroyers just sank it."

Kyle leaned forward to get a look out of the cockpit windows. He thought he could see a trail arcing from one of the heavily-armed destroyers; a faint whisper of smoke that suggested it had fired something at the sinking ship.

"Kid," the pilot growled. "You think maybe you could get that gun out of my fucking face please? I'm flying the damn chopper aren't I? All you're doing at this point is pissing me off."

Kyle flushed and lowered the weapon. Behind him he heard a snort of amusement. Tom.

He turned to face his brother, and felt hostility rushing through him, desperate for an outlet. Maybe it wasn't right, maybe it wasn't even fair, but Tom had fucked everything up. He had been right about Wildfire but wrong about everything else after all. There was nothing they could have done to stop it. They should have gone to ground, should have found a place to hide and ride out the apocalypse. Tom had lost himself in dark fantasies, and Kyle's guilt had allowed him to drag them both down, and now there was nowhere to run and they were both almost certainly about to be executed.

"Got any bright ideas?"

"I'm sort of still focused on the fact that we just escaped from a fucking *monster*, Kyle. Whatever this is, it hardly seems to matter. Trouble's been brewing on these ships for weeks." He shrugged. "Nobody knows what's going on. Some people are starting to realise they aren't getting paid, and everyone is pissed off. Maybe that ship tried to make a break for it and that's how Sullivan deals with mutineers."

Kyle rubbed his temples.

"In that case I can only imagine how he's going to deal with *us*," he said. "I don't think he's going to be happy that Sanderson isn't with us. What's our story when he asks? Got a smart answer for *that*?"

Tom slipped a pistol from a pocket and stared at it lovingly.

"Something short and to the point," he said absently, as though the gun had hypnotised him.

Kyle gritted his teeth in frustration, and was about to shake his brother out of it—physically, if necessary—when the helicopter began to drop sharply toward the deck of the *Conqueror*.

35

Rule one when it came to holding a sword, Michael had discovered, was keeping hold of the damn thing after you plunged it into somebody. Learning the rule by actually *losing* your sword was, he guessed, inevitable. Believing that didn't improve the situation one bit.

"Go!" He screamed, turning from the creature that collapsed away from the broken window, taking the sword with it. He was relieved to see the Claire hadn't waited for his prompt: she was already pounding her short legs and crossing the restaurant's small dining room with surprising speed, through a pair of swinging doors that presumably led to the kitchen, and hopefully to the rear exit.

Michael took a step after her, and crashed to the floor as strong fingers reached through the window and clasped the makeshift rucksack on his back.

The impact as his backside met the floor sent a shockwave of white-hot pain travelling up his spine, and for a fraction of a second the terrible prospect that he would once again slip into paralysis made him whimper in terror.

With a grunt he shrugged out of the rope straps and away from the rucksack, scrambling back to his feet and offering a silent prayer of thanks when he found they still worked; pausing only to slide the rifle from the pack and smash the butt of the weapon into the ruined face of the creature that loomed at the window once more.

The creature fell away again, and Michael figured he had a second or two at most before it once again tried to scramble through the window.

He turned and bolted across the dining area, crashing through the doors, and almost colliding with Linda. To his left he saw Pete and Claire hiding behind a large refrigerator, their eyes painfully wide.

"Why aren't you running?" Michael gasped.

"The back door is locked," Linda replied grimly.

Michael dropped his gaze and saw the carving knife clutched in her trembling hand, and understanding uncoiled in his mind, dark and terrible.

This isn't an escape.

It's a last stand.

Somewhere behind him, Michael heard shards of glass clattering onto the floor.

Heard a thump as something heavy followed it a moment later.

Michael stared at the rifle dumbly.

Five bullets.

He pressed the butt of the gun into his collarbone and aimed it at the doors.

And waited.

*

Rachel grabbed Emma's clammy hand and hurried to the rear exit of the cottage. Somewhere behind her, she heard another thud; louder this time. Either the Infected had heard them inside or somehow sensed that hunting inside the cottage would bear fruit.

Whatever the case, it was just a matter of time before the creature stopped beating on the wooden panels and focused on the large pane of glass set into the door and—

The sound of *cracking* glass suddenly became the sound of *shattering* glass; an almost harmonious twinkling of fragments rattling on a tiled floor.

Rachel had hoped to spend a moment studying the road outside the rear of the cottage, but moments had become valuable currency, and her purse was empty.

As the sound of the glass raining down on the floor inside the cottage reached her ears, Rachel took a deep breath and pushed the door open.

She stepped through, pulling Emma along behind her, muscles tensed and ready to flee for her life. Once outside, a quick scan of her immediate surroundings revealed no movement, and she closed the door softly behind her, sealing the creature inside the cottage and praying that it hadn't detected the soft clicking of the closing door.

The shriek that erupted on the other side of the wood, just inches away from her face, told her that luck was in even shorter supply than time.

Please, let that be the only one. Please, don't let any others hear that shrie—

An answering shriek, to her left.

Judging by the volume of the noise, the creature was about fifty yards away.

Without pausing, Rachel bolted to her right, trusting that Emma was following and expecting that at any moment she would feel hands clutching at her, dragging her to the ground, and then teeth...

As she ran, Rachel felt a scream building in her lungs, but it wasn't a scream of terror, though there was plenty of that. No, this was a scream of rage and frustration, a primal roar that had been building inside for days. A scream that had wanted to be unleashed since the moment she saw her damaged brother pounding John's head into the ground and knew that all hope was lost.

Little Jason. The shy guy who didn't know his own strength, the kid who had always needed the protection of his big sister despite his intimidating size.

Harmless little Jason.

St. Davids' *gentle giant.*

He's killed us all.

She heard the rattle of footsteps on the street behind her and risked a look over her shoulder.

Emma was about ten yards behind Rachel, struggling to keep pace and slowly falling further behind. Beyond her, Rachel saw the Infected rounding the corner onto the street, and felt her heart leap. She counted six...no, *seven.* A couple of whom she recognised instantly as some of the young women that had survived Darren Oliver's reign of terror at the castle.

They had survived Annie Holloway, too. In the end it had been Rachel's own brother that had brought death to their door. After everything that had happened, after surviving Victor and Darren and Annie, nobody was going to survive Jason.

Rachel turned away and poured every ounce of energy into pumping her legs, praying that the uneven cobbles would not betray her.

Seven Infected.

Her mind immediately ran to a more terrible number.

Four.

The amount of bullets she had left in the revolver.

This is the end.

Get off the street.

Small boutiques and coffee shops blurred past as she ran, and her legs began to burn. Nothing offered itself up as a means of escape. Getting into one of the buildings might offer her a faint chance, she thought, but pausing to try a door only to find it locked would get her killed for sure.

Gasping for air, Rachel twisted her neck again, hoping to see some sign that she was pulling away from the Infected.

What she saw instead was Emma, now forty yards back, collapsing to the ground and *exploding*, her abdomen ripped wide open by clawing fingers and snapping teeth.

A shocking spray of blood erupted across the cobbled street. A glistening rope of something arced behind it; something that Rachel couldn't identify for moment, until her mind finally offered up the obscene answer with a horrified scream: *intestine.*

She had seen the devastating effects of a human being encountering a single Infected, and they were horrific, but watching seven of the creatures bringing one young girl down was something else. Like a pack of starving hyenas, each desperate to tear away its fill before the meat ran out.

Rachel saw Emma open her mouth to scream; saw one of the Infected driving its snapping jaws down onto the girl's lips. It was a kiss drawn from the depths of a nightmare. A kiss that ended with Emma's tongue hanging limply from once-human teeth, torn out at the root.

Another jet of blood spurted into the air, painting the window of a nearby clothing store a grisly shade of red-black.

So much blood, Rachel thought dimly, but the blood wasn't the worst part. Emma was still alive, still trying to scream as her eyes began to cloud over with a deep angry crimson and the virus raced with the Infected to claim her.

Still human until the last terrible second.

Without realising what she was doing, Rachel suddenly found the revolver in her hand, and she blindly loosed a couple of rounds at the seething mass of violence on the street, letting her rage at the obscenity of Emma's death overcome her. For a moment she felt as blinded by emotion as the eyeless creatures that tore at the poor girl's warm corpse, and the fog in her mind only lifted when she saw the Infected drop Emma's body back to the cobbles, whipping their heads toward the deafening roar of the revolver.

Well done, Rach. Smart move.

With a chilling shriek, the Infected left Emma's ruined body on the cobbles and lurched toward Rachel.

She turned to run with a heavy heart and aching legs, knowing that escape was impossible; unable to do anything other than *try*.

The small buildings huddled along the street became a blur once more, though less so this time. Rachel had spent a lot of time over the years jogging to keep fit, but she was built for endurance rather than speed. Maintaining a steady pace for many miles was one thing;

terrified energy-sapping sprints another entirely. Already she was beginning to slow.

To her left, a small art shop with a single large pane of glass comprising its frontage caught Rachel's eye, and without thinking she fired the gun one more time, shattering the window and hurtling through, praying there might be a door she could lock inside. Something—*anything*—to slow the creatures that hunted her.

There was nothing. Just an open-plan space designed to mimic a tiny gallery. Lots of paintings and small sculptures adorned the walls; local art that focused on the grim, desolate beauty of the Welsh coastline; art that no one would ever buy because art was history now. Like everything else.

The rear of the gallery held a small stockroom, but there was no door. Hanging beads divided the stockroom from the shop itself.

Beads.

Fucking hippies.

It was almost funny. Almost enough to split Rachel's mind in two.

She came to a stop, panting for air, and heard the chorus of shrieks outside. Approaching fast.

There was only one thing left to do. The thing that she had promised Michael she would do if things ever went as bad as they possibly could.

The thing she had promised *herself.*

You won't take me.

Rachel pressed the barrel of the revolver to her temple and turned to face the creatures that had chased her relentlessly, right up to the bitter end.

One bullet left. More than enough.

The first of the creatures appeared, bolting into the gallery, and Rachel squeezed her eyes shut, unwilling to look at the horror that streaked toward her. Her mind shrieked at her finger, demanding that it pull the trigger before it was too late.

Do it. Do it. Do it. Do—

The tearing fingers and teeth she expected to feel on her flesh did not arrive. Instead she heard a strange sound, a strangled *yelp* and a thud, and a huge shadow fell across her, and after an eternity Rachel pried open her eyes in disbelief and the scream that had been building inside for days finally burst from her.

*

Inch by tortured inch, Ed helped Shirley shrug out of the damaged pack, taking great care to cup his remaining good hand over the ragged tear, clasping the packets and cans inside that desperately wanted to fall out and ring a dreadful alarm around the small alley. His other hand had been heavily bandaged by Linda until it was no more effective than a stump.

In another time it might have looked like the two men were trying to act out some sort of comedy sketch; as if they were part of a movie that was being advanced frame-by-frame.

The rest of the world wasn't moving in slow-motion, though.

Ed caught a can of soup as it slipped through the hole in Shirley's pack and lowered it gently to the ground, and from the corner of his eye he saw another blur of motion at the narrow entrance to the alley.

Another of the Infected, streaking past toward something—some *person*—that was unfortunate enough to have attracted its full attention.

Poor bastard, Ed thought, and shuddered as he realised that he might as well be referring to himself. It was just a matter of time before one of the Infected stumbled across the two men cowering in the alley.

This is taking too long.

He focused intently on the ground, placing another errant can down noiselessly as it slid from the pack, and saw a shadow fall across the cobbles.

He froze.

It seemed to take an eternity to persuade his eyes to wrench themselves away from the ground.

At the entrance to the alley, another of the Infected had appeared, but this one wasn't heading away on some bizarre and grisly mission. Nothing had attracted this one's attention. Not yet.

The creature paused.

Swaying oddly.

Like it was trying to gather more data; to confirm that it had in fact just heard something nearby.

Paralysed by terror, Ed and Shirley stared directly into the creature's empty eye sockets. It was a matter of feet away from them.

Ed held his breath, but knew that it was a temporary solution. Already the air in his lungs felt like it was catching fire. Soon enough, it would evacuate explosively. With each passing second, the effort of holding in the toxic oxygen increased the pounding of his heart.

It's going to hear my pulse.

Ed had listened to Michael's heartfelt speech back at the castle; he really had. *Don't panic.* How could a simple two-word command be so impossible to follow?

With each beat, his heart seemed to get louder, and it began to feel like the various parts of his body were going to betray him all at once. He felt an overwhelming urge to cough, as though a lifetime of knowing how to breathe just fine had abruptly ended, and now it had become a task that required his full attention.

I'm choking. Can't breathe.

I have to cough.

I'm going to die.

Ed's eyes slowly fell back to the ground. As they travelled, they spent a half-second pointed at Shirley, and Ed had a moment to absorb the man's fearful expression; the faint shake of the head as the biker realised what Ed was doing. Ed hadn't even realised himself; not until his eyes landed on the can at his feet again, and his fingers clenched around the cool metal almost involuntarily.

Before Ed could decide whether the course of action he had opted for was a *bad idea* or a *terrible idea*, the time for debate was over. He whipped the can forward, putting every ounce of strength he had into the throw.

The can sailed through the air.

The creature whipped its head up.

And then it crumpled toward the ground as the can caught it square in the forehead with a soft thud.

Ed stared, amazed, and part of him wanted to yell out his disbelief.

Great fucking throw!

But things were still falling, still making the journey toward the ground and the inevitable noise of landing.

Oh shit.

The now-dented can hit the cobbles with an impossibly loud metallic *crash*, and Ed's breath finally forced its way explosively out of his lungs.

Shirley flung the remains of the ruined pack from his back, oblivious to the clatter as the rest of the contents rattled on the cobbles like a medieval alarm system, but Ed saw none of that.

He was already running.

The buildings that lined the narrow alley became a fear-drenched blur as Ed rocketed past them, focusing only on keeping one foot in front of the other. In a strange way, he had never felt so alive; so in tune with the rhythm of his body. He could almost feel the individual muscles working, the fibres twitching. Each movement was a perfect symphony, a hundred different parts of the miracle that was the human body playing the same frantic song.

And then one of the windows set high in a building overlooking the alley erupted, showering glass into Ed's path.

Not just glass.

Something else.

A whimper escaped Ed's lips, riding the current of painful breath that tore itself from his lungs, and he slammed to a halt.

A dark shape exploded into the alley. Right in front of him.

Huge.

Covered in blood.

Wielding a pipe.

Ed wanted to scream and laugh and cry in relief, but there was no energy left. Only enough fuel in the tank to stumble past Jason, and to turn and see the big man start swinging.

*

As Jason decimated the Infected that had been bottlenecked in the alley, Ed felt a presence beside him, and turned to see another figure climbing through the broken window that Jason had burst through seconds earlier.

A slight figure with eyes that burned with dark intensity.

Rachel held out a hand toward him as she clambered awkwardly across the broken glass.

"Little help would be nice," she said with a crooked grin.

Ed nodded dumbly and offered her the hand that still had fingers, letting Rachel balance herself against his arm as she dropped from the window to the cobbles.

Once she was in the alley alongside him, Ed turned to see Jason dropping the last of the Infected that had poured into the narrow space with a blow that almost cleaved the creature's head in two.

"Are you okay?" Ed asked a little hesitantly.

Rachel grimaced.

"I've been better. Emma's dead. A few others from the castle, too. I saw them...turned, I guess. Changed. You know."

Ed didn't know what to say, and so he simply nodded. Rachel delivered the news with a matter-of-fact detachment, but he could tell from the shimmering intensity in her eyes that Emma's death had meant a lot more than nothing.

For the first time as he looked at her he felt something other than intimidation. Something that seemed a little more like sympathy.

She must have been through a hell of a lot, he thought, *to be able to deal with this so calmly.*

"Uh...is *he* okay?" Ed asked, pointing at Jason.

The big man was busily smearing Infected heads across the cobbles with mighty blows of the lead pipe, and seemed unaware that all of the creatures were already dead. He swung remorselessly, like a machine, until the bodies piled at his feet were reduced to little more than a horrific paste.

Rachel's expression hardened, but Ed thought he saw something else in her eyes. Something broken.

"He hasn't been okay for a long time," she said hoarsely.

For a moment Ed, Rachel and Shirley stood and watched Jason silently, as if a dark spell had been cast over them. The big man, for his part, seemed utterly unaware of their presence.

"Okay," Rachel said breathlessly, shattering the awkward silence, and staring pointedly at Ed and Shirley. "Where's Michael?"

The answer to her question floated on the air, carried like driftwood on a fast-moving stream.

Gunshots.

36

As the helicopter touched down on the deck of the *Conqueror*, Kyle toyed with the notion that he should once more jam the barrel of the rifle into the pilot's neck and demand that he take off again.

It wasn't the two armed men scurrying toward the chopper as the whine of the rotor blades began to lower in pitch that made his heart leap; hell, *everyone* seemed to be armed these days. Kyle had managed the best part of thirty years without ever seeing a gun; five minutes ago he had been threatening to blow somebody's head off with one.

No, it wasn't the guns that scared him. Not anymore.

It was the bodies.

In the distance, behind the approaching men, he saw a stack of bodies, like something from some grisly old photograph depicting the hideous result of a brutal war.

What the fuck happened here?

He stepped out of the chopper, half-wondering if somehow the game was up, and Sullivan knew he had two interlopers in his bizarre private army. Maybe the two men running toward the chopper were here to execute Kyle and his brother. Certainly Kyle couldn't imagine them doing any *arresting*. Law and justice was *definitely* a thing of the past, and not a matter that Sullivan had overly concerned himself with even when it *had* meant something.

True to form, Tom remained in the chopper, presumably hoping that he could somehow make himself invisible and avoid the inevitable shit-storm to come.

And you thought you were going to kill *Sullivan*, Kyle thought bitterly.

He had often felt guilty for labelling his brother *delusional*, but not where that was concerned. Two men with no military experience and one gun that neither of them could fire with any degree of accuracy were never going to get anywhere near Fred Sullivan.

Kyle lifted his arms aloft in surrender as the two men reached the chopper, and grunted in surprise when the younger of the soldiers pushed him aside and leapt aboard.

"Wait," Kyle said, "What's going on?"

His answer was an ear-splitting roar, and he turned in astonishment to see one of the nearby destroyers unleashing a devastating salvo of rocket fire at a ship further to the west. Another huge explosion tore the air over the North Sea apart.

Even more incredibly, a second or so later, Kyle heard the noise of another crunching impact and felt a sudden tilting of the deck. No more than a degree or two, barely noticeable. Kyle wouldn't have noticed it but for the fact that *nothing* caused the *Conqueror* to tilt. Previously, he had suspected it would have taken a tsunami wave to make the gigantic ship feel like it was actually at sea.

But he saw no tsunami.

"*That's* going on," the younger soldier growled, as the older one—clutching an assault rifle identical to Kyle's own—hauled himself into the helicopter.

"The mutation is free," the older soldier said. "And I think it's just arrived."

"*Here?*" Kyle said in astonishment. "But we just left it on the other ship."

"You were on the McIntosh ship?"

Kyle nodded.

"Well," the older man said. "A lot's happened since then. It's already been through two ships that we know of."

"In *five* fucking minutes?"

"Yeah," the younger soldier snarled. "Nice chat. Now get on the chopper or don't, but *you*"—he jabbed the barrel of a pistol into the pilot's neck—"get this fucking thing back in the air *now*."

The pilot bristled.

"That's the second gun I've had pointed at me in-"

"Then I guess you're just unlucky, mate. Pilots are pretty valuable at the moment. Trust me, the way things are going on this ship, you're going to have someone pointing a gun at you one way or another. You'll be glad it was me, because I *really* don't want to have to pull this trigger."

The pilot stared at him, his eyes narrowing, and sighed. He fired the engine again, and the rotor began to howl.

"I don't have much fuel. Where is it you want to go?"

"Not far. We're landing on the fastest ship out there, and then we're getting the fuck out of here before Sullivan kills us all."

The pilot pouted almost comically.

"Well," he said. "You could have just *said* that."

Kyle heaved himself back onto the helicopter, and moments later he felt the deck of the *Conqueror* fall away. As the chopper rose into the sky, he stared down at the enormous ship. At a glance it looked quiet and still, and it was difficult to believe that anything at all was happening beneath the surface.

*

Jake stood in a shallow lake of blood, and felt a certain amount of disappointment.

The destroyer he had torn through like an Act of God hadn't been the challenge he had hoped for after all, and after charging through two vessels without meeting meaningful resistance he had expected that the largest ship in the fleet—an enormous aircraft carrier—would also have the largest crew.

As fatigue began to set in it had taken him two attempts to punch through the thick steel hull, which was a little disconcerting, and what he had found inside was mainly corpses. It was as if the humans aboard the carrier had been aware of his imminent arrival and had formed some sort of mass-suicide pact.

All the bodies looked peaceful; unmarked, almost as if they had all just decided to go to sleep. As ever, the enormous energy expended by Jake's preternatural movement had taken a massive toll, and the first thing he did was take a huge bite out of one of the bodies.

He spat the meat back out in disgust.

The blood of the dead had been poisoned. If this was the old man's attempt to prevent the inevitable, Jake thought, it was poorly planned.

He wandered cautiously through the piles of bodies, until finally he registered some actual living humans nearby, and he made straight for them, tearing them apart eagerly and shuddering in ecstasy at the powerful rush of energy their blood provided. Yet there were only a handful.

Puzzling.

At least, once the energy began to course through him, he was able to move faster, but still Jake found himself hesitant to proceed. The ships and the humans he had encountered thus far had been entirely predictable in their reactions: they fired their ineffectual weapons until the bullets ran out, and then they died in spectacular fountains of blood that made Jake feel giddy.

Yet this was different.

Surely the old man would be on this ship: the biggest in the fleet; the one at the centre. Sitting at the middle of things like a fat spider on an enormous web.

Unless, just like a spider's web, the aircraft carrier was a trap; just a big piece of irresistible bait to lure him in.

Jake had underestimated Sullivan once before, and the result had been catastrophic. The old man was cunning and ruthless. Charging forward blindly might well end in disaster and darkness and the horrific noise that had made his nerves shriek in agony.

The incessant need that burned in Jake's twisted mind urged him forward, relentlessly exhorting him to give in to the monster that he had become, and to blindly pursue the blood and violence he craved so desperately.

Only the part that remained vaguely human held him back. The part that had once been a simpering coward that he detested with all his soul.

Controlling his impulses had always been a problem, but in the past it had been one that he had learned to overcome when necessary. He had never been the sort of lunatic that was completely blinded by their lust. Those sort of killers were sloppy; easily apprehended. Detachment and the intelligence to see the bigger picture were vital, he had always believed, if you were to forge out a successful life in the business of serial murder.

The thought that he was now in thrall to his own twisted genes and the addiction to the narcotic rush of human flesh; helpless as a shivering junkie, mortified and enraged him.

This is a trap.

You should run away.

Shut the fuck up, coward.

With an enormous effort, Jake forced himself to move slowly, creeping through the belly of the ship on high alert and conserving the energy that leaked away from him with such appalling ease.

The ship was gigantic, but he could sense the presence of humans not too far away. Somewhere above him. Fighting to suppress the dark desire that screeched in every cell of his mutated body, and refusing to acknowledge the familiar voice in his mind that told him to flee, Jake began to ascend.

37

Sweat trickled down Michael's brow, making him itch, and he had an overwhelming urge to brush it away before it ran into his eyes, but his fingers were locked around the rifle, and they didn't appear to be keen to let go for anything.

Staring down the barrel at the door, he expected it to burst open at any moment, but instead he heard a familiar sound, one that took him right back to his first encounter with the creatures that had destroyed everything.

Sniff...sniff.

The creature was unaware of the people cowering in the next room, and was stumbling blindly around the restaurant's dining area, trying to locate the prey that it knew had been there only moments before. With an effort, Michael pried his fingers from the rifle, and pressed his forefinger to his lips.

Maybe if we remain quiet. Just maybe...

He breathed in softly through his nose. Overwhelmingly he could smell coffee and cooking oil that had been re-used one too many times. By the smell of the place, the restaurant had done a rocking trade in bacon sandwiches and fried sausages, and the scent of the meat seemed ingrained.

He heard a screech of wood on tile. From the sound of it, the creature in the dining room had stumbled among the tables, and had bumped into a chair. Beyond the door, he heard a faint rushing noise; an expulsion of air that reminded him a little of a horse snorting out a breath.

The thing in the dining room sounded...*disappointed.*

Michael felt a chill running down his spine.

How human are these fucking things? He thought. *How much do they* think?

As if in response to the question, he heard a shattering of glass on the dining room floor.

It could simply have been the creature bumping into a table and knocking a wine glass from it, of course, but the image in Michael's mind was of the thing sweeping an arm across the table and sending the glass to the floor.

Frustration.

He let out a breath, long and slow; a breath he hadn't realised had been held in for several long moments, and slowly twisted his neck to face Linda and the children. With an effort he tore his left hand from the barrel of the rifle and held it up. One of John's simple gesture commands.

Wait.

The swinging doors that separated them from the horror in the other room had no means of locking, but they did have handles. Just wide enough that Michael thought he could slip the rifle through to bar the doors.

And what then? Even if you can do that without making a noise, there's no way out of this kitchen without the keys.

Michael's mind boiled with frustration as he desperately tried to decipher the best course of action. Sooner or later the creature outside was bound to stumble into the doors and then it would be right on top of them, and the only options left would be shooting at point-blank range or dying.

Rushing out there to kill it—even if he could do that without resorting to firing the rifle—would surely mean making enough noise that more of them would come.

Barring the door was the only option. If the creature heard the rifle being inserted through the handles it would be battering at the door immediately, and would probably be joined by more of its ghastly brothers in no time, but Michael could see no other option. Moving carefully, he aimed the barrel at the handles, and began sliding it through.

Just like that old board game, he thought, *the one where you operate on a man, and if your hand trembles a buzzer goes off. Except that this time, the buzzer will be the last thing you ever hear.*

Michael heard another thump in the room beyond, and then an ear-splitting shriek, and he froze. His heart hammered against his chest.

In the dining room he heard what sounded like a scuffle, and then a loud *thud*. Moments later he heard a *voice*, whispering his name.

"Michael?"

Stunned, Michael motioned at Linda and the kids to stay put and cautiously cracked open the door.

In the dining room, swaying a little uncertainly and clutching a large rock stained with blood, he saw Gareth Hughes, and Michael felt his jaw slacken.

He stepped into the dining room slowly, scanning for any other movement and seeing none. On the floor to Gareth's left, he saw the prone body of the infected creature, and finally allowed himself to breathe easier.

"It's okay," he whispered back into the kitchen, and moved toward Gareth with a grin.

"I guess you're one of the good guys, now."

Gareth smiled a little sheepishly.

"Any of the others with you?" Michael asked, and Gareth nodded. "A few, hiding next door. I saw it follow you guys in here, and I figured I had to...you know."

Michael clapped Gareth on the shoulder.

"You did great, mate," he said. "I honestly wouldn't have thought you had it in you to kill one of those things."

Gareth grinned.

"Neither would I," he said. "I just shut my eyes and swung. A bit like when I played cricket at school. Never did make the team."

Michael felt a laugh building in his throat, but there was something else building too. An apprehension that quashed all the humour.

Just one swing.

It could still be—

Michael span around just in time and far too late simultaneously. A fraction of a second later and he would have missed it: the infected creature—stunned and most definitely *not* dead—lurching upright and sinking its teeth deep into Pete's calf as he stepped out of the kitchen.

"No!" Michael roared, but the word was lost in another scream, high-pitched and horrified, a young boy's scream that twisted until it became a familiar bloodcurdling shriek. It was a sound that Michael thought he would hear in his nightmares for the rest of his life, however long that might be.

With a hoarse cry of despair, Michael aimed the rifle and squeezed the trigger, destroying the face of the creature on the floor.

When he looked up, he saw Pete's eyes for the last time, clouding with blood and seeming to swell in their sockets.

And then the boy reached into his skull with his forefingers and ripped them out with a grunt of terrible *relief.*

Michael was still screaming; oblivious to the noise and the Infected that might hear it; a wordless roar of pain and despair as he lifted the rifle once more and did what had to be done.

*

Rachel moved through the streets warily, pulling along her giant brother by the hand. It felt like leading a horse. Jason was compliant but apparently unaware. He had slipped once more into what she thought of as his *standby* mode.

As heartbreaking as the emptiness on his face was, Rachel was glad that he had become so quiet. Her brother was able to detect the presence of the Infected somehow, she was sure. Just as Gwyneth had been. If Jason had once more retreated into his shell, it at least allowed her to believe that the immediate threat had passed.

At what cost?

As the small group headed back toward the river—and the sound of gunfire they had heard moments earlier—Rachel tried not to look at the corpses that littered the ground, but there were many she vaguely recognised, and soon enough she found herself examining every single body that she passed, dreading seeing a face that was more familiar to her.

Some of the dead she had seen only briefly before they met their grisly end: sad, silent men and women with haunted eyes that had arrived at the castle with Annie Holloway.

Some others, Rachel knew a little better: the young girls that Darren Oliver had harvested from Caernarfon to be his playthings. There was no sign of Michael.

Please be alive.

When they reached the river, right back at the spot that they had been gathered at when all hell had broken loose just a few short minutes earlier, Rachel found the ground awash with blood, and the town seemed eerily still.

She resisted the urge to shout Michael's name. Jason might be able to detect the presence of the Infected, but Rachel had no idea how far such an ability extended. Maybe not as far as her voice would carry.

And besides, Jason's response to the Infected was to draw them straight to him. If that happened again, Rachel didn't think anybody would survive. At least, not anybody other than Jason. She pictured her brother alone, wandering the countryside like a ghost killing and killing, and felt bitter tears sting her eyes.

"There," Shirley whispered suddenly, pointing at a restaurant with a smashed window to their left. Rachel watched as the a dark shape appeared at the window and Michael climbed out, followed by Linda, Claire and one of Holloway's men.

Tears streamed openly down Michael's face, and Claire's narrow shoulders heaved with heavy sobs, and

Rachel realised who was missing, and felt a lump in her throat.

38

All told, eighteen people had survived the disaster on the riverbank in Caernarfon. More than half of the people that had set out from the castle had been killed outright, or had been executed by Jason once they had turned.

A trip that had been full of fear and trepidation now felt marked more by sadness and weariness. A pall of despair hung over the group. Seventy-five miles to travel, and their number had been cut in two before they had even travelled *one*.

They huddled together by the riverbank for a while and no one spoke, but Michael had an idea that they were all thinking the same thing.

We can't make it.

He stared forlornly at Claire, who had buried her face in Linda's coat. The sobs that had heaved through her had quieted, but Michael could still hear her snuffling.

It could have been her, he thought. *It was just dumb luck that it* wasn't *her.*

Michael had felt like slamming the butt of the rifle into Gareth's face after he had been forced to execute Pete, but the feeling faded quickly. It wasn't Gareth's fault. It was his own. He had let his guard down for just a second; long enough to overlook something so simple and so devastating.

He hadn't been able to keep Pete safe. Nor John or Gwyneth or any of them. Even the ones still alive, like Rachel and Jason, had been damaged or broken entirely. Linda had once pleaded with him that the survivors needed Michael to lead them, but what good was he if he couldn't even protect a child standing no more than a yard away from him?

The darkness that lived in his mind clawed at him, revelling in the moment.

All your fault, Mike.

Claire will be next.

And now you're just sitting here, waiting for the power station to blow and end it all, because that is the easiest way out, isn't it?

Michael blinked away tears that burned his eyes and tore his gaze away from the floor to find Rachel staring at him.

"We have to go for the bus," she said flatly. "Darren's bus. It's our only chance, Michael. The noise of the engine might draw the Infected, but so what? They attacked the bus when Darren was driving and he made it. Nothing has changed. We get to Liverpool, get a boat and *go*."

Michael stared at Rachel for a while and tried to find some hope in her words. Didn't manage it.

"The bus probably doesn't work. We don't have the keys."

"Then we'll find something else," Rachel snapped. "Goddammit, Michael, snap out of it. We have to *go*."

Rachel was right, but Michael felt anger burning inside him nonetheless.

"And what about *him*?" He snapped, jabbing a finger at Jason. The big man sat apart from the rest of them, apparently oblivious to their presence.

"What about him?" Rachel said, surprised. "He comes with us, of course."

She shrugged.

"Rachel, he's not Jason anymore, don't you see that? I'm not even sure he's human! All he cares about is the Infected. He *drew* them to us, Rachel. He did that. He got people killed. Almost got *all* of us killed."

Fire burned in Rachel's eyes. Hot enough to melt steel.

"And what if he knew they were out there? What if he only did that because he knew there were Infected in the town? What if he was trying to keep us safe?"

"Then he failed," Michael spat. "What happens next time? How many times is Jason going to get to keep us *safe* before there's none of us left?"

Rachel opened her mouth, and snapped it shut again without speaking. Her eyes drilled into Michael furiously until he spoke. When he did, he found that that the brief flash of anger he had felt had already begun to dissipate.

"Rachel, you *know* he can't come with us. Even if we take him now, sooner or later you'll have to leave him behind. If Australia is free of the virus, and if by some miracle we can actually get there, do you really want to take the virus *with you*?"

"I'm not leaving him here, Michael. After the guy has just saved my life—maybe *all* our lives, I can't believe you want to either."

Michael sighed.

"Of course I don't *want* to. I don't *want* any of this," he said bitterly. I wanted to be a husband and a father, and to spend my life helping people. I wanted to be a good police officer and have a normal life. This is as far from what I want as it's possible to get. I-"

"He's my fucking *brother*. He's coming. Unless you're prepared to kill *him*?"

Rachel's eyes flashed dangerously, and the emphasis in her words was unmistakable. *Gwyneth.*

"You'd better be prepared to kill me as well if that's the case."

Michael's shoulders slumped.

And then went rigid.

In the distance, somewhere to the west, a huge rumbling noise ripped apart the tense silence, roaring for several terrifying seconds before dying away, like an advance warning of an impending earthquake.

Wylfa.

Michael stared at the sky above the castle. Somewhere beyond it, something on Anglesey was pouring a thick column of black smoke into the darkening sky.

She's right. We have to move.

After a moment Michael stood, and glanced around the group.

Everyone was looking at him with hope on their faces. Waiting for him to tell them what to do.

Relying on me.

"Darren Oliver left a bus at the outskirts of town. Our best hope is to find it and get the fuck out of here. If we can't find it, we'll find another. Find *something*. Anything bigger than a car, something that won't fall apart if—*when*—we have to drive through some Infected."

All those faces staring at him. All those eyes.

He couldn't help but wonder how long it would be until he saw them being torn out.

"Let's go."

39

"The creature is on board the ship, Sir."

Fred detected a tremble in the soldier's voice, and felt it replicated in his own aged nerves. It had been a long time since he had felt anything resembling actual *fear*. The sensation was almost as bewildering as it was infuriating.

Two of the ships in the fleet were now slowly sinking to the bottom of the ocean, but the second time he had ordered a destroyer to fire on its own people the protests over the radio had been long and loud. They had acquiesced, finally, but had made it clear that there wouldn't be a third time.

Fred's position had been weakened irrevocably, and his obsession with Jake McIntosh had taken his eye off the ball. He had no control over the soldiers now; no leverage. The end would be weak and humbling. Mortifying. Even worse than the prospect of McIntosh tearing him limb from limb was the reality that the days of Fred's orders being followed were officially over.

Already several of the smaller ships in the fleet were fleeing. Precious few knew anything about the mutation, but they didn't need to; the only knowledge required was that the world had gone to shit and now the destroyers that were supposed to protect them had instead begun to sink them.

At least Isabelle is on one of those ships.

The thought surprised Fred a little. His daughter was a deluded imbecile, raised by money and parental absence to remain a selfish child forever. If she was to be his legacy, after everything he had accomplished, then his failure truly was monumental. The fact that he actually hoped she would survive merely underlined the hopelessness of it all.

"Sir?"

Several of the crew that had been on the bridge of the *Conqueror* had already fled. The couple that remained were, Fred suspected, not loyal so much as paralysed by their own stupidity. A life of following orders had left them unable to think for themselves. Doubtless, they were praying that Fred would order them to join the evacuation that they so dearly wanted to be a part of.

Fuck them.

"I want my helicopter ready to go in ninety seconds," Fred barked.

"Uh...there aren't many pilots left, Sir."

"I only need *one*," Fred snapped. "Where are they?"

His voice was rising in pitch, slipping away from his control. The sound of it in his own ears made him cringe. He sounded weak and pathetic. Frightened.

The soldier pointed silently at the window.

Outside, Fred saw a couple of choppers and a handful of the Harrier jets lifting off.

That's where the pilots are. Fleeing. Leaving me to die.

"What about you?" Fred snarled. "Can you fly a helicopter?"

The soldier shook his head slowly.

"Then what fucking good are you to me?" Fred screamed, and he pulled out his revolver and put a hole in the man's sweat-drenched forehead. Turning sharply, he pointed the gun at the only crew member left on the bridge.

There was no point asking if the man could pilot anything; Fred knew exactly what the response would be.

Still got one hand left to play. All in, old boy, and let the chips fall where they may. Impetuous, indeed.

Fred moved to a glass cabinet on the wall next to the door and smashed it with the butt of his revolver, withdrawing a gas mask and slipping it over his face.

"Turn on the gas," he snarled. "And stay out of the lower decks if you want to survive."

The soldier stared at him in open-mouthed astonishment.

"Sir, shouldn't we all be evacuati—"

Fred turned on his heel and strode from the bridge before the man could finish.

"I said turn on the gas," he snarled over his shoulder. In all likelihood, he thought, it was the last order he would ever give.

So be it.

It was a long walk to the engine room, and Fred knew that McIntosh was down there in the dark somewhere, prowling around the maze of steel corridors like the mythical Minotaur, so he moved cautiously at first, and only began to quicken his pace when he heard the hissing of the poisonous gas that seeped from the air vents.

The gas would clear McIntosh out of the lower decks, he was certain. At least for long enough to allow Fred to make his way to the twin nuclear reactors that powered the ship. Long enough to arm the device that represented Fred Sullivan's final move in the great game.

Death wasn't to be feared; death was *nothing*. Being bested—especially by a sub-human creature like Jake McIntosh—was another thing entirely. A legacy of failure. Utterly unacceptable.

The final word would belong to Fred Sullivan.

It always had.

*

Gas.

The old fucker was cunning all right, but it seemed he lacked a true understanding of just what Jake *was*. His ears caught the clicking of the air vents almost before it happened, and he heard the first puff of the toxic air as it wheezed from the ship long before it had any chance of reaching his lungs and doing any damage.

Somewhere high above him, Jake heard the clamour of humans and smelled the fear upon them, a ripe stink far stronger to Jake's sensitive nose than Sullivan's invisible attempt at an execution.

No point in conserving energy now.

With a grunt, Jake squatted low, tensing the muscles in his calves, and launched himself upwards, bursting through the ceiling and onto the deck above. His feet barely touched the cool metal floor before he pounced again, using his extraordinary momentum to drive up through the decks of the aircraft carrier like a spear thrown up from the depths of Hell itself.

Somewhere below him, the gas slowly expanded into the vacuum, as slow and pointless as a lifetime. Nothing Fred Sullivan did could threaten Jake. Not now. Gas was a pathetic last resort. A weapon that even a human could outrun if they saw it coming.

With a roar, Jake exploded into the open air and landed on the flight deck to see humans scurrying before him like insects; delicious in their terror; fleeing for the aircraft that could not possibly save them.

Some of the aircraft were already airborne; beyond his reach, but he saw a helicopter lifting off slowly and launched himself toward it, catching the vehicle's skids in one massive hand and dragging the thing back down, launching it across the deck like a dart at a row of parked jets.

Screams.

Explosions.

Delightful.

Jake let out a high-pitched shriek and began the dance, crashing around the deck like a pinball fired from a rocket launcher, tearing and biting and killing. It was like moving through a field of statues. Many of the soldiers on the deck died before their expressions had even changed from confusion to fright.

It was killing for the sake of killing, and Jake barely derived any pleasure from it. There was no enjoyment in the feel of their pulsing organs or the warm torrents of blood that drenched his hands. Jake had never been what the authorities termed a *mission killer*; there was no underlying purpose to his murders, nothing beyond the burning desire to open up the human body and play with the innards; to inflict pain because pain was so much damn *fun.*

This, though, was different, and the murder of dozens of soldiers was tainted; ruined by the mission he now felt compelled to complete.

He ripped the head off a fleeing woman and tossed it across the sea at one of the distant retreating ships like cannon fire and bellowed in frustration.

"Sssssssssulllivannnnnnnn!"

The old bastard wasn't on the ship; probably he never had been. He had out-thought Jake once more, luring him toward the obvious target and now he was out there somewhere, on any one of a dozen or more ships that scattered like dust on the wind. Even with his astonishing speed, Jake knew he could not hunt down all of the vessels. The blood that sustained him was like sucking in a lungful of cocaine; the energy burned bright and fast. It needed to be replenished constantly to operate at the level he required to destroy an entire fleet. Maybe he could decimate a handful of the ships, but by the time he had worked his way through them, the others would be gone; adrift on the vast ocean and lost to him forever.

An atomic blast of rage rocked through him at the notion that he, too, would be left to drift, too far from land to swim without fatigue overcoming him. Mindlessly, shrieking like one of the pathetic Infected that had inherited the Earth, Jake began to strike out, smashing holes into the deck and destroying the remaining aircraft.

"A temper tantrum. What a waste of such enormous potential, *Misters* McIntosh."

The voice behind him made Jake freeze. Deep and gravelly, grooves cut deep into the tone by the decades.

He turned slowly, expecting to find that the old man had cornered him in some unforeseen trap after all, but all he saw was Fred Sullivan, alone on the deck and still wearing a ridiculous silver suit, pointing a pathetic excuse for a firearm at him.

Fred saw the trembling of his hand; saw the barrel of the revolver shaking. If he had any intention of firing the weapon, it might have been a cause for concern.

The mutation rumbled a laugh.

"Do you know how many bullets I've had fired at me today, Sullivan?"

"More than the six I have, I'm sure. I—"

Fred blinked.

The hand that held the pistol out in front of him was gone. The whole *arm* was gone. The realisation hit before the pain did; the sickening knowledge that he hadn't even seen the creature *move*, and yet there it stood, twenty yards away, gnawing at his dismembered arm like it was a strip of jerky.

Fred collapsed, darkly fascinated by the stump where his left arm had been; by the *jet* of blood that spurted from it. It looked like all the blood a human body could possibly hold.

And suddenly the mutation was hovering above his face, leaning in close, breathing the stench of death and rotten meat across Fred's face, making him gag.

"Well, come on, then," Fred snarled. "You move fast. So get it over with."

The mutation laughed, and regarded Fred with inhuman eyes that seemed incapable of displaying mirth.

"You get to go *slow*, old man. Your sanity will be long gone before I let *you* die."

Fred tried to pull away in horror as the creature reached its massive, deformed hand slowly toward his face, and only when he felt an almost tender pinching at his hairline did he understand, and he began to scream as Jake McIntosh slowly and precisely peeled his face off.

Fred felt his mind beginning to break as he watched the creature consuming his flesh and realised that the reason he couldn't shut his eyes to block out the hideous sight was because his eyelids were gone; torn away, leaving him powerless to avert his gaze.

Fred laughed.

A high-pitched giggle that hadn't been the tone he had aimed for, but which had the desired effect. McIntosh reared backwards a little. Fred thought he saw confusion on the fearful features; as much as the twisted muscles of the creature's face would allow.

"Such a *fast* mover," Fred wheezed through the blood in his mouth. "Extraordinary speed in every muscle except the one that counts. I wonder if there's anything on Earth you *can't* outrun."

As final words went, Fred thought they were unremarkable, petty and vindictive, but it wasn't his words that mattered, not now. It was the small remote control in the palm of his remaining hand. The one that had only a single button.

Fred's thumb was on the button; had been from the moment he stepped out onto the deck and took what he knew would be his last breaths. He had seen the future of humanity, and he had taken steps to ensure that the terrible future brewing for the denizens of Earth would be averted, but now, at long last, he was done.

Let the fuckers fight over what remained. Wildfire wasn't going anywhere; Wildfire was all there was now. Just Wildfire and Fred Sullivan's determination to ensure that a deformed monster like Jake McIntosh didn't wind up as the winner of *anything*.

As the mutation's eyes widened in fearful understanding, Fred released the button on the tiny, insignificant piece of plastic clutched in his palm, and the explosive charges that were his ultimate contingency plan drove teeth of fire into the *Conqueror*'s nuclear engine, and the world became pain and bright, unending white light.

*

Kyle Robinson was standing on the deck of the decommissioned destroyer *Portsmouth Charger* as it travelled southwest at full speed, staring back at the scattering fleet when the *Conqueror* became a searing ball of light. By the time the roar of the detonation reached his ears, the flash had already blinded Kyle, burning the nerves in his eyes to a crisp before he could even think to look away.

The explosion was enormous, engulfing several of the ships that had been too slow to flee, creating a chain reaction of smaller explosions, and giving birth to a tidal wave that smashed against the hull of the *Portsmouth* several seconds later.

Kyle began to fall as the ship rode the huge wave, before hands caught him in the sudden darkness and hauled him upright.

"Got you, brother."

Tears streamed down Kyle's face.

"I'm blind," he sobbed, and heard a grunt of acknowledgement.

"I'd say that puts you in the majority, now."

Kyle couldn't decide if the noise that ripped from his throat in response wanted to be a laugh or a sob or a *fuck you.* Maybe a little of each.

He could still feel the staggering heat of the explosion, racing along the waves behind the *Portsmouth,* but falling behind as the ship powered forward, heading south.

Nothing could possibly have survived the destruction of the fleet's core. In a way, Tom's mission had finally been accomplished. Project Wildfire—whatever the hell it had twisted into at the end; something insane—and those behind it, had been wiped from the face of the Earth. Only its pitiful creations remained, and they too would surely die out in time.

After a moment he felt Tom guiding his hands to the rail, and Kyle steadied himself against it. He could feel his brother's presence right next to him, staring out to sea, but Kyle could not make out anything against the dark canvas that had been draped across his eyes: no shapes, no colours; not even the flash of movement as Tom held something aloft to catch the fading light.

"It's beautiful," Tom whispered softly. "Perfect."

Kyle thought he detected something strange in his brother's tone; something troubling. It didn't sound like he was talking about the view.

"Come on," Tom said. "Let's get you inside and have a doctor take a look at you."

Kyle nodded and let Tom lead him slowly away from the deck.

40

It took around half an hour to find the bus that Darren Oliver had mentioned.

The vehicle was abandoned at the northern outskirts of town, presumably because it was far too large to successfully navigate through the narrow, winding streets of Caernarfon. Michael recalled his attempts to steer a police car around similar streets in St. Davids, and the bittersweet memory of Carl's frustration each morning at the delays in getting him to what he called 'a proper breakfast' made him smile sadly.

The survivors had moved slowly and cautiously through the streets, pausing every few yards so that Michael could check Jason's blank face for some sign that there were Infected nearby. Jason remained impassive, staring at whatever horizon his eyes saw, and Michael slowly allowed himself to accept that Caernarfon had been cleared of the monsters at last.

For a while, at least. More would come. They always did.

When they found it, abandoned in the middle of the road that led to the east, the front of the bus was covered in blood. It was just as Darren had described it: his journey to Caernarfon had included Infected throwing themselves in front of the vehicle, but the bus was sturdy enough to survive the suicide attacks and didn't look too badly damaged. When the number of Infected had threatened to finally overwhelm the bus, Darren had got lucky, stumbling across a mutation that might have saved them all if the man could have brought himself to treat it like a sick human rather than an animal.

Michael had blamed Darren for that at the time, but things had become more complicated since then, and the notions of *right* and *wrong* he had struggled so desperately to cling to had become slippery; as elusive as smoke. He wasn't sure any of it was important now. Only survival mattered.

The door at the front of the bus stood open and Michael stepped inside cautiously, letting the barrel of the rifle lead the way. He had three bullets left, and hoped more than anything that he wouldn't need to use them.

The bus was empty.

The keys hung in the ignition.

Michael felt like punching the air.

"Okay," he said, "It's safe. Everybody on board."

As the survivors filed onto the vehicle, Michael surveyed the empty road behind them, expecting at any moment to see Infected charging toward him or to hear shrieking in the distance, but Caernarfon was a town of the dead now; a massive open grave.

Just like St. Davids and Aberystwyth.

Michael wondered if there were any places left out there that hadn't been reduced to stark monuments to a dead past, and couldn't help but shudder at the thought of what might be waiting for them in Liverpool. A city with a population of over a million. In a way, he hoped there was nothing to find there but more death and emptiness.

Not that it should matter: the plan did not involve sightseeing. If it were possible, Michael intended to drive the bus right to the waterfront and get everybody on board the first suitably large boat they could find, leaving the UK behind forever.

He let the thoughts of Liverpool dissolve. No point thinking about the city when just getting there was a task that might prove to be impossible to accomplish.

Just wing it, he thought, and he smiled. John would have approved.

When everybody was safely inside, he pulled the door shut, painfully aware of how flimsy it was. The bus would offer safety as long as it was moving, but if it came to a stop; if they ran into a herd...

No point thinking about it.

He settled into the driver's seat, taking a moment to familiarise himself with the controls and dragged in a deep, shuddering breath.

Once he twisted the key there would be no turning back. The town looked clear, but the virus would not be too far away, stumbling around out there in the dark fields, listening intently. The roaring of an engine would bring them quickly. The only hope was to be moving by the time they arrived.

Fuck it.

He twisted the key and the engine stuttered loudly for a terrifying moment before roaring into life.

"Buckle up," Michael said grimly to nobody in particular, and he stamped on the accelerator, turning the huge wheel smoothly and putting the picturesque town of Caernarfon in the rear view mirror.

*

A single wide road would take them all the way to Liverpool: one long highway that snaked right across the northern coast of Wales and into England to the east. For the most part, the road was empty, and Michael found himself giving thanks that the virus had attacked so early in the morning, long before the roads could clog up with traffic.

There was very little sign of the Infected. Occasionally a lone creature would stumble onto the road and throw itself ineffectually against the side of the passing bus, and the people on board would freeze as the thing's shriek of frustration gradually receded when Michael floored the accelerator.

A couple of times they appeared directly in front and Michael yelled at his passengers to brace themselves, but the isolated impacts did not trouble the huge vehicle unduly. Beyond the surprise of the steering wheel trying to tear itself from his grasp a couple of times, Michael could almost believe that he was running over nothing larger than a rabbit or a fox.

After about twenty miles, when Michael felt more reassured that the bus could handle the scattered

Infected, the worst part of the journey seemed to be the fraught atmosphere aboard the bus.

Claire must have felt it too, because she was the one that broke the tension when she burst suddenly into a shaky rendition of *the wheels on the bus go round and round*. After a few stunned moments another voice joined her, and then another, and soon the whole bus was singing, like children heading off on an exciting school trip.

Michael couldn't help but smile. For weeks these people had lived under an oppressive cloud of silence, terrified that even the slightest noise they made might mean a terrible death for them. Now, they belted out a simple song at the top of their voices, and it felt like it was a necessary release for all of them; like a heartfelt *fuck you* to the horror of the world outside the windows.

He had been driving for around an hour when he saw the first signs for Liverpool, and slowly he began to allow himself to believe that they might just make it.

Twenty miles to go.

Fifteen.

Ten.

Five.

And then, without warning, the engine cut out abruptly and Michael looked down at the dashboard in horror as the bus began to coast toward a stop. A couple of the dials on the dashboard were cracked, and he hadn't paid them enough attention. Hadn't checked them properly.

Behind glass that was little more than a spiderweb of fractures, the fuel gauge sat and taunted him for his stupidity and for daring to believe.

Empty.

41

For a long, dreadful moment Michael stared at the flimsy door to his left. At the darkness beyond it. Then he turned to find Rachel staring at him, her eyes as wide as his own felt.

"How long since we saw Infected?" She whispered breathlessly.

Michael felt like telling her the time for whispering was over. Every creature for miles around would have been following the roaring of the engine, closing in on them inexorably.

He stared at the dashboard, but the clock was smashed; stuck at 05:29am. It could well have been, he realised, the time at which the bus had encountered the Infected for the first time. The moment at which the driver had smashed his head into the dashboard, immortalised forever.

"I'd guess maybe eight or nine minutes," he said.

"Then we'd better move, and hope most of them are somewhere behind us," Rachel said.

Michael hoisted the rifle.

"Everybody off," he barked. "Silent. Single file. *Fast.*"

With that Michael swept back the door and let the night air in.

It brought snapping teeth with it.

Michael fell backwards, stunned, jabbing blindly with the butt of the rifle and sending the creature that leapt toward him crashing back through the door.

Move.

He sprang forward, catching the creature once more on the forehead as it charged at him, oblivious to the weapon. Didn't catch it flush, though; just a glancing blow, and suddenly the creature was on top of him and only the rifle was blocking the snapping teeth and Claire was screaming and—

The creature's head collapsed, crumbling inward like a controlled demolition as the lead pipe swung through the air only inches away from Michael's face. He felt the air the swing disturbed, and a second later the terrible weight was lifted from him.

Paralysed once more, Michael could only watch in stunned amazement as Jason squeezed his huge bulk through the door without a word and moved outside to begin killing.

On the bus, drenched in the heavy darkness, the passengers sat and listened for what felt like an eternity to the melody of death; the shrieks of frustration and the wet snapping of bone, until finally Michael shook himself out of the trancelike state he had fallen into.

More would be coming. Maybe a *lot* more. And Jason could only do so much.

Michael stood on legs that trembled as badly as they had the first time he heaved himself out of the wheelchair, and motioned to the people huddled on the bus.

Follow.

*

Rachel exited the bus to see Jason felling the last of the creatures that had streamed toward the vehicle in the darkness. When the body crumpled to the floor, Jason stood and stared down at it blankly. It was almost, Rachel thought, like he couldn't see them either. Not really *see* them.

She took his huge hand in hers, and led him away from the pile of eyeless corpses that littered the ground at his feet, directing him back to the bus.

In the distance, Rachel heard the sea.

No, not the sea. A river.

The Mersey.

So close.

It was as she was focused intently on listening to the sound of the water that she heard it. Somewhere behind them. A faint rumble of rolling thunder. The sound was odd, though. It didn't seem to fade away as thunder normally did; didn't recede as the atmosphere drew in its breath to bellow once more.

Rachel came to a dead stop.

It wasn't thunder.

Shit.

*

Michael bristled when he heard footsteps approaching him hurriedly. Logic told him that Jason had killed all of the Infected, but still, as he turned to see Rachel approaching fast, he felt himself tensing up as if he expected an imminent attack.

"You hear that storm?"

Michael nodded. "It should help cover the noise of our movement, we'll have to run the rest of the w—

"That's no storm."

Rachel fixed him with a meaningful stare.

"Listen," she hissed.

Michael's stomach lurched. She was right. The noise he heard didn't have the undulating quality of thunder. The rumbling was enormous. Constant.

Getting louder.

Footsteps. Hurtling toward them.

"There must be *thousands*," he breathed in a horrified whisper.

Rachel nodded.

"It's getting louder, Michael. That's the only reason I realised it wasn't thunder. At first I thought the noise was behind us, but now it sounds like it's *everywhere*. Listen."

Rachel cocked her head for a moment, and jabbed a finger into the darkness.

"West."

Jab.

"South."

Jab.

"East."

Michael's eyes widened.

"We've driven into the middle of a fucking county-sized herd. They're coming straight for us," Rachel said.

For a moment Michael felt like his mind was a computer, and somebody had just hit the reset button. It was taking him some time to reboot.

"Do you know where we are? Where, *exactly*?"

It was a simple question, and one to which Michael had no ready answer.

"Not exactly," he said. "The last sign I saw was for a town called *Mold*. I think that is pretty near the English border, just south of Liverpool. Hang on."

Trying to make as little noise as possible, Michael stepped back onto the bus and searched the various compartments dotted around the driver's seat, sighing in relief when he discovered a roadmap.

He hadn't needed to check a map while driving the bus: the roads were all clearly marked and well travelled. Getting to Liverpool had been a matter of just following the signs.

But on foot, and with the knowledge that there were Infected all around them, navigation became a different matter entirely. Following a road blindly now could well see them walking in the wrong direction and running headlong into danger.

He squatted, stifling a grunt as his back shrieked in complaint, and spread the map out on the floor, focusing the beam of his flashlight on it. After a moment, Rachel crouched down next to him.

"That would put us around here, right?" She said, pointing.

Michael followed her finger and nodded.

"This is the road we're on," he agreed. "And the last sign for Liverpool said it was five miles away..."

"Which means we're here," Rachel repeated, jabbing a finger at the map.

Michael followed her gesture and saw a peninsula that jutted from the Welsh coast, rising north until it was parallel with Liverpool. The peninsula offered a single way to reach the city, and as Michael realised what that route was he felt anxiety rising in his gut.

The Mersey Tunnel.

Three miles of claustrophobic underground darkness. One way in, and one way out.

Michael would have liked to avoid taking the tunnel even if he had still been behind the wheel of the bus. The risks were simply too great. There was no way of knowing if the tunnel was clear or not, no guessing what might be waiting for them at the exit. The only way to survive an encounter with the Infected on anything other than the smallest of scales was to run or to hide, and the tunnel severely limited the chances of either of those options being successful.

Now there was no choice, and no time.

Just go.

Michael straightened, and turned to the frightened group of people that huddled by the bus, their confident singing long forgotten.

"They're coming," he hissed. "Follow me. Run!"

He didn't stop to look back. Grabbing Claire's hand and pulling her into motion beside him, Michael tried to ignore the shattering pain in his back, and put his head down to the wind, running blindly, panicking because it was the only thing left to do.

Behind him, he heard footsteps clattering as the group followed his lead, and further back still, a wall of noise that approached indefatigably. Two miles to the tunnel. Three miles through it.

Michael blanked the thoughts from his mind; blanked out everything except a single all-consuming directive.

Right foot.
Left foot.
Right foot.
Faster.

42

The Mersey Tunnel connected the town of Birkenhead to Liverpool, running deep beneath the Mersey Estuary. When Michael saw it looming in the distance, he had already been running for nearly two miles, and the pain in his back had consumed his entire being. Nothing seemed to penetrate the wall of agony: no emotion, even fear, found a way through.

Until he saw the yawning blackness of the tunnel entrance, and his pace began to falter.

Birkenhead was a ghost town, as the entire peninsula appeared to be. That wasn't surprising: the virus would have ripped through the isolated stretch of land in no time, and the Infected would have been forced to move south to find more prey.

Or north.

Into the tunnel.

Into the impenetrable darkness.

A handful of the group had flashlights; a couple of them had mobile phones taken during the raid on Caernarfon: pocket-sized communications miracles that were now useful only for the soft light the screen provided. When the batteries ran out, the phones would become fossils. The days of recharging anything were finished.

The thundering of footsteps behind them had maintained its volume, and was still heading north. Michael imagined the entire peninsula heaving with the Infected, scrambling across each other to get to the fleeing group of humans, a seething mass of death that stretched from one coast to the other.

Not helpful, Mike.

He felt the group begin to slow behind him, and heard the clicking of flashlights being turned on. Felt the fear, too, radiating off the people in sickening waves.

In the tunnel they would be as blind as the Infected. The monsters would have a clear advantage.

They need your courage now, Mike. They need somebody to follow.

Michael gritted his teeth, pushing back the agony and the terror, and beckoned to the group to pick up the pace.

Thirty seconds later he plunged into the tunnel, and the world was reduced to darkness and writhing shadows.

*

The world was pools of light that danced across an endless dark, but Claire could feel the walls of the place even without seeing them. The air in the tunnel felt still, and heavier somehow than it had outside.

All the flashlights did was confirm that they were underground; none was powerful enough to truly light the way forward.

Claire had been underground in the darkness once before, trapped inside a car when the power died. Things had moved in the darkness then. Things that still terrified her and tormented her dreams.

She felt like screaming.

The tunnel was wide, and when lit it had probably appeared unremarkable; white-tiled and sterile. Just another road. In the darkness it became something else; filled with intent, like the blackness wanted to wrap invisible hands around her throat. Like the air itself was alive with something dangerous.

After every few steps, Claire hesitated, until finally Linda stumbled into the back of her, and it was all Claire could do to keep the scream from bursting out of her throat. She felt Linda's hand on her shoulder. The woman gave a reassuring squeeze, and Claire began to move forward again.

Far beneath the estuary, the tunnel curved and snaked toward Liverpool, and Claire could no longer see the frail light of the stars behind her. In front there was only darkness.

Darkness and emptiness, until the silence gave way to a faint grunting sound on the road ahead, and Claire suddenly crashed into something.

*

Michael had held up a closed fist, but of course no one had seen it. Everyone that had a light had it pointed outwards like a searchlight, as though scanning for the iceberg that might sink them at any moment. He gritted his teeth as Claire ran into him, and heard the ripple effect as it moved through the group. The faint whispering of frightened bodies coming into contact. Nobody spoke. There wasn't even so much as a grunt of surprise.

We might just get away with that, Michael thought, and he froze, straining to catch any noise in the dark space ahead. He was sure he had heard something. A soft *grunt*.

His flashlight had a range of about thirty yards, and Michael could only properly pick out detail for fifteen of those, but he thought he saw something further along the road. A shape moving in the darkness.

He crept forward, and saw it after five steps, and his mouth dropped open.

Another grunt.

The rhythmic movement was unmistakeable.

It can't be...

He took another step.

About twenty yards ahead of him he saw two of the Infected, pressed together. Thrusting and bucking. Mating.

No, not *mating*, Michael realised in growing horror. Breeding.

Breeding.

The hideous truth of Project Wildfire rolled out endlessly before him, and he saw it all with a sudden, piercing clarity.

The Infected would not just die out. They wouldn't starve. Survival for humans was not just a matter of finding a safe place and *waiting* for the apocalypse to pass. It had been there in front of his eyes all along. The creatures were evolving. A new species a matter of weeks old. They were genetically wired to kill humans, but there was nothing supernatural about them; they were just mammals. They would adapt, they would procreate. Some had learned to communicate; some guided those less advanced than themselves. Some could swim.

A species in its infancy, rising inexorably, learning and adapting to the environment that they had inherited.

He understood suddenly just why the creatures were compelled to kill those who had been their blood relations before they turned. The virus compelled them to kill off their old family so that they could replace it with a new one. The world belonged to them and they weren't going anywhere. They were *thriving.*

Even the animals could contract the virus. Wildfire was everything now, and everywhere; a part of the planet itself, as ubiquitous as water and air and death.

The world hadn't ended. Hadn't been destroyed.

It's just been transformed. And there's no place left in it for us.

It took only a moment for Michael's brain to run through it all, but it was long enough. Just enough time to distract him from the fact that there *was* a noise behind him now. A pounding of heavy feet.

Jason charged past Michael, hefting the pipe and killing the first of the Infected with a single blow, but he wasn't quick enough. Even as he pulled the pipe clear and began to swing again, the second Infected creature registered the sudden noise in the tunnel.

And shrieked.

The noise ended a moment later with an abrupt liquid *crunch*, but it seemed to echo off the walls of the tunnel forever, taking on a life of its own.

Michael held his breath and began to count.

One.

Two.

Three.

He expected the darkness to be split by an answering shriek, but there was no sound. He exhaled a long, slow breath and drew in another, shuddering.

"Bet you're glad we brought Jason along now, huh?"

Rachel breathed the words into Michael's ear and he jumped. He hadn't noticed her moving alongside him in the darkness. He trained his flashlight on Jason, and even as he opened his mouth to speak he saw the big man stiffen suddenly, as a faint shriek reached his ear.

Fourteen.

"That was fourteen seconds away. Behind us," Michael growled as Rachel's eyes widened. He turned to the group that he couldn't see, but which he knew were clustered behind him the darkness, holding flashlights that all poured in the same direction for once, bathing Jason and the dead Infected in a wide pool of light.

"They'll be coming," he hissed into the darkness. "They're not far away. They'll come *fast*. We have to run."

He half-worried that there might be debate or at least terror to slow them down, but Jason provided a dreadful punctuation that underscored his argument.

With a grunt, Rachel's giant brother began to strike the road at his feet with the lead pipe like a metronome.

Clang.

Clang.

Clang.

It's up to you now, Rachel, Michael thought, and with that he turned, grabbing Claire's small hand, and began to run once more.

*

You can do this, Rach.

John's final words blazed in Rachel's mind clearly, as if bright sunlight poured across them and brushed away the shadows that had obscured their true meaning.

His message hadn't been about Annie Holloway, or the Infected or Project Wildfire. It hadn't even been about her survival, at least not directly. John had been talking about Jason. The one thing that he had known she would have to do if she was to have any chance of living.

Rachel remained frozen as the others began to sprint forward, leaving her alone with her giant brother. She studied his empty features, his eyes pointed at the unending darkness implacably, as though that was all they had ever seen.

You can leave him. You have *to leave him.*

Somewhere behind her the single shriek had become a wall of static; a meaningless cacophony that grew louder with each passing second. Soon the noise would enter the tunnel like a speeding train, and Jason would be there to meet it.

A huge sob wracked her body.

"I love you, Jase. I'm so sorry."

It might have been her imagination, maybe just a mirage spotted in the desert of her mind. Just wish fulfilment, John would probably have called it, but as Rachel sprinted away from her brother, leaving him behind forever, she thought she had detected a flicker of something in his eyes. A vague flash of terror and loneliness that made her heart break.

*

By the time Jason began to swing, cutting into the tide of Infected that split around him like water crashing over a rock in the black tunnel, Rachel's footsteps had long moved beyond his hearing. She was gone, and what remained of Jason Roberts wasn't certain she had ever existed in the first place. Yet with each skull he crushed, there was a part of him, a fractured part buried deep somewhere that felt glad that she ran.

43

When Michael saw a patch of lighter darkness up ahead, he almost screamed in relief.

The tunnel seemed to have curved around under the water for an eternity, until ridiculous notions surfaced in his mind that there *was* no exit after all; that the Mersey Tunnel was just some terrible joke played on the people of Merseyside.

No light reached him from the city, of course, but he saw faint starlight, and he redoubled his pace, struggling to keep up with the others. In a different time Michael would have bet on himself in a race against any of them, but in the terrible present, it was all he could do to give silent thanks to whatever god might be listening that his legs still obeyed his commands.

He exploded from the tunnel to find the others had stopped running, and he came to an abrupt stop, panting for oxygen and searching frantically for Claire. Only when he saw her, bent double and heaving air into her small lungs, did he relax a little.

But only a little.

Behind him he heard the terrible echoing of death approaching. The Infected had reached the tunnel, and there was no way Jason would be able to stop them. They had a few minutes at most.

"Why have you stopped?" He panted, as he pushed his way through the bodies, but nobody answered. There was no need.

Rachel pointed ahead silently.

Around fifty yards ahead, Michael saw a row of huge stakes driven into the gardens of the houses, spread out at intervals of around ten yards.

On each stake, an eyeless body had been hung like a grisly Christmas decoration. Even at this distance, Michael could see the banner that had been hung across the road. Foot-high letters daubed in blood.

WELCOME TO LIVERPOOL.
POPULATION 113.

People.

He felt a hand clutching at his shirt, and a moment later Rachel's voice breathed into his ear.

"What the fuck is this?"

Michael shook his head at her. He was about to say that it didn't matter, that the docks weren't far away and they should just run through the grisly fence that had been erected around Liverpool and make their escape, when a sudden thought occurred to him.

Stifling the urge to grunt in pain, he bent low to pick up a small stone from the ground near his feet. A trick he had learned the very first time he had encountered the Infected. A simple test.

He hurled the stone toward the hanging creatures, and when it landed with a harsh *click* on the road, the fence burst into life. Ragged panting. Eyeless faces twisting left and right, searching for the source of the noise, before once more lapsing into silence.

An alarm system.

The horror of it drove needles of terror deep into Michael's heart. The Infected were horrifying, but looking at the fence and wondering at the insanity that had caused somebody to build it, Michael realised that the most frightening thing about them was that they had once been human. Nothing was worse than humans. Maybe nothing ever would be.

Three miles behind and closing fast, a herd of killers raged through the tunnel like a pyroclastic flow. The herd would destroy everything in its path, and the hundred-and-thirteen sick bastards left in Liverpool, whoever they were, were about to discover that their time was up.

The only thing that mattered was that they didn't get a chance to interfere with the survivors of Caernarfon before the surging river of death washed over them.

"Single file," Michael whispered. "Straight through the middle. No noise. Move slow. Once you're clear, you run. Don't worry about anybody else, just *run*. The docks should be to the left. Whoever gets to a boat, get on it and go. Don't wait. Got it?"

Michael stared around the group and saw frightened eyes staring back at him, but he saw understanding, too. The road into Liverpool was the point of no return. The choice had always been between death or survival, and the time had come to make it and suffer the consequences. No more hiding.

Silently and slowly, ignoring the screaming of his nerves that death was chasing him and that he should run for his life, Michael began to pad forward. One step at a time, barely daring to breathe.

The plan was doomed to fail.

Michael should have known it, but he was so focused on moving without making a sound, creeping forward by inches, that he had forgotten.

He was standing right between two of the horrific fence posts when he heard the noise that told him the game was up.

Sniff.

Sniff.

A shriek split the air right next to him, and then suddenly the entire world seemed to be screaming, as the fence came to life.

In the distance to his right, Michael heard a man's voice shout: "People at the fence! Go!"

"Run!" Michael screamed, and he veered to the left, pouring every last drop of energy into pumping his legs, heading for the docks in the distance.

He was overtaken almost immediately. Even the larger guys, like Shirley and Gareth Roberts, men that he would once have beaten in a race without breaking sweat, swept past him, and Michael cursed his legs. After everything that had happened, his back was going to get him killed after all, right before he reached the finish line. It was so cruel, it seemed almost funny.

He watched the others disappearing toward the docks, and pounded onward, but he felt like a marathon runner in the final few paces of the race, hitting the wall.

He had to stop.

Had to draw in some oxygen.

"Michael, come *on.*"

Rachel's voice.

He looked up in horror to see her coming back for him.

"Rachel, go," he snarled. "I said don't wait for anyone. Keep Claire safe."

She stared at him hesitantly.

"Go!" He screamed.

He turned away from her. In the distance he saw shapes moving in the darkness, but the animal gait he had come to expect from the Infected was absent. This was a different sort of threat. Far worse.

Panting for air, he pulled the rifle from his back and took aim.

The shot rang out like thunder.

He had missed, of that he was certain. He had never been a good shot to begin with. But the roaring of the gun had stopped their approach. Michael counted ten men; maybe twelve, scattering for cover behind parked cars on the dark road.

"They've got a gun," he heard a voice say, and Michael's face split in a savage grin.

Well, not really, he thought.

Two bullets left.

He fired off another round when he saw the distant shadows creeping out into the road once more, and when they ducked back into cover, Michael drew in a huge lungful of air and turned away, pumping his legs through a thick lake of fire.

A few hundred yards to the docks.

It wouldn't matter. The others would be gone by now, on a boat and heading out to sea. All that did matter was that Claire was safe. He just wanted to see the boat; to know that she was gone.

Footsteps behind him again.

Gaining ground.

He turned and fired his last bullet.

No more cards left to play, Mike.

Tossing the rifle aside, Michael focused all his thoughts on his legs once more.

And ran.

*

He heard the engine of the boat before the dock loomed into sight, and his heart sank. It sounded close. Far too close, like it had taken them a while to find a boat with a working engine and to get it started.

When he finally saw it, Michael's heart leapt into his mouth. In the darkness, the boat was lit like a beacon, but it wasn't far out at sea as he had hoped. It hadn't moved at all. The engine churned the water and light spilled from every window, but it sat in next to the dock wall like it had not even been unmoored.

They don't know how to move it, he thought in despair. He should have known; should have expected that it would all end so feebly. *Get a large boat,* he thought. *So simple. Unless no one knows how to actually operate a large boat.*

Michael slowed to a stop about twenty yards from the boat, and turned away from it. He waited on the dock, standing in the narrow alley that ran between large shipping containers and parked trucks. Only a second or two passed before the group of men that had been chasing him burst into his line of sight.

He saw knives.

Clubs.

Feral grins.

Michael balled up his fists. He couldn't stop them getting to the boat, but he would make sure some of them didn't get past him. Hell, he was going to make sure some of them didn't go anywhere ever again.

The man at the front of the pack laughed savagely.

"Just you is it, mate? Everyone else on board the jolly roger over there?"

The man dropped his gaze to Michael's fists.

"All out of bullets, too. Hope you've watched a lot of *Jackie Chan* films, fella. Or this is going to get pretty ugly for you. And for all them pretty girls you're travelling with."

Michael gritted his teeth as the man took a step towards him.

And then his jaw dropped in astonishment as the man's head exploded and a deafening roar split the night air. Michael watched, stunned, as the headless corpse crumpled to the ground.

"Not just him. Me, too. And I've got plenty of bullets."

Rachel stepped out of the shadows to Michael's left, pointing the revolver at the group of stunned men.

"And we've all got plenty of knives. I even have this lovely *mace.* Any of you fuckers have a *mace?*"

Shirley appeared next to Rachel, grinning widely.

And then Michael saw Gareth Hughes. Linda. Ed. All of them.

Michael saw glinting knives and dead-eyed stares loaded with threat. He wouldn't have believed them capable of it.

"Next one of you to so much as blink is going to end up in the same mess your mouthy bastard friend there found himself in," Rachel said amiably, sweeping the revolver left and right. "Now we're going to get on that boat, and be on our way. It's up to you how many of you are left to wave us off."

Michael saw hesitation on the faces of the men from Liverpool. Saw a couple of them take a faltering step backwards and his face split in a grin.

"I thought I told you not to wait for me," he said as the men began to retreat.

"Yeah," Rachel agreed. "You're an idiot sometimes."

*

Rachel kept her gun pointed at the road long after the group of men had slunk out of sight, and was still aiming it as the boat chugged slowly away from the docks.

"Good job you still had that thing," Michael said, joining her on the small deck to the rear of the boat.

"Good job I still had one bullet left," Rachel replied with a sly grin.

Michael's mouth dropped open, and he shook his head in disbelief.

"Balls of steel," he whispered in admiration, and Rachel laughed.

"You think we'll make it?"

Michael shook his head ruefully.

"On this thing? To Australia? Honestly, no I don't," he said. We barely got this thing moving and no one has any idea how to steer it, let alone how to navigate. Getting to the other side of the *planet* doesn't seem likely."

Rachel nodded sombrely.

"Oh," she said.

"We'll find somewhere. A small island. Somewhere safe. As far away as we can get."

Michael shrugged.

"It's all I've got."

Rachel nodded.

"We'll make it," she said, and Michael almost believed her.

"Vessel to starboard, Sir."

"Range?"

"One kilometre, Sir."

Nathan's ears pricked up. It had been several hours since the *Portsmouth* had fled the waters north of Scotland. He had spent most of that time on the bridge, explaining the events of the recent past to Captain Bertrand. It was made abundantly clear to Nathan that he was a guest of the captain's, and that he had no rank on this ship.

He was fine with that.

He spent a long time persuading the Captain that the rumours about Australia were true. It was Sullivan's rally point. A place to flee if disaster struck the project. Once the Captain had heard enough, Nathan was told to remain in his seat, and the journey became a procession of uneventful miles that passed slowly.

The sighting of another vessel was the first bit of excitement he'd had in hours.

The captain scanned the windows with powerful binoculars.

"Pleasure yacht," he said, and Nathan thought he detected a little disdain in the man's tone.

"Should we fire on them sir?"

Nathan looked at the radar operator in horror, and flicked his gaze back to the captain. He knew what Fred Sullivan's answer would have been. He hoped the man that ran this ship might turn out to be different. So far Bertrand had been businesslike and aggressive, with a ruthless air that made Nathan edgy, but he hadn't seemed like a maniac.

Outside the *Portsmouth*, in the far distance, a small yacht bobbed on the choppy waves of the Irish Sea, lights flickering in the dark like fireflies, and apparently making little in the way of progress in any direction.

"What the fuck is wrong with you, Soldier?" The captain snarled, and Nathan heaved out a relieved sigh. "No we should not *fire on them*. This is over, don't you get it? All this secret mission bullshit is done. What we're doing now is surviving. There is no us and them."

He pointed behind him, back toward the dark shape of the mainland that had all but disappeared from sight.

"There's us and *them*. Understand?"

The soldier flushed and nodded.

"Sound the horn. And get a lifeboat out there. Tell the medical crew to be ready. We're taking on more passengers."

*

The *Portsmouth* made steady progress, but the trip to Australia would be long, Michael had been told. They would give the land as wide a berth as possible, so they wouldn't be taking the fastest possible route.

Adding extra time to the feeling of calm safety that being on the ship gave him didn't seem like such a bad idea to Michael. Already he was beginning to wonder what they might find when they reached the only country on Earth that was supposed to be unaffected by the Wildfire virus. Nobody really knew if it was true; for all anybody knew they could make land and walk right into the very same horror they were running from.

He wouldn't have minded staying on the ship forever.

After two days the power station at Wylfa finally collapsed upon itself, and the sky behind the *Portsmouth* was lit briefly, like a poisonous second sun had appeared, burning itself out in seconds.

Michael realised he couldn't even be sure it had been Wylfa. Could have been any number of power stations around the UK. Might even have been an explosion tearing apart a different country altogether. France, maybe; Spain. It barely mattered. All around them, the land itself would burn as the remnants of civilization began to decay.

This fire would burn for decades. Centuries, maybe.

The fallout from the destruction of the nuclear industry might well kill off the Infected, but there was no way to know for sure. The creatures' genes were a mystery, and might now remain so forever. Michael hoped so.

He leaned on the rail and stared at the endless peaceful ocean. They hadn't seen land for a while. He smiled when he felt Rachel's presence next to him.

"G'day, mate," she said with a wide grin.

Michael arched an eyebrow.

"Figured I should practice the lingo," she said with a shrug. "We're all going to be Australians now, right?"

Michael cracked a smile.

"Oh, I don't know," he said. "When there's only one place left, is there any point giving it a name?"

"It'll just be *home*, then."

Michael couldn't disagree with that.

"I guess we're still running," Rachel said a little wistfully.

"I look at it more as regrouping," Michael replied. "Australia's a big place, but it won't be long before it feels small. One way or another, we're going to have to take this planet back."

Rachel nodded thoughtfully, and stared down at the waves that washed gently against the hull of the ship.

"One way or another," she agreed finally.

Michael followed her gaze and watched the sea passing underneath the *Portsmouth*, and wondered how long it would be before he saw land again. Saw people again.

He flinched a little in surprise when Rachel slipped her hand into his and squeezed gently. For too long, Michael's thoughts had been dominated by fear of humans; by the overwhelming urge to put as much distance between himself and others as possible.

After a moment's hesitation, he squeezed back.

Epilogue

Brad heaved his board across the damp sand, panting at the effort it took to make progress under the energy-sapping heat of the blazing sun above. The surf had taken it out of him, more than he could ever remember. The waves had been fantastic, high and regular, each one persuading him that the fire in his muscles should be ignored for just one more run, and he had been powerless to resist the lure of the waves until finally he began to cramp and had no choice but to return to the beach.

A lot of people didn't understand the narcotic rush of surfing. Brad felt sorry for them. Something about being carried along by the ocean made him feel humble and powerful; giddy and focused all at once. There was nothing quite like it, and on a day like this, when the sun that seemed to scorch the skies over Australia incessantly decided that it would be okay for the wind to get involved too, Brad would have bet that anyone—even the most ardent anti-surfer—would feel a twinge of addiction if they just *tried* it.

When he was about fifty feet away from the clear waves that lapped at the beach, Brad stripped his wetsuit to the waist and collapsed onto the soft, powdery sand, letting the warm breeze dry his hair and body.

He stared up at the empty sky, feeling his vision swim a little as his aching muscles engaged his mind in a heated debate about the wisdom of taking a nap.

Other than the whisper of the waves, there was no sound.

It had been like that for a couple of months, and no one in Australia seemed to know why. TV, radio and internet had disappeared simultaneously one day, and in the weeks that followed, as speculation reached fever pitch, the general sentiment in Australia was that something terrible had happened out there, beyond the endless crystal sea.

Nobody seemed to have heard from their relatives in the US or the UK, and even the closer countries—Japan, New Zealand—had fallen silent.

Brad had heard plenty of rumours: that some awful disaster had befallen the world—a war, perhaps; or maybe the day of reckoning had finally arrived and God had spared only Australia.

It was all nonsense, of course. The only rumour Brad paid attention to was the one about the military sending out recon flights that never returned, and even then only because his brother was in the military. If Shane said there was something to the rumours, then Brad figured he should probably listen.

Finally there was a rumour of a single plane that *did* return, bringing back a cargo of extraordinary tales about a world burning, lapsed into shocking violence, as though nuclear war had broken out across the rest of the globe all at once, and everything everywhere was affected.

Brad wasn't sure he believed it, but he supposed it was plausible enough. The TV news—back when there had been TV news—was always full of some country squabbling with another, tearing each other down and delivering threats like schoolyard bullies.

Brad thought the world would have been a much better place if all those idiots in suits could just spend a little time out there on the surf, letting the rolling waves wash away their problems.

He shrugged mentally. It didn't much matter to him what happened to the rest of the world. Australia could survive just fine on its own: very little of the country's goods and services were imported because the place was just so damn far away from everywhere else that it made shipping most things impractical and inordinately expensive. The only thing they had really lost was the news and the internet, and in some ways the loss of communications had actually improved life.

He let his eyes close, daydreaming about catching up with Kimberly later for a barbecue. And the rest: today was Brad's birthday, and he knew Kim had procured some special lingerie for the occasion.

Life was good.

He dozed.

*

Brad woke with a start sometime later, when the sun had passed overhead, and his first thought was that he hadn't applied sunscreen, and that he should know better than to fall asleep on a blazing hot afternoon. He didn't burn much, not anymore. But there was always the threat of skin cancer.

He reprimanded himself as he sat upright, and only then did he begin to wonder what might have caused him to wake so suddenly.

His mouth dropped open.

When he had fallen asleep, Brad had been alone on the beach. It was often like that: Australia practically had more beautiful beaches than it had people; there were plenty to go around.

But he wasn't alone now.

An enormous battleship sat just offshore; long and sleek and laden with enormous guns that looked like they could blow a hole in the universe. Much closer, he saw a small boat powering its way to the beach, and realised that it was the noise of the engine that had caused him to stir.

He stood on the hot sand, swaying a little, filled equally with curiosity and apprehension.

What the fuck?

There were seven people on the boat. As Brad watched, six disembarked into the shallow water and splashed toward the beach, and the boat turned around and made its way back toward the distant ship. Further back, Brad could see similar boats approaching. It looked like the ship was unloading all its passengers, and pretty soon the beach was going to be crowded.

Brad trotted forward, open-mouthed, his surfboard forgotten behind him.

The first of the people to reach dry land was a man with a serious expression and a slightly underfed look about him. A woman followed behind, petite and attractive and with intense eyes that Brad found almost hypnotic.

"Is this Australia?" The man asked gruffly in an accent Brad could not quite place.

The question threw Brad a little.

"What? Uh...yeah, of course this is Aus—Dude, is that a fucking *battleship*? What's going on?"

The serious man turned to the woman and grinned wryly.

"Looks like John was right about Australia being clear."

The woman nodded and smiled wearily.

"Clear? Clear of what?" Brad stuttered. "Where the hell did you guys come from?"

The man grimaced.

"I think we're what's left of the rest of the world," he said flatly.

Brad's mouth had only just managed to shut. It dropped open once more.

"The rest of the world? What happened?"

The man shook his head ruefully and laughed, as if he didn't even know where to begin.

"The end," he said finally.

Printed in Great Britain
by Amazon.co.uk, Ltd.,
Marston Gate.